THE HAUNTED COLLECTION

VOLUME I

LEE MOUNTFORD

INSIDE: PERRON MANOR

Sign up to my mailing list to get the FREE prequel...

In 2014 a group of paranormal researchers conducted a weekend-long investigation at the notorious Perron Manor. The events that took place during that weekend were incredible and terrifying in equal measure. This is the full, documented story.

In addition, the author dives into the long and bloody history of the house, starting with its origins as a monastery back in the 1200s, covering its ownership under the Grey and Perron families, and even detailing the horrific events that took place on Halloween in 1982.

No stone is left unturned in what is now the definitive work regarding the most haunted house in Britain.

The novella, as mentioned in Haunted: Perron Manor, can be yours for FREE by joining my mailing list.

Sign up now.

www.leemountford.com

HAUNTED: PERRON MANOR

BOOK 1

CHAPTER 1

Back, after all these years. Back to Devil's House.

Chloe Shaw took a breath and held it as she looked around the entrance lobby of Perron Manor. She had lived here for close to a year when she was a child, but had never set foot inside since. And now, after the passing of her uncle, it was hers.

Well, hers and her sister's. And it would be the perfect family home, history be damned.

The space around her was impressive, and much different than she was used to. A marble-tiled floor was firm underfoot, and just ahead of her was a grand set of oak stairs. The bannisters and spindles were a deep brown, and the timber treads had discoloured slightly over time. The stairs ran up to a half landing, which then split off both left and right before they turned back on themselves, creating walkways that gave access to the corridors upstairs.

Given the lobby was a double-height space, it made the entrance feel suitably majestic. The walls were covered with oak panelling up to mid-height, and after that cream wallpaper—which had peeled and yellowed over time—took over.

As majestic as it was, years of neglect were apparent. The wall panelling had scuffed and cracked in areas, and the varnish on the wood had stained. The air was stuffy as well, and the smell of something rotten permeated the air. Rectifying that would be only one of the many jobs that lay ahead of them.

'Cosy,' said her husband Andrew, making no attempt to hide his sarcasm. He held on to Emma, their eighteen-month-old daughter, who was asleep in his arms and had her face snuggled into his upper chest. Andrew was not as enthused about the place as Chloe was. She had known that ever since they had made their first visit up here to view the house, when his face had been a persistent frown. But, he'd agreed to move here—albeit a little reluctantly—and this was their home now.

'Cosy isn't the point,' Chloe said. 'Not with a place like this.'

She was still a little in awe of her surroundings. When they had first come up here, Chloe had not been able to remember much about Perron Manor, given she'd been only six years old when she'd left. But now, after being back inside for a little while, pangs of recognition had started to bloom: the intricate carvings of the stair balustrades, the ornate ceiling high above with detailed coving around the edges, and the pattern of the marble floor—overlapping squares and rectangles, a mixture of greys, whites, and dull yellows. They all hit home and pulled some long-forgotten memories back to the surface. She remembered running through here a lot, and had always loved the pattering echo her feet made on the tiled floor.

She turned back to Andrew and couldn't help but smile. 'Honestly... what do you think?'

He paused, looked around, and then scratched at the stubble on his chin with his free hand. The grey in his facial hair had long since spread to the receding hair atop his head. Andrew's normally serious blue eyes again settled on Chloe. He shrugged.

'Workable, I suppose,' he replied, then added with a grin, 'though it smells like someone died in here.'

She shot him a scowl. 'Don't push it,' she warned. Chloe knew he was only teasing, but she didn't want him going down that road. He was well aware that people *had* died in this house.

Her estranged uncle, for one. Though that was just the tip of the iceberg.

But that didn't matter, it was all in the past. And the past couldn't hurt them.

Andrew held up his free hand in mock supplication. 'Fine, fine,' he said. 'Not another word. I guess it has… potential.'

'It's got *huge* potential,' Chloe corrected. And it did. Perron Manor, for all its history, was a massive property, far too large for Andrew and her to have afforded on their own. And yet it had been gifted to her and her sister, along with a not-insubstantial inheritance.

The grounds around the house alone made her giddy with excitement, and the possibilities about what she could do with them were endless. Sure, the gardens and lawns and all looked shabby and overgrown now, but with a little tender loving care, they could be transformed into something beautiful—just like the house itself.

It was a project Chloe could not wait to get started on. First, however, she knew they would need to get the important things in order. A transit van full of their essential belongings was parked outside, and two more trucks from a removal company were due to arrive later that same day. And then, of course, there was her sister.

'So, when is Sarah due to get here?' Andrew asked, as if reading her mind.

'Later today.'

'Well, then,' he went on, 'shouldn't we get to work claiming the best bedroom before she steals it?'

Chloe laughed. 'That sounds like a good idea.' Andrew started to walk over to the staircase before them, but she stopped him. 'Not so fast. Let's take a look around the ground floor. We have a little bit of time.'

Andrew glanced at the sleeping child in his arms. 'This one will be waking up soon,' he said. 'I think we should at least get her crib set up, first.'

'It'll be fine,' Chloe said with a dismissive wave of her hand. Her excitement to take in their new home was simply too great, so the unpacking could wait a while. It would do them good to explore the house a little and take a moment to savour their new home.

With Andrew following behind, she made her way off to the left of the entrance lobby to one of the heavy-looking oak doors. Chloe pushed it open, and it creaked horribly. A hallway was revealed beyond, the floor of which was lined with a faded patterned carpet of predominately reds and blacks. The walls, like the main foyer, were half-height wood panelling and the same cream wallpaper above. There were no external windows here, so most of the space was cloaked in darkness. Chloe hit the brass light switch to her side, and the single light fitting in the corridor—a black, iron chandelier—sputtered to life, casting a dull yellow hue not quite powerful enough to fill all the corners.

That will need to be replaced, Chloe thought.

The corridor was not a long one, and turned ninety degrees to their right just up ahead. She knew that by following the hallway, it would bring them out into what was called the great hall.

I own a house with a fucking great hall!

And from there they could look out into the rear courtyard.

I own a house with a fucking courtyard!

Chloe was giddy, there was simply so much to get excited about.

Straight ahead, set in the wall before them at the point where the corridor snapped to the right, was a door that led into a good-sized dining room. That door was open, even though Chloe was certain she had closed all of them during their last visit. *Obviously not.* The darkness of the room looked heavy. Chloe poked her head inside as they passed and saw that the thick curtains had been pulled closed. *Weren't they open when we left?*

'Something wrong?' Andrew asked.

Chloe shrugged, deciding she was simply misremembering in her excitement.

'No, let's keep going,' she replied. Chloe was just about to turn away and pull the door closed, when something in the dark caught her attention. She had to squint, and it was hard to make out, but when she looked toward the far wall, Chloe could swear there was a humanoid shape within the black, little more than a shadow itself. She stared more intently, taking in the unmoving form but unable to make out any firm details. A slight chill worked its way up her spine. However, the more she stared, the harder it was to see, and eventually she realised there was nothing there at all.

Chloe quickly reached her hand inside the room and felt for the light switch. The illumination was slow at first, but soon flickered to life.

There was nothing. No shape. No figure.

'What is it?' Andrew asked from behind her.

Chloe shook her head. 'Nothing,' she replied, deciding her mind was playing tricks.

Faces in the fire.

She switched the light off and pulled the door shut again. 'Come on, let's keep going.'

Her excitement returned. This place was going to be perfect for them. She just knew it.

CHAPTER 2

THE TASTE of the coffee was almost as delicious and comforting as the smell itself. It was a hazelnut roast, and the fragrance the drink cast off from the plastic carry-out cup was divine.

Sarah Pearson smacked her lips together after taking another long slug of the hot liquid. Chloe would no doubt turn her nose up at the taste, given the woman—for some crazy reason—detested hazelnut.

'Good?' the barista asked.

Sarah smiled and nodded. 'Better than good. It's perfect.'

She hadn't expected to find such a good coffee shop in a place like Alnmouth. Though, in truth, she had no idea what to expect, really. Sarah knew it was a small town, but that was about all she had found out before travelling. For some reason, she had expected it to be a little... backwater.

Instead of heading straight to Perron Manor—her new home, and a place she hadn't even seen yet—Sarah had wanted to make a quick stop in the local town first and pick up a few bottles of alcohol to celebrate moving-in day. After all, if she couldn't celebrate being given a Goddamn mansion, then when *could* she celebrate?

And the first thing Sarah had seen after parking her car in the quaint town centre was a shop named *Hill of Beans*. Evidently a coffee shop and cafe. It had a plate glass frontage that was surrounded by sleek black framing, and actually looked quite modern. The smell from the shop pulled her inside immediately, calling to her—especially since it had been over two hours since her last cup.

It was quite busy inside, but not bustling, and the atmosphere was nice and calm. The only sounds were that of the chattering patrons and the hissing of the coffee machines. Sarah had feared the worst from Alnmouth, but her first impression was a good one.

Sarah took another sip of her coffee. 'Is there anywhere around here I can grab a few bottles of wine?' she asked.

The barista was a young woman with dark hair, which was mostly hidden behind a black cap embossed with the shop's logo. The girl couldn't have been much older than twenty, but seemed so quick and efficient at her job that Sarah guessed she could have worked there for years. She was shorter than Sarah, who herself stood at five-foot-seven, but had similar blue eyes.

'Sure,' the barista said. 'A few places, really. There is a convenience store just across the road that will have a good selection. It's directly opposite this place. You can't miss it.'

'Cool,' Sarah replied, but immediately regretted saying it. Even though she was only thirty-seven, the word sounded forced coming out of her mouth.

That's a young person's word, Sarah, and you aren't young anymore. You've only old age to look forward to now.

It was a sobering thought, and one that had tended to plague her more and more as the years advanced.

The barista smiled, but it was almost condescending. *Oh, look at that old person trying to be hip. Bless her heart.*

Or maybe that was just Sarah being paranoid.

Sarah thanked the girl for her drink and left the shop, stepping outside into the crisp, clean air. Her shoulder-length dark and wavy hair blew across her face, forcing her to tuck it back behind her ears.

The centre of Alnmouth was quaint, and Sarah guessed it was the kind of town people moved to when retired, given the average age of the people seemed to be around fifty or so. The architecture was predominantly Victorian, with lots of terraces and mismatching facing materials: bricks, stone, and even some renders. A small church sat on a lush green field, surrounded on one side by neatly kept trees. The stores in the vicinity seemed a mix of local companies and more well-known commercial chains. Hell, behind the church, a few hundred yards away, Sarah could also make out a small lake with a stream running off from it. It was very picturesque.

Whatever preconceived notions Sarah had about this place, she realised she had been wrong. She wasn't against roughing it, given the career and life she had just left behind, but Alnmouth seemed rather more upmarket than Sarah had first feared.

As hard as it had been, leaving her old life was the right call. The thought of staying after what had happened to Tania was far worse than leaving the military behind.

Sarah wanted something different out of life now. Trouble was, she didn't know what that was.

The trip to the convenience store was a quick one, and she grabbed a few bottles of red for her and Chloe to share, as well as a bottle of whiskey for Andrew. There was also a section of child's toys, and she chose a stuffed bunny that looked cute. The animal wore an endearing, dopey grin, and held a bright orange carrot, which was stitched to its paws. She hoped Emma would like it.

Sarah had never considered herself very maternal, so perhaps this was as close as she was ever going to get. Being the cool aunt. She was okay with that.

The drive to her new home—something she could still scarcely get her head around—took about fifteen minutes, the road bringing her out of the centre of Alnmouth and to the outskirts. Here it was all fields and trees, and the only pocket of civilisation she could see was in the town centre in her rear-view mirror. A small, country lane led her up a hill, between more trees, and then, eventually, to Perron Manor itself.

It took her breath away a little.

This is the place I've inherited?

Sarah had previously done a little digging about the house, of course. She knew a bit of the history, and found a few photos online, but they didn't give much away. Chloe, who had been here once before already, had previously given Sarah a description, but it was nothing like seeing the place in person.

Sarah was still a distance away, but the road ahead was a straight one, flanked by hedges and trees, and she could see the open, wrought-iron entry gate set into a high stone boundary wall. Beyond that lay the house itself.

She could make out a little of the detail, such as the steps up to the front door and the angled canopy above that, which ran the full width of the front elevation. But at this distance it was the floors above that were more visible, given they stood proudly over the top of the wall.

The external walls were constructed from buff stone blocks, built up in a random pattern with no uniform mortar joints to speak of. The windows—four to the middle floor and three to the top—all had arched heads, and thin white frames. One of the most distinct features Sarah could see was the three peaks to the roof at the head of the building, the central one being the most prominent. They all cut into the normal eaves line of the building's main roof facade, which ran in a perpendicular direction.

Central to the building—and lining up with the middle peak—was a shallow outward step in the building's footprint, one that brought a sense of character to the symmetrical design.

And the house was *big*. Sarah had never in her wildest dreams thought she'd own a home of this size. It just wasn't in her future. She wasn't sure what the technical distinction of a mansion was, but if Perron Manor wasn't actually classified as one, then it had to have been close.

Sarah carefully navigated her vehicle through the open gate and entrance pillars, then onto the property's grounds. She had no idea as to the age of the house, or how many modifications had been made over time, but it didn't strike her as an aesthetic that was from any one particular era. At least, none that she could discern. Not that Sarah was an architect or anything, but she did have a passing interest in building design and history, given she had been seriously considering following a career in that field before joining the military instead.

Was it too late to rekindle that interest and push for a new kind of career?

You're thirty-seven. Of course it is.

Not exactly old, but not young enough that the world was her oyster anymore.

Now that she was within the confines of the grounds, Sarah could see more of the ground-floor canopy. Its angled roof was slate, and the central section of it came together to form a ridge, with a smaller peak mirroring the larger ones above. Two grand columns ran down either side of the entrance door, and the windows lined up with the ones on the floors above it, making the front elevation seem very ordered, and almost simplistic in design. Had it not been for the canopy, slight central outcropping, and the three ridges at the head, the building might have looked quite boring. As it was, it had just enough character to be interesting without being chaotic.

As she drove down the gravel driveway, Sarah noticed that the grounds around her were clearly uncared for, but impressive in their size, with garden areas as well as long stretches of lawn.

Up ahead, she saw a few transit vans near the house, where the gravel driveway opened out to a considerable parking area. Sarah also saw Chloe and Andrew's metallic-blue SUV. A much bigger car than her own, and Sarah was happy with what she had. Her Mini had less bulk, but with that came more pull and speed, especially given the sports engine.

Sarah's own possessions, the ones that weren't packed into the small car with her, would be coming the following day. But it was a fraction of the amount Chloe and Andrew had to unload. Being in the army, and away from home most of the time, meant that Sarah hadn't really built up much in the way of material possessions. She liked that. It was easier to pack up and move on if needed.

She pulled her car to a stop away from the cluster of other vehicles and got out, leaving her bags, cases, and boxes inside for the time being. She could unpack everything later, after she'd greeted her family. The only thing Sarah did grab was Emma's stuffed toy.

A bulky man with a flat cap, his face glistening with a sheen of sweat, flashed her a polite smile as he trudged his way over to the tall removal van and hopped in the back. Sarah walked up the stone steps that led up to the entrance door, taking it all in. The house towered above her, and looking up at it made her feel dizzy and somehow… unworthy.

A lot of the steps beneath her were cracked, which was yet another sign that Perron Manor had not had the required love and attention needed over the years. That then begged the question: would the three of them—she, Chloe, and Andrew—be able to maintain it any better than her uncle had?

Sure, three people could do more than one, but with a place like this it seemed a whole staff would be required to keep the house in good order.

Chloe had previously assured Sarah that it would be fine. Her specific words being, 'It does need a lot of work, I won't lie, but it's manageable. And it can't hurt to try. Worst comes to worst, we just sell it.'

Sarah had agreed with her sister. In truth, she was actually looking forward to diving into a project, as it was something she could focus on to occupy her mind. She hadn't seen the inside of the house yet, of course, and she knew it could be in an even worse state of disrepair than the outside. But it was something to work on together.

Even if it was only temporary.

Sarah knew that she couldn't live here with Chloe, Andrew, and Emma forever. They were a family, but eventually both she and they would need their own space.

For now, however, fresh out of the army and with no other calling in life, it happened to come about at the perfect time.

As she reached the top step, Sarah briefly thought about the man who had left all of this—the house, and a quite generous sum of money—to them. It had been a gift from an uncle she had never even met and never would.

Vincent Bell.

To say the whole situation was surreal was an understatement. But Sarah was, in a way, used to the surreal. Being dropped into the harsh landscape of Afghanistan, knowing each day could be her last, had certainly been surreal.

And scary.

So living here, even if there was hard work ahead, would in truth be a luxury.

From the porch area, Sarah peered inside of Perron Manor for the first time and took in the sight of its entrance area, seeing the staircase rise up and then split off both left and right from a half-landing.

Very grand.

She also noticed the double door—which was currently open—that was made from heavy-looking stained oak, with glass panels to the top sections of each door leaf. On one, Sarah saw a brass knocker: a frowning lion's head with a circular ring hanging from its mouth. It wasn't quite to her tastes—too old world—and something she would quite happily get rid of in the near future. Sarah took hold of the brass ring and lifted it. It was heavier than she had expected. There was a squeaking of metal, and Sarah let it fall. A sharp *clank* rang out as the ring struck the door's brass fitting.

Quirky.

Sarah then stepped inside, and the fresh air outside was immediately replaced with something heavier. A distinctly damp smell caught her off guard. She heard slapping footsteps approach from a corridor to her left. Then, her sister appeared through an open door. Chloe paused at first, then a huge smile broke out over her angular face.

She was taller than Sarah, more lithe—she always called herself bony—and was certainly beautiful. She was blessed with gorgeous, long dark hair and hazel eyes, though she always had the appearance of looking slightly tired, something Sarah had noted could be common amongst mothers. At the moment, Chloe was dressed in a purple t-shirt with a light grey cardigan over the top with her sleeves rolled up to the elbows, as well as tight-fitting jeans and flat, black shoes.

'Hey, Sis,' Sarah said, returning Chloe's smile. She then made a show of looking around their surroundings. 'Does this make us upper class now?'

Chloe laughed and shook her head. 'I don't think any amount of money could get us into high society.'

'Speak for yourself, commoner,' Sarah shot back. 'I could get used to the high life.'

Maintaining her smile, Chloe strode over and the two embraced in an affectionate hug. Sarah could smell Chloe's lavender shampoo, which was a scent that she always associated with her sister.

'It's going to be great here, Sarah,' Chloe said to her. 'I promise.'

CHAPTER 3

'Well, look what the cat dragged in,' a male voice called out.

She pulled away from her hug with Chloe to see Andrew enter the room. He was dressed in a simple light-blue t-shirt, jeans, and trainers, and Sarah could see developing sweat patches beneath his armpits. Given how fastidious Andrew was about his appearance, and how professional he always tried to present himself, the sweat was a clear sign he had been hard at work.

Andrew came towards her with a friendly smile and arms out for a hug. This was now their normal way of greeting—which Sarah had insisted upon, knowing it had initially made him uncomfortable. Now that he was more at ease with it, though, it had lost its appeal to her.

This time, however, she held up a hand, stopping Andrew in his tracks.

'We can hug after you shower,' she said, pointing to the patches beneath his arms. He frowned, confused at first, then looked down. 'What happened, Andrew?' she asked with a playful smirk. 'You always used to take such pride in your appearance.'

An embarrassed smile spread across his lips. 'Working hard getting things unpacked, I guess.'

Sarah laughed and pulled him in for the hug anyway. 'Sure, sure, sweaty boy.' She pulled free of him and turned to Chloe.

'So, where's Emma?' Sarah held up the stuffed rabbit and shook it.

'Oh that's adorable,' Chloe said. 'She's just down for a nap.' Chloe then took out a baby monitor from her pocket and showed it to her sister.

The image was a mix of black shadows in the distance and a blue hue that illuminated little Emma as she lay in a large cot-bed with side railing. It had been over half a year since Sarah had last seen her niece, and the child had been less than a year old then.

'Look at how big she is!' Sarah cooed. She had seen photos that Chloe had uploaded on social media, of course, but it still hit home just how long it had been since she had last seen and held Emma.

'She's been down for a while,' Andrew said. 'We could wake her if you want?'

'No,' Sarah said, shaking her head. 'There will be plenty of time to make a fuss of her. Let her wake up in her own time. I don't want to be the reason she's all grumpy.'

'Strange,' Andrew said, raising his eyebrows. '*You're* usually the reason the rest of us are grumpy.'

'Hilarious,' Sarah replied before sticking out her tongue and shooting him the finger.

'Do you have any stuff with you?' Chloe asked. 'Or is it all coming tomorrow?'

'I have a little of it with me. Not much, though.'

'Should we fetch it?'

'Later,' Sarah said. 'I want a quick tour of our new house first.'

'Sounds good,' Chloe agreed, wearing a big grin. 'Might wanna prepare yourself, though. This place is something else.'

'You got that right,' Andrew said. 'Wait till you see the basement.'

'We have a basement?'

'Yeah,' Andrew replied. 'A really creepy one. Used to be used as a prison, apparently.'

Sarah paused for a moment. 'No way.'

He nodded. 'The cells are still there.'

Sarah turned to Chloe for confirmation. Chloe rolled her eyes, though she nodded as well. 'He's making it sound worse than it is. There aren't any iron bars or anything. Only the old walls. It's just a cool little feature.'

'The furnace is down there too,' Andrew added. 'When it starts up it sounds like a bloody—'

'Enough, Andrew,' Chloe cut in with a polite yet stern smile.

But Andrew went on. 'Oh, and there is a whole section on the top floor that is completely locked off and we can't even access. Don't forget that.'

Chloe's expression turned to a scowl.

'Wait, really?' Sarah asked.

'We just haven't found the right key yet, is all,' Chloe told her. 'But we will. It'll be around here somewhere. If not, we just take the doors off the hinges. No big deal.'

'Alright, then,' Sarah said with a laugh. 'Anything else I should be aware of?'

'Mobile phone signal is spotty at best,' Andrew told her. 'So, until we get the internet sorted and installed, you're not gonna be very connected to the outside world. Oh, there's also the whole history of the house, of course.'

'Andrew, please!' Chloe shot back. It was clear to Sarah that Andrew wasn't as enamoured with the house as Chloe was.

'That's no problem,' Sarah said. 'I think I know as much as I need to about the house's history, anyway.'

'Fair enough,' Andrew answered, holding his hands up in defeat.

It was fair to say the house they now owned *did* have a checkered history—at least the small amount Sarah knew of it, which basically consisted of the events that took place in October of 1982. Chloe had been present for those events, though Sarah's older sister didn't remember anything of the chaos that took place back then. Sarah missed everything, of course, as she hadn't been born until the following July.

If it didn't bother Chloe, and she was excited about living here, then it sure as hell wasn't going to concern Sarah. All places had history. With her role in the army, Sarah herself had been to many countries that had violent and bloody recent pasts. That didn't mean they were inherently bad.

'Come on, then,' Chloe said, taking Sarah's hand. 'There's loads to see.'

Sarah was initially shown the ground floor as they first headed through a short corridor. The walls of the hallway were lined with cream wallpaper above wooden panelling, and patterned red carpeting lay over the floor. A dining room and a storage room were accessed off that corridor, which took a ninety-degree turn, and then led to a large, open area that caused Sarah to gasp.

'This is the great hall,' Chloe said, sweeping her arm grandiosely in an arc.

And 'great hall' wasn't a bad description of the area. While it wasn't the size of something out of Hogwarts, it was still impressive for a stately home. A long dining table with twelve seats was dwarfed by the free space around it. The walls in the room were covered with a deep green wallpaper lined with golden patterns. Hung on the walls were oil paintings and a large mirror with an ornate, gold frame. The ceiling above was plaster with intricate and detailed panelling, and solid white columns that ran from ceiling to floor added to the grand ambience of the hall. Lastly, stone-tiled flooring underfoot lent the space an almost medieval feel.

The only natural light that spilled in was from the large, glazed double-door that sat in the centre of the rear wall. It looked out into a courtyard space, which was in itself flanked by the two rear protruding wings of the house's rear, forming a rough 'U' shape. There were doors on either side of the rectangular great hall as well, and Chloe informed Sarah that the one to their left opened into the kitchen and the ones to their right accessed a toilet. There were also some steps that led down to the basement as well. The damp odour had lessened in this large area, yet it still smelled very musty.

'This is unreal,' Sarah said, unable to hide her smile. It was so far beyond what she was used to—either bunking down in barracks, or her old, rented flat—that it made her head swim.

Also accessed from the great hall were the two wings at the back of the property, and each consisted of two bedrooms off a short corridor. It was clear that, while still old, these wings were definitely newer than the main house.

The group of three then looped around, taking a different door off the great hall on their way back. They passed a living room and library before ending up again in the entrance lobby, accessing it from the opposite side from which they had left. They then took the stairs up to the middle floor, which consisted of a maze of corridors, bedrooms, storage rooms, and bathrooms. Chloe made sure to point out the rooms they had claimed for themselves and Emma.

'You'll have to pick your room as well,' Chloe told her. 'Sorry we jumped in and nabbed ours before you were here, but we needed to start putting stuff away.'

'It's fine,' Sarah said. 'I'm sure one of the many, *many* others will work for me.'

The top storey was accessed from a different set of stairs, and consisted mostly of bedrooms, though this time they were set into the roof space, so there were sloping ceilings, and windows cut into the main roof. The views this high up allowed Sarah to see for miles beyond the house's boundary walls. Sarah was then shown one of the two locked doors set in the looping corridor, both of which blocked off the same area.

This door, and the cross wall it was set into, did not match the quality of materials and construction workmanship elsewhere in the house. It looked strong, certainly, but it was plain, with only a basic wood veneer finish and nothing in the way of panelling or detailing. A brass handle and lock were the only distinguishing features.

'We have no idea what is beyond here,' Andrew said.

Chloe shrugged. 'Probably just more bedrooms, like everywhere else.'

'Then why lock it off?' he asked.

'I don't know,' Chloe admitted. 'We can find out when the key turns up. It's no big deal.'

'Can you remember if it was locked like this back when you lived here?' Sarah asked.

Chloe paused for a moment, clearly trying to remember. She shook her head. 'I don't know. That was a long time ago. To be honest, I don't remember a great deal of that time. Now it's just more feelings of nostalgia than anything actually specific.'

That made some sense to Sarah, as she herself couldn't remember a thing about being six years old.

'So the only thing left is the cellar, right?' Sarah asked. 'Definitely looking forward to seeing that.'

But then the baby monitor that Chloe was carrying crackled to life, and Emma's cries came through the speakers.

Chloe sighed. 'Doesn't look like I'll be joining you for this one.'

'That's okay,' Sarah said, 'I'd rather go see my niece anyway. The basement can wait.'

The trio then descended the stairs to the level below and entered the room that had been designated as Emma's, sitting right next to Chloe and Andrew's.

The inside of the room was very stately and traditional in appearance, with blue wallpaper on one feature wall. The others were painted an off-white, with cream carpet, decorative coving around the perimeter of the high ceiling, and a window that looked out over the front of the property. White cupboards, drawers, and a change unit had been placed against one of the walls, but there was little else in the way of furniture, other than the cot-bed Emma lay in. It made the room feel a little bare. And it seemed cold inside as well, with a distinct cabbage-like smell emanating from one corner in particular, next to the door. But almost as soon as Sarah had moved farther into the bedroom, the temperature seemed to return to normal, and the offending smell gave way to a more pleasant scent given off by an air freshener plugged in at the wall.

Sarah looked down at her niece, who was now standing up in her bed with her hands wrapped around the top bar of the side railing. Emma's hair was a dark, fuzzy, and untamed mop, and she had the same big brown eyes as her mother. The same pale complexion as well.

Emma gave Sarah a big, toothy grin.

'Oh my God, she has most of her teeth now!' Sarah exclaimed.

Chloe smiled. 'She does. It wasn't a whole lot of fun while she was getting them, though. Lot of sleepless nights.'

'I bet,' Sarah replied. Emma then balanced herself and held out her arms in Sarah's direction.

Chloe looked at Sarah expectantly. 'Well, aren't you going to pick her up? She seems eager to see you.'

'I'm surprised she remembers me. It's been a while,' Sarah replied.

'She'd never forget her cool aunt Sarah,' Chloe told her. Sarah reached down to scoop Emma up, giving the little girl a great big hug and nuzzling her cheek against her niece's hair.

'Oh I've missed you, baby girl,' Sarah said. Then, she detected another sharp odour that made her pull her head away.

'Someone needs changing!'

Chloe laughed. 'You up for that?'

But Sarah just shook her head and handed the child back. 'Cool aunty duties end with cuddles and snuggles, I'm afraid.'

Chloe shook her head and took Emma from Sarah before walking over to the change-table.

'I'll need to feed her next. Andrew, why don't you show Sarah the basement now?'

'I could,' Andrew replied, 'but think I should probably help the removal guys out a little more. We kinda just left them to it.'

'That's fine,' Sarah cut in, 'I need to get my stuff anyway. I'll check the creepy cellar out later.'

'Want a hand with any of your things?' Andrew asked.

Sarah shook her head. 'Thanks, but there's not much to get. I can handle it.'

'Might wanna claim a room first,' Chloe told her. 'And let us know which one you pick.'

'Given how badly Andrew snores, it'll probably be one over on the other side of the house,' Sarah responded. It was now Andrew's turn to shoot her the finger.

'Fair enough,' Chloe said, laughing. 'A lot of the rooms on this level have en-suites, and a private bathroom is always nice.'

'Noted,' Sarah said. 'I'll catch up with you three when I've gotten settled in.'

And with that, Sarah and Andrew turned and left, letting the door click shut behind her.

'Good luck finding anywhere nice,' Andrew whispered. 'All the rooms are pretty much the same. Old and cold.'

'Not thrilled to be here, I'm assuming?'

He shrugged. 'I'll give it a chance, like I promised.' And with that, he then strode off down the corridor before turning out of view.

Trouble in paradise, Sarah thought to herself. She then looked down the hallway to the many doors set into its walls.

'Now,' she said. 'Which one of you is going to be mine?'

CHAPTER 4

'Kid, you have more of this smeared across your face than you do in your belly.'

Chloe ran a wet-wipe around Emma's mouth, cleaning away the mashed strawberry that clung to the child's skin, making her look like a freaky infant-zombie that was mid-feast. Emma pulled away as her face was cleaned, cranky at being fussed over.

'Well you shouldn't make such a mess, then,' Chloe told her, smiling, as Emma continued to squirm in her high-chair and babble angrily.

Andrew walked into the kitchen, carrying a large and heavy-looking box with him. He dumped it on the counter and took a few deep breaths. Chloe's husband always kept himself in shape and had an athletic physique, but it was clear he was pushing himself hard to get as much done as possible today.

'Have a quick break,' Chloe said, feeling a little guilty. Taking care of Emma was the priority, of course, but she really wanted to throw herself into it and help out as well.

Andrew turned and leaned back against the kitchen countertop. 'Maybe a couple of minutes,' he said.

One of the removal men, Tony, entered the room shortly after. He was a stocky young man with a shaved head and goatee, and was carrying a box full of kitchen utensils.

Emma turned her eyes to him, then pointed. 'Man!' the infant said through a mouthful of food. Tony smiled.

'Don't mind her,' Andrew said with a chuckle. 'It's a phase. She does it with most men she isn't familiar with.'

'Yeah, every now and again she just blurts it out,' Chloe added.

'It's no problem,' Tony said, then raised the box up a little and gently shook it. 'Anywhere in particular I should put this?'

'Anywhere,' Andrew said, and Tony set the box down on a countertop and left the room, giving Emma a little wave as he did. Emma chuckled and waved back.

Chloe turned to Andrew and noticed his eyes wander around the kitchen, taking it all in. This was a change for him, she knew. He was used to modern ways of living: town centres, big flatscreen TV's, energy-efficient light fittings, and solar panels. That was what they had left behind. And he had agreed to that... for her.

The kitchen itself summed up just how different Perron Manor was to their old place, with block walls that were painted an ugly and sickly shade of yellow, high windows, rustic stone-slab flooring, and a kitchen table that was long and well worn. The table could well have been as old as the house. The cooker was huge and wrought iron, looking like it had been installed many years ago with the intention of feeding scores of people—which made sense, given the size of the property. But, apart from the horrible yellow that would have to be changed, the features were precisely what Chloe loved about the house. It just screamed history and character, something that could stand the test of time, as opposed to the generic, small boxes contractors were now throwing up and calling them houses.

But to make this work, compromises would need to be made. Andrew had done his part by moving here in the first place. It was many miles from where they used to live, so she couldn't accuse him of not trying. Thankfully, the move wouldn't interfere with his business, where he acted as a consultant in the construction industry, helping professionals and contractors acquire the health, safety, and sustainability qualifications they needed. He'd built his business from the ground up, and worked from home when he wasn't out visiting clients.

Given his clientele were dotted around all over the country, his base of operations didn't really matter.

Chloe knew that many of the features she liked in Perron Manor—such as some of the old, classical wallpaper, and the patterned carpets—would eventually need to give way to more modern decoration.

'You'll get used to it, you know,' Chloe told Andrew as he continued to look around.

He smiled. 'I know. It's just bigger and colder than I'm used to, you know? It feels empty. It'll just need an adjustment period.'

'Trust me, once Emma gets older, it might not feel big enough.'

'Maybe not if she has a little brother or sister.'

Chloe paused. 'Is that in the cards?'

Andrew shrugged. 'Maybe. I'm not getting any younger. So it's something I've started to think about.' He was smiling as he said it.

Chloe didn't know what to say. It was true they were both advancing in years, with him being forty-three, and her a year older at forty-four, but they were still young enough to add to the family if they acted quickly. The thought of it made Chloe happy.

But her heart quickly sank.

'Do you think we would get so lucky again?' Chloe asked.

They'd not spoken about trying again due to the problems they'd had conceiving Emma. The fact was, the couple hadn't expected her to come along at all, given the news they had received from the doctors many years ago.

You can keep trying, but given the low sperm count, the odds are against it happening naturally.

Andrew's smile faltered. 'Well, if we both want it, we could consider other options.'

'And you would be okay with that?'

Chloe remembered all too well the issues Andrew had had back when they found out children were unlikely for them. How his mood had darkened and enthusiasm for just about everything had waned. He blamed himself, and his pride had been dented. It took a couple of years before he seemed himself again. But he was never comfortable with any *outside help,* as he put it. A sperm donor was not an option for him, and the cost of IVF was prohibitive. Then, years after that, the miracle happened.

But the chances of that happening again, and quickly, were stacked against them.

'I don't know,' Andrew replied. 'Maybe. Just been thinking a lot recently that if we don't do it now, it'll never happen. I know it might not anyway, but if we don't even talk about it, then any chance we *do* have will just pass us by. And… I don't know if we would regret that.'

'Okay,' Chloe said, still searching for the appropriate words. The whole conversation had blindsided her. 'Well, we can talk about that.'

He walked over to her and placed a gentle kiss on her forehead.

'I'm going to try with this place,' he said to her. 'I know I complain a lot, but I will give it a proper shot. I promise.'

She looked up at him. 'Thank you.'

Both Chloe and then Andrew jumped as an electronic noise sounded from the table. She whipped her head around to see the baby monitor was active, and the noise they both heard coming from it sounded like a long, distorted exhalation.

'I thought I switched that off,' Chloe said, picking up the small, rectangular monitor. The image was the normal blue and black, and showed Emma's empty bed.

'Strange sound,' Andrew said. 'Interference or something?'

'Must have been,' Chloe agreed, still staring at the image. Nothing moved, so she eventually switched it off.

'Right, I'm going to get back to work,' Andrew said, and kissed her on the head again. 'I'll leave you with this little monster.'

'Thanks,' Chloe replied with a laugh. 'I'd be happy to swap with you, if you want?'

'Nah, I got this. Your job looks more stressful.'

Chloe looked to Emma again. Though her mouth was now clean, the meal of cut cucumber, strawberries, blueberries, a little cheese, and some ham had been half-devoured and half-smeared around the highchair's table, as well as up Emma's arms and across her bib.

'You got that right,' Chloe agreed as Andrew left the room. 'Come on, then, little monster, let's get you cleaned up.'

CHAPTER 5

Sarah's unpacking was complete, so she took a moment to lie down on the four-poster bed in her chosen room. The mattress was firm beneath her, which she liked, though she knew she was lying on a bed that was likely older than she was, and it had kicked up a small cloud of dust when she settled into it. God knows when the thing had last been used. The sheets and blankets would need replacing, at the very least.

The descending dust particles that fell onto Sarah didn't bother her, even though she knew there was likely dead skin mixed in with the particles. During her time in the army, she had been covered in far worse than just a smattering of dead skin.

She paused briefly and thought of Tania, then quickly shook it off. She didn't want to succumb to sadness, guilt, or nausea. Not now. Today was supposed to be positive.

Sarah was pleased with her choice of the room—number fourteen—figuring if things didn't work out with it she could easily enough switch to a different one. It wasn't like there was a shortage of spare rooms in the house.

And even though she had joked with Andrew about picking one well away from him due to his snoring, that was actually what happened, with her choosing one directly opposite and on the other side of the manor. If Sarah opened her door, she could see the other occupied rooms at the far end of the corridor.

And there wasn't much between the two rooms other than distance, either. Midway down the joining corridor was a window on one side that looked out over the rear courtyard, and opposite that was the stairway that led up to the floor above.

Sarah was initially going to pick either a front-facing or a rear-facing room, figuring the views would be better. However, she'd ultimately decided on one on the side of the house, picking one that had an en-suite and was one of the largest on offer.

She had seen a lot in the world, and taken in views that had stolen her breath, but living in luxury would be new to her. She wanted to try going all in to see how it fit.

One thing she hadn't chosen the room for, however, was the current decor, which would need to be changed as quickly as possible. That, however, was true of most rooms here.

The wallpaper, for one, was hideous. An overwhelming mix of patterned reds, yellows, and whites that was so jarring it made her feel dizzy. It might have been slightly more bearable if the timber floor had been left exposed, but instead it was covered with a rug that had a similar pattern to the wallpaper, only a deeper shade of red. The whole decor just felt rather oppressive.

But that would only give her the impetus and drive to get it refurbished to her liking in short order. And, in truth, it didn't need a whole lot: throw out the bedsheets and rug, strip off the wallpaper, a new lick of paint to the walls... and that was pretty much it.

One thing she did like, though, was the fireplace. It was very ornate, with an oak mantelpiece. Most rooms in the building seemed to have a fireplace set in them, which was evidence of how the house used to be heated before the black, cast-iron radiators had been fitted.

The other thing Sarah liked was the furniture that had been left. On the opposing side of the room to her bed was an oak display unit, which was the height of a wardrobe and had glass set into its doors. Inside, Sarah could see shelves that held ornaments and old pictures of people she didn't recognise. The pictures were creepy, to be sure, but the oak unit itself was very nice, with intricate carvings cut into the frame. In the glass, she could see her own faint reflection from her position on the bed.

There was also a small dressing table in the room, which seemed to have been crafted with as much care as the display unit, and a set of drawers and two large wardrobes. Sarah figured the furniture alone could have been worth quite a bit of money. Though, given the inheritance she had just received, plus what she had saved from being in the army, she was in the fortunate position of not having to worry too much about her finances. At least not yet. However, Sarah knew she couldn't just loaf around for the rest of her life.

The problem was, she didn't know what direction to take beyond this adventure at Perron Manor. But, she reasoned, at least she had time to figure all that out.

She took a deep breath and was about to heave herself from the bed, when three quick and hard knocks on the door startled her.

'Hello?' she said, snapping her head over to the door.

There was no response.

'Chloe? Andrew?' she called, but again got nothing back.

Sarah sighed, got to her feet, and walked over. However, when she opened the door an empty hallway was all that greeted her. She poked her head out farther, then looked left and right. Nothing.

'What the hell?'

She was baffled. The noise sounded like someone had rapped on the door, but there was clearly no one around to have done so.

'Weird.'

Sarah shook her head, knowing there were likely going to be lots of strange noises and quirks to get used to in a building as old as this one. Since her unpacking was done for the moment, it was time to rejoin the others and help out if needed. Or, preferably, indulge in a cup of coffee. She grabbed a packet of hazelnut beans from her bag and headed downstairs.

CHAPTER 6

'Can't believe you drink that,' Chloe said, making a face. 'Even the smell is revolting.'

'You're such a weirdo,' Sarah shot back. She then took another sip of her drink. 'It's divine.'

Chloe felt like she might vomit. The thought of that flavour was awful enough. But Sarah seemed to be enjoying it, taking yet another gulp and smacking her lips in satisfaction.

Chloe was pleased to see that her sister seemed happy and healthy, and Sarah's most recent deployment had left her with a healthy tan. For the most part, the Pearson family—Chloe *definitely* included—were generally pretty pale in complexion, but Sarah didn't seem to suffer from the same affliction, and years on deployment in sunnier climates had only helped in that regard. It was something Chloe envied her sister for.

'You have odd taste, Sis,' Chloe told her.

She then saw Sarah look back over to her with a cocked eyebrow, before she gestured towards Andrew with a nod. 'You're one to talk,' Sarah said.

'Thanks,' Andrew added sarcastically. 'I always could count on you to raise my spirits.'

Chloe set the snacks she had prepared down on the kitchen table, which was one they had brought with them. Though the actual dining room and great hall both had existing tables, gathering in the kitchen had always been something of a tradition with Chloe and Andrew.

It had been a whirlwind of a day, but their work was now done. The removal men had finally left, and as much unpacking was finished as was going to be. Chloe didn't want to push things too quickly. There was still plenty of work ahead, but no reason not to pace things out sensibly.

The family were all seated around the table, with Emma in her highchair again, and they picked at the assortment of nuts, crisps, and dip that Chloe had laid out.

'Just something to keep us going,' she said. 'We should order take-out later. Put Emma down for the night then have a nice big feast to celebrate.'

'And wine,' Sarah added. 'I brought alcohol, so we can *really* celebrate.'

Chloe chuckled. 'One or two glasses couldn't hurt.'

'And I even brought whiskey for the unrefined neanderthal over there.'

Andrew grinned and raised his cup of tea in a gesture of thanks.

There were a few moments of silence between the three of them, and Chloe sensed the other two were reflecting in their own way. She could definitely see Sarah's mind ticking over about something.

'Okay,' Sarah began, 'I know we've talked about it before, but... you really have no idea why this Uncle Vincent left us the house? I mean, he never even met me, and hadn't seen you since you were, what, six?'

Chloe shrugged. 'No idea at all. The only thing I can think is that we are his only surviving relatives, so if he had no one close to him, who else would it have gone to?'

'I guess,' Sarah replied. 'Did you know much about him?'

Chloe shook her head. 'Nope. Like I said, don't remember too much from back then. And Mum and Dad didn't really speak about him.'

'That's true,' Sarah said. 'All they said was that he was an odd man who liked to keep to himself. Did you ever speak to Mum and Dad about Perron Manor?'

'No. I tried to when I was in my teens and I found out what happened here in '82. Crazy to think it all happened while I lived here.'

Andrew cut in. 'How many people died that night?'

'I don't know exactly,' Chloe admitted.

'Wasn't that the night the house got its nickname?' Sarah asked. Then, as if as an afterthought, she said, 'Devil's House.'

Chloe nodded. 'It was. A newspaper ran a story about what happened and named it that. And it just stuck, apparently, even though it was a hotel at the time, not a house.'

Sarah let out a disbelieving laugh. 'I still can't get over the fact we live in a place called Devil's House. It's crazy.'

'Tell me about it,' Chloe agreed. 'Whenever I brought it up with Mum or Dad, they always evaded the subject as best they could. Said something terrible happened, but not to worry about it. Not my problem. Dad once told me that, 'Bad things happen, but sometimes it's best to leave things in the past.' And I never got much more out of them.'

'I remember him saying that,' Sarah chimed in. 'He told me the same when I started asking about it. Must have been his go-to response.'

'And your parents had no idea you two were in Vincent's will?' Andrew asked.

'It would appear not,' Chloe answered.

Andrew crossed his arms over his chest and leaned back in his chair. 'You know the locals are going to think we're weird as hell for living here, given what happened.'

'Let them think that,' Chloe replied with a shrug. 'Besides, no one really knows *what* exactly happened. Yes, a lot of guests died—'

Andrew cut her off. 'They didn't just 'die' from what I read, Chloe. It was almost like they were… butchered.'

'Fine, whatever. The owner back then was a crank, anyway, obsessed with the occult. The most likely theory is that it was some kind of ritualistic thing, and everyone who attended was in some kind of cult. It was horrible, of course, but sometimes shit like that happens.'

'It happened while you were there, Chloe,' Andrew went on. 'I don't mean to belabour the point, but are you sure you're okay living here knowing that?'

'How many times do I have to repeat myself?! Yes, I'm fine with it!'

Chloe snapped, feeling exasperated by the turn the conversation had taken.

It was one she'd already had with Andrew, so it had been adequately covered in her mind. There shouldn't have been a need to go over it again.

But, apparently, that wasn't the case.

'Look, I don't remember a thing,' she went on. 'I was asleep the whole time, and Dad carried me out of the house. I didn't wake up until I was outside with him, Mum, and Vincent, I think. Then we left. I didn't see anything bad happen, and didn't find out about it all until years later, because they had kept it hidden from Sarah and me. It doesn't matter. Sure, I'd prefer it if this place didn't have baggage, but does that really affect anything? We've gotten a *huge* house for nothing. Something we could never have dreamed of affording has literally been dropped into our laps, along with a nice little chunk of money.' Chloe noticed Andrew's face turn into a scowl at the mention of the money, but she went on, 'It would be stupid to turn it all away.'

'I know,' Andrew said, crossing his arms over his chest.

'So why keep going over old ground? Nothing is going to change what happened or how I feel.'

'I...' Andrew paused, then sighed. 'Fine. I'm sorry.'

Silence resumed. Chloe knew it was awkward, especially with Sarah here, but she was starting to get frustrated with her husband, as he just wouldn't let anything go, even after agreeing to move here.

And yet, only a few hours ago, he'd promised he was going to make a go of it. Even spoke of having another child.

As if sensing the atmosphere in the air, Emma began to squirm in her seat and held her hands up to Chloe.

'Out,' she said.

Chloe lifted her daughter out of the highchair and set her down, letting Emma toddle around the floor.

'So... this is fun,' Sarah said, draining her coffee. 'If you two could try not being at each other's throats for the rest of the day, that would be great.'

Chloe looked at Andrew, waiting to see his response to this.

He looked back at her. 'I already said I'm sorry.'

'Fine,' Chloe eventually replied, knowing it wasn't really fine, and the issue was not settled. But it could wait.

'Worst make up ever, but okay,' Sarah added. 'So, which room was Uncle Vincent's anyway?'

'Room 6,' Chloe said. 'Same floor as ours, but towards the back, in one of the rear wings.'

'You been in there much?'

'Once. Poked my head in to have a look. It's small. Not sure why he settled on that one, especially if he lived here alone. But there you go.'

'Does he have much stuff to get rid of?'

'Not sure. Didn't look to be a lot, since the room was really basic, but I guess we'll have to clear out his wardrobes and the like. Why do you ask?'

'Just curious about the man that used to live here. I think we should go check out his room a little more.'

'Now?' Chloe asked, raising an eyebrow.

'Why not? You at least met him, but I don't even know what he looked like.' Sarah then got to her feet.

'Why don't we do it tomorrow?' Chloe asked.

'Because I want to make a start on my room tomorrow. And there will be loads to do. We don't have anything pressing right now.'

'I have an engineer coming out tomorrow as well,' Andrew added. 'He's going to look at that furnace downstairs. See if we can't get it working a bit better.'

'See,' Sarah said, gesturing toward him. 'Andrew has an engineer coming out. That could take all day… wait.' She turned to him. 'Tell me we still have heating. The furnace *does* still work, right? I mean, I imagine this place gets pretty cold at night.'

'Oh the heating works,' Andrew said. 'We tested it before you got here. It's just… well, I'll put it on later and let you hear for yourself.'

'Sounds ominous,' Sarah said, then turned back to Chloe. 'So, why not now? Not like we have anything else to do.'

'Fine,' Chloe said. 'I'll run Emma's bath while we're up there, then put her down for the night.'

'Awesome,' Sarah said, clapping her hands together. 'But, if we find any hidden gold or jewellery, I have dibs.'

Chloe laughed. 'You'll have to fight me for it.'

CHAPTER 7

'THIS IS... FUNKY,' Sarah stated.

Vincent's room, just as Chloe had said, did not have much in it at all. There was a single metal-framed bed, with a thin, red quilt, a set of drawers sat opposite the bed, a window on the side wall, and a full-height black cupboard.

And that was it.

There weren't even any pictures on the walls. The dirty-white wallpaper was peeling, and the hardwood floor was stained and a little sticky underfoot.

'Told you there wasn't much here,' Chloe said. 'He seemed to keep it pretty basic.'

'And didn't bother cleaning,' Andrew added.

Given the size of many of the other bedrooms in Perron Manor, it was indeed odd that Vincent had chosen one of the smaller rooms to sleep in. With the three of them all inside, plus Emma in Chloe's arms, the space felt extremely cramped.

Sarah began looking through the drawers, working from the top down.

'Anything of interest?' Andrew asked.

'Just a few clothes. I was hoping he'd have a picture or something. I wanted to see what he looked like.'

'Doesn't this feel like snooping?' Chloe asked as Sarah moved over to the wardrobe. 'A bit disrespectful?'

'Of course not, we need to sort through all this stuff anyway, so we aren't seeing anything we wouldn't see eventually.'

Sarah then pulled open the doors on the black-painted wardrobe, and inside she saw a few hanging clothes: a frayed jacket, some shirts, and three pairs of trousers. Above the clothes was a high shelf, which contained a few small boxes. However, it was what was on the back of the wardrobe that drew Sarah's attention.

Scratches.

She slid the hanging clothes out of the way to get a better view, and Chloe and Andrew crowded round as well to look inside. 'Did an animal do that?' Chloe asked. Sarah wasn't certain, but doubted it.

Frantic claw marks had been cut into the back face of the wardrobe, mainly around the centre of the panel, though many pulled down closer to the ground. The natural, creamy colour of the timber showed through where the paint had been scraped away. While an animal could indeed have done that, Sarah was quick to spot something that made her think otherwise.

She didn't want to touch it, so instead pointed at the remnant of a fingernail stuck in one of the gouges.

'Oh that's disgusting,' Chloe said, backing up.

While in the army, Sarah had been shot in the arm, which had certainly hurt. A *lot*. However, potentially getting shot again, while unwelcome, never really unnerved her too much, nor did it get under her skin. But the thought of a nail being torn out, exposing the raw nerve endings beneath made her shudder.

'Creepy,' she said. 'What the hell got into him to claw at this like a dog?'

'No idea,' Andrew answered. 'Maybe he was mentally ill.'

'It doesn't matter,' Chloe added. 'We'll throw that wardrobe out. Chuck away everything in here. Decorate the room and make it nice. It'll be like… that,' she gestured to the markings, 'never happened.'

'Fine,' Sarah said, 'It's just strange, is all.'

'Well, like Andrew said, he could have been ill. We don't know what happened here, so let's just ignore it.'

Sarah caught Andrew's attention, and raised an eyebrow. Andrew, in return, rolled his eyes.

'We'll ignore it, then,' Sarah said, before looking up to the shelf above. The boxes on it were covered with dust, and she pulled out the first one she could reach—which was a box not much bigger than the palm of her hand. She opened it.

'It's a key,' Sarah said, retrieving the metal object and holding it up for the others to see. It was long, and made of black iron, with decorative spirals at the head.

Chloe looked at it, then shrugged. 'So what?'

'Well, if it's a key, then surely it…' She trailed off as something clicked, suddenly making sense to her.

She knew of a lock that could be a perfect match. With a grin, Sarah said, 'I think we have a way to see what's been locked away upstairs.'

CHAPTER 8

'Let's just check it out tomorrow,' Chloe said. 'I need to bathe Emma, and it's getting late.'

But Sarah shook her head. 'No way. I can't wait on this until tomorrow. It's too exciting!'

'How is it exciting?' Chloe asked. For her, the whole thing was annoying and an inconvenience—especially what they had found in Vincent's room. But to Sarah, it seemed like some kind of childish adventure.

'Oh lighten up, Sis,' she replied. 'Aren't you even the tiniest bit intrigued?'

Perhaps part of Chloe was, in truth, but mostly she was worried about what might be uncovered up there. She knew Andrew's hesitation with the house would only grow every time an unexpected issue was thrown up. They'd already had to deal with things like the furnace, the hideous decor, the poor mobile phone reception, and those scratches at the back of Vincent's wardrobe. All things Andrew could no doubt use as an excuse if he ultimately decided this place wasn't for him. Chloe didn't want anything else added to that list.

'I'm too busy to be intrigued,' Chloe eventually replied. 'I have Emma to take care of.'

It was just an excuse, of course. Emma could wait a few more minutes—it wasn't particularly late for the child—but she *really* didn't want to go up there.

'Then I'll go up on my own.'

'I'll go as well,' Andrew added.

Chloe sighed. The two of them going without her was an even worse prospect.

'Fine,' she said. 'But let's make it quick.'

They all made their way up to the top floor. Sarah first, then Chloe with Emma, and Andrew bringing up the rear. The area was decorated similarly to the floor below, and directly to their left after coming up the stairs was the first locked door, which barred entry to the corridor beyond. If they had turned right at the top, they could have followed the hallway round in a loop, and would eventually reach the other locked door to the sectioned-off area.

Chloe watched as Sarah slotted the key into the lock before her. It fit perfectly. Sarah beamed and turned the key and heard the faint clunk of sliding metal. With a turn of the handle, the door drifted open.

'Ta-da!' Sarah exclaimed.

The way ahead was dark, the only illumination coming from the artificial light that spilled in from the hallway they were currently in.

The now-opened door revealed another corridor beyond, or rather a continuation of the one they were in. Sarah tried a nearby switch, but it was clear that the light fixtures here were not working. And with no external windows, the way ahead would be tricky.

In response to the problem, Sarah quickly flicked on her phone's flashlight feature. The newly opened area was a lot more ominous than the other hallways of the house. Though decorated in a similar fashion, the wallpaper here peeled heavily, and a thick layer of dust lined the bare, untreated timber floor. There were cobwebs aplenty, and Chloe knew there would be scores of scuttling spiders running loose up here. She smirked. Arachnids had never bothered her, but she could already sense Andrew tensing up.

Yet again, Sarah led the way, and they moved into the dark hallway with the torch from her phone lighting their path. Up ahead, the corridor branched off both left and right. To the left, they could see the other locked door that would take them back out into the main area. There was also another door close to it that, if it repeated the layout of the floor below, would give access to a bathroom. To the right were two doors, both of which looked like bedroom doors, but neither had numbers on them.

'Shall we?' Sarah asked. Chloe rolled her eyes and hugged Emma a little tighter, as it was noticeably colder here than elsewhere in the house. Sarah didn't wait for an answer, and pushed open the nearest door, one that looked like it led to a bedroom. She cast her light around the room, allowing the beam to highlight the area.

'Are you fucking kidding me?!' Chloe asked through gritted teeth, momentarily forgetting her rule about not cursing in front of Emma.

'Oh my God!' Sarah exclaimed as well, but there was a hint of humour in her voice. She clearly found this more than a little funny. 'This is wild.'

Though it was difficult to take in the full details of the room, Chloe could still make out its purpose.

It was a study, of sorts. And a spacious one.

As Sarah's light moved steadily around the area, Chloe saw that it was actually two rooms converted into one. She also realised, given their location on the right-hand side of the building, that they were directly above the bedroom Sarah had chosen.

While joining two rooms together and having a space used as a study was far from odd or noteworthy, it was the *contents* of the room that caused Chloe to bristle.

Firstly, there was the thing on the floor, which Sarah's light had illuminated first. A faint symbol, drawn in something white—possibly chalk—on the timber floorboards. That was the reason for Chloe's initial outburst.

An honest-to-God fucking pentagram.

Old candles stood at each of the symbol's five points, rising up from puddles of hardened wax. And smeared across the marking was a dark stain that had discoloured an area of the flooring.

But there was more to the room beyond the pentagram: display cabinets, bookshelves, chests, and desks all filled the space. Each was a dark oak, matching the panelling on the lower section of walls.

The bookshelves were packed with old-looking leather-bound tomes, and even glass jars filled with small animal bones. And the display cabinets had within them all kind of strange artefacts and parchments, and even some daggers. With the pentagram linking all of these items and artefacts together, it didn't take a genius to work out the occult theme that ran through the room.

Chloe heard the click of a light switch, and she turned to see Andrew trying the brass fitting on the wall next to the door. However, like those in the corridor outside, the lights in the room refused to work, with the bulbs obviously having long since given up.

Sarah began inspecting some of the books that filled a shelf, and Chloe again felt the cold. Emma began to shift in her grip, and let out a discontented whine. The child then shook her head and snapped, 'No!'

Emma clearly didn't like it up here.

That makes two of us, kid.

'Can we go?' Chloe asked. 'It's cold in here and creepy as hell.'

'It's amazing,' Sarah argued, like she was a kid looking around a toyshop. She moved over to a prominently positioned, waist-high display cabinet with a glass top. Even from her position on the other side of the room, Chloe could make out a single book, set against a plush red and cushioned interior. The cracked leather of the book's cover looked extremely old—even ancient—and it bore a title that was etched in faded gold. However, the words made no sense to her.

Was that Latin?

There was no author name that Chloe could see, but in each corner of the cover were odd-looking markings.

'How old do you think this is?' Sarah asked in something approaching wonder.

Andrew walked over and gazed through the glass. 'God knows.'

Emma's frustration grew, and she began to cry.

'Right!' Chloe snapped, having seen enough. She then grabbed Andrew by the arm and pulled him towards the door. 'Enough of this. Emma needs her bath.' She turned to Sarah. 'You finished here? How about you come and spend some time with your niece.' Chloe's tone was firm and annoyed.

Sarah's eyes widened a little in surprise. 'Calm down, Chloe. I was just looking around, for God's sake. And don't try and guilt me with my niece. I swear, you're such a control freak.' Sarah then shook her head and stomped past Chloe, walking out into the corridor.

Chloe immediately felt bad, and knew that Sarah had a point.

But then, Chloe had a point too. It *was* cold and dusty up here, and not a good place for Emma to be in for too long.

Chloe locked the room up, and then did the same to the door in the corridor, closing off the whole area again. Then, they all proceeded downstairs without saying another word.

The little spat between Chloe and Sarah would need nipping in the bud. Given things between her and Andrew seemed to be a tad up and down at the minute, Chloe didn't want things to be frosty with her sister as well—especially not when it was supposed to be an exciting time for them all.

Chloe got the chance to put things right not even a half-hour later. Emma was splashing happily in the bath when Sarah came into the room. As she entered, Chloe flashed her a small, apologetic smile.

'Sorry,' she said.

Sarah just rolled her eyes. 'If this is gonna work, Sis,' she began, 'then you are going to have to loosen the reins a bit. You know that, right?' She then moved over to them, kneeling down next to Chloe to watch Emma in the bath, who was laughing as she dunked a plastic duck under the water.

'I know,' Chloe admitted. 'It's just, well, I really want things to work here. Andrew is on the fence about it, at best, and I don't think it'll take much to push him the wrong way. That room we found upstairs... well, let's just say that isn't going to help matters.'

'Really? I think it's cool as hell,' Sarah said. After a slight pause, she then went on to ask, 'So, what is it he doesn't like about the house? The history? Or that it's old?'

'A bit of both, maybe,' Chloe said. 'But I don't think either of those is the main issue.'

'Then what is?'

She paused, but then went on. 'It's that *he* didn't provide the house for us.'

Sarah cocked an eyebrow. 'What do you mean?'

Chloe just shook her head quickly. 'Nothing. I shouldn't have said anything. But, if we get this place just how we like it, he might come round. I know we could be really happy here.'

'Can I ask...' Sarah went on. 'What makes you so sure? I mean, don't get me wrong, it *is* an amazing place, but it's also kind of a novelty. Do you actually think it'll make a good family home?'

'Of course I do,' Chloe replied, turning to her sister. 'Why wouldn't it?'

'Oh, it *could*. But isn't it a little... big, for just us?'

'Not really. I think you get used to the space around you. It will be odd at first, but it'll soon become normal.'

'Fair enough,' Sarah replied. 'So what is the draw for you? Just that it's big and not the norm?'

'Not really. I think this place made an impression on me when I was little. I don't remember too much, but I do know that I was happy while I was here. It always felt so rich with history. Beyond the obvious, anyway. I think houses like this just have more charm and character.'

'Oh yeah,' Sarah said with a grin. 'I remember that old Victorian dollhouse you used to have. You loved it.'

'Exactly,' Chloe replied. 'I never thought I'd actually get to live in a place like that, and then one just fell into our laps. Plus, imagine all we could do with it!'

'How do you mean?'

'Well, Emma isn't going to need this much attention forever, so in the future we could... I dunno... turn it into a guest house or hotel or something. It would give me a project to focus on, I guess.'

'Running a hotel? Really? Given what happened here last time—'

'Don't,' Chloe said sternly.

Sarah laughed and held up her hands in defence. 'Fair enough. But running a hotel... really?'

Chloe shrugged. 'It could be nice. I mean, I love being a mother, I do, and I wouldn't swap it for anything. And I also don't regret leaving the corporate world behind. But sometimes, with Emma, it's sort of... all-encompassing, you know? It's like, this is your role and your life, you're a wife and a mother... and sometimes I feel like that other part of myself, the one with the ambition, kind of gets drowned out. I suppose that's why I'm so eager to get started fixing up this place. It gives me something else to focus on except being a mum.'

'I get that,' Sarah said after a brief moment of thought.

'Really?' Chloe asked, then looked at Sarah a little sheepishly. 'It doesn't sound like I'm being a little selfish?'

'Fuck no! It doesn't make you a bad mother just because you want to focus on yourself from time to time.'

Chloe smiled, feeling a little relieved. 'Thanks.'

Logically, she knew there wasn't anything to feel guilty about in the first place, but that didn't stop her feeling that way sometimes, or questioning herself endlessly.

'So... I take it there are no plans to give this little one a sibling?' Sarah asked as she looked down at Emma, who continued to splash the duck around in the water. 'Cos that could derail your plan of a guest house pretty quickly. I mean, I know you two struggled with Emma, but you never know... wait, why are you smiling?' Sarah frowned in confusion.

Chloe chuckled. 'It's just... Andrew actually mentioned that earlier today.'

'Really?'

'Yeah.'

'Bloody hell. So, are you guys gonna try?'

Chloe shrugged. 'Not sure, we didn't go into much detail.'

'Well, that would *definitely* put the whole hotel thing on ice.'

'It would,' Chloe agreed. 'But who knows what's gonna happen. Nothing is decided or anything. Plus, you know, even if we wanted to, it might not happen. But that's all for the future, I guess. All right, time to get this little one dried, fed, then put to bed.'

'And then we get drunk!' Sarah announced, holding her arms up in celebration. Emma looked up at the sudden movement and giggled.

'*You* can get as drunk as you want,' Chloe said. 'I'll just have a couple of glasses of wine.'

Sarah stood to her feet. 'Aw come on, Sis, cut loose. You only live once.'

'Maybe three glasses, then.'

'Wow,' Sarah said, completely deadpan. 'Wild.'

Chloe gave her sister a playful bat on the leg, then lifted Emma out the bath, quickly carrying her over to the change-table and laying her on the already placed towel. She wrapped the infant up in a bundle to keep her warm, then began drying her off. Once Emma was changed, Sarah left the room, and Chloe carried Emma to the child's bedroom. As Chloe entered, a sudden surge of cold ran through her, and she made a mental note to check the furnace in the basement. It was an old heating system, but the only one they had. Why Vincent had never had it replaced was beyond her.

However, almost as soon as she had felt the chill, and after taking a few more steps inside, Chloe's body temperature quickly normalised. Which, she guessed, was one of the problems with living in an old house: lots of air leakage and cold spots.

Chloe then walked over to the rocking chair they had set up in the corner of the room closest to the window, took a seat, and began to feed Emma. The child's eyes grew drowsy as she suckled. And it was just as the little girl slowed her feeding, and was about to fall asleep, that a sudden and awful odour assaulted Chloe's senses. Something... rotten. Once again, a cold draft drifted down onto the back of her neck, causing the hairs there to stand on end.

Chloe quickly stood up, holding Emma carefully, and turned to look over her shoulder, but could see no reason for the draft. The seat was close to the window, but not so close as to allow a breeze that strong to reach her, unless it had been open. And besides, the closed curtains weren't moving or blowing either, indicating no draft was coming through. Also, the feeling of cold had seemed to emanate directly behind the chair she had sat in, right in the room's corner.

She felt Emma's little body slacken in her grip, and Chloe looked down to see her daughter start to gently snore. Chloe then lifted her head back up and realised that smell had disappeared, as had the feeling of cold.

Suppose I gotta get used to that, she told herself. The scope of the work ahead started to seem a little daunting.

Chloe then set Emma down in her cot-bed, checked the baby camera was still in position on top of the wardrobe, and then picked up the accompanying portable monitor. She whispered good night to her daughter, then left the room, turning off the light as she did.

Sarah's previous idea of getting drunk was starting to sound a bit more appealing.

CHAPTER 9

AFTER CLEARING AWAY the last of the plates and throwing out the rubbish, Sarah poured herself a hearty measure of wine.

The meal, while not mind-blowing, had certainly been good. Enough to fill the emptiness in their stomachs, at any rate. Once they had decided on Indian food, the actual ordering process had been a chore, given the lack of consistent phone signal in the house. Sarah was forced to go outside to order.

But, it had all worked out in the end.

Sarah, Chloe, and Andrew all sat around the kitchen table, enjoying a well-earned drink, with Sarah and Chloe on the red wine and Andrew indulging in a glass of the whiskey Sarah had bought him.

After taking her first sip, Sarah was pleased to discover the brand she had chosen was delicious, with a smooth taste, long finish, and slightly peppery undertones. She was far from a wine connoisseur, but had drunk enough in her time to know the good from the bad.

And this one was definitely good. Chloe appeared to agree as well, letting out a long moan of satisfaction after her first mouthful.

'So, you all set with your room, Sarah?' Chloe asked. 'I mean, as much as you can be?'

'Yeah, I guess,' Sarah replied. 'I swapped out the sheets with some I brought with me. But, other than that, and packing away some clothes, there isn't much more I can do just yet. Are you guys all set?'

Chloe nodded. 'Enough for tonight, anyway. But plenty to get through tomorrow.'

'Let tomorrow wait,' Sarah said. 'Tonight, we drink!' She didn't want the fun to be derailed by any worries of the future. And, on that note, she raised her glass. 'A toast, to Perron Manor—our new home. It may be weird as hell, but shit... what an opportunity.'

Chloe raised her glass as well, and was reluctantly followed by Andrew. 'Here, here,' Chloe said. She then twisted the baby-monitor around to glance at Emma.

'She okay?' Sarah asked.

'Fine. Sleeping like a... well, you know.'

Andrew took a sip of his amber-coloured drink, then looked up to Sarah. 'So, you've left the army for good now?'

Sarah nodded. 'Yup. All done. No more tours.'

'Aren't you going to miss it?' he asked. Sarah knew he wasn't prying, or being insensitive as to what happened. He was genuinely curious.

'Oh yeah, of course I'll miss it,' Sarah told him. 'But it was the right time.'

'We were really sorry to hear about Tania,' Chloe added.

It was a nice sentiment, and it came from the right place, especially since Chloe and Andrew hadn't seen her since it all happened. However, Sarah still felt her body tense up at the mention of her best friend. Thinking about what happened in Afghanistan wasn't what Sarah needed at the moment. She just wanted to forget.

'Thanks,' Sarah eventually said, more dismissively than she had intended. 'But I'm okay.'

Chloe gave a sad smile and nodded before changing the subject completely.

'So, what time is that engineer coming tomorrow to look at the furnace?'

'Sometime in the morning,' Andrew replied. 'Don't have an exact time. Hopefully he can at least figure out what's wrong with it. I'll see if he can quote for a completely new system as well, strip that old thing out.'

'What was the deal with the furnace, anyway?' Sarah asked, recalling the earlier conversation about it.

Andrew laughed. 'It screams when you start it up.'

Sarah paused. 'It fucking *what*?' She looked to Chloe, fully expecting it to be a joke, but Chloe gave an embarrassed nod.

'Well,' she added, 'it doesn't *actually* scream, but when you light it up and the steam starts running up through the pipes, it does sound a little like it.'

'A screaming furnace? For real?'

Andrew nodded and got to his feet. 'I need to go down and have a look at it now, actually, since it's starting to get cold in here. The bloody thing might have gone out again. Come with me, if you want. I'll show you.'

'You don't have to—' Chloe began.

'Fuck yeah,' Sarah said, cutting her off and quickly standing up. 'This I gotta see.'

'Why doesn't that surprise me?' Chloe asked. 'Well, I've seen it, so I'll let you two run along. I'm warning you though, Sarah, if you don't hurry back, I'm finishing this wine on my own.'

Sarah laughed. 'Fair enough. We'll be back before you know it.'

CHAPTER 10

'Jesus, this place is creepy,' Sarah said, looking around.

The basement was partially illuminated by dirty-yellow lighting from fittings in the ceiling above, but there were deep pockets of shadows where the light could not reach.

They'd had to use light from their phones to guide themselves down, as the light switch was, frustratingly, at the bottom of the steps.

The floor around them consisted of old and uneven stone slabs, and the walls were bare stonework with some areas of water leakage. Sarah guessed the size of the basement was probably half the area of the storey above.

To her right, Sarah could see internal stone walls which formed a line of small rooms, each no bigger than a tiny bedroom. While there were no doors, Sarah knew what they were. Or, rather, what they used to be.

The cells.

The other main feature down in the basement was set against the far wall: a large, industrial-looking furnace. It was made from strong black iron, and was far larger than she had expected it to be.

'Bloody hell,' she said. 'We could both fit inside that thing.'

'Not what you were expecting?'

She shook her head. 'I'll say. It's huge. Though I guess that makes sense, considering the size of the house.'

The furnace stood taller than both Sarah and Andrew, and was split vertically into two sections. The top was a little wider, and the bottom had three hatches to the front, with two adjacent to one another and the third centrally below them. It gave the impression of a rudimentary face, with eyes and a mouth. Given their size, any of these hatches could be used to gain access if someone so wished. And each hatch had a door to it that would conceal the heat inside when closed. The furnace was also longer than it was wide, with thick, ribbed fins that ran along its side.

Thick and circular metal ducting—made from the same rusted-black metal as the furnace itself—ran off the large unit, snaking up the wall behind it before disappearing through the floor above. In addition, there were piles of black coal mounded close to the huge appliance, as well as a few smaller piles of chopped wood. Sarah could also see that some of the old cells were piled up with coal as well, leaving pools of fine black dust on the ground around them.

'Not the most efficient system, is it?' she asked, pointing to the coal. 'Bit of a bitch having to load it up just to get the house warm.'

'Tell me about it,' Andrew agreed. 'Not like it was back home, where we just flipped a switch.'

Sarah sensed the frustration in his voice, and remembered the conversation she'd had with Chloe up in the bathroom earlier. Though it wasn't her place to get involved, she did feel a duty to help out her sister.

'I know it isn't easy,' Sarah began, 'but this is all fixable. The furnace can easily be replaced.'

'Yeah, but at what cost? This house is huge, so any new heating system is going to cost an arm and a leg.'

'But we have the inheritance,' she said. 'I'm sure we can easily cover the cost of it.'

Sarah saw him tense up at the suggestion, and he didn't respond. Instead, he opened one of the three hatches in the front of the furnace, peeked inside, then grabbed a nearby shovel that lay on the ground. He scooped up a mound of coal and thrust it through the opening.

'It's definitely stopped working again,' he muttered. 'Fucking thing. I'll have to start her up.'

The level of rust on the once-black metal gave an indication of just how infrequently the furnace had been cleaned during its lifetime.

Andrew continued to shovel coal inside. He was depositing it in the lower, central hatch, which made it look like he was feeding some kind of giant, metallic infant. Andrew stopped after only six loads.

'Will that be enough?' Sarah asked.

'It will for now,' he replied. 'I'm just topping it off.'

'So... how does it work?'

'Basically, the coal burns, and that heats up the top unit,' he pointed to the higher, wider section now. 'That one is full of water. The water turns to steam, and the steam is then fed through the house via these pipes to the various radiators.'

Sarah watched him turn some of the valve handles on the side of the main unit, as well as a circular wheel on the main ducting that protruded from the top of the furnace. The wheel was quite high up, and he had to climb to reach it. Lastly, Andrew threw a piece of chopped wood inside before grabbing a strip of old, dry cloth, from the pile on a stool close to the furnace. There was a box of matches with the cloth, and Andrew lit one, using it to ignite the end of the rags he held. Sarah could smell the burning material, and Andrew then carefully held the flaming cloth in through the opening for a while until some of the wood and coal inside began to take.

'Should work,' he said, dropping the material inside and closing the door. 'But we won't know for a little while.'

The furnace was truly a fascinating piece of equipment, one that gave a brief glimpse into a prior way of life. Sarah could certainly understand Chloe's obsession with things like that. However, having to go through all that work just to get the heating going was certainly going to be a chore.

'And that's all there is to it?' Sarah asked, trying to make her sarcasm obvious. Andrew laughed. They then stood in silence for a little while, just waiting.

Eventually, Sarah heard the crackle of flames getting stronger inside the iron unit, and the temperature gauges started to slowly rise.

'Getting there,' Andrew said.

'Do we have to wait around for it?' Sarah asked.

Andrew shrugged. 'Probably not, but I just like to make sure the water is at least boiling. I've read that these things can go out pretty easily if you don't watch them carefully.'

'Fair enough,' Sarah replied. She felt the wine upstairs calling her, but it didn't feel right just leaving Andrew alone down here on his own. As the crackling inside continued, Sarah soon detected another sound, one that was faint and almost intertwined with the sounds of burning coal.

It almost sounded like... a moan. However, it quickly faded, and Sarah thought herself stupid—only to then hear it again.

'Is that just my ears playing tricks?' Sarah asked. 'Or can you hear something inside of there?'

Andrew looked puzzled. 'All I hear is the burning. But that isn't what's special. Just wait until the water starts steaming, and then you'll see.'

It didn't happen straight away, and Sarah continued to pick up what she thought was intermittent groaning within the metal furnace. Then, when the temperature and pressure gauges were higher, she could tell the liquid in the top section had started to boil. It quickly turned to gas and was then pushed through the ductwork.

It was at that point a sudden and horrible sound caused Sarah to jump.

Andrew began to laugh. 'Catches you off guard, right?'

'You're fucking right it does,' she replied, still reeling. *It* does *sound like a fucking scream!*

'It's just the steam forcing its way through the pipes,' he said. 'There is air inside that is pushing its way along. Some of it is no doubt getting out through a crack or some gaps in the pipework. That's all it is, like the sound old kettles used to make. But it's pretty freaky.'

In all honesty, Sarah didn't need the explanation; her mind had quickly formed a similar conclusion itself. But she had to admit that just as Chloe and Andrew had told her earlier, the sound did indeed initially resemble a sharp and sudden scream.

'That is freaky,' Sarah agreed after the noise had completely dissipated.

'Not a bad feature, is it? A screaming furnace. Think we could get people to pay to listen to it?'

Sarah laughed. 'Probably. Ghost hunters and the like would have a field day with it. With the house in general, I suppose.'

'You might be right. Anyway, things *should* start to warm up now, but we'll need to see how it goes. I want to make sure it doesn't kick out too much heat during the night.'

Sarah nodded.

She wanted to go back to her point about having enough money for a replacement, and tell him this was all just a temporary issue. That they were family, all in it together, and that the problem would quickly get resolved.

But she also remembered Chloe's words about why Andrew hadn't been overly enamoured with the house in the first place.

Because he didn't provide it.

That wasn't an issue she wanted to deal with right now. It was for Chloe and Andrew to work out between them.

'Come on,' Sarah said. 'It's dark and depressing down here, and there is alcohol waiting for us upstairs. Let's go.'

Andrew gave her a thumbs up, then followed her back upstairs.

CHAPTER 11

THE THREE OF them spent the rest of the night drinking and talking, and the mood was a positive one.

Earlier, Sarah had briefly raised the topic of the weird study on the top floor, but Chloe had made it clear that wasn't something she wanted to discuss at the minute. That was fine for Sarah, who was happy to move onto a different topic, but she knew it could not be ignored indefinitely.

And Sarah certainly had questions.

For one, whose study was it? Obviously it would have belonged to Vincent, the whole house had, but was he the one responsible for the weird collection? Or had he just been the most recent custodian? Could it have maybe been the man who owned Perron Manor when the events in 1982 occurred? Sarah remembered his name from an article she'd read online: Marcus Blackwater.

At eleven-thirty, Chloe suggested they call it a night. Sarah could have easily continued, but Andrew agreed with his wife and Sarah did not want to keep on drinking alone. So, they all went up to the middle floor together, said their goodnights, and entered their respective rooms.

Given it had been a long day of driving and carrying boxes around, Sarah felt a little grimy, so she decided to wash before she got into bed.

The room's en-suite housed a deep metal bath, which stood on four legs, all of which were shaped like lion paws. There was no shower—which was a shame, given it would have been quicker—so instead Sarah started to draw a bath. She figured her room was far enough away from the others for the noise not to disturb them.

Thankfully, the heating in the room still seemed to be working, and the water ran hot. Once Sarah had the bath full enough, she undressed, leaving her clothes in a pile on the floor. She then dipped a toe down through the surface of the water. It was hot.

Not quite scalding, but just right for her. Her skin would no doubt be bright red when she got out, but that didn't bother her in the slightest. Sarah then stepped fully inside and carefully let herself slide down, submerging herself up to her shoulders and leaning her head back into the curved rim of the bath.

The room around her swirled with a layer of building steam, which was exacerbated by the lack of a window. There didn't seem to be an extractor fan either—something else that would need to be rectified when Sarah eventually got a shower fitted in the room.

The en-suite wasn't huge, but it was certainly big enough, and housed the bath, a vanity unit with washbasin, and a toilet. The walls were clad with simple white tiles, and the floor was similarly tiled as well, though with a light grey finish. Nothing fancy, but the decor worked. There was a large mirror above the vanity unit as well, that had completely misted up.

The aches of the day began to melt away, seeping out from her bones and into the hot water around her. A welcome feeling of relaxation started to consume Sarah. She was well aware she'd consumed a reasonable amount of alcohol, so didn't want to relax too much and fall asleep. Even now, after only a few minutes of stewing in the water, Sarah felt her eyes grow heavy. She let them close for a moment, enjoying the warmth around her. But it was getting late, and she knew she should make this quick, especially given there would be another full and hectic day tomorrow. Her bed was calling her.

She opened her eyes and poured some shower gel into her hands from the bottle she'd set on the bath's edge. Casting a look to her side and towards the vanity unit, she paused, seeing an unclear dark mass in the mirror's glass surface. It appeared to show something on the opposite side of the bath, but after turning her head Sarah saw nothing behind her at all. She again looked back to the mirror. Whatever the figure-shaped mass had been, it was no longer there. Sarah frowned, unsure if she'd even seen anything in the first place.

She then proceeded to wash, finishing off with her hair. After completely submerging to rinse off the suds, Sarah felt a sudden cold between her legs and gasped and pulled in a mouthful of water. She quickly sat up, coughing and spluttering, heaving out the warm water she had swallowed. Panic seized her, and she frantically looked around.

But there was nothing that could explain the sudden sensation of intense cold beneath the surface of the water that had settled over Sarah's crotch. It had felt like someone with ice-cold hands had roughly grabbed her groin.

Despite the warmth of both the water and the room, goosebumps formed on Sarah's arms. After she got her coughing under control, and wiped the water from her eyes, she looked around the bathroom. Whatever had caused the sensation, it clearly hadn't come from anyone's hand, given she was still alone.

Sarah sat in the water for a little while longer, letting herself calm down and forcing her breathing into a slow and steady rhythm. She would not let irrational fear get the better of her.

During her career, she had been in situations that were truly terrifying—and life threatening—and she'd come through them by forcing her mind to focus and push the fear away.

This was nothing. *Literally* nothing. Just her getting spooked by something that was likely very explainable—even if she couldn't actually explain it at the moment. And yet, she still felt anxious.

Get a grip, you fucking idiot.

She stood up and grabbed her towel, then wrapped it around her shoulders. Sarah used her toes to fish around under the water, snagging the chain between them, and released the plug. She then stepped onto the bathmat and began to dry herself off. After brushing her teeth and using the toilet, Sarah gave the bathroom another glance over—seeing nothing out of the ordinary—before flicking off the light and closing the door. She was finally feeling a little more relaxed, and it wasn't long before she fell asleep.

That night, however, she slept fitfully, and her dreams continued to replay her final moments with Tania.

The wrong step. The explosion. Sarah thrown to the ground from the blast. And then feeling the hot mush that was once her best friend coat her.

Something was different, however. Through it all, Sarah could hear an odd whispering. It wasn't in a language she recognised, but she still somehow understood the intent.

The whispering got louder and louder and louder, and then the dream changed. She was falling... no, being dragged down into the ground...

When Sarah snapped her eyes open, there was only darkness around her. It took a few seconds for her mind to pull itself from the horrible dream—being pulled through a hole in the earth, into an existence of agony. All the while, horrible, taunting whispers echoed around her. And for a moment after waking, that insidious whispering was still present.

Soon, however, everything grew quiet, and Sarah started to fully wake up, even if she was still tired. She reached for her mobile phone, and the screen showed it was only three-thirty.

After rolling back over, Sarah stared through the dark at the ceiling above her, remembering her vivid dream. Remembering Tania.

Sarah had been supposed to take point that day. But she didn't. And Tania had died because of it.

Sarah cried, and didn't sleep any more that night.

CHAPTER 12

Oliver Tripp was a local heating engineer Andrew had found online, one who had mostly positive reviews. He arrived mid-morning, and Andrew greeted him at the door. The man was well into his fifties, heavily balding, and had a thick, grey moustache under a pronounced nose. He was also rake-thin, and had fingers that had yellowed and stained, no doubt caused by years of smoking. Dressed in navy blue trousers, and a matching polo-shirt that had his company name embedded in gold across the upper-left side, he looked professional enough as well. Andrew immediately liked Oliver, as he seemed amenable and friendly.

However, after showing the man the furnace, Andrew could tell that fixing it was beyond Oliver's skill.

Andrew had switched it off early that morning, so that he could show Oliver exactly what they were dealing with. As expected, the noises that came from the furnace had startled him. Regardless, Oliver had taken a good look around, but did so with constant shakes of his head and a confused rubbing of his chin. Finally, they moved back upstairs to the kitchen.

'I've never heard anything like it before,' the engineer said as he took a drink of his coffee, which Sarah had made for him. Oliver, Andrew, and Sarah were all gathered around the kitchen table, while Chloe had left them to go up and get Emma, who had just woken from her nap.

'Takes you by surprise, doesn't it,' Sarah stated.

Oliver nodded. 'Just about shit myself,' he said, causing Sarah to chuckle.

'So, can you do anything with it?' Andrew asked Oliver. 'Even if it's just to check and see if everything's running okay?'

The engineer rubbed his chin again and shook his head. 'Sorry to say, but the system isn't something I'm familiar with. It's just too old, and I wouldn't really know what to look out for. Not much I can do beyond what I already have in checking the seals and everything. Wasn't anything too in-depth, to be honest.'

'Fair enough,' Andrew replied just as Chloe reentered the room with Emma in her arms. The child looked around, spotted Oliver, then pointed.

'Man!' she exclaimed.

'Yes,' Chloe responded to her. 'It *is* a man.' She then looked apologetically over to Oliver. 'Sorry, she keeps doing that.'

Oliver just laughed. 'Don't apologise, she's just curious. Isn't that right, little one?' He then gave her a playful wave, but Emma just turned away and began to play with the small plastic car she had with her.

Andrew wanted to turn things back to business. 'Hopefully what you've done will help for the time being,' he said. 'What if we were to look at replacing the whole thing, and putting in a more modern system? Is that something you can do?'

Oliver's eyebrows raised excitedly. 'Sure is,' he said. 'I'd need to pull in some help, given the size of the house. Also, I suppose you know it wouldn't just be a standard boiler that you'd need. House this big would need a commercial-sized system. But I could get it designed for you and install the whole thing. Only trouble is,' Oliver's enthused expression dampened a little, 'it would cost a pretty penny. I don't say that to dissuade you, and I'd keep my price as keen as I could, but I want you to be aware of that upfront.'

'No, I understand that,' Andrew replied. 'But it certainly needs doing. It's just no good having to fire the old thing up and wait an age just to get warm.'

Oliver nodded, his smile returning. 'Then yeah, I'd love to price it up for you. I'll need to pop back at some point to get a full measure of the house, if that's okay? Don't really have time to fit it in today. That way I can get a designer I know to come up with a full system, and get a cost back over to you.'

'And how long would that take?'

Oliver rubbed his chin yet again as he pondered the question. 'I could get back out in a few days to measure up. Say a couple of weeks or so to get the design done, then I'd need to cost it. Given a job of this size, and the labour I'd need to pull in, I'd make it a priority, but it would probably be a month or two after we agree on price before I could start. Would that work?'

Andrew looked to Chloe and Sarah, who in turn cast each other a glance before turning back to him and nodding.

'Okay,' Andrew said. 'Get the price over and I will consider it. We can go from there.'

'Sounds good!' Oliver said. He then took a look around the kitchen, drinking it all in. 'You know, I never thought I'd be working up here at Devil's House.'

Andrew had to fight to stop from cringing at the man's words. 'You know about this place?'

'Of course, everyone in town does. My uncle actually came up here once. He was a plumber. Saw something that spooked him pretty badly, I heard. Never said much about it to me, but my cousin said he was really freaked out.'

'Really?' Andrew asked. 'Well, I'm not sure what he saw, but I can assure you there is nothing here that—'

'Oh, don't worry,' Oliver cut in. 'I don't put much stock in stuff like that. All a bunch of nonsense.'

Andrew smiled. 'Glad you think so. Wouldn't want you getting spooked about working up here.'

'Don't worry about that,' Oliver said before he downed the last of his coffee. The man then got to his feet. 'This would be a hell of a job for me: putting a full new system in a place as big and famous as this house. It'd be a hell of a thing for my business.'

Andrew shook his hand. 'Sounds good. Get the price over, first and foremost. And hopefully we can get things moving.'

'Will do,' Oliver said. He then turned to Sarah and pointed to his now-empty mug. 'Hazelnut roast, you say?'

Sarah nodded, smiling. 'That's right. Did you enjoy it?'

'Loved it!' he replied. 'I'll have to get me some of that.'

Andrew saw Sarah turn to Chloe and stick out her tongue. He then stood up and ushered Oliver towards the exit. The engineer waved to both Chloe and Sarah as he left.

Just as Oliver stepped over the threshold at the main door, he turned back to Andrew.

'I'm assuming you will be seeking alternative quotes as well?'

Andrew nodded. 'Probably,' he admitted. 'No offence, but I'd be silly not to.'

Oliver shook his head and held up his hands. 'No need to apologise, I totally understand and would do the same in your situation. But, can I ask: if you get something comes in cheaper, can you let me know and give me the opportunity to shave a bit more off? It's not like my price would be high, or anything, but I'd certainly look again at areas I could save, if it meant getting the job.'

Andrew didn't answer straight away, as he wasn't sure how comfortable he was with that. In his head, the price should just be the price—no second bite of the cherry if you missed out the first time. 'I'll consider it,' he eventually said, then held out his hand.

Oliver looked down for a moment, clearly expecting a different answer. However, he still shook. 'Thank you,' Oliver said. 'I'll be in touch soon about coming back out to measure up.'

After he'd gone, Andrew walked back to the others in the kitchen and sat down. 'What do you think?' he asked Chloe and Sarah.

'He seemed nice,' Sarah said.

'Think the job may be too big for him, though,' Andrew added.

'Suppose we won't know that until he starts and it all goes wrong,' Chloe added. 'But he seemed to know his stuff. Although… would he be okay stripping out what's here if he isn't familiar with it, do you think?'

'I think so,' Andrew replied. 'Ripping stuff out is a lot easier than maintaining it. I just don't know if we would be better suited getting a larger company in. A commercial one. But that would cost us a lot more.'

'I think we'd have enough to cover it,' Sarah offered, and Andrew felt himself bristle. Just because they had money now didn't mean they had to waste it. Besides, that money wasn't earned, anyway. But he tried to keep his annoyance in check.

'No reason to let costs spiral, though,' was all he said.

'So let's get some other prices in, then,' Chloe said. 'That way, we'll know where we stand. Can't hurt to look around a little.'

Andrew nodded. 'I agree.' He then looked to Sarah for her confirmation as well. It was every bit as much her house as it was Chloe's, so she had a say.

Even more so than Andrew did, in truth.

'Yeah, I'm okay with all that,' she agreed.

'I'll arrange for us to get some other quotes,' Andrew said. 'Hopefully, I can get them here before I go away.'

Sarah frowned. 'You having a holiday without us or something?'

'Nothing so fancy,' Andrew replied. 'I need to get back to work, I've taken enough days as it is. I have to head down to London to meet with a client, so I'll be out and about for a few days.'

'The Big Smoke? Nice,' Sarah replied. 'But have you even set up an office yet?'

Andrew shook his head. 'No, that's next on my list. I also need to get the bloody internet sorted out, though I don't think that'll be done before I leave.'

'I can't believe Vincent didn't even have any kind of connection here,' Chloe chimed in. 'Imagine not being connected all those years.'

'Sounds like that's the way he wanted it,' Sarah offered. 'Besides, we've lived without the internet before, when we were kids, and it didn't do us any harm.'

'I guess,' Chloe replied. 'Still feels like we are cut off a little bit.'

The sound of the doorbell ringing brought the conversation to a close.

Sarah stood. 'I'll get it.'

CHAPTER 13

Upon opening the front door, Sarah was met with a smiling man whose grey eyes—which widened upon seeing her—sat behind black-framed glasses.

'H-hello,' he said, his tone uneven and slightly nervous. He then thrust his hand out to be shook, but moved so quickly as to make Sarah flinch. 'Sorry,' the stranger quickly said. 'My name is David, David Ritter.'

There was an awkward pause, and Sarah waited for him to give a little more information. None was forthcoming.

'Okay, David Ritter,' she said. 'Is there something you need?'

He pursed his lips and looked to the ground. 'Well, what I am going to say may come off as a little… strange.'

Sarah wasn't surprised to hear that, as he seemed a little bit strange himself. However, she wasn't unnerved by him in the slightest. More amused at his uncertain demeanour.

The man before her had brushed-back grey hair that framed a square face. However, though his hair was grey, he only looked a similar age to Sarah herself. He wore a black jacket over a dark shirt, as well as blue jeans, old scruffy trainers, and a backpack slung over one shoulder. He had a certain nerdish quality to him, and if Sarah were to guess at his job, she'd have gone with some kind of role in I.T.

'Go on,' she said, somewhat intrigued.

'Well, I live in the area… and I'm a paranormal investigator.'

'No fucking way!' Sarah blurted out, unable to help herself. Then, she quickly brought a hand up to her mouth. 'Sorry,' she said. 'I just… really didn't expect that.'

He gave a nervous laugh as his cheeks flushed red. 'Not the sort of thing you tend to hear when a stranger knocks on your door, I guess.'

'No, it isn't. Certainly not something to open with, anyway.'

He gave an embarrassed nod. 'Fair enough, I suppose. But it was relevant.'

Sarah smiled politely, but crossed her arms over her chest. 'Okay, David Ritter, paranormal investigator, I'm gonna have to ask you to start from the beginning here.'

'Understood. It's about the house you now own. See, it is a place I know a lot about.' David reached into his backpack and pulled out a pristine-looking paperback book, then handed it over to her. She looked down at the cover and the title: *Inside: Perron Manor*. And the tagline read: *Investigating Britain's Most Haunted House*. Sarah's eyes widened. *He* was the author.

'Wow… you wrote a book about my house?'

He nodded enthusiastically. 'I did. A few years ago now. You can keep it if you want.'

'Thanks,' Sarah said, trying—and failing—to find a tone to match his enthusiasm. She imagined that he likely had boxes and boxes full of unsold copies of this book at his home.

'It's well researched, and goes into a bit of detail about the history of the place. I like to think I uncovered quite a lot.'

'Okay. So are you here to tell me my house is haunted, David?' Sarah gave a playful smile.

'Erm… kind of,' he replied.

Sarah laughed. 'Is that so? Well, sorry to burst your bubble, David, but I really don't think it is. I haven't seen any ghosts or heard any clanking chains in the night.'

'Well, it doesn't really work like that. It's more—'

'David,' Sarah cut in, rather sternly, but she still couldn't hide her amused smile. The exchange was odd enough to almost be endearing, but she still had no clue what the hell this strange man wanted. 'Can we get to the point of the matter, please?'

'Yes, of course. See, if you read that,' he pointed to the book in Sarah's hands, 'you will see it also details an investigation I carried out here with my team in 2013. The results blew us away. I mean, the things we saw... it was phenomenal.'

'Is that so?'

'It is. Honestly, please read the book. It's all true. And it will amaze you, I'm sure.'

'So... what? Is this a warning about my new house, then?'

'Excuse me?'

'Have you come here to warn me the house is haunted?'

'Well... kind of. But, you see, after my initial investigation, the prior owner never let us back. I don't know why, but he just cut us off.'

'Wait... you mean Vincent Bell?'

'That's right,' David said.

'You knew him?' Sarah asked, suddenly interested in what the man had to say.

'Not quite. I met him, of course, and we spoke a few times when he let me and my team stay here for a weekend.'

'What was he like?'

'Mr. Bell?' David paused for a little while. 'Cranky,' was his response. 'Sorry,' he added quickly. 'I don't mean to speak ill of your deceased uncle, it's just—'

'How did you know he was my uncle?'

David shrugged. 'It's public record who inherited the house, if you know where to look. That's how I found out it was willed down to his surviving nieces.'

Sarah took half a step back. 'This is getting a little stalkery, David.'

'No!' he said, and his hands came up defensively, palms facing her. 'It's not that. I just have a great interest in the house. I researched what happened here in '82, and I know that your parents, and uncle, all escaped. And... are you Chloe?'

'Chloe is my sister.'

'Ah,' he said. 'So that would make you...'

'Sarah,' she finished for him.

'Sarah, right. Pleased to meet you, Sarah.'

He offered his hand again, no less awkwardly than the first time. Sarah didn't take it.

'As fun as this has been,' she said, wanting to bring everything to a close, 'I really am very busy.'

'Oh, of course.' His face fell. 'Can I just ask you to consider something for me? I would be eternally grateful.'

'Care to get to the point?'

'Yes. Certainly. See, Vincent never let us back in here, and I'd like to ask if you would consider allowing me and my team back in, at some point? To, you know, carry out another investigation.'

Sarah was momentarily lost for words—a rarity for her. She soon found her voice. 'Are you serious?'

'Yes, of course.'

She laughed. 'We've *just* moved in, David. Couldn't you have at least waited a few months to ask?'

'Oh… I didn't mean—'

'Look,' she said firmly. 'That isn't something we'd be willing to accommodate, to be honest. This is our home, not a public attraction. So I'm going to have to say no. But, thanks for asking.'

Sarah saw a look that boarded on heartbreak cross his face, and she couldn't help but feel bad for letting him down so abruptly.

'I see,' he replied, sounding like a child who had been told he couldn't have his favourite toy. 'Is there no way…'

'Sorry, David, but we don't believe in things like that, and letting people run around our house hunting imaginary ghosts would just be intrusive. I'm sure you understand.'

He nodded slowly. 'Okay. Please, though, keep the book. It might be of interest.'

'I will,' Sarah said with a smile, waving the book in her hand. 'But I've got to go now. It was nice to meet you, David.'

'You too,' he replied, 'but one more thing. If you do see anything in there, and ever need any help… please let me know.'

Yet again, his hand thrust forward. This time, however, it was holding a small rectangular piece of card. Sarah sighed, but took it, and read what was written on the front: *David Ritter, Paranormal Investigator.*

He has an honest-to-God business card. 'Okay, I promise I'll call you if I see anything. But I really have to go now,' Sarah said, trying not to laugh. She still couldn't get over the fact he had gotten business cards made up. She waved, then closed the door on her strange new acquaintance.

Sarah quickly walked back through to the kitchen and saw Chloe fixing up dinner. 'Where's Andrew?' she asked.

'He's gone to start setting up his office. Who was at the door? And what's that book?'

Sarah pulled her sister away from the food she was preparing, moving her over to the kitchen table.

'You are not gonna fucking *believe* the conversation I just had.'

CHAPTER 14

3 Days Later...

'Why the hell are you reading that thing?' Chloe asked her sister.

The sisters were curled up in the living room, which was situated at the front corner of the house and looked out over the front lawn and driveway. They were seated on the leather sofas Chloe had brought with her, with Chloe on one and Sarah on the other.

Sarah had a blanket wrapped over her legs, and she sipped at a hazelnut coffee. The television was playing a documentary about Orca whales, but Chloe felt distracted and found it hard to concentrate. Her own cup of tea was close to being empty. And while it wasn't exactly late in the evening—a little after eight—Chloe still felt tired.

'Actually, it isn't too bad,' Sarah told her, looking up from the pages she had been so engrossed in. 'If half of this is true, then Perron Manor has one fucked-up history.'

Chloe just chuckled. 'We already knew it had a fucked-up history. I was here for some of it,' she said, before adding, 'whether I remember it or not.'

'No, I mean before that,' Sarah replied, '*Way* before that. It was built back in the 1200s as a monastery, apparently, and the stuff that has supposedly happened since is... unreal.'

'I'm not sure I even want to know,' Chloe said, turning back to the television.

'Really? It's fascinating. Though it's definitely not something I should share with Andrew. Don't need to add more fuel to his fire about this place.'

Chloe nodded. 'Agreed.'

Fortunately, Andrew wasn't with them that night and was down in London on business, leaving Chloe, Sarah, and Emma alone for a few days of quality girl time. Chloe was used to him going away every now and again, but still missed him every time he did.

'Does it say anything about why we have Satan's study upstairs, then?' Chloe asked.

Sarah laughed but shook her head. 'No, but I haven't gotten into modern history yet. Still covering the 1800s, so no mention of it.'

'That book you're reading could all be bullshit, you know.'

'It could, I suppose, and I'm sure the stories of ghosts and the like *are*. But I think a lot of the events it covers are factual.'

'I still can't believe that creepy guy turned up on our doorstep and wanted to use this place to hunt bloody ghosts. It's weird.'

'I know,' Sarah said with a chuckle. 'Harmless enough, though.'

Chloe's attention was turned to the side-table, where the baby monitor sat. The sound of Emma mumbling in her sleep was coming through the speakers.

Chloe watched her daughter, bathed in blue, as she rolled over, then quickly settled down again.

'I just don't want our house becoming some kind of freakshow,' Chloe said.

'I get that,' her sister replied. 'But come on, it's known as Devil's House. And bad shit happened here. It's always gonna have that stigma, and there isn't much we can do about it. If this is going to work for you, I think you need to come to terms with that and accept it.'

Chloe didn't like that notion, as true as it was. 'It just feels like a black stain on what we're trying to do. This place would be perfect, otherwise.'

'Yeah, but it's a small price to pay for getting a free mansion, Sis. If that is the only drawback—that, and the ungodly amount of work that needs doing—then it still isn't a bad deal, is it?'

'I guess,' Chloe admitted, but still wished she could snap her fingers and make everyone forget about the irrelevant past. Had she been naïve in thinking a history like that would have no bearing on their lives here?

'You'll get used to it,' Sarah said. 'Just don't let it get you down.'

'Easy for you to say, you seem to love it all,' Chloe replied, pointing at the book. 'When we found that study upstairs, you were practically giddy.'

'Of *course* I was,' Sarah exclaimed. 'It's as far from normal as anything possibly can be, so why wouldn't I be interested in it? One thing I'll say about this place: it certainly hasn't been boring so far.'

Chloe sighed. 'Boring would have suited me fine.'

But Sarah just stared over to her sister and narrowed her eyes. 'That's a lie.' Chloe had no response to that.

More noises from the baby monitor caught her attention again. Emma was now standing up, hands resting against the side rail, and was chattering to herself.

'She's awake, then, I take it?' Sarah asked.

'Yeah. I'll give her a minute, see if she settles back down.'

Then Emma paused, and Chloe saw her point to something out of view of the camera. It wasn't unusual for her to point at things, but something had clearly gotten Emma's attention.

'Man!' the child said.

Chloe paused and felt a small chill run down her spine.

Sarah looked over to her. 'Did she just say…?'

'Yeah,' Chloe confirmed with a frown. 'Probably just jabbering.' Even so, Chloe felt the need to go up and check. She grabbed the monitor and got to her feet.

'Want me to come with you?' Sarah asked, but Chloe shook her head.

'Nah, it's nothing. You enjoy your book.'

Although in all likelihood it was indeed nothing, Chloe still kept a close eye on the monitor as she made her way upstairs. Emma continued to stare off-camera, standing in silence. Chloe put on a burst of speed, and practically jogged all the way to Emma's room.

Upon entering, she saw her daughter was still standing, but there was no one else present. However, it was cold, and that horrible odour Chloe had previously noticed in the room again lingered for a few moments. She quickly checked the room over, to satisfy herself there was nothing to worry about.

Chloe then laid Emma back down and ran a hand through her daughter's fuzzy hair. 'Kindly do me a favour, kid, and stop freaking me out like that.'

Giving one last look around, and realising that the nasty smell had dissipated completely, Chloe turned the radiator up a touch and left Emma alone, closing the door behind her.

She knew that fixing the smell in Emma's room would need to be a priority.

As Chloe walked back downstairs, she kept stealing glances at the monitor. Thankfully, Emma remained lying down and settled.

'All okay?' Sarah asked as Chloe re-entered the living room.

'All okay,' Chloe confirmed, and took her seat again.

The sisters then sat in silence for a little while, with Sarah still engrossed in her book and Chloe watching the whale documentary. Chloe's hand kept wandering to her phone so she could check social media or surf the internet. However, given the Wi-Fi wasn't yet installed, and the signal in most of the house was terrible, it proved futile.

Over the last few days, she had found that annoying desire to idly waste time on her mobile phone had begun to wane, which was a good thing. Chloe, like so many others in today's world, had definitely developed an annoying habit of having her face constantly buried into the screen, letting social media devour every spare moment she had.

That was something Chloe respected about Sarah, who obviously still owned a phone, but never seemed to get drawn into the time-sucking loop of browsing and scrolling.

They remained in the living room for a couple more hours, until Chloe started to feel tired. She yawned and stretched. 'I'm done,' she said. 'Going to turn in.'

Sarah closed her book. 'Yeah, me too.'

The two women double-checked the ground-floor doors to make sure they were all locked before moving upstairs and bidding each other goodnight. Chloe then looked in on Emma again, who was still sleeping soundly.

She then went into her room and readied herself for bed, quickly paying a visit to the en-suite in order to brush her teeth and answer the call of nature.

Just as she got into bed and pulled the covers over her, Chloe heard something that startled her.

While it wasn't particularly loud, the noise was still very audible. And it caused an instant pang of anxiety to rise up from her gut.

She sat up in bed and checked her phone, seeing it was a little after ten at night.

And then she heard it again. A knocking—no, a banging—on the front door downstairs.

What the hell?

She climbed out of bed, feeling a sense of building dread, similar to the apprehension experienced when getting a phone call late at night: it could never be good news.

Who the hell could be knocking at this time of night?

Chloe slung a dressing gown around herself, then grabbed her keys, as well as her phone, just in case an emergency call was needed. She then quickly stepped out into the hallway, wondering if she should find something to arm herself with.

When she looked down the corridor, Chloe saw that the banging had obviously disturbed Sarah as well, who was now standing outside of her own room dressed in a blue tank top, grey jogging bottoms, and was barefoot. She had, however, armed herself with a baseball bat.

Chloe had no idea that her sister had packed a bat, but in that moment, Chloe was grateful for her having it.

Bang, bang, bang.

The two sisters ran to each other. 'Who the hell could that be?' Chloe asked, trying not to let the panic she felt come through in her voice. She had images of going down to see police officers standing outside. *'Ma'am, I'm afraid it's about your husband.'*

'Maybe it's my new friend coming to get his book back,' Sarah joked.

While her dilated pupils indicated she was far from relaxed, Sarah did still exude a level of calm Chloe could not match. Not surprising, given Sarah's training.

'Should we answer it?' Chloe asked.

Sarah nodded. 'I think so. Just follow me.' She then held up the bat. 'If you see me start to swing, run up to Emma, then call the police. Got your phone?'

Chloe raised and shook it as confirmation. 'I have my keys to unlock the front door.'

'Me too,' Sarah said.

The pair then navigated the hallway to the upper section of the entrance lobby. They quickly looked over the rail, and down to the front door. Chloe was not able to make anything out through the glazed panels, as there was only darkness beyond. That in itself was strange, given Andrew had installed security lighting. If someone *was* outside, then it should have tripped the sensor.

Unless the visitor had already run off.

But that idea was quickly disproven, as three more quick bangs sounded out. They were hard enough to rattle the solid door on its hinges and loud enough to make both Chloe and Sarah jump.

Though the glass in the door was frosted for privacy, Chloe still couldn't make out any movement beyond it. Sarah then started to walk towards the staircase.

'We need to answer it,' she said, 'otherwise they're just going to keep banging on the fucking door and wake Emma.'

Chloe didn't like it, but Sarah had a point. So the two sisters slowly made their way down, each step causing an ominous creak underfoot. Once at the bottom of the stairs, they approached the front entrance, with Sarah taking the lead.

She moved to the door, drew in a breath, then yelled, 'Who is it?'

Silence.

'Maybe they've gone,' Chloe offered, hoping it was true but not really believing it.

Sarah slowly moved her face closer to the glass panel and peered out.

'Can't see anyone,' she said. Then, she called out again, 'Hello?'

Nothing.

'Let's just ignore it,' Chloe said. 'Whoever it was has obviously left.'

But instead, Sarah retrieved the keys from her pocket and slid the correct one into the lock. There was a click as it opened, and Chloe felt her breath catch in her throat.

Sarah slowly pulled the door open a crack and peeked outside. For Chloe, the silence as her sister looked about felt like an eternity. Sarah then pushed her head farther out and the security light flicked on, illuminating more of the outside space and pushing back the shadows. After scanning the area thoroughly, Sarah pulled her head back inside and closed the door.

'Well?' Chloe asked.

Sarah shook her head. 'No one.'

Chloe felt a wave of relief wash over her. *Thank Christ for that.* Though the thought that someone *had* been there was still hugely unnerving.

'Who the fuck was it, then?' Chloe asked.

'No idea, but it might be an idea to get a security camera fitted.'

'Yeah,' Chloe agreed. 'I like the sound of that.'

'I'm going to check the back door as well,' Sarah said. 'You can go back upstairs if you want.'

Chloe's heart was still beating fast, and thoughts of sleep seemed a million miles away. 'No, I'll come with you.'

The two women then walked from the entrance lobby through to the great hall. From there, the rear glass doors that looked out into the courtyard could be seen. The security light there remained off. They walked up to the door and peered out, but no one could be seen.

'All clear,' Sarah confirmed.

'Do you think we should call the police?' Chloe asked. 'I mean, we still don't know who it was. I don't like the idea of someone creeping around out there. It's a long trek for someone to make without a good reason.'

Sarah seemed to be considering it, but then shook her head. 'It's stopped, so whoever it was has likely gone. If it happens again, then maybe.'

'But how do we know they've gone?' Chloe asked. 'They could still be on the grounds somewhere.'

'Then let's check,' Sarah replied.

Chloe was confused, and a little worried that meant actually going outside. But instead, Sarah led the way upstairs into an unused and rear-facing bedroom. There, they both looked out of the window to see the courtyard and rear gardens. The view was bathed in darkness, but they could just about make out the edge of the property, close to the boundary wall.

'Can't see anyone,' Sarah said. They then checked a few more rooms as well, looking out either side of the house, as well as the front.

There was no one.

'I honestly think we are okay now,' Sarah said.

'Fine,' Chloe conceded, though she still would have felt safer calling the police.

'Try and get some sleep,' Sarah told her. 'We can discuss it more in the morning, maybe file a report or something then. Pointless dragging anyone out here now.'

'Fair enough,' Chloe replied. The two sisters hugged, and said their goodnights for the second time. Chloe then checked Emma again before finally getting into bed herself. She let out a long sigh.

Bang, bang, bang!

Her eyes went wide and her body locked up. Another banging, again from the front door.

Bang, bang, bang!

Chloe was quickly up again and out into the hallway, pushing herself forward despite the fear she was feeling. As expected, Sarah was just leaving her room as well.

'This has got to be a fucking joke!' Sarah seethed, marching towards the stairs. Her face was twisted into a look of pure anger, and the bat was again in hand. 'I am not having some fuckwit mess with us like this. Come on!' she called to Chloe.

Chloe had her phone in hand, ready to call the police, feeling her heart hammer in her chest. But her screen showed no signal. Chloe jogged along in order to keep up with Sarah, though she didn't like the idea of going back down again.

The house felt colder now, somehow.

Bang, bang, bang.

Bang, bang, bang.

Sarah gripped the bat tightly in two hands as the sisters emerged again onto the walkway of the entrance lobby. They both again looked over the side railing.

Like before, the security light was still off, and they couldn't spot any shapes or movement beyond the privacy glazing in the door panels.

Sarah quickly ran down the stairs.

'What about the police?' Chloe shouted, following her sister on shaking legs.

'Later,' Sarah snapped. 'First, I'm going to wrap this bat around their fucking heads, whoever the hell they are.'

She strode over to the door, took in a breath, set herself, then yelled out, 'I'm giving you one last warning, you fucking creeps. Get the hell out of here before I rip your Goddamn lungs out!'

Chloe's eyes went wide. She had never seen such aggression from Sarah before, and from the expression on her sister's face, Chloe didn't doubt Sarah intended to follow through with her rather graphic threat. Aggression had been part of her job, of course. But still, for Chloe to see her little sister unleash it in such a way was unnerving.

Sarah was still slow and steady, however, as she reached a hand towards the door handle and once again pulled open the front door. She had the bat cocked back, ready to strike, and she slowly inched her way outside while checking left and right. Once fully out, and her bare feet planted on the paving stones, Sarah stood ready, bat still poised. Just as she stepped outside the security light above her clicked on, washing Sarah in a cold, white light.

'I don't believe this,' she muttered.

'No one there again?' Chloe asked, realising she was hugging herself —both from the cold and the anxiety.

Sarah looked around, but her body started to relax, and the bat lowered.

'I don't understand it,' she said. 'The light is clearly working. So how come it didn't go off when we heard the knocking?'

Chloe shrugged. 'I have no idea. But, can we please call the—'

Bang, bang, bang.

The quick, hard banging this time came from somewhere else in the house. It was duller this time, like a strong thumping on thick glass.

'The back door!' Sarah exclaimed.

'Sarah, wait!'

But it was no use, and Chloe yet again had to follow her sister while experiencing an ever-growing feeling of panic. Chloe checked her phone, but there was still no signal. The only place she'd been able to consistently get any inside of the house was up on the top floor, towards the front of the building.

The two women ran into the great hall and flicked on the light. Sarah once again readied the bat, but no one was outside.

This time, however, the security light above the door *was* on, washing the courtyard out back in a yellow hue that reached to the end of the two protruding rear wings of the house. Though it was not quite enough to see the back of the boundary wall.

Given the light from both outside and within the great hall, Chloe saw their own reflections in the glass door as they approached it. Hers specifically looked tired, with messy hair in a loose ponytail, and brown eyes so wide they looked like they were about to pop out of their sockets. Despite being a quite tall five-foot-ten, she looked more like a scared child, especially next to her shorter but more determined-looking sister.

'Sarah,' Chloe whispered, trying to find some steel in her voice, 'I really want us to call the... oh my God!'

Sarah quickly turned to Chloe with a frown of confusion, but Chloe kept staring straight ahead. Sarah then whipped her head back around, and a gasp of surprise indicated she had seen it, too.

A person was standing outside, just beyond the illuminated area and mostly covered in shadow.

'Who the fuck is that?' Sarah shouted, taking a tentative step closer to the door.

It was hard to see much of the stationary figure that stood at the edge of the light. From what Chloe could see, it was a man, based only on the fact he was very tall—easily over six feet. They could also make out that he seemed to be wrapped in dark robes, but had the hood pulled down.

'What... what the hell is up with his face?' Chloe asked, feeling a sudden increase in her anxiety.

Though it was difficult to make out, the face in question seemed... off... somehow. As well as being deathly pale, the man's nose was bent and twisted, and there looked to be painful sores and scars on the skin. The eyes were lost in pools of shadow.

The man, whoever it was, did not move an inch. He just continued to stare at them.

Sarah dug one of her hands into her pockets and pulled out her phone.

'Police?' Chloe asked, relieved.

'Picture,' Sarah replied, unlocking the screen. 'And I wanna use the zoom on the camera to see—'

But when they looked up, the figure was gone.

'What the hell!' Sarah growled.

Chloe looked around frantically, but could not see him. The only explanation was that he'd stepped back into the darkness, because now all they saw was the empty courtyard, and their own reflections in the glass.

Then, the security light clicked off.

'Enough,' Chloe stated, shaking her head. 'We are calling the police right the fuck now.'

Thankfully, Sarah agreed. 'Yeah, I think that's a good idea.'

The two women then quickly moved up to the top floor again, and Chloe grabbed Emma on the way. The little girl cried incessantly, but there was no way Chloe was going to leave her daughter when a stranger was lurking around outside.

Once on the top floor, Sarah managed to find enough signal in one of the front bedrooms to make the call.

CHAPTER 15

It only took the police car fifteen minutes to show up.

'Well, we've had a good look around,' the policewoman said, her thumbs hooked into her black, standard issue stab-vest. 'But can't find anyone on the grounds. They must have run off.'

Sarah wasn't surprised. Even if the stranger had been hanging around, the police arriving surely would have scared him away.

She was a little ashamed of herself for getting so spooked, but there was something about the man—a feeling she got after looking out at him which she couldn't quite place, yet had truly unnerved her.

Sarah had been in war zones before, so a man creeping around outside should have been way down on the list of things that should get under her skin. But after seeing him, she couldn't deny that sneaking fear quickly overrode her previous desire to confront him.

Something about the whole thing just felt wrong.

Sarah, Chloe, and the two police officers—PC Andrea Taylor and PC Terry Rollins—were all gathered in the great hall, with Emma asleep in Chloe's arms. After arriving and speaking with the sisters, the officers had checked the full exterior of the property before coming back inside to speak to them.

'I'd recommend getting a security camera installed,' PC Andrea

Taylor said. She had blonde hair pulled back in a tight bun, a square-set jaw, and a stocky build.

'Yeah,' Chloe replied. 'It's on the to-do list, now. But who do you think it was? Just someone trying to fuck with us?'

'We can't be sure,' PC Terry Rollins replied. He was taller and thinner than his female counterpart, and had a neatly trimmed black beard and brushed-back hair. 'We could only speculate. However…' he trailed off, seeming to consider his next words.

But Sarah had an idea what he was going to say. 'It's the house, isn't it?'

PC Taylor raised an eyebrow in confusion. 'How do you mean?'

'It's pretty well known in the area, so it's not a stretch to think it could attract a bit of attention.'

'It could be,' PC Rollins confirmed with a nod. 'Most people around here know of this place—'

'They do?' his colleague cut in.

He smiled. 'Well, those of us who aren't new to the area do, yeah.' He then turned back to Sarah. 'I've seen a few cases of people coming up here just because they're intrigued by it, in all honesty. Mostly youths, but it has never been anything sinister.'

'Well, this guy definitely wasn't a kid,' Chloe said. 'Not from what we could make out.'

'And he was wearing robes, you say?' the female officer asked.

Chloe nodded. 'Yeah. Not exactly normal clothing when out exploring at night, is it?'

'No,' PC Rollins admitted. 'But, if I may, the house doesn't always attract people who are *normal*.'

Sarah and Chloe looked at each other, then turned to him with a frown.

'Oh God,' he said, holding up his hands. 'I didn't mean you two. You live here. I'm talking about the people who want to come up and see the house where people have died. They're sometimes a little… eccentric.'

Sarah thought of David Ritter, and realised the officer had a point.

'So… nothing to worry about?' she asked.

'I don't think so,' he replied. 'But, I'd obviously advise you to stay vigilant. Think about getting some cameras installed, like we said, and if you do see anyone else, don't hesitate to call.'

'Be *very* vigilant,' PC Taylor added. 'Sorry, but if someone is running around knocking on doors when they *know* someone is inside, that isn't just a person curious about a building. That's deliberate. Probably messing around or for kicks and actually *trying* to scare you.'

'I guess,' the other policeman conceded. 'Maybe they thought they were being funny. I still don't think you are in danger, but like my colleague says, best to keep an eye out.'

Not very comforting, Sarah thought. But the policewoman had certainly made a good point, and Sarah was glad of her candid advice.

However, she knew there was little more the police could do now.

After finishing up, the officers bade Sarah and Chloe goodnight, and then left. The sisters watched the police drive their squad car down the long, gravel driveway.

When they were gone, Sarah took a step forward. 'I'm gonna follow them down and close the gate,' she said.

'Are you sure?' Chloe responded.

'Of course. You can't take Emma down there. Go ahead and put the kettle on. I don't feel like sleeping at the minute.'

'Why don't we leave the gate until morning.'

Sarah turned to her, and forced a smile. 'Honestly, Chloe, it's fine. I had to walk down there to open it for them in the first place. And that didn't bother me.'

However, that wasn't necessarily true. The long walk in the dark so soon after seeing that stranger had certainly been an unsettling one.

What the fuck was it about that man that freaked me out so much?

The lack of explanation was infuriating Sarah. Perhaps it was the way he had looked—so pale and... *unnatural?*

Was that the right word?

Just thinking about him and those pools of shadows over his eyes caused a creeping feeling of cold to work its way up her spine.

Push it out of your head.

Sarah didn't give Chloe any further chance to change her mind, and set off down the driveway, the gravel crunching under her now-slippered feet. She called back over her shoulder.

'Hazelnut coffee for me. Feel free to make one yourself, Sis.'

She could only imagine the face Chloe was making at the suggestion.

'You sure you want coffee this late?' Chloe asked. 'You won't sleep.'

'I'll be fine,' she replied and kept walking.

Though Sarah tried to force all thoughts of the watcher from her mind, it was difficult, and as she got farther and farther away from the safety of the house, the more she felt isolated and exposed. She half expected to suddenly see the man in the shadows—or worse, to turn around and see him right behind her, following her up the driveway.

That didn't happen, of course, and Sarah reached the security gate without incident. She pulled the gate shut, replaced the padlock, and dropped the bolts that slotted into a concrete base-pad. It was an old gate, which would also need replacing at some point, preferably with an automatic one so they wouldn't need to open and close it on their own.

The return trip to the house was equally creepy, especially when she heard her crunching footsteps in the otherwise dead silence, but also equally uneventful. Sarah was grateful when she eventually got back inside to the relative warmth of Perron Manor. She headed straight to the kitchen and found Chloe sitting at the table with two drinks.

However, the coffee had been ignored, and two glasses of red wine sat ready.

'Perfect,' Sarah said approvingly. 'Did Emma go back down okay?'

'Yeah, she was asleep anyway. Just hope this doesn't cause her to be tired and grouchy tomorrow. I did the right thing getting her, didn't I?'

'Of course,' Sarah replied, taking the glass that was offered. 'Better to risk her losing a bit of sleep than anything bad happening. We didn't know what was going on.'

'I guess,' Chloe said, and took a long drink. Then she shuddered.

'Not good?' Sarah asked.

'What? Oh... no, it's not that. The wine is delicious. It's just... you know, thinking about that guy.'

Sarah took a gulp of her own drink. 'Try not to dwell on it,' she said.

'Easier said than done,' was Chloe's reply, and it was one Sarah fully understood. Though Sarah's advice had been good, it wasn't exactly something she could keep herself from doing either. Her mind was especially drawn to the way he had just stood there, totally unmoving.

Watching.

After each sister took a few more sips in silence, it was Chloe who went on. 'What the fuck am I going to tell Andrew?'

'What do you mean?' Sarah asked.

'Well, if I tell him what happened, then that's it for this place, isn't it? He's not going to entertain staying here if it's dangerous.'

Sarah considered her answer, as she knew Chloe had a point. If Andrew wanted a way out of this place, and he wanted an excuse where he couldn't be blamed for not giving the house a fair shot, then this was it.

Andrew would no doubt decide that strangers showing up in the middle of the night was sufficient to get out.

But, then again, it *was* a valid reason.

Sarah saw disappointment etched on her sister's face as Chloe stared at the ground while sipping her wine. Sarah's heart ached for her a little. It was clear just how much Chloe wanted this to work.

'Look,' Sarah eventually said. 'We can't hide this from him, it wouldn't be right. But, we can... I don't know, maybe... *frame* it a certain way.'

'What do you mean?'

'Well, we tell him what happened, but we play it down. Just say some idiot was knocking on our door then running away, being a nuisance. Don't let on that we were a little freaked out.'

'A *little* freaked out?' Chloe asked with a smile.

'Well, maybe more than a little. But, you have to make sure you're happy with that.'

'Happy with what?'

'I mean... would you still feel safe here? Do you think it's safe for Emma? Is staying here the right thing to do?'

Chloe paused for a moment. 'I... I don't know.'

Sarah understood the uncertainty. She was feeling it herself, but the more time that had passed since the incident, the more she'd started to think the whole thing ridiculous.

'Then let's think it through. What really happened here?'

'Some creepy guy tried to scare us.'

'Probably,' Sarah agreed. 'But no more than that. He knocked on our door. Is that really worth us losing a house like this over? I do think the history is something we need to keep in mind, as it might attract a few oddballs. But once we get some cameras set up, and maybe look at improving the boundary walls, electric gate... hell, even more security lighting on the grounds, that should stop strangers coming up here for a snoop around.'

'You think?' Chloe asked, and Sarah nodded. She *did* think that, more so now than earlier. It was a ridiculous notion to give up your home just because of the actions of an idiot.

Hell, harassment could happen anywhere. Even in the most populated of areas.

'We aren't going anywhere,' Sarah stated. 'Like I said, you need to tell Andrew, since it isn't right keeping it from him. But, you know...'

'Frame it,' Chloe repeated with a laugh.

Sarah clinked Chloe's glass with her own. 'Exactly.'

CHAPTER 16

1 MONTH LATER...

Steam filled the room, and even the open window failed to adequately ventilate the air.

'Can't see why you just didn't want to leave it as it was,' Sarah said to Andrew while nodding towards the wall's covering. 'This wallpaper has character.' She then slid the edge of her scraper utensil under the paper and cut away another strip of it.

The hell it does, Andrew thought.

He was holding the steamer machine to a separate area, letting the heat and moisture seep into the fabric of the wall lining, which made it easier to pull away. It also turned the room into a makeshift sauna with the steam it was kicking out.

'I hate the wallpaper,' he replied. 'You can have it everywhere else, if you want, but if this is going to be my office, then I need it how I like it.'

And that was their task today: to strip the wallpaper and carpet, which would allow the room to be re-plastered in a few days. Then he could decorate as he saw fit.

Earlier that morning, they'd humped out all of his equipment—computer, desk, filing cabinet—and moved them into a temporary office. Next, they had ripped out the carpet. Now all that remained was the hideous wall coverings.

'You're only going to plaster the whole thing then paint every wall white,' Sarah said with a grin. 'That's so boring.'

'Well,' he replied, 'I might go crazy and have a feature wall. You never know.'

'Oh, what colour?' Chloe asked.

Andrew shrugged. 'Probably some kind of pastel.'

Both Chloe and Sarah laughed. 'Absolutely *wild*,' Chloe joked.

They carried on stripping the paper and loading the rubbish into black bin-bags as the steam continued to clog the room. In truth, it was probably overcrowded with the three of them, but with Emma down for her midday nap, Chloe had insisted she wanted to chip in.

And, in fairness, the two girls had already set about fixing up the other parts of the house. Given Andrew had to work a lot, he'd expected the refurbishments to take an age, but he had underestimated just how much the sisters were looking forward to the monumental task ahead of them. With the help of sub-contractors and specialists, they had all managed to get a lot done. The internet was up and running—though it still tended to drop out quite a bit—and they had replaced the front entrance gate with an electronic one. Security cameras had been fitted to the front and rear doors, which also sent a feed to all of their mobile phones. Additionally, they'd finished the redecorating of their bedrooms, including Emma's. They had even started on renovating the garden and surrounding grounds.

The damn furnace still hadn't been replaced yet, but that was hopefully in hand and they were just waiting on a start date from Oliver. Andrew desperately wanted that thing replaced. Only a few days ago he had tried tightening a pipe that seemed to be leaking in one of the rooms. The water that dripped steadily from the heating pipe must have been mixed with rust, as it had a distinct crimson colour to it. When he'd cleaned it up, it had smeared across his fingers and left them smelling like copper.

However, even though Andrew still had his reservations about Perron Manor overall, he did feel like things were looking up.

That hadn't been the case when he'd found out about Chloe and Sarah being harassed—some idiot trying to scare them, apparently—

and that had made him see red. But in the end, Chloe and Sarah had put things into perspective.

Would they have left their last house because of the same thing?

The answer to that, he was forced to admit, would have been *no*. He and Chloe had then had a long conversation, where she again stressed her desire to make living here work. She also raised the point that he had promised to try, so his sniping and jibes at the house and the situation weren't helping. She also said that if he never intended to really commit, he should have never agreed to live here in the first place.

It took Andrew a little while to see things from her point of view, since he was initially defensive, but he'd eventually apologised.

She was right.

The truth was, he'd never *really* tried since moving in, and had just been going through the motions, waiting for an excuse to get out.

The possibility of another child had also been talked about again. They'd agreed that Chloe would come off the pill, and then they would see what happened over the next few months.

Thankfully, there had been no more instances of trespassers on the property.

The baby monitor—which was set on the floor in the room—crackled over the hissing of the steamer. Chloe leaned over to inspect it.

'Nothing,' Chloe said to them. 'She's still asleep.'

They carried on with their work, but another bout of light static came from the device, again drawing their attention. This time, however, Andrew could detect something within the crackling noise, though he wasn't certain what it was.

Sarah laughed. 'Jesus, that sounded like someone was whispering.'

Chloe was staring at the monitor. 'It did a little bit, didn't it? Strange.'

While it was true there was an odd sound on the monitor, he certainly didn't think it was anyone whispering.

'Pareidolia,' Andrew stated.

The girls turned to look at him. 'In English, please?' Chloe replied with a raised eyebrow.

'It *is* English,' Andrew told her, grinning. 'It's when you see or hear things that aren't there. You hear something odd, and your brain makes a connection to explain it, likening it to something you understand.'

'Is that so, Doctor?' Sarah asked.

'Yes, that is so,' Andrew confirmed with a playful smile and nod.

'Sounds like something they'd yell at Hogwarts while swinging their wands around.'

'I wouldn't know about that. But the 'whisper' was likely just more static, probably at a different frequency or something.'

'Scientist as well as a doctor, now?' Chloe teased. 'Full of surprises.'

Andrew chuckled. But then, all of their phones chimed at the same time.

It was the signal that indicated one of the motion-detection security cameras had been activated. Andrew pulled out his phone and saw an alert, then quickly checked the feed.

'Anything?' Chloe asked.

He shook his head.

'That thing is far too sensitive,' Sarah added. 'It goes off at the slightest thing. Probably just a bug flying past.'

'I'll have a look at it,' Andrew said.

The three of them managed to strip the last of the wallpaper before Emma woke, which then left Andrew and Sarah to bag up all of the remaining rubbish and take it out back. After throwing the last bag into the large bins outside, which were set within a timber bin-shed, Sarah let the bin lid drop shut.

She shook her hands off. 'Urgh, I definitely need a shower.'

'True,' Andrew replied. 'You stink.' Sarah flipped him the bird, but he ignored it and went on, 'How are you finding it here?' he asked her.

She let out an exhale. 'Where to start? It's certainly different.'

'Do you like it?'

She paused briefly, before giving a firm nod of her head. 'I do,' she stated, then narrowed her eyes at him. 'But you aren't a fan, are you?'

'It wouldn't have been my ideal forever home, put it that way' he admitted.

'I know that, Andrew, but Chloe—'

'I'm not about to start complaining again,' Andrew cut in, raising his hands in defence. 'Honestly, I'm going to make a go of it. I just wanted to know what you thought of it here as well. After all, there are three of us involved.'

'And are you okay with that?' Sarah asked.

'What? There being three of us?'

'Yeah.'

'Why wouldn't I be?'

'Well, I don't suppose you ever expected to have to share your forever home with your sister-in-law, did you?'

He laughed. 'No, I guess not. But the house is so big I don't think it will be an issue. Are *you* okay with it, though?'

'I am,' she said. 'For now.'

He frowned. 'What's that supposed to mean?'

'Meaning I'm well aware it can't stay like this. I might end up starting my own family one day. Hell, I've even been thinking about travelling for a little while. This place should just be for you guys in the long run.'

'Erm… have you spoken to Chloe about that?' he asked.

Sarah gave a guilty shake of her head. 'Not yet. I was going to, but she just seems so happy. I guess I didn't want to ruin that just yet.'

'Okay. But don't you think you need to have that conversation?'

Sarah nodded. 'Yeah. And I will. But there's no rush. It's not like I'm just going to pack up and go tomorrow. I think staying here for the foreseeable future will be good for me, at least until I figure things out.'

'What things?'

Sarah paused, then smiled. 'Life.'

'Life is a pretty big thing.'

'It is. I just… don't know what I want out of it yet. Everything was clear and straightforward in the army. And the future was always so far away. Now… it just feels like it's right on top of me and breathing down my neck.'

'Sneaks up on you, doesn't it?'

'It does! And soon I'll be old and grey like you. Then what is there to live for?'

He smirked and shook his head. 'Always a pleasure, Sarah.'

She did a curtsy, which looked strange coming from her. 'Thank you. Now come on, let's go. I need to get cleaned up.'

'Doing anything exciting today?'

'Nothing concrete, just going to head into town for a little bit. Been cooped up in the house for days and I want a break.'

'Just you?'

'That's the plan.'

'Take Chloe,' he said. 'That is, if you don't mind. I'll watch Emma.'

'Really? You don't have any work to do?'

'I *always* have work to do,' he said with a grin. 'But it's Saturday, and I've earned a day off. You two have a few hours out of the house together.'

'Cool,' Sarah replied. 'Sounds great. We'll bring back some food.'

'And some whiskey, if you don't mind,' he added. 'I'm running low.'

'I'll see what I can do.'

The two then walked back inside, with Andrew finally optimistic about the house.

CHAPTER 17

'Well,' Chloe began as she sipped on her tea, 'we know Alnmouth has some nice shops, but for a proper shopping trip we're going to have to go farther afield.'

'Yeah,' agreed Sarah. 'It's good for the basics, and nice coffee, but that's about it.'

Chloe made a face as her sister took another large mouthful of that revolting hazelnut coffee.

They were seated in *Hill of Beans*, the lone coffee shop in town. Chloe liked the establishment. It was quaint, with a gentle stream of people moving in and out, and had a modern decor.

Sarah was facing the entrance, and Chloe's position gave her a view of the seating area and serving counter. The smell of coffee beans was strong and pleasant.

Chloe definitely felt better being out of the house for a little while, especially since the work there had overtaken all of their lives recently.

That had been expected, of course, but it didn't mean it wasn't tiring, with a rinse-and-repeat cycle of sleep, work, eat, work, eat, work, sleep. The only variable was Emma and the attention that she needed.

So this was a welcome distraction.

'We're making good progress with the house,' Sarah said. 'I mean, still a long way off from finishing, but the essentials are getting there.'

'Yeah. Hard work, though.'

'And how are you feeling about it all? Is it starting to seem like home yet?'

Chloe thought about that for a moment, before eventually nodding. 'It is. I think it's easier to settle into a smaller house, to be honest. The Manor is so big and it's hard to make it feel like a home. That will change, though.'

'Yeah, I get that,' Sarah added. 'Seems like a place you go for a quiet weekend away, like a retreat in the country or something.'

'Exactly. But it is getting more and more familiar. And I *do* love it. Every day I wake up and am excited that it's mine. Sorry… ours.'

Sarah laughed. 'That's right, Sis, *ours*. Remember to share.'

'You know what I mean.'

'I do.'

'And how do *you* feel about the house?' she asked Sarah.

There was a pause, but Sarah finally responded, 'I like it.'

Clearly there was something else to be said. 'But?' Chloe asked.

'No, no buts, I like it. Honestly.'

'Somewhere you can see yourself living, then?'

Sarah smiled at her, but it was almost false, as if disguising something.

'Sarah, just tell me if—'

'There isn't anything wrong with the house, Sis,' Sarah insisted with a smile. 'It's fine, I swear. It's just… I'm struggling to sleep, is all.'

'How so?' Chloe asked.

'I don't know,' Sarah replied with a dismissive shrug. 'I'm having trouble getting a full night. Odd dreams. I keep waking up in the early hours of the morning a lot of the time.'

'Strange,' Chloe said.

'Just adjusting, I guess. I've certainly slept in worse places.'

'I bet. Though, you've never really told me much about that side of your life.'

'Not a whole lot to tell,' Sarah said quickly, then a playful smirk drew over her face. 'You've seen Rambo, right? Same thing. I was just like him.'

'Of course you were,' Chloe said with a laugh.

'Anyway,' Sarah went on, and Chloe got the impression she was quickly changing the subject, 'there is something about the house we need to discuss.'

'Go on...'

'A certain room that we need to get sorted. One I think you're avoiding.'

'Vincent's?' Chloe asked.

'Okay... I guess there are two rooms.'

Chloe sighed. 'That fucking study.'

'Have you been back in since we found it?'

'No,' Chloe answered, shaking her head. 'You?'

'Briefly. I know you hate it and all, but I wanna go in there and take a good look. I mean, Andrew seems committed now, don't you think? I don't see any reason why we need to ignore the room like it doesn't exist. Some of the stuff in there seemed fascinating.'

'It looked macabre,' Chloe corrected.

'Those things don't have to be mutually exclusive. I'm just saying we can't keep ignoring it, unless you wanna keep that room as a kind of creepy museum forever.'

Chloe considered that for a moment, then rolled her eyes. 'Fine, we can move onto that one next.' Sarah gave an excited clap, and Chloe laughed before adding, 'You're so weird. And, *speaking* of weird, did you finish that book you were given?'

'Yeah,' Sarah said with a nod. 'It was really good. A little farfetched in places, obviously the whole thing about the ghosts is bullshit, but the history of the building is certainly cool. Wanna read it?'

'Nah,' Chloe replied. 'You can give me the highlights sometime. That man hasn't been back to the house again, has he?'

'No,' Sarah said with a grin. 'I'm pleased to say I haven't seen him since...' Then Sarah's face fell, and her jaw hung open.

Chloe frowned. 'What? What is it?'

'You know the saying: speak of the Devil and he shall appear?' Chloe's eyes went wide, and she turned her head as Sarah went on. 'Not that he's the Devil or anything, but that ghost hunter just walked into the fucking shop!'

Chloe scanned the entrance and quickly noticed the man that had just entered. He had grey, brushed-back hair, black-rimmed glasses, and was dressed in a black coat, jeans, and scruffy trainers.

'So that's the ghostbuster?' Chloe asked quietly.

'That's him,' Sarah confirmed.

David Ritter glanced around the shop after entering, and his gaze fell on the sisters. His eyes went wide. Both Chloe and Sarah immediately looked away, but the act was so obvious it had to have looked ridiculous.

'He's seen us,' Sarah whispered.

No shit.

'What do we do?' Chloe asked, looking down at her nails and pretending to inspect them.

'I... uh-oh. He's coming over.'

Chloe looked up again and saw that Sarah was correct. Though he looked nervous and moved awkwardly, the strange man was weaving between tables as he made his way over.

'Sarah?' he said as he reached the table and stood between the two sisters. Then, he looked down at Chloe and gave an uncertain smile.

'Hi, David,' Sarah said. 'Nice to see you again.'

'You too,' he replied.

Chloe braced herself, certain he was once again going to try and get inside their home to hunt his ghosts.

'I'm glad I bumped into you,' he said. 'I... erm... I think I owe you an apology.'

'You do?' Sarah asked, sounding as surprised as Chloe felt. That was not what she had expected to come out of his mouth.

'I do,' he confirmed. Then he cast his eyes down to the ground. 'I shouldn't have just shown up at your house like that, just after you'd moved in, to ask for access. It was insensitive. I... I tend to get carried away with things like that. And I'm truly sorry.'

He seemed sincere, and Chloe felt a little bad for branding him 'strange' without ever having spoken to him. It still might have been an accurate description, but even so...

'Thank you, David,' Sarah replied. 'I appreciate that.'

An uncomfortable silence fell, with no one seeming to know what to say next. David looked over to Chloe and his hand shot out, causing her to jump a little. She soon realised that it wasn't an aggressive move, but it had still caught her off guard.

Jesus, fella, don't move so suddenly!

'You must be Chloe Pearson,' he said. 'I'm David Ritter.'

She shook his hand. His grip was gentle, bordering on limp. 'It's Shaw now,' she told him. 'I married.'

'Oh, I see,' he replied, holding on for a little too long. It wasn't in any kind of creepy way, she knew, more that he seemed socially awkward and just didn't realise when to release. So Chloe pulled her hand away instead.

'David hunts ghosts,' Sarah said with a grin.

'So I've heard,' Chloe added, keeping her answer brief.

'Well,' David cut in, 'only in my spare time. My day job is an I.T. consultant.'

Chloe heard Sarah snigger a little, so she turned to see what was so funny. 'You were mentioned in David's book, you know,' Sarah said, pointing at Chloe.

'You read it!' David exclaimed with a big smile.

'I did.'

'Wait, what did it say about me?' Chloe asked, now interested, though 'concerned' would have been more accurate.

'Nothing much,' Sarah told her. 'Just that you, Mum, Dad, and Vincent were the only survivors back in 1982.'

'Oh,' Chloe said, still not comfortable with being discussed without her knowledge—and in a bloody *book* of all places.

'What did you think of it?' he pressed. 'If you don't mind me asking.'

'It was good,' Sarah replied. 'I found the history of the house really interesting.'

'I knew you would.' He seemed almost giddy. Then, he turned apprehensive. 'And... the end? The section about my investigation.'

Sarah then made a face, wearing a condescending smile. 'Well, that part didn't do it for me.'

'Oh,' he said, looking crestfallen.

'Don't take it badly. It's just, well, I really don't believe in that kind of thing.'

'Every word was true,' he insisted. His cheeks were now flushed red.

But Sarah, it seemed, was not about to simply humour him.

'Don't take offence, that's just my opinion. It's like if someone were telling me that Santa was real. It's the same thing.'

'It... it *isn't* the same thing, though.'

'To me it is,' Sarah insisted. 'But hey, I wasn't there. I'm just going on what I personally believe.'

David looked as if he wanted to debate the point farther, but instead gave a nod. 'Okay. That's fair enough.' He gave a short pause, before adding, 'But I'm not making anything up. Hasn't there been anything happen there that was a little... odd?'

Chloe turned to Sarah and gave her a death stare.

Don't you dare.

Chloe knew there was a plethora of weird shit Sarah could use by way of example: the smells, the noises, the creep who had knocked on their door in the middle of the night. And, of course, that occult study upstairs, which was a black mark that needed to be scrubbed away.

'Nope,' Sarah eventually answered. 'Sorry, but we haven't seen anything.'

Chloe breathed a sigh of relief.

'Well... that's good,' David replied, though he didn't look pleased with the answer.

'It is,' Sarah went on. 'Hell, Chloe has a daughter living there. Little Emma, my niece. And *she* is absolutely fine.'

David's face quickly darkened. 'There's a child living at the house?'

'There is,' Chloe stated firmly as she turned more towards him. 'Why is that an issue?'

David paused, his face twisting a little. He clearly had something he wanted to say, but was resisting. Or, he might have been trying to find an appropriate way to word it.

'Look,' he began, 'I know you don't believe in the things I'm telling you. And that is fine, I can totally understand that. And I'm not saying this to deliberately scare you or anything. But... you need to be careful. Especially with your daughter. It's dangerous in that house for anyone, but especially for a child.'

Chloe felt a pang of anger and quickly stood to her feet. 'Enough!'

she snapped, loud enough to draw attention from all those around her. David visibly shrank back. 'You have no right to harass us like this.'

'I'm not harassing!' he stressed, palms held out and his eyes wide in shock.

'You pester my sister to run some kind of bloody ghost-hunting expedition. Then, when that doesn't work, you come over under the guise of apologising, only to use the safety of my child to... what... find an angle? Are we supposed to panic now that you've given us your warning? Are we to ask you to come save us?'

'Honestly, that wasn't my intention. I—'

'No!' Chloe snarled, cutting him off. 'You've said enough. Now leave us alone and don't ever bother us again.'

The man actually had the nerve to look hurt, almost close to tears. But Chloe didn't care. She just wanted him gone.

He took a breath, looked her in the eye, and quietly uttered, 'I'm sorry.'

With that, he left, not even bothering to get whatever he'd come in for. After he'd gone, Chloe allowed herself to retake her seat. She was shaking a little, and had to keep from grinding her teeth together. She glanced up at her sister, who looked both shocked and amused.

'Wow,' Sarah said. 'You know, if we hurry outside now, we might actually see him cry. I'm guessing floods of tears, what do you think?'

'Don't,' Chloe said.

'Come on, Sis, don't you think you went a bit far, embarrassing him like that?'

'*I* went too far? Are you serious?'

Is Sarah really taking his side here?

'Look,' Sarah began, 'I know what he said was bat-shit crazy, but he wasn't nasty or anything.'

'Sarah! He brought my daughter into this. Tried to use her as a pawn to get his own way.'

Sarah held up her hands. 'Fair enough,' she said. 'Although, I honestly don't think he was looking for an angle. I think he believes the things he is saying.'

'Then he's an idiot,' Chloe snapped.

Sarah laughed. 'Probably. Anyway, come on. Let's get back before you make anyone else cry. Oh, and for the record, I totally guessed he would be an I.T. consultant.'

CHAPTER 18

Emma's electronic cries came through the monitor on the nightstand, and Chloe slowly sat up in bed.

She wasn't ready to be pulled from a well-earned sleep just yet, and she felt her body protesting. There was a temptation to just lie back down and drift off again, but she knew she couldn't do that.

The room still smelled a little of fresh paint. It had been given a makeover recently where they had put in carpets, fitted wardrobes, and redecorated the walls, providing the room with a much lighter and airy feel.

Chloe yawned, stretched, then checked the monitor, already knowing she would have to get up and tend to her daughter. Chloe had learned quickly to distinguish between the different cries and mutterings that Emma made, and she knew which ones could be ignored and which ones required attention. These were the latter, and the child was clearly upset. On the display, Chloe saw that Emma was standing, propped up against the side of her cot-bed, and wailing. Chloe then looked at her phone to check the time.

Three-twenty-seven.

Perfect, she thought to herself with a hint of annoyance.

She glanced over to Andrew, who snored lightly, undisturbed by the sound of his daughter. Chloe then got out of bed and padded her way to

Emma's room next door, shivering a little as she passed through a pocket of cold air in the entryway. The child, with tears running down her face, looked visibly relieved to see her mother.

'Come here, baby,' Chloe cooed, and lifted Emma up, bringing her in for a protective hug. She was surprised to feel the child clinging to her tightly. 'It's okay,' Chloe whispered, nuzzling her cheek into Emma's fuzzy hair. 'You hungry?'

Chloe took a seat in the wooden rocking chair in the corner of the room and brought Emma in to feed. Chloe then looked around the room in the dark, feeling pleased with its transformation. While it was true that she quite liked the traditional wallpapers and features found throughout the house, she agreed with Andrew that the room needed to be both more modern and more child friendly. The walls had been stripped, re-plastered, and painted, and Chloe had even added a hand-painted mural on one wall, showing some of Emma's favourite cartoon characters. It was basic—Chloe classed herself as a competent artist, though no more than that—but gave the room life. The other walls were a very light grey, and to complement that, there was a thick light-grey carpet on the floor.

The black cast-iron radiator certainly looked out of place, but that would have to stay until the furnace and heating system had been replaced. Hopefully, that would eradicate some of the random cold spots that seemed to pop up throughout the house with no rhyme or reason to them.

As Emma fed, Chloe felt her eyes grow heavier, and it was only when she felt a sudden chill from behind—almost as if an icy hand touched the back of her neck—that she jolted fully awake.

Emma grumbled for a moment, and then carried on feeding.

'Sorry, kid,' Chloe whispered, and shuddered, feeling warmth once again run through her.

Fucking cold spots.

It didn't take long for Emma's suckling to cease, and Chloe heard tiny, adorable snores come from her little girl. Gently, as to not wake her, Chloe got to her feet and set Emma back down into her bed. She then tiptoed from the room.

Once out into the hallway, she turned and moved back to her own room, but stopped just outside when she was suddenly hit with a feeling of being watched. Chloe turned to look down the long, dark corridor behind her. At the far end, she could see the door to Sarah's room, which was slightly open. However, she could see nothing inside, except for thick and impenetrable darkness.

Then, the door glided shut, punctuated with the audible *click* of the latch snapping into the mortise.

Chloe stood motionless for a moment, and a sudden and oppressive feeling hung over her. Had Sarah been watching her? If so, why close the door like that?

It struck Chloe as extremely odd. She did consider ignoring it and just going back to bed, but curiosity got the better of her. She began to make her way slowly down the hallway to her sister's room, deciding not to flick on any lights in fear of waking anyone.

A squeak of floorboards under her bare soles sounded after every few steps.

She arrived at the stairs that led to the top floor, then glanced up. It was dark, and the shadows seemed even heavier up there.

Then she paused, and her body froze. For a moment, Chloe could have sworn there was a figure at the top of the stairs, merging with the darkness. But after staring for a few seconds, it became obvious that wasn't the case. There was nothing.

Pareidolia, she thought to herself as she moved on, soon reaching Sarah's room. She stood outside the door and listened, not really sure what to expect. If Sarah *was* up and awake, she would likely make some kind of noise.

At first, Chloe could hear nothing.

Then... whispering. Though the words themselves were unintelligible, Chloe knew the voice was Sarah's.

'Sarah?' she quietly called through the door. There was no response, just a short pause in the whispering before it quickly resumed again. Try as she might, Chloe could not pick out or understand any of the words being uttered.

It was then Chloe realised that her sister could just be talking in her sleep.

She had a protective impulse to check on her little sister, which was ridiculous, knowing the kind of person Sarah was; she certainly wasn't someone that needed protecting. However, Chloe was still the big sister, so she gently twisted the brass handle and pushed the door open.

It took a few moments for her eyes to adjust to the gloom and blackness in the room, but she was soon able to make out Sarah's form in her bed. Her sister lay still, eyes closed and breathing steadily—very clearly asleep. The covers looked like they had been kicked away, and lay crumpled and twisted around Sarah's lower legs.

The room, like Chloe's own, had been freshened up from its original state, but Sarah had elected to keep the same wallpaper as before, as well as most of the original furniture.

After a few moments, Sarah's mouth moved, and again those gentle utterances escaped, a kind of babbling Emma would have been proud of.

But... was it really babbling?

Chloe paused, and realised that it actually sounded more like a different language than random gibberish. She wasn't versed in anything other than English, but this had a certain familiarity to it, something she had at least heard before.

Perhaps Latin?

As Sarah continued to whisper, she began to slowly turn her head as it lay on the pillow, moving it right and left. Sarah scrunched her already closed eyes even tighter.

Whatever dream was taking place in her mind didn't seem a pleasant one. Chloe was tempted to wake her sister and relieve her of the mental torment, but decided against it. Fitful sleep was perhaps better than no sleep at all.

Instead, she walked round to the other side of the bed, took hold of the discarded sheets and pulled them, wanting to cover up her sister. However, she found resistance, which was confusing, given there was nothing there for the sheets to get snagged on. Chloe pulled again, and this time the duvet complied.

Chloe then dropped the sheet over Sarah and tucked the top up around her chin. Hopefully it would keep her warm, since the room had a noticeable chill to it. Chloe then sat on the bed next to her sister, and placed a comforting hand over her forehead, feeling a light layer of perspiration.

'Night, Sis,' she whispered. Chloe then detected a faint, but rank odour in the room, as if something were rotting and fetid. It came out of nowhere, and Chloe could only assume it was perhaps standing water in the heating pipes. An ongoing issue, and something else to fix.

Chloe sat back, ready to stand up, knowing there was nothing she could do about it now. However, as she leaned back, her gaze moved over towards the glass-fronted cabinet opposite Sarah's bed.

She froze.

In the dark reflection, Chloe was able to make out a terrifying sight. There was something else in the room with them. A woman. And she was on the bed, right next to Chloe.

Through the reflection in the cabinet, Chloe could see the woman was haggard and twisted, with dark hair that was pulled tightly back into a bun. Her face was lowered over Sarah's head, mouth to Sarah's ear, and she wore what looked to be a dirty, once-white cotton blouse, one that had a high neck and was form-fitted to the thin figure. The woman also wore a long black skirt that covered her legs, complementing an outfit that looked to be from a different era.

It was her horrifying face that truly scared Chloe. Pale skin was pulled tight over the skull, and it had thin purple veins running through it. The deeply sunken eyes looked blank, fully white, with no pupil to speak of. One eye sagged lower than the other, its lid half-closed. Any skin that had existed around the mouth had rotted away, leaving exposed, raw, and red flesh as the strange woman's mouth hung open.

The last detail Chloe took in was a gash of red across the throat, accompanied by a drizzle of crimson liquid that stained the neck of the woman's top.

And in the reflection, Chloe saw the hideous stranger move, slowly lifting her head up and bringing it millimetres away from Chloe's, who suddenly felt an even more intense cold radiate from the space next to her. The woman's head turned from Chloe, towards the reflection in the glass cabinet, and their gazes locked.

It was only then that Chloe was finally able to gain control of her body and cry out in absolute fear. She whipped her head around, expecting to see that horrible sight directly before her. But she did not.

Sarah sat upright in her bed, hair a mess and eyes drowsy.

'What... what the fuck?!' was all she managed to say.

However, Chloe couldn't concentrate on her sister at the moment, and she simply stared ahead of her, at where that horrible woman *should* have been.

But there was nothing.

She quickly turned back to look at the reflection again. But there was no woman.

The only reflections in the glass now were of Chloe and her sister.

'Chloe?' Sarah asked in a groggy voice, squinting through tired and confused eyes. 'What is it? Did you just scream?'

Chloe was unable to answer. Fear had resumed its grip on her voice, and she was shaking uncontrollably. She turned back to Sarah, whose face became a picture of concern.

'Sis?' she asked. All Chloe could do was break down and cry.

CHAPTER 19

Sarah's mind was reeling.

Upon opening her eyes, she'd spotted Chloe sitting on the bed. Her sister had a look of fear on her face as tears rolled down her cheeks.

So, naturally, panic flooded through Sarah, too.

Something's wrong. Is Emma okay?

But that worry was mixed in with grogginess and confusion at having been woken so abruptly. A portion of her mind still swam in her dreams, and she still heard the echoes of that horrible voice.

Dede!

Soon, however, she was able to fully focus, and she sat up on the bed, taking hold of her sister's hands.

'What is it?' Sarah quickly asked, trying to keep calm.

Chloe's eyes turned and fell on Sarah. Her breathing was quick and ragged. 'I… I…' but she was unable to continue.

That did nothing to ease Sarah's rising panic. She had never seen her sister like this before, which meant that whatever had happened was serious. Sarah brought Chloe close and hugged her, hoping to calm her enough for her to explain what had happened.

'It… it can't have been real,' Chloe whispered.

'What?' Sarah asked. 'What can't have been real?'

It took Chloe a few moments to compose herself enough to speak, and she cast Sarah a desperate look. 'Please tell me you'll believe me.'

That caught Sarah off guard. 'Of course I will,' she quickly replied, surprised Chloe would even have to ask. There wasn't a thing in the world Sarah wouldn't believe her sister about—she trusted Chloe completely.

Then, Chloe told Sarah what had happened: about waking in the night, coming into Sarah's room, and seeing a strange woman crouched over her.

Sarah paused, unsure how to reply.

As it turned out, for the first time in her life, she *didn't* believe her sister. Well, perhaps that wasn't true; she didn't doubt Chloe believed what she was saying, but that didn't mean it was factually correct.

Because what she was saying was physically impossible. People didn't just vanish into thin air. Could it be possible that the altercation with David Ritter was simply playing on Chloe's mind and caused her to have a very life-like dream?

Sarah considered her next words carefully, not wanting to hurt or offend her sister, who was clearly upset.

'Wow, that's... unreal. Are you okay?'

Chloe shrugged. She had stopped sobbing, but was still visibly shivering. 'I just don't know what to make of it. It seemed so real. But it can't have been... can it?'

A wave of relief washed over Sarah. Sanity and reason, it appeared, had taken hold. Maybe she didn't have to hurt Chloe by dismissing her story. Chloe was already questioning the whole thing on her own.

'Well, no,' Sarah replied. 'But that's a good thing, because I *really* don't want some creepy ghost-woman watching me sleep, thank you.'

Chloe offered a small smile.

Progress.

'I guess not,' she said. 'Guess I'm just losing my mind.'

'Nah, you're just stressed. There's a lot going on, and this isn't exactly a normal situation we're in, is it?'

'True,' Chloe replied. 'To be honest, I've felt a little on edge here since that night a while back...'

'Ah, when the weirdo came a-knocking?'

Chloe nodded.

And it started to all make sense now: the pressure Chloe was putting on herself to make Perron Manor work for them all, the work involved in refurbishing it, Andrew not being a team player at first, the study of the Devil upstairs, David Ritter's ramblings and warnings, and the fright they both had a little over a month ago… how could it all *not* affect her?

A stressed mind could very easily play tricks on its host. Sarah was well aware of that. In the months after Tania's death, she'd woken up in the night more than once only to see her friend at the end of her bed, yelling, *'Your fault!'* before exploding into a sea of crimson mist. But Sarah knew it was nothing more than a guilty vision left over from her subconscious mind.

Perhaps it was the same with Chloe.

Sarah then relayed the story of seeing Tania—something she had *never* shared with anyone before—to Chloe. It wasn't something she wanted to do, but felt it might help provide clarity and perspective.

'Shit, Sarah,' Chloe said. 'I had no idea you were going through that. I mean, I know you and Tania were close, but I didn't know you felt so guilty about it. It wasn't your fault, though.'

Sarah took a moment. 'But it was.'

'What do you mean?'

'She was on point, and stepped on a mine. That was supposed to have been me. But I… something just felt *wrong* about the whole day. I hesitated after being selected, resisted even… I've never done that before in my life. Following an order was never an issue for me, dangerous or not. So, Tania volunteered to help me out. I didn't want her to, but…'

'Jesus,' Chloe uttered.

Sarah nodded. 'Yeah.'

'Why didn't you tell me that before?'

Sarah looked away and twisted up her mouth. 'Dunno. Haven't really told anyone about it. I'm not exactly proud of killing my best friend.'

'That isn't what happened!' Chloe stated firmly. 'It was a horrible situation, but it wasn't your fault. That's pretty clear to me.'

'It's hard to see it that way, Chloe.'

'But it's the facts, regardless of how it looks to you. It wasn't your fault, Sis.'

Sarah waved a hand dismissively, 'Anyway, it doesn't matter. I just wanted you to realise that, just because I saw her doesn't mean she was really there. The mind can be a funny thing, and it can fuck you up if you let it.'

'And make you believe things that aren't really true,' Chloe added. 'Maybe we both need to remember that.'

'Maybe,' Sarah said, though she knew the guilt over Tania would never go away. Nor should it.

CHAPTER 20

'You sure you want to go up there?' Sarah asked, and Chloe nodded.

After how foolish Chloe had been the previous night, she felt like she needed to prove to herself there was nothing odd about the house.

Well, that wasn't the best way to put it, because there was plenty *odd* about Perron Manor. The room they were in was a prime example.

But she needed to convince herself that there was nothing more to it than that.

Sarah had mentioned that she wanted to go back up to the study, so Chloe had insisted she go as well, which was clearly a pleasant surprise to her sister.

Emma had been put down for her mid-morning nap, so Chloe, Sarah, and Andrew ventured up to the top floor.

They stood in the previously hidden section of hallway, with its discoloured wallpaper, dusty floors, and dark surroundings. This time, Andrew had come prepared, and set about replacing the old bulbs in the antiquated light fittings. After trying a switch, the darkness was washed away.

'Let there be light,' he said, waving his arm in a sweeping gesture.

'You're such a nerd,' Sarah said to him.

'A nerd who lit the way,' he retorted. 'These bulbs should work in the study as well, so we can finally get a good look at what we're dealing with.'

'Where do we even start with all of that stuff?' Chloe asked. 'Do we just throw it all out?'

'Hell no!' Andrew shot back. 'We don't know what's in there. Some of it may be valuable. Hell, the least we should do is donate it all to a museum or something.'

'First, we have to see what's there,' Sarah reasoned. 'It might all be junk.'

Chloe and Andrew both nodded in agreement, and they once again entered the bizarre study.

Andrew set about his task of replacing the bulbs, and was aided by the torchlight from Chloe's phone. There were four wall fixtures to replace, and two in the ceiling.

Once done, he flicked the switch and—just as it had with the hallway outside—dull light illuminated the area.

The first thing Chloe noticed again was that damn symbol on the floor, and the dark stain within.

Sarah was looking at it as well. *'That,'* she said while pointing, 'is fucking ridiculous.'

'It is a little... hokey,' Andrew agreed, clearly struggling to find the right word.

With more light at their disposal, Chloe could easily make out more of her surroundings, and was quick to move her attention away from the pentagram on the floor.

With more light, it was easier to see the wallpaper now, and Chloe could now make out the odd, faded pattern of intermingling burgundies and creams, which actually meshed rather well with the dark oak panelling below it. However, all the colours still lent the room an overbearing and oppressive feel, only exacerbated by the amount of junk crammed in here.

The bookshelves were overflowing with old-looking tomes, all packed into any available space. Piles of cardboard boxes seemed to have been dumped haphazardly on the floor, and the display cases were laid out without any real thought or form.

It wasn't a space to showcase the items it held, and was obviously just a storage area.

However, one thing seemed to have been given both respect and room: the glass-topped, waist-high display cabinet Sarah had seen during their last visit. It drew her attention again now, and she stood before it, gazing through the glass.

Chloe walked and joined her sister in peering at the thick, ancient-looking book that lay on the red, cushioned base inside the cabinet. The gold title of the book, set against the black leather, read: *Ianua Diaboli*.

Chloe had no idea what that meant, and really didn't want to know. She watched as Sarah traced a finger down the glass lid that protected the book. Her eyes had a longing expression in them, which Chloe found odd.

'Piqued your interest, has it?' she asked.

Sarah blinked, then turned to her sister and her eyes slowly regained focus. 'I guess. Just looks interesting.'

Sarah had a point.

There were strange markings—all set within small, concentric circles—in each corner of the front cover. And while most of the leather looked aged and cracked, these golden symbols and the small areas around them somehow appeared to be pristine.

One of the markings was an eight-pointed star, and another a simple cross. The lower left was a triangle which had another inverted triangle set within it, and the final symbol, in the bottom right, resembled the eight lines on a compass, all pointing off to their respective directions.

Close to the book they were inspecting sat a beautiful, old-style mahogany writing desk. There was a large, brown-leather ledger upon it, and though it still looked older than Chloe, it could well have been the youngest item in the room. An elegant fountain pen was slotted into a metallic base next to it.

Chloe took a step towards the desk, but stopped as Andrew spoke up.

'So... should I state the obvious?'

Both girls turned to look at him. 'Which is?' Sarah asked.

'1982? I mean, look at this place. Pentagram on the ground, with what is quite clearly blood in it, and then items that are obviously occult in nature. I mean, Aleister Crowley would have been in his element here. Wasn't there a theory that what happened back then was some kind of cult suicide or something?'

'*One* of the theories,' Chloe said, having heard it before. 'But I don't remember the guests here being part of a cult.'

'Maybe they just hid it well. Or maybe someone went off on a rampage, fuelled by stuff like this,' he said, and cast an arm about the room.

Then Sarah threw in something else. 'What about Vincent? If that is true, do you think he was involved?'

Chloe shook her head.

Her memories of the man were limited, but their uncle had always seemed nice and genuine as far as she could recall. However, there was another person back then whose impression upon Chloe had been a little... darker. 'Maybe the owner, if anyone,' she said. 'Marcus Blackwater. He committed suicide that night, so it's a possibility, I suppose.'

'That's a lot of people to kill on your own, though,' Andrew replied.

'It doesn't matter,' Chloe snapped, feeling agitated. 'The police looked into it all, and it was up to them to figure out what happened. It's not our problem.' She then looked at the stain within the pentagram. 'They could have cleaned up the blood, though,' she added.

'Not surprised they left it,' Andrew said. 'Especially back then. Once they were finished with the house, I can imagine it was up to the owners to clean everything up.'

'Vincent inherited the house,' Sarah added. 'So he just left it all like this all these years?'

'I'd guess that he was the one who locked this area up, too,' Andrew said.

'Maybe he wanted to just forget about it all,' Chloe offered. 'I can certainly understand wanting to ignore it. Regardless, it doesn't matter anymore. We can clean it up now, and scrub it all away from history.'

'Agreed,' Sarah said.

Andrew nodded as well.

'So,' Chloe began, 'how do we start? Just sorting through all of this is going to take a *lot* of time. Do we put the rest of the house on hold until it's done?'

'I don't think we should,' Sarah replied. 'We can spend a little bit of time each day just working through it, I guess. Slow and steady, when we have any spare time. Start with the smaller stuff, and get it all boxed away, then stack it with the things that are already packed.' She then pointed towards the piles of cardboard boxes.

'Which is fine,' Andrew cut in, 'but wouldn't it be wise to get someone in to have a look at it all first? Just to see what the hell we're dealing with, and if any of it is valuable?'

'Do you know anyone who deals in this kind of thing?' Chloe asked.

'Hell no,' he replied. 'But I do know my way around the internet. I'm sure we could find someone.'

Chloe and Sarah cast a look at each other. Andrew had a point.

'Fair enough,' she said. 'We can pack away what we can for now, I guess, and get someone here to look through everything. But… Andrew?'

'Yeah?'

'Can you get someone here quickly? I'd like this stuff gone as soon as possible.'

Andrew nodded. 'No problem. In fact, I'll start looking today and try and have someone at least lined up before I go away.' Andrew gave Chloe a kiss on the cheek and walked from the room, shouting back, 'I'll be in my office.'

He was due to leave again in two days, heading up to Scotland this time.

Once he was gone, a dull clicking sound caused Chloe to turn around. She saw that Sarah had unlocked the display cabinet she had been looking at.

'What are you doing?' Chloe asked.

'Just having a look,' Sarah replied, and once again had the same longing look in her eyes. With the glass barrier released, she was able to run a finger over the leather cover of the book and trace around the title.

But Chloe didn't see the appeal. It was just an old book.

Sarah opened it and began to carefully leaf through the yellowed, fragile-looking pages. The handwriting within was written in block columns; the penmanship was extremely neat, with elegant curves.

And not a single word in English that Chloe could see.

On some pages were detailed sketches of things she could have done without seeing.

There were diagrams of the human form, such as the flesh, the skeleton, the muscle, even certain organs. In addition, inked on the pages were a plethora of other occult-looking symbols, along with drawings of things that appeared to be... inhuman.

Terrible things, clearly born from a terrible mind.

Sarah stopped flicking through the pages close to the centre, and then stared at the foreign text on the page. There seemed to be a title at the top: *Impius Sanguis*.

To Chloe, there didn't appear to be anything special about this section of the book, at least compared to some of the others.

'Something interesting, Sis?' Chloe asked.

'Huh?' Sarah responded without looking up. 'No... just...' Her voice sounded distant.

Chloe clicked her fingers before Sarah's face, causing Sarah to blink quickly and shake her head. She looked like she'd been pulled from a nap.

'What?' Sarah eventually asked.

'I was asking why you found this'—Chloe pointed to the words on the page before them—'so interesting.'

Sarah glanced down, then gave a confused look. 'I don't. I can't even read it.'

'Then why... Forget it,' Chloe said, rolling her eyes. 'Come on, we can make a start on this another day.'

'Okay,' Sarah agreed, but didn't move away from the book.

While it was an interesting artefact, Chloe wanted to know why it had beguiled Sarah so much. She had an idea to quickly flick to the back and see if there was any information about the writer—though even if there was, she doubted she'd be able to read what was there. She moved next to Sarah and took hold of the book herself.

After turning through to the rear pages, she saw the last section was titled: *Claude Ianua*. It was similar to the other passages, and had accompanying sketches as well. One was of a mirror, and one of what seemed to be hideous reflections on a liquid surface. But, beyond that, nothing. The book just seemed to end abruptly.

With a shake of her head, Chloe heaved the full thing shut. She then closed the glass lid and turned the small key to the front of the cabinet, locking it once again.

Sarah followed Chloe from the room, though Chloe noticed her sister glance back once more as they left.

CHAPTER 21

2 Days Later...

'I could have just come on my own,' Chloe said, dropping the carton of baby tomatoes she held into the shopping trolley.

'Well, I can't just leave you to do the grocery shopping all the time, can I?' Sarah responded. 'Seems a bit lazy. Plus, I wanted to get out of the house for a little bit.'

The supermarket was large, which was surprising for a small town like Alnmouth. The aisles inside were packed with goods, and the trolley Chloe pushed squeaked across the laminate flooring underfoot. The high ceiling above them consisted of corrugated metal sheeting and exposed steel purlins.

Emma sat in the built-in child's seat at the rear of the trolley, happily looking through one of her sturdy board-books, one about a dog who had gone missing just before dinnertime. As they passed an elderly man, who walked on his own, Emma pointed at him.

'Man!'

Chloe gave the old man an apologetic smile, but he just chuckled and gave Chloe a friendly wave. The girls moved on, browsing the isles.

For weeks, Chloe had taken it upon herself to fulfil the weekly task of shopping, but today Sarah had been keen to come along as well.

And Chloe was quick to notice that her sister looked tired.

'Still not sleeping too well?' she asked.

Sarah shook her head. 'Not really. It's getting a little worse now, to be honest. It seems like I'm waking up every single night.'

'Always at the same time?'

'Yup, roughly between three and four in the morning.'

'Well, don't take this the wrong way but... why don't you try speaking to someone?'

Sarah picked up a packet of chocolate bars and looked them over. 'What do you mean?' she asked before setting the chocolate back.

'Well, isn't not sleeping a symptom of going through some kind of trauma?' Chloe wasn't a psychologist, but it certainly sounded right to her.

Sarah whipped her head around and frowned. 'Dealing with trauma? What the hell are you talking about?'

'You know what I mean,' Chloe replied. 'What happened with Tania. Maybe something isn't sitting right, and talking about it could help.'

'I don't think so,' Sarah stated dismissively. 'I'm fine.'

'Fair enough,' Chloe said, deciding to drop it. For now. But she knew Sarah was not *fine*.

The two women then moved on to the frozen section, and the air around them dropped in temperature. Chloe was picking through the frozen meats when she heard a jingling tone emit from her phone.

Sarah's too.

It was the camera system they had installed at the house. Detecting movement was a regular occurrence, and nine-times-out-of-ten, it was a false alarm, set off by God-knows-what.

Both girls pulled out their phones and flicked on the live-feed application, which displayed the full-colour stream from the activated camera. It was from the rear door, and looked out over the courtyard of Perron Manor.

'Nothing,' Sarah said. 'I swear to God, that thing is so sensitive the fucking light from the sun could set it off.'

And that was true enough. They'd had an engineer check the system over, but all he'd said was that it was configured correctly. But the amount of notifications they were receiving, which showed nothing of interest, had definitely worn on them.

Only this time, Chloe spotted something that her sister had not. In the distance, standing close to a large hedge, was the form of a person peeking out.

It was little more than a dark mass, but Chloe was able to see the rough shape of a head and a body, which was covered in a thick-looking material. She felt herself seize up.

'Who the hell is *that*?' Chloe asked, showing her phone screen to Sarah and pointing to the figure. Sarah frowned, then looked to her own phone.

'Oh shit, I missed that.'

The coldness around Chloe seemed to grow heavier at the sight of this stranger and her thoughts ran back to the night they had been harassed by someone knocking on their door and running away.

Chloe hit the record button on the streaming application, so they at least had a record of what they were seeing.

'Is he just… covered in shadow or something?' Chloe asked, feeling an ominous sense of panic start to emerge, like grass-shoots breaking through the soil above.

'Looks like it,' Sarah confirmed, though she sounded less than convinced. Chloe understood why: there didn't seem to be any other shadows near him. 'And it's definitely a person?'

'I… I think so,' Chloe said, but started to doubt herself. 'Can't be certain, since he's standing so far back. Could be a trick of the camera. Maybe.'

Sarah then clicked her touch screen, and cycled to the feature that allowed her to transmit her voice out of a speaker near the camera.

'Excuse me,' she said into the phone, 'care to tell us who you are?'

The girls stared at their respective phones, but the person—if it truly *was* a person—made no movement at all. They just continued to stare, and Chloe got the distinct impression the stranger was looking directly at *them* through the camera, like it knew they were there.

'We should call the police,' she stated.

'But we don't even know if anyone is actually standing there. It's kinda hard to make out.'

'Better safe than sorry,' Chloe stated, remembering the last time they'd needed officers there. She had regretted not calling sooner.

She clicked off the feed, knowing Sarah still had hers going, and made the phone call. Once connected, Chloe started to relay what was happening to the call handler. Sarah nudged Chloe and showed her the phone screen, which was still displaying the feed but with no sign of the shadowy stranger anymore.

Where is he? Chloe mouthed.

Sarah shrugged and whispered, 'Just vanished. I looked back at my phone and he'd gone.'

Frustration rippled through Chloe, but she carried on with the call, still wanting the police to get over to the house and check everything out. The woman she spoke to confirmed that a squad car would head over as soon as possible.

'We better get back,' Chloe said once she had ended the call. 'And meet them there.'

'Fair enough,' Sarah said, but pointed at the trolley full of food. 'Do we pay first?'

'No time, we should just leave it. Come on, let's go.'

Chloe drove them back to the house as quickly as she could without breaking the speed limit. She was certain the person from the video feed was the same one who had tormented her and her sister.

And she wanted the fucker caught. No more of this nonsense. Whoever this freak was, he would *not* scare them out of their home.

However, she couldn't deny how strange it had been that, the longer they looked at the image on the feed, the more the visitor seemed to almost dissipate. She started to question if he had even been there in the first place.

The police arrived at Perron Manor only moments after Chloe and Sarah, and the squad car followed the sisters down the long driveway to the house. They all disembarked, and Chloe recognised one of the two officers as the female policewoman who had attended last time.

The other officer was someone different this time: a short, clean-shaven man, with broad shoulders and thick frame.

'Mrs. Pearson,' PC Taylor said. 'I understand you have another unwelcome visitor.'

'Yes,' Chloe confirmed. 'We have a camera system installed now, and while we were out we saw someone out back on the video stream.'

The policewoman nodded. 'Now, am I correct in understanding the house is locked, and there should be no one inside?'

'That's right,' Chloe said.

'Okay, we'll check it out.' She then gestured to her partner. 'This is PC Walters. I'd like you two to get back in your car while the two of us have a look around the grounds.'

Chloe didn't particularly want to retreat back into her vehicle, and would have rather accompanied the two officers on their walk-around. She knew the police would never agree to that, though, so she and Sarah did as instructed.

Once they were back inside the SUV, they sat in wait.

'Should we show them the footage?' Chloe asked.

Sarah paused. 'Honestly, I'm not sure. It isn't exactly clear cut. They could say it's nothing, and I'd rather they kept taking us seriously, just in case this happens again.'

It was a fair point, so Chloe decided to keep the recording to themselves for now.

They waited for about fifteen minutes before the two police officers emerged from the other side of the house. Chloe could tell by the expressions on their faces that the officers had found nothing of note.

PC Taylor, on her approach to the car, shook her head, confirming Chloe's gut feeling. Chloe and Sarah disembarked.

'All clear,' PC Taylor said. 'We didn't find anything out of the ordinary.

'To be expected,' Sarah added. 'They probably ran when they heard the cars approach.'

The police officer nodded in agreement. 'Yeah, if not before that. There were no signs of a break-in or forced entry, either. Obviously, you should take a good look around inside to make sure nothing has been taken. We can stay and help with that if you want?'

'You don't need to do that,' Chloe said, feeling her frustrations grow. She wasn't frustrated at the police, of course, but at whoever was hounding them like this. 'They didn't get inside. The alarm would have gone off.'

PC Taylor nodded, then paused for a moment before speaking. 'Look, I know this is an annoyance for you, given this is the second time

I've been up here, but like I said before, stay vigilant. Call us if you need to. Don't let people like this scare you.'

'Oh, don't worry,' Chloe said, 'I'm past being scared now. Just angry.'

'Well, in that case, also remember not to do anything stupid. Let us handle what we need to. Don't go and get yourself in trouble, understand?'

Chloe nodded. 'Understood.'

Soon after, the officers left Chloe and Sarah alone again, and the two sisters—along with Emma—went inside. As they did, Chloe tried to keep a lid on her bubbling anger. After heading over to the kitchen, she started to make herself a cup of tea, and a coffee for Sarah, but set the cups down so hard on the kitchen countertop as to almost shear off the handles.

'It's okay,' Sarah said. 'I'm angry too. And that's good. Better to be angry than to be scared. But… just make sure it's channelled correctly. Otherwise…'

'Otherwise what?' Chloe asked.

'Otherwise you may end up breaking my favourite mug, and then I'd have to give you a beating,' Sarah responded with a grin. Chloe smiled. Sarah went on, 'And you'll drive yourself crazy. I'm willing to bet our little visitor is just someone obsessed with the house and its history. When we catch him, and we will, I'll make it clear to him that he isn't welcome here. And I guarantee he won't come back then.'

Chloe frowned at her sister. 'Didn't you hear what the policewoman said about not doing anything stupid?'

Sarah smiled. 'I won't do anything that gets us in trouble. But he won't bother us again, I promise you that.'

Chloe finished making the drinks and took a sip of her hot, bitter tea. 'You know,' she said, handing Sarah her drink, 'we keep referring to our visitor as a *he*. Could be a woman, for all we know.'

'I guess it's possible,' Sarah replied, 'but not likely. It tends to be men who play the obsessive stalker card.'

'Fair enough,' Chloe replied. Her mind quickly jumped back to the thing she had seen in Sarah's room a few days ago, the thing that had been crouched over her sister. That was a woman…

And that *was all in your head,* Chloe scolded herself. *Enough!*

Sarah let out a yawn and stretched her arms above her head. Chloe noticed just how tired her sister looked, with purple patches beneath sleepy eyes.

'Go take a nap,' Chloe offered.

'No, I'm not a napping person. I'll sleep tonight. The coffee will get me through.'

Chloe knew it was pointless trying to persuade Sarah to do something she didn't want to, so she left it.

Instead, she took out her phone and played back the footage from earlier, which showed the shadowy stranger standing outside in the courtyard. Chloe wanted to see the exact moment he disappeared. Then, a notion occurred to her.

'I'm going to check something,' she said, and walked from the room. Sarah followed, and they moved out to the great hall, then over to the glazed rear doors, which gave a clear view out over the courtyard.

Chloe played back the recording.

The stream showed the figure. Try as she might, however, Chloe could not make out any detail beyond a dark mass that was quite obviously humanoid in its shape. It was also tall, especially when actually looking at the hedge outside, which helped put things into perspective.

'Big guy,' said Chloe.

'Yup,' Sarah agreed.

'Still think you can put him in his place?'

Sarah just nodded confidently. 'It doesn't matter how tall a man is, if he gets kicked in the balls, he's going down.'

They continued to watch the footage, with the stranger not moving an inch. Chloe eventually speeded up the playback a little, but even then there was no jerking or flickering from the black mass, no swaying of any kind, as would be natural from a person standing for so long.

Eventually, Chloe reached the section where the mass disappeared. She rewound, then watched it back in real-time twice more.

'That's weird,' Sarah said, stating out loud what Chloe was thinking.

The visitor on the footage didn't step out of the shot, nor did he just blink away. Over the course of several frames, the shadows around the mass seemed to fully consume it, then melt away into the surroundings.

'What the fuck!' Chloe exclaimed. 'That makes no sense.'

'Maybe it wasn't a person after all?' Sarah offered. 'Just a shadow that kind of disappeared as the sun moved, or maybe as some clouds had passed over?'

Chloe turned to her sister, with a look of scepticism.

Sarah shrugged. 'Do you have any other explanation?'

Chloe did not.

CHAPTER 22

3 Days Later...

'Big job, but high profile,' Oliver Tripp said to Steve Davis, one of the plumbers he'd drafted in to help with the project. They stood outside of Perron Manor, where they were joined by the other three that would be helping, as well as the client, Andrew Shaw.

'Won't argue that,' Steve replied. 'Everyone around here knows this place. As kids, we used to come up here and dare each other to go inside.'

'Did any of you ever do it?' Andrew asked.

Steve—a painfully thin man in his mid-fifties with thin red hair and speckles of stubble—shook his head as he took a drag from the roll-up cigarette between his thin, chapped lips. 'Nope. And that was before what happened in '82,' he said. 'We didn't come up here at all after that. Place always gave me the creeps... no offence.'

'None taken,' Andrew replied with a smile. 'You should try living here.'

As much as Oliver was happy his client was being friendly with the help he had pulled together, he didn't like the way the conversation was going. Maybe it was natural for a place like Perron Manor, but he wanted the whole thing to be a positive experience for the family that lived here. Given the start date had slipped a little due to design complications, Oliver now aimed to exceed all expectations and didn't want anything else to sour the service he offered. He worried Steve's wandering mouth could do just that.

'Forget all that,' Oliver said. 'I think we can agree we're all too old for ghost stories, anyway. Some of us more than others, eh, Steve?' Oliver prodded Steve in the ribs before turning back to the house. 'First, we get started on the strip-out. Careful as we go, of course. All the iron we rip out goes in that skip.' He pointed to the large, blue metal container that had been placed on the gravel drive. 'Everything else, in the other one.' The other was a faded yellow container, roughly the same size as the first.

One of the ways Oliver was able to get his price low was by knowing he could sell all the waste iron from the pipework, radiators, and the furnace itself. Given the size of the house, he anticipated there would be a lot of metal, and it was something he could fetch a good amount of money for when weighing in at the scrapyard. The client was well aware of this, and the man seemed too astute to be taken advantage of—not that Oliver would ever try. Mr. Shaw had actually been impressed at Oliver's ingenuity in pricing and finding a way to drive his cost down.

'Okay, then,' Andrew said. 'I'm taking the girls out for a little while today. We're going to pick up a few portable hot water tanks, then go to the park to spend a bit of time outside. Should only be a few hours, but I figure it'll give you guys some time and space to get started without us getting in your way.'

'Perfect,' Oliver said. 'Though you don't need to worry, we'll be able to work around your family. We'd just need to coordinate when we need access to certain rooms.'

'We can work with that,' Andrew said. 'But you get a few hours' free rein, which should help anyway. And remember what I said about that room up on the top floor.'

Oliver nodded. 'Don't worry, we won't need to be in there today. Though we probably will need access in a couple of days to stay on schedule.'

'That's fine,' Andrew stated. 'There's just a *lot* to get through in there.'

'Left in a bit of a state, was it?' Oliver asked, and received a chuckle in response.

'Like you wouldn't believe.'

Less than twenty minutes later, the family had left, and Oliver and his team were alone at the house.

The team Oliver had gathered were all self-employed, but people he knew and trusted enough to bring on board.

There was Steve, who had been doing this longer than Oliver had, even working on a few commercial-sized projects such as hotels and care homes for larger contractors.

The other three were Cal Wilks, Ashton Mitford, and then the youngest among them, Art Steward.

All competent enough, but Oliver intended to watch them all as closely as possible, especially the more inexperienced Cal and Art, just to make sure there were no hiccups. While work had been steady recently, it hadn't exactly been booming. However, if the client here had the kind of connections in the construction industry that Oliver suspected he did, then who knows what kind of other opportunities the job could lead to.

First, though, he had to impress.

While gathered in the entrance lobby, Oliver gave out his instructions.

'Right, this morning is going to be a tour of the building so I can show you what we have ahead of us. The more you know of the house before diving in, the better prepared you'll be. So, we walk around and get the lay of the land. Okay?'

'Fair enough,' Steve said, taking a long drag from his cigarette before blowing out a cloud of yellowy-cream smoke. Oliver coughed.

'Put that stinking thing out before we start,' he said. 'We'll make our way down to the basement first, see the furnace, then work our way up.'

'What's the deal with the room upstairs?' asked Cal—a stocky, good-looking lad in his mid-thirties.

Oliver chuckled. 'Think the previous owner left something of a mess up there, from what I understand. Lot of junk that needs sorting through. We can ignore it for now; the client has it locked up anyway.'

Oliver had already seen the space, and could attest that it *did* need clearing out, but he wouldn't necessarily call it 'junk,' despite what he'd said to the others. Some of it looked potentially valuable, if a little macabre. He knew the client intended to catalogue it all and get it checked out before any of it was removed. Apparently, someone was coming out the next day to look it over.

But he had labelled it all as junk merely to downplay any interest the lads might have taken in it. Though he trusted them, you could never be too careful. And he didn't want anyone wandering off to rifle someone else's belongings. Even if the area had been locked off by the client, wandering hands could always find a way.

Oliver led his band of merry men through the side corridor, which was devoid of any windows or natural light, and into the great hall.

'Hell of a place,' Steve said. 'Like something off one of them Victorian shows the wife watches on T.V.'

'Victorian shows?' asked Art.

'Yeah, where they all prance around like lords and ladies in big houses, dressed in fancy suits and gowns. You know the type of stuff.'

'Can't say I watch it,' Art replied with a grin.

'Me either,' Steve was quick to clarify. 'Like I said, the wife does.'

'Sure, sure,' Cal added with a smirk. 'You just happen to always be there while she's watching it, huh?'

'Ah fuck off, the pair of you,' Steve shot back, shaking his head.

'This way,' Oliver said, keeping the focus on the job at hand. He led them through a side door and into a small area where stone steps ran down into the dark basement below.

'No lights?' Art asked.

Now it was Steve's turn to smirk. 'Are ya' scared, lad?'

'No!' Art shot back. 'Just don't want to tumble down there and break a leg.'

'Lights are at the bottom,' Oliver stated. 'Wait here.'

He then began to descend the steps, feeling the temperature drop as the darkness overcame him. The existing heating system had already been switched off, but houses like this were funny beasts. The thickness of the stone walls usually retained heat quite well, but they were a bitch to get warmed up in the first place. The ground-floor had actually felt relatively comfortable, but in walking down here, there was a noticeable dive in the temperature. He could also detect an ever-so-slight breeze, which was odd.

He reached the bottom and held out a hand, feeling along the stonework wall beside him while he searched out the light switch.

A quick skittering noise from deep within the black void drew his attention, one that sounded heavy but quick on the stone floor. Oliver shuddered.

That sounded like a big fucking rat!

And as much as normal creepy-crawlies didn't bother him, rats were different. Horrible, disease-ridden things.

His fingers eventually found the metallic fixture and Oliver flicked the switch. There was a quick strobe effect as the lights in the basement slowly flickered to life, causing a dancing of shadows that confused Oliver, giving the impression of movement close to the furnace.

As if something had ducked behind it.

But he knew it was just a trick of the brain as his eyes adjusted. Within moments, the bulbs settled into a steady stream of light, and they cast a dirty orange hue over the area.

Oliver could see the form of the old cells, as well as block pillars used to support the floor above. The furnace was at the far end of the space, and Oliver could also make out the piles of coal and wood that were used to fuel it.

The sound of footsteps behind him indicated the others had started their descent, and soon the group of five spread out into the large area, all eyes on the archaic metal furnace.

'Jesus,' Steve said, running a hand over his head. 'Never seen anything like that before. How old is it?'

'Who the hell knows,' Oliver replied.

'Going to take some heaving out of here, though.'

'It will, but I figure we strip it down first and take it out in chunks.'

'We got time for that?' Steve asked.

Oliver nodded. 'I allowed a few days for it.'

Then Cal cut in. 'How are the clients going to live here with no heating and hot water for so long? Don't they have a little 'un?'

'There are fireplaces all over the house,' Oliver replied. 'So they're going old-school.'

'And the hot water?' Cal asked. 'How will they bathe?'

'He's getting a few portable hot water tanks. They'll fill them up, plug them in, and use them to heat up water. They'll do for bathing and washing up and the like for a little while.'

'So… slumming it,' Art said.

'For a little bit, I guess,' Oliver told him. 'Which is why we need to work as fast as we can.'

Oliver then gave the group a quick tour of the next floor up, then finally the top storey—at least, as much as they could get access to. By the time they were done, it was a little past midday.

'Everybody happy?' Oliver asked with a clap of his hands.

'It's a *lot* to strip out, Ollie,' Cal said with a frown. 'The pipework alone will probably be a nightmare. If we go over the agreed time, I'm gonna have to bill you extra, mate.'

Oliver gave a dismissive wave of the hand. 'It'll be fine. Besides, I can come in on weekends on my own to keep things moving. You don't worry about anything, just concentrate on doing a good job. If we do run over, I'll see you're looked after. So, I ask again… everybody happy?'

The crew looked to one another, each searching for guidance. It was Steve who finally nodded his consent.

'Aye, Ollie, we're all happy.'

'Good. You guys go eat your lunch. I'm gonna go down to the basement and figure out how to take the furnace apart.'

CHAPTER 23

THE PUZZLE LOOKED solvable to Oliver.

He'd carefully inspected the furnace, and could certainly see areas where dismantling the unit could work. He also knew where to start.

Disconnecting the protruding pipework would be job number one, and then the heavy-looking top section could be unfastened and lifted off—a job that would likely take all of their combined strength. But, from there, it seemed like the metallic beast could be further stripped down, reducing it to handleable chunks.

Now he needed to figure out if the furnace should come out first, and then work up, or if it was best to disconnect the radiators and work back down. Given a good portion of the top floor was currently off-limits, that essentially made the decision for him.

Oliver had eaten his sandwiches while he planned out his approach, as having lunch on the go was normal for him. He wanted the lads to have more structure, and dedicated breaks, even if they hadn't truly gotten going yet. Though he was self-employed, and usually had no people working under him, Oliver knew that a well-fed and appropriately rested workforce was a happy one. He'd learned that pretty quickly when working on building sites as a youth.

So, he gathered up his sandwich wrappers, and prepared to go up and brief the others.

The lights above him suddenly blinked out.

Great, Oliver thought to himself. Perhaps a power-surge had tripped the circuit board switches—the only explanation for all the lights down here going out, rather than a single bulb.

The lights then flickered again; they were still functioning, apparently, but not at full power. There was a strobing effect that carried on for a few moments, quickly flashing the area in light before cutting it back to brief darkness, over and over again.

Then, a prolonged darkness once again settled in. Oliver could hear the buzz of electricity flowing above him, but for now the lights remained off, and he could see very little besides the glow from the light at the top of the steps.

At least he could follow that to make his way out.

'For the love of God,' he muttered, agitated. This was *not* the start he needed.

'Help.'

Oliver's body locked up, and he twisted his head.

It took him a few moments to realise that what he'd heard was a voice. Meek and quiet, almost wheezy, coming from a space ahead of him, over near the furnace.

But it couldn't have been.

His first thought was that perhaps one of the others had come down to mess with him, but none were particularly light on their feet, and Oliver was sure he'd have heard them descend the stone steps.

Or maybe he'd heard nothing at all, which was the more likely explanation.

Going mad, old man.

But the 'old man' soon heard it again, uttering a different word this time.

'Please.'

A foul odour then drifted over to him, one that vaguely reminded him of barbecued meat, though this had a sickly, sour tinge to it. Oliver then heard wheezed and ragged breathing off ahead. It was faint, but definitely there.

'It... hurts. It... always... hurts.'

'Who's there!' Oliver demanded. No response. 'Cal? Art?'

Still nothing.

There was a long sound of squeaking metal, like an old door swinging on its hinges. The only thing it could be, Oliver knew, was one of the doors on the front of the furnace.

He grabbed for his phone, which he could use to at least cast some light on the situation. However, he had been more panicked than he thought and snagged his thumb on his pocket while pulling his phone out. The device slipped from his grip and skittered off across the stone floor, into the black.

Shit!

There were a few more moments of silence, followed by a shuffling sound, and more of that sharp, ragged breathing. Oliver took a step back, feeling genuine fear start to course through him.

It has to be one of the lads. They've snuck down here to try and frighten me.

'Stop fucking around!' he yelled sternly. 'I'm serious, otherwise you're off the job. The lot of you!'

The voice returned, and though it still sounded pained, like the act of speaking was a struggle, it had a more sinister, threatening tone to it. 'It'll... hurt... you... too.'

There was another flicker of the lights. Just before he was again thrust into darkness, Oliver saw something struggling towards him, walking with stuttering and awkward movements, like a hideous marionette, and he would have screamed if his voice hadn't gotten lodged in his throat.

Its skin was a mesh of charred black areas that had crisped over, along with weeping and angry red flesh where open wounds bled freely.

Misshapen fingers were fused together, and some of the meat from the arm that had been reaching towards Oliver had been burnt away to the bone. Though Oliver was sure this... thing... was male, given its rough form and voice, there were no distinct sexual organs dangling between the legs; instead, there was just a melted and twisted mound of skin.

And then there was the head and face: mouth hanging loosely and pulled down to one side, the lips stripped away to reveal teeth and gums behind, and a single, sagging, milky eye. The other was missing, replaced by a congealed pocket of black flesh. In addition, there were no ears that Oliver could see, and only a few strands of hair in with the seared red and black skin of the scalp.

The lights then cut out once again.

'I'll... take... you... through... the... door,' it wheezed in the dark, and something approaching a cackle escaped it. 'Come... through... with... me.' It laughed again.

Oliver let out a whimper and began to back up quickly, moving away from the shuffling thing and toward the faint glow of light from the steps. As he did, he felt his heel clip on a raised section of stone slab, and Oliver fell hard to the ground, hitting the back of his head against the hard surface.

He let out a grunt. The shuffling sound before him suddenly grew quicker, and the wheezing more frantic and excited. Suddenly, the thing was on him, and Oliver felt a searing pain around his wrist as a hard and scabby hand took hold of him.

A bellowing scream erupted from Oliver, one that had been building since he'd first laid eyes on... whatever the hell this was. The smell was now overwhelming, causing him to gag and heave.

'Ollie?' someone called out from the top of the stairs. 'You okay?' Even in his fear-stricken mind, as Oliver fought against the impossibility that lay on top of him, he was able to hear Steve call down to him.

'Help!' Oliver screamed desperately. 'Help me!'

He then heard multiple feet quickly thunder down the steps. And, as they did, the weight above him, as well as the smell and the horrible breathing, vanished. The lights blinked back on, and Steve and the others came into focus, all wearing looks of confusion and worry.

'What the hell is wrong?' Art asked. 'What happened?'

Oliver took a few moments, trying to get his breathing back into a regular rhythm and calm his erratic heart.

'Did... did you see it?' he asked.

'See what?' Steve questioned, raising an inquisitive eyebrow. The man's eyes then widened a little. 'What did you do to yer arm?'

Oliver looked down and saw the skin around his wrist was angry and red, like a surface-level burn.

'Tell me you saw it!' Oliver screamed, feeling a sudden burst of despair run through him.

However, it was clear as the group looked at each other in puzzlement they had no idea what the hell he was talking about.

Oliver suddenly realised that they wouldn't believe him, anyway. They'd think he was nuts.

But it *had* happened!

He'd seen that burnt monster come at him. Smelled its stench. Felt its touch. And there was also physical proof of that—the angry welt across his wrist.

The house, he suddenly realised. *It's true.*

What happened to his uncle all those years ago wasn't just a crazy story.

'Calm down,' Steve said. 'Your eyes look like they're gonna pop out of your head. Just tell us what happened.'

'You might wanna pull yourself together as well,' Cal said, frowning. 'Mr. Shaw's car just pulled up, think the clients are home.'

Fuck the clients!

How could he work here now, after having seen and experienced *that*?

Oliver pulled himself up to his feet, and took a moment to himself, as his legs felt like jelly. He looked over to the furnace. One of the doors was now open, though he was certain it had been closed when he'd first come down.

'The hell with this!' he spat, then pushed Steve out of the way, grabbed his phone from the floor, and quickly ran up the steps.

Andrew went around the back of the car and pulled open the boot, looking at the portable water tanks they had just bought. They sat beside a brand-new coffee machine Sarah had insisted on getting. The next few weeks were going to be rough, he knew, but worth it for the luxuries the new heating system would bring.

Movement from the doorway of the house caught his attention, and Andrew saw Oliver storm from the house with a wild-eyed look etched on his face.

Chloe, who had just lifted Emma from her car seat, turned to the engineer. 'Hi, Oliver, how are you getting on?'

But Andrew could tell from the man's quick pace, set jaw, and balled fists that something was definitely wrong. He seemed extremely agitated.

'I'm leaving,' Oliver stated through gritted teeth, and quickly strode over to his van and pulled open the door. The members of Oliver's crew appeared at the front door as well, looking just as perplexed as Andrew felt.

'Excuse me?' Andrew asked. 'And *where* are you going?'

'Away from here!' Oliver shouted, surprising Andrew. 'I'll not set foot in that blasted house again. Ever.' He then turned to his colleagues. 'You lot coming?'

'What do you mean you won't set foot inside?' Andrew asked, raising his own voice and taking a step forward. 'You're under contract.'

'Fuck your contract!'

Andrew stopped short and raised eyebrows in shock.

'Ollie, what the hell's going on?' Art asked. 'What about the job?'

'Job's off,' he replied as he got into the driver's seat of his vehicle. 'Now get in, or I'll leave you here.'

Andrew strode up to the van and put his hand on the open door, preventing Oliver from closing it.

'I think you owe me an explanation. If you don't finish what you've signed up for, you know I can sue, right?'

Oliver leaned over to him, and Andrew saw something in the man's eyes that was beyond mere agitation, or even anger. It was fear.

'Then fucking sue me,' came the snarled reply. Oliver shoved Andrew back and closed the door. He leaned out through the window. 'I'll get the skips picked up, but I'm not coming back. You do what you have to do. I don't care.' He then cast a worried look back to Perron Manor. 'I'm not going back.'

Eventually, Oliver managed to get his dumbfounded colleagues into the van as well, and he drove off, leaving Andrew confused and furious.

'Erm, what the hell just happened?' Sarah asked.

Andrew had no idea how to answer.

CHAPTER 24

'F%%%!' Andrew snapped, and threw his mobile phone down onto the kitchen countertop.

'Still not picking up?' Sarah asked, feeling the anger radiate from him.

'No. What the hell's wrong with that man?'

'I don't know,' Chloe replied. 'I understand you're angry, but can we please stop the cursing in front of Emma.'

Andrew nodded, looking a touch embarrassed. 'Sorry. Won't happen again. It's just... I don't get it. He seemed over the moon when I gave him the job. And now he quits and doesn't even have the courtesy to tell us why?'

'But he's under contract,' Chloe said. 'You said so yourself. Isn't he bothered about being sued?'

Andrew shook his head and shrugged. 'No idea. Though, in fairness, the contract just protects both parties against losing money. Like if he wrecked the house, then he'd have to pay for it. Considering he didn't even start, and isn't asking for any money, we can't really claim anything. We could try, but I doubt it would lead anywhere.'

Sarah took a seat at the table next to Chloe, and started to play peek-a-boo with Emma, who was toddling around the floor, dragging a toy trailer along behind her. After getting back into the house after the altercation with Oliver, they had again gravitated to the kitchen area, despite Perron Manor having a dedicated living room, a study that doubled as a snug, and even a library, which they had barely used since moving in.

The kitchen had become the hub for their activity during most daytime hours.

She was as baffled as the other two as to why their engineer had abandoned them, but it wasn't something Sarah was going to lose her cool over. Yes, it meant they were stuck with that bloody furnace for a while longer, but it was hardly the end of the world.

However, she knew Andrew wouldn't see it that way, as it was the principle of the matter for him.

After a little while of playing with Emma, Sarah got to her feet, and then unpacked her brand-new coffee machine. She set it on the countertop and plugged it in, happy with the purchase. It wasn't often she indulged on material goods, but when she saw this thing in the store, it seemed like a no-brainer.

Andrew was still bemoaning the situation to Chloe and Sarah was beginning to feel restless. So, she grabbed the key for upstairs from the utility drawer and left her sister and brother-in-law to debate their options going forward.

But what options were there, really? They just had to find someone else to do the work.

That was the end of it.

Rather than get involved, Sarah wanted to go back up to the study on the top floor and once again look at the treasures within.

They had boxed away a lot of the items up there, which had been a unique experience, especially seeing Chloe's face when handling a liquid-filled bottle that also contained a cluster of rodent foetuses floating within. Most of the belongings upstairs were ready for the arrival of an antiques dealer Andrew had found online.

The book and its display case, however, had been left as they were.

Once on the top floor, Sarah unlocked the door to the corridor and entered the study. It still looked cluttered, even though many of the books had now been pulled from the shelves and boxed up. Many of the artefacts were left out as they had been, for fear of damage, so the whole room had the feeling of a job half-finished. Looking at some of the strange objects, Sarah couldn't help but feel a sense of wonderment, and part of her ached to know the actual age of the things around her.

In one cabinet, there were amulets, sigils, a dagger that looked to be made of bone, and rolls of parchment. One of the sigils had a rather demonic-looking face etched into its metallic form.

Whoever Andrew had found to come and look through all of this stuff was likely to have a field day. Or a heart attack, depending on their disposition.

Sarah had never been one to have an interest in the occult, but she couldn't deny the appeal of the treasures this room held, especially up close. But there was one thing in particular that intrigued her more than any other item.

Ianua Diaboli.

After turning the small key in the edge of the cabinet's frame, Sarah lifted the glass top, then took hold of the book and brought it up to her face. She could smell the aged leather, and felt its substantial weight in her hands.

Open it.

She set it back into its cradle, then slowly and carefully opened the cover to the first few pages. The writing scribed in black ink was beautiful, but unreadable to her. Even so, she got the sense that the words here held power, through great wisdom and knowledge. The desire to learn its secrets was hard to ignore.

Sarah worked through the pages, searching for something—though she had no idea what. It wasn't until she saw the heading of *Impius Sanguis,* midway through the book, that she stopped.

She stared at the unintelligible text. There was no reason these pages should have held her interest so, especially when compared to the others, and yet she could not get herself to look away. Sarah found herself mouthing the words as best she could as she read through the text.

Enim sanguis clavis est.

When she eventually did turn to another page, Sarah noticed that it didn't hold the same interest to her. Neither did the next one. That pattern continued as she leafed through the book, even if some on the surface should have looked more interesting. Indeed, a page with a sketch of something covered in shadow was startling to look at, but it still did not hold the same mystery and sway as *Impius Sanguis*. And, when she flicked to the back and saw the title of *Claude Ianua*, something close to revulsion overcame her. She looked away and quickly closed the book.

Strange.

Sarah then closed the cabinet lid again and continued to look around, slowly walking over to the old writing desk that held a thick ledger. The cover was plain except for symbols drawn onto the leather, similar to those on the cover of *Ianua Diaboli*. Sarah opened the ledger and saw handwriting on yellow, lined paper. This time, the writing was very much in English, though the penmanship left a little to be desired. The first page had only a few lines of text written on it, and seemed to be an introduction of sorts.

These transcriptions from Ianua Diaboli *are as accurate as I can make them, given the use of 'Old Latin' in with the more classical use of the language.*

While the original author of the book remains unknown, its purpose, and the purpose of the texts therein, are very clear. They all pertain to a very specific phenomenon that is able to exist in our world, one that is very relevant to Perron Manor.

This house is special.

It is, I believe, alive. And Ianua Diaboli *could very well be a way to harness what exists here, for those brave enough to do so.*

- A. Blackwater.

Sarah pondered the name. A. Blackwater? From what she understood, the previous owner before her uncle was a man named Marcus Blackwater, who died in 1982. Could he have had an unknown Christian name beginning with the letter 'A'? If not, then this was written by someone else.

Suddenly, Sarah realised she had a way to make sense of *Ianua*

Diaboli. She looked back to the book in the case, and a pang of excitement sprang up in her.

The ledger is a book of transcriptions!

Sarah then quickly shook her head. *Why is this rubbish entrancing me so much?* It was interesting, sure, but to actually make her excited…

'You okay there, Sis?'

The sound of Chloe's voice startled Sarah, who jumped and let the cover of the ledger fall shut. 'Jesus,' she said, looking to her sister. 'You scared the hell out of me. Why are you sneaking around like that?'

'I was hardly sneaking,' Chloe replied. 'And I've been calling you as well. Are you deaf? And what were you grinning about?'

Sarah cocked her head. 'Grinning?'

'Yeah. When I came in here you were smiling like a madwoman, staring off into space. You feeling okay?'

That took Sarah by surprise. 'I'm fine,' she said after a few moments.

Chloe narrowed her eyes, before shrugging her shoulders. 'If you say so. We're going to order food in again tonight, so I thought I'd check what you wanted.'

'Anything,' Sarah replied. 'Something spicy.'

'Spicy works for me.'

'So… has Andrew calmed down yet?' Sarah asked.

Chloe smiled but shook her head. 'Not really. But it is what it is, I guess. Strange that Oliver just ran off like that, though. Andrew still can't reach him. Seems like we'll just have to look elsewhere.'

'Yeah. It'll get sorted out, no need to stress or panic about it.'

There were a few moments of silence. Then Chloe asked, 'Why do you think the engineer bolted?'

Sarah shrugged. *How am I supposed to know that?* 'God knows. You have any ideas?'

Chloe chewed the side of her mouth for a moment. 'Well, can you remember when we first met him? He mentioned that his uncle worked up here way back in the day.'

The story did ring a bell with Sarah. 'Sure.'

'Apparently, Oliver's uncle saw something that freaked him out, and he ran. And with Oliver running out the way he did… I don't know, it just seems a bit strange. Maybe history has repeated itself.'

'So you think Oliver saw something that scared him?'

'Well… possibly. I mean, doesn't it fit? He looked terrified. Something had spooked him enough to give up the job entirely.'

'I guess,' Sarah admitted. What Chloe was saying did kind of make sense, but Sarah didn't like where the line of thinking would take her sister. If Oliver had gotten himself spooked over nothing, then fine, but Sarah didn't want Chloe to go down a path of believing there was more to it.

The incident of waking to find Chloe trembling in Sarah's own room, swearing she had seen an old woman had not been forgotten.

'But if that's the case,' Sarah said, 'then he's an idiot. It's an old, creepy house, and he shouldn't have let himself get so paranoid over nothing.'

Sarah maintained strong eye contact with Chloe.

Thankfully, Chloe seemed to grasp what had gone unspoken. 'You're probably right,' she said, then turned. 'I'm going to go back down, I'll catch up with you in a little bit.'

'Wait up,' Sarah replied, walking over to Chloe. 'I'm finished up here anyway.'

CHAPTER 25

'No!'

Chloe's eyes snapped open, and she gripped the sheets of her bed with tightly balled fists. Her breathing was rapid and shallow—she was almost panting. She then batted a hand to the side of her head but found only air. Chloe got the distinct impression something had been close to her head, whispering in her ear.

It was a dream. Just a dream!

Even so, her body was locked rigid, and it took a moment for Chloe's aching muscles to relax.

Just a dream...

And it had been a dream. Looking round, Chloe could clearly see that she was no longer downstairs in that dark, horrible basement anymore. She remembered the feeling of biting cold on her back, as well as the extreme heat that flowed over her front as she had stood in front of the raging furnace. Something she could not see had been holding her from behind: something ancient, strong, and malicious. It whispered things into her ear that she could not understand, and she could smell its foul breath. The flames and heat from the furnace before her, with its open doors, had seared her skin.

The walls around the basement were no longer stone, and had

instead looked like a horrible meld of skin and flesh, smattered with roving eyeballs and mouths that puckered and moved.

And a tall, pale man had been standing next to her. He'd been dressed in old clothing and had an almost skeletal face that wore a sinister grin. Wide and manic eyes without lids had watched as he held a squirming and crying infant in his grip.

Emma.

He had been reciting nursery rhymes in mocking tones, enjoying the panic in both mother and child.

Then, as Chloe screamed in desperation, the evil old man had thrown her child into the fiery depths of the furnace.

It was just a dream!

Even so, the panic that surged through Chloe was still intense, and she felt tears born of rage, helplessness, and failure bubble from her eyes.

Then she heard a voice on the baby-monitor beside her.

'Round... and round... the garden.'

Chloe snapped her head around, but the image she saw was just of Emma sleeping peacefully. Safely.

Her mind swam, still reeling. Was the voice simply another lingering memory from the nightmare?

She then cast a glance to her other side, where Andrew snored lightly beside her. She quickly rolled from the bed and stood, the feeling of the cool air pleasant on her sweaty and sticky body. Dressed just in her light-blue silk nightie, Chloe quietly walked from her room and into Emma's. She needed to see her daughter with her own eyes, just to make sure her child was safe.

Though the room was a touch cold, and that horrible odour from the old heating system was faintly detectable, all else was as it should be inside of the child's bedroom.

The wave of relief that washed over Chloe was palpable. The emotions were so strong that she had to take a seat in the rocking chair, and put her head into her hands, letting the feelings run their course.

Just a dream.

After sitting in the dark for over ten minutes, just listening to Emma breathe, Chloe decided it was time to go back to bed and try to get some sleep. However, that seemed unlikely, considering how awake she now was thanks to the adrenaline that pumped through her.

She stood to her feet and took a breath. The house felt oppressive. Heavy. Smaller than it should, considering its size. In truth, for reasons she couldn't explain, it had started to gradually feel smaller day by day, ever since that night when she and Sarah had heard the banging on the door.

And despite what her sister had insisted, Chloe couldn't completely ignore the possibility that there was something wrong here. Things she had previously passed off as just being in her head now seemed entirely possible.

Especially in the dead of night, surrounded by nothing but shadows, all of which felt like they were watching her.

Chloe felt guilty about dragging her family out here and insisting that living in a place with a such a history could actually work.

Another breath.

Don't let your imagination run away with itself.

Despite how she currently felt, part of Chloe knew that, logically, Sarah was probably right. She just hoped things would seem different when the sun rose, and she could think things through in the warm light of day.

Chloe walked from Emma's room and gently closed the door behind her. After making her way back towards her own bedroom, Chloe stopped short, detecting movement from the other side of the long corridor opposite her door. She gasped, and the image of a naked woman slowly walking towards her sent a chill up her spine.

Just as she was about to scream, however, she focused on the woman. The scream settled, retracting back down her throat. Confusion now overshadowed the fear she had been feeling.

'Sarah?'

Her sister did not answer, just continued her slow and steady walk, eyes half shut.

She's sleepwalking! Chloe realised.

Sarah stopped midway along the hallway, held her position for a moment, then turned her head to the side. Her body followed, and Sarah then began to ascend the stairs up to the top storey of the house.

Chloe let out a long sigh. She had no idea Sarah was prone to sleep-walking, though she was glad the figure had only been her sister, not something else.

While Chloe had heard that you weren't supposed to wake someone who was sleepwalking, she didn't want to just let Sarah wander around naked and possibly hurt herself, so she decided to retrieve her sister and get her back to bed.

She padded her way to the bottom of the steps and got there just in time to see Sarah turn from the top and move further into the darkness. Chloe climbed the stairs as well, surprised at the increasing pace. When she reached the top, the door that was usually locked now hung open.

Wasn't that locked?

Chloe caught a glimpse of Sarah as she disappeared into the study that Chloe detested so much.

'Oh for the love of God,' she said with a sigh. Chloe really didn't want to go back in there so late at night.

Regardless, Chloe followed, and she found Sarah standing before the display case again, hands on its glass surface, staring at the book inside through half-closed eyelids.

'Sarah,' Chloe said quietly, using as soothing a tone as she could muster. She didn't want to startle her sister, but still aimed to get her out of here quickly. She walked over to Sarah and took hold of her arm, which was surprisingly warm—even hot—considering the girl was totally naked. 'Come on,' she whispered.

Chloe was able to gently pull Sarah away from where she stood. Thankfully, Sarah was compliant. Chloe then guided her from the room and carefully back down the stairs to the storey below. Though it took a little while, the pair eventually reached Sarah's room.

Once inside the room, Chloe noticed discarded shorts and a tank-top on the floor. She realised Sarah had gotten undressed before leaving for her little expedition.

Still, what did it matter? People were prone to doing strange things when sleepwalking, Chloe knew, and she was just thankful she hadn't found her sister peeing in a cupboard or something. As Chloe laid Sarah down, she quickly cast a look over to the cabinet opposite the bed.

Apprehension filled her, but there was nothing in the reflection except the two sisters.

Thankfully.

Chloe then pulled the covers over Sarah and tucked them in tight before leaving the room. Once back in the hallway, she allowed herself a moment.

What a night.

The thought of sleep seemed even more elusive, and the idea of just lying in bed, listening out for noises within the house did not seem appealing.

However, a cup of hot chocolate certainly did. It was her go-to staple when unable to sleep, and the warm, tasty cocoa was usually enough to help relax her body and mind.

That meant going downstairs alone, of course, which was another unappealing thought. But, if she was going to make Perron Manor a success for them all, she would need to get over the fear she was developing about the house.

She thought again of that horrible old man tossing Emma...

Just a dream!

With a renewed sense of determination, Chloe quickly ducked back inside her room and retrieved a robe to help ward off the night chill. She then headed downstairs and made her way to the back of the house, towards the kitchen.

Perron Manor at night was a strange and unsettling beast. The silence seemed to have an oppressive weight to it, and was punctured only by intermittent creaks in the huge structure, and even the slight rattle of old pipework.

In addition, the feeling of being watched made Chloe increase her pace until she finally reached her destination, though she couldn't help but glance back over her shoulder once or twice en route, fearful she was being followed.

But no one was there, obviously. It was just her mind playing tricks.

Again.

Chloe could have used Sarah's new coffee machine to make her hot chocolate, but instead she boiled the kettle and used jarred powder. She was used to the taste of this brand, and wanted familiar comforts at the minute.

Once the drink was prepared, she took a seat at the table and cupped her hands around the warm mug. The lighting in the kitchen had the same dirty feel to it as most of the other old lights in the house, which were a far cry from the energy-efficient lighting they had left behind in their previous house. However, the lighting here felt a little warmer to Chloe—less clean and clinical.

The yellow light spilled out through the two windows in the room, both of which looked out the side of the house. There, she could see a little of what was beyond the glass, but the majority of what Chloe saw was the light bouncing back and the reflection of the kitchen that was cast in the glass.

It took her eyes a few moments to determine exactly what was outside, and what was just a reflection.

Ever since Chloe had seen that... thing... reflected in the cabinet in Sarah's room, she had always felt at least a little apprehension when looking through windows or into mirrors. Thankfully, this time there was nothing out of the ordinary, which went some way towards soothing her mind.

She took another sip and tried to enjoy the peace and quiet. The gentle tick-tick-tick of the wall-mounted clock, which read three-twenty-two, was the only thing to break the silence.

Her drink was close to half-gone when she started to feel relaxed again, even sleepy. She looked forward to climbing back into bed again.

Bang, bang, bang.

Chloe's body seized up at the sudden noises from the back door.

CHAPTER 26

Chloe didn't want to go and look.

All she wanted to do was flee back upstairs. Those dull reverberations from the glass of the rear door were identical to the banging she and Sarah had heard months ago.

She didn't want to go through the same kind of fear again. Especially not alone.

Chloe couldn't help but consider who was making the frantic noises. Was it truly someone obsessed with the house, toying with them? Or someone—or some*thing*—a little more… unnatural?

Both options terrified her.

She could just cut through from the kitchen straight to the dining room, given there was an adjoining door, and then make her way back to the staircase that way. It would negate the need to move through the great hall, where she would be forced to look at the back door.

However, another part of Chloe refused, and was ashamed at her own cowardice. She was a mother, and had a duty to protect her family. Given how close Chloe was to the source of the knocking, then she had to at least look to see what she was dealing with.

Bang, bang, bang.

She gasped.

Chloe wasn't certain if the banging was loud enough to wake Sarah or Andrew upstairs, but she knew she couldn't wait for them to come down and help her.

And she refused to just hide away in the kitchen.

So, Chloe got up, which caused the chair legs to screech loudly on the hard floor as it slid back. She then timidly moved over to the kitchen door and rested her hand on the doorknob, the feeling of the brass cool to the touch.

But Chloe hesitated.

Fear played a part, but she also wanted to wrench open the door at the exact moment she heard the knocking again. That way, whoever it was would have no time to hide.

After a wait which seemed to stretch on forever, the sound returned.

Bang, bang, bang.

Fighting through the hesitation and anxiety, Chloe quickly pulled open the door.

The large space of the great hall was dark, which only accentuated the glow of the external security light that came in through the rear glazed door. Something had tripped the sensors. And yet, despite Chloe opening the kitchen door the instant the banging sounded, she could see no one outside at all.

Impossible.

Chloe's breathing got quicker, but she still took a determined step into the hall and flicked on the light. Then, she made her way over to the glass door, forcing herself to inspect further. But, as she was midway across the hall, the security light outside powered down, plunging the external area into darkness.

The light was on a timer, and would not stay on very long without movement to keep its sensors activated. Now, Chloe could see a little more through the glass door than pockets of the reflected area she stood in.

She waited, unsure of what to do next. Even squinting to focus her vision, Chloe was unable to see anyone lurking outside.

After a few moments, the light clicked back on. But again, no one was there.

In amongst the reflection of the great hall, Chloe was now able to see the stone paving of the courtyard outside, as well as the two protruding wings of Perron Manor that enclosed it. However, there was nothing out there that would have caused the light to turn on again.

She waited, still holding her breath, slowly walking forward. Eventually, the light cut out once again.

Chloe saw herself in the glass face of the door. She could also see the reflection of the great hall behind as well. She felt like something was playing with her, toying with her fear. She wanted to call out, to demand this all stop, but didn't dare. The utter silence was almost overwhelming, and a creeping sensation made its way up her spine.

Almost predictably, the light came back on again, illuminating the area outside.

This time, however, someone *was* standing there, right on the edge of the light spill. However, the person—who appeared to be male—was mostly hidden by the darkness of night, and he was absolutely motionless.

Chloe's breathing sped up yet again, and she began to hyperventilate. A tiny whimper escaped her.

Once more, the light went out, and she was unable to see the strange man anymore. Chloe wanted to take a step backwards, then sprint upstairs, but she couldn't move. Her legs felt like dead weights.

Then, the moment she had been dreading. The light came back on. She let out a gasp and began to shake.

The man was now directly outside of the door, close to her.

In an instant, Chloe noticed many of the tall man's details as he stared at her with a wide—almost manic—gaze. Pale skin, bald head, and one eye surrounded by bloody and tattered flesh with no eyelids, making the eyeball appear to bulge from the socket. His expression was blank. Whoever he was, the stranger was dressed in dark, basic-looking robes, almost monk-like, that hung down to the floor. His arms were folded at the abdomen, hands hidden within the interlocking sleeves, and the light from outside somehow seemed to pass through his form.

Chloe's heart hammered in her chest as unrelenting panic rose inside of her.

It had taken a moment for her vision to adjust when the light blinked on, and she had taken in all the details in an instant. But now, Chloe realised the man was not standing outside the courtyard and looking in.

Rather, she was looking at a reflection of someone standing behind her.

CHAPTER 27

CHLOE COULDN'T HELP the scream that erupted from her.

She instinctually clasped her hands over her eyes—unwilling to look on this horror any longer—and survival instinct kicked in, allowing her to take control of her limbs once again. She spun, then ran blind towards the rear wall, feeling the cold sensation suddenly increase, as if she had passed through a chiller. By the time she reached the door to the hallway, guiding herself by peeking through her fingers, the cold blast had faded.

Panic-stricken, she pushed the door open and fled from the room. However, she could not help but give one last glance back over her shoulder into the great hall. In truth, despite being so overcome with panic, she had expected the figure to be gone, given what had happened previously in Sarah's bedroom.

But he wasn't.

Chloe screamed again as the spectral monk simply stood stationary. However, he had now rotated his body and was glaring directly at her. He stood directly beneath a light fitting that shone down over him like a spotlight, and Chloe could make out the horrible detail of the damaged area around his left eye: angry, red flesh and torn skin.

Chloe bolted through to the entrance foyer, then thundered up the stairs to the floor above. The whole way, the feeling of someone right behind her, gaining ground, was palpable. It was almost overwhelming, to the point she just wanted to drop, curl up into a ball, and scream. However, each time Chloe cast a tentative look back, she saw nothing.

She followed the corridor to her room, terrified and panicked in equal measure, and feeling the blood pumping through her veins as her heart slammed against her chest. But just as she reached her room, Chloe stopped, and another cry fell from her mouth.

A figure stood in the corridor that ran perpendicular from her room.

As before, it took a few moments for her to realise it was Sarah. Again, she was naked. Just as she had been earlier.

The door behind Chloe opened, and she almost fell into her room, but instead dropped back into someone's grasp. Her body tensed and she expected some unknown thing to spin her around so she could stare into its undead eyes.

Instead, the arms that circled her were warm.

'What's going on?' she heard Andrew say.

Chloe spun around in an instant. She had to see his face. She had to *know* it was *him*.

Andrew was dressed in a plain white t-shirt and baggy blue boxer shorts. His eyes were still sleepy, but the frown on his face was one of concern. 'Are you okay?' he asked.

Chloe didn't answer, she simply buried her face into his chest and cried.

'Jesus, Chloe, what's wrong? What happened?' After a few moments, he added, 'Is that Sarah?'

Still sobbing, Chloe twisted her head, still pressing herself into Andrew's form and his strong embrace. She saw that Sarah was once again making her way upstairs to the top floor and disappearing from view.

Chloe felt firm hands grasp her upper arms, and Andrew slowly moved her away from him, just enough so she could make eye contact.

'Tell me what's happening, Chloe.' His voice was low, but firm. 'Is it Emma? Is she okay?'

Emma.

Chloe quickly broke from his grip and ran to her daughter's room, terrified of what she would see standing over the child's bed. She burst into the room and flicked on the light, braced for whatever may be waiting. Other than Emma, however, the room was empty. The baby rolled from her front to her back and blinked her eyes in surprise.

The light was flicked off, and Chloe felt herself pulled from the room.

'What the hell is going on?' Andrew asked in a hushed but stern tone as he held onto her arm.

'I… I…'

But Chloe didn't know how to answer.

Should I tell him the truth? But he'll think I'm crazy.

A weird man dressed as a monk appearing in the kitchen? She could just imagine the look of surprise that would cross his face, immediately followed by a sceptical frown. And she didn't know if she could bear that right now.

But she didn't have a choice. It *had* happened. She was certain about it.

'I saw someone downstairs,' she said.

Andrew's eyes went wide.

'What? When?'

'Just now, in the great hall.'

She saw his body tighten up. His jaw clenched. 'Watch Emma,' he said. 'And get your phone and call the police.'

He turned and pulled away from her, but Chloe held on tight, gripping his t-shirt.

'Don't go!'

Andrew placed his hands on her shoulders. 'It'll be fine. Call the police.' He then released himself from her grip.

Chloe panicked. This wasn't like a normal intruder. It was something else. Something much more… unnatural. And, in truth, Chloe didn't want to be left alone again. But Andrew moved too quickly, and before she could try again to stop him he was jogging head-first into the unknown.

Which was absolutely stupid of him.

'Andrew!' she called, but he had already turned the corner and was out of sight.

CHAPTER 28

OTHER THAN THE light being on in the great hall, Andrew could see nothing out of the ordinary. Certainly no intruders in the house. He went on to search the entire ground floor, looking in every room and cupboard, and checking that all doors and windows were locked. He even had a quick walk around the courtyard outside, as well as the area outside of the front door.

The initial rush of adrenaline that had run through him began to wane with each area he searched. The living room was the last room he checked downstairs; however, even before entering, he'd already resigned himself to the fact Chloe had somehow been mistaken.

There was no one here in the house with them.

Throughout his search, Andrew still wasn't able to shake the image of Sarah heading to the top floor, naked as could be.

He made his way back upstairs, feeling the chill in his bones from being outside in so little clothing. He found Chloe sitting on the floor with her back pressed against the door to Emma's room.

She looked pale and was still trembling. Whether anyone had actually been downstairs or not, *something* had clearly freaked her out. He sat down next to her and put an arm over her shoulder, pulling her into him.

'Emma's asleep again,' Chloe whispered. 'I keep checking on her, but she's okay.'

'She's a good sleeper,' Andrew said and kissed Chloe on the top of the head. 'Just like her old man.'

There was a moment of silence between them, before Andrew asked the question that was on his mind. He tried to keep all scepticism from his voice.

'What was it you saw, Chloe?'

She didn't answer immediately, taking a few beats before speaking. 'I... don't really know. I could have sworn there was someone standing in the hall.'

'All the doors and windows are still locked,' he replied. 'No one has broken in. What made you go downstairs in the first place? Did you hear something?'

She shook her head. 'No. I just... I was awake and couldn't sleep. Bad dream. So I went down, rather than just lying in bed. That's when I...' She trailed off.

'Did you call the police?' he asked.

Another pause. 'No.'

In all honesty, Andrew was relieved. It would have been a wasted trip.

He then heard movement on the floor above, and he felt Chloe immediately tense up.

'Sarah,' he said. 'What the hell was she doing?'

He felt Chloe relax a little. 'Sleepwalking,' she told him. Her voice sounded quiet, almost distant.

'She sleepwalks?'

'Apparently.'

'Naked?'

'Apparently,' Chloe repeated. There was a tiny hint of amusement in her voice, which was a good sign. She went on, 'I saw her doing it earlier, just after I got up. She went up to that horrible study, so I brought her back down.'

'Sounds like she's back up there. Should we go get her?'

Chloe seemed hesitant. But whatever had frightened her *must* have been imagined, or at least something normal that had been twisted in her head.

'I'll come with you,' he confirmed. 'But you'll need to dress her, or cover her over with something. I've already seen too much. She'll never be able to look me in the eye again if she finds out.'

'Okay,' Chloe finally said.

Andrew got up, and pulled his wife to her feet as well. He cupped her face before gently kissing her. She still looked scared, but also embarrassed, and she cast her eyes down and away from him.

Regardless of what she may or may not have seen, Andrew didn't want her feeling bad about this. His wife did so much for them, and put so much pressure on herself, that he refused to add any more burden to what she was feeling.

'We'll get a dressing gown from her room,' Chloe said. He nodded and led the way. Chloe reached inside of the room and grabbed a fluffy blue robe from the back of the door. They then made their way to the stairs, but Chloe hesitated at the bottom.

He stepped up first and took hold of her hand. 'It's okay,' he said, and gently pulled her along. Chloe came tentatively, and they headed up to the study.

Inside, in the dark, Andrew could see Sarah standing before a display case, her hand on the surface. She was mumbling something that sounded like gibberish.

'Go cover her up,' he whispered to Chloe. 'Then we'll take her back down.'

It took a gentle nudge from him to prompt his wife to step into the room, but she quickly hurried over to Sarah and draped the garment over her sister's shoulders. Chloe then took Sarah's hand, and Andrew heard a gentle, 'Come on.'

Sarah allowed herself to be led away, and Andrew followed the two of them back downstairs, where Chloe put Sarah back to bed while he waited out in the hallway. After closing the door behind her, Chloe looked sheepishly to Andrew. He smiled, rubbed her upper arms, then brought her in for a hug.

'Weird night, huh?'

'I'll say,' she quietly replied.

'Come on,' he said, taking her hand. 'Let's go back to bed.'

Though Andrew slept soundly beside her, Chloe simply could not drop off. The vision of what she'd seen downstairs still plagued her thoughts. It had seemed so *real*.

But Andrew had found nothing, and now she was battling with herself, simultaneously doubting her own sanity and also feeling an overwhelming need to get out of the house to save her family.

She was also scared to think how Andrew, and particularly Sarah, would react if she told them the *whole* truth about what she had seen.

With her covers pulled up to her chin, Chloe kept checking the baby-monitor that sat on the nightstand beside her, and then looking over to a particular dark corner of the room close to the window. She needed to make certain Emma was safe, but her gaze was also drawn each time to the deep shadows at the room's edge. She could see nothing there, but for some reason it gave off an ominous aura, and she half-expected some spectral form to suddenly lurch out of the black, pale hands outstretched and ready to grab her.

That didn't happen, though she still couldn't help but constantly stare, certain something within the pool of darkness was looking back at her.

She didn't sleep much more that night.

CHAPTER 29

SARAH FELT EXHAUSTED, like she hadn't slept a wink all night, and she was plagued by the memory of her strange dreams.

Plunging down through a hole that seemed to stretch on forever, surrounded by earth and rock, which eventually turned to... flesh, meat, skin. Within these seemingly living surroundings, she saw wandering eyes, moving limbs, and gaping mouths. An abstract nightmare. And the farther she fell, the worse the horrible screaming sounds became.

She thrust a forkful of warm eggs and toast into her mouth, savouring the salty flavour and trying to forget those horrible visions.

Something else was troubling her as well. *Why the hell have I woken up stark naked?* She certainly hadn't gone to sleep that way.

The smell of frying bacon filled the kitchen. Chloe was working frantically, insisting she make everyone a slap-up breakfast. She looked exhausted as well, with her usually immaculate hair just pulled back into a messy ponytail, and heavy bags under her eyes. Chloe turned and put down a plate stacked with thick, fluffy pancakes.

'Hun,' Andrew said. 'This is too much. We won't be able to eat it all. Come on, you sit down and eat some yourself.'

'I'm okay,' Chloe replied. 'I just want to keep busy.'

But it was clear to Sarah that her sister was definitely *not* okay. She was close to being manic.

Emma, who was seated in her high-chair next to Sarah, handed her aunty a blueberry from her own plate. She smiled, clearly pleased with her attempts at sharing.

'Thanks, kid,' Sarah said, taking the berry and popping it in her mouth. She chewed it loudly, making an exaggerated show of rubbing her belly. 'Mmmmmmmm.'

Emma laughed and picked up another blueberry. 'Again,' she demanded.

As Sarah pacified her demanding niece, she kept an eye on Chloe. Without knowing what had happened, she could only guess that perhaps she and Andrew had fought during the night.

Chloe wasn't making eye contact with anyone, though Andrew was. He kept sneaking awkward glances at Sarah, only to quickly look away again when caught.

'Okay, what's going on?' Sarah demanded. 'Have you two been bickering?'

Andrew sat up straight, and Chloe turned around, looking confused.

'What do you mean?' she asked.

'Something's out of whack this morning. You are running around like a madwoman, Andrew keeps looking at me weird, and I could cut the atmosphere with *this*,' she said, holding up a spoon.

Andrew looked at Chloe. 'I think we should tell her,' he said. Chloe frowned angrily and shook her head.

'Tell me what?' Sarah asked.

'It's nothing,' Chloe said.

Sarah rolled her eyes. 'Well, clearly it's not noth—'

'You were sleepwalking last night,' Andrew interrupted.

Sarah's mouth hung open a little bit in shock. 'I was... I was what?'

'Sleepwalking,' Andrew confirmed. 'You did it twice. Kept going up to the top floor, to that study.'

She didn't know how to respond. 'Really?' she asked.

He nodded, then his cheeks flushed a little. 'And you were... erm... not fully dressed, shall we say. Well, that's not quite accurate. You weren't dressed at all.'

'I was sleepwalking naked?'

Andrew nodded. Sarah's eyes went wide, and she pointed at him. 'Did you see anything?'

He shuffled in his seat. 'Not much, honestly. Chloe covered you up. But… yeah, it seems you like to walk around in the buff while you sleep.'

'Well shit,' was all Sarah could say. 'I didn't realise.'

'Has it happened before?' he asked.

Sarah shook her head. 'Not that I know of.'

Chloe still wasn't looking at either of them, having gone back to cut up more fruit. Sarah was confused as to why it was such a problem for her sister. Maybe the whole sleepwalking thing was a little odd, but certainly nothing to cause an issue between them. Hell, if anything it was funny.

'Is there something else?' she asked, staring past Andrew to Chloe.

After a silence, her sister turned. She was still frowning, and cast a scowl towards Andrew.

He shrugged apologetically. 'I was only going to mention the sleepwalking. That was it.'

Sarah was growing tired of the whole charade. 'What else happened last night?' she demanded.

Chloe chewed the side of her mouth for a few moments before sighing. 'I thought I saw someone. Out there,' she hooked a thumb over her shoulder, 'in the great hall.'

'Someone was in here?!' Sarah asked, incredulous, rising to her feet. 'Why the hell didn't you tell me sooner?'

But then, Sarah considered the way Chloe had worded the statement.

She thought *she saw someone.*

And Sarah also remembered the night Chloe *thought* she saw an old woman's reflection, as well.

'I looked,' Andrew said, 'but couldn't find anyone.'

Sarah kept her eyes on Chloe. 'So what happened?' she asked. 'Was there someone here or not?'

'We don't think so,' Andrew confirmed, but the cloud of anger that formed over Chloe's face indicated she wasn't on the same page.

'Who did you see?' Sarah asked.

Chloe's jaw was set, and her top lip curled a little. She set down the knife she was holding and began to walk from the room. 'I need to use the toilet,' she snapped, bringing everything to a close.

But that wasn't good enough for Sarah; she wasn't going to be left in the dark. So, she got up and followed Chloe out of the room, leaving Andrew to look after Emma.

'Hey,' she called as she and her sister paced through the great hall, Sarah a good few steps behind. Chloe ignored her, so Sarah repeated herself, louder this time. 'Hey!'

Chloe stopped and quickly turned around. 'What?' she asked curtly.

Sarah kept walking until she was close to her sister. 'Just tell me what happened last night. What's gotten into you?'

'Nothing,' Chloe snapped, rolling her tired-looking, red-rimmed eyes. She tried to turn away again, but Sarah quickly shot out a hand and grabbed her by the upper arm.

'Talk to me!' Sarah insisted.

Chloe stared back angrily. 'Would you please just let me go for a piss.'

'You don't need to pee,' Sarah shot back. 'I'm not an idiot.'

Chloe took a deep breath. Eventually, however, the tension in her jaw eased, and her features softened a little. She then began to talk.

'Honestly... I'm not sure I know. I swear I saw someone down here, standing roughly where we are now. So I ran. But, like Andrew says, when he came down he couldn't find anyone. And there were no signs of a break-in.'

'And what did this person look like?' Sarah asked.

Chloe shrugged. 'Just a person.'

'Man or woman?'

A sigh. 'It was a man.'

'Good. And what did the man look like? Short, tall, big nose... what?'

'Why does it matter?' Chloe asked, throwing her hands up in the air. 'He apparently wasn't even here to begin with.'

'Tell me,' Sarah insisted.

Chloe looked away for a few moments, but finally went on. 'He was tall. Bald. And wearing some kind of robes, or a cloak. He had a weird injury over one of his eyes. And... he kind of reminded me of the guy we saw on that security footage a little while ago.'

'Did he do anything?' she asked.

Chloe shook her head. 'No, just stood there, staring at me.'

Now Sarah was worried. Not because there could still be an intruder loose in the house or anything like that, but because she feared for her sister's sanity.

'You know there was no one standing here, right?' Sarah asked. Chloe looked hurt at the statement, but Sarah continued. 'It was just like when you thought you saw that old woman in my room. None of it really happened.'

'This was different,' Chloe replied, but her tone was hardly convincing. 'It wasn't just a reflection. I *saw* him. He was real.'

'Okay, then answer me this, and be truthful. Do you think he broke in just to stand and look at you in plain sight?'

Chloe shook her head and turned again, but Sarah caught her arm for the second time. 'Answer me,' she demanded. 'Do you think someone broke in here last night?'

A moment's pause. 'No,' Chloe admitted.

'So, that means no one was standing here in this room, doesn't it?'

Sarah knew what her sister really meant, and what she really thought this strange man was. Not an intruder, but something else.

It was ridiculous. An impossibility. Sarah wouldn't let her sister—regardless of any stresses she was going through—be weak-minded enough to believe in such things.

But she wanted Chloe to realise it on her own. Hopefully, that would be the first step in getting past this nonsense.

'Do you agree no one was here?' Sarah repeated after not receiving an answer.

Chloe looked up and stared Sarah dead in the eye. 'No,' she stated. 'Someone *was* here.'

Sarah shook her head in disbelief. 'Is that so? Okay, so no one broke in, but someone *was* inside the house. Explain that to me, please. Did they have a fucking key?'

'You know what it was,' Chloe said.

'I want you to say it.'

'Why?'

'So you can hear how stupid it sounds!'

'It isn't stupid,' Chloe insisted, yanking her arm from Sarah's grip. 'You weren't there.'

'So the house is haunted? And you're okay believing rubbish like that?'

Chloe strode away from Sarah and yelled back, 'Just leave me alone.'

But Sarah would not, and called after her, 'Careful no ghosts get you while you're taking a piss.'

Chloe didn't turn around, just raised a hand and flipped Sarah the bird. 'Fuck you!'

There was venom in her voice—real, seething anger. Chloe disappeared from the room, and it wasn't until after she was gone that Sarah started to feel bad for pushing so hard. And she was confused as to why she felt the need to do so.

'Shit,' she said to herself. *Nice going, dipshit.*

Then, the doorbell sounded.

CHAPTER 30

Andrew opened the front door, Emma cradled in one arm, and was greeted by a short man who looked to be in his sixties. He was wrapped in a green farming jacket and wore a flat cap, burgundy trousers, and loose-fitting moccasins. Grey hairs protruded from under the cap, and the visitor stood with a straight back and strong posture, his chin tilted upwards. A scuffed leather satchel was slung over one shoulder.

'Hello, can I help you?' Andrew asked.

The man cocked a bushy eyebrow. 'I should hope so. *You* asked *me* to come.'

Andrew paused for a moment, then realisation dawned on him. 'Mr. Mumford?'

'The very same,' the man replied with a half-smile. He then held out a hand. 'But you may call me Isaac.'

Andrew shook, but was a little hesitant. 'Mr. Mu... sorry, Isaac. You are a little early.'

'Nonsense,' Mr. Mumford said with a wave of his hand. 'We said ten-thirty. I hardly think five minutes before that classifies as *early*.'

'It wouldn't, normally,' Andrew agreed. 'But we said *eleven*-thirty.'

The man shook his head dismissively, and Andrew had to keep from letting his small pang of annoyance grow into something more.

'No,' Isaac replied. 'Ten-thirty was the time. Am I to take it you are not available for our appointment, then?'

Isaac's grey-blue eyes—one of which looked to be slightly off centre—stared expectantly at Andrew. He had a good mind to tell the man to get lost, but thought better of it.

'I can accommodate you coming early,' Andrew said, stepping aside. Isaac made as if to argue the point, but Andrew cut him off. 'Come on in. I'll take you up to the study.'

Isaac stepped inside, put his satchel down, and then removed his coat, thrusting it into Andrew's free hand. He had a thick, green, wool jumper on underneath, with the collar of a white-and-burgundy-check shirt protruding out from the neck. 'Is there anywhere you can put the little ankle-biter while we do business? Best if we can concentrate unhindered on the job at hand.'

Andrew's jaw dropped. *Ankle-biter?*

'Everything okay?' Sarah said, appearing in the room. She walked over to them, and Andrew noted Chloe wasn't with her. He guessed the conversation between them hadn't gone too well.

'I think so,' the visitor said, and held out his hand. 'Isaac Mumford. I've come to inspect the items you inherited, to see if any of them are worth anything.'

Sarah shook his hand but cast Andrew an amused smile.

'Pleased to meet you,' she said.

'I take it you're the wife?'

Sarah's eyes widened, as did her amused smile.

'I'm the sister-in-law, actually,' she told him. 'And I also have a name. It's Sarah.'

'Delightful,' Isaac replied, not sounding the least bit interested. 'Would you kindly watch this one?' He pointed squarely at Emma, his finger inches away from the child's nose. 'Children tend to get in the way. Things will go much more smoothly if he isn't bothering us.'

'*She,*' Andrew corrected, sternly.

Isaac took a closer look at Emma, narrowing his eyes. 'Really?' he asked, then shrugged. 'If you say so.'

Andrew's fists balled up, and he turned to Sarah, with his eyebrows raised in disbelief. Sarah, in turn, looked like she was fighting the need to burst out laughing. But what could Andrew say? It was *he* who had found this strange man and arranged the appointment in the first place.

Andrew just hoped this Isaac Mumford knew his stuff as much as his reputation online seemed to indicate.

'Tell you what,' Sarah replied. 'Since I'm one of the inheritors, how about I come up with you and listen to what you have to say. My sister, *the wife*, will want to be there as well. I'm afraid you'll just have to put up with the child.'

Isaac let out a sigh. 'If you insist.' He then turned to Andrew. 'Would you keep it quiet, though, old chap?'

Andrew gritted his teeth together. He was about to respond, but at that moment Chloe walked into the room.

'Chloe, this is Isaac Mumford,' he said. 'He's here to look at the stuff upstairs. He's early, but that's okay, we can accommodate. Let's go and get this over with.'

'No need to sound so curt,' Isaac said, hooking his satchel over his shoulder again. 'And I *wasn't* early.'

Sarah watched Isaac slowly walk around the large study as he took everything in.

'You packed a lot of the items away, then?' he asked, gesturing to the full cardboard boxes piled up on top of each other.

'We had to make a start,' Chloe said. 'They had been cluttering the room for long enough.'

'Cluttering the room?' Isaac asked, incredulous. 'If these things are authentic, then they are far from clutter.'

Chloe's expression was flat. 'I don't care,' she stated.

Isaac shook his head. 'Unbelievable.'

He then continued with his inspection, peeking inside boxes, studying the tomes that lined the bookshelves, and gazing at the various artefacts still on display.

Sarah could feel anger radiate from her sister. Some of it likely directed at her. She tried to make subtle eye contact to draw Chloe's attention, but to no avail.

Why the hell was I so hard on her?

Chloe was clearly stressed out and struggling with things at the minute, it was written all over her face, and Sarah *knew* that. Normally, she'd have discussed things rationally with her sister... but that hadn't happened back in the great hall.

'Anything of interest?' Andrew asked.

'Possibly,' was Isaac's one-word reply.

Moving at his own leisure, the man finally settled on the book in the display case. It was the most obvious item in the room, given its placement, and one it seemed Isaac had deliberately left until last.

'My,' he began, and lifted up the glass lid. He then let his fingers run over the book. 'This looks interesting. Very old.' He opened it, nipping the front cover between his fingers. 'Seems to be wooden bindings wrapped in leather. Could be medieval... or older.'

Sarah, Chloe, and Andrew all gave each other a look, and Andrew's eyebrows raised up. Sarah knew what he was thinking, as something that old would clearly be worth a pretty penny.

Isaac put his satchel down, then opened its flap, pulling out some white, cloth gloves. He slipped them on and then began to carefully flick through the pages.

'Hand-written,' he said. 'And in Latin. Not my area of expertise, but it seems to be authentic, whatever it is. Certainly an original.' Isaac quickly flipped the cover over again and read the title out loud. '*Ianua Diaboli*. Hmmmm, not something I've heard of. But I can certainly look into it.'

He slipped off his gloves and delved back into his bag, retrieving a notepad and pencil he used to scribble some notes. He then brought a digital camera from the satchel and snapped a few pictures. The flash was so bright that Sarah's view swam with motes, and she had to blink repeatedly to clear her vision.

'I assume I'm okay taking pictures,' he said without looking at them, then shot off a few more.

Sarah couldn't decide if she detested this man or absolutely loved him. He reminded her of a senile uncle who had no filter... or manners.

'So,' Chloe began, 'do you have any idea if this is all just junk?'

Isaac chuckled and shook his head. 'Define '*junk*,' he replied. 'You may think all of this is rubbish, but someone else would value it highly. And the things I value, you might just disregard as clutter. It's all in the eye of the beholder.'

Sarah saw Chloe clench her teeth. 'Then tell me, does any of this have monetary value?'

'Possibly,' he said. 'There is a lot here. Most of it seems to have an inclination towards the occult and the dark arts, which isn't surprising considering the house it's stored in.'

'You've heard of this place?' Andrew asked. 'I thought you lived a few towns over?'

'I do,' Isaac replied. 'But that town isn't situated under a rock. A house with a history like this… of course I know of it. I'd also heard of the museum of the occult that was rumoured to be kept here. Until now, I didn't know if that was true.'

'You have an interest in this macabre crap too, then?' Chloe asked.

Another chuckle. 'Heavens no. Not my field, really. But I know people who can help, if I feel any of these items have merit. Which… I believe they might.'

'What *exactly* have you heard about Perron Manor?' Sarah asked, wanting to pull the conversation back to something that sparked her interest. 'And what did you mean by a *museum of the occult?*'

'Well,' Isaac began, as he continued to look around. 'This place has quite a history, as I'm sure you are aware.'

'Yes, we know what happened in '82,' Chloe said.

'And the rest,' he replied. 'That is just the tip of the iceberg. This house, it is said, often drew people to it who have a fondness for the darker things in life. That begs the question, why do *you* wholesome folks live here, hmmm?' He waggled his bushy eyebrows and laughed to himself.

'The owner of the house in the late eighteen-hundreds was a man named Alfred Blackwater. He had a similar profession to mine, and traded rare artefacts. However, it was well known he had a certain interest in things like this.' Isaac cast his arm around the room.

'And he used his quite successful business to fund his acquisitions. When he had the chance to buy Perron Manor, which he viewed as the biggest occult artefact one could own, he snapped it up and continued building his collection. After his death, the house was passed to his son, Timothy, who left it empty but kept it in the family name. And when *he* died, it was then passed to Marcus, Timothy's son. Marcus had very similar tastes to Alfred, and continued his grandfather's work. And word spread of his collection, but no one was ever certain if any of it was true.'

'And what was your take on what happened that night under his ownership?' Sarah asked.

'Do we *have* to go over that?' Chloe asked with a sigh.

'Yes,' Sarah said, surprising herself at how curt she sounded. She then turned her attention back to Isaac.

'No one knows for sure,' he said. 'Just a lot of dead people. Butchered. If you ask me, the survivors had to have been in on it. How else do you explain the whole thing? I mean, look around.' He gave another gesture to the items in the room. 'The kind of people that own and collect these kind of things... is it such a leap to think they could have been swayed to act out some kind of ritualistic killing, or some such nonsense?'

Sarah saw that Chloe was shaking, and her fists were tightly curled, the knuckles white. Sarah could understand why Chloe was upset, as the man was unwittingly implicating their parents.

'The police didn't seem to think that was the case,' Andrew said, though Sarah could tell it was more to appease Chloe than anything.

'Bah,' Isaac responded with a flippant wave. 'Useless flatfoots. Especially in the eighties. Couldn't join the dots between two points to save their lives.'

'You don't buy the stories that the whole thing was somehow... supernatural?' Sarah asked.

She knew she shouldn't have said anything, but she wanted Chloe to hear it from someone else. It would no doubt cause another fight, but so be it.

Isaac's bellowing laughter at such a suggestion was all Sarah needed, and she saw Chloe's cheeks turn a deep red.

She felt an instant pang of guilt. *Why are you pushing this so hard? What's wrong with you?*

'Good God no,' the man said, wiping away a tear. 'A little too old for fairytales, I believe. And not so weak of mind as to fall for nonsense like that. Although, people *do* believe in that kind of thing, and I know that can lead them to do strange and horrible things. Like what happened in '82, in my opinion. Or that Chelmswick fellow, in the nineteen-thirties. You know of him, right? Killed a bunch of children in here, supposedly singing nursery rhymes at them as he did. It's true there have been a lot of... unpleasant... tragedies happen at Perron Manor down the years, but considering the age of the building, is that so surprising?'

Sarah looked over to her sister, expecting Chloe to have a face like thunder. However, Chloe's expression was... something else. Worry? Shock? Sarah wasn't quite sure.

'Are you about finished, Mr. Mumford?' Chloe asked, not hiding the annoyance in her voice.

'Not really,' he replied, continuing to nose around.

'Then allow me to word it differently,' she said to him. 'Get the fuck out of my house. Now.'

Everyone in the room paused in shock. Isaac's expression was the most surprised of all.

'Excuse me?!' Isaac asked incredulously, his face turning red. 'How dare you—'

'Shut up! Just shut up and get out now. You've been nothing but a boor since arriving, and I'm sick of listening to you. We don't want to do business with you, so go. And don't come back.'

'Listen here, missy,' he replied.

But Chloe, it appeared, was in no mood to listen at all.

'No!'

She marched up to him and got right in Isaac's face. 'I have zero problem throwing you out of the house myself, if needed.'

Sarah immediately felt a flush of guilt. The exchange, and Chloe's outburst, was all her fault. Why had she pushed it so much?

Isaac's frown wavered, and the prospect of Chloe following through on her threat clearly ran through his mind.

'Fine,' he eventually said and started to pack up his things. 'Heathens, the lot of you. Good luck getting any money for what you have here, because make no mistake, I will blackball you to the local dealership community. *No one* will deal with you.'

'Less talking,' Chloe said. 'More hurrying up and getting the hell out.'

Isaac slung his satchel over his shoulder and stomped from the room like a child, muttering to himself the whole way back downstairs as the others followed him. Andrew handed him his coat, which Isaac snatched, then opened the door for him. Isaac moved to the threshold, then turned back to Andrew.

'Your wife is a rude woman,' he said. 'You should keep her on a leash.'

That was the last straw.

Chloe charged the man with a roar, and was far too quick for either Sarah or Andrew to stop her. She shoved their guest, and a look of complete shock registered on the old man's face as he toppled backwards, trying—and failing—to keep his footing. Isaac fell backwards, landing with a thud, inches away from the stone steps.

Chloe was over to him in an instant, standing above him.

'Leave it!' Andrew shouted, but Chloe just glared down at the grounded man, who held up a defensive hand and turned his face away.

'I will *not* tell you again, little man. Leave!'

Isaac looked as if he were going to say something again, clearly unused to not having the last word. Thankfully, however, he thought better of it. Instead, he gathered himself up and hurried away.

They watched him go, and Sarah saw Chloe was breathing heavily, hands still curled into fists. Finally, Chloe turned and walked back towards the house. She stopped at Sarah, and the look she gave her was one Sarah had never seen before. Almost like Chloe wished death upon her.

Sarah broke eye contact and looked down to the ground.

CHAPTER 31

Chloe sat on her bed and sobbed. She wanted out.

Perron Manor was done to her now. Finished. Her dream of the idyllic mansion with its beautiful grounds had been shattered.

She felt bad about it, given she had been the driving force to get people together to live here in the first place. It was *she* who had put the idea to Sarah that selling the house wasn't the right thing to do. That it would make a perfect place to live.

She'd also spent no small amount of time and effort convincing Andrew, who had gone along with it out of his love for her and nothing more.

So, she would have to bear the brunt of tearing it all down. Andrew may well be happy with the situation, but she had a feeling Sarah would react differently.

Though, in truth, she did not care in the slightest how her sister took the news. Not now.

Fuck her.

Chloe used to think she could talk to Sarah about anything. But after trying to share her recent experiences… Sarah just seemed like a different person.

Granted, they were pretty fantastical events, but Sarah's attitude had not just been disbelief—she had tried to belittle and humiliate Chloe.

Chloe couldn't remember a single time in her life where she had ever been this angry with Sarah.

But whether her sister believed her or not, Chloe just didn't feel safe here. Even now, alone in her bedroom during daytime hours, she still felt on edge, as if someone were watching her. Part of her just wanted to go back downstairs and join the others, if only to feel a little safer.

But she couldn't do that. At the moment, Chloe needed time and space. And facing Sarah again now would just result in an argument.

Chloe was feeling angry and hurt and scared and ashamed... and a million more negative emotions. So, for now, she just needed to pull herself together in her own space.

She remembered what Isaac Mumford had said about the man who killed children in the house. That story, regardless of anything else that had happened, probably scared her the most. The event in '82 was horrible, but as far as Chloe knew, the victims were all adults. But this...

There was also the comment about the killer reciting nursery rhymes to the poor children he slew. She remembered the previous night, and the thing she'd heard on the baby monitor after waking.

The thing she had convinced herself at the time was nothing but her imagination.

Round and round the garden.

There was a light tap on the door, and immediately Chloe tensed up. She imagined the tall monk standing outside of her room, rapping on the door. But a voice soon followed.

It was Sarah.

'Sis, it's me. Can I come in?'

'Go away,' Chloe replied. She was in no mood to talk with anyone, least of all her sister. The door opened anyway, and Chloe let out an audible sigh. 'Are you deaf?'

Sarah closed the door behind her, but didn't make eye contact. She seemed almost meek, which was a new look for her.

'I'm sorry,' she said, fidgeting with her hands and picking at the nails. 'I really am.' Sarah finally looked up, and her blue eyes settled on Chloe. The expression she wore was an earnest one.

'I don't care,' Chloe replied. Sarah didn't deserve to have her apology accepted. Not yet. Things were still too raw.

'I understand,' Sarah added. 'I deserve that. But I wanted to say sorry anyway. I overreacted. And, honestly, I have no idea why. Don't get me wrong, I don't believe there is anything wrong with the house like you do. But that was no reason to push you and try and embarrass you like that. I don't know what came over me and... I'm sorry.'

Whether intended or not, the line about still not believing Chloe stung, and didn't help her feel any less crazy. But the apology was welcomed, even if Chloe didn't want to admit it.

'I just don't get why you went at me so much. You've never done that before.'

'I know,' Sarah agreed. 'It's just... and don't get angry here... I felt that it was weak to think like that. To let your imagination run away with itself. And it made me angry, even though it shouldn't have. I don't know... I guess I've just been feeling tired a lot lately, and it's all getting to me.'

'Maybe all the sleepwalking is interfering with your rest,' Chloe offered. 'Like that isn't strange enough, anyway.'

'Don't,' Sarah said, closing her eyes and raising a finger. 'It's not a big deal. Don't make more out of it than it is. How many people in the world sleepwalk? Do they *all* live in haunted houses?'

Chloe stopped. She *did* think that Sarah's nighttime strolls the previous evening were strange, but couldn't really argue the point her sister had made. She was right. Lots of people did it, and it didn't usually mean anything.

Usually.

But that didn't change anything. Chloe's mind was made up. She should have really spoken to Andrew first before having this out with Sarah, but she proceeded anyway.

'I'm not going to live here anymore,' Chloe said. 'I can't. I'll speak to Andrew, and we are going to leave.'

Sarah's face fell. 'What?! You can't be fucking serious.'

'I am. I know you don't believe me about this stuff, and that's fine. But I know what I saw. And I'm not prepared to stay here and put my family in danger just because you think it sounds a little farfetched.'

'A *little* farfetched? Jesus Christ, Chloe, it sounds absolutely fucking insane. And now you're going to jump ship because of it? After *you*,'

Sarah jabbed her finger at Chloe, 'were the one to persuade everyone to live here in the first place.'

Chloe had fully expected Sarah's response. 'I know. But it is what it is.'

Sarah had come here offering an apology, which was good of her, but Chloe knew there was another fight incoming.

And Chloe was fine with that.

'You selfish bitch!' Sarah snarled. 'I gave up my life for this. For *you*. And now you're running away?'

'*What* life?' Chloe asked—and immediately regretted it.

Shock, then hurt, registered on her sister's face. Sarah's top lip curled and her teeth clenched together in an angry grimace. She then took a step forward, and Chloe genuinely thought her sister was going to punch her.

Instead, Sarah marched right up to Chloe and dipped her head down, so they were eye to eye, with Chloe still seated on the bed.

'Fuck you,' she said in a low, nasty tone. 'Go. Fucking run away. You're nothing more than a pussy who's scared of your own shadow. You've always been the same. An utter. Fucking. Coward.'

Chloe jumped to her feet, and the two sisters stood toe-to-toe. The rage that surged through Chloe felt uncontrollable—almost unnatural. How had things so quickly spiralled to this?

'Get out,' Chloe said, trying her best to control the bubbling anger.

Sarah simply looked at Chloe like she was shit on her shoe, then shook her head and left the room.

Chloe was shaking, and she sat back down on the bed, breathing deeply. She tried to push down a rage she had never felt before, especially towards Sarah.

She needed to speak to Andrew and get him on board. Then they could look at getting out of this place as quickly as possible.

Sarah could do whatever the hell she wanted.

But despite all that, Chloe still felt a need to prove she was right, that she *wasn't* crazy. And in order to do that, she needed to know more about what was going on.

She needed that reassurance for her own sanity.

Even though her mind was made up, a small, lingering doubt

remained. Who the hell could she turn to for that kind of help? Who would believe her?

Then, a name popped into her head. Someone who *would* believe her. However, it was someone she would need to apologise to first.

David Ritter.

CHAPTER 32

'I DIDN'T THINK I'd hear from you again,' David Ritter said as he approached Chloe. She was seated in *Hill of Beans*—the same shop where Chloe had so quickly berated David for simply telling the truth.

Emma, who was seated in a highchair next to Chloe, looked up at David and pointed. 'Man!'

Chloe offered David a smile. 'I think I owe you an apology.'

'So you said in your message,' David replied and scratched at the back of his neck. He was dressed in loose-fitting jeans, scruffy trainers, a grey t-shirt with the Atari logo branded across, and a charcoal-coloured hoodie. Standing above them, he looked awkward and hesitant.

'Please... take a seat,' Chloe said, gesturing to the empty chair opposite.

David looked around at the coffee shop first. There were only a handful of patrons, and Chloe could tell he was more than a little uncomfortable.

Probably trying to think if anyone here recognises him from when I publicly embarrassed him.

Thankfully, David sat down.

'Can I offer you a drink?' Chloe asked.

He smiled and shook his head. 'No, it's fine—'

'I insist,' Chloe stated. She got to her feet. 'I'm getting one anyway. What do you want?'

'Coffee. Black,' he conceded. 'Thank you.'

Chloe stood up and approached the counter, which was only a few steps away. While waiting for the barista, Chloe considered again if the whole thing was crazy.

After her argument with Sarah—once she had calmed down—the first thing Chloe had done was to seek out her husband and lay everything out for him. Andrew had been shocked, and she could see the doubt plastered across his face when she told him everything. He didn't believe her, she knew; however, he did say he would support her if she wanted to leave. Which wasn't surprising.

One thing he had said, though, was that Chloe should smooth things over with Sarah before firming anything up.

But Chloe wasn't ready for that.

Next, she had looked up David Ritter online and found an email address through his paranormal research company website. He had responded soon after, and a meet up for that afternoon was arranged. David had been hesitant in his initial response, but Chloe had pressed the urgency of the situation, promising to explain it all.

Too late to back out now.

She just hoped that David was capable of providing some answers. After all, he had been to the house and claimed to have experienced some kind of paranormal phenomena himself.

Should have read his book, she thought to herself.

A barista approached with a big and friendly smile. After placing her order, Chloe moved back to her seat.

'They'll bring everything over as soon as it's ready,' she told David. 'I've ordered some cakes and biscuits as well, so feel free to dig in.'

'You didn't have to do that,' he said, and she noticed he had tucked his hands into his jacket pockets.

'No, it's fine. It's the least I can do after going off on you last time we were here.'

He offered a closed-mouthed smile.

Chloe went on. 'Look, David. I'm sorry for the way I acted. I had no right. For whatever reason, I was angry at what you were insinuating, and I just lost it. I shouldn't have. And again, I'm sorry. I really am.'

'Appreciate that,' David eventually said, and she saw his body visibly relax a little. 'I know the kind of things I was saying are hard to believe, so I don't blame you for thinking I'm nuts.'

'Well, that's just it. I *don't* think you are nuts. Not anymore.'

He frowned, then his eyes widened in realisation.

'Oh,' was all he could manage to say at first. After a few moments, he followed it up with, 'Is everyone okay?'

'For the moment,' Chloe replied. She appreciated that his first question was checking her wellbeing, rather than asking what had happened.

'But you have experienced something?' he followed up.

Chloe nodded. 'Yes. Though I wish I hadn't.'

A waiter approached the table—a young man with fluffy, wispy stubble and messy hair. He set the drinks and cakes down, and the smell of coffee along with the sweet food made Chloe's stomach growl loudly in anticipation. Too loudly, it seemed, and David looked up at her with wide eyes.

'Sorry,' she said with an embarrassed grin. 'I haven't eaten much today.'

David took a sip of his drink as Chloe grabbed a slice of caramel cake and bit into it. The taste exploded on her tongue, and she couldn't help but let out a small moan of appreciation.

'Mine!' Emma insisted.

Chloe turned to her and saw that her daughter had her arm outstretched, waiting for some of the delicious food as well. Chloe didn't normally like giving her daughter too much sugar, but couldn't very well deny her now.

Once the waiter had left them alone again, David leaned forward, placing his elbows on the table. 'Can I ask what happened?'

She nodded, then told him everything she could think of, starting with the events of the previous night but also her strange dreams of being pulled down through a hole in the ground—falling into an eternal abyss—as well as seeing the old woman in Sarah's room. She even told him about the hidden study. It felt good to unburden herself of it all.

At the mention of the room upstairs, David's eyes widened. 'I had no idea about that,' he said. 'The area was locked off when we carried out our investigation.'

'Well,' Chloe said, 'it really is something to see. But I think that pretty much brings you up to speed. So, tell me, do you think my family and I are in danger?'

She held her breath. The last time she'd met David, his word had been worth nothing to her. Now she was waiting for his judgment on the whole situation, ready to take his response as gospel.

'Quite possibly,' he replied. Chloe felt her stomach drop.

CHAPTER 33

'These things are complicated,' David went on. 'I've studied paranormal phenomena all my life, experienced some things I would have scarcely believed, and I still can't understand it all. But, after what I saw in Perron Manor, there is one thing I am sure of: that place is evil.'

'One that you want to investigate again, though,' Chloe cut in. 'So can it be too bad?'

'I have my reasons,' he replied. 'And I'd like to think I would be prepared enough to be safe. But the difference is, you and your family are living there, and are therefore in the house pretty much all the time. Given what I know about the history of the building, that kind of exposure never ends well.'

'Do I dare ask you to expand on that?'

'If you want to. It's all in the book I gave to your sister.'

'I didn't read it,' Chloe said. 'Though I might now.'

'Well, the important thing to note is that the cycle of tragic events has been repeated over and over for as long as Perron Manor has stood.'

'But my uncle lived there for many years, and nothing happened to him.'

'That's true enough,' David admitted. 'Like I said, these things are hard to explain and comprehend. I believe that these... spirits... for want of a better word, work on energy. It flows and pulses. Sometimes the power is stronger, and other times it isn't, so the manifestations are less potent. I have a theory that their actions are all tied to the living people they can draw on from the house. Maybe your uncle just wasn't a good fit for them.'

Sounded like a pretty flimsy explanation to Chloe. 'And the rest of us are?'

'Possibly,' David said. 'After all, you *are* experiencing heightened phenomena, are you not?'

Chloe stuffed a slice of shortbread into her mouth and chewed it quickly, considering David's words. They sounded ridiculous when spoken out loud, but it was the best she had to go on right now.

'Can we stop it?' she asked after she'd swallowed.

He hesitated in his response, looking uncertain. 'Hard to say. Normal hauntings can be tricky enough to cleanse at the best of times. Perron Manor is anything but normal. For example, I don't just think you are dealing with ghosts. I think there is something... darker... behind it all.'

Chloe hesitantly asked, 'What do you mean?'

David took another long sip of his steaming coffee. 'Well, towards the end of our investigation we saw something. And this was after already witnessing supernatural phenomena, and even seeing some spirits, which was a first for me. But things didn't stop there... they only got worse. At the end, we caught a glimpse of what I believe is the centrepiece of Perron Manor. The thing which was the puppet master to all the trapped souls within. A demon.'

Chloe just stared at him, unsure what to do with that information. On the one hand, it terrified her, but on the other just hearing the term *demon* sounded ridiculous.

'Stupid question, but having a demon... that's bad, right?'

David nodded. 'Extremely. Spirits can be bad enough, but this is a different level. Some believe demons have the power to twist and bend the souls of the dead to become their servants, to an extent, so those unfortunates are trapped in their own kind of eternal purgatory.'

'To an extent?'

'Yeah. There are differing views on this kind of thing, from a paranormal academic point of view.' *Paranormal academic*—those were two words Chloe would never have put together. But she let him continue. 'One school of thought is that demons are able to poison the souls of the dead and control them, but when left unchecked the tainted spirits act on their own free will. It's kind of like a warden controlling patients in an asylum. If not watched closely, the inmates run free.'

'Brilliant,' Chloe said. 'So, how do we get rid of the demon?'

'I'm afraid that is complicated. From what I understand, it isn't an exact science, and there are no guarantees. But I think an exorcism is the best bet. That could possibly banish the entity and free the souls of those trapped inside the house.'

Chloe slumped in her chair, feeling like she'd walked into a bad horror film. 'And how does one go about getting an exorcism performed?'

'You need to contact a vicar or priest to start the process. But it is a slow one. I know one local priest, Father Janosch, fairly well, and he has a little bit of experience in things like this. But ultimately, all he can do is verify the claims and then move the case up his chain of command, so to speak.'

'And how long does that take?' Chloe asked, but David's hesitant smile told her everything she needed to know.

'How long is a piece of string? I'd say months, at the very least.'

Great. We'll be dead before that happens. 'So I need to get my family out of there,' she stated.

'That might be your only option. At least for now. If you want, I can speak with Father Janosch and try to get things moving?'

Chloe paused.

Her instinct was just to go, flee, and leave the house to rot. But that would then mean they'd need to sell it, and that could be... difficult. Plus, Sarah didn't look like she would leave, anyway, and getting both Sarah and Andrew to agree to having an exorcism performed seemed unlikely. They would both think Chloe was losing it if she even suggested such a thing.

She closed her eyes. Her chest started to feel tighter. Chloe had never suffered panic attacks before, though she had an idea this could be the onset of one.

Everything seemed to be happening too fast and was spiralling out of control. It didn't seem too long ago that she was as happy as she'd ever been, looking forward to their new life in the perfect house. And now... now she was in a position where arranging a fucking exorcism seemed like a sane and reasonable step.

'I... I need to talk to my husband and sister about it,' she told him. 'They aren't exactly as open to this whole thing as I am. In fact, Sarah pretty much gave me the same treatment as I originally gave you.'

'I see,' David replied. 'Then you need to convince them. This isn't a joke, and the longer it goes on, the worse it will all get. Especially given you already have a history with the house.'

Chloe cocked her head. 'What do you mean?'

'Well, you spent a little time there when you were young, right?'

'Yeah.'

'And you were there in '82?' Chloe nodded, and David went on, 'So the house, and the demon... it knows you. You got away once. It won't want to let that happen again.'

'Are you serious?!'

'Afraid so,' he replied. 'I've heard cases where demons can latch on to people instead of places, and they are relentless. Once they have contact, it can be hard to break, until the person is, well...' He trailed off.

'Dead,' Chloe finished for him. 'And I've walked right back to it.'

David gave a nod. 'Yeah. I could be wrong about all of this, of course. Like I keep saying, it isn't an exact science. But, considering these events started happening relatively quickly after you moved in, when sometimes they can take years to manifest, it stands to reason that whatever is there is using you to draw from. You mentioned your sister is acting a little strange, and sleepwalking. Could be that she is susceptible as well, and the demon is targeting her to get to you.'

Chloe leaned back in her chair. If her head had been spinning before, now she was completely reeling.

'So... this is all my fault?' she said, with a horrible realisation. Because *she* had brought her family in harm's way.

'Don't say that,' David quickly replied. 'You didn't know—how could you? It's just one of those things. You aren't to blame.'

But Chloe knew she *was* to blame. Regardless of whether the demon was focused on her or not, it had still been Chloe who had railroaded the others into coming to Perron Manor in the first place.

She had been the catalyst for the move. And now they were all going to pay the price.

'Can I ask?' David went on. 'What do you remember of your time there as a child? And do you remember much of *that* night?'

'Not a lot,' Chloe answered. 'I was six. How much can you remember from being six?'

'Not a great deal,' David admitted. 'But, with respect, I never went through what you did.'

'I wasn't even awake for most of that night,' she said. 'I have a vague memory of being outside with my uncle, and then my parents showed up, but I just seem to remember their panic at the time. Nothing more. I didn't actually see anything. While growing up, the whole thing was kinda hidden from me, never spoken about. I only really learned what happened after I looked it up myself. So, as bad as that night supposedly was, it never really affected me. That is why I was so comfortable going back there to Perron Manor. To me, it was just ancient history. Gruesome, yes, but it didn't change the fact I had inherited an absolutely beautiful house and didn't have to pay a penny for it. In my head, it was more foolish to turn it away. I never dreamed that it would be…'

She couldn't complete the sentence out loud, but her inner voice finished things up for her.

Haunted.

She contemplated her situation, trying to determine the best course of action. All roads seemed to point back to fleeing.

However, before that could happen, Chloe needed to have a long conversation with her husband and sister. Even then, it wasn't likely they could just leave straight away. She looked up to David.

'I have to ask,' she began. 'Given you know so much about it, even wrote a book, what is with your obsession with Perron Manor?'

David hesitated—taking another drink—and then lifted up a biscuit from the plate. 'I dunno,' he said. 'This kind of thing has always fascinated me. And since I'm local to the area, Perron Manor was probably the first place I became aware of that was rumoured to be haunted. I was only young at the time, but the stories always stuck. So, having such a fantastic location so close to me, which I was never able to access for the longest time, made it a bit of a 'white whale.' Even if only half the stories are true, I would say it's still the most haunted house in Britain.'

'Brilliant,' Chloe said, deadpan. 'And I'm living in the fucking thing.'

CHAPTER 34

SARAH'S LUNGS BURNED, and her feet were sore from pounding the tarmac. She would be back at the house soon but felt like she still had too much negative energy to burn. With gritted teeth, she pushed her jog into a sprint.

Anything to help snuff out the anger inside.

In truth, just getting outside again had helped a little. She had avoided Chloe after their fight, where at one point Sarah was close to taking a swing at her sister. Thankfully, Chloe left to go somewhere, which afforded Sarah space. Still, Sarah wanted to focus her anger into something at least semi-productive. So, she'd changed into her sportswear—a tank-top with a thin, cotton jacket over the top, lycra sports leggings, and a pair of running shoes—and went out for a long run.

The route had taken her down long and winding country lanes, before skirting the fringes of the town of Alnmouth. Finally, she was working her way back. It had been close to an hour and a half already, and Sarah was enjoying once again pushing herself physically. Ever since she'd moved in, her fitness had been neglected and taken something of a nosedive.

The scenery, too, was a welcome change to the relative gloom of Perron Manor. The beautiful sky above was beginning to burn orange at the onset of dusk.

While it felt good to be out of the house, she still had no intention of leaving it permanently. If Chloe was going to run, then she was a fool.

Sarah turned back into the driveway to Perron Manor and saw those distinctive three peaks at the head of the front elevation. She also saw Chloe's car was back.

She jogged up the steps in a few long strides, then stopped at the front door, checking her pulse. Sarah glanced at the brass knocker again: the frowning lion's head with a circular ring dangling from its mouth. She hadn't been overly enamoured with it upon first laying eyes on the thing, but it had certainly grown on her and helped add to the charm of the house.

Once inside, Sarah made a beeline for her room straight away, not wanting to see or interact with her sister. She showered, and as she was changing Sarah heard a gentle rap on her door.

'Sarah?'

Closing her eyes, she tried not to clench her teeth together too tightly. Chloe's muffled voice from the other side of the door was *not* welcome right now.

No doubt she just wanted to talk again about how she was going to run away, like a coward. Sarah didn't want to hear that. What she wanted to do was grab Chloe and shake her, and tell her she *had* to stay. She belonged here at the house.

They all did.

Sarah felt like she *had* found herself here, especially over the last few days. She knew where she needed to be.

Force her to stay.

Sarah had a sudden resolve to make Chloe see things the same way. Her sister called out again.

'Sarah, can we talk?'

Perhaps speaking with Chloe right now wasn't such a bad thing.

'Come in,' she called back, slipping on a powder-blue wool jumper, one that wasn't too thick or heavy.

Chloe entered the room.

Sarah had expected her to be ready for an argument—a frown and set jaw, shoulders square, ready for combat. But the half-smile Chloe wore was almost apologetic.

'What is it?' Sarah asked firmly.

'I spoke with Andrew,' Chloe replied. 'Went over a few things with him.'

'And how does he feel about his wife believing in fairytales?' Sarah asked, her tone thick with sarcasm. However, the point was ignored, and Chloe continued on as if Sarah hadn't said anything.

'We're going to look for another place,' she said. 'Both permanently and something in the short term. We might even rent. And we're going to try and find a hotel or bed and breakfast that can fit us in for tonight. Andrew is making some calls right now.'

Sarah's jaw hung open. 'You can't be serious.'

'I'm not sure if we will find anywhere close enough on so little notice, but I want to try. I just don't feel safe here anymore. And I… want you to come with us.'

A humourless laugh escaped Sarah before she could stop herself. 'You've lost it,' she said. 'Absolutely lost your Goddamn mind. I'm not going to follow you while you scamper away like a gutless coward.'

Sarah thought the barb might have at least angered her sister a little, but instead Chloe just stepped forward, hands clasped together at her belly.

'Please,' Chloe said, 'just consider it. Even if it's just for a night at first. Get away from this place and clear your head.'

'No!' Sarah shouted. 'I'm not leaving. And you shouldn't either. Jesus Christ, Chloe, just think about what you're doing.'

'I know it's hard to believe,' Chloe told her. 'I get that. I also know I'm asking a lot. But, well, I'm not just asking. I'm *begging*. I spoke with the guy who wrote that book you read—'

'Who?' Sarah cut in. 'That whacko you yelled at in the coffee shop? *You* spoke to *him*?'

'Yes,' Chloe answered.

'And he got you believing this place is haunted, didn't he.'

'*He* didn't, Sarah. The things that happened to me made me believe it. But David did tell me it's dangerous to stay here, that the house wants me after I got away from it when I was little. And, without an exorcism—'

'Exorcism?' Sarah asked, bringing her hands up to her head in disbelief. 'Are you fucking for real?!'

'That's the only way to release the souls that are trapped here...' Chloe paused, then shook her head. 'Never mind, none of that is important. But, we need to leave.'

'Enough!' Sarah snapped, thrusting her fists down to her sides and gritting her teeth together.

Within moments, Andrew appeared at the door, Emma in his hands. He gave Sarah a half-smile, and it occurred to Sarah that she'd not spoken to him properly since all of this madness started.

'Can you believe this?' she asked him, pointing at Chloe. He didn't answer, so she pressed further. 'Tell me you don't believe this rubbish as well?'

'Look, Sarah,' he said, defensively, 'there's no need for you guys to fight. We need clear heads here.'

'Clear heads?' Sarah asked, incredulous. 'Clear heads do not believe in ghosts, Andrew.'

He looked away, almost embarrassed. Sarah knew he didn't really believe his wife either. And yet, he was still going along with her crazy demands.

'Sarah,' Chloe began. 'Please. Just come with us tonight.'

'Actually,' Andrew cut in, 'about that. I haven't been able to find anywhere with any space on such short notice.'

Sarah saw Chloe's face fall. Was she really so scared to spend just one more night in the house? If so, it was pathetic.

'There has to be somewhere,' Chloe said, but Andrew just gave an apologetic shrug.

'I'm sorry.'

Sarah folded her arms across her chest. 'Okay,' she said with a smirk. 'How about this. We stay *here* tonight. If something happens, and I see it, then I'll believe you. If nothing happens, then you consider the fact that whatever *is* happening could all be in your head, and you are upheaving all our lives for no reason.'

'No,' Chloe said softly, shaking her head.

'Chloe,' Andrew began, 'there isn't any other option for tonight, we need to stay here. Unless you want us to sleep outside. But I don't think Emma would thank you for that.'

The muscles in Chloe's jaw tensed, and then she stormed out of the room.

'You obviously can't be that scared if you're happy enough to go off on your own,' Sarah called after her, and Andrew shot her a scowl. 'Oh come on, Andrew, why are you humouring her here? Is it just so you can get your way and get out of this place? It's all clearly bullshit and you *know* it. You're just using it to your advantage.'

'I'll tell you what I know,' Andrew said, with a surprisingly stern tone. 'I know that my wife—your *sister*—is really struggling at the moment. No, I don't think the things she is saying are physically true, but I can see something is weighing on her. I've never seen her like this before, so I'm worried about her. And, given how close you two always were, I'm surprised you can't see it, either. Or do you just not care anymore?'

Sarah's mouth was already open to fire back when she caught herself and paused, considering his words. Her body relaxed a little, and her posture slumped as guilt washed over her.

He was right.

Regardless of what Chloe was saying, it was clear something was very wrong. And instead of helping her sister, as she normally would have, Sarah's reaction had been to try and mock her, shame her, and beat her into submission. Sarah's defences had come up straight away, as if any slight towards Perron Manor was somehow aimed at her as well.

It wasn't like her, especially when it came to Chloe, the person she was closest to in the whole world. Sarah felt nauseous as the realisation came over her, and she started to leave the room.

'Don't,' Andrew said. 'Another fight isn't going to help anything.'

'We aren't going to fight,' Sarah replied. 'I promise.'

She then went looking for Chloe, searching the middle floor. And finding her in Vincent's old room surprised Sarah.

Chloe was seated on the end of the bed, looking at the floor, and had tears running down her face. Her hands gripped the bedsheets so tightly that her knuckles were white.

Seeing her sister like this, almost broken, only served to increase the shame Sarah felt.

'Hey,' she said, her voice little more than a whisper.

Chloe didn't look up. 'Hey.'

Sarah didn't know where to begin with her apology, but she sat on the bed next to Chloe and put an arm around her. Thankfully, Chloe leaned in.

'I'm sorry,' Sarah said. 'I don't know what's been wrong with me lately.'

'Well, I'm sorry for fucking this all up for us,' Chloe replied. 'You're right. I *was* the one who persuaded everyone to come here, and now I'm the one who wants us gone.' She sniffed, then wiped the back of her hand across her face, smearing tears across it. 'What the fuck is wrong with me?' Chloe asked, and she broke down again, her shoulders shaking as she sobbed.

'Nothing,' Sarah insisted, then hugged her tightly. She then turned Chloe to face her. 'Listen to me, Sis. If you want to go, then we'll go. Tomorrow, we'll find somewhere to stay, then leave.'

'But… you don't want to. You don't believe any of it.'

That was true, but what was really important here had suddenly been brought into focus: Chloe's wellbeing.

Screw the house.

'I believe that you need to be away from this place, for whatever reason. So, we'll do it. I'll come with you, and we can figure the rest out from there. I know we'll need to stay here for tonight, but come tomorrow, we're gone. All of us.'

The sounds of the pipes within the walls suddenly beginning to rattle startled them both, and Sarah heard a faint screeching that sounded like expanding metal. However, everything soon settled into silence again.

Sarah then saw that Chloe had tensed up, so she smiled mischievously at her sister.

'Guess the house doesn't want us to go, huh?' she joked.

Thankfully, Chloe smiled as well. 'I guess not.' Then Chloe added, 'Are you sure you're okay coming with us?'

'Of course,' Sarah replied, happy to see the relief on her sister's face. 'Are you gonna be okay staying here for one more night?'

Chloe shrugged but was still smiling. 'Looks like I'll have to be.'

CHAPTER 35

It had just turned nine o'clock in the evening, and darkness had set in outside.

Chloe, Sarah, and Andrew were all gathered together in the living room. Emma was up in her room, asleep. Chloe hated that her daughter was alone, and it made her even more on edge.

They had tried to keep the child downstairs with them, to placate Chloe, but Emma had refused to sleep with the others in the room. She just thought it was playtime. The child fought against her obvious tiredness and, eventually, her weary yowls turned into a full-on screaming fit. It was then Andrew suggested that they put her to bed, but keep a close eye on the monitor. Given he didn't really believe there was any danger, his primary concern at that point was that his child get the sleep she needed.

Chloe didn't want to agree, but Sarah had assured her that they would all be close by, and at the first sign of trouble all three of them would be able to get upstairs quickly to help. She had explained everything in a kind and gentle manner, with no mocking or condescension. Chloe appreciated that, though she still felt like a child being talked down to by the grown-ups.

That only served to make Chloe question her sanity even more. Was she just losing it? Had the events of the previous night actually been perfectly explainable but she had just twisted them out of all proportion in her own, tired mind?

Previously, she had been certain of what she had seen. No question. But now...

Instead of concentrating on the film on the television with the others, Chloe spent most of her time looking at the baby monitor, watching Emma sleep soundly, clouded in the blue hue of night-vision.

Andrew had managed to get the fire in the room going, which kicked out a lot of heat and a pleasantly smokey smell. He was seated next to Chloe, with an arm draped over her and her head rested on his chest. Sarah was on the sofa adjacent to them, wrapped up in a blanket.

On any other occasion, it could have been a wonderful and cosy night in for them all.

But for Chloe, it was simply a case of counting down the minutes until she could go up to bed. She was seriously considering sleeping on the floor of Emma's room tonight, though she knew Andrew would likely not be happy with that.

It was hard not to replay the events of the previous night, and also to call her memory into question. *Was* there a way it could have been explained?

Emma let out a moan, and Chloe fixed her eyes on the screen. However, the child was just shuffling about in her sleep. Perfectly safe.

Sarah let out a yawn from her place on the adjacent sofa. 'Sorry, Andrew,' she said, 'but you have the worst taste in films.'

'This is a classic,' he protested.

'It's garbage,' Sarah replied.

Chloe actually found their playful bickering nice. Like a small return to normality.

'Back me up here,' Andrew said, prodding Chloe in the ribs. She jolted a little and smiled.

'Sorry, hun,' she said, turning to him, 'but I'm not a fan.'

'Bah,' Andrew huffed, making a show of throwing up his free hand. 'You're both heathens.'

Chloe chuckled, then turned back to check on the monitor again. Emma was still safe.

In fact, even after the film finished and the three of them decided to go up to bed, nothing untoward happened. Chloe and Andrew bid Sarah a good night—Sarah even hugged Chloe tightly—and then they quietly checked on Emma.

Still safe.

Chloe and Andrew then readied themselves for the night and climbed into bed. The monitor, as ever, was positioned on the nightstand, not far from Chloe's head.

With the lights off, Chloe lay motionless, just watching the dark shadows in the room and feeling the stresses of the day catch up with her. But all was well… or as well as it could be. Nothing was happening. And that was enough.

Eventually, Chloe fell asleep, knowing that this would be her last night ever in Perron Manor.

CHAPTER 36

CHLOE WAS HELD DOWN, *unable to move. Everything was dark around her. The voice that came from above was vile and inhuman, sounding like the purest form of hate she could imagine. A smell followed it—a disgusting stink of rot and death.*

'We are going to kill your baby.'

Chloe fought with everything she had. Large, cold hands grabbed her head. She still could not see. Her neck twisted and then began to snap as she was killed in absolute darkness.

She woke with a gasp, gripping the sheets of her bed, her body locked tightly.

That voice, and the smell, was still with her. A feeling of cold emanated close to her ear.

'Kill... your... baby.'

Chloe quickly managed to regain control of her body to turn her head in panic, but saw nothing beside her, only the blue hue of the monitor.

Just a dream. Another horrible fucking dream.

Her breathing was rapid, and she couldn't help but take short and shallow breaths as anxiety gripped her. The sheets around her felt damp with sweat. Andrew snored loudly beside her.

Calm down, Chloe told herself. *Control your breathing.*

She tried to do just that. Eventually, her body relaxed.

Another horrible dream.

But in the end, she knew it was just that—a dream, and nothing more. Chloe wiped a little of the sweat away from her forehead and turned her body so she could squint at the monitor. Emma was seemingly in a deep sleep, lying blissfully unaware of anything except her own dreams. The digital clock next to the monitor showed the time was a quarter past three in the morning.

Chloe rolled over to her back and let out a sigh. *Get a grip on yourself.*

She then allowed her eyes to close again, hoping she could relax enough to fall back to sleep.

However, a noise from the corner of the room—a faint and brief clicking sound—drew her attention.

The only light afforded was the dull glow from the baby monitor, as well as the faint bits of moonlight that managed to penetrate the thick, dark curtains. Most of the room was heavy with darkness, and Chloe's vision could scarcely stretch over to the far wall. There was one corner in particular, however, that seemed much darker than the others, where the shadows were heavier.

Chloe could not see where the walls met, but it was where the sound seemed to have originated.

She squinted, but couldn't make anything out. Then there was another sound, one that made her body lock up again: a long and loud exhale, coming from the same place.

Chloe lifted herself up to her elbows, eyes wide, and tried to process what she had just heard. Could it be that someone was standing in the corner of the room, lost in the shadows?

She didn't know what to do, so when she whispered a faint, 'Hello?' she immediately felt stupid. Did she really expect some kind of response?

And yet, that is exactly what she got.

The response was a hoarse whisper, male, and sounded almost pained.

'Chloe...'

Her heart seized. She wanted to elbow Andrew hard in the back and scream his name, just so he could witness this. But she couldn't find the strength to move.

Then, she saw something emerge slightly from the black. It was the form of a man, though she could see little more than his facial features, the body below still hidden.

Chloe gripped her sheets tighter. She struggled to breathe while gazing at the smiling face that was framed with dark, brushed-back hair. The man's eyes were bloody and mangled holes. Tendrils of blood ran from the wounds, lining the face like horrible tears, even streaking his exposed teeth. His jaw was square and chiselled, and the throat beneath had a yawning slash across it which opened up the flesh. Blood ran freely from that wound as well.

Though she didn't know how, the man's face seemed familiar, somehow.

'We've... missed... you,' he said. Each word seemed to be a struggle, though his mouth never moved. Blood pumped from the open neck wound.

Go away, go away, go away, Chloe begged.

This couldn't be real. *Couldn't be!*

And yet, she could see it. No matter how much she willed the horrifying image to disappear, it simply would not. The man continued to smile and stare.

A noise escaped her throat, but it was barely comprehensible—neither a word nor a scream. More like a mewl.

Then, the man retreated in one swift and fluid motion, once again disappearing into the darkness.

Chloe fought to try and push her fear back enough that she could move, or at least scream.

However, another noise came from beside her, and was enough to force Chloe to turn her head. She looked to the baby monitor. The sound was crackly, but sounded like a heavy breath.

'No!'

The word fell out of her, an instinctual reaction to the thing on the screen. It wasn't her daughter anymore, but a face so close to the camera as to be washed out in white.

She could make out a set of cracked and misshapen teeth, given the mouth was so close to the camera. Thin lips were pulled back into a hateful smile as the mouth tittered. The skin was pulled tightly over the skull beneath it, but the eyes were out of the frame.

And then, words spilled from the monitor in strained and breathless tones.

'Round... and round... the garden...'

Finally, the fear that held Chloe prisoner was broken as sheer panic that exploded within. Whatever that thing was, it was in there with Emma.

'Andrew!' she shouted and jumped out of bed. In her peripheral vision, she saw her husband start to stir, but she was out of the room before he'd fully woken up.

Please be okay, please be okay, please be okay, Chloe repeated the mantra over and over again as she burst into the hallway, praying for the best. The thought of her defenceless and innocent daughter alone in her room with that... *thing* embedded a new level of terror inside her that she didn't know was possible.

She thrust the door open and hit the light switch, illuminating the room. Emma's fuzzy head started to move, and the child rolled over with a look of surprise on her little face.

Chloe's eyes darted around, first looking to the camera, then checking everywhere else. She was scared, more than she had ever been in her life, and confused beyond belief, but the need to protect her daughter made her fight through the fear. She quickly checked under the bed, in the wardrobes, and even behind the curtains.

But she found no one.

'Chloe?' she heard Andrew call in a tired and confused voice. 'What is it?'

She didn't respond but instead scooped Emma up out of her cot-bed, then checked her over. Other than being a little disgruntled at being woken, Emma seemed fine, and she rubbed at her eyes with small, chubby hands. But Chloe's heart still hammered in her chest, and she knew she had to get the little girl out of that room.

Hell, out of the house.

Then, Chloe saw Emma look past her, over her shoulder, and Chloe felt an intense cold radiate from behind.

Emma pointed.

'Man!'

Spinning around, Chloe let out a shriek. The thing that towered over Chloe, blocking the door, was indeed a man, but not the one she had seen in her bedroom. This one was different: thinner, older, and much, much taller.

The stranger's skin was the colour of ash, and his eyes were milky, with small pupils dead centre. There were no eyelids, so the stare he gave was a manic one, with his eyes almost bulging out of their sockets. His face was almost skeletal, and his bared teeth were cracked, chipped, and misshapen. Wispy and patchy white hair jutted out from his cranium at wild angles.

In addition, she saw that the man was dressed in a dirty and ragged black suit, one that looked to be from a different era.

A horrible stench wafted over Chloe, like rotten meat, and a large and pale hand reached out for her.

CHAPTER 37

SARAH'S MIND swum back to consciousness, and she sat upright in bed. Everything was confusing. Shards of abstract images—leftover fragments of her dream—replayed in her mind.

Tania. The bomb. Sarah bathing in what remained of her friend, grasping the sloppy remains and rubbing the glistening red flesh over her own body. *Such... pleasure.*

However, screaming had pulled her from the dream. She lifted her head from the pillow and felt something like a breath on her face. Not just a breath, however, but a spoken word.

Dede!

She shook her head again, and it did not take long for her waking mind to fully take over and push the horrid dream away, banishing it to a vague memory that quickly dissipated. A sudden feeling of urgency brought Sarah's senses back to full alert.

Though the screams sounded far off, they were still very audible.

Chloe!

She quickly scrambled from her bed, planted her bare feet on the floor, and ran from the room, dressed only in the white tank top and grey shorts she had been sleeping in.

The corridor outside felt cold, as if all the windows on the floor had been left open during the night. She saw Andrew appear from his room, and the two made brief eye contact. He looked as confused and panicked as Sarah felt. He stopped at Emma's room, the source of the screaming, and Sarah then realised that she could hear Emma crying as well.

Her heart dropped.

Please God, don't let anything have happened to her.

Andrew frantically tried to open the door to Emma's room but was met with resistance.

'Chloe, what's happened?' he yelled and banged his fist against the thick wood. 'Let me in!'

The only response was another scream, so he began thrusting his shoulder into the door in an effort to force it open. Andrew threw himself at the door again and again, but it did little more than rattle its hinges. Emma continued to wail.

Sarah was next to Andrew a few moments later and pushed him aside.

'Chloe!' she screamed. 'Let us in!'

She tried to force the door open as well, and kicked against it, thrusting the sole of her foot hard against the weak point where the handle and latch were. The door shook. Another kick. And another. Then, with a scream, Sarah flung herself shoulder first, again aiming for the weak point.

Nothing.

Andrew began to help, and the two of them hit the door with their bodies, one after the other, in quick succession.

The wood of the door dented and cracked, and it was forced open ever so slightly.

They kept going, yelling out for Chloe, but getting no response. Andrew looked inside through the small gap they had made, where the door met the frame.

'Jesus, someone's in there with her,' he exclaimed, and Sarah pushed her head in to see as well.

A large figure, easily over seven feet tall, loomed over Chloe, who was sitting on the floor with her back pressed against the far wall, Emma clutched to her chest.

The man who was slowly approaching her, almost gliding, suddenly turned and gazed at Sarah and Andrew as they peered in. Sarah let out a gasp at those wide eyes and their dead stare. She knew instantly that the thing was not human.

Chloe was right!

All along, Chloe had been right.

'Leave her alone!' Sarah screamed, but was not able to sound nearly as commanding as she wanted or needed to be.

Keep going, a voice inside told her, the one she relied on when she needed to face dangerous situations.

'I'm coming, Chloe!'

Of course, Sarah had no idea how to help when she finally got into the room, given what they were facing, but still she had to get to Chloe and Emma. Sarah backed up, tensed herself, and again thrust a strong kick into the door.

Thankfully, this time, the door opened, as if whatever force had been holding it shut instantly disappeared.

Sarah just about fell in the room, with Andrew close behind. Chloe was still on the floor, sobbing, and pressing herself against the far wall. Emma wriggled and cried in her arms.

But Sarah could see no-one else. She looked around the room as Andrew ran over to his wife and child. Checking the wardrobes and under the cot-bed yielded no results. Whoever—or *what*ever—had been in here, was now gone. Sarah then rushed over to her sister and niece and dropped down next to Andrew.

She locked eyes with Chloe, who looked defeated and terrified in equal measure, with tears streaked down her face. Sarah put a firm hand on Chloe's shoulder, knowing they were not out of the woods by a long shot. She didn't pretend to even remotely understand what was happening, but she knew they were still in danger.

'Sis… we need to go. We need to get you and Emma out of here. Now.'

CHAPTER 38

EMMA WAS PRESSED TIGHTLY to her chest, but Chloe didn't dare relax her grip any. They were running down the main stairs, with Andrew on one side of her and Sarah on the other.

No one was talking, only panting frantically as they moved.

Given what had happened up in Emma's room, Chloe didn't need the others to admit they believed her now. They had seen the entity with their own eyes.

The thought of that dead man still terrified her, and she could not shake the feeling of his icy touch from when his hand had lain on her shoulder. At the time, Chloe had turned away to shield Emma, but the sound of the door to the room being kicked open had quickly drawn her attention.

The tall man was gone, but Sarah and Andrew had emerged. They came to her. Soon after, they all ran.

Sarah was holding Chloe's upper arm tightly as they turned onto the half-landing, guiding her. They then thundered down the remaining flight of stairs, towards the entrance door.

A horrible banging sound erupted from all around, like something was trying to break through the very walls of the house. Chloe felt thick reverberations in the steps beneath her feet.

So sudden was the onset of violent sounds that she jolted, and Emma almost slipped from her grasp. Her reactions were quick, thankfully, and she managed to keep hold of the child. But the close call still made her heart race even more, if that was possible.

Emma's cries only made the frantic situation they found themselves in even worse. The child was confused and scared—the same as the rest of them. Chloe felt like a failure in every respect.

When her foot made contact with the marble floor, the continuous crashing sounds ceased instantly, though they still echoed in her ears. Then, the front door slowly creaked open on its own.

The fleeing group drew to a quick halt as the door finished its swing. There was no one outside. All Chloe could see was the front steps leading down into the night.

Who the hell opened the door?

'What do we do?' Chloe asked, her voice a scared whisper.

'We run,' Sarah replied, sounding determined.

Chloe didn't have time to argue, as Sarah again grabbed her and pulled her along. Andrew followed, and they all quickly moved towards the now-open door. Chloe didn't like it, though. Something was very wrong.

Her concerns were quickly realised when a bloody hand appeared from outside. Its fingers curled around the side of the door frame, taking hold from its position close to the ground. The group stopped again and Chloe shrieked. She heard a low moan, and a dry sliding sound as a disfigured *thing* pulled itself into view.

It was once a man, but the head had been brutally battered and misshapen. Large, tumour-like bulges protruded from one side, and both eyes were covered over with a stretch of solid skin.

It was his mouth that drew Chloe's attention first, with the jaw completely removed. Blood ran freely from the ripped and jagged flesh at the sides, and another pained groan came from him. The horrific entity pulled itself farther into view. One arm was cut and lacerated, but the other was just a deformed and withered stump from the elbow.

'This can't be happening,' Andrew said, wide-eyed in sheer terror. He took a step back, pulling Chloe with him. The rest of the monstrosity at the door came into view, though there wasn't much more to see given it was cut off at the midsection. A severed spinal cord was dragged behind, wrapped up in spaghetti-like entrails.

The crawling monster reached out towards them with its good hand, and its tongue lolled and writhed like a snake.

Chloe screamed. The three turned and ran, ducking into a side corridor.

'The back door,' Sarah commanded, breathless, sounding distinctly less determined than before.

CHAPTER 39

CONCENTRATE ON GETTING OUT. *Nothing else matters.*

The things Sarah had witnessed were enough to drive her insane. But she knew that if she gave in to that line of thinking, then it was all over for them. So, she pushed the need to rationalise everything completely out of her mind.

Just focus on the next step.

The next step was getting to the great hall, and then getting the hell out through the back door. Then they could escape.

Unless something else was waiting for them there, of course.

Sarah led the others through the corridor safely, and out into the great hall. It was dark, so Sarah switched on the lights upon entering. They flickered a few times before hitting their full strength.

A shriek from Chloe drew Sarah's attention, and she looked to the glazed rear door. Sarah felt her body freeze.

Standing in front of the door—perfectly still and blocking the exit—was a woman. She was dressed in an old, black dress with a high collar. White hair was pulled up into a loose bun.

The woman looked ancient and had sagging, wrinkled, and ashen skin. Black teeth were revealed as her cracked lips spread back in a menacing grin. Where her eyes should have been were instead black pits that ran with blood. The muscles in her throat moved, and Sarah heard a croaked, vile-sounding chuckle.

The woman lifted up her arms to them, and Sarah saw that the fingers were skeletal, with only small patches of dark and decayed flesh on the bone.

Shit.

Then the banging noises started again, accompanied by horrible wails and screeching. It sounded similar to when they started the furnace, only amplified in intensity.

'We can't go that way!' Chloe exclaimed, stating the obvious.

Sarah was always prepared for a fight if the situation called for it, but how the hell were you supposed to fight *those* things?

A pressure built in her chest and Sarah realised her focus was waning. Fear was taking over.

'Back the way we came,' Andrew instructed. However, even before they turned, Sarah felt a blast of icy-cold air across her back.

Someone was directly behind them.

When they spun, Sarah saw a young, blonde-haired man, who was completely naked, his stomach cut open from navel to breast. He was only a few feet away, and intestines ran out from the stomach wound over his gesturing hands. The man looked at the group through milky, blank eyes, with an almost confused expression.

'*Help,*' he whispered.

The banging continued around them, getting louder and louder. The group sprinted away from the staggering man, who shuffled after them, still holding his rope-like intestines.

'This can't be real!' Sarah shouted, desperate to cling to sanity. But she was finding that difficult.

Only one exit seemed to be unobstructed, and they moved towards it—the door down to the basement. Sarah pressed her palm to a nearby wall as they ran, in an effort to keep her balance as Chloe fell into her. As Sarah's hand touched the wall, she felt something warm and wet. Glancing at her hand, she saw it was streaked red.

Blood was trickling down the wall.

'What the fuck...'

Chloe looked as well, then let out a cry of fear. The walls were actually *bleeding*. And what's more, Sarah was certain that she saw texture beneath some ripped wallpaper that didn't seem right. Was that... *skin?*

'We need to keep going,' Andrew stressed, but it was clear he was as scared as the rest of them and looked close to tears. Through it all, Emma continued to cry.

Even through her panic, Sarah knew they should try and loop around again towards the front door, as the basement offered no way to escape. However, the half-man they'd seen at the entrance was dragging himself through the other door that led to the front entrance, his tongue trailing across the floor as he moved.

The door to the basement hung open, inviting them in.

'There!' Andrew said, pointing to it. 'That way!'

He ran ahead, pulling Chloe and guiding them towards it. Chloe, in turn, pulled Sarah.

No, she thought. *This isn't right. We're being shepherded.*

She tried to stop them as they crossed the threshold into the small room that housed the steps, and pulled at Chloe's hand. However, something cold and firm grabbed her from behind.

Sarah didn't even see what it was, but it caused her hand to slip from Chloe's.

Her sister looked back, confused, and then the door between them slammed shut.

She was then spun around, and the thing that held Sarah pushed her hard up against the now-closed door.

'Sarah!' she heard her sister call out from behind. But as Sarah stared into the demonic yellow eyes before her, she knew it was hopeless.

'Chloe! Run!'

CHAPTER 40

'We need to go,' Andrew urged, breathless. He pulled Chloe along with him towards the steps that led down.

'But what about Sarah?' Chloe argued. 'We need to get her!'

Andrew shook his head without making eye contact. 'We *need* to keep moving. Whatever those things are, they'll be through soon.'

Emma's crying was relentless as Andrew guided Chloe over to the top of the steps. She didn't know what to do. Leaving Sarah like that didn't seem right, but then, she needed to get Emma away from danger.

They descended, Andrew leading the way. It occurred to Chloe that it should have been pitch black down in the basement, but she could see a faint and flickering orange glow.

The farther down the steps they got, the more Chloe could make out the distinct crackling of a fire. It was only when they reached the bottom that she saw it: the furnace at full blaze. All of its front doors were open and the flames within were roaring. They stopped in their tracks.

'Andrew, we need to go back,' Chloe cried.

Over the noise of the fire, Chloe could hear something else as well, something coming from *inside* the inferno. Cries of pain. She also saw movement—a black form that writhed within the fire and moved to the front of the furnace.

It was a man. Hideously burned, with blistered, blackened, and melted features.

'*Help!*' he cried, reaching an arm through one of the openings. Chloe saw that the fingers of the hand had been fused together, one of his eyes had been melted away, and there was a sickening smell of cooking meat suddenly around them.

She turned around and pulled Andrew with her, but both quickly stopped.

Someone was standing on the stairs behind them. And Chloe immediately recognised the face and brushed back hair—as well as the gouged-out eyes and slashed throat. It was the man she had seen in her room earlier, the one who had peeked out from the shadows.

Once again she had the impression she vaguely recognized him.

Andrew let out an involuntary cry of panic, and the two backed up. The man on the stairs laughed. He was dressed in a dark suit with a black shirt beneath. The chest of the shirt was wet with his own blood, which spilled freely from the yawning hole in his throat.

'Hello... Chloe,' the man said in a strained voice.

Seeing his fine—if ruined—clothing and hearing his voice again, though distorted, ignited something in Chloe's memory. From a time when she was very young.

She knew who this man was now. *Marcus Blackwater!*

He took a heavy step down towards them, emitting an insidious chuckle.

Chloe and Andrew continued to backpedal until Marcus—or what *used* to be Marcus—stood in the basement with them, barring the only exit. Emma writhed in Chloe's arms, still crying. Chloe didn't know what to do. She felt the heat from the great furnace behind her.

She then jumped as Andrew let out a fierce roar, and he charged at the entity blocking their escape. Chloe didn't even have time to call out his name before her husband reached Marcus. The grinning monster held up its arm, and planted its palm directly into Andrew's oncoming chest.

Andrew let out a pain-filled cry, and his body was thrown back like a rag doll, landing over ten feet away. He crumpled to the ground and rolled over, ending up in a motionless heap.

'No! Andrew!' Chloe cried out, unsure if her husband was even alive.

Marcus Blackwater just continued to cackle.

The screaming of the man trapped in the furnace suddenly ceased, and that alone was enough to draw Chloe's panicked attention. She quickly turned her head to see that the burned figure was still inside the roaring fire, but now seemed unconcerned with the searing flames. He peeked out through one of the holes, focusing on her with his one good eye, seemingly unconcerned by the heat and fire that continued to ruin his body. He reached a hand out again and curled its fused fingers inwards in a beckoning motion.

'Give me... the baby.'

Horrible, mocking laughter burst from the unmoving mouth.

Chloe ran over to Andrew, unsure what else to do with Marcus blocking the stairs and the horrible burnt thing in the raging furnace. Emma continued her desperate screams. Chloe touched Andrew's arm. It felt ice cold, but he was still breathing.

'Get up, Andrew,' she begged, but he was unresponsive.

She then felt cold hands grab her by the shoulders—although 'hands' wasn't the right word. The fingers were long and sharp, more like talons, and the tips pierced her skin. She screamed, but whatever it was held her firm, easily overpowering her. The cold and the stink that flowed from behind Chloe was overwhelming.

A shadow fell over her front. She looked up to see someone standing before her, looming over both her and Emma, while she was held from behind.

'Ring... a ring... o' roses...'

It was the old man in the filthy suit. The one with the wide, lidless eyes, and almost skeletal features.

And he plucked Emma from Chloe's arms.

CHAPTER 41

Sarah opened her eyes, and it took her a moment to realise where she was: still in the great hall, but sitting on the floor with her back against the door that had cut her off from her sister.

She twisted her head both left and right, but the thing that had grabbed her was now gone. However, its ice-cold touch still lingered on her skin.

Sarah realised she must have blacked out, but *why* exactly, or for how long, she had no idea. She could not shake the image of the face, twisted and inhuman. Or its burning yellow eyes.

It had been different than the other entities she'd already seen. Something ancient and evil.

A demon.

Sarah's heart pounded violently in her chest, and she couldn't help from shaking. As cowardly as it made her feel, she wanted to flee. The idea of staying here to help her family caused her stomach to churn. Despite all the life-threatening situations she'd been in throughout her career, Sarah had never experienced fear like this.

Everything was just so unknown. The rules of engagement were non-existent, and the enemy seemed as unbeatable as it was unknowable.

Getting to her feet seemed like a herculean effort and left her feeling weak and exposed. Though she could see nothing else around her in the great hall, it felt like a million eyes were watching and waiting, ready to pounce when the time was right.

She knew she should run downstairs to help Chloe, Emma, and Andrew. However, Sarah couldn't bring her body to move. She remembered what her sister had said in their fight the previous day, something about the house wanting Chloe because she'd gotten away from it once before.

That was probably why it had stopped them from leaving. But it had her now. It had what it wanted.

Sarah looked to one of the doors that led to the front exit. Perhaps it was an opportunity for her while the house was busy. It shamed her beyond words, but that exit now looked *very* appealing.

CHAPTER 42

THE HORRIFIC SCREAMING of his wife was the first thing to register in Andrew's mind as he slowly regained consciousness.

He opened his eyes, but his vision was spinning and blurred. He wanted to vomit.

What the hell is happening?

His body felt like it had been frozen, and an intense cold radiated out from his chest in waves. It took a moment for his memory to catch up, and he was reminded of the impossible things he and his family were currently facing.

The last thing he remembered was charging at the man with the slashed throat. Then, he'd been hit with a flash of cold so strong that he thought his heart had stopped. Weightlessness followed, then... darkness.

His vision began to clear, and he was met with a sight that threatened to stop his heart again.

Chloe was held captive by some dark, hideous abomination of vaguely humanoid shape, though twisted into something else entirely.

But that was not the worst of it.

A tall, old-looking man held his child, his poor baby girl Emma. He was carrying her towards the roaring furnace, where a burning man waited within the flames.

Hoarse whispers escaped from the old man, who glided slowly forward as Emma howled frantically.

'*A pocket... full... of posies...*'

Andrew tried to crawl forward, but he could barely move his limbs. His strength did seem to be returning, but far too slowly, and he knew he wouldn't be able to act in time.

The old man with his baby girl moved closer and closer to the furnace.

'*A-tishoo... A-tishoo...*'

'Noooo,' Andrew weakly cried out.

But the hideous old man kept going and finished his awful nursery rhyme. '*We all... fall... down...*'

CHAPTER 43

Chloe struggled for all she was worth, writhing her body as violently as she could against the inhuman grip. But no matter how hard she tried, it was impossible to break free. She saw Andrew was now moving, pulling himself forward, but his progress was incredibly laboured.

She sensed other bodies emerge from either side of her, feeling their cold. These spirits of the dead, with pale, expressionless faces, all watched on as the old man carried Chloe's daughter to the furnace. There was an old woman with her throat cut, the monk with the ruined eye, and a plethora of other horrors, including Marcus Blackwater.

All had come to watch the sacrifice.

Tears streamed down Chloe's face, and she screamed her voice hoarse. The old man was at the furnace now with her daughter. This was it. He pulled the child back, ready to throw.

'Noooooo!'

Chloe whipped her head to the side. The guttural cry had come from a voice she recognised. Rapid footsteps pounded off the stone floor, and soon Sarah broke through the darkness, sprinting for all she was worth, a feral and angry expression etched on her face.

She wove through the motionless undead crowd, and flung herself at the man holding Emma. Chloe's breath was caught in her throat as she watched Sarah grab Emma from the old man's clutches. In one fluid motion, Sarah turned herself mid-air and landed on her back, protecting Emma from the fall.

Demonic roars of outrage thundered from the gathered crowd. Sarah hauled herself up, holding the crying child protectively. She backed up and turned her body to keep Emma shielded from the spirits that had begun to slowly advance towards her as one.

Chloe felt the cold grip from behind release her. She quickly turned and saw that there was no longer anything behind her. Which meant she was free.

However, when Chloe looked back over to Sarah, she saw that something stood behind her sister, merging with the darkness and only partially visible. It was a tall and yellow-eyed demon, skin cracked and obsidian, and its facial features twisted and melded together to be more monstrous than human.

'Sarah!' Chloe screamed. 'Behind you!'

Sarah quickly turned, then scuttled backwards with a scream upon seeing the demonic thing that stood so close to her.

'Run!' Chloe ordered.

She was unable to get through the throng of bodies between her and her sister, but did see there was enough room in the basement to skirt around the mass of drifting apparitions.

Her sister noticed it too, and Sarah ducked to her side, then sprinted towards the edges of the room. Sensing her chance, Chloe bent down to Andrew and pulled him.

'Get up!' she screamed. 'We have to run!'

He groaned and tried to move, but he was slow and sluggish. Chloe wrapped an arm over her shoulder, letting him brace his weight on her. She managed to get him to his feet.

'Just... go,' he said weakly.

'Come on!' was all she said in reply, and forced herself to backpedal with him away from the danger. He stumbled with her, his skin still cold to the touch, though warming slightly.

Chloe saw Sarah arc around the floating mass, and then make a beeline towards the pair. She quickly unloaded Emma to Chloe and took over supporting Andrew.

'Give him to me,' she said, her voice thick with urgency. 'And run!'

The relief that surged through Chloe at once again holding Emma in her arms was immeasurable, though she was very aware that they weren't safe yet. The three of them moved as quickly as possible back towards the steps that would lead them upstairs again, but they were greatly slowed by Andrew. Chloe could hear the groans and moans from the horrors that she knew were following but did not dare look back to see.

They reached the bottom step, but just as they did, the flickering light from the furnace cut out in an instant. This time, Chloe could not help but look back… and saw only darkness.

No advancing entities, no raging inferno, and none of the horrible sounds that had been ringing in her ears only moments ago. Just a dark and empty basement. The only noise was their own panicked breathing.

'What… what happened?' she asked, confused.

'It doesn't matter,' Sarah said and pushed Chloe forward. 'We just need to get out.'

Chloe led the way, running up the stone steps and holding Emma tightly, with Sarah and Andrew following closely behind.

CHAPTER 44

With Andrew's weight on her, progress for Sarah was slow. Though the entities down in the basement had vanished in an instant, panic still flooded through her, and she was desperate to get out of the house.

The whole situation was maddening. They were being hunted by things that just should not exist. And on top of that, Emma had been so close to…

Sarah couldn't finish the thought.

She still felt eternally ashamed for even considering leaving her family behind when the opportunity had presented itself. She just hoped the well of courage she'd found would help see them through to an escape.

By the time they had reached the top of the steps, Andrew was moving more freely and holding most of his own weight. Whatever had happened to him was apparently wearing off, at least to the point where he could hold himself up. Sarah still let him lean on her, but by the time they had cut through the great hall and were into the connecting corridor, it was easier to let him move completely on his own again.

The whole time they were running, Sarah was on edge, fully expecting something to reach out of the darkness and grab them. But the house remained silent, and they ran into the entrance lobby. The closed door was only a few feet away now, and escape was within reach.

Why the entities downstairs had suddenly disappeared and let them go, Sarah didn't understand. Right now, she also didn't care. Just as long as they broke free of the house.

She let Chloe and Andrew approach the exit first, and Andrew released the thumb-turn lock. He pulled the doors open and saw that the way ahead was clear.

Andrew then pushed Chloe and Emma out first, then he followed, with Sarah close behind.

This was it. They were going to be free…

But no.

Just as Sarah was about to cross the threshold, she felt her body lock and something take hold. No matter how hard she fought against it, some unseen power held her still, like a statue.

'Chloe!' she managed to cry out.

As her sister turned around, Sarah felt herself savagely pulled back, and she shot through the air, rising higher as she went. She could do nothing but scream as her body slammed against the far wall of the entrance lobby, and she then hung in mid-air, over the half-landing. She was about eight feet above the landing, held by something she could not see.

Sarah could see Chloe outside, and she looked horrified. Then, Sarah's legs were forced together, and her arms pulled out to her sides, her body forming the shape of a crucifix.

Disembodied wails and roars then rose up around her.

CHAPTER 45

CHLOE HAD no idea what she was supposed to do.

She had gotten Emma free, Andrew too, but now her sister was trapped inside Perron Manor, held above the ground by an invisible force while she screamed in agony.

'We... we need to go,' Andrew said, his voice shaking. 'I'm sorry, but we need to get Emma to safety.'

But Chloe couldn't do that. As scared as she was, there was no way she could abandon her sister. After all, it was Sarah that had saved Emma from those... things downstairs. She had saved them all, in fact, and Chloe would be damned if she was going to now leave Sarah behind in her time of need.

So, she thrust Emma into Andrew's arms. He had finally regained his strength and could carry the baby. She then grabbed his shoulders and looked her husband directly in his eyes, and they widened in surprise and worry.

'Go,' she instructed. 'Get Emma out of here now. Get off the grounds and don't stop until you are free of this place. Don't turn back.'

'But—'

'There's no time!' Chloe snapped. She loved that he was protective of her, but he needed to get their daughter away from danger. 'Do it. We'll follow.' She then grabbed his head and kissed him hard before pushing him away. He reached for her, but Chloe ducked away from him. 'I love you,' she said, then barked, 'now go! For Emma's sake.'

Chloe backed up, not giving Andrew the chance to argue further. She knew he wouldn't let anything happen to Emma, and even though it must have been killing him inside, he began to walk away.

Thank you, she mouthed to him, then turned around. Sarah was still inside, hanging in mid-air, and her screaming had increased in both pitch and magnitude. Still in the crucifix position, there was obvious tension in her arms and legs, as if they were being stretched out.

A protective instinct to save her little sister took over, and Chloe bolted back inside of the house.

However, once she had crossed the threshold, an army of ghostly entities revealed themselves to her. All motionless and standing watch.

They were everywhere, dozens of them, crowding around the perimeter of the lobby as well as up either side of the stairs. They had left Chloe a direct route up to her sister.

More of the rotted and twisted spirits watched on from the walkways above as well, peering over the edges. The cold that filled the room was intense, causing Chloe's breath to fog up the air before her.

'Go,' Sarah pleaded, weakly.

But Chloe would not. Instead, she began walking towards her sister, and the pale faces of the dead turned, following her movements as she went.

She was exposed and vulnerable, and Chloe knew that at any minute the things could pounce and kill her. But she kept going. Not quite able to break into a run, she still managed to tentatively push herself forward.

When she placed her foot on the bottom step, Chloe fully expected to be swarmed. They could simply crowd round her now and box her in, leaving no room for escape. But they didn't, and instead let her climb the stairs.

What are they waiting for?

She reached Sarah on the half-landing, and her sister's bare feet hung down directly before her. Chloe looked up, and Sarah's face was etched in pain. She still groaned in agony, and Chloe could see a tension in her sister's arms and legs as they were being pulled away from her body. Something was ever-so-slowly ripping Sarah apart.

'Run,' Sarah again pleaded. 'It's doing this just to get to you.'

But Chloe didn't care. If Perron Manor wanted her soul, then it could come and take it. She was *not* leaving her sister. She grabbed Sarah's ankles and pulled.

'Let her go!' Chloe cried out.

The gathered dead *still* did not approach, and simply stood by as a mere audience. Whatever was holding Sarah was strong, and Chloe was not able to free her, but she continued to desperately yank at Sarah's legs anyway.

'Please,' Sarah whispered between cries of pain.

'No!' Chloe shouted back, to the house rather than her sister. 'Enough! You won't take her, you hear me? You can't have my sister. I'll burn this fucking house to the ground before I let you have her. Now… Let. Her. Go!'

Chloe pulled again, and to her surprise, Sarah fell, her body dropping hard onto Chloe. They both fell backwards and tumbled down the long flight of stairs.

The world was a spinning blur, and pain erupted as Chloe bounced down the steps, hitting different parts of her body: her back, her knee, her head, even the back of her neck, which twisted a little at an awkward angle.

She hit the marble floor and rolled twice, skidding to a stop. Her mind reeled and body ached. Disoriented, Chloe tried to turn her head to seek out Sarah. Her vision was blurry, and there was a terrible pain in her neck and head, enough that she felt like vomiting. But she managed to find her sister, who lay close to her. She was moving, but slowly, and was groaning in pain.

Chloe also noticed through blurry eyes, however, that the souls of Perron Manor had disappeared.

It felt like the house was toying with them, dangling the promise of freedom as a false hope, ready to pull it away again. Chloe could see no other options—they had to run.

She grabbed Sarah's arm and heaved herself up, pulling her sister with her. Chloe felt like she could topple over at any moment, but adrenaline and sheer desperation drove her forward.

'Come on,' she said through gritted teeth, limping back towards the open door. She felt battered and bruised, the fall down the stairs taking more out of her than she'd initially realised. But her vision, while still blurry, was focused on the exit.

Sarah hobbled with her. The house was quiet except for their panting and occasional pained groans. The door grew closer, step by step until the threshold was upon them.

Please, Chloe begged to herself. *Just let it be over.*

She tasted the fresh air, even felt it on her skin as her foot passed over to the porch outside. Sarah was beside her the whole time... and then she wasn't.

Chloe's sister was suddenly thrown forward, pushed outside to the ground.

And instead of being flung with her, Chloe was instead held by something, and cold, sharp claws dug into the skin of her upper arms.

Chloe screamed and was then pulled back inside while her feet slid helplessly across the marble. Still upright, she came to a stop just before the bottom of the stairs again. She could feel a radiating cold from behind, as well as a gut-churning and sulphuric smell.

The demon had her. Sarah turned from her position on the ground outside and cried out for Chloe, who felt the large talons now take hold of her head and force it to twist around to one side.

But her body did not move in the same direction.

Perron Manor had her now, she realised in her last moments. Her neck was then slowly and deliberately broken.

CHAPTER 46

FROM HER POSITION OUTSIDE, Sarah saw the life drain from her sister's eyes and turn into a blank death-stare. Her neck was horribly twisted to one side, and Sarah had even heard an audible *crack* as Chloe's neck broke.

She screamed.

The thing that held Chloe then dropped her lifeless body to the floor, and it fell into a crumpled heap. Chloe's face was turned towards Sarah, who continued her pained cries, unwilling to accept what her eyes were showing her.

Her brain hadn't fully registered the situation, but Sarah was quickly back on her feet, and she ran as quickly as she could back towards her sister. The demonic creature stood above the fallen girl, and its monstrous mouth was twisted into a grin.

However, before Sarah could get back inside, the doors of Perron Manor slammed shut, cutting her off from her sister. She banged on the door, repeatedly, desperately, kicking and punching the surface. But it would not open. Eventually, after throwing everything she had at the door, Sarah collapsed to the ground, hyperventilating. The overwhelming pain and sadness at seeing her sister's death was too much to take.

It can't be. It can't be. Chloe can't be dead.

And yet, as much as her mind refused to believe it, somewhere inside she knew it to be true. If Perron Manor did indeed want Chloe—the girl who had escaped all those years ago—it had her now.

Sarah cried, her heart broken, and she thought of Emma and Andrew. A mother and wife, the best of each, stolen from them by this house of evil.

Sarah sat in front of the door to Perron Manor for close to half an hour, sobbing and wailing, unable to let what had happened sink in. Then, the door behind her clicked open of its own accord.

She turned and saw Chloe's body lying alone on the cold floor. Everything was silent. Sarah rushed over to her, and took Chloe in her arms, hugging her, still feeling her lingering warmth. She could smell the lavender scent of Chloe's hair.

Sarah knew that the house could very well take her too, now, but she didn't care.

But nothing came for her. Eventually, the realisation dawned on her that she needed to go to Andrew and tell him what had happened. And that meant leaving her sister... which she just didn't want to do.

After another fifteen minutes of sitting with Chloe in the dark, Sarah gently laid her head back down, and got to her feet.

'I'm so sorry, Sis,' she whispered.

Sarah then slowly walked from the house. She began to trudge her way down the long driveway, feeling the harsh, painful stones under the soles of her bare feet.

After getting only a few feet from the building, a sudden sensation washed over her, like she was being watched. Sarah spun and examined the house. The door was still open, and Chloe was inside as before, but nothing else looked out of place... until she looked up to one of the mid-floor windows. Sarah's breath caught in her throat.

Chloe!

But it wasn't the Chloe she knew. Even at this distance, Sarah could make out that the features were twisted and distorted, with milky eyes, sunken and pale skin, and matted hair. And her expression was one of pain and sadness.

This version of Chloe put a hand up to the window, pressing her palm flat against it. Though no words could be heard, Sarah was easily able to read what Chloe mouthed.

Help me!

CHAPTER 47

2 Weeks Later...

The casket was one Chloe would have liked. It had been picked out by Andrew, and had a dark mahogany veneer to it with shiny brass handles. A few handfuls of dirt lay on the closed lid.

Chloe's body was inside.

Thankfully, the dark clouds above had not unleashed the torrent of rain they'd been threatening, with the worst of it being a mild shower at the start of the funeral.

It felt weird for Sarah to be back in her hometown again after so long away, and to see her extended family—none of whom she was close to.

She was just thankful that both her parents had passed, so they didn't have to see or feel this moment. It would have broken them—God knew it was breaking Sarah.

The graveyard was well kept and pleasant, and the traditional stone church stood large and imposing behind them. Chloe had not updated her will and testament since moving to Perron Manor, so as per her last wishes, she was laid to rest here.

But she wasn't at rest at all, Sarah knew. And certainly not at peace.

Sarah stood above her fallen sister, looking down and crying uncontrollably. She was supposed to be paying her respects, but Sarah couldn't focus on anything other than what she'd seen the last time she was at *that* house. The image of Chloe, upstairs and alone, begging for help.

While Chloe's earthly shell lay below Sarah, she knew without question that the essence of her sister was still back at Perron Manor. Trapped and suffering.

And would be for all eternity. Unless...

She felt a hand on her shoulder and knew instantly it was Andrew. He stood beside her, dressed smartly in a dark suit. His face was streaked with tears as well, and he offered her a sad smile. Emma was with his parents, who stood on the other side of him. The poor little girl had no idea what was happening.

Probably for the best.

Sarah returned Andrew's smile. She felt bad for him. More so for Emma.

The night Chloe died, Sarah had eventually walked to find Andrew, and explained what had happened. He had reacted angrily, which was natural. He'd said he needed to see her, and no amount of arguing could persuade him. So, Sarah had to stand in the night with Emma while he ran back to the house. Eventually, he returned with an armful of blankets, and his face was still full of rage. But the house had not taken him, and no harm had come to him. In fact, he claimed to have seen nothing.

He'd also told Sarah that he had called the police, as they couldn't just leave Chloe like that. Sarah had agreed, but asked how they would go about explaining what had happened.

In the end, they had lied.

They stated that Chloe had woken them all up during the night to the sounds of someone else in the house. They had tried to flee, and Chloe had tripped and fallen while running down the stairs. She'd landed on her head, and they heard a horrible crack.

Sarah hated herself for having to lie about the death of her own sister like that and pretend like it was some freakish accident. The police investigated, and advised they found no trace of a break-in, but they said they didn't discount it as a possibility. In the end, they accepted the cause of death as an accident.

A light breeze circled Sarah, carrying with it the smell of wet grass as the priest said his final words. It was time for them to leave. Sarah again looked down at Chloe's casket, and though she spoke no words, made a vow.

She would not let Chloe suffer for eternity.

Afterwards, Andrew had arranged for a get-together at a local country pub, where people could gather and drink and eat, like it was all some kind of party. Sarah didn't want to be there. She wanted to be getting on with things, with the job at hand, but felt obligated.

Sarah gave it a couple of hours, and right as she was getting ready to bid her farewells and leave, Andrew approached her with Emma. The child looked as cute as could be in a little dark dress and adorable big white bow in her hair. Earlier in the day, Sarah had heard the little girl asking for her 'Mummy,' and that had broken her all over again.

'You look like you're getting ready to leave,' Andrew said to her. 'You keep glancing over to the exit.'

'Sorry,' Sarah replied. 'I'm just not comfortable here. Not comfortable with this whole thing, to be honest.'

'Me either,' he agreed. There was a pause between them. 'Emma and I are going to be staying with my parents for a little while, until we find somewhere to live.'

'Okay,' Sarah replied.

'You are welcome to stay, too. Their place is pretty big.'

'I'll be okay.'

'Well, you're always welcome to come see Emma. Anytime you want. You know that, right?'

She smiled. 'I do. And thank you.'

Another pause, then he went on, 'I suppose it goes without saying that neither I nor Emma will ever set foot back in that place again. I don't want anything to do with it.'

'Of course,' Sarah replied, giving an understanding nod. Legally, in the event of any of them dying, the house was to fully transfer its ownership to the surviving sister, as per the stipulation in the original will. And, given they had no time to change any of those stipulations before Chloe had died, that meant Sarah was now legally the sole owner. 'I'll put it up for sale,' she said. 'And if I manage to sell it then you and Emma are getting half the money.'

'We don't need—'

'It's non-negotiable,' Sarah said, cutting Andrew off. 'And I can promise you, I'm never going back to that fucking place again, either.'

But that was a lie.

CHAPTER 48

1 Week Later...

The hazelnut coffee Sarah sipped was piping hot and full of flavour. Chloe would have hated it.

The last time Sarah had been in this place—the *Hill of Beans*—was with her sister. The man she was now due to meet had received a tongue lashing, and all because he had delivered a warning they should have heeded.

David Ritter entered the coffee shop and quickly spotted her. He gave her a sad, sympathetic smile—followed by a wave—then walked over.

'I'm sorry to hear about what happened to your sister,' he offered.

Sarah just gave a tight-lipped smile and small nod in return, then gestured to the empty chair opposite. He took it.

'It was an accident,' Sarah told him, lying once again. She didn't want him to know the full details of the story, nor the full dangers Perron Manor actually posed. Not when she needed something from him.

'So it *was* the fall that killed her?' David asked, seemingly a little surprised. 'I'd heard that was the case, but thought maybe...'

'No, that much was true,' Sarah told him. 'But before the fall, things happened we didn't tell the police about.'

David gave a solemn nod, but one with no hint of an 'I told you so' smugness.

'So,' he started, 'you said in your message you wanted to talk to me about something?'

'Yes.' Sarah took another sip of her drink. 'Chloe and I got into a fight that day, before everything happened. She believed what you told her about Perron Manor, and I... well, I had a hard time with it. But she did let something interesting slip. According to you, the only way to free the souls trapped in there was... with exorcism?'

'Possibly,' David said. 'But it was more an educated guess, to be honest. Why?'

Sarah took a breath. 'After Chloe died, I saw her again in the house. Upstairs. And she was in pain.'

David just nodded. 'The house has her,' he stated.

That threw Sarah. She thought her revelation might have been more of a surprise to him. *Does he know more about that place than he's letting on?*

'I believe it does, yes,' Sarah continued. 'But I can't let it keep her. I won't allow it.'

David paused for a moment. 'So... you want the place exorcised.'

'That's right,' she said, then added, 'and I need you to help me do it. Will you?'

David didn't need to consider the question for very long. 'Yes,' he said enthusiastically. 'I'll help you.'

Sarah felt a wave of relief, then smiled. 'Good.'

I'm coming for you, Chloe.

The End

HAUNTED: DEVIL'S DOOR

BOOK 2

CHAPTER 1

JANUARY 1982.

'It's big,' Ray Pearson said, looking up at the house before him.

'And our home for the foreseeable future,' his wife Rita added, sounding almost hesitant. She stood beside him, and her brown eyes were squashed into a frown. 'Do you think we'll be able to handle it?'

'I hope so,' he replied.

It did seem an imposing task, but right now they were acting out of necessity.

'I like it,' their six-year-old daughter said. Chloe stood in front of her father, smiling, showing the two missing teeth from the top row. Ray's big and calloused hands rested gently on her shoulders. 'It's like a mansion,' she said.

Ray gave her shoulders a squeeze beneath the thick red coat she wore. Both he and his wife were well wrapped up, too, given the biting January cold. The clouds above were dark and threatened rain, and the gravel underfoot was wet from an earlier downpour. Their car—an old, burgundy Ford that had barely made the journey up here—was behind them, parked at the head of the long driveway the family now stood on.

Rita was right. The house, which was bigger than any Ray had seen, was to be their home now. The thought of living here was difficult to comprehend. He was used to small, terraced houses with families living practically on top of each other, where things were noisy and chaotic, yet warm. Here, they could live at different ends of the house and rarely see each other.

He didn't like the thought of that.

At the top of the walls in front of them—high above and over three stories up—were three distinct peaks cut into the roofline. They offered character to the front elevation of the building, and a symmetry Ray liked. The house was predominantly stone, but the craftsmanship of the stonemasonry was definitely something he could appreciate. The windows were taller than they were wide, with thin wooden frames and arched heads.

They sure didn't make them like this anymore.

'Suppose we knock?' Rita offered, which seemed the only reasonable course of action, given no one was coming out to welcome them. Ray had thought perhaps the noise of their car would have alerted the owner to their arrival. But, apparently not.

Rita took the lead, as she so often did, and started to walk up the steps before her, towards the front door. Whether she felt it or not, Rita never showed any signs of nerves or fear in social situations. Conversely, Ray wanted nothing more than to crawl back into his car and light up a smoke. And that was just at the thought of meeting the owner of Perron Manor.

Marcus Blackwater.

With his hands buried into his pockets, Ray traced a nicotine-stained finger over his tobacco tin inside, feeling the pull. But he couldn't roll one up now. Rita had earlier warned him that first impressions counted, so he didn't want to have a rolled-up cigarette hanging out of his mouth for the first meeting with their new boss. Instead, he followed his wife, who was dressed in a smart, figure-hugging grey coat and matching wool beret. Beneath the long coat, legs wrapped in tight jeans poked out, and she had calf-high tanned boots on her feet.

Mid-way up the steps, Rita stopped and turned back to him.

'Well come on, then,' she said, quickly flapping her hand in a *come here* motion. He was dawdling... deliberately so.

Chloe skipped ahead and her long brown hair flowed behind her. The distinct red coat Chloe wore was as stylish as her mother's, and cost more than Ray had been comfortable paying. His own clothes—an old navy blue jacket, faded jeans, and boots—were simple but adequate in comparison. However, they did the same job and cost a fraction of the price.

He reached the top and stood by his girls, letting Rita take the lead. She was better at the social game than he was, and if first impressions did indeed count, then Rita would do well. To Ray, she was stunning, smart, and highly professional.

Ray held his breath. This was it: the first day of living in a mansion. And their job was to turn it into a hotel for the owner.

Rita used the brass door knocker—a lion's head, with a large ring hanging from its mouth—to signal their presence. After a few moments, Ray heard someone approach on the other side and saw a shape moving through the privacy glass set within the door. The door opened, and there stood Vincent Bell, Rita's older brother.

Ray had always found Vincent something of a flake, though he could be nothing but grateful to the man for casting Ray and his family a lifeline when they needed it most.

In truth, however, Ray didn't really understand the relationship between Vincent and Marcus, so he was interested to see what the situation here actually was.

'Sis!' Vincent exclaimed, wearing a big smile that showed his teeth. His thick, unkempt beard coupled with his long, slightly greasy hair, gave him a grungy sort of look. It was a shame, as even Ray could tell that under it all, Vincent could have been quite a good-looking man. Although, he looked a lot paler than Ray remembered, and much more gaunt.

Vincent's less-than-pristine appearance was completed by a frayed beige shirt, unbuttoned to the chest, corded blue trousers, and soft loafers.

He pulled Rita in for a hug, and Ray could tell his wife was a little surprised at the forwardness. It had been over seven years since they had last seen each other. It had been at their mother's funeral, and Ray didn't recall Vincent hugging Rita that day.

'How are you, Vinnie?' Rita said after pulling away. She wore a big smile as well, one that would have fooled most people.

Except for Ray.

He knew that it was, in fact, her business smile. It showed plenty of teeth, but to him seemed forced, and it wasn't nearly as warm or beautiful as her real one.

'I'm good, I'm good,' Vincent said. 'And I'm really glad you guys are all here. The house is amazing. You're going to love living here.'

Vincent then looked over to Ray and held out his hand.

'Nice to see you too, Ray. You're looking well.'

'Thanks,' he replied, 'you too.' Ray didn't exactly mean it, but didn't want to be rude. Besides, he knew that he wasn't exactly an oil painting either. 'Listen, Vincent, I want to thank you for this. For letting us stay here and helping out. We really appreciate it.'

'Ah, don't mention it,' he replied. 'Besides, it was Marcus who agreed to it all, I just put the idea forward. You're good with your hands, and Rita here has run a hotel before. You two are perfect. With your help, we'll have this place up and running in no time.'

'Thanks for the vote of confidence,' Rita said.

Vincent looked past them to their car on the driveway. Boxes were piled in the boot and back seat, which had forced Chloe to make the long drive up to Perron Manor riding on her mother's knee.

'You fit all your stuff in there?' Vincent asked.

'We travel light,' was all Rita said. 'So we won't take up too much room here.'

Vincent laughed. 'Room is one thing we have an abundance of.' He then stepped aside, revealing a grand entrance area inside, with a marble-tiled floor and wide oak stairs. 'Come on in and meet Marcus before you unpack.'

Ray and his family all walked into the foyer. It was double-storey space, with ceilings high up above giving a hugely grandiose feel to the entrance—which was no doubt what the original designers were shooting for. A plush carpet lined the centre section of the timber stair-treads, and the lower half of the walls had wooden panelling, which was the same dark oak as the stairs. The whole area had an odour of old wood and lingering varnish, which Ray appreciated.

Chloe started to click the heels of her shoes on the marble, giggling at the echoing sound. The smile on her face grew wider. Ray knew that the young girl was in love with the house already, and she'd barely seen any of it. To a six-year-old, this must have all seemed like one big adventure.

Vincent must have noticed the way they were all looking around in awe. 'Takes your breath away, doesn't it?' He then held his arms out to his side. 'Ladies and gentleman, I give you… Perron Manor. Or, as it will soon be known, the Blackwater Hotel.'

Ray wasn't sure what Vincent expected them to do after the cheesy little announcement. No doubt Vincent had intended it to be significant and grandiose, but it only came off as… forced. Was a round of applause in order? Instead, Ray just gave a small smile and nod.

'So where is the owner?' Rita asked.

'He should be along shortly,' Vincent replied, and then as if on cue Ray heard a door open to one of the walkways above. He heard footsteps move along the gantry until a figure appeared above them as it turned onto the stairs.

While Vincent's appearance was rather grungy, Marcus was the polar opposite. He had dark, brushed-back hair with no signs of grey, blue eyes beneath dark brows, a slight tan to his skin, trimmed stubble, and wore what looked to be an expensive black shirt and pressed dark trousers. To Ray, the man reeked of money and confidence, and he wore a charming grin, likely to show off his perfect white teeth.

'Ah,' Marcus said, his voice deep. 'The hired help!'

Ray assumed that was supposed to be a joke, even if it was mostly true, so he offered a polite chuckle. But Marcus Blackwater had yet to even look at Ray. His gaze had been focused purely on Rita and there was a wolfish, almost predatory look in those bright blue eyes.

Marcus started to descend the steps slowly, taking his time. He still wore the smile that had at first been charming, though now it seemed just a little off to Ray.

First impressions count, Rita had told him. Whether it was just Ray's own insecurities clouding things or not, his first impression of their host wasn't a great one.

Though he did like the fact that Marcus was much shorter than him, looking about five-foot-seven at best. Given Ray himself was six-foot-two, it offered him a little comfort to be able to tower over Marcus as the man stepped out onto the marble floor to join them.

Marcus walked straight over to Rita, keeping his eyes on her. He took a hand that wasn't offered before planting a slow kiss on it.

'Pleasure to meet you all,' Marcus said, keeping his unblinking gaze fixed on her.

Rita quickly pulled her hand away and gave a forced smile. 'You as well, Mr. Blackwater,' she replied. She then turned and held an arm out to Ray. 'This is my husband.'

It was only then that Marcus finally turned his attentions away from Rita. 'Ah yes... Raymond, am I right?' He held out his hand. Ray shook. Marcus' grip was strong and tight.

'Just Ray,' he replied.

Marcus nodded, still smiling. 'Of course.' Then he turned and looked down to Ray's daughter. 'And you must be Chloe?'

Chloe giggled. 'Yes, sir. Pleased to meet you.'

Marcus gently ruffled her hair. 'You too.' He then looked back to Rita, but appeared to address them all. 'Now, I'm sure you are tired after your long drive, so how about we get you settled into your rooms first? Then we can go about getting you all fed. How does that sound?'

Rita nodded. 'Sounds good to me.'

'Excellent,' Marcus replied, clapping his hands together. 'Well, let's get your belongings from the car.'

They all walked out to the car, Ray staying by Rita's side the whole way.

CHAPTER 2

'WHAT DO YOU THINK?' Rita asked as she hung one of her blouses inside the wardrobe.

Unpacking their essentials was taking a while, but it was a job she wanted done quickly—one less thing to worry about later.

'Think about what?' Ray asked. 'The house, or our host?'

Rita smiled. She'd seen Ray tense up the moment he'd laid eyes on Marcus. But, in fairness, their new boss *had* been a little singular in his attentions while he blatantly focused on Rita. She hoped it wouldn't develop into a problem.

'Let's start with the house,' Rita said.

'It's beautiful,' Ray replied. 'And huge.'

'*I* love it!' Chloe added from her position on the bed, her legs dangling off the edge and swinging to-and-fro. Rita was glad about her enthusiasm, as Chloe not acclimatising to her new environment had been a big concern. Chloe had her large stuffed doll on her lap. The doll had button eyes and red, stringy hair. Chloe had named it Emma, and it was by far her favourite, even though it was starting to show its age and fraying at the edges a little.

After meeting with Vincent and Marcus earlier, they'd all gone back to the car to retrieve the family's belongings. Then the four of them—

with Chloe helping where she could—had carried everything over to the two rooms designated for Rita, Ray, and Chloe.

The whole time, Marcus had not been shy at looking Rita over, though she didn't think Ray had noticed, thankfully.

Her husband tended to be a little insecure at times, though not to a degree where it was ever an issue. She just wished he could see his own worth and his own attractiveness. He was a large and broad-shouldered man, with a square jaw, cleft chin, and dark eyes under thick black hair which was always worn in a simple side-parting. And he had a kind smile that lit up his whole face.

The family had been put towards the back of the house, on the middle floor, and both rooms were on one of the protruding wings that ran out into the rear grounds. Chloe's room was set at the end of a short corridor, with Rita and Ray's just next to it. Those were the only two rooms in the short corridor.

Both bedrooms were nice and very traditional in their décor, befitting a manor such as this one. Rita and Ray's room had a dull but thick brown carpet, pale green walls, black cast-iron radiators, and high ceilings with ornate coving and chandelier lighting. The furniture was dark oak—a theme that seemed to run through the house—but the centrepiece was, without doubt, the four-poster bed. The frame was dark wood, with cream fabric hanging down from the canopy, and the sheets and pillows were a mix of reds and whites. Rita had never slept in a four-poster bed, and none of the previous hotels she'd worked at had ever had them.

Very fancy.

Chloe's room was similar in style and layout, but the carpet had a checkered pattern to it, and the walls were a plain white, which made the room feel lighter. Chloe had a four-poster bed as well, and upon seeing it her eyes had lit up.

Rita continued to unpack, but she felt Ray's eyes on her.

'Do you think we'll be able to do what they're asking?' Ray questioned. 'I mean, just the four of us to run a hotel… surely we need more hands.'

Rita shrugged. 'I honestly don't know. Depends on how quickly business picks up, I guess. Suppose we won't know until we try.'

She was trying to be optimistic but could understand Ray's reservations. The deal was that they come and live here and help get the hotel ready for launch, then help run it for as long as the Pearson family wanted to stay. How long that would be, exactly, Rita was unsure, but the offer had come at a time when they'd needed it most.

Ray's work as a labourer and handyman had been intermittent at best recently, and Rita had lost her job as a hotel manager after a recent takeover. They had no actual income, and the little bit of savings they did have squirrelled away was fast running out.

And then, out of the blue, Vincent had gotten in touch with an offer of a job. The stars had aligned, and there was no way they could refuse.

Negotiating pay had been a quick process: Marcus had a figure in mind that he would pay them both and wouldn't budge from it, even though Rita—through Vincent—had tried to haggle for more. However, their combined wage meant they would actually be making more in total than they had in a long while. That, plus the fact that they didn't have to pay for their housing, made it an easy decision.

At the very least, Perron Manor was a place where they could get back on their feet, even if things didn't work out long term. They made the leap, as well as the long drive up to the far north, to the outskirts of a town called Alnmouth.

'Well,' Ray went on, 'let's hope for the best. At least we have a roof over our heads for now.'

They eventually finished unpacking and setting up both rooms, with the task taking close to two hours in the end. Chloe had helped with arranging her own room, taking great pride in setting out her scores of books. When done, Rita felt ravenous and was looking forward to some food. They had arranged to meet Marcus and Vincent in the great hall at four-thirty, which gave them just over half an hour to kill.

'Why don't we go explore?' Chloe asked. 'We've hardly seen anything of the house so far.'

'Not yet, hun,' Rita told her. 'I think we should wait until we've been shown 'round first. It's only polite. You'll have plenty of chance to run around here later.'

Chloe made a face and continued to play with Emma's stringy hair.

'Can't hurt to have a little look around,' Ray cut in. 'Nothing else to do. And besides, we live here now. We can't be prisoners in our rooms the whole time.'

Rita mulled it over for a few moments. Ray did have a point, and it couldn't do any harm as long as they didn't go snooping anywhere they shouldn't.

'Fine,' Rita eventually said, getting a cheer from her daughter. 'How about we throw on our coats and have a quick walk around outside, see the gardens?'

'Sounds great!' Chloe said, hopping down from the bed. 'I'm gonna go get my coat.'

After putting on their shoes and cold-weather wear, the family walked along the mid-floor corridors before making their way down the stairs and into the entrance lobby. They then stepped out onto the paved area beyond the front door, and Rita breathed in air. It had rained recently and she could smell the wet grass. Rita could also see the tall house behind her in the puddles on the ground.

Though the skies above were grey and the air was cold, the house felt so private and remote that Rita was filled with a sense of peace. It was a sharp contrast to the terraced streets she was used to, packed with cars and neighbours chatting out on the pavements. She was now surrounded with dew-lined lawns, bushes, shrubbery, and even some plants that were enduring the winter. The many trees, on the other hand, had all lost their leaves, and the naked branches clawed at the air like spindly, skeletal fingers.

'This way!' Chloe called out and hopped down the steps before them. Ray linked arms with Rita, and they followed their daughter down before making their way along a pathway around the side of the house.

The rain had caused a light mist to crawl across the ground. That, plus the onset of dusk, lent their surroundings a serene quality.

Everything was so *quiet*.

'I could get used to this,' Rita said. 'Walking the grounds of our home every day.' She leaned her head onto Ray's shoulder. 'It's lovely.'

'It is,' Ray agreed. 'And it'll be even better in summer, with nicer weather.'

That was probably true, but Rita had always liked the winter. The bite of the cold made her feel more awake and alert, and the world resetting itself for the bloom of spring had a unique beauty to it.

At the rear of the house, the ground dropped away from the external courtyard in tiers until it met the back garden, where there were lawns, lines of hedges, planters, and even a fountain: a stone woman with a water jug on her shoulder. Nothing ran from the fountain at the moment, but the rain had filled the circular base with dirty, stagnant water.

Rita and Ray stood at the top of the tiered steps and watched Chloe as she excitedly explored her new surroundings. She seemed happy, enthralled at the new adventure. Rita then turned to glance over at the courtyard, which sat between the two rear prongs of the house behind them. The ground there was paved with cobbled stone, and around the edges sat a line of planters. Other than that, however, the area was pretty plain. There was certainly an opportunity to liven it up and make it more of a feature.

After sensing movement in her peripheral vision, she glanced up at one of the top-floor overlooking windows. It was, like most others in the house, taller than it was wide with thin white frames.

Behind the glass, Rita saw a figure looking out at them.

Since she was three stories down, it was difficult to make out much of the person, other than their general form. Whoever the person was, they quickly stepped from view.

Rita could only think that perhaps it was Marcus or Vincent up there, looking out on her family. Her initial instinct had been the person was female, though, given their rather thin frame and wider hips.

They all stayed outside for a little while longer, until the sound of a cough behind drew their attention.

Rita turned, her attention drawn to the rear glazed door of the house. It was open, and Marcus stood outside, smiling. He had changed into something a little less formal, wearing a dark sweater—rolled up to the elbows—and grey trousers.

'Enjoying the grounds?' he asked, calling over to them. 'Quite something, aren't they?'

'They are indeed,' Rita agreed. 'Sorry, we got finished unpacking early and Chloe wanted to explore a little.'

Marcus waved a hand dismissively, and even from this distance, Rita could see the blue glint of his eyes. 'Don't apologise,' he said. 'This is your home now. You can all explore most places here at your leisure.'

'Most places?' Ray asked.

Marcus just nodded. 'We'll get to that later. But for now, if you're hungry, come inside. I've fixed us up something to eat.'

He didn't wait for a response, and instead just turned and walked back into the great hall, leaving the door behind him open.

'I guess we're going to eat,' Ray said.

CHAPTER 3

THOUGH RAY WAS a little loath to admit it, the food was delicious, and every mouthful was packed full of flavour.

They were all seated at the long table placed within the great hall. Since there were only five of them, and the table seated twelve, they had all clustered at one end, with Ray seated next to Chloe, Vincent and Rita opposite, and Marcus at the head of the table.

The atmosphere felt formal, almost like a job interview, and Ray kept looking over to Rita for reassurance, mimicking her movements as best he could: taking a sip of wine as she did and keeping his mouthfuls of food small when all he wanted to do was shovel the food in until his cheeks bulged.

He continued to put on a front, remembering what Rita had told him about impressions counting. Rita always handled herself so well, with an endless amount of class. She was from a working-class background, the same as Ray, but hid it so much better.

Her makeup—light lipstick and a touch of eyeshadow—was always subtly applied and used only to accentuate her already beautiful, angular features. Her long, wavy hair was currently worn down, and there was a sweep of fringe coming close to her left eye. But, as beautiful as Ray thought she was, Rita always seemed to carry a frown of concern, as if she were constantly bearing the weight of the world.

The great hall they were in certainly lived up to the name, with a deep green wallpaper covered by twisting golden patterns, a stone-tiled floor, and four square support columns spaced evenly around the room that ran up to an ornate plaster ceiling. A variety of expensive-looking paintings hung on the walls: portraits, landscapes, even some biblical imagery, as well as a large, gold-framed mirror.

The meal was served in a bowl and consisted of large chunks of chicken—still with the skin—marinated in a delicious sauce which had hints of garlic and wine. Marcus had announced it was a French dish, called *coq au vin*, which Ray had never heard of before. However, he agreed that it certainly *sounded* French. Chopped mushrooms and tomatoes floated in the brown sauce, and they only accentuated the flavours.

'Hope it's to your liking,' he said as everyone devoured their food.

'It's delicious,' Rita replied, dabbing her mouth with a napkin. She then took a sip from her glass of red wine. In truth, Ray wasn't much of a wine enthusiast, and this one didn't do much to change his mind on that front. A good beer would definitely have been preferred. The other three certainly seemed to enjoy it, and Chloe was clearly happy with her lemonade.

Marcus then turned to Ray, with eyebrows raised, seemingly waiting for his approval as well.

'I love it,' Ray replied, not knowing what else to say.

'Excellent,' he said in reply. 'So, everyone is happy with the arrangements here, I assume?'

'We are,' Rita said. 'It will be a lot of work, though, given a skeleton staff of just the four of us.'

Marcus nodded and took a slow sip of his wine. 'I understand that. And, to make matters worse, I'm going to be honest and say I won't be contributing a whole lot. I have other matters that will keep me busy.'

'Oh.'

'You can call on your brother as you need to, of course,' Marcus added.

Ray turned to Rita and squinted his eyes in confusion. Rita went on, 'Well, that is your choice, obviously, but running a hotel is a huge undertaking. We need bodies so we can stay on top of things.'

'The way I see it,' Marcus said, 'is that we just start small. There will likely only be a few guests while we build things up. Things should be manageable that way. If it gets out of hand, then we can look at pulling in more help. The thing is, while I want this venture to work, I don't have an endless pot of money to throw at it.'

Ray again looked to Rita, who was chewing the side of her mouth. 'Fair enough,' she eventually said. 'We can see how it goes. But, we'll need to set up a reception area close to the entrance lobby. And I'll need a space for an office.'

'Done and done,' Marcus replied. 'You have the run of this place, for the most part, so use whichever rooms you see fit. I have no issue with that. See, Rita, the thing is… I want you to take ownership of this project. The hotel is now your baby. Grow it and make a success of it, and I promise you will reap the benefits. As far as the business side of things go, you are in charge… until I see a reason for you not to be.'

Ray didn't consider himself the smartest man in the world, but he knew that Marcus had just issued his wife a pretty clear challenge. And, given what had happened at Rita's previous hotel—where she had been discarded without a second thought despite still being the best person for the job—he knew it would be a challenge she would relish.

'There won't ever be a reason,' she replied confidently. 'I guarantee it.'

'Excellent,' Marcus exclaimed, and a wolfish grin spread over his face.

'But what about supplies?' Rita asked. 'I understand you want to keep costs down, but there are still things we'll need.'

'There is a business bank account set up, with a deposit of money in to get you going. You will have access to that account. All the money we make goes in, and it is up to you to manage everything from there. You will pay yourselves the agreed wage, I will get a dividend, and you will also manage the stock and inventory. Like I say, this is your place to run.'

Rita widened her eyes in surprise. 'That's a lot of responsibility,' she said. 'Don't get me wrong, I'm up to it. But it should also have had a bearing on my wage.'

'And it will. Eventually,' Marcus told her. 'If this place does well, then so will you. The only ceiling to your success would be your own failings.'

Ray felt a little lost, like he was just going along for the ride, but he certainly saw a fire in Rita's eyes. This wasn't just a stop-gap lifeline to her anymore; it was a chance to prove herself again.

But, to Ray, something about the whole thing seemed… off. However, he couldn't put his finger on why. He hated feeling like things were just happening without his involvement. So, he spoke up, if only for the sake of speaking.

'What kind of improvements do you want to make to the building before opening?'

Marcus was slow to take his eyes off Rita, but eventually looked over to Ray and shrugged. 'I don't think we need to do an awful lot in that regard. A few tweaks and a freshen up. It would be good to get the gardens into a nicer state to suitably impress the guests. But have a good look around the place and see what you think needs to be addressed. This is your project too, Ray.'

'Okay, no problem,' Ray responded. It was all he could think to say in reply.

'And when are you looking to get the hotel open for business?' Rita asked.

'As soon as possible. I think a couple of months should give us plenty of time to be ready. Do you think that's feasible?'

Rita nodded. 'Yes. I think we can do that. But we should start putting the word out now, and also try and get a little coverage in the local press.'

'That shouldn't be hard to do,' Vincent cut in. 'This house has something of a history and is well known in the area. I'm sure if people found out it was opening up to the public that would create a buzz of its own.'

'History?' Ray asked. 'What do you mean by that?'

'We can go over that another time,' Marcus said, again waving a dismissive hand. 'Trust me, we'd be here for hours. But, Vincent is right. I believe it should be quite straightforward to generate interest. However, one thing to note, and something that is quite important: the top storey is strictly off-limits. Both for guests and also yourselves, at least for the time being.'

'Wait, are you serious?' Rita asked, frowning. 'Why?'

'Because I said so,' was all Marcus offered in reply, grinning playfully.

'But that is cutting off how many rooms we can rent out,' she shot back. 'Do we really have to lose a *whole* floor?'

'Not permanently,' Marcus answered. 'But there are two rooms in particular that I will be using on a permanent basis up there. We can look at blocking that area off in time, which would then open up the rest of the floor.'

'The sooner, the better,' Rita argued. 'Given our own bedrooms are out of use anyway, cutting off the top storey as well will only hurt our revenue.'

'Noted. But that is how things stand for now.'

Ray could tell his wife was not completely happy with that arrangement, but she relented. 'Fair enough. But what's up there that is so private?'

'Another time,' Marcus said, and he then finished the rest of his wine. 'Why don't you enjoy the house? Explore. Make yourselves at home and feel free to indulge in any food or drink in the kitchen that tickles your fancy. For now, however, I have business to attend to.' Marcus then dabbed his mouth with his napkin and stood up. 'Leave your plates and glasses. Vincent here will clean everything up.'

And with that, he gave a small, courteous nod and walked from the room. Ray couldn't quite believe it. He turned to his wife, eyebrows raised. *Is he for real?*

Rita, in response, just gave a shrug of her shoulders. Even Chloe watched on with a confused frown.

'We'll clean up after ourselves, Vinnie,' Rita said. 'It's no trouble.'

'Oh, it's fine,' Vincent replied, getting to his feet. He then began to stack the dishes. 'You do as Marcus suggests and have a look around the house; get acquainted with your new home. There's lots to see, but just be careful down in the basement. The light switch is at the bottom of the stairs, which can be a pain. The furnace is down there as well. Ray, you might want to familiarise yourself with it.'

'Will do,' Ray told him.

Vincent picked up the pile of plates he'd gathered and smiled at the others. 'Then I'll bid you goodnight. I have to assist Marcus as well, so I may not see you again until morning. But just enjoy yourself. Tomorrow we can start planning how to make this place a success.'

He then walked off, leaving the great hall via a side door to what Ray assumed was the kitchen. Ray and Rita looked to each other.

'Thoughts?' she asked him.

He shrugged and shook his head, unsure what he was feeling about the whole thing. 'Honestly, hun, I have no idea. I guess we just have to roll with it for now. It isn't like we have any other options, right?'

'I guess not,' she replied. 'But I think there is an opportunity here, if Marcus was being honest. I can make this place a success, Ray, I know it.'

He smiled. 'I know you can too. I don't doubt it for a second.'

'So what are we going to do now?' Chloe asked.

'I don't know, sweetie.' Rita said to her daughter. 'What do you want to do?'

'I want to explore some more!'

Rita chuckled. 'Not a bad idea. Can't hurt to start getting used to the new house.'

CHAPTER 4

'Well,' Rita began. 'This is as creepy as all hell.'

Ray couldn't help but agree. Their first port-of-call had been to walk down to the basement, because Ray was keen to see what kind of heating system he would be dealing with in the house.

'Do you think it's haunted?' Chloe asked, a sense of excited wonder in her voice.

'I don't think so,' Ray replied. 'No such thing as ghosts.'

'And how do you know?' Chloe asked, putting her hands behind her back and making a smug face. 'You can't say for certain, can you?'

'I'm certain enough,' was his reply. Ray then moved over to the large, metallic structure of the furnace. It was tall and quite deep: a mix of ribbed iron and sprouting pipework, almost gothic in its architecture and design. Rita hated it as soon as she saw it.

'What do you think?' Rita asked, nodding to the huge appliance.

'Out of my league,' he replied. 'Hopefully it works okay. If not, we'll need to call somebody in.'

Ray saw Rita hug herself. It was certainly cold in the basement, and smelled of damp and coal. He didn't foresee Rita spending much time in the basement if she could help it.

The walls around them were bare stone, and streaked watermarks ran down to the uneven floor. A dull orange hue from the light fittings in the ceiling above was not strong enough to illuminate the whole area, leaving pockets of shadows. Piles of coal and wood were dotted around the space, and the only other feature of note was the line of what appeared to be old cells against a far wall. All were open to the front, and some were full of more fuel for the furnace.

It was dirty and horrible down there, and certainly no place for Chloe.

'How about you come back down here later?' Rita suggested. 'I'm sure there are nicer places for us to explore tonight. Vincent or Marcus can show you how to work *that* thing another time,' she nodded towards the nightmarish furnace.

'Yeah,' Ray agreed. 'Besides, we need to get out of here before the *ghosts* get us!' He then widened his eyes and zombie-walked over towards his daughter, groaning as he did. Chloe squealed and giggled, then quickly ran away from him.

'Careful you don't fall,' Rita admonished, but was unable to keep her tone serious as Ray grabbed his daughter and scooped her up.

They made their way back to the stairs, with Chloe going first, followed by Rita. Ray was last, so he hit the switch, killing the lights. Rita looked back down at him just as Ray placed a foot on the first step. As he did, he quickly turned his head back to stare into the dark.

What the hell was that?

'Everything okay?' Rita asked him.

'I... yeah, I guess,' he said, though he shook his head in confusion. 'Thought I heard someone whispering.' He then chuckled and turned back to her, then waggled his eyebrows. 'Maybe Chloe was right.'

They moved on and looked around the rest of the ground floor, taking in all the rooms, including the large kitchen—which had a large cupboard full of wines, whiskeys, and rums—a dining room, living room, and even a library.

'There are so many books!' Chloe exclaimed while inside. And it was true. Ray wasn't much of a reader, but even he was impressed with the space. It had dark wooden bookshelves along two of the four walls, all filled with leather or cloth-bound books. There must have been hundreds of tomes in there.

'I'm going to read them all,' Chloe said, smiling, eyes lost in the treasures before her.

'Well, we're going to have to vet them first,' Rita replied. 'Some of them might not be suitable for you.'

Chloe made a face and stuck out her tongue.

The floor of the library was polished hardwood, and there was an ornate recliner with pale green cloth and golden edging sitting near to the window. Given the room was to the front of the building, it provided nice views out over the long driveway, front lawns, and the boundary gate in the distance.

There was a musty smell of old wood and paper, and the single chandelier lit the space: golden with elegant and intricate patterns to it.

The room was impressive, and Ray could certainly see why Chloe would be so enamoured with it.

'This would be good for the hotel,' Rita said, taking everything in. 'A nice, peaceful reading room for those who want it. Lends the place a lot of class.'

'So you don't want me to rip the bookcases out?' Ray asked with a smile.

'God no!' she replied. 'This definitely stays as it is. Maybe a few more chairs or something, make it a little more cosy. But that's about it.'

The library was accessed both directly off the entrance lobby and also from an adjoining corridor, and even Ray saw that it could become a nice focal point for guests. It even had a fireplace, and he could imagine some of the higher-ups in society in here at night, reading by firelight with a glass of scotch or port.

Rita turned to leave. 'So far, so good. I can really do something with this place, Ray. I just know it.'

Shortly after, they made their way up to the floor above. That one consisted mostly of bedrooms, as well as some toilets and storage rooms. The bedrooms, while decorated in slightly different ways, all had a similar feel to them, with grand four-poster beds, classically patterned wallpaper, and thick carpets.

Including the four bedrooms on the ground floor, Ray counted a total of sixteen rooms, not including any on the storey above. If they took away the rooms already allocated for those that lived in Perron

Manor—the Pearsons, Vincent, and Marcus—that left twelve available to guests.

Ray mentioned that point to Rita as they ventured down a corridor at the back of the house. He then asked, 'Do you think that's manageable for us?'

'Probably,' she replied after giving it a few moments of thought. 'At capacity we might be stretched, but we need to get the bedrooms upstairs in use as well. That is just going to hold us back.'

They approached a flight of stairs that ran up to the top-floor. Ray could hear very faint voices, which he recognised as Marcus and Vincent. 'Speaking of which, what do you think is going on up there?' he asked, pointing a finger to the stairs.

Rita shook her head and rolled her eyes. 'No idea.'

Ray looked up and saw that the small section of the hallway up there seemed identical in decoration to the one they were in, with pale green wallpaper above wooden panelling, and a high, decorative plastered ceiling. There was no obvious reason Ray could see why the floor above could not be used for guests. That meant Marcus had something up there he didn't want people to see, or know about.

'I'm sure we'll find out in good time,' he said.

'We better,' Rita added. 'I don't like working with one hand tied behind my back.'

The family of three then made their way back to their own rooms to change for the evening. Ray had a mental list of things he could start working on the next day, and after slipping into a thick but comfortable chequered shirt and a fresh pair of jeans he scribbled the items down onto a scrap of paper. It consisted of small tasks, mainly, like changing the odd fitting or bulb, and making some adjustments to stiff or squeaky doors. He'd consult Rita on some of the bigger jobs, however, so that they were on the same page and his work would fit in with any plans she was formulating.

For tonight, however, they planned simply to relax. The lounge on the ground floor looked cosy and had a television in there that Ray thought may have been a colour set. They all headed down together, and Ray got the fire going with fresh logs that had been stacked on the fireplace, ready for use.

Rita switched on the television. It had wooden veneer surround and two large knobs on the front—one that controlled the channel and one for volume. After quickly adjusting the aerial, a picture emerged from the static, and Rita cycled through the three available channels, settling on the BBC station. It was showing a talk show that she liked.

Rita then took a seat next to Ray on the sofa that sat against the far wall, and Chloe took her place on the other one in the room, which ran perpendicular. Their daughter snuggled under a blanket with Emma and one of her books, one that featured a kind-hearted giant.

With the heat and flickering light of the fire, Ray felt extremely relaxed. He concentrated on the skies outside more than the television, watching the already dark blues turn to black. Clouds blocked out any stars that may have shone through, but it was still nice to look out into the dark and see a little of the grounds that were close by. The peace and quiet was far removed from anything he was used to, and something he could certainly enjoy. However, he did consider one problem: if the rooms here were all to be used by guests when the hotel was up and running, then what were they supposed to do with their free time? They couldn't stay barricaded in their own rooms all the time when off duty, and Chloe would need to be able to roam and play. He considered bringing it up with Rita, but decided against it for the moment. It could be sorted out later, and he just wanted to enjoy the feeling of calm and warmth. All that was missing was a glass of scotch.

I can fix that.

'I'm going to go to the kitchen and get us a drink. Red wine?'

'That sounds fantastic,' Rita said, leaning over to kiss him on the cheek.

'Any brand in particular?' he asked.

'Just see what is there,' she said, with a shrug. 'Dealers choice.'

Ray turned to Chloe. 'Do you want anything?' He already knew what the answer would be.

'A cup of hot chocolate!' she exclaimed with a big grin.

Ray got to his feet with a groan and ruffled her hair. 'I'll see if they have any. If not, I can fix you some warm milk.'

'Thanks, Daddy,' she replied. Ray realised that she hadn't stopped smiling since they arrived at Perron Manor. The place certainly met with her approval. Considering the two-bedroom, rented council house they had come from, he was pleased to see it—even if he was a little worried she would develop a taste for the finer things in life he would scarcely be able to provide.

Still, it was an adventure for her, and he decided it wouldn't hurt to try and look at things the same way.

Ray left his two girls and navigated through to the kitchen, cutting through the great hall on his way. The echoing of his footsteps on the tiled floor was unsettling in the otherwise dead silence, especially since he was used to the soft patter of carpet.

The kitchen—vastly larger than any he had owned before—was quite something. Though the shade of yellow paint on the walls wasn't to his liking, the abundance of cupboards was impressive. There was also an honest-to-God larder. The floor slabs underfoot were a rustic stone with splashes of natural browns and yellows mixed in with a dark grey. An old, strong-looking wooden table sat central to the room, and there was a cast iron cooker against the far wall, with eight burners, which looked like it could feed a platoon.

This will come in handy when we have the hotel up and running.

Ray dug through the cupboards and kitchen units, looking for the one that housed the alcohol. When he eventually found the double-height unit flanked by a fully stocked wine rack, he was amazed at the choice inside.

There were scores of bottles. And the colours of the liquids inside ranged from ambers to browns to clear, and even purples. Thankfully, they were all categorised into the alcohol types, and he quickly found the scotches, selecting an already-open eighteen-year-old blend. After pouring himself a drink and selecting a random red wine for Rita, he managed to find a tin of powdered hot chocolate.

Perfect.

Ray gathered up the drinks and made his way towards the door that led from the kitchen to the great hall. He then crossed the main hall. En-route, he stopped at the glazed rear door. Movement in his peripheral vision, from outside, had drawn his attention. However, when staring out into the night, he could see nothing. Whatever movement he had registered had only been fleeting, likely a bat or something whizzing past the glass.

Thinking no more of it, he set off again—but halted immediately when he heard a quick and light rapping sound on the door. Again, he looked outside but was met with the same result.

Nothing.

He walked closer, bringing his face close to the glass, though he could only see the reflected image of the great hall behind him mixed in with the black of the night outside.

He shook his head and then turned away, satisfied that it was nothing of importance. Just an old house making strange noises. Or even bugs hitting the glass—certainly no cause for concern.

Ray headed back to his family, ready to enjoy a cosy night in front of the fire.

CHAPTER 5

Rita had awakened early, a little before six, and padded through to the en-suite to bathe, letting Ray sleep a little longer.

She was an early riser anyway, but today she felt especially motivated. Marcus' speech last night had certainly lit a fire, and Rita no longer saw the work ahead as just a stop-gap to keep the family afloat.

While she didn't really know Marcus or his motivations, if he was true to his word, then they could really make something of the hotel. And make some good money themselves while doing it.

The water in the bath was close to scalding—at least that's what Ray would have told her. But it was to her liking. She enjoyed showers the same way: to the point of turning her pale skin red. It helped burn away any leftover morning grogginess. Not that there were any showers to enjoy in Perron Manor: it was a bath or nothing.

Today she hoped the red-hot water would also scrub away completely the already fading memory of last night's dream—one where she was being dragged down through a hole in the earth while awful moaning and screaming sounded around her.

It was very strange, especially since Rita wasn't usually one for nightmares.

She slipped into the water, wincing a little, but then let the water settle around her. Her mind was alive with ideas: coming up with endless lists of tasks and trying to sort them by importance. The reception desk and office area would be two of the first things to focus on, as they couldn't run a hotel without either.

She didn't want to set anything up in the entrance lobby: it was a magnificent space, so preserving its original aesthetic and grandeur would be important. However, the reception area would still need to be close to the entrance, as asking guests to travel too far before being welcomed would run the risk of them getting lost and confused.

First impressions count.

Two rooms were accessed directly from the entrance lobby that could be used as a reception area. First, there was the library. But just like that lobby, it would need to be left as it was. Even if it ended up being rarely used, the fact it was there added a great deal to the building, lending an authenticity to its original roots as a manor. Rita would make sure every guest saw it on their initial tour, knowing it would be a great area to follow up with after the entrance lobby. And then, with the great hall to follow, she had no doubt the patrons would be sufficiently wowed.

The other room was a study and was directly opposite the library. It currently contained some seating, a writing desk, and a half-full bookshelf. That space didn't really add anything to the house, so it would be the perfect choice. They would just need to add in a reception counter to the front of the room, and the area behind could be used as the office. It would be easy enough for Ray to add in a wall to separate the two areas and hide away the office, Rita assumed. Then, all that would be needed was some signage out in the lobby to point guests the right way.

Perfect. One decision made.

Next was sourcing the supplies they would need. To do that, Rita would need to find reputable and dependable retailers. She would require sheets, towels, plates, glasses, bathmats, toiletries, and food, at least, and getting supply-chains in place was critical.

Rita felt that the rough deadline of two months' time was eminently achievable. That meant she also needed to think about how to start getting the word out and build a little bit of buzz about the opening. The thought of getting started with the PR side of things excited her.

She hadn't felt this motivated since being promoted to manager at the last hotel she'd worked at—The Fenton.

Rita's mood soured as she remembered how that had turned out. She began to scrub her hair and scalp hard with shampoo. All her best-laid plans and efforts had been wiped away by the new owners, ones who had their own man in mind for the role of manager.

So Rita was gone without ever being given a proper chance to prove herself, and her previous sterling work had been ignored completely.

Thanks and goodbye.

But this would be different. Though she couldn't say she trusted Marcus completely—after all, Rita barely knew him—he simply had no reason to bring anyone else in now to replace her. At least not yet.

She had an opportunity. One that she planned to seize.

After finishing with her bath, Rita dried off and walked back into the bedroom, with only towels wrapped around her. Ray had woken and was sitting up in bed, hands clasped together behind his head as he stared out of the window.

'Did I wake you?' she asked.

He yawned and shook his head. 'Not at all, hun.'

'Good. The bath is free.'

'Isn't there anywhere to get a shower around here?'

'Not that I know of.'

Ray had never been one for taking a bath, preferring the in-and-out speed of a shower. She smiled. 'We could put some bubbles in and get you a rubber ducky if it helps?'

Ray laughed and got out of bed. 'Soap and water will be just fine.' He then walked into the bathroom, leaving Rita to ready herself for the day.

Given the cold weather outside—and even *inside*—she slipped on a pair of nylons over her legs and covered them with black trousers. She then put on a tan blouse and gathered up her hair into a neat bun. Subtle lipstick, concealer, eyeshadow, and some heels completed the look: professional and all business.

Rita then strode out into the corridor and rapped on Chloe's door, hearing her daughter yell, 'Come in,' in response.

Rita entered and saw that her daughter was wide awake. The young girl was lying on her bed and reading one of her books.

'Been awake long?' Rita asked.

Chloe shrugged. 'A little while.'

'Hungry?'

'Very!' Chloe replied with a nod of her head.

Rita smiled. 'Come on then. I'll give you a bath, and then we will go down for food.'

Once the family were all ready, they made their way down to the kitchen to figure out what to eat. The cupboards were well stocked, and since Marcus had told them to treat the house as their own, Rita set to work making a breakfast of crispy bacon, poached eggs, and French toast. She and Ray both had coffee to accompany it, and Chloe slurped down an orange juice. Though the great hall was just next door, they decided to stay in the kitchen to eat. The hall was impressive, but it lacked intimacy and warmth.

Halfway through breakfast, they were joined by Marcus and Vincent.

'Why are you hidden away in the kitchen?' Marcus asked as he entered wearing a dark polo-neck jumper, and jeans with flared bottoms. Rita had to keep from bristling, thinking that the look which was so obviously meant to be stylish just seemed pretentious.

Vincent, in contrast, was in a simple, light-blue shirt—again, open to the chest—with the beginnings of sweat patches beneath each arm, dark blue cord trousers, and scruffy trainers.

'It's a little cosier in here,' Rita replied. 'There are some eggs and bacon ready if you want some.'

Marcus looked over to the remaining food keeping warm on the stove, and his nose wrinkled up. 'Thanks, but I'll fix something else a little later.'

Rita could not stop herself from growing annoyed a second time, but made no comment. Vincent, however, stepped forward and grabbed a plate. 'Don't mind if I do,' he said, heaping on rashers of bacon and spoonfuls of eggs. He took a seat next to Ray, and then poured himself a coffee.

'Have fun,' Marcus said. 'Take a few days to get your thoughts together on this place, and how you intend to take it forward. I'm sure you both have some ideas already, but we can sit down soon enough and get a plan of action together. For now, I need to head out for a few hours.'

Marcus didn't wait for a response before he left, but he did make a point of meeting eyes with Rita. His gaze was a hungry one. She didn't like it at all.

Ray took a long sip of his coffee, then turned to Vincent, who had a mouth full of food, some of which had dripped onto his bushy beard. 'Your friend is a little… different,' Ray said. 'If you don't mind me saying so.'

Vincent chuckled, nodding his head in agreement. 'I guess so. He's eccentric… but he's also very intelligent. Even brilliant, in some ways.'

Hearing her brother speak about Marcus that way, almost in reverence, didn't sit well with Rita. She hadn't seen Vincent in a number of years prior to coming here—they weren't exactly close—but even so, Rita still cared for him. However, she got the impression that Marcus only saw him as a lackey.

'So, what is he to you?' she asked her brother. 'Like… a friend? Or a boss?'

'What do you mean?' Vincent asked, tilting his head.

'Well, it's pretty clear he calls the shots.'

'Of course he does. This is *his* house.'

Rita shook her head. 'I know that, but what do *you* get out of the arrangement between you two?'

'Other than living rent-free in an amazing building?' he asked as if that should be answer enough.

But it wasn't. 'Yes,' Rita stated. 'Other than that.'

Vincent paused and frowned, but continued to loudly chew his food. 'We're friends,' he eventually said. 'We share interests. And we have the same outlook on life. So why *wouldn't* I take him up on his offer to live here?'

'Fair enough,' Rita replied, holding her hands up. She didn't want to upset him and rock the boat so soon after moving in.

'So,' Ray said, picking up the conversation for her. 'How did you meet him?'

'We've known each other since university,' Vincent replied. 'We shared a class and got to talking. Hit it off from there.'

'So… friends for a long time?'

'Yeah,' Vincent confirmed.

Ray nodded. 'Fair enough.' He then added, 'Vincent, I still want you to know we appreciate you getting us in here. I promise that we won't let you down.'

A big smile broke over Vincent's face. 'We know you won't,' was all he said in reply.

CHAPTER 6

It was a little after lunchtime and Chloe was relaxing in the library. She was reading one of her own books since her mother had told her not to take one from the bookshelves until they had all been fully approved. She might have only been six, but Chloe fancied she could read any of the thick books in there, though they did look *quite* dull and boring.

The house still excited her, and the sense of adventure was still fresh. However, she knew there was a wrinkle waiting in the wings to put a damper on all the fun. Before the move, her parents had found Chloe a place in the local school, and she was due to start next week. She wasn't against going to school at all—it was something Chloe usually enjoyed—but being the new girl wasn't something to look forward to.

However, that was next week's problem. A lifetime away.

An approaching car drew her attention, and Chloe sat up from the lounge-chair she was sprawled out on to look out of the nearby window.

The car that rolled down the gravel driveway looked like an expensive one. It was black, with a long front and high grille, which had two headlights on either side, giving four in total—something she hadn't seen before. Light bounced off the polished body and silver trims.

It looked like Mr. Blackwater had returned.

The car made its way to a covered carport and pulled to a stop. Her father's car was also in there, but tucked away at the back and out of sight.

Mr. Blackwater got out and walked towards the front door, wearing a long, black, wool coat. He had a small pack of books tucked under one arm, about four in total, and they all had dark brown, leather bindings. They looked old and well worn. Mr. Blackwater then disappeared from view, and Chloe heard the front door open.

She was intrigued by the owner of Perron Manor, though she hadn't seen a whole lot of him since moving in. Granted, Chloe and her parents had only arrived the previous day, but even so, Marcus Blackwater always seemed to be hidden away on the top storey of the house. She then heard dull footsteps on the stairs and knew instantly that was where he was going again.

Her curiosity was piqued. And while she knew she shouldn't, Chloe had a strange desire to sneak upstairs and see what held Marcus and Vincent's attention so much.

A moment's trepidation held her, because Chloe was not normally one to do something she knew could get her into trouble. However, the excitement of the new adventure was still coursing through her, pushing her to be more daring. Chloe set her book down and got up to her socked feet. She padded over the hardwood floor of the library, satisfied with how quiet she was being. She was confident she could be stealthy enough to get upstairs without being heard, and then maybe she could see a little of the upper floor.

But did she dare?

With a smile, Chloe decided that she did indeed dare, and she left the library to make her way to the foot of the stairs. She listened, hearing no movement above. Satisfied that no one was close—and knowing her parents were busy in the dining room, she placed a foot on the bottom step and pushed herself up. The stairs were strong and sturdy, and none of them creaked under her steps. Perhaps an adult would have made more noise—Marcus certainly had—but Chloe moved almost silently.

Once on the mid-floor, Chloe snuck around the corridors until she reached the stairs that led up to the top storey. As before, she waited at the bottom and listened. She could just make out muted voices, but only barely. With a tingle of excitement at doing something she knew she shouldn't, Chloe moved up to the first step. Then the next. And then, confident she would not be caught, she silently moved to the top. The hallway she found herself in was decorated just like the ones below it: wooden panelling on the lower half of the walls, pale green wallpaper above, and ornate plaster ceilings that had a woven pattern to it—like plaited hair—running around the edges.

The stairs had led up to the back of the house, where a window in the wall before her gave fantastic views out over the courtyard and even beyond the boundary wall. She listened again, detecting the voices coming from somewhere towards the front.

Chloe felt like she was on forbidden ground, but was surprised to find there was a certain thrill that came with it. That thrill pushed her forward along the hallway, tiptoeing as she went. Chloe then discovered that both Mr. Blackwater and Vincent were gathered in one of the corner rooms to the front of the building.

The door to the room was ajar, but only a little, so she couldn't see much of what was inside. Chloe kept her distance and pressed herself flat against the wall at an angle where she was confident she was safely hidden from view. Unless, of course, someone came walking out. Holding her breath, Chloe tried to tune in to the conversation taking place. Given Mr. Blackwater had the deeper voice, she was easily able to distinguish between the two men.

'I agree,' she heard Mr. Blackwater say, but Chloe was unsure what he was agreeing with. 'But I'm not sure they'll reveal anything we didn't already know.'

'May… may I read them?'

That sounds like Uncle Vincent.

'When I'm done,' Mr. Blackwater replied. 'For now, I'm going back to the translations. Leave me alone for a while.'

'Okay,' Vincent replied after a pause. He sounded a little disappointed. 'But I'm not sure why you don't trust your grandfather's work.'

'Latin is a difficult language, and translation is not a straightforward process. Things can often be open to interpretation, and I can't let that—'

A noise cut him off, and it also made Chloe jump. It had come from the corridor she was standing in. A door close to her which had been open had somehow been blown closed.

But there is no breeze up here.

However, the sound had obviously caught the attention of Marcus and Vincent. She heard footsteps coming from their room, and panic seized her. Without thinking, she quickly turned and ran, trying to be as quiet as possible while she headed back towards the stairs again. She was completely out of sight before she heard the door creak open and was confident she hadn't been spotted. But she needed to keep going, so she quickly descended the stairs, her heart beating rapidly.

Chloe didn't stop until she was back in the library, where she jumped into the lounge chair again and snatched up her book. She was breathing heavily and felt a film of sweat develop on her forehead.

Maybe the whole thing hadn't been such a good idea. Chloe expected the owner of the house to burst into the library at any moment, to point to her and yell, 'You were spying on us!'

But that didn't happen.

Ten minutes passed, then twenty, then an hour. And eventually, Chloe was satisfied that she'd gotten away with the whole thing. The relief she felt was palpable, as was the returning excitement.

Sneaking about had been fun.

CHAPTER 7

'Ray, wake up!'

The sound of his wife's voice pulled him from sleep. He blinked a few times, feeling a little disoriented, but he quickly got his bearings. Ray then rolled over to see his wife sitting on their bed—on top of the covers—leaning over him and pressing a hand onto his shoulder. She had gone to bed wearing just a black nightie but was now covered with a light blue dressing gown.

His first thought was that he'd slept in. However, given it was still dark, he knew that wasn't the case.

'What is it?' he whispered back before glancing at the bedside clock that sat on the nightstand. He had to squint to read the two black hands in the dark but saw that it was close to three-thirty in the morning. He felt Rita shake him, and he turned back to her.

'Listen!' she insisted, bringing a finger up to her mouth, signalling for him to be quiet. He did as instructed. He didn't hear anything at first.

Then quick and heavy footsteps passed by the door to their room from the hallway outside.

Ray sat up.

They were too heavy to be Chloe's.

Then, abruptly, the footsteps stopped.

'Who the hell is that?' he said, pulling back the covers and swinging his legs from the bed. Ray suddenly stopped as the noise repeated, sounding like it was coming back the other way. A few quick, heavy steps... then silence once again.

Ray stood up, but Rita tugged on the shoulder of his white t-shirt.

'I already checked,' she whispered. 'But there was no one out there.'

He turned to her with a frown. 'You should have woken me up right away,' he replied, 'not checked yourself.'

'Well, you're awake now, so what does it matter?'

Ray shook his head, but then made his way over to the door anyway. The chill was only slightly warded off by the thin t-shirt and long pyjama bottoms he wore, and he felt goosebumps form on his bare forearms. All Ray could think was that perhaps Marcus or Vincent were pacing around outside, though he couldn't even begin to guess why.

He took hold of the door-handle and turned, pulling it open. Ray then poked his head out, looking both left then right, and saw a dark yet quite empty hallway.

Strange.

After a few more moments of staring into the shadows, he stepped back fully into his room and pushed the door shut. Rita had one eyebrow raised.

'No one there?' she asked, though it was close to being less of a question and more a statement.

'No,' he replied, shaking his head in confusion.

'I heard it three times before I checked,' she went on. 'But I didn't see anyone either. After I came back to bed, I heard it again. That's when I woke you.'

Ray then looked up to the ceiling. 'Maybe someone is moving around upstairs,' he offered. 'Thin ceilings, no insulation between the separating floor... the sound could travel and make it seem like the footsteps were outside.'

Rita shrugged but looked less than convinced. 'I guess.'

Ray considered his own suggestion. He knew he was grasping at straws. However, while unlikely, it *was* a possibility. In truth, it was the only explanation they had.

But, then again... those footsteps had sounded like they were *right* outside. Ray moved back over to his wife and sat on the bed with her. 'Something to remember for the to-do-list,' he told her.

'What do you mean?'

'If the noise travels like that, it's going to disturb the guests.' He chuckled. 'Can you imagine how people would react if they heard other guests getting it on? I don't suppose it would go down too well with the stuffy, well-to-do types.'

Rita laughed. 'Fair point. I guess we need to do something about it.'

'Insulation between the floor joists should help,' Ray said. 'We'll go in from above, take the floorboards up. Don't want to ruin the ceilingwork by going in from underneath. I'd never be able to replicate the detailing they have.'

Rita looked up at the ceiling. She nodded. 'Good point.' She then lowered her head and stared into his eyes.

'Tell me,' she started, 'do you think we're being crazy by coming here?'

He shook his head. 'We're doing what we need to.'

'I know that, but… you really think we can make the hotel work?'

He took her hands in his and caressed the backs with his thumbs. 'With you leading the charge, I *know* we'll make it work. Trust me, this is going to be the most popular hotel for miles around.'

She smiled. Even though her big brown eyes looked a little tired, Ray couldn't help but appreciate just how beautiful she was. 'Thank you,' she said, and placed a gentle, lingering kiss on his lips.

As she pulled away, he felt something stir. He then brought a hand up to the back of her head and kissed her again. Passionately. His tongue found hers. Rita pulled away a little, but only so she could again look into his eyes. There was a hunger there, an intensity that excited him more.

She gave him a coy smile. 'Should we? I mean, I don't want to wake everyone in the house. Especially if the sound travels—'

Ray brought a finger up to her lips. 'Then we'll be quiet,' he whispered. Rita giggled, and the sound was the sweetest Ray had ever known. She fell into him as they rolled onto the bed.

CHAPTER 8

2 Days Later.

Rita, Ray, Vincent, and Marcus had all gathered in the great hall and were seated around the table there. It was a little before midday, and though it was cold out, a strong winter sun shone brightly, melting away a morning frost sprinkled over the grass outside.

For Rita and Ray, the past couple of days had been spent acquainting themselves more with the house. Especially for Ray, as he wanted to figure out how much manual work lay ahead of him. A recent trip down to the basement had proven eventful, where Vincent had shown both Rita and Ray how to start up the furnace and heat the building. The noise that the huge metallic unit had given off when starting up had been... surprising, to say the least.

Rita, for her part, had been formulating and coming up with her plan of action, and she now took the time to relay it to the owner of the house.

Marcus had before him a leather-bound notepad and an elegant fountain pen in hand, scribbling down notes as Rita went over her ideas and plans for Perron Manor—a place that would soon be known as the Blackwater Hotel.

In one sense, Rita was surprised how much interest Marcus was taking during this briefing. He had been aloof at best since their arrival, always hidden away up on that top floor. It was something of a concern that he hadn't taken a great deal of interest in what Rita's plans were. She had suspected the whole endeavour was something of a game for him: a whim, with no real drive to see it succeed.

But he was now listening intently and making extensive notes, which gave her confidence.

Rita finished her ideas and let Ray chip in on the maintenance and repair side of things. Then they waited for Marcus' response. He finished scribbling down the last of his notes, then set down his pen, clasped his hands together, and made direct eye contact with Rita. His face was unreadable, at first, but he soon broke into a large grin.

'Excellent!' he exclaimed. 'I love what I'm hearing. And, I'm on board with it all.'

He then reached into the pocket of the smart black jacket he wore and pulled out an envelope, which he then slid over to Rita.

'These are the details of the business bank account so you can start withdrawing money and placing your orders. Time to make it all happen, Rita.'

She couldn't contain her smile. Marcus' comments felt like validation. 'Thank you,' she replied, picking up the thick envelope. Her already high motivation was suddenly supercharged.

'And if you agree,' Marcus went on, 'I think we can look to open in March.' His eyebrows were raised, waiting for confirmation.

'Yes, we can definitely achieve that.'

Marcus clapped his hands together. 'Then let's get to it!' With that, he stood to his feet.

Meeting over, Rita assumed, and she stood up as well, along with Ray and Vincent. Marcus' lingering smile was tight-lipped, and he walked with the others as they moved out of the room. Rita felt a gentle hand tug at her elbow, and she turned to see him motioning for her to stop, with Vincent and Ray still a few steps ahead.

'I want you to know,' he said in a low, soft voice, 'that I am extremely impressed.'

'Thank you,' Rita said again. 'I'm glad to hear that.' Ray stopped up ahead and turned to face them as well. But Marcus then leaned in so only she could hear him speak.

'If you stick with someone like me, I think you could go far.' The smile he wore was not a happy or pleased one, anymore, but something else entirely. Something more predatory. She felt his thumb, still on her elbow, begin to caress the skin through the silk material of her blouse.

The revulsion and anger that overcame Rita was hard to keep under control. Her skin crawled at his touch, and at his self-assured grin. She had a sudden impulse to slap him hard across the cheek.

She didn't. Instead, she quickly moved her arm away and gave him a humourless smile while she kept her eyes serious. When she replied, her voice was low, ensuring her words were only for him. 'While I'll carry on with the job at hand, Marcus, I need you to know that I'll be sticking with my family and my husband. I trust that's clear?'

His expression didn't change, which infuriated her even more. But, he at least nodded his head in confirmation. 'Of course.'

'Good,' Rita stated, then turned and walked away, keeping the envelope tucked tightly under her arm.

Ray was frowning in confusion as she passed him. 'Everything okay?' he asked.

'Fine,' was all Rita said in response.

CHAPTER 9

3 DAYS LATER.

Chloe's heart was racing. A slight sweat had formed on her brow, and she tried to subtly dab it with the back of her hand. Her chest felt tight.

She wanted to be away from this place—to be anywhere but here.

But she was trapped. And *that* moment was coming.

'And,' Mrs. Taylor began, from the front of the class. 'We have a new student today.'

Here it is. Chloe wanted the ground to swallow her up in that moment.

'Chloe Pearson,' Mrs. Taylor announced with a big smile. The older woman had frizzy brown hair and glasses that dangled from a chain down over a heaving chest hidden beneath a thick cardigan. 'Would you please stand up?'

Chloe's face flushed a shade of red so deep she could have been mistaken for a tomato. Nevertheless, she did as instructed and timidly stood to her feet. Chloe could feel the eyes of all the other students on her.

She didn't like the classroom she had been assigned to. Not the people, necessarily, as she didn't really know anyone yet, more the room itself. The flaky paint on the walls was a sickly yellow covered in lots of areas with large swathes of black sugar paper. That paper, in turn, was mounted with drawings from her new classmates. The floor was a beige, sticky vinyl, and the ceiling was lined with square tiles, some with evident water stains. The only windows in the room were high up—close to the ceiling—and were long and thin, making the room feel dark, dank, and oppressive.

The students were all seated at tables that faced towards the front of the room, and the chairs were hard plastic and not very comfortable. Chloe, thankfully, was seated towards the back and shared a table with two other children—a boy and a girl—though she didn't know their names yet.

'Why don't you tell us a little about yourself, Chloe?' Mrs. Taylor asked, though it was clear it was a command, not a question.

No! Chloe thought. *How about I don't!*

But she took a breath, slow and steady, and tried to force away the nerves she was feeling. 'I'm Chloe,' she started, her voice cracking as she began. She coughed and pushed on. 'I'm six, and I like to read. I just moved here and don't know many people yet.' She paused. 'And that's all I can think to say.'

'Very good, Chloe,' the teacher said. She then looked around the room, hands held out wide. 'Now, does anyone have any questions for their new classmate?'

Chloe sincerely hoped they did not. To her disappointment, however, a hand went up from the little girl seated next to her.

'Yes, Alice,' Mrs. Taylor said. 'What is your question?'

Alice, who had long, dirty blond hair, with a narrow black headband wrapped over the top, looked up to Chloe.

'Do you live in that scary house?'

Chloe frowned, confused at the question. The teacher cut in. 'That isn't the type of question I meant, Alice. Does anyone have any specific questions for Chloe that are about *her*.'

Another hand went up, this one belonging to a boy across the room.

'Andrew, go ahead.'

'Have you seen a ghost there?' he asked.

A small ripple of giggles permeated through the class, making Chloe feel like she was outside of a shared joke. The kids obviously knew about the house she lived in and had a certain opinion on it.

'It isn't haunted,' she snapped.

'Alright,' Mrs. Taylor said, bringing up her index finger to her lips. 'That's enough. If no one has any *real* questions, then we can move on. Chloe,' the teacher said, looking over to her, 'you may take your seat.'

Chloe sat, and her face felt hot and flushed. Mrs. Taylor went on with the lesson, holding court to a less-than-rapt class while she taught some basic division. The girl next to Chloe, Alice, leaned over.

'I didn't mean to make you angry,' the little girl whispered.

'You didn't,' Chloe lied, not looking back at her. She kept her voice low.

'It's just *everyone* says Perron Manor is haunted.'

'It isn't,' Chloe said flatly.

Alice paused, then nodded. 'Okay,' was all she said, seemingly happy with Chloe's answer.

Chloe tried to concentrate on what Mrs. Taylor was saying, but struggled to focus. She was not happy with how her school life at Alnmouth Primary School had started. If all the kids here thought her house was weird, that would probably make them think less of her, in turn. And all without even getting to know her.

Just after ten o'clock, the class broke to allow the children out into the large playground. Kids from all different age groups and classes could mingle, but with no circle of friends to gravitate to, Chloe kept to the edges of the yard. She leaned against the metal boundary fencing, her hands tucked deep into the pockets of her red, wool coat. She stared down at her black, shiny shoes, feeling utterly alone. Chloe didn't remember her first day of school back home being like this.

Until today, the move to Perron Manor had been exciting for her. An adventure to be enjoyed. Now, however, the realisation of all she had left behind—her friends and her old way of life—was beginning to sink in. It had been brought into sharp focus today as she now stood alone while other kids laughed and played.

A football bounced off the fence near to her, causing Chloe to jump. A short boy with shaggy black hair ran over to retrieve it.

'Sorry,' he said earnestly, and punted the ball back over to his friends. He then jogged away.

In truth, Chloe would have preferred to have been back inside her classroom. At least there she had a place to sit and a lesson to concentrate on. Out here, she felt lost and exposed.

'Hi,' a voice said, approaching from her left. Chloe looked up and saw Alice walking towards her. She had on a dark blue coat that was similar in style to Chloe's.

'Hi,' Chloe replied, not wanting to be rude. At least someone was talking to her, which would stop her from looking like a loner to everyone else.

'Are you okay?' the little girl asked. 'Not nice being the new girl, is it?'

Chloe got the impression that Alice was speaking from experience. She shrugged. 'I'm okay,' she lied once again.

'I just started a little while ago, too,' the girl went on to say, confirming Chloe's suspicions. 'Haven't made many friends yet.' Alice then offered Chloe a smile, and she noticed the girl was missing the same two top teeth as Chloe was.

Chloe smiled in return, not really sure what else to do. Then, a question came to her, one she really wanted to know the answer to.

'Why does everyone say the house I live in is scary?'

Perron Manor had never been scary to Chloe, not in the short time she had been there. It had been *amazing*.

Alice shrugged. 'I've only heard other kids talk about it, but that's what they say. Might just be because it's old and creepy.'

'It isn't creepy,' Chloe stated defensively.

'But it's *definitely* old,' Alice replied with a big grin.

Chloe smiled too. 'Yeah. It's old. I just don't get why the others would say it's haunted when they don't even know.'

'Well, I've heard them tell stories about it. One of them was about an old man who killed a load of kids up there.'

'That didn't happen!' Chloe snapped. 'It's probably just a stupid story.' Chloe had no way of knowing for sure, but refused to believe that could ever happen in her perfect new home.

Alice just shrugged. 'Just what I heard.'

'When was it supposed to have happened?' Chloe challenged.

'Dunno. A lot of years ago, I think.'

'Well... *I* don't believe it.'

'Okay,' was all Alice said in reply.

The bell then sounded, bringing an end to their break-time. Chloe made her way back inside and Alice walked beside her. 'I hope we get to read now,' the girl said. 'I love reading.'

'Me too,' said Chloe, feeling like she was at least starting to make a friend.

CHAPTER 10

'Don't listen to them, honey,' Ray told his daughter. He was trying to placate her, but something about what she'd said didn't sit well with him.

'So they were just lying?' Chloe asked.

'Well,' Rita began, 'it's just kids telling scary stories, that's all. And because this house is kind of out of the way, and big and old, it's probably a bit of a mystery to the kids in your school. That's why they make up stories about it. We used to do it, too.'

Chloe considered that for a moment. 'But I don't like it,' she said, her face full of sadness.

The family of three were in the library. Chloe had run straight to it after getting home from school. Ray and Rita had followed her in, knowing something was wrong, and she had told them both what the other kids had been saying about Perron Manor.

Initially, Ray assumed it was just kids being kids. But that story about the old man killing children here seemed a little too… specific. Though maybe he was reading too much into it.

'I know,' Rita went on. 'but it'll pass when they get to know you. And then you can just tell them all about how great the house is.'

'Can I get them to come over?' Chloe asked hopefully.

'Maybe,' Rita replied. 'We'd have to just check with Mr. Blackwater. But I don't see why not.'

That seemed to satisfy Chloe, but Ray had his doubts. Other guests wouldn't exactly be happy with an army of kids running around. He again considered if Perron Manor was going to be good for Chloe, or if it would restrict and isolate her.

Not that there was any choice in the matter. They had come here out of necessity.

Ray and Rita both gave Chloe a hug. 'Are you okay?' he asked her, laying a gentle hand on her shoulder.

She smiled and nodded. 'Yeah, I'll be okay, Daddy.'

'Good,' Rita said. 'You can go up and read your books for a little bit if you want, and I'll call you when it's time to eat.'

Chloe grinned, then grabbed up her school bag, walked from the library, and headed upstairs to her room. He was happy to see there was more of a bounce in her step than when she had first come home.

Ray and Rita then walked back to the study opposite the library, the one that was going to be converted into an office and reception. The jobs he'd done so far had all been small, but the task ahead felt like the first semi-substantial project, one he could really sink his teeth into.

Once inside, he turned to Rita. 'What did you make of all that?'

Rita shrugged her shoulders. 'Just kids being kids.'

'Yeah, but... the thing about children being killed here? That seemed a little more graphic than the standard ghost story to me.'

Rita laughed. 'Kids are different than when we were young, Ray. They're exposed to a lot more. I wouldn't worry.'

'I'm just saying, we don't really know anything about this house. And most stories and legends are based on some kind of fact, aren't they?'

'I'm sure it's nothing, honey,' his wife said, laying a hand onto his arm. She was probably right, but even so...

The sound of the front door opening drew their attention, and Ray poked his head out into the entrance lobby to see Vincent standing inside with a shopping bag in each hand. He was wrapped up in an old, green polyester coat and his cheeks burned red from the biting cold outside. He saw Ray and raised his eyebrows in greeting.

'Just been out to get a few things,' he said, raising up the plastic bags. Then, with a frown, he added, 'You didn't want anything, did you?'

Bit late to be asked now, Ray thought. But he answered with, 'No, we're fine.'

Vincent nodded, then started to walk forward, but Ray stepped out of the study. 'Hey, Vincent,' he began, 'let me ask you something.'

'What's that?' Vincent replied. He stopped and turned round to face Ray. Ray could see the handles of the plastic bags digging into the skin of Vincent's fingers, turning them red, so he tried to be quick.

'Chloe heard a story today at school,' he started. Rita quickly stepped out beside him.

'Come on, Ray,' she said. 'We don't need to go over that. It was just a story.'

'And I'm only asking a question,' Ray told her. He then turned back to Vincent. 'She heard that an old man killed a bunch of kids up here a while back. Any truth to that?'

Vincent didn't answer immediately, but his slightly shocked expression was all the answer Ray needed.

'Well…' Vincent began, but then trailed off, clearly searching for the words.

'Oh my God!' Rita exclaimed. 'It's true?!'

Vincent took a step back, shrinking away. 'It's an old house,' he eventually said. 'Lots of things have happened here. But it's nothing to worry about.'

'Jesus, Vinnie!' Rita spat. 'Why did you never mention it to us?'

'Would it have made a difference?' a voice asked from the top of the stairs.

Marcus started to descend to the half-landing. Today, he was dressed in a pair of dark-brown loafers, black, pressed trousers, and a black, thin jumper with sleeves rolled up to the elbows. He definitely had a preferred colour palette when it came to his clothing.

'Well,' Ray replied, 'it would have been nice to know. Might have made a difference when making our initial decision to come up here.'

Marcus cocked his head and smiled, showing no warmth in his eyes. 'Is that so?' He then looked to Rita. 'So, if you knew that the house had a history, as most old houses do, then you would have… what? Become homeless instead of travelling up here?'

Ray felt a swell of anger. More so because the man had a point. That knowledge wouldn't have changed anything, because Ray and his family had been desperate.

Marcus continued down the remaining flight of stairs and stepped out into the lobby, then walked over to them. 'Consider a house that has stood for centuries will have seen war and famine, and a plethora of other tragedies. None like this stand without having some kind of death attached to them.'

'Yes, but there's a difference,' Ray shot back. 'Most others won't have had a man kill little children in them.'

Marcus just stared at Ray with a less-than-impressed expression. 'But they may have had other equally despicable acts carried out there. And to think otherwise is just naïve.'

'So what else has happened here that we aren't aware of?' Ray challenged. He felt Rita's arm on his shoulder, and knew her intent. *Leave it alone before you get angry.* But Ray just wanted a straight answer.

Marcus let out a small chuckle. 'Where to start? The house was built in the twelve-hundreds, so the number of souls it has seen come and go boggle the mind. I could give you *scores* of stories, if not hundreds. But, again, I have to ask… does it matter?'

Ray took a breath and eventually shook his head. 'Probably not,' he admitted. 'But I'd still be interested to know.'

'Then you can!' Marcus replied, with surprising enthusiasm. 'I'd be more than happy to tell you. Both of you.' He looked at Rita now as well. 'The house does have a bit of a local reputation, but the history is long and fascinating, far beyond what most people realise. If you are both genuinely interested in hearing about it, how about we have dinner tonight in the great hall. All of us. I can tell you a little more then.'

'Is it something Chloe can hear?' Ray asked.

Marcus paused. 'Good point. Caution might be the best way forward there. After all, we don't want the poor girl scared of her own home. How about we have drinks after she is in bed, then? We can gather in the dining hall at the front of the house instead. Somewhere a bit more intimate.'

Ray would have suggested the living room, since it was a little more comfortable and informal, but regardless, he was interested to hear just what Marcus had to say. He looked to Rita to see what she was thinking, and his wife gave him a subtle nod.

'Fair enough,' Ray told him. 'We'll meet for a few drinks. Sounds good.'

'Excellent!' Marcus exclaimed with a clap of his hands. He then looked over to Vincent. 'Put those away would you?' he said, nodding towards the bags Vincent was struggling with. 'Then fix some dinner. I'm ravenous.'

Vincent nodded then trotted off like a dutiful dog. Ray frowned at Rita. Marcus and Vincent certainly had a curious relationship.

Marcus gave them both a polite smile and started to walk through to the kitchen after Vincent.

'Don't let me keep you,' he called back. 'I'm sure you have lots to be getting on with.'

CHAPTER 11

MARCUS TOPPED up Ray's glass of whiskey, and Ray did not protest, despite already feeling lightheaded.

They were all seated around the polished, rectangular dining room table, and in its centre was a silver tray that held bottles of scotch, spiced rum, and red wine.

Ray and Marcus were sharing the delicious whiskey, which had a smoky finish. Vincent enjoyed the rum, and Rita was on her second glass of wine.

The family hadn't spent much time in this room since moving in. Not that Ray didn't like it, of course, it was just that the living room was a little more comfortable, and a little more... *them*.

While it wasn't as grand as the great hall, the dining room was certainly impressive, and quite formal. The walls had a dark oak covering, giving the room a slightly heavy and oppressive feel to it. The plush red carpet underfoot only added to the traditionalist style, and the room smelled of sandalwood, which was given off by the scented candles Marcus had lit before starting. He obviously preferred to set the mood with them rather than using the electric chandelier overhead.

Whenever their drinks had run low, Marcus had taken it upon himself to refill them, which surprised Ray. He'd assumed that was just something he would have tasked Vincent to do, as it seemed to be the case with everything else. However, Marcus was clearly making an effort as host tonight and took great relish in telling his stories about the house's long history.

Ray had to admit, it was all very impressive to hear. If a little disturbing.

There seemed to have been—from what they'd been told—a disproportionate amount of death inside these walls. But, as Marcus had put it, they had only been discussing it for a little while, and the history spanned *centuries*. Was it really so strange? Of *course* it was going to sound a lot when condensed into such a small time-frame.

Even so, the very first story, where Marcus recounted the time when the building was a monastery, had creeped Ray out a little. All of the monks that lived here were, apparently, slain by one of their brothers, someone Marcus referred to only as 'the Mad Monk.'

But there were other tales of slaughter and murder as well—such as in the thirteen-hundreds, when the building was known as Grey House and was under the stewardship of Edward Grey. That man had constructed the basement level used back then as a jail. He'd captured prisoners from the war with Scotland, and those prisoners were taken downstairs to be tortured. Grey eventually went mad, it was said, and killed all the prisoners before then taking his own life.

Marcus then went on to tell them that it was in the fifteen-hundreds that the building had gained the name of Perron Manor, when it was taken over by the illustrious Perron Family. Again, however, a similar tale was weaved, where almost a century later the last surviving heir passed away. There were stories of Robert Perron's devotion to the 'Dark Arts,' and when the house was investigated after his death, a horrific scene was uncovered: scores of dead bodies strewn about the house, many strung up, while others looked like they had been used in some kind of occult rituals.

In addition, the building had also been used as a sick house, as well as an orphanage, and other strange events had supposedly taken place during those periods as well.

Marcus had been talking for close to an hour and a half before he finally got to the story Chloe had heard at school: in 1936, a vagrant had been found in the house after killing six children. He was arrested, of course, but always maintained he was being controlled. As he had killed the children he had sung nursery rhymes to them, to both try to soothe their fears, and also to block out their screaming.

'Well,' Rita said after Marcus had drawn his storytelling to a close, 'that is certainly a lot to take in.'

'I'll say,' Ray added in agreement, and took another long sip from his whiskey. The pleasant burning sensation was soothing, and Ray was well aware he'd hit the point where the alcohol was wrapping his mind in a nice, comforting fuzz. Marcus had divulged a lot, but Ray was certain their host had only scratched the surface.

'Now, just to be clear,' Marcus went on. 'The reason none of this was brought to your attention earlier was because I simply didn't think it was relevant to your decision. As you can see, I have absolutely no qualms telling you anything you need to know about Perron Manor. I certainly don't want this to be an issue.'

Ray supposed he could see that point of view, as much as he didn't really want to admit it.

'Okay,' Rita said. 'Like you said, it isn't going to make a difference. But it would have been good to know, so we could have thought about how it would affect Chloe. If this house has a reputation locally, then it stands to reason that would get back to our daughter.'

Marcus considered her words, cocking his head to one side. Then he nodded. 'Understood,' he replied. 'That was not something I had considered. But, any other questions you have, just ask. Please. I'd be happy to answer them.'

Then, before Ray's filter could kick in, he blurted out the question that had been on his mind for a while.

'Why is the top floor out of bounds, then? What are you two doing up there all the time?'

In his peripheral vision, Ray saw Rita's eyes go wide, as if that line of questioning was taboo. Maybe it was, but Marcus had just said they could ask anything.

Their host just smiled and ran a finger around the rim of his whiskey glass. 'Fair enough,' he said, 'I suppose I do owe you an explanation on that one.' He then took a few moments before continuing on. 'I conduct my business up there. And I need a private area to do so.'

'What *is* your business?' Ray asked, genuinely curious.

'I have carried on in my grandfather's footsteps. He was a trader of rare and valuable artefacts, and I have continued his legacy. So, as you can imagine, I have quite a few items up there I need to keep secured.'

'You could have told us that from the beginning,' Ray said.

'Forgive me,' Marcus rebutted, 'but I did not know you or your family at all. Vincent had spoken highly of you, especially Rita, and it made sense to invite you up here given my plans with the hotel. However, I am not in the habit of broadcasting what I do or what kind of things I keep in my possession. As you can imagine, it would be quite the temptation for someone to try to—'

'Hold on,' Ray interrupted. 'You thought we might *steal* your stuff?'

'I didn't know one way or the other,' Marcus replied firmly. 'So, I held off from telling you. Quite frankly, it was none of your business, anyway. This is *my* house, after all.'

'He didn't mean anything by it,' Rita cut in. 'But I can promise you, Marcus, we would never snoop or steal any of your belongings.'

Ray thought that point should have been obvious. He and his family weren't rich, but they certainly weren't *thieves*.

'No, I understand that,' Marcus eventually replied. 'Which is why I am happy to share that information now. Even though you've only been here a little while, I trust you all.'

Ray looked over to Rita and saw her frowning at him. He took another drink, feeling it best to keep his mouth shut for a little while.

'Can I ask?' Rita began. 'If your business is trading, then why the desire to turn Perron Manor into a hotel?'

'A good question,' Marcus replied. 'The simple answer is… why not? Perron Manor is a big place. Far bigger than I need. I have my space and privacy to attend to my personal affairs, but the rest of the house feels like it is going to waste. If we can get the hotel up and running, and make it the success I know you can, the extra revenue will be most welcome to me. Of course, you will get a share of that as well.'

'So this whole endeavour is a serious venture, then?' Rita asked. 'Bit late to ask, of course, but I need to know you won't throw the whole thing away on a whim.'

'It is serious,' Marcus confirmed. 'I can promise you that. The only way things will change is if the hotel fails and I cannot financially support the endeavour any longer.'

'Then let's make sure we keep the money coming in,' Rita said with a smile, raising her glass. The others joined her as well, though Ray was a little slow on the uptake. He felt warmth in his cheeks and realised he might have had a little too much of the beautiful amber liquid, which was starting to have more and more of an effect. But then again, what did it matter? Ray didn't drink a whole lot, other than the odd glass at night, and he couldn't remember the last time he'd gotten even a little tipsy, let alone drunk.

'If the locals all know of the house,' Ray said, hearing his own words slur ever-so-slightly, 'do you think they'll even come and stay here?'

Marcus shrugged. 'Maybe. Maybe not. Depends on how well we market it.'

'Well, I think we also need to target people farther afield,' Rita offered. 'We also need to make it clear that the hotel is a perfect relaxing getaway. We are going to be targeting a certain level of clientele, I think: those that enjoy weekend breaks to country manors. This place would be perfect for them.'

'I like it,' Marcus said, grinning. 'Clearly something you've thought about.'

'Of course,' Rita said. 'If we do that, the history of the house won't be an issue.'

'Or,' Ray cut in, 'you could make the history a focus.' He then took another drink. When he lifted his head, all three of the others were looking at him, and Rita had one eyebrow raised in confusion.

'What do you mean by that?' Marcus asked, curiosity evident in his voice.

'Well, you know... Chloe said all her friends thought the house was haunted and that grisly things have happened here. Play up to that.'

Rita shook her head. 'I think you've had too much whiskey, dear,' she said, curtly. 'We are *not* turning this place into some kind of cheesy haunted-house attraction.'

Ray shrugged. 'Fair enough. Just an idea. You're the expert on these things. But, imagine how much interest you could generate if you... I don't know... had a big event over, say, Halloween. The place would be jam-packed with people who are into ghosts and that type of thing. It could be huge.'

'Thank you for the input, darling,' Rita said, letting out a chuckle that bordered on condescension, 'but leave the planning and marketing to me, okay?'

'No, wait,' Marcus said as he held up his hand. 'You might be on to something there, Ray.'

Ray lifted his eyebrows in surprise, then turned and shot a smug grin over to his wife.

Rita rolled her eyes and shook her head. 'I don't think that is fitting for a place like this,' she said. 'You want to exude class, not use cheap, corny tactics.'

'But as a one-off-event, Ray is right. It could be huge. Trust me, *everyone* has at least some interest in the darker things in life—especially the upper classes, from what I have seen. An event like that could draw great interest. Imagine the number of bodies we could pack in here over that weekend.' He then cast a glance to Vincent, who had remained pretty much silent the whole night. Marcus rubbed his chin. 'Something to think about.'

'How about we use that as a fallback plan,' Rita argued. 'If we aren't filling this place up week-in, week-out, then we could consider it.'

Marcus pondered for a while. 'Let me think about it. Like you say, something to keep in the back pocket, at least. Great idea, Ray.'

Ray smiled, even though he was perfectly aware Rita was currently scowling at him. He took another drink, enjoying it.

This whole marketing thing was easier than he'd thought.

CHAPTER 12

Rita peered through the dark at the ticking clock on her nightstand.

Three-twenty-seven.

She rolled over to her back again and looked up to the ceiling, letting out a sigh.

Another broken night of sleep.

It was becoming a common thing, and something she could do without. Her eyes felt tired and itchy, and rubbing them only made the sensation worse—as if tiny granules of sand were lining the fleshy orb.

The side of her face felt cold, specifically her inner ear, as if an icy breeze had been flowing over her while she slept.

It was again a certain dream that had woken her—one of being dragged down into the earth as she fought and screamed against an unseeable thing that pulled her down against her will. The tight hole she was sinking into had at first been made up of earth and rock, but that eventually gave way to a different kind of material that reminded her of flesh and skin. Rita caught glimpses of eyes and mouths within the constricting walls; her own screams were lost, overpowered by those that bellowed around her from an unknown origin.

Through it all, she had still been able to make out a strange whispering, one that seemed to burrow into her skull. It repeated the same thing over and over. However, Rita was unable to properly understand the word, given it was definitely not English. It sounded more like gibberish, concocted from her own tired subconscious.

Dede!

Rita had never been one for such visceral nightmares before, nor had she ever suffered from such a constant stretch of broken sleep, at least not since Chloe was a baby. Back then, she'd been woken by the cries of her daughter, whereas this was all the doing of her own mind.

She could only assume it was because of the self-imposed pressure she was under to make things work at Perron Manor. Once again, Rita felt she had to prove herself, to know for sure she was as capable as she thought.

Being let go from her last position, even though Rita felt it unwarranted, had certainly made her question her own abilities.

What if they were right?

She closed her eyes again and waited, listening to Ray's snoring. She hoped the exhaustion that throbbed behind her eyes would soon seep into her mind, quiet it, and allow her to get some sleep. But after over ten minutes of lying with her eyes closed and feeling nothing but agitated, Rita quietly got out of bed.

Rita could think of nothing but the hotel and the work ahead. That, and Ray's stupid idea which he'd floated earlier—one that threatened to turn the hotel into some kind of ridiculous haunted-house attraction.

That idea was something she planned to derail. Quickly.

She padded quietly to the desk in the corner of the room and picked up a pen and her planning binder. She then threw on her dressing gown and headed out into the hallway outside, quietly closing the door behind her. It was cold, and the unreliable heating system had obviously ground to a halt. Rita headed down to the kitchen, where she fixed herself a cup of warm milk before moving on to the living room. It was a place she could sit in comfort and work for a while. If she grew tired, Rita figured, then all the better, she could just return to bed. If not... then tomorrow was going to be a very long day. But at least that night would have been productive.

Given the chill in the air, Rita decided to get the fire going. There looked to be enough coal in the fireplace, and the warmth might help relax her again.

Once the fire was lit, a pleasant smokey smell began to fill the room. Rita took a seat at the small, circular table close to the window and set down her pad. She was facing the television, which was positioned in the corner of the room, as well the fireplace, and the crackling flames in her peripheral vision were soothing. The thick, royal-green curtains were pulled closed across the window, and they helped ward off the cold that seeped through the single-glazed glass panes.

Picking one of the more simple tasks to focus on, Rita started to think of any signage she may need, such as direction plaques, room numbers, reception sign, a welcome sign outside the front door and also at the boundary gates. Given there may be long timescales for delivery to consider, Rita wanted to get a handle on the signage quickly.

After listing down her items, she set the pen down and took a drink, cupping her hands around the warm mug. She then let her eyes wander around the room. Her gaze passed over the television set, then to the fire… and then back to the television, where something seemed out of place.

It was an instinctive glance back, with her mind not quite sure what had felt wrong. Rita focused on the blank screen, and it only showed a somewhat dulled reflection of the room she sat in. In it, Rita could see herself, holding her cup, as well as the table. She could also see the sofas in the room, even the pictures on the wall.

But why is the reflection so troubling?

And then she noticed it, and immediately drew in a quick breath.

Her vision locked on to the reflection of the doorway. While the door itself was open, the space was filled by the shadowy form of a person.

The outline was too blurry to make out too much clearly, but Rita could certainly distinguish the shape of a head, arms, torso, then hips and legs. The figure also seemed to be naked, from what she could tell.

Rita instantly whipped her head around in fright… but saw nothing out of the ordinary.

She then turned her head back to the television set, half-expecting to see the doorway clear this time.

The figure was still there, face blank—or at least too blurry to be readable—and standing absolutely motionless. Rita felt a cold, creeping sensation, like icy fingers crawling their way up her spine.

She quickly stood, and the chair beneath her screeched as she pushed it back. However, when she looked over to the door, it once again did not match the reflection in the television. It was empty. Rita felt her heartbeat start to quicken.

Get a grip; it's probably nothing. She braced herself while turning her head back to the reflection in the televisions screen, only this time the strange form had gone.

Whipping her head back and forth, like she was watching a live game of tennis, Rita repeatedly checked the doorway and the television set. Whatever it was she had seen was no longer there.

Still, that feeling of foreboding hung in the air, like a heavy cloud had descended over her. Suddenly, Rita wanted to be back in her room and in bed with her husband.

Had she really seen anything? Whatever the truth was, she could admit to herself that she was scared. She felt on edge and jumpy, like at any moment she expected *something* to happen.

So Rita got up and quickly placed the solid-iron fireguard over the opening of the fireplace to cut off the air supply. She didn't plan to wait around and watch the fire die out, and instead gathered up her binder, then trotted from the room while casting another look into the television screen.

Thankfully, the coast was clear.

As she stepped out of the living room, a chill ran through her, like she had stepped into a refrigerator. Rita broke into a run, feeling rising goosebumps pinprick her skin. She moved, and the temperature around her normalised, but she pushed on, not daring to look back. Rita made her way through into the entrance lobby, then took the stairs up two at a time.

Rita hurried upwards, feeling anxious. The house around her seemed oppressive. She kept having to look back over her shoulder, for some reason fully expecting to see someone behind her.

Stop it, the rational part of her brain admonished. *You're freaking yourself out over nothing.*

When Rita was close to her room she happened to glance out of one of the windows. As she looked, something hit the glass with an awful bang, making her jump and cry out in shock. However, even though it had initially surprised her, Rita had seen enough of the object to know what had happened. She'd even heard the tiny squeak after impact.

It was a bat, and it had swooped full speed into the glass pane. Though much of the motion had been a blur, Rita did see the animal drop after impact and fall to the ground below.

She now stood motionless, breathing heavily, clutching her binder to her chest for protection.

Calm down, it was nothing to panic about, she told herself. *Just a bat. You saw it yourself.*

Regardless of that being true, Rita's anxiety level shot up a hundredfold. Then, another sound startled her, this one the opening of a door. She breathed a sigh of relief as Ray poked his head out from their bedroom, eyes still half-closed and his hair a wild mess.

'What is it?' he asked in a groggy voice, squinting at her. 'Did you shout or something?'

'I... a bat hit the window,' Rita said, pointing to the point of impact. When she looked closer she saw a small crack in the windowpane.

Ray frowned, then stepped out into the corridor to look at the glass. His sleepy eyes widened. 'Strange, don't often hear of bats colliding with things. Don't they have sonar or something?'

Rita had no idea if that was the case or not, but this one certainly had suffered a mishap. So she just shrugged. Ray ran a finger over the crack.

'This will have to be repaired,' he said, then turned to her. 'What are you doing up, anyway?'

'Couldn't sleep, so I went downstairs to do a little more work.' Rita then held up the binder.

Ray looked at the folder, then back to Rita. 'Get much done?'

'A little,' she replied.

'The bat thing scare you?' he asked. 'You look as white as a sheet.'

Rita considered telling her husband what she had seen—or what she *thought* she had seen. But, it sounded crazy even in *her* head, so she had no idea how Ray would react to such a fantastical tale.

'It made me jump a little,' she finally said. 'But I'm okay.'

He held out a hand, and she gratefully took it. 'Come back to bed,' he told her. 'Try and get some sleep.'

She did, eventually managing to drift off after another half-hour of lying awake and staring at the shadows in the corner of her room.

CHAPTER 13

MARCH.

Today was the day—the grand opening of the Blackwater Hotel.

'Grand' wasn't exactly an apt term. After all, only three rooms had been booked out.

Ray knew it wasn't the start Rita had been hoping for. Despite her best efforts to get the word out—even garnering some press coverage in the local paper—the buzz hadn't really taken hold. Rita had been dismayed to read the newspaper report she had worked so hard on actually focus on the notoriety of the building, instead of keeping the story on the upcoming opening.

The reporter had even used the phrase, 'the purportedly haunted building,' which enraged Rita further, causing her to toss the newspaper into the bin and label it a tabloid rag.

The hotel certainly looked the part, and Ray was pleased with how he'd managed to convert the old study into the office and reception area. The separating wall he'd constructed was basic, but he'd managed to make it look fairly seamless, save for the break in the original's ornate coving, something he was not able to replicate.

That day, Ray was dressed in a smart suit that Rita had bought for him, but he thought it made him look like a butler. Maybe that was the point, but he hated it. He also hated that he had to pretend to be something he was not.

But Rita needed the opening day to be perfect, regardless of the low guest count, and Ray didn't want to get in the way of that. So, he went along with it in the hopes that the first impressions to the guests would be good ones. Rita's aim was that despite the low numbers the guests would at least pass on good recommendations to their friends.

From their position in the office, adjacent to the entrance lobby, both Ray and Rita heard the rumble of a car engine approaching the house.

'They're here,' Rita said, her voice full of nervous energy. She strode from the room, waving Ray after her, and headed out into the entrance lobby. Rita suddenly turned to Ray and straightened out his collar, then brushed off his shoulders, even though Ray knew they were clean—mainly because she had been brushing them off intermittently for the last half an hour.

He took hold of her by the elbows. 'Rita... stop fussing. Everything will be fine. You'll be charming, I'll carry the bags, and the guests will have an amazing time.'

His wife took a deep breath, but he could feel her shake slightly in his grasp. She eventually nodded. 'It will. It will all be great.'

She sounded like she was trying to convince herself, rather than really believing it, but Ray didn't doubt her. All of the nervous energy would dissipate the instant she needed it to, and Rita would transform into the consummate professional with a kind smile and courteous demeanour.

Rita led Ray outside to stand at the top of the steps out front of the house. The weather was crisp and clear, with the beginnings of spring starting to show: shoots of new yellow and white flowers had begun to bloom, and the green nubs of leaves had started to appear on the formerly bare trees.

The couple watched with big, forced smiles as the car drove over to the carport. After it was parked, Rita and Ray trotted over as the visitors inside disembarked. The couple were fairly advanced in years.

'Welcome,' Rita said, sounding calm, polite, and professional, just as Ray knew she would. 'I hope your drive up here was pleasant?'

The lady was small with angular facial features, and had dark, curly hair without a grey in sight, meaning it was probably dyed. The guest smiled at Rita. Her lips were decorated in bright red lipstick, and they pulled back into a smile that revealed gleaming white dentures. Thick makeup covering her sagging skin and a heavy layer of blue eyeshadow completed the look of someone desperately fighting against the never-ending march of age. She wore a tan shawl over a smart white and black tartan jacket, and black trousers beneath.

'Oh yes, it was indeed, dear,' she replied in a light Irish accent. 'Very tranquil.'

'This is a lovely area,' the gentleman added, with the same accent as his wife. If Ray were to guess, he'd say the man was a bit older than his wife, due to the bald head that was smattered with liver spots. He also bore a trimmed, white moustache that hung under a rather pointed nose, and his eyes were a pale, dulled blue. The man wore a tan dinner jacket, white shirt, and cream trousers, a look that Ray found gaudy, though he assumed was the norm for people of wealth. The couple were quite obviously wealthy, and their car was a clear indicator of that: a pristine, oil-blue Bentley convertible which gleamed in the daylight. Ray felt a pang of jealousy looking at the sleek automobile.

Oh how the other half live.

The old man was holding a hand to his lower back and gave a wince of pain, and Ray noted the gentleman hadn't quite fully straightened up yet. 'Bit of a drive, though, not good on the old back.'

'Then let me get your bags,' Ray said, stepping forward.

'Thank you,' the man replied, and popped open the boot of the car. There were three suitcases inside, which Ray after a bit of adjustment managed to gather up in one go. He held a bag in each hand, and the smallest was tucked under his right arm.

'So, Mr. And Mrs. Lancaster,' Rita began. 'If you would care to follow me, we will get you checked in and then settled into your room, which I am sure you will love.'

Rita then led the couple up towards the house. Ray had read the arrivals for the day but had no idea how Rita knew these were Mr. and Mrs. Lancaster. All guests were able to check-in from 2 o'clock onwards, so it could have been any of them, given all three rooms were booked out to couples.

'Lovely building,' the man said, staring up at the hotel.

'It is,' Rita agreed as she began up the front steps, guiding the guests while Ray brought up the rear. The bags Ray was carrying were heavy, though manageable. Rita went on, 'It was built in the twelve-hundreds, believe it or not, and was first used as a monastery.'

Ray couldn't help but smirk, given Rita hadn't been exactly thrilled when she'd heard the history of the house, though she was now happy using it to impress the guests. He also noted that she conveniently left out the part about the 'Mad Monk' going on to kill all of his brothers.

'Fascinating,' the lady said as they entered the great hall. 'This is quite something.'

Ray could see Rita allow herself a small smile—the two guests were suitably impressed. An excellent start to their stay.

'Now,' Rita began, motioning towards the door that led to the newly formed reception area. 'If you please come this way, we'll get you checked in. My husband Ray will take your bags up while we deal with the formalities. Then we can give you a tour of the building if you'd like.'

'Sounds wonderful, dear,' Mrs. Lancaster said. Rita gave Ray a look—his indication to scuttle off with the suitcases. He already had the key to their room, which was one that overlooked the front of the property. Ray gave them both a polite smile, which he hoped didn't look as awkward and forced as it felt, and climbed the stairs. As he did, he felt the solid plastic handles of the cases start to chafe his fingers.

Once he got to the room, Ray set the cases down and unlocked the door, nudging it open with his foot. He then carried everything inside and set the luggage down next to the bed, which he'd made up only that morning. Ray then double-checked the bathroom to make sure the towels and other toiletries were all present and correct, and when he was happy everything was ship-shape he headed back downstairs.

Rita was just finishing off with the checking-in process, and after that was complete the four of them began the tour. Rita led the way and used some tidbits of the house's history that Marcus had divulged.

Again, the more morbid and controversial details were obviously left out.

The stairs to the top floor were also pointed out to the guests, though only to clarify that they were currently out of bounds. There was also now a red rope across the opening to the stairs, with a 'no entry' sign. Rita used the excuse that the floor above was still being renovated and wasn't fit for the public to see just yet. That seemed to be enough to satisfy the guests' curiosity.

Once Mr. and Mrs. Lancaster were settled into their room, Ray and Rita made their way back down to the office area. When Ray checked the time, he saw that he had just over an hour before he needed to go pick Chloe up from school, and he hoped the other guests would be checked in by then—otherwise Rita would be carrying the bags up herself.

'How did you know which couple they were?' he asked his wife. 'Did they give their car registration or something?'

Rita shook her head. 'I recognised Mrs. Lancaster's voice from when she made the booking,' Rita replied, impressing Ray with her attention to detail.

'Well, I think they were suitably charmed, hun. First ones down, two more to go.'

As if on cue, they heard another car approaching. Rita and Ray walked outside to see this couple were younger than the last—in their mid-to-late thirties—but clearly still quite well off. The husband had brushed-back, dark brown hair, and the woman—dressed in a tight-fitting dress that showed off her curves—had long blonde hair that looked to have been expensively styled.

The last of the guests arrived shortly after as well. These were the oldest pair of the three, with the husband being a retired Royal Infantry veteran. In fact, Rita had to pull Ray away and scold him for talking the guest's ear off and asking about the man's old war stories.

Everything went perfectly that day. All the guests made use of the facilities to relax: reading in the library, walking the gardens and grounds outside, and drinking coffee in the great hall while looking out over the courtyard. In the evening, Rita and Ray prepared the meals, and the guests seemed to enjoy the food—Ray even received a few compliments on his friendly service when dishing out the food. The last to retire for the night was the younger couple, who got a little tipsy on the cocktails Rita served. However, they caused no trouble, and Ray and Rita managed to climb into bed a little before midnight.

The couple had even managed to carve out time to spend with Chloe; each had taken turns to deal with any guest requests that came up. Making sure Chloe wasn't starved of attention was something of a concern for Ray. But, so far, it all seemed to be working.

It wasn't until the next morning that the perfect start hit something of a snag.

Mr. and Mrs. Lancaster, the first guests to check in, were also the first to check out, deciding to skip breakfast. Ray arrived at the reception desk at six in the morning, prompt. The two guests came down—fully packed and suitcases in hand—by six-ten.

They immediately demanded to speak with Rita, who came down as quickly as she could.

'Check us out immediately,' the lady snapped, slamming her key down into the reception desk. Rita looked stunned.

'Of course,' Rita replied, maintaining her calm. 'Is everything alright?'

'It most certainly is not,' the husband answered. 'I don't know what kind of place you are running here, but if it is a place where people are allowed to run around in the nip, that should have been made known.'

'The nip?' Rita asked from behind the desk. Ray stood next to his wife, just as confused as she clearly was.

'You know... *nude*. Is this some kind of swingers resort? It is not what we expected.'

Ray hadn't heard that colloquialism, which was possibly an Irish thing, but he was confused at the accusation about the hotel. Even Rita —normally unflappable—struggled to find her words. 'Sir... I... I'm not quite sure what you mean. This isn't that kind of establishment at all.'

'Well,' the man replied haughtily, 'you might want to tell your *other* guests that.'

'What happened?' Ray asked, unable to keep quiet.

'I'll tell you,' the woman took over, jabbing an angry finger at Ray. 'I was woken up in the middle of the bloody night by one of the other guests. I don't know how, but he'd managed to get our door open. Probably picked the lock. And he just stood there in the doorway, watching us sleep, naked as the day he was born!'

Ray heard a small gasp from Rita. 'Oh my lord,' she said, bringing a hand up to her mouth. 'I'm... I am so sorry about that. We really had no idea. I can promise you, though, this is not that kind of place. Do you know which guest it was? I will, of course, speak to them and—'

The husband just held up his palm. 'No need,' he snapped. 'We don't want to hear excuses. And no, we don't know which one it was, so don't ask. But now I can't get the image of his pale bloody body out of my mind. It was quite disturbing, being watched like that. I told him to scram, but the pervert just stood there, watching. He didn't vanish until I turned on the light and got out of bed. He was quick on his feet then, I can tell you. I didn't even see him move. He was just gone. Probably afraid of what I was about to do. So, as you can imagine, we've seen enough of what the Blackwater Hotel has to offer and will be taking our leave now.'

'How about I deduct some money from your bill,' Rita suggested. 'For your distress. It's the least we can do.'

The two guests did not seem interested, however, and were already gathering up their cases.

'Deduct money?' the man said with a scoff. 'I'm not paying a single red cent. Not after that fiasco.'

Ray felt a small pang of anger. He had previously suggested that all guests pay upfront, but Rita argued that it was better for them to pay on check-out, to show confidence in the services.

Ray opened his mouth to speak, feeling their stance was grossly unfair, but Rita raised a hand and placed it on his chest.

'I understand,' she said to the couple.

Ray didn't like it. After all, it wasn't *their* fault one of the guests had a penchant for naked strolls in the night. He also had no clue how the guest had managed to pick the lock.

No more than ten minutes later, Mr. and Mrs. Lancaster had driven away in anger, leaving Ray and his wife dumbfounded.

'Who the hell was watching them sleep?' Ray asked, but Rita shook her head.

'I have no idea. Maybe the younger guy?'

It seemed a logical guess, given the brief description, and Ray doubted it was the veteran. But then, the younger man was hardly pale in Ray's estimation, which went against what Mr. Lancaster had said.

'So... do we confront him?' Ray asked.

Rita shrugged. 'I don't see how we can. Without knowing for certain who it was, we can't level something like that at him. It's not like Mr. Lancaster is still here to identify the guy.'

'Jesus fucking Christ,' Ray said with a sigh. 'What a start. And how the hell did he get the door open?'

Neither had an answer, so Ray went up to check. However, he couldn't find anything wrong with the lock, or any sign of forced entry. In fact, something sprang to mind that he should have mentioned earlier. The doors all had pull-chains across, and if that was on its latch, there was no way someone from the outside could have gotten the door open. So what the hell had happened?

Perhaps the Lancasters were just spinning a lie in order to get out of paying, which only angered Ray more.

While Rita maintained her impeccable air of professionalism for the rest of the day, Ray could tell the less-than-stellar experience of their first guests was bothering her.

The opening of the Blackwater Hotel had been rocky, to say the least, and Ray just hoped for Rita's sake things wouldn't continue that way.

CHAPTER 14

April.

Rita watched the young couple she had just checked in follow Ray as he led them up to their rooms. He would then carry out the tour on his own.

Only two rooms had been booked for the whole weekend, which simply wasn't good enough. Rita rubbed her tired and sore eyes. The dull headache, which was turning into a constant annoyance, threatened to blossom into something much worse. She needed sleep. But every night, Rita's own body worked against her, waking her in the dead of night like clockwork.

She retreated to the closed-off office and took a seat, leaning herself back and letting out a sigh before propping her feet up on the neat and orderly desk before her.

They were a month in, and though there had been guests in that time, the stream had been underwhelming—more like a trickle at best.

That had meant adjusting to their new life here had been relatively easy in some respects, as balancing time with Chloe hadn't been too much of an issue. On the other hand, the stage of needing to bring in more staff seemed to be a million miles away.

To make matters worse, when Marcus had gone over their recent progress he'd once again raised Ray's idiotic idea for an event in

October as something to think about. Unfortunately, Rita couldn't really afford to look down her nose at the idea anymore, considering her own efforts had been lukewarm.

And yet, try as she might, that elusive 'ah-ha' brainwave or spark of inspiration that would transform their fortunes had simply not come. The more Rita focused on the problem, the more it festered and ate at her. It seemed impossible to overcome.

On top of all that, spending so much time inside the house seemed to be getting to her as well, and she felt like cabin fever was setting in. Rita always had the sense of being watched, and she was often uneasy late at night, though she'd never had another incident like the one two months ago where Rita had thought she'd seen something in the television's reflection.

Looking back on it, she knew it was only her mind playing tricks on her.

Rita had half an idea to nap for an hour or so, but a knock on the door to the office startled her. She looked up to see Marcus standing in the doorway, dressed in a dark blue wool sweater, blue jeans, and suede loafers.

'You look exhausted,' he said.

'I'm fine,' she replied, swinging her feet from the table. She felt slightly embarrassed that he'd seen her laid back like that. Though Rita had always worked hard for him—for them all—she hated the idea that anyone may think she was lounging around.

'If you say so,' Marcus shot back, smiling as he entered the room. 'How are things going? Not many guests so far this weekend, I've noticed.'

'No,' she admitted and got to her feet. 'Bit of a quiet one.'

'They all seem quiet ones, don't you think?'

Rita paused, feeling like she was under a spotlight. 'Maybe,' she admitted. 'But you have to build to success. It doesn't just happen overnight.' That was an excuse. She knew it was. While the statement was true enough, Rita had still been expecting far better of herself.

'Fair point, I suppose,' Marcus went on. 'Have you given any more thought to the event in October?'

This again. 'Not really,' she replied. That wasn't necessarily true. Rita had thought about it *a lot*, but purely in terms of how to avoid it.

'Well, I think we start making plans for it,' Marcus stated. It wasn't a suggestion.

Rita felt her defences go up. 'I really don't think that's a good idea. We are building something here, Marcus. An establishment that screams class, not cheap gimmicks and parlour-room tricks. It won't help us, believe me.'

'Well, I think we try it,' Marcus insisted. 'I have little doubt we could fill this place up for the weekend if we did, and the word of mouth would help.'

'I understand what you're saying, but—'

Marcus held up a hand, stopping Rita in her tracks. 'I appreciate your point of view, Rita,' he said. 'I do. But we aren't screaming 'class' at the minute, are we? We are screaming 'empty.' So please, indulge me. We move ahead with this. I'll speak to you later this evening about how we go about it. Plenty of time to get things prepared.'

Rita clenched her teeth together. 'Well, we can't very well fill this place up when the top storey is *still* off-limits, can we?'

She then took a breath. She'd thrown that point up in pure frustration, and while it was true, they hadn't even come close to needing those extra rooms. Still, if he wanted this event on Halloween to fill up the hotel, then the top floor would indeed be needed.

'That is another good point' Marcus said. 'And something I intend to rectify. The top storey will soon be opened up for use. I will need to keep two rooms back, so I want to speak to Ray about a conversion that will help. But the rest of that floor will be available to the public.' He then smirked and added, 'If you even need them, that is.'

Rita had nothing else to say to that. She was still angry at being railroaded into the Halloween idea.

'So…' Marcus went on. 'Do you want to see it?'

Rita frowned. 'See what?'

'What it is that I'm doing upstairs.'

Rita was caught off guard, given the privacy Marcus had demanded over his activities up there.

'Is there something specific you want to show me?' she asked.

'Kind of. And I think it will be of interest.'

What could Rita realistically say to that? So, she simply nodded her head.

'Excellent!' Marcus exclaimed. 'We'll wait until Ray returns, since I want him to see it, too.'

CHAPTER 15

'JESUS CHRIST,' Ray said when shown the room on the top floor. He didn't know what he was looking at, exactly, but it was equal parts impressive and... creepy as hell.

The large room he, Rita, Marcus, and Vincent had all gathered in was near the front of the building, clearly originally used as a bedroom. Now, it was a storage area for things Ray didn't really comprehend.

'Quite something, isn't it?' Marcus asked, the grin he wore wide and proud.

'It... really is.'

The space was jam-packed with bookshelves, display cases, and boxes that all contained—as far as Ray could see—things that were... *odd*.

Ray could see strange artefacts in some of the display cases: weird sigils, daggers, and unrolled parchments. There were even small, dead animals floating in jars full of yellow liquid, forever preserved.

'You two haven't been sacrificing goats up here, have you?' Ray asked, unable to help himself.

Thankfully, Marcus took the remark in good humour and bellowed out a laugh.

'No,' he said. 'No sacrifices, I can promise you that. However, it may or may not surprise you to know this: Perron Manor isn't a stranger to such things.'

Both Ray and Rita turned to look at him. 'Sacrifices?' Rita asked, shocked.

Marcus nodded. 'Yes. You see, when I divulged some of the history of this house to you, I may have left a little bit out. Partly due to time, and partly because I wanted to ease you into it.'

'You're going to have to explain that further,' Rita replied as she started to walk around the room. She squeezed herself between boxes and bookshelves, taking an interest on what was on show.

'Understood,' Marcus said. 'You see, while Perron Manor has a… shall we say… bloodier than average history, for its age—'

'Hold up,' Ray cut in. 'I thought you said *all* houses like this have dark elements to their history. Now you're saying it's bloodier than the average?'

'What I said was certainly true,' Marcus replied. 'But yes, this house has seen more than its fair share of darkness. I believe a lot of it is self-perpetuating, of course, given the early years. Word travelled about the murders that took place here when the building was used as a monastery. The house gained a reputation and attracted a certain type of person to it. People like Edward Grey, and especially Robert Perron. Those who had an interest in the darker things in life.'

'Would you add yourself to that list?' Rita asked, stopping at a waist-height display case, one with a glass top and a plush red lining inside. It contained a single book, bound in black, creased leather, and had gold symbols and wording on the cover. Ray walked over and looked down at it as well.

The title isn't written in English, he noted.

'Well, it is my stock and trade,' Marcus replied, casting his arms about the cluttered room. 'But, of course, there is a difference.'

'Which is?'

'In my view, people like Robert Perron absolutely believed in the things they were studying.'

'And you don't?'

'No, I don't,' Marcus confirmed, shaking his head. 'I find it fascinating, for sure, seeing how the uglier side of human nature can manifest.

But do I believe human sacrifice has any material bearing on the world? No, of course not. Other than people ending up dead.'

'Wait,' Ray jumped in. '*Human* sacrifice? I thought we were talking about goats and stuff?'

'Well, I suppose there could have been some of that. But many of the tragedies that have befallen Perron Manor are borne from the wrong kind of people being attracted to the house. People known to go to the extreme.'

'And it just so happened to fall into your family's possession?' Rita asked. She continued to stare at the book. Ray even saw her run a finger over the glass case.

'It wasn't by chance,' Marcus said. 'My grandfather wanted this place precisely *because* of what it was. Given its past, it became well known among his colleagues. And since I've followed in his footsteps, why would I ever sell up? It was just a shame it stood empty to rot while my father was in possession. It wasn't really his kind of place. He was far too… short-sighted. Thankfully, he was wise enough to keep it in his possession, knowing its value would only increase. I suppose I'm grateful dear old Daddy had at least that much sense.'

'You don't sound very fond of your father,' Ray noted, and Marcus shook his head.

'No, I don't believe I am. Don't get me wrong, he wasn't a bad person by any stretch. In fact, his problem was the total opposite. He was quite vanilla and pedestrian and… well, *boring*. He didn't really make the most of life. And I don't have much time for people like that.'

'So why show us this room now?' Rita asked. 'I'm sure you didn't really bring us up here to talk over your daddy issues.'

Ray was a little shocked at how confrontational Rita was being. He'd noticed a small change in her demeanour recently, but put it down to exhaustion and stress. However, she'd always toed the line with Marcus. Until now.

Marcus narrowed his eyes. 'Indeed not,' he replied, flatly. 'I came to show you what this house is *really* all about. I believe one of the reasons you are struggling to attract guests is because of some preconceived notions people have about the house. And I think Ray hit on something when he said we'd be better served embracing its true nature.'

'Well,' Ray began, 'I don't think I put it *quite* like that.' He didn't want this to come back on him, given Rita was dead set against it.

'Regardless,' Marcus said, 'you were correct in your assertions. Let me tell you both something—I have dealt with a lot of people doing what I do. A lot of *wealthy* people. All are very intelligent, and all are very successful. But one thing many of them had in common was that any time discussions turned to the occult or the... dare I say, supernatural... their ears all pricked up. Interest heightened. I believe that is because to be successful you need something of an edge. And that is what we're currently lacking with the Blackwater Hotel. That edge, which would separate us from the norm.'

'So, people will come here to look at all of *this*?' Rita asked, gesturing to the macabre treasures within the room.

Marcus took a moment and rubbed his chin. 'Well... in all honesty, I hadn't considered that. I was just thinking of playing up to the house's reputation. But I suppose we could put some of these things on show. Another good idea. Of course, anything of true value will need to be safely locked away.'

'But don't you see,' Rita argued back. 'There isn't a large market for that kind of thing—otherwise, it would have been done before. Even if October is a success, it won't sustain the hotel long-term. We need a solid brand so the business can grow organically.'

'We've tried it your way,' Marcus said, with finality. 'And now we will try it mine. If it doesn't work, then we will see where we land. For now, I want you to focus your efforts on October, and making this happen.'

'And if I say no?'

Marcus smiled, but his eyes contained only anger. 'Then I'll thank you for your service thus far and we can part ways.'

An awkward silence descended over them all. Vincent looked to the floor, seeming like a lost puppy, and Rita had a face like thunder. Marcus continued to stare at her, neither giving any ground.

'So, in the meantime,' Ray cut in, hoping to play peacemaker. 'Can we try and build the business as Rita suggested? See how things grow? Then, come October, we have the event and see where we're at. We might surprise ourselves and find we're filling the hotel up every day of every week by then.'

Marcus eventually broke his strong eye contact with Rita and looked over to Ray. He rubbed at his chin again with his thumb for a moment, then nodded. 'Seems like a fair compromise.' He turned back to Rita. 'Agreed?'

Just agree, Ray pleaded internally. Thankfully, Rita nodded as well.

'Good,' Marcus said. 'Now, Ray, I need to speak to you about a few modifications I want to make up here. As you can see, space is a little tight, so I want to convert two rooms into one.'

'Okay,' Ray said. 'That should be no problem.'

'I'll leave you to it,' Rita cut in, her voice curt. 'I have things to be getting on with.' She then walked away, leaving Ray in limbo. He desperately wanted to stand up for his wife, but at the same time he didn't want to make them homeless.

'Don't worry about her,' Marcus said. 'She'll come around.'

Ray shook his head. *You obviously don't know my wife very well.*

CHAPTER 16

Once Ray had left them, Marcus walked over to the display case that contained *Ianua Diaboli*.

The Devil's Door.

Vincent approached and stood beside him, an ever-present shadow. One that had its uses, of course.

'I thought my sister was going to quit right there,' Vincent said, his voice soft, mumbling… pathetic.

'She won't quit,' Marcus replied, still eyeing the precious book. 'They have nowhere else to go.'

'I suppose. How are the translations coming?' Vincent asked.

Marcus lifted the lid and then picked up the thick, heavy book. 'Getting there. We should have plenty of time, though. I believe my grandfather had been largely accurate… for the most part. Such a shame he didn't have the courage to make use of the knowledge he had.'

Vincent just nodded uselessly. 'And… it's going to happen *then*? In October?'

'Yes,' Marcus confirmed. 'I think Ray stumbled upon a good idea with that. It should give us the bodies we need.'

'And my sister…'

'Is proving less than compliant,' Marcus finished. 'I'll need to change that.'

CHAPTER 17

'IT'S A JOKE!' Rita spat, struggling to keep a handle on the rage that bubbled through her.

'I know,' Ray agreed, 'but what can we do?'

She wanted to scream. Ray was right, there was nothing they could do. They were trapped here, and she *hated* it.

The whole venture suddenly felt like it was spiralling and collapsing down around her. After being tasked with putting together a fucking haunted house tour, Rita might as well have been working at a carnival.

She and Ray were back in the office, tucked away from anyone else in the house. Rita checked the clock and saw that it was close to three in the afternoon, which meant one of them would soon need to go pick up Chloe from school.

'I guess we just have to bend over and take it,' Rita snapped. 'All because you couldn't keep your mouth shut.' She saw Ray's face fall. She knew her words hurt him, but it didn't stop her. 'Next time, leave the ideas to me, got it?'

Ray's shoulders slumped and his head dipped a little. In an instant, Rita felt terrible for taking her anger out on her husband like that. All he'd done was put forward an idea. Granted, it was a stupid one, but it was Marcus that had picked up the idea and run with it. *He* was the one imposing his plan of action onto Rita, whether she agreed with it or not.

And *that* was the real root of her anger. Early on, Marcus had insisted that this was Rita's show. However, he'd been quick to enforce his will when it suited.

Her early enthusiasm had been stamped out. Rita now realised Marcus was no different from the other men who'd screwed her over—all that mattered to them was what *they* wanted and what *they* thought was best.

Everything else was just lip-service.

'I'm sorry,' Rita eventually said to her husband.

Ray shook his head. 'No, you're right. I *should* have just kept my mouth shut and let you do your thing. I'm an idiot.'

Rita walked over to him and placed a hand on his cheek. 'You're not an idiot, Ray. I'm just tired and angry, and I'm taking everything out on the wrong person.' She cupped a hand under his chin, raised his head up, and looked into his eyes. 'You are *not* an idiot,' she repeated.

Then, she kissed him. Hard. Before Rita knew it, she was clawing her nails through Ray's thick, black hair. A sudden surge of desire ran through her, and Rita wanted desperately to find some kind of release to her frustration. She started to undo the buttons on Ray's shirt.

She didn't want to use sex as a way to brush over the apology she'd just given, but right now the need to feel him inside her was just too strong.

Ray pulled away a little, visibly shocked. 'Do we have time?'

She just nodded and kissed him again. 'We'll make time.'

Ray was then pushed onto the desk, and Rita climbed atop him.

'Erm... hello?'

Both Rita and Ray stopped at the sound of a voice from the entrance lobby. Her teeth were still clamped over Ray's top lip. She released him and turned her head.

'Yes?' Rita shouted back, feeling a sting of frustration. She had recognised the voice, and it belonged to Mrs. Tenant, one of the few guests they currently had staying.

'I... I have something of a problem that I need you to have a look at.'

'Shit,' Rita whispered. Then, louder, she called over to the waiting guest. 'I'll be right out.'

'Guess we'll need to pick this up later,' Ray said.

'I guess so. Come on, let's go and see what the issue is.'

'You go first,' he replied. 'I'll follow up in a few minutes.'

Rita frowned in confusion. Ray then raised his eyebrows, and Rita felt his hardness against her.

'Ah,' she said, realising his issue. She laughed. 'Okay, you take a few minutes to calm down first, and then you can follow us up there. It's room ten.'

'No problem,' Ray replied, and Rita climbed down off him, making sure to give him a teasing squeeze with her hand as she did.

CHAPTER 18

'Yes, I can certainly smell it,' Ray confirmed. 'But I'm sorry, I have no idea what it is.'

After calming down, Ray had made his way up to the room and arrived just in time to hear the end of the complaint from the guest.

Mr. and Mrs. Tenant were a couple in their mid-forties. He was a tall, broad-shouldered man who had a few inches even on Ray, and she was the polar opposite—petite and lithe, with long dark hair, heavy makeup, and a tight top that accentuated her breasts.

Their room was one to the rear of the house, with pale green wallpaper, white curtains and throw pillows, and a runner that was a slightly darker green than the walls. The room also had an adjoining en-suite, which all four of them were currently squeezed into.

The smell in question was potent and not an odour that was easy to distinguish. Close to rotten cabbage, but a little sweeter.

'We will of course move you to a new room straight away,' Rita said. 'And I apologise for the smell in here. It wasn't something we were aware of. If we had been, we would have never put you in here.'

'I'll take a look at it,' Ray confirmed, knowing it would have to be done after he picked up Chloe. If the guests were changing rooms, that would tie Rita up, meaning he would be on school-run duty.

'No problem,' the large man said, rolling a thick, golden ring around one of his pudgy fingers. The couple seemed amenable and perfectly pleasant, which was a relief to Ray. Often, when guests had a complaint, they *really* let you know about it.

'Something else you may want to look at,' the woman offered, 'is that there is sometimes a draft in here. I noticed it earlier when I first picked up on the smell. I felt what I thought was someone breathing on my neck. It was the weirdest thing. Obviously, I think you may just have a crack in the walls or something where the air was getting through. It really gave me the shivers, though.'

'Thanks for letting us know. I'll definitely make sure it gets taken care of. And, again, I'm sorry. We do inspect the rooms thoroughly before check-in, so we must have missed it.'

'Oh it's fine,' the lady said with a wave of her hand. 'Don't worry too much about it.'

'I'll still look into it,' Ray promised. The smell in the en-suite was undeniable—and unpleasant. So much so that he wanted to be out of the confined space and get a little fresh air.

'How about we move you into a similar room, just on the opposite side of the house, would that be okay? You'd still have a private bathroom.'

'That's fine,' the man said. 'Absolutely no trouble.'

'We'll move your bags over,' Rita added. 'And a few drinks on the house are in order, I think. So, if you'll follow me…'

Rita led the couple out of the en-suite. Ray was pleased by the agreeable demeanour of the guests. They certainly could have made things more difficult.

Just as he was leaving the bedroom himself, however, Ray felt a sudden gust of air roll over his cheek. As it did, that vile smell suddenly intensified, and Ray's cheek tingled from the cold.

He looked around, puzzled, and felt the air with his hand. However, he could not detect any further breeze or airflow.

The guest was right. And it *had* felt like an exhalation of breath on his skin. But there was no one around, and the horrid smell soon dissipated as well.

At a loss, Ray closed the door behind him and left, knowing he could come back to this later. For now, Chloe was waiting.

CHAPTER 19

May.

It was their fifth month of living at Perron Manor and Ray was getting more and more concerned about his wife.

There were times that she would drift off and just stare at nothing, in a zombie-like state, and wouldn't come out of it unless he shook her or repeatedly called her name. She was also starting to look gaunt, with sunken cheeks, and she had to wear heavier makeup to hide the bags under her eyes.

After Ray had finished converting the two rooms on the top floor for Marcus—which involved knocking out the separating wall and a bit of redecorating—he had been allowed to convert one of the bedrooms on the mid-floor into another living area, this one for him and his family to use in the evenings. The living room downstairs was now used by the guests exclusively… when they had any.

The mid-floor living room, situated on the opposite protruding rear wing to their bedrooms, contained only a black-and-white television and some sofas and side tables, and was basic but adequate.

The family was gathered in the newly converted mid-floor living room, with Chloe reading on her own sofa and Rita snuggled up with Ray. If any guests needed them, then there was a note at reception to either come up to this room or, if it was late and there was an emergency, dial a direct number to Ray and Rita's bedroom. Thankfully, it hadn't been needed as yet. Still, he found it difficult to truly switch off and relax.

Rita was looking over at the television, though she wasn't really watching it. It was close to nine in the evening, and normally Ray liked to have Chloe in bed by then. Given Rita was looking exhausted as well, he decided they should all turn in. Only two nights ago, he had woken to see that Rita wasn't in bed with him, and he found her sleepwalking down the corridor outside of their room. He hoped not to have a repeat performance of that tonight.

'Come on,' he said, kissing Rita on top of the head. He then stood up and stretched out, feeling his vertebra give a satisfying pop. 'I think we should all call it a night.'

'Awww,' Chloe complained, 'can't I stay up a little longer?'

Ray shook his head. 'Not a chance. You have school tomorrow. We've already let you stay up late enough as it is.'

'Fine,' she huffed playfully, slapping her book closed. Ray walked over to the television set and clicked it off. He turned back to Rita, who was still staring blankly at the screen.

He moved over to her and gave her a gentle shake on the shoulder. Rita blinked a few times, and then her brown eyes focused onto him. 'Everything okay?' she asked, her voice distant.

He laughed. 'Yeah, but we're going to bed. Come on.'

Holding her hands, he pulled his wife up to her feet, then the family walked over to their rooms. Ray put Chloe to bed after reading her a few chapters from her story—one about a secret society of witches.

Once back in his own room, Ray saw that Rita was already under the covers, lightly snoring.

Good. I'm glad she's getting some rest.

He used the toilet then brushed his teeth, changed into pyjama bottoms and a t-shirt, and finally climbed into bed next to his wife. He lay in the dark, running over the family's situation in his head, wondering if there was a way to move away from the hotel and start again, should they need to. He didn't get very far, however, as sleep soon claimed him.

It felt like he'd only just drifted off when he was woken by an urgent ringing sound. Confused and disoriented, he lifted his head from the pillow. Fragmented remnants of a dream clung to him, though they were hard to piece back together. He could only remember the feeling of falling. Or, rather, being dragged down. Had he been underwater? No, everything around him had seemed too solid for that.

Other than the ringing, which he soon realised was coming from the phone in the room, everything else seemed quiet. He checked the clock, squinting through the dark.

A quarter past three.

If a guest was calling this late at night, that meant there was a problem. A *serious* problem.

He got up and walked over to the nightstand on Rita's side of the bed. Rita didn't seem to be stirring, which was a blessing. However, Ray knew that there was a good chance he was going to have to wake her anyway. The cold in the room bit at his arms, and there was the faintest of odours that seemed... off.

Ray lifted the receiver and brought it up to his ear. 'Hello?' he said into it, trying to hide the grogginess in his voice.

He then waited for a response. There was none initially, but he could hear heavy breathing down the line, so thick that it gave off a crackling effect with it. Ray waited a little longer before asking, 'Anyone there?'

'*Yesssssss*,' came the throaty reply. '*I'm... here.*' That was followed by a giggle. Ray felt a chill, and could only think that one of the guests was drunk and making a prank call.

'Is everything okay?' Ray asked, attempting to stay professional. Another long pause. Too long. 'Hello?' Ray went on.

'*I... want... you,*' the voice eventually replied in a hoarse whisper. The line was crackly and distorted. '*We... want... you... Ray.*'

Ray gritted his teeth and held his breath. He was certain it was a drunk caller now—some woman who was feeling randy with no inhibitions—though he wasn't sure which guest it was. Ray wasn't sure he wanted to find out, as he had an intensely uncomfortable feeling about the whole thing.

'*Do... you... want... me... Ray? Do... you... want... us?*'

He didn't know what the hell she was talking about. *Us*? Did this woman have multiple personalities? Or was she referring to another guest involved?

'I'm going to end the call now,' Ray said. 'This isn't appropriate. So, go back to bed and sleep it off.'

He then replaced the handset. The cold air around Ray felt heavy, unusually so, and his skin was lined with goosebumps. He realised that the call had him a little freaked out, though he wasn't certain why. Sure, it had been unusual, but even so, it was just some idiot who'd had too much to drink. So why had it unnerved him so?

He looked down to Rita, who still lay asleep—which he was thankful for. In truth, he was surprised the ringing of the phone hadn't woken her. As Ray turned to walk around the bed again, keen to lie down and put the call out of his head, the phone rang again, loud and urgent.

Ray sighed, clenched his teeth, then picked up the receiver once more, desperate not to wake his wife. He knew who was on the other end of the line, of course, and didn't even bother to say anything as he placed the receiver against his ear.

When the voice spoke this time, it was male.

'Helloooo, Ray.'

A drunken husband, or boyfriend, perhaps?

'Who is this?!' Ray asked through gritted teeth.

'We... are... friends,' the man replied. Like his female counterpart, he spoke in a whisper. 'Come... with... us. Through... the... door.'

'Look,' Ray snapped. 'I don't know what you're talking about but I'm warning both of you, you and your girlfriend, hang up the phone, go to bed, and don't call me back. Guest or not, I won't put up with shit like this. Understand?'

The only response was a mocking titter, one that rose in frequency until it became indistinguishable from the rising static that surrounded it. Soon, there was a clicking sound, followed by the long tone which signified the call had ended.

Perhaps Ray's threats had worked. He again replaced the handset but stood by the phone, watching it and waiting for it to ring again. After a few minutes of nothing but his wife's deep breathing, he was satisfied the couple had called it a night. He then turned to walk back around the bed. As he did, however, Ray stopped dead.

The door to the room was ajar.

Ray hadn't heard the handle move, or any squeak of the wooden door swinging on its hinges. There was no way a door as heavy as this one had simply drifted open of its own accord. Ray had made sure to click the thing shut after coming inside. Although, he wasn't certain if he'd actually pulled the security chain across.

But someone else had clearly opened it.

Ray's sense of unease only grew. He realised that someone could be standing just outside the room right now. The most obvious suspect was the woman he'd spoken to first, given the door had most likely been opened while he was talking with her partner.

If they were playing games like this they were either stupid or maybe a little unhinged. And that thought scared him. Had they brought Chloe into a potentially dangerous environment?

Ray strode out into the corridor, fists clenched, only to find it empty.

He quickly moved to his daughter's room but saw that the door was still closed. Ray didn't want to take any chances, so he quietly opened it —she wasn't allowed to use the security chain in case there was an emergency—and peeked inside. He saw Chloe fast asleep and under her covers.

That meant his late-night visitor had run off in the other direction.

Ray then quietly closed Chloe's door and walked back to his own room, stopping just outside of it. He could go back to bed and hope that whatever fun the couple was trying to have was now finished with. However, that did not sit right with him at all. He needed to make sure it was over, and the only way to do that was to confront the culprits and put a stop to this nonsense himself.

But first, he needed to figure out who the culprits actually were. Ray closed his eyes and tried to remember all of the people currently staying at the hotel.

He wasn't great with names but recalled there was a little old lady staying, though she was alone so Ray could rule her out. The other three rooms in use were taken up by couples, so they were the obvious candidates.

The first was occupied by two men, who said they were staying for business. However, Ray could tell it was anything but business. Instead, their rendezvous seemed like something they were hiding away from people, which Ray felt was a shame for them.

So, given the call had been from a woman *and* a man, those two gentlemen could also be checked off the list. The next couple were in their mid-to-late sixties, and prank calling didn't seem like something they would do.

Which left only one other pair, and the most likely culprits. Ray was far from Sherlock Holmes, but to him, his process of elimination had been solid. It was the only viable explanation.

Ray tried to remember the surname of the younger married couple. Was it Watson or Wilson... something like that. *Screw it*, he thought, *I'll just go with 'Sir' or 'Ma'am.'*

He'd guessed the couple to be in their thirties, and they were at the hotel for a romantic weekend away. Ray noticed earlier that they had been enjoying their evening drinks quite a bit, laughing and giggling together. If they had kept that pace going after Vincent had taken over the evening shift, they may have ended up quite soused.

He would still never have guessed they'd be the type to go on and act like naughty children in the middle of the night, but they were certainly the most likely candidates. They were staying on the same floor as Ray, but on the opposite side of the house.

He started towards their room, trying to keep as quiet as possible, but still walked with purpose—and still simmered with annoyance and anger.

He decided to try and keep it polite... at first. If they didn't listen, well, then he intended to get a little more stern.

Don't do anything stupid, a voice inside warned. Wise words, but Ray didn't intend to go in swinging. He would just make sure their behaviour improved.

When he reached the door to their room, he saw it was closed. Everything was quiet. Ray moved his head closer and listened through the thick wood, trying to pick up anything: movement, whispering, giggling, any sign of life. He heard something, but not what he'd expected.

The man inside was clearly a snorer—a loud one—and the rumbling came in constant and steady waves. Ray seriously doubted that whoever had made the call would have had the chance to legitimately fall asleep in such a short time. Which meant either the guy was faking, or it hadn't been him in the first place.

If he knocked, and it turned out the couple had genuinely been asleep, then he would have to explain himself.

But, if Mr. and Mrs. Wilson, or Watson, or whatever the hell their names were, *had* been responsible, and he just left it alone, then they would have gotten away with it. That would give them confidence to start up their shit again.

As he was internally debating the issue, quick and sudden footsteps made Ray jump. He turned his head and heard the sound continue again, from around a corner up ahead. He realised someone was heading towards the stairs of the entrance lobby.

Ray quickly hurried in that direction as well, hearing whoever it was thunder down the stairs, not making any effort to be quiet in the dead of night. That only angered him further.

Ray then broke through to one of the high-level walkways in the lobby and looked over the rail, hoping to see the person he was chasing. But the rapid footsteps had already moved out of view, and he heard a door below him slam closed. Ray followed as fast as he could, but always seemed too slow. For someone he'd assumed to be drunk, this stranger could certainly move fast.

When Ray broke through into the great hall, he stopped and looked around. The area was dark, with the night outside visible through the rear glazed doors. All was quiet. No running footsteps, no doors opening or closing… nothing. Only the sound of his own breathing. That meant the person he'd been chasing was down there with him now.

Ray looked around the space for any kind of clue and noticed all doors except the one to the basement were closed.

If a guest had gone down there in the dark, then they had put themselves in danger running down a steep flight of steps.

Stone steps, no less.

Also, all the guests were made aware that the basement was strictly out of bounds.

Ray was through fucking around.

He marched over to the open door and stepped through, into the small room that housed the steps. It was a small area, with nothing else of note except the drop to the level below. He looked down into the dark, which seemed infinitely deeper than that of the ground floor. The shadows were thick and heavy, looking almost impenetrable. The light switch for that lower level was at the bottom of the steps and had not been flicked on yet.

Ray descended, taking slow and steady steps. There was no other route out of the basement, so he was now in no rush. They couldn't get away.

The air grew colder the lower Ray got, rolling over his exposed arms. An intense chill ran up through his bare soles as they pressed down on the hard stone steps.

When Ray reached the bottom, he held out a hand and felt along the wall until his fingers crept across the light switch. He flicked it, and the lights above slowly blinked to life.

Once his eyes adjusted to the light, he looked around the now-lit area, searching for the wayward guest.

He saw the furnace, piles of wood and coal, the small cells... but could see no one down there with him.

At first.

It was only when he turned away from the cells and back to the furnace that he caught a glimpse of a face peeking out from behind the giant metal structure. The sudden sight made Ray jolt in shock.

He didn't get much of a look before the head pulled away out of sight, but it seemed to Ray that something was wrong with the person's eyes. They just looked... blank. Devoid of pupils. But that could have just been because of the distance and the poor lighting. Regardless, Ray could not dwell on that point for long, as he intended to put a stop to the whole thing now. However, no sooner had he taken a step forward did the lights cut out and again plunge him into darkness.

Ray was unsure if the bulbs had blown or if the electricity had been tripped, but he could see nothing now. Not even his own hands that he raised up before his face.

All he could do was to listen. After a few moments, Ray heard something: breathing, which was slow and laboured, almost exaggerated. It was coming from directly ahead of him, though it was hard to pinpoint the exact distance. Maybe ten feet away, he guessed.

'Hello?' Ray called out, hearing his own voice echo. He received no response and heard only the continued breathing. Ray backed up and felt for the light switch again. Once he found it, he tried it a few more times, flicking the switch back and forth. Nothing happened.

Anxiety began to creep up, and his skin started to crawl. Some primal sense inside warned of imminent danger, and his heart began to beat faster and faster.

That horrible odour he'd experienced throughout the house recently again made itself known—a sickly sweet smell, foul and rotting. Ray moved his foot back again, and his heel made contact with the lowest step. He knew he could simply turn and scramble back upstairs.

But before he did, another sound made his heart seize.

From up ahead, Ray heard a throaty cackle, immediately followed by rapid footsteps that slapped against the stone floor. They moved towards him, quickly getting louder and louder, and they moved so fast Ray scarcely had time to turn around before the sounds were right on top of him. Ray felt a blast of cold air slam into him, followed by something much more... solid.

A body. After the impact, Ray was thrown backwards. He landed hard on the steps behind him and let out a grunt of pain as his shoulders collided with the edge of a step. He felt something move over him, and those quick footsteps started again, running up the steps to the level above.

Ray turned to his front and looked up the flight of steps, hoping there was enough light to make something out, but he could see nothing beyond faint movement in the darkness.

He suddenly had a desperate need to be out of the basement, but that meant following the stranger. That thought filled him with dread. Ray couldn't fully explain what was happening, and that allowed his fear to rise.

Who the hell was that person? A guest? Someone else?

He hadn't gotten a good enough look to know for certain.

Regardless, Ray pushed himself up and ascended the stairs as quickly as he could. He stumbled a couple of times on the way and banged the front of his toes on one of the steps edges, causing him to yelp in pain. He kept going, but was limping now, thinking he may have cracked a few toes. He soon reached the top and hobbled back into the great hall.

'What are you doing?' a weary voice asked, causing Ray to jump in shock. However, he soon saw his wife standing alone in the great hall, a light-blue dressing gown wrapped around her and a confused frown nestled on her sleepy face. 'Were you just down in the basement?' she asked.

'I... yes, I was,' Ray eventually replied, unsure of how to explain what had just happened. He was breathing heavily.

'Why?' Rita asked.

Ray took a breath, steadied himself, then recapped the night's events, starting with the phone calls.

When he was done, Rita raised a sceptical eyebrow.

'I didn't hear the phone ring,' she stated. 'Are you certain it did?'

'Of course!' Ray exclaimed. 'Twice. I had *two* conversations... if you can call them that.'

'Okay, okay,' Rita replied defensively, 'it's just something that would have normally woken me.'

That was true, but Ray had assumed it was Rita finally catching up on some much-needed sleep.

'So... you didn't find whoever was down in the basement, then?' she asked.

Ray shook his head. 'No. Well, I saw *someone*, I think, but the lights went out, and they got past me and ran up here.'

'Well I didn't see anyone,' Rita stated. 'No one came running up before you did.'

Ray couldn't explain that, unless the mystery person had gotten out of the hall before Rita entered. Ray's head hurt trying to make sense of it all. He knew there had to be a logical explanation for it all, and still put it down to one of the guests causing mischief.

'Come on,' Rita said, 'let's go to bed.' She held out a hand, and Ray walked over to her and took it.

'So why are you down here, anyway?' he asked her.

'I woke up again—another bad dream—and saw you were gone. You weren't in the bathroom, so I came looking for you. I was a little worried. You normally sleep like the dead and never stir.'

'True enough,' Ray agreed, and they headed back upstairs. Ray kept himself alert, looking and listening out for anyone who may have been up and skulking around the hotel. But there was no one. Now that everything seemed to be calming down, Ray had a feeling that this was a mystery he would not solve.

CHAPTER 20

June.

The translations were now complete.

Marcus looked over the ledger with a sense of pride. Indeed, his grandfather had put in the bulk of the work transcribing the ancient book, but there were some areas that Marcus had improved upon, making things more accurate.

He'd also added his thoughts to the back of the ledger his grandfather had started all those years ago, and was now satisfied he could move ahead with the plan in a way that was safe.

At least, safe for him.

He closed the ledger and got to his feet. The room around him, formerly two rooms, now offered more space for his collection thanks to Ray's improvements. It was hard to imagine how he'd managed when it was just a single room. Though it was still cluttered, he at least had space to properly display his most prized possession.

The *Ianua Diaboli*.

Marcus moved over to the case it was stored in, lifted the lid, and then took hold of the precious book—one that contained knowledge and power beyond what most people could comprehend.

The black leather of the cover was worn, but at each corner there were pristine, gold-embossed symbols, each different from the others.

The top left marking was an eight-pointed star. The top right, a simple cross. The bottom left symbol was a triangle with another inverted triangle set within it. Finally, in the bottom right, was eight intersecting lines, arranged like the lines of a compass.

Marcus knew what these symbols were. Not just decorative markings; they had a purpose. They had *power*.

They protected the book from the influence of forces that lay beyond the natural world. Forces that may try to destroy the book, given what was inside. The protection offered by the symbols went beyond just warding off any supernatural entities, but also extended to any people that may be possessed.

Of course, as well as a dangerous and sacred knowledge, there were things written in the book that would be of great interest to those same forces. *If* they were to become aware of what the incantations could do.

After a moment's admiration, Marcus set the book back down and locked the display case again. He then made his way downstairs to the office, hoping to find Rita there. Preferably alone.

He walked down to the entrance lobby and over to the reception area, where he saw Rita checking out some guests: three women, all in their thirties. They may have been businesswomen, and were dressed in suit jackets, professional skirts and heels. Marcus stared lustfully at the women, who had their backs to him, appreciating their lines and curves.

Very nice.

Rita noticed him over their shoulders and offered a curt nod to acknowledge his presence. She still wasn't happy with him, but he didn't care. She would wear down soon enough.

She'd never really liked him, but he aimed to change that. And, luckily, Rita was very easy on the eye. She would do nicely for what he needed.

At least, he hoped she would. There were no guarantees with a plan like this.

Marcus listened in to the conversation that Rita was dealing with, and he heard one of the women talking animatedly. She was shorter than the others, and her skin the colour of burned butter.

'Well,' the woman said, 'we didn't really want to wake you and cause a fuss. But I've never smelled anything like it before in my life. It's like there was a dead animal in the room.'

'Again,' Rita said, 'I'm so sorry for that.'

'And it was *so* cold,' the tallest of the women went on. 'I mean, when we woke up it was like we were in a fridge. We could see our own breath.'

The last of the women finally noticed Marcus and turned around. She was dark-haired with Latin features and high cheekbones. Her hazel eyes fell on him, and Marcus held a confident smile.

'Hello?' she said with a frown.

'This is Mr. Blackwater,' Rita said as the others turned to see him as well. 'The owner of the hotel.'

The dark-haired woman's expression immediately softened. 'Oh, pleased to meet you. In that case,' she continued, 'I suppose you need to know that your hotel needs work.'

'How so?' he asked, feigning a genuine interest.

Another of the women spoke up, the tallest of the group. 'Last night, we were woken by someone running up and down outside our room, for one. And the radiators weren't working so the room was stupidly cold. And the smell…' She wrinkled her nose and stuck out her tongue. 'Urgh.'

Marcus forced his eyes wide, putting on an expression of shock. 'Oh dear,' he said. 'That is no good at all.'

They were so oblivious. What the group had experienced were actually *signs*, indications pointing to the presence of other entities. The women would have been safe enough, of course. While the spirits of the dead trapped in this house could influence the living, given enough time, Marcus had taken steps to ensure no person could be physically harmed in the bedrooms.

That had been done by having protective symbols drawn onto the floorboards beneath the beds, completely hidden from sight. Those markings were similar in nature to the ones on the cover of *Ianua Diaboli*.

In addition, Marcus had taken extra precautions in his own room, as well as Vincent's, by marking the Eye of Horus onto the floorboards there as well. That would ensure his and Vincent's minds remained uninfluenced.

The rest of the house, however…

Still, Marcus didn't feel like the building was quite 'alive' enough. Certainly not enough to cause anyone any true harm. Yet.

'Tell you what,' Marcus said. 'We'll knock fifty percent off your room hire. How does that sound?'

The women looked shocked but pleased, and after casting a look to each other to make sure they were on the same page, they all nodded.

'That seems fair,' the taller woman said.

It was more than *fair*, and Marcus knew it. But he didn't care. Rita seemed bothered, however, and shot him an angry frown. Obviously, her offer of compensation would have been much more restrained.

'Excellent,' Marcus went on. 'And we'll look into the smells and the cold, I can promise you that.'

'And you might want to keep your guests in check,' the woman with Latin features added. 'Get them to stop running round in the night.'

'Will do,' Marcus confirmed.

The guests soon finished their business with Rita, checked-out, then left. Ray went with them, helping with the bags, leaving Marcus and Rita alone together. He followed her back into the office after she tried to walk away without another word.

'Fifty percent was too much,' she said, circling her desk to get to her seat.

'Fair enough,' Marcus replied. 'I'll leave that to you in the future. Just trying to help.'

She shot him a look that told him his help was not wanted. Even angry, Rita had a certain allure. One he wanted to act on.

Needed to act on… in time.

'The thing about the guest running around outside of their room concerns me,' Rita said.

'How so?'

'A little while ago Ray said he heard the same thing. It would have been strange enough if it happened just *once*. But multiple times?'

'Strange,' Marcus said with a nonchalant shrug. 'Something to keep an eye on, I guess.'

'I guess,' Rita repeated, but she narrowed her eyes. 'I have to ask, it isn't you or Vincent, is it?'

'What do you mean?'

'I mean… is it the two of you that people are hearing in the night?'

Marcus laughed. 'What, you think we get up and play 'tag' when everyone else is asleep?'

'I don't know *what* the hell you two do,' Rita shot back.

'Well, I can't speak for Vincent, but I can assure you that I'm asleep in my room during the night. Not running around the hallways like a child.'

Rita continued to cast him an accusing glare, but it soon softened. 'Fair enough,' she eventually said, and then began busying herself with a file on her desk. 'It's still strange.'

'I definitely agree. Now, I came down here to speak to you about the event we have coming up in October.' He saw her jaw tense up, and he held up his hands defensively. 'I know, I know, it isn't something you're too enamoured with. *But*, I did want to check up on how the preparations are shaping up.'

'They're ongoing,' Rita replied flatly.

Marcus paused, expecting her to go on. When she did not, he prodded a little further. 'Care to go into detail?'

She sighed. 'Well, I've blocked those dates out of the diary, so we don't make any cross bookings.'

'And that's it?'

'Look, Marcus, we have bags of time until the event. We can't start building hype too early or things will fizzle out. And other than getting the word out and taking bookings, there isn't much more we can do.'

'So you've done *nothing?*' He didn't hide his disappointment. At the same time, he didn't show his true anger, either. Not yet.

Rita took a deep breath, held it, then slowly exhaled. Marcus had to fight from snarling. He took exception to her acting like he was an annoyance. She was in his own house, no less—where *she* worked under *his* employment.

After standing up, Rita walked over to the filing cabinet and pulled out a thin blue file. She then walked back, sat down, and set the file on her desk, opening it up to a series of handwritten notes on the first page.

'I've made a list of all the local newspapers and magazines where we can advertise, or at least start some stories running to help get the word out. I also have details of the editors and journalists at those publications. I've looked into magazines that deal in the paranormal and things like that, and begun to make some inroads. I'm sounding out the reporters and trying to get on friendly terms. It's no good trying to hound them for page space if they don't know who you are. So, I'm busy putting myself on their radars. When the time comes, I can then leverage those relationships. And not just for October's event, but for the hotel in general, if needed.'

Rita flicked over to another page. 'I've also done some research into paranormal groups in the surrounding areas as well, which hasn't been easy. But, I've found a few. I have to be honest, I was surprised to see they're primarily made up of older people in the upper class, so you were right about that. I have the contact addresses of the people who run these groups, as well as telephone numbers. When the time comes, they will be perfect to target with a leaflet drop and follow-up phone call. I've also—'

But Marcus cut her off. 'Alright, alright, I get it,' he said, raising his hand. 'You've done a lot of work. I don't know why you didn't just tell me all of that when I asked.'

'Because I hate people looking over my shoulder when I work,' Rita told him. 'You hired me to do a job here, so just let me get on with what needs doing.'

Rita took another breath, then pinched the bridge of her nose with her fingers and squinted in pain.

'You okay?' Marcus asked.

'Headache,' she stated. 'Comes and goes. Probably because I'm feeling a little run down. It's nothing to worry about, though.'

'You're working too hard,' Marcus told her, and he walked over to her desk.

'If I don't work hard, then I can't get this place where I want it to be.'

He came and stood behind her, looking down at the nape of her neck, which was just visible behind her ponytail. Rita rubbed a hand over the area where her left shoulder met the upper trapezius muscle, working out an obvious ache.

'Rita, I probably don't say this enough, but you really are doing a good job here.'

She let out a humourless chuckle. 'I wouldn't call it a 'good job.' The place has been more than half-empty since opening. I'd call that a piss-poor job.'

'It's a work in progress,' Marcus offered. 'Rome wasn't built in a day. You'll get us there. I have faith.'

'Faith enough to push the Halloween thing on us, even though I don't think it's a good idea?' She then turned to look at him, wincing as she did. Rita again began to rub her neck.

'Humour me with that one,' Marcus replied. 'Please. You might be surprised. If you don't mind me saying, you look tired. Not sleeping well?'

She shook her head and turned back to her paperwork. 'Not really. I wake up just about every night.'

Marcus smiled but didn't let her see it. 'Any particular reason?'

She shrugged. 'Bad dreams, I guess.'

'Sounds like stress.'

'Maybe. It always seems to be between three and four in the morning, as well. It's weird, and annoying as hell. I can't get more than a few hours of unbroken sleep.'

Excellent, Marcus thought to himself. *That will help make her much more compliant.*

'A stressed mind can do funny things,' he told her, then tentatively laid his hands on her shoulders. He felt her immediately tense up.

'What are you doing?' she asked.

'Nothing inappropriate. Just relax.' Marcus then began to firmly massage her neck and shoulders, pressing his thumbs deep into the muscle and tissue. Rita let it continue, if only for a moment. But it was a little longer than he had expected, which was a good sign.

'That's okay,' she eventually said, batting his hands away and slipping out from her seat. She turned to face him. 'Thank you, but I'm fine.'

He held up his hands in submission. 'As you wish. I was merely trying to help, but appreciate you may not be comfortable with it.'

There was an uncomfortable silence, which Rita eventually broke. 'Well, I have a lot to catch up on, so… if that is all?'

Marcus smiled and gave a polite nod. 'Indeed it is, at least for now. Have a good day, Rita.'

And with that, he left her alone, happy with how things were going.

CHAPTER 21

JULY.

Ray stretched, feeling the heat from a sliver of sunlight that had penetrated through a crack in the curtains. He yawned and slowly opened his eyes, ready for another day—another day where his wife continued to deteriorate and drive herself mad with stress.

When his eyes adjusted, however, he was shocked to see Rita standing just next to the bed, looking down at him. Her eyes were half-closed, and she swayed ever so slightly, as if in a trance.

'Rita?' he asked, quickly sitting up. 'What's going on?'

She didn't answer and just continued to stand. He quickly realised she was still asleep, but had obviously been sleepwalking and decided to stop close to him. The image of his wife looking dazed and unresponsive like that was more than a little unnerving.

Ray put a hand on her side. 'Rita,' he whispered. 'Wake up.'

He still got nothing in response. So, Ray pulled himself out of bed and tried guiding her back to her own side. She came willingly. As he led her, he glanced at the clock and saw that it was a little after six-thirty. Rita's skin felt cold to the touch and he wondered just how long she'd been standing there like that, watching him.

After helping her into bed and pulling up the covers, Ray watched Rita slowly close her eyes completely. It was only then that her body seemed to relax a little more. After a few moments, she started to breathe deeply, and he was satisfied she was completely asleep.

Ray didn't plan to wake her now. The hotel would run under his supervision today—all day, if it needed to. He would stumble his way through while his wife was resting. There was a knot of worry in his gut. Ray had already been concerned about Rita, given her exhaustion and obvious stress, but now it seemed she had taken to walking around in her sleep—hardly the sign of a contented and healthy mind.

Something had to change.

For now, though, Ray knew he needed to get ready. Chloe needed to be dressed and taken to school, and they had to be ready for today's guests as well. So, Ray took a quick shower, readied himself, and then went to check on his daughter, happy to let Rita continue to sleep.

Chloe was already sitting up in her bed, which Ray wasn't surprised to see. Nor was it a shock to find her reading. She looked up at him and smiled.

'How you doing, kiddo?' he asked. 'Been up long?'

'A little while.'

'Well, we need to get you ready for school. I'm letting your mum have a lie-in today, as she has been working really hard recently.'

'Okay,' Chloe replied and hopped out of bed. She then paused and crinkled her face. 'Is she okay?'

'She's fine,' Ray said. 'Just tired.'

That seemed acceptable enough to Chloe, and they both prepared for the day before getting breakfast. They then jumped into the family car and set off for school.

En route, Ray wanted to get more of a feel for how Chloe was coping with life at the minute.

'How's school?' he asked as a segue.

'Okay,' she replied.

'Really? Just I know you had a rough start, with kids telling you stories about the house and everything.'

Chloe just shrugged. 'They still do, and they ask about it all the time as well. But they're mostly my friends now, so it's fine.'

'Mostly?' Ray asked.

'Well, yeah. Some of them are just 'okay,' I guess. Not really friends.'

'But no one is bullying you or anything like that?'

She looked at him, frowned, then shook her head. 'No. Why?'

'Just checking up on you, kiddo, that's all.'

'Okay.'

'And what about living at the house?' he went on. 'Still think it's cool?'

The grin that broke out over Chloe's face told the whole story even before her words did. 'Oh yeah! I love it. It's like a castle!'

Ray chuckled. 'Well that's good,' he said.

In truth, though he—and more specifically Rita—had been feeling the effects of running a hotel full-time, Chloe had always seemed to enjoy it.

It was good this adventure of hers hadn't lost its shine just yet. Though Ray wasn't certain how much longer it could continue, as he wasn't prepared to let his wife continue to suffer. In truth, he'd been considering getting his family out of there anyway. *Especially* after the previous month's experience where a guest had been running around in the night. Ray hadn't felt comfortable in the building since then. But, after seeing his wife this morning, Ray knew he had to broach the subject of their long-term plans with Rita sooner rather than later.

They still had nowhere else to go, of course. Ray would just have to figure something out.

Marcus and Vincent might not be too happy, but if Ray was being honest, he didn't give a fuck what they thought.

CHAPTER 22

Rita scrubbed her skin with the coarse washcloth as firmly and quickly as she could. The water she sat in was lukewarm at best, since she hadn't had the time to run the bath correctly.

How could I have slept in for so long? And why had Ray let me?

It was past midday when Rita had opened her eyes, still feeling tired, and with a thumping headache. But when she'd sat up and saw that she was alone in the bedroom, Rita instantly knew something was off.

She checked the clock… and panicked.

Once finished in the bath, she all but leapt out, then dried herself off as fast as possible. She hurriedly changed into her clothes and threw on some makeup before running down to the reception area. There, she found Ray behind the reception desk, dressed in his suit as normal. There was no one else around, which meant she could give it to him full-force for not waking her when he had gotten up.

She marched up to him, teeth clenched and jaw set. Ray smiled when he saw her, but that smile faltered when he noticed her demeanour.

'What the hell are you doing?' Rita snapped as she walked around to the back of the desk, standing over him.

'What'd you mean?' he asked, sounding genuinely confused. *How could he be so dense?*

'It's half-past-*fucking*-twelve, Ray! Why the hell didn't you wake me up?'

He frowned and shook his head, somehow surprised at her attitude. 'Because you *needed* it,' he replied. 'Jesus Christ, Rita, I woke up this morning and found you standing above me. Do you even remember that?'

Rita stopped in her tracks, and the mountain of anger she was readying to unleash was momentarily held back. 'What the hell are you talking about?'

'This morning,' he repeated. 'I woke up, and you were standing next to my bed, looking down at me.'

'That didn't happen,' she snapped back with a frown. However, deep down, Rita knew there must be some truth to it. Ray wasn't the type to make up things like that.

'It did happen,' Ray stated calmly. 'I don't know if you were sleepwalking or what, but I put you back to bed and you dropped off almost instantly. So, like I say, you *needed* the sleep. God knows how long you'd been standing there like that.'

Rita was stunned. She had no idea. 'Jesus,' was all she could mutter.

'Tell me about it,' Ray said, then got up from his seat and guided Rita into it instead.

Her mind sprang into action. 'But what about the guests that were due to arrive?'

'Two lots are already checked in and up in their rooms,' Ray said. 'The rest haven't arrived yet.'

'And what about Chloe?'

'At school. She's fine.'

She let out a sigh of relief, but then had to wonder why Chloe was the *second* thing she had worried about, after work matters.

'Look, Rita,' Ray began, 'I think we need to have a long talk about what we're doing here.'

She looked up at him. 'What do you mean?'

'Well... is this place good for us?'

Rita wasn't quite sure what he was getting at. 'It's kind of essential, Ray,' she replied. 'We need it so we don't end up on the street. You know that.'

He nodded. 'Yes, I know, but is it *healthy* for us? For *you?*'

The point then registered, but Rita didn't like what he was implying at all. 'Are you saying I can't handle it?'

Ray quickly shook his head. 'No, that isn't what I'm saying at all.'

'Yes it is,' she shot back. 'That's *exactly* what you are saying, isn't it? Just admit it,' she challenged.

'Rita, when is the last time you had a proper night's sleep? You always look exhausted. We spend more time working and looking after strangers than we do our own daughter. And now you're getting up and wandering about in the middle of the night. How can I not ask the question? I'm worried about you. About all of us.'

Rita stood up, furious. A sharp and sudden anger cut through her, tearing its way to the surface. 'Bullshit, Ray!' she snapped. 'You're just like all the others, aren't you? You don't think I can do this at all. Do you think I'm incapable? Is it because I'm a woman, Ray? Is that why I can't do it?'

Ray looked genuinely stunned, but Rita didn't care. She knew what the truth was now.

'That isn't it at all,' Ray replied. 'You're the most capable person I know. It's just this house, the hotel… I think it's a lost cause, and I don't want you killing yourself trying to prove it's not.'

'I'm not going to kill myself, Ray,' Rita snarled. 'But I *am* going to prove you all wrong. We are *not* leaving this house.'

'Rita, listen to reason, for God's sake,' he went on, but they both had to stop when they heard the front door open.

'Just keep quiet,' Rita told him. 'More guests are here. I don't want to talk about this again, understand.'

She expected a subservient nod in response. Instead, he just stared back at her, incredulous.

Four new guests entered the reception area, and Rita greeted them with a beaming smile. 'Hello. Welcome to the Blackwater Hotel.'

CHAPTER 23

Two Days Later.

Chloe was bored.

She lay on her bed and stared up at the plaster ceiling above her, admiring the intricate patterns to the edging.

Given Chloe had read all of her books countless times before, she was starting to grow a little tired of them; it was still a little while until her birthday, where she could ask for more. Television didn't intrigue her, and it was raining outside, heavily, which kept her from going out to play in the gardens again.

What Chloe really wanted to do to help pass the time, however, was to explore more of the house. It seemed like a cruel torture to live in a place like this but be confined to only a few rooms.

The house was a mansion—like something out of one of her stories—yet she hadn't seen half of it in any great detail. And there were many places she hadn't seen at all. Going down into the basement appealed to her in a spooky kind of way, and when she'd told her friends at school about it, their eyes had lit up.

'Is that where the ghosts live?' Trevor had asked. And she had to tell him yet again that the house wasn't haunted. Even so, the one time she had been down there with her dad, it was cold and uncomfortable, so it would have been an ideal spot for a ghost.

Chloe decided that she wasn't brave enough to venture down there on her own. And besides, her mum and dad would probably ground her if they found out she had gone against their strict instructions to stay away from the basement.

There was still the rest of the house, but her parents had given Chloe similar warnings about running around. It was fine before the hotel had opened up, but not any longer.

With a house like this and all the secrets it must have had hidden away, it was hard for her to accept.

She had snuck around the house once already, without being caught. So, if she was careful, she could probably have another little adventure and relieve the boredom.

She bristled with excitement. Regardless of the consequences, the appeal was just too much. Chloe reasoned that her mum and dad were either too busy with guests, or too busy ignoring each other at the moment to really worry about her. She knew that something had happened between them recently. They didn't fight often, but when they did the two tended to keep away from each other and not talk until one of them saw sense. Even Chloe knew that wasn't the best way to resolve a disagreement, but what could she do?

In truth, she was a little worried about them—particularly her mother, who always seemed tired and cranky recently.

Chloe jumped off her bed and grabbed Emma before running over to the bedroom door. She pushed it open and peeked out into the hallway. No one was around.

She set foot outside and felt her excitement rise, trying to decide where to go first. The ground-floor had the library and great hall, as well as the kitchen, but she had seen those rooms more than enough times already. She craved something new. The floor she was on contained mostly bedrooms, which were predominantly empty, so she could try and explore those to see if there was anything cool hidden inside.

That was as good a plan as any.

She set off, creeping through the halls and checking doors, but only after listening through them to make sure the rooms were empty. Much to her disappointment, however, all doors she tried were locked.

So that just left the top storey.

Chloe knew she shouldn't go up there, but then again she shouldn't have been wandering around at all, so if she was going to break the rules, why not go all-in?

She brought Emma up to her face and looked into the two button-eyes of her doll. 'Should we do it?' Chloe asked. The stitched, permanent smile from her friend was all the answer Chloe needed. 'I agree,' she said. 'Let's go.'

On tiptoes, Chloe snuck around towards the stairs that led up to the top floor, then placed her foot on the bottom step. She took a breath and started her climb, being as light on her feet as possible. As she continued up, she knew that if anyone turned the corner at the top there would be no hiding at all. Thankfully, she made it without detection and stepped up to the top storey for only the second time since moving in.

Chloe worked her way around to her right after exiting the stairs, and at the end of the corridor saw something that hadn't been there before: a new wall that blocked off the way. It ran the width of the hallway and had a door set in it.

The wall was not like the old ones and consisted of basic plasterboard, but without wallpaper, and it had no detailed coving at the head. The door did not look as ornate or heavy-duty as the rest, either, and Chloe could only assume her dad had installed both but had not quite finished.

She knew the way ahead led to the room she'd heard Vincent and Mr. Blackwater in the last time she was up here. Listening now, she could hear something through the door—a muffled, but steady and rhythmic scratching. No, that wasn't quite right. It was more like a *scrubbing* sound.

She took hold of the handle on the door and slowly turned it, certain it would have been locked.

Instead, the door swung open smoothly and soundlessly, revealing more of the hallway beyond. With the door now ajar, the scrubbing sound became louder. Intrigued, Chloe crept onward. She saw the room Vincent and Marcus had been in last time, but that door was now shut, and the sounds she heard were coming from farther away—from another room up ahead and just around a corner. Chloe snuck around and saw that another wall and door had been put in as well, which boxed off a front corner of the house completely.

The scrubbing noise drew her attention further, and the door to the room it was coming from hung open. Chloe crept over to it and peeked inside.

She saw Vincent on his hands and knees on the floor, a rag in hand and bucket of soapy water next to him.

The bed had been pushed aside, and the carpet was pulled back across most of the room, revealing the floorboards beneath that Vincent was rubbing with a wet rag. His shirt was damp and clung to his skin, and he appeared to be scrubbing away what looked like an old, painted pattern on the floorboards.

That looks like a symbol.

A crudely drawn eye looked up to a top eyelid, though there wasn't much else left to see.

Chloe could make out the very edge of another symbol farther along, but the carpet had not been pulled back far enough to completely reveal that particular one.

The ends of Vincent's fingers looked raw and scabby. Chloe's first thought was that he was scrubbing too hard and had cut his fingers up, but the scrapes around his nails looked old.

Looking around the room, Chloe quickly figured out that it didn't belong to Vincent, since none of the clothing looked like what he wore. The outfits were mostly dark and a mix of suits, blazers, crisp shirts, and pressed trousers—a far cry from the type of clothing Vincent always wore, such as the frayed chequered shirt and chord trousers he had on now.

Chloe realised it was Marcus' room. And it seemed Vincent was doing some kind of cleaning.

He suddenly paused his movements and looked up. Chloe was too slow in ducking back behind the door jamb and was seen.

Annoyed with herself, and now panicked, she looked back down the corridor and considered running away. She could just deny everything to her parents when Vincent inevitably told on her.

'Chloe?' she heard her uncle say softly from inside the room.

She held her breath, considering her options while dreading the telling-off that was no doubt coming. But, running away was pointless. Chloe knew it would solve nothing. Her father had always told her that running away didn't make anything better; it just put off what was coming anyway. So, she might as well face up to what was in store.

'Yeah,' she replied and stepped back from around the door frame, head hung low.

'What… what are you doing up here?' he asked, still gripping the wet and stained cloth.

Chloe shrugged. 'I was just bored,' she admitted. 'So I came up here to explore. I know I shouldn't have.'

He squinted his eyes, then nodded. 'Okay. I bet it's a little bit boring for you here sometimes, huh?'

'Sometimes,' Chloe admitted. 'It's an amazing house. But I always have to stay stuck in the same old rooms all the time.'

Vincent leaned back on his heels. 'I get that.'

'Isn't it boring for you, living here?' she asked. 'You always seem stuck up on this floor all the time.'

Vincent chuckled, then shook his head. 'Boring? No. One thing about this house, if you know what to look for, is that it's never boring.'

'Really? But you've lived here for a long time, haven't you? Doesn't that mean you've seen everything?'

'I haven't seen everything yet. I can promise you that.'

She smiled, but it quickly faded. 'Are you going to tell my mum and dad I was up here?'

Vincent cocked his head to the side. 'Don't you want me to?'

'Well, I'll get in trouble because I'm not supposed to wander around like this. But it's my own fault, I guess.'

'Hmmm, that's true,' Vincent said. He then smiled, but it wasn't a happy smile. To Chloe, it was more mischievous. It looked like the tiger in one of her books, one who came and ate all the food a family had in their cupboards. 'You know,' Vincent went on, 'I could just keep it all a secret.'

'Really?' Chloe asked, surprised.

'Really. As it happens, I'm not really supposed to be in here either.'

'In Mr. Blackwater's room?'

Vincent nodded. 'That's right. He doesn't like it when people come in here without him knowing.'

'So… why *are* you in here?'

'Cleaning. You see, Mr. Blackwater isn't the neatest person in the world. He has gunk like this on the floorboards,' Vincent gestured to the markings on the floor, which to Chloe looked like more than just 'gunk.' 'I'll bet it's been here for years and has never been cleaned up. So… I'm just helping him out. Of course, he probably wouldn't appreciate it. Which is why I've come in here while he's out. Understand?'

Chloe nodded. Though, if she were honest, it didn't make a whole lot of sense. What did it matter if there was something on the floorboards, especially since the carpet covered it anyway? But Chloe wasn't about to look a gift-horse in the mouth, and had a feeling a compromise was about to be offered.

'I guess so,' she said.

'Good. So, how about this: you don't tell anyone you saw me up here —and I mean *anyone*, not your parents, and certainly not Mr. Blackwater—and I won't tell anyone that I saw you, either. It can be our little secret.'

Chloe nodded enthusiastically. 'Yeah, I can do that.'

'You have to promise me now,' Vincent added sternly. 'If we promise each other, then you can't go back on it. Do we have a deal?'

'We do!' Chloe said.

Vincent held a hand out towards her, and Chloe frowned in confusion.

'Shake on it,' he said.

'Huh?'

'You know, 'shake on it?' If you make a deal with someone, then you have to shake hands to seal the deal. It makes it unbreakable.'

'Oh,' Chloe replied, unaware of the tradition. She put her own hand into his—it felt warm and sweaty—and he shook.

'There we go,' he added, smiling. 'Now it's a *real* promise. So, you have to keep it. Forever.'

'That's a long time,' Chloe said with a laugh.

He just shrugged. 'Depends on your perspective.'

Chloe frowned, not really understanding his comment in the slightest. She then just giggled. 'You're funny.'

'Well, I do try,' he replied, and let go of her hand. 'Now you run along and I'll get finished up in here before Mr. Blackwater gets back.'

'Okay,' she said, then turned away to leave.

'And Chloe,' Vincent added, causing her to turn back. She saw him make a motion over his mouth like he was pulling a zipper closed. He then mimicked turning a key at the corner of his lips.

'Don't worry,' she said, realising what he meant. 'I won't say anything.'

'Excellent,' he replied. 'That's a good girl.'

Chloe skipped away, heading straight back to her room. She was confused at the interaction with her weird uncle, but definitely glad she had avoided getting into trouble.

CHAPTER 24

September.

Rita's head hurt. A lot.

It was another dead weekend—not a single guest. The hotel was dying, and it made Rita feel like she was trying to push a river of water uphill. Nothing she did worked and nothing was good enough.

Ray had suggested, given the weather was nice, that they spend the day outside in the garden. They worked on tidying up the space a little, which was a welcome reprieve from being stuck inside the house all the time.

She had agreed and was now kneeling on a foam pad, trowel in hand while she churned over a soil bed that surrounded one of the lawns. She picked out any weeds that she could find as she went. Given the heat, Rita was dressed in only a light summer dress—which was strapped at the shoulders—and sun hat. Though it wasn't a lot of clothing, it still felt like too much, and her brow was sweating.

Ray was manning the riding lawn tractor up and down one of the long stretches of grass, and the machine gave off a constant and annoying hum as it rolled along. Chloe was playing outside as well, free to roam around the gardens as she pleased.

Vincent and Marcus, as ever, were tucked away up on the top floor.

After scooping up another pile of dirt, movement in the soil drew

Rita's attention. In the dirt, she saw the frantic wiggles of a long and thin worm as it desperately tried to burrow its way back into the muck. Creepy-crawlies had never bothered her, but looking down at the pathetic, writhing thing, she had a sudden urge to bring up her trowel and split the fucker in half. In fact, her trowel was already rising up when Rita caught herself.

She instead reached down and pinched the small worm between her gloved fingers, then dropped it farther along the soil bed, in an area she had already finished. That would allow the little guy to burrow back to safety.

She and Ray still weren't on the best of terms. It had been close to two months since the fight, where Ray had brought up the idea of leaving the Blackwater Hotel. He wanted to cut and run like a coward.

He'd tried to push the idea a few more times as well, coming at her with what he called 'logic and reason.' Each time it had happened, she'd cut him off, telling him in no uncertain terms that they *weren't* leaving. If he wanted to, he could go alone.

Rationally, Rita knew she should try and find a way to patch things up with her husband. However, she couldn't bring herself to do it. She felt like he'd betrayed her by not believing in her abilities. It was only a few days ago that he'd insisted she 'wasn't herself at all, acting like a completely different person.'

Well, maybe she was a different person. Maybe she had become a person who was tired of being walked on.

No more.

Rita would make the Blackwater Hotel a success if it took her the next ten years. Hell, they had a fantastic home here that they didn't even have to pay for. *She* had provided that for them. Granted, it was because of her brother, but what had Ray done to help their situation in the last few years? Nothing. He was an archaic creature, lost in the new world, and fumbling around like a big, useless mammoth—aimless and ready for extinction.

Rita caught herself again, realising just how harsh she was being on Ray. *Do I really think so little of him?*

She thrust the trowel into the dirt again, angrily, though she wasn't quite sure who the target of her bubbling rage was: Ray, the world, or herself?

Rita carried on churning the muck and picking out the unwanted weeds, building more and more of a sweat as the hot sun burned in the clear blue sky. After another half hour of solid work, Rita leaned back and stretched out her spine, feeling a dull ache from being hunched over for too long. It was then, when she looked up to the back of the hotel, that Rita saw a figure looking out from one of the top-storey windows. The sight of the person shocked her for a moment before she realised it was Marcus. He raised a hand and waved.

Rita returned the gesture.

Marcus had been acting differently lately—less aloof, more engaging. It was a side to him she liked. Marcus then stepped out of view slowly but watched her the whole time; Rita realised she was smiling. She shook her head and got back to the job at hand. The sound of the lawnmower cut off, and she looked up to see Ray jump from the vehicle and start to walk over to her. She tensed up as he approached.

'Want some juice?' he asked. 'I'm pretty parched, so I'll go get some.'

'Sure,' Rita replied but offered nothing else.

After a few moments of expecting a little more in the way of a reply, Ray eventually nodded. 'Right, then, I'll be right back, I guess.'

He then trudged off. She knew she was being short with him, and also that she should feel bad for it. But she just… didn't.

He soon returned with a jug of orange juice and some glasses. The jug glistened, and droplets of condensation ran down the glass, reflecting in the sun.

He had three glasses pinched between the thick fingers of his other hand, which she hoped to God he'd washed. She had a feeling that wasn't the case.

Rita took the glass he offered, seeing the smudge of a fingerprint on the side, then let him fill it up. She took a long gulp of the tangy, refreshing juice, and it practically exploded with flavour on her dry tongue.

'Good?' Ray asked, eyebrows raised. She knew he was waiting for some kind of thanks, so she decided to throw the dog a bone.

'Very nice,' Rita said, nodding and smacking her lips together. 'Thank you, Marcus.'

She finished the rest of the drink and handed him back the empty glass. Ray didn't take it. Rita paused when she noticed his frown.

'What's the matter with your face?' she asked.

'Don't you realise what you've just done?'

She had no clue as to what he was talking about. 'I didn't *do* anything,' she replied.

Ray's frown deepened. 'You just called me Marcus.'

'What? No I didn't,' she argued.

'You did.' His voice was flat but certain and his stare unblinking.

Rita tried to remember the words she'd used, but couldn't be sure one way or the other. If she had said it, then it had certainly not been intentional.

'Well... I didn't mean it,' she eventually shot back defiantly. She then thrust the empty glass back into his hand. 'Go and give Chloe her drink, will you? It's hot out, and I don't want her to get dehydrated.'

And with that, she turned around, knelt down, and got back to work, not giving her husband the chance of a rebuttal.

Her head still pounded in pain, like something within her skull was trying to break its way out.

CHAPTER 25

Ray was seething.

Having stormed off, leaving the lawn unfinished, he headed back inside to the kitchen. He needed time to try and process what had just happened.

Ray couldn't remember ever being disrespected by Rita like that before. *Not ever.*

But ever since the day he'd expressed his concern over her wellbeing, she'd treated him as little more than the shit on her shoe.

This latest incident, however, when she'd actually referred to him as *Marcus*, was a new low.

He grabbed a whiskey glass and started digging through the cupboards. He needed something to scratch the itch. Towards the back of one of the cupboards, he found a twenty-five-year-old scotch that was unopened. Possibly one Marcus was saving for a special occasion.

Fuck it.

Ray twisted the cap free and took a sniff. He got hints of oak mixed in with the strong-smelling alcohol. He poured himself a hearty measure and drained the glass in one go, wincing as the whiskey burned on the way down. In that moment, he sincerely hoped Marcus *had* been saving the bottle. He poured another drink.

It was hardly a mature or productive way to deal with what had happened, but Ray felt like he had hit a brick wall every time he tried to speak to his wife about anything important recently. His opinions and concerns were simply dismissed out of hand. Worse, he was then accused of lacking belief and trust in his wife, which was the farthest thing from the truth. As far as he had seen, *no one* could turn this place around. Maybe it truly was cursed.

And now he had a fresh concern. Maybe his wife's slip of the tongue *had* been a simple mistake, with no further implications behind it. Or maybe... there was an underlying reason. Had she been thinking of him?

Or was he just being stupidly paranoid?

Regardless, Ray knew they couldn't go on like this. It felt like a pivotal point in their marriage, and there was too much at stake—Chloe, their mental wellbeing, and their very relationship—to let petty pride cause things to spiral further.

He was now certain they needed to leave this place in order to make things work. The house was toxic, and its poison was seeping into their pores.

Ray downed another whiskey—wincing again as he did—then replaced the bottle. He decided to try and speak to Rita again, though this time he would not let her divert the conversation. But, he would wait until that night to do it.

He was alerted to the sound of someone approaching, and Marcus entered the room.

The last person Ray wanted to speak to right now.

'Oh, it's you,' Marcus said, looking visibly disappointed. 'When I heard someone come in, I thought it may have been Rita.'

'Something you need to speak to her about?' Ray asked, trying his best to keep his voice neutral.

'Just... business stuff,' was the reply.

Just business stuff—as clear a lie as Ray had ever heard.

'Such as?' Ray asked. 'Maybe I can help.'

Marcus paused for a moment, then shook his head, almost as if the question had taken a few seconds to register. He seemed a little spaced-out. 'No, that's okay. Thank you.'

There was something different about Marcus recently, something

Ray had been noticing more and more over the past month. For one, his impeccable appearance was starting to slip ever-so-slightly: his normally brushed-back hair was now a little frazzled, and his clothes hadn't been quite as pressed or pristine as usual. Plus, he looked tired as well—a lot like Rita—with dark bags beneath his eyes.

Ray wondered if the lack of success the hotel was having was beginning to take its toll on the owner as well. Marcus had always come off like money was never an issue, but maybe the hens were coming home to roost.

'Where is she?' Marcus went on to ask, referring to Rita.

Ray shrugged. 'Not sure,' he lied. 'But if I see her, I'll say you were asking after her.'

Another slight pause, then a nod of confirmation. 'Good. Thank you.'

Marcus then turned and walked away, leaving Ray more certain than ever that he needed to get his family out of the house.

CHAPTER 26

AFTER FINISHING up in the bathroom, Rita walked back into her bedroom, only to see Ray sitting up in bed with his nightlight still on. She couldn't help but feel a pang of disappointment; she had deliberately taken her time, all in the hopes he would have fallen asleep. Then they wouldn't have to indulge in any small talk.

What the hell is wrong with you? This is your husband.

The dissenting voice was brief, and quickly pushed back down by the irritation she felt towards Ray.

He was a weight around her neck. Hell, if he could have even just looked a little more professional, then the guests may have accepted this hotel as a classy place. But no, all they saw was a gorilla dragging his knuckles.

How she wished that Marcus could make himself more available, if only to lend a little sophistication to proceedings.

Rita!

And there was that voice again, the one that was always getting in the way. Always holding her back.

'Hun,' Ray began. 'I think we need to talk.'

'Can we not?' Rita replied, padding over to the bed and slipping in next to him. She kept a healthy distance, however. Rita then reached over to her nightstand and grabbed a tube of hand cream. She applied some to her palms, and then started to rub it into the skin on the back of her hands. It smelled of butter. 'I'm tired,' she went on. 'And I have a pounding headache, so I just want to try and get some sleep.'

She hoped his silence was an indication of agreement. *Maybe he'll turn off the light and go to sleep.*

'I'm sorry,' he eventually said, shaking his head, 'but that isn't good enough.'

She turned to him with a scowl. When she spoke, her voice was laced with sarcasm. 'Oh, I'm sorry, is my exhaustion and suffering *inconvenient* for you, somehow?'

'No,' he replied. 'And that's exactly what I want to talk about.'

She shook her head. 'Not this again.'

'*Yes*, this again,' he said, but his tone was steady and soft, not confrontational. 'Honey, things aren't right here. They haven't been for a while now.'

'Things are fine,' she shot back. 'Maybe a little hard, but that's just life. If things get tough, you don't just quit and run. What kind of lesson would that be to Chloe?'

'I dunno,' he said with a shrug. 'Maybe one that shows there are more important things than work and money. Like your own health. That's a good lesson, I think.'

Rita couldn't help but grit her teeth. 'Spoken like a person who has never had to worry about either work or money, isn't that right, Ray?'

'What do you mean by that?'

'Since when have you provided either to this family? You've had a few odd jobs every now and again... when was the last time you brought us a steady, reasonable paycheque? Let's be honest; you're *hardly* the great provider.'

A dark expression clouded his face, and Rita knew her barbs had landed as intended. However, the brief flashes of anger she'd seen quickly dissipated.

'I don't want to fight, hun,' he said, turning away from her. 'I just want to make sure you're okay.'

'I *am*,' she stressed. 'So I wish you would stop going on about it.'

He again looked to her, then set a large, warm hand on her shoulder. Rita moved to shrug it off, but Ray's grip strengthened. Not to the point that he hurt her, but enough that she couldn't easily brush him away. Ray then sat forward, closer to her.

'Do you hate me?' he asked.

'What kind of question is that?'

'An honest one,' he replied. 'For the past two months, things between us have been terrible. I've tried to build bridges, but you just keep pushing me away. And I can't believe this all stemmed from me checking if you were okay.'

'No,' Rita snapped. 'That's not what you did. You wanted us to pick up sticks and move, just because *you* were having a tough time adjusting.'

'I'd stay here forever for you, Rita, if I thought it was good for us. I'd do it whether I liked it or not. And you *know* that. I don't know where this guard of yours is coming from, but can you let it down long enough for us to get this sorted out?'

'I'm done,' Rita said and tried to turn away again. His grip, however, remained firm. Using both hands, he twisted her round enough to fully face him.

'What the hell is going on, Rita?!' he pressed, raising his voice. She shook her head petulantly, desperate to be away from him. She didn't want to give him an answer. What was the point? He wouldn't understand, anyway.

But then that voice inside popped up again. *Understand what, exactly? What are you expecting of him?*

'Look, Rita,' he went on, 'if you don't love me anymore, and you don't want to be with me, then that's okay, it's your choice.' Ray's voice cracked. She turned back and saw that tears were building in his eyes. 'Even though it would kill me, I'd accept it. But you need to think about yourself. *And* your daughter. When was the last time you played with her or gave her any attention that wasn't squeezed in-between work hours?'

'I've been busy, Ray,' she shot back, but the sight of his tears starting to fall broke something inside of her.

'If you can't find time for Chloe, then you're *too* busy. It isn't working. She needs you, Rita. We both do. But you just seem to be getting lost inside the house, sinking farther away from us.' He was sobbing now. 'You're driven and determined, Rita, but while you're here, you're also angry. You've never been that way. So I *know* you aren't happy here.'

'I... I *am* happy,' she whispered, but even as she spoke, a feeling of guilt rose up, washing away whatever misplaced anger she had been feeling. 'I am.'

Ray shook his head. 'You don't smile anymore, either. Not really. And it's definitely not the smile I know.'

That was true. She didn't.

Rita *was* miserable here. Completely and utterly broken. The walls she'd built fell away, and Rita started to cry as well. In an instant, Rita's recent attitude made no sense to her: the way she'd spoken to Ray, the neglect of her daughter, and not realising she'd been falling into a pit of self-loathing and depression.

'What the hell is wrong with me?' she asked quietly in between tears.

Ray took her in his arms, hugging her tightly. 'Nothing is wrong with you, Rita,' he said. 'You've just taken on more than anyone should, and it's been overwhelming.'

That might have made sense, logically, but Rita couldn't believe it. She'd been in prolonged and stressful situations before with other jobs, but she'd never become so isolated and angry during those times. This seemed different, somehow, like she'd been on autopilot and someone else had been at the controls. Someone she didn't like.

Rita pulled back a little and looked deep into Ray's brown eyes. She saw a lingering hurt there, a pain that *she* had caused.

'You're right about this place,' she told him. 'It's a cancer. The hotel isn't going to work, and I'm tired of being... tired.'

Ray smiled. He looked visibly relieved.

Rita felt a release as well. The weight that lifted from her shoulders made her feel physically lighter.

She went on. 'You're right, we should leave. Start over somewhere.'

He nodded enthusiastically. 'Where?'

'We'll figure something out,' she replied. 'As soon as we find somewhere, and have a plan in place, we're gone.'

Ray pulled her in again and hugged her tightly. She could feel the relief in him through his powerful hold. 'Chloe isn't going to be happy,' he said. 'She loves it here.'

'She'll understand. She's a smart kid.'

He nodded. 'She is,' Ray agreed, pulling away. He brought a hand up to her cheek. 'I'm glad to have you back.'

Rita kissed him. There was still so much for her to process after her realisation, and she needed to figure out how she'd allowed things to spiral so much, but right now she was just happy to have seen the light. And she hoped that might even lead to a good night's sleep.

CHAPTER 27

Down.

Farther down.

Rita fought and fought, but those hands—grasping hands she couldn't see—continued to pull her through the earth.

She wanted to scream, but something covered her mouth. The rocky ground Rita continued to fall into changed its consistency. Soon, it was not earth that engulfed her but glistening skin. In it, mouths moaned and eyes rolled. However, even the skin that surrounded her soon changed, turning into exposed meat and flesh. The temperature continued to rise, as did the incessant stench.

And then Rita woke up to find she was standing in the dark. She wasn't in her room anymore, and she was completely naked.

It took Rita a moment to figure out just where she was, since she couldn't see anything. However, her first clue was the cold, hard ground underneath her bare feet. She felt rough and uneven stone beneath her soles. Rita could also feel a light circulation of cold air around her, and it bit at her exposed skin.

It had to be the basement.

Rita turned her head, looking around, but saw nothing beyond blackness. She was encompassed by it. *Smothered* by it.

How the hell did I get down here?

Rita had been asleep only moments ago, so there could be only one explanation. But as she was now alone in the dark, panic surged through her, further fuelled by the confusion she felt.

'Ray, are you here?' she called out desperately, hearing a meek echo accompany her words. The lack of response indicated she was alone. Rita held her arms out before her, feeling the air, but couldn't even see her own hands. She had no memory of coming down here. And to wake actually standing up... she must have been sleepwalking.

Rita was shivering, the cold around her having seeped into her bones. *How long have I been down here?*

She tried to keep her ever-rising panic under control and think logically so she could get herself back upstairs. The problem was, she had no way to navigate back to the steps.

She debated screaming, hoping her cries would draw the attention of someone above. However, if it was still the middle of the night, then her voice would have to travel up through at least two solid floors, and then wake a sleeping person.

Think.

She had to move, as staying put simply wasn't an option. If she couldn't see, Rita knew she could at least feel. Therefore, it seemed like the only option was to try to find a wall, and then work her way around until she found the steps.

So, Rita started to move forward, taking small shuffles, sliding her soles across the ground so as not to trip. Her hands were still held out before her, fingers moving and feeling, ready for contact of any kind.

It was so fucking *cold*.

After a few moments of incredibly slow progress, Rita felt her fingertips finally brush against something hard. After an initial shock, she then let her hands run over the object, soon realising it was made of wrought metal. She squatted, feeling her way down, finding that the metallic object ran all the way to the ground. It didn't take Rita long to figure out it was the furnace.

If the furnace was in front of her, that meant the stairs should be behind, just off to the side a little.

That was good.

At least now Rita was oriented. She turned around and began to sidestep to her right, eventually finding the side wall. From there, she started to follow that wall, moving forward, knowing she would soon find the steps. However, no sooner had she taken a few steps did Rita hear something from behind—a dull thud from *within* the furnace.

Her body seized, and her hands instinctively balled into fists.

'Hello?' she called out.

There was no reply. *Get a grip*, she told herself. The noise from the furnace could have been anything—the metal contracting in the cold, or even a rat that had gotten inside. *Don't let yourself lose control.*

That was easier said than done when stripped of her sight. Fear was the easy and obvious option.

Rita began to move forward again. She knew that she just had to keep calm long enough to reach the steps, and she refused to let herself think of anything else.

As she moved, the temperature around Rita dropped, seemingly with every steady step forward. To compensate, Rita tried to concentrate on how warm and comfortable it would feel when back in her bed, wrapped up in the thick duvet.

Then, sounds of whispering in the darkness made Rita stop in her tracks.

The whispering had come from her side, a few feet away from her, and she let out a gasp.

And it wasn't just one voice she heard… but multiple.

Fear gripped her, tightening her chest and making breathing difficult.

'Hello?' Rita called out again. This time, however, she heard something in response—more whispering, though the actual words were too quiet to make out.

Oh Christ, oh Christ, oh Christ.

Who the hell could be down here with her? Perhaps Vincent, Marcus… Ray?

But that didn't make any sense. If it had been any of those, they surely would have responded. Hell, none of them would have been hiding down here in the first place.

'Who's there!' Rita managed to muster. She waited. Then there was a quiet, child-like giggling.

'*We're... here,*' a young, male voice whispered back. Rita screamed.

Rita ran, no longer concerned with moving carefully, driven now by fear and adrenaline. As she sprinted, her shoulder bounced off the wall next to her and she felt a sting, but she kept going, knowing she would be soon at the steps... though she'd likely slam her feet and shins into them. Rita didn't care. She needed to keep moving. Especially when she heard more giggling from the unseen children. This time, the sounds had a distorted, almost demonic quality to them. Definitely inhuman.

Shit, shit, shit!

This couldn't be real. Couldn't be happening. There was no way...

She suddenly cried out as the toes on her left foot collided with the solid bottom step, and an intense pain exploded up through her foot.

Rita then fell face-first into the stairs, the impact driving the wind from her. She quickly became disoriented, feeling like the dark world around her was spinning. Her foot continued to ache, and Rita thought she might have broken a toe. In addition, her shins were scraped to hell, and her face throbbed where it had bounced off the corner of a step. However, she was so close to getting out, so she pushed the pain away and started to scramble quickly upwards... until something grabbed her ankle.

She screamed.

The tight grip was unrelenting, and Rita could feel only three appendages on the hand, each with sharp ends. The grip brought with it a fierce cold, and it made the skin of Rita's ankle feel like it was burning. She tried to kick against the thing that gripped her, but couldn't even move her leg. Whatever had hold of her was infinitely stronger.

'No!' she cried out, terror and panic now completely gripping her. 'Help me!'

Rita felt a nauseating breath roll over her back, one that was accompanied by a sour-smelling odour. Something was leaning over her. The whispering from the unseen children continued in the background, but now it sounded fearful. She heard the quick pitter-patter of small footsteps moving quickly—running—farther away from her.

'Please,' Rita begged, but she was then pulled savagely backwards, away from the steps and deeper into the darkness.

CHAPTER 28

'Rita?' Ray called out from his position in bed.

At first, he thought she was maybe in the en-suite, but he could hear no movement from within the adjoining bathroom. He got up and checked inside, but it was empty.

Strange.

The clock showed the time to be a little after eight in the morning, so Ray dressed himself for the day, keen to find his wife after last night's breakthrough. It felt like the real Rita had returned, and he was glad to have her back.

They'd talked late into the night, not settling down to sleep until it was close to two in the morning. He felt much better for it, especially after listening to his wife talk about her confusion over how she had been acting.

Once they were away from this house, then they could start again.

Of course, they had to find somewhere to go first, and that would not be an easy task. He and Rita had discussed using the savings they'd built up while working at the hotel, which would hopefully cover them for a few months. Rita said she would reach out to her old contacts to try and find something—*anything*—for now.

He would do the same, but also resolved to apply himself better. Whether Rita was acting like herself or not, she had made a good point about him not providing. He'd tried, of course—God knows he tried—but the skillsets of a handyman seemed to be in less and less demand these days.

That meant he would need to adapt, for the good of his family.

Once dressed, he used the toilet and brushed his teeth, and then went looking for his wife. There were no guests due that day—the same as the previous day—so the hotel was empty except for his family, Marcus, and Vincent.

Ray walked over to Chloe's room and lightly knocked.

'Come in,' his daughter called, and he pushed the door open. She was inside, reading again, but was alone.

'Have you seen your mother this morning?' he asked.

She shook her head. 'Nope, not yet.'

'Huh. Okay, you read a bit longer. I'm going to find her, and then we'll all get breakfast.'

'No problem,' Chloe said, then went back to her book.

Ray considered broaching the subject of them leaving with Chloe, but decided against it. Both he and Rita needed to be present for that, and there was no need to ruin his daughter's day so early on.

He tried to think of where Rita could be. It was doubtful she would have started work so early, given the conversation last night plus them not having any guests, so the office seemed unlikely. The kitchen was a possibility. If she hadn't slept well, then maybe she was down getting a coffee—something he suddenly craved. If she hadn't already eaten, Ray could fix them all breakfast as well.

Ray made his way along to the entrance lobby and descended the stairs. As he did, he heard voices, male and female, both of which he recognised.

They were both coming from the office area.

Ray quickly made his way down, not quite believing his ears—the unseen pair actually seemed to be discussing the upcoming Halloween event, and they were speaking with clear enthusiasm.

It can't be. Not after last night.

But his suspicions were confirmed as he walked into the office. His heart dropped.

Rita was seated at a desk, and Marcus was planted on the table next to her leaning over her as they both looked through some paperwork she had laid out on the desk.

'What's going on?' Ray asked, his tone reflecting his confusion.

But the pair kept talking between themselves, and Ray felt like he was invisible.

'I think we can count on this guy to put a story out,' Rita said, tapping a handwritten name on one of the loose sheets of paper. 'He seemed quite amenable. And if I press, I think I can get some good press in his newspaper.'

Rita was back in her business clothes—black jacket over a navy blouse, and her hair was immaculate. She looked tired, which seemed to be a normal thing these days. But today seemed particularly bad. Her skin was practically ashen, and her cheeks had sunken farther seemingly overnight.

Marcus, too, had dark circles under his eyes, though he was dressed stylishly in a black suit with a silk, navy-blue shirt beneath.

'Excellent,' he said. 'I think we move on this straight away.' He then patted Rita on the shoulder, like a pleased owner. Ray noticed that his hand lingered on after the pat.

'But I'll have the story worded as though space here is running out. Scarcity breeds interest,' Rita added.

Marcus nodded. 'Good idea.'

Ray coughed loudly, and eventually drew the attention of the pair.

Rita gave a half-smile. 'Morning. Sleep well?'

'I guess,' he said. 'What are you both up to?'

'Planning the October event,' Rita answered with an enthusiastic smile.

'We've agreed that we need to get moving on it,' Marcus said. 'I think we've all let things slip recently, so it's time to ramp up our efforts in order to make the weekend a success.'

Ray was reeling. Surely Rita wasn't *actually* going along with this so willingly, not after their talk the previous night. He wondered if she was perhaps just humouring Marcus, to throw him off the scent of their new plan to leave. It was a possibility, but he needed to get her alone to find out for sure.

'Can... can I talk to you for a moment, Rita?' he asked. 'In private.'

A frown crossed her face. 'Well, I'm a little busy with Marcus at the minute, dear. Can you give me a little time and I'll come find you later?'

Ray didn't know what to say. He wasn't sure if Rita was playing a game here with Marcus to keep up appearances, or if something had drastically changed since the previous night.

He was unsure as to whether he should comply. His first instinct was to decline and insist on a moment with his wife. He chewed at his lip.

'Sure,' he eventually said, deciding to trust her for now. 'Come find me when you're done, okay?'

Rita nodded but was already looking at the paperwork again with Marcus. 'We need to start with the leaflet drops as soon as possible as well,' she said.

'I know someone who can get them produced quickly for us,' Marcus told her. Ray walked out of the room.

What the hell is going on?

He left it a couple of hours, but Rita did not come and find him as promised. Ray had even seen Marcus head back to the top floor alone, but his wife was nowhere to be seen. After another fifteen minutes of waiting, he reached the end of his tether and walked back down to the office.

There she was, still seated at her desk, with the phone receiver tucked between her jaw and shoulder as she spoke and scribbled down notes at the same time.

'Thank you,' she said to whoever was on the other end of the line. 'I really appreciate it. We'll look out for the story. And yes, Mr. Blackwater will be able to sponsor your event in return, no problem.'

She then hung up the phone and continued with her notes.

'Rita?' Ray said, stepping inside.

She briefly looked up to him before she quickly turned back to her writing. 'Hi,' was all she said.

Is she trying to piss me off?

'I thought you were gonna come find me when you finished with Marcus. You know... so we could talk.'

'Oh, sorry,' she said, still not looking up. 'It completely slipped my mind.'

She carried on working as if nothing at all were wrong with that statement. Ray took a moment, hoping she would just look up and say, *'Just joking! Now, how do we get out of this place?'*

But she continued scribbling her notes, almost feverishly.

'Are you fucking serious?' Ray snapped, unable to hold it in.

Rita lifted her head, and actually had the nerve to look shocked. 'What did you just say to me?'

'I asked if you were serious,' he repeated angrily.

'About what?' Rita's own tone was defensive.

How could she be so dense?

'About what you're doing,' Ray replied, exasperated. 'You're ploughing ahead with that stupid thing on Halloween!'

'It isn't going to plan itself, Ray.'

'Fuck it!' he said. 'Why are you planning it at all? Do you even remember our conversation last night?'

A look of realisation then washed over her face, and she eventually nodded. 'Ah, now I see,' she answered, and gave a tight-lipped smile— one that was almost condescending.

'About that... I've been thinking,' she started, but Ray couldn't believe what he was hearing.

'Don't you dare,' he cut her off.

'Look, I wasn't thinking straight last night. If anything, I think you blindsided and manipulated me when I was feeling down.'

'What?! You can't be serious.'

'I am.' Her tone was forceful and certain. 'And I'm *not* leaving this place, not when there is so much to be done.'

Ray walked over to her, standing on the opposite side of the desk, and set his palms down on the surface. He then leant over his wife. As he did, Ray detected a strange but faint smell, one which he thought was coming from Rita. Not body odour, exactly, something more... musty.

'Tell me this is just some sort of joke,' Ray said. 'I can't believe you could flip so much in the span of one night.'

'I'm not joking,' Rita said and stood up to meet him, staring him down.

'It's Marcus, isn't it?' he asked. 'He's said something to you that's scared you, made you change your tune.'

Rita shook her head. 'Marcus has been nothing but supportive,' she said. 'Actually, you could do with taking a leaf out of his book. If you can't do that, then just stay out of my way.'

Rita then walked around the desk and past him.

'Where are you going?' he asked, struggling to keep his voice even remotely calm.

'To run an idea past Marcus, I'll see you later.'

Rita walked out of the room and closed the door behind her, leaving Ray alone, raging, and in utter disbelief.

CHAPTER 29

Vincent watched on in silence as his sister spoke with Marcus. They were on the top floor, tucked away amongst Marcus' artefacts.

Vincent's fingers felt sore, and there was a raw pain from where some of his flesh had been scraped away. He kept his hands hidden in his pockets.

Rita had just informed them both of what had happened downstairs with Ray, and how he wanted to leave. Marcus was then a shoulder to cry on and was currently comforting her with an arm wrapped around her waist.

'Then he's an idiot,' Marcus said.

'He is,' Rita agreed, nodding. 'He doesn't understand me or what I want to achieve here.'

'Some people have no vision,' Marcus soothed, and laid a hand on her upper arm, gently squeezing it. Rita did not pull away. In fact, she smiled.

It was all happening before Vincent's eyes: everything Marcus thought he wanted.

Destroying the seal in Marcus' room had clearly worked. His thoughts were not quite his own anymore.

'I'll give you two a moment alone,' Vincent said and left the room.

The pair didn't even notice; they were too busy staring into each other's eyes. With the door shut behind him, Vincent took in a deep breath, feeling both fear and electricity buzz through him.

It was small relief to Vincent knowing he wasn't ignorant to what was happening around them. Not like Marcus, who thought he was still in control of his own actions.

From his left, Vincent heard the sound of rasping breathing coming from down the hallway. He turned his head and only just kept from yelling out in fright.

There stood a woman at the very end of the well-lit corridor. She wasn't trying to hide her presence, grotesque as she was. Vincent knew she *wanted* him to see her.

The strange woman's hair was long, patchy, and scraggly, and what strands she did have were greasy and shiny. Her skin was mostly pale but smattered with dark-purple blotches. She wore a short, filthy, and torn nighty that covered little of her rake-thin frame. One shoulder-strap was undone, and a drooping and twisted breast popped free. Her legs were bent inwards at the knees, and her feet were black, with toes missing from each.

Through strands of long hair, Vincent could see her blank and milky eyes looking at him, staring with a wide gaze. Her nose was bent to one side and she had a cleft lip, which showed some yellowed teeth behind. Her breathing sounded like that of a person close to expelling their death-rattle.

What he was looking at was her soul. Or rather, a twisted version of it. And it terrified him.

Vincent looked up to the ceiling above and addressed the house, rather than the horrifying vision at the end of the hall. 'I did what you asked,' he whispered, voice shaking.

The woman then took an unsteady step forward.

'Please,' Vincent begged, close to wetting himself. He then repeated himself. 'Please... I did as you asked.'

The woman drew closer, but Vincent knew he could not flee. It would do no good. In fact, it would make things worse. The twisted hag shuffled her way to his side. Her stench—one of rotted and fetid meat—

overcame him. She brought her mouth to his ear, and he felt an icy chill radiate over him.

The woman began to whisper to him… and Vincent nodded his understanding.

CHAPTER 30

Marcus' hand was cupped behind Rita's head, and his fingers gripped a handful of hair. He tilted her chin up towards him, pulling her mouth closer. Her eyes were smouldering. She wanted him.

And he wanted her.

It was quite the turnaround, considering how things had started between them. Marcus was a man who was used to getting what he wanted, though usually without as much resistance. However, this woman had rebuffed him, even challenged him, and had been a tough nut to crack.

However, he wasn't naïve enough to think he'd actually cracked it himself. Marcus could see it in her attitude now. Hell, he could even smell it on her. Rita wasn't herself anymore. But that suited him perfectly, as Marcus needed a much more subservient Rita than the one who had first set foot in Perron Manor.

'Are you sure you want this?' he asked, and brought his other hand up to her mouth before running his thumb over her bottom lip, then gently down her chin.

She nodded. 'I do.'

'What about your husband?' Marcus' voice was a teasing whisper.

'He...' Rita took a moment, struggling with the answer. 'He isn't important,' she eventually replied, though the pause annoyed Marcus.

He'd seen a look of doubt and resilience flash across her eyes. It quickly vanished, however, and her carnal lust returned. The real Rita was once again quashed, replaced by a puppet.

A puppet for the house. One where he controlled the strings.

'Tell me how much you want me,' Marcus pushed, enjoying the control.

'I ache for you,' she whispered.

'And you'll stay here with me? And do as I ask?'

Rita gave a slow, deliberate nod.

'Excellent,' Marcus said, sliding his thumb back up to her lips. She took the digit into her mouth and lightly sucked on it, maintaining strong eye contact the whole time.

Her compliance was an important step. Marcus needed to ensure her servitude was upheld until the time was right.

In the meantime, however, he'd earned himself a little fun. Marcus knew he could have *lots* of fun with her until his plan finally came to pass.

He grabbed her hair, hard, and kissed her. Rita's tongue darted into his mouth, and he yanked at her jacket, pulling it down so he could slide it from her arms. Marcus then got to work on her blouse, lost in his desires.

They were soon on the floor, both completely naked, and Marcus mounted her.

As they fucked, neither saw the dark figure with burning yellow eyes watch them from the corner of the room.

CHAPTER 31

EARLY OCTOBER.

The eggs Chloe was eating were slightly overdone, and the accompanying bacon was soggy and stringy. That definitely wasn't the norm from her mother.

At least, it didn't *used* to be the norm. Over the last couple of months Chloe had noticed that her mum hadn't been putting in the same effort, care, or even love that normally came with her cooking.

It was the weekend, which meant no school, and Chloe's father had promised to take her out into town and then to a park, saying the fresh air would do them both good.

Her mother was too busy to go, apparently.

All three were currently in the kitchen, eating breakfast in silence. Another recent normality that Chloe didn't like.

Her parents weren't the same anymore, and she was scared for them.

'When you're ready, we'll get going. Make a full day of it,' her father said after draining the last of his coffee.

'We do have guests this weekend,' Chloe's mother said. 'Marcus and I could do with your help carrying their bags up to the rooms.'

'You and Marcus can cope on your own,' her dad said. His voice was stern, and Chloe couldn't help but note he never used to speak to her mother that way.

'Fine,' her mother shot back, before shovelling more food into her own mouth and swallowing without chewing. 'You two enjoy your day. I'll just keep the hotel going on my own.'

'You do that.'

No eye contact was made. Chloe's mother then got up and left the room without another word. She looked sickly, Chloe thought. Thinner than normal, and paler, too. Chloe wasn't sure if her mother was brushing her teeth correctly, either, given her breath always had a weird, metallic smell to it.

'Is Mum okay, Dad?' Chloe asked, a little afraid of what the answer might be.

Her father didn't respond straight away, but he looked at her with sad eyes. He took a breath. 'I honestly don't know, kiddo. We're just under a lot of stress at the minute, that's all.'

It perhaps wasn't the answer Chloe was looking for, but at least it was truthful. She could always count on that from her father.

'Are you two going to split up?' Chloe asked.

She couldn't help herself. The thought had been playing on her mind recently, so she had to ask.

He gave her a smile. A false one. 'We'll work it out, don't worry.'

The answer terrified Chloe. Because, for the first time that she could remember, she could tell that her father had just lied to her.

'Come on,' he then said, getting up. 'Let's go try and have some fun.'

The autumn breeze in the park had a chill to it, but Ray had made sure both he and his daughter had wrapped up warm. She was wearing her thick, red cotton coat, a grey skirt with white tights beneath, and a black beret hat. Ray was in his standard jeans, boots, and navy jacket.

While not bustling, the park was far from quiet, with couples walking, children playing, and dogs running free through the fallen, golden leaves. Up ahead, Ray saw a play area for kids, with a climbing frame, swing set, see-saw, and some balance beams.

'You can go play in there if you want,' he offered, hoping to break the silence between them. As they had been walking, he'd noticed Chloe carrying an expression of concern, one that had been more and more frequent recently—like the weight of the world was on her small shoulders. It reminded him of Rita.

The old Rita.

'It's okay,' Chloe said, kicking at a pile of leaves. The whole situation was breaking his heart, and it was clearly taking a toll on their daughter. Ray didn't know how to fix it.

'Nope,' he said, putting on a big smile. 'Afraid I can't accept that. I'm making it an order.'

Chloe gave a half-smile in return, but her eyes said she wasn't up for it. He knew she was about to politely decline again, but he instead scooped her up.

'Let's go!' he ordered and carried her over to the play areas.

'I don't think I want to,' she said, looking over at the swings. 'I think I just want to walk for a bit instead.'

But she didn't take her eyes off the play equipment, and Ray saw through the false reservation.

'We can walk soon enough; I think your legs need a rest!' He tried his best to sound enthusiastic and then set off running as he carried her. Chloe jiggled up and down in his arms, giggling as he pretended to trip and jostled her more vigorously. 'Oops, best make sure I don't do that again,' he joked before giving another exaggerated stumbling step. Chloe laughed again.

Ray quickly reached the swings, and out of the three that were there, only one other was in use. He carefully let Chloe drop into the free one nearest the frame. Her legs dangled through the gaps in the plastic seat, and he trotted around behind her.

'Now,' he said, 'you best hold on tight, 'cos I've got a lot of energy to burn, so I'm gonna make sure you go *really* high. Are you ready for lift-off?'

Another giggle, and the sound started to warm his soul. It may have been temporary, but for now it was a welcome reprieve.

'Ready!' Chloe exclaimed, letting the brief happiness and excitement overcome her as well.

Ray grabbed hold of the seat that supported her and pulled it back. The chains squeaked as Ray lifted her higher, all the way up to his chest.

He then held Chloe stationary for a moment. 'Three,' he bellowed playfully, beginning the countdown. 'Two...'

Chloe started to laugh, but Ray didn't wait for the 'one' and pushed her down early to surprise her. It worked, and his daughter cackled and shrieked with joy as she went sailing forward in the swing-seat, hitting the apex of her climb and getting as high as Ray's own head. Before her descent back the other way, he saw Chloe kick out her feet with a laugh, and then she came swinging back. He pushed her again, keeping the momentum going.

'Higher,' she ordered, still laughing. He did as instructed, pushing harder. Her beret flew backwards off her head after one particularly strong push, and she squealed, slapping her hand to her head but missing the hat. Ray was quick, however, and caught it with his free hand.

'Got it!' he announced, stuffing it into his pocket while using his other hand to keep her momentum going. Chloe's brown hair flowed behind her as she moved through the air, and Ray couldn't help but feel that he was having an important and much-needed moment with his daughter.

Rita should be here for this.

He tried not to ruin the time they were having. *Concentrate on the here and now.*

It was strange to think that blocking his wife out of his thoughts was a way to actually make him happy. But that had become more common since the day she'd reneged on her promise to him. Since then, it was like she'd plunged even further into the abyss after she'd come up for a moment's clarity.

'Keep going!' Chloe shouted. Ray realised he'd missed his cue, and she had started to slow.

'Aye, aye, captain,' he said, and pushed her again when she swung back to meet him.

While Ray would be crushed if he and Rita split up, he knew the one who would be hit hardest was the one they both cared about most. If Chloe wasn't worth fighting for, then nothing in this world was.

Surely Rita would come back to them for her?

Ray and Rita had been together for what felt like forever, so what was a few months on the rocks compared to all those years of happiness?

But there was only one thing that scared Ray. One thing he wasn't certain they could come back from. Rita had been spending a lot of time with the owner of the hotel recently... and that worried him. In the early days, Marcus had almost been a phantom presence in their lives. Now, however, it seemed like Rita spent more time with him than she did her own family. And if the two of them were...

Ray didn't even want to think about it. He'd always trusted his wife completely. Surely she wouldn't be so selfish as to do something like that, regardless of any trouble they were having?

After ten more minutes on the swing, Chloe decided her time was up. 'I'm starting to feel a little sick,' she said.

Ray wasn't surprised; she'd been going non-stop for quite a while, so he caught the swing and slowly lowered her down to a stop before lifting her out. She was a little unsteady, legs wobbling a little, but soon found her footing.

'You okay?' he asked, squatting down to her level. After she took a few deep breaths, the colour started to return to her pale cheeks.

'I'm fine,' she said with a toothy smile.

'Glad to hear it. How about we go into town and get a cup of hot chocolate?'

Her enthusiastic nod was answer enough, and Chloe skipped ahead as they walked back to the car.

The day out with her father had been a great one, and Chloe didn't really want to come home. As much as she loved the house, things were always frosty and cold there now.

No one seemed to smile or laugh anymore. Even her father, who had been chatty and happy all day, had quieted down again as they drew closer to the house.

The car rolled down the long driveway, and Chloe could hear the gravel crunch and shift beneath the tires. The sight of the building was still something Chloe savoured, especially from this distance. Its three peaks stood tall and proud against the backdrop of the security wall and the hills and trees beyond.

With all that was going on between her parents, she felt like their time at the house was drawing to a close. Chloe dearly hoped her parents would fix things so they could go back to how things were when they first moved in. But, she knew that wasn't likely.

When they drew closer to the house, Chloe noticed something in a window on the top floor. It was a figure, looking out—possibly Marcus, her Uncle Vincent, or even her mother. Whoever it was, they were too shrouded in shadow to make out clearly. It did confuse Chloe why the person just stood motionless like that and didn't wave. Chloe considered waving first, or even pointing the person out to her dad, but after staring for a few more moments, the strange figure simply wasn't there anymore. They hadn't stepped from view, just blended into the darkness, which made Chloe unsure if she had even seen anyone there in the first place.

Obviously not.

Her father pulled the car to a stop in the carport and switched off the engine.

'Ready to go back in?' he asked her, forcing a smile.

'Yeah,' she lied. Chloe wanted nothing more than to go back to the park with her dad.

CHAPTER 32

LATER THAT MONTH.

Marcus was busy with Vincent's sister again. Vincent heard them fucking in Marcus' room when they no doubt thought everyone else was asleep.

But Vincent didn't sleep too much anymore.

Which, he knew, was true of Rita and Marcus as well. Vincent knew *exactly* why that was, though the other two were ignorant to the truth.

While Marcus was... occupied, Vincent took the opportunity to sneak into the room upstairs, using the keys he had stolen from Marcus' room earlier. He moved to the door of the locked-off area, noticing the walls Ray had recently put up were still undecorated.

The Halloween event was quickly approaching, and while the hotel wasn't full, the majority of rooms had been booked out. Hopefully, the number of souls staying that weekend would be enough for what was needed.

Vincent unlocked the door and opened it, moving to the area where Marcus stored his collected treasures. Vincent flicked on the light.

The true value of the many artefacts inside was probably far in excess of even what Marcus had estimated, especially when considering the true power contained within the room. Vincent had been made aware of the power mainly by the house itself. It spoke to him nightly through its avatars, their words like worms burrowing into his brain and infesting his thoughts.

There was one thing in particular that the house was interested in. One which spoke to its true nature.

Ianua Diaboli.

He walked to the display case that contained the book, lifted the lid, and took it out. Not for the first time. There was something about the tome, something that drew him back again and again; a compulsion just to hold it and touch it that Vincent couldn't explain. The author of this ancient book was, as far as Vincent knew, unknown. As was the book's place of origin. That it was written in Latin was probably some clue, of course, but neither he nor Marcus had been able to find out much in the way of its history, beyond what Marcus' grandfather had uncovered.

Vincent leafed carefully through the pages, knowing which in particular he was headed to, without actually being able to understand what was written.

Marcus had never let him near *Ianua Diaboli* before, so he always had to sneak in here in the dead of night just to be near it and fulfil the compulsion. He was allowed to inspect and study all other artefacts in the room, but not the book. Vincent had respected that at first, even gone along with it, as he was just so happy to be learning more under Marcus' tutelage.

He was thrilled to be in a house like Perron Manor—one that was alive with spirits from beyond. It was both terrifying and liberating. Knowing there was more to life than just death gave Vincent purpose. Over time, he'd actually begun to have experiences with entities and had seen spirits roaming the halls. But he soon also felt their insidious nature, as well as their cold presence. Vincent had even laid eyes on the more powerful and evil things that existed in the house as well. Not just the souls of the dead, but demonic beings that had never truly lived. Not in this world, anyway, even though they desperately wanted to.

Through snippets of what Marcus divulged, Vincent had slowly learned more of the nature of the house and how it tied directly to *Ianua Diaboli.*

Vincent had needed more. He grew resentful of the fact that the most powerful artefact in Perron Manor was being kept from him. It wasn't *fair*.

It was an incident in the basement, midway through the previous year, that changed things for him. Vincent had been down in the depths of the house alone, hoping to catch a glimpse of the burned man who lived in the furnace; he was the one who screamed in agony every time the equipment was fired-up as it boiled his blood. Instead, he saw something else. A yellow-eyed demon, only partially visible from the shadows. It spoke to Vincent without moving its mouth, but said its name was Pazuzu.

It was a demon Vincent had heard about.

He had been terrified in that moment, but the entity put forward a proposition that offered knowledge, as well as eternal life. Vincent just had to destroy the protective seals in his room.

Vincent had struggled with the offer for days after, knowing there were inherent dangers, but he was equally frustrated at being held at arm's length by Marcus. Blackwater had cast doubt over his ability and aptitude regarding the dark arts.

Eventually, even though it filled him with terror, he had eventually complied. From that point on, his room was no longer protected from Perron Manor. The effect of the house, subdued so far thanks to the Eye of Horus keeping it at bay, was unleashed, like water finally surging past a broken dam. Perron Manor had already tasted both him and Marcus, so with the last obstacle removed, its subsequent hold on them was quick to tighten.

Vincent was well aware he was possessed. Evidently, the house did not care that he knew. Was Vincent so subservient and easily controlled he wasn't considered a threat? Marcus, in contrast, seemed ignorant to his situation.

Soon after Vincent's compliance, he started to see more and more of the spirits in the house, and the demons as well. Though the entities terrified him, they never tried to hurt him.

Slowly, the spirits began to speak to Vincent. His dreams changed. He realised what he had to do.

It was at that point Vincent had gained the courage to go against Marcus' wishes and look at the book.

Vincent recalled the very first time he held *Ianua Diaboli*. He was instantly beguiled, though he understood nothing of the foreign language written within its pages. After leafing through the book, he'd stopped at a section titled *Impius Sanguis*, immediately realising there was something special about it. He'd then moved on to the back of the book, and when he got to the last passages titled, *Claude Ianua*, a sudden revulsion overcame him.

Just looking at the words, as well as at the drawings that littered the pages—mirrors and pools of water all with horrible things in their reflections—was enough to make him nauseous. He was forced to close the book as a sudden and unexplainable *hate* rose up within him, aimed at those particular pages and the simple ritual narrated on them.

However, that made no sense, given he couldn't even understand the words.

Vincent knew it wasn't really *his* hate that was being channelled, but that of the house. He was compelled to rip out the offending pages and destroy them, but was physically unable to. Something stopped him. A protection on the book, of some kind, tied to the symbols on the cover.

Over the months that followed, he'd tried many times to tear out those pages, or alter the markings on the cover, but could not. The symbols on the cover stopped any who were possessed from destroying or altering the book.

Out of curiosity, Vincent flicked to the back of the book again to try once more, though the result was as expected. He took one of the pages and tried to pull... but his body did not respond.

So instead, Vincent just continued to enjoy being in the presence of the book. It lent him a sense of peace he couldn't seem to find anywhere else in the house.

He knew he could not indulge in that peace for long. Marcus and Rita would be finished soon, and preparations for the ritual of *Impius Sanguis* needed to be carried out. Vincent had no doubt that Marcus would seek *him* out to complete the more menial tasks involved.

Vincent set the book back in its case and laid a loving hand on top. He noticed that his fingers were beginning to look worse. One nail on his left hand had come away completely, and angry red flesh showed through where strips of skin had been rubbed away. Vincent knew he should stop the scratching, but just couldn't. It was too much of a release.

He left the room and walked back to his small, sparse bedroom. Only twenty minutes later, there was a knock on his door.

'Come in,' he called, already knowing who it was. The door opened, and Marcus stepped inside, wearing a dark blue t-shirt and black jogging bottoms. His feet were bare, and his normally pale cheeks were still slightly flushed. Marcus moved into the room and closed the door behind him before walking over to Vincent and sitting down next to him. Vincent couldn't help but notice that his 'friend' smelled of sweat and sex.

'How are you doing, Vincent?' Marcus asked.

'Okay,' Vincent replied.

'Glad to hear it. I wanted to come by on the off-chance you were still awake.'

'I don't sleep much,' Vincent said in response.

Marcus nodded. 'Me either, at the moment. I've tried to figure out why, and I think it is because of what is coming. I suppose I'm nervous. And excited.'

You're a blind idiot, Vincent thought, and wanted to say it aloud. While they were both puppets now, at least Vincent could see his strings.

The actual response he gave was much more sympathetic. 'I guess that makes sense. You know… you never did tell me the full extent of what is going to happen here.'

'I know,' Marcus said, looking ahead, his eyes lost in thought. 'But the time has come to indulge you, I think. I need your help to see it through.' He then turned to Vincent. 'Will you help me?'

'Of course,' Vincent said.

'I'm glad to hear that. I think you know that the book I treasure so much—*Ianua Diaboli*—has a connection to this house. Or, rather, for places like this house. The book was written to utilise a power that exists at certain points in our world. Points that have a connection with—'

'Hell,' Vincent finished.

Marcus looked surprised. 'That's right. How did you know that?'

Vincent smiled, then lied: 'The translation of the title. Or, at least, one of the possible translations. A Devil's Door. I've heard of such things.'

The house. The house has shown me.

'Impressive,' Marcus said, eyebrows still raised. 'Maybe I underestimated you and your knowledge. But yes, that's right. The house is built on one of those gateways. That is why it's special.' Marcus then looked at the walls of the room, admiring the structure around him. 'My grandfather only learned what this place truly was after finding *Ianua Diaboli*, and that is why he moved ahead with buying the house. But… he was too afraid to use the power himself. I will make no such mistake. That is the reason we turned the house into a hotel.'

'To get bodies in here,' Vincent said in confirmation. 'Souls the house can feed off of.'

'Correct. Even if it is just tiny bites, for now, the constant stream of fresh souls are enough to keep things building and growing. And that is needed for a ritual in the book. *The* ritual, as far as I'm concerned. Vincent… I need you to know something. I won't be here after the ritual is done.'

'You won't be at the house anymore?'

'That's… complicated. However, as a thank you, I've added you into my will. You are to be the sole heir of the house, which you will inherit after I'm gone.'

Vincent made a show of looking surprised. 'Wait… are you saying you intend to die? Is that part of the ritual?'

'It is. And it is unavoidable,' Marcus said. 'I have to go through with it. Though, I can promise you it won't be the end for me. Even so, I need someone here in the house to keep it safe. A gatekeeper, if you will, until the time is right. That gatekeeper is you.'

'Thank you,' Vincent said. 'You have no idea how much that means to me. But, Marcus… does it have to be that way? I mean, dying is a big price to pay.'

It was all lip-service. They were both just acting out a charade, even dancing to the same tune, but Marcus wasn't actually aware of it. Vincent could only assume the house controlled people in different ways, and the strong-willed were easier to fool if they believed they were still in control. Not so with himself, he knew, as he had submitted out of fear.

'Believe me when I tell you,' Marcus went on, 'the price is *nothing* compared to the reward.'

'So, what can I do to help?' Vincent asked, though he already knew the answer.

'We need to get the boundaries for the ritual set up. To do that, we need to mark the house with certain symbols.' He reached into his pocket, pulled out a crumpled piece of paper, and unfurled it. It showed a hand-drawn circle, which had a large dot in its centre.

'A circumpunct,' Vincent said.

'Correct.'

'I thought that was a sign of God. Order withholding chaos.'

'It is. And that is why it needs to be drawn on the *outside* of the house. The dot represents the chaos of the house, and the outer ring would represent the outer world.'

'So we contain the chaos within.'

'You're quick on the uptake,' Marcus said. 'I need you to draw this at specific points. But, there is one more thing… each marking will need blood added to it. Just a drop, from a pinprick in your finger or something.'

'That is no problem,' Vincent said, taking the paper.

'Also, the protective markers in most rooms—besides mine, yours, and the study upstairs—will need to be removed.'

'I can do that.'

'Excellent. Now, I have to ask something else. Are you feeling okay?'

Vincent lifted a confused eyebrow. 'What do you mean?'

'Well, we need to be sure we are… pure, for the ritual to work as expected. My blood will be spilt, and your blood is being used as well.'

'What do you mean by pure?'

Vincent knew *exactly* what Marcus meant, but played dumb in order to keep this dance going and make sure Marcus still felt in control.

'I've ensured our rooms are protected in this house, as you know, so that our minds are not poisoned by the house. My plans could get a little… derailed… if it turns out either of us are not fully in control of ourselves. Do you understand??'

Vincent gave him a look of realisation, then nodded. 'I understand,' he said. 'But I'm fine. I still feel myself. Do you?'

Marcus nodded with misplaced confidence. He even gave a condescending chuckle. 'I'm fine, dear boy,' he said, patting Vincent on the back. 'I know what I'm doing. Believe me, I'd know if something was wrong.'

It took everything Vincent had to keep from laughing at the poor, misguided fool.

'Then I'll get to work,' Vincent said, standing up and waving the scrap of paper.

'Now?!' Marcus asked.

'Perfect time. No one is awake to see me doing it. Best not to raise any suspicions with Rita or Ray.'

'Good thinking,' Marcus said and stood up as well. He held out his hand. 'Thank you for everything, my friend.'

They shook. 'No problem,' Vincent replied, almost taken aback by the man's ignorance. 'It has been my pleasure.'

CHAPTER 33

O***CTOBER*** 29***TH***.

The weekend was upon them.

Rita and Marcus had worked so hard to reach this point and now it was time.

Ray had intentionally kept out of it recently; his focus instead had been on reaching his wife again. Mostly. However, he'd failed to reconnect with her and had been routinely ignored. Every now and then he'd seen flashes of regret and sorrow in her eyes, but they had been brief.

She had given him a promise, however, though he didn't put much stock in that.

'Just let me get Halloween out of the way,' she'd said. 'Let me make a success of at least *one* thing in this hotel, and then I'll be happy. After that, we can hand our notices in to Marcus and leave here. I promise.'

She hadn't been as emotional and readable as that night the previous month, where she'd broken down crying; instead, she appeared guarded and robotic, but at least it was something. It was a promise Ray could cling and hold her to. So, he'd reluctantly agreed to that.

It was early, and they had all gathered in the office—even Vincent and Chloe, who had tagged along out of interest. Marcus stood before the group with his hands behind his back and serious expression on his face, like a general about to give orders to his men.

'This is it,' he said, wearing a prideful smile. 'All we've worked so hard for. We may not be fully booked, but thanks to Rita's ingenuity, guile, and persistence, we have more guests staying this weekend than ever before. So,' he looked directly at Rita, who was beaming, 'I want to say a big and personal thank you to you, Rita. This is all because *you* made it happen.'

Marcus then started clapping enthusiastically, clearly wanting everyone to join in, but it just came off as awkward. Still, Ray didn't want to simply stand with his arms folded while another man showed appreciation to his wife, so he joined in as well. Chloe followed, as did Vincent, though he seemed less than enthused. Since Ray's arrival ten months ago, he hadn't really seen too much of Vincent, probably even less than Marcus. Even though Vincent was Rita's brother, he'd been little more than a ghost to them, popping up every now and again but always staying in the background. A non-entity of a person, in Ray's eyes.

Still, Ray preferred him to Marcus when all was said and done.

'Now,' Marcus went on, raising a hand to bring the applause to an end, 'we need to stay focused. All the hard work needs to continue for just a few more days. Later this afternoon our guests will start to arrive, and things are going to get busy. There will be a lot of requests and demands for you all to deal with. I myself will take the lead on the events we have planned.'

Ray raised an eyebrow. 'What kind of events?'

'It was Marcus' idea,' Rita replied with a smile. 'Give the people what they want. This is a paranormal weekend, after all, and since Marcus and Vincent have a huge amount of knowledge in that field, Marcus will be running workshops and tours.'

'Workshops?' Ray asked, still not quite understanding.

'You know,' Marcus cut in, 'Ouija board sessions, vigils, and I'll even go over the history of the house and its supposed paranormal influences.'

'But you said you didn't believe in any of that rubbish,' Ray retorted.

'I don't,' Marcus snapped, and Ray saw him bristle. 'But like Rita said, we must give the guests what they have paid for. Understand?'

Ray shrugged. 'I suppose so.'

Marcus glared at Ray for a moment, then turned to the others and forced a smile. 'So, I want everyone looking their best and ready to roll no later than two o'clock this afternoon. You need to be energised and battle-ready.'

'We will be,' Rita replied, looking at the hotel owner like he was some kind of fucking idol. It sickened Ray seeing his wife act like a cheerleader, and he wasn't naïve enough to fully trust she would go through with her promise.

But he had to give her the benefit of the doubt... for now. If it turned out to be a lie, then he knew their marriage was truly in the gutter. There would be no way back, despite how much he didn't want that to be true.

Ray had also needed to stifle a laugh when Marcus had instructed everyone to look their best.

The nerve of it.

While their boss had access to some truly nice clothes, they didn't hide that the man still looked ill; he was gaunt, pale, and absolutely exhausted. But, the same could also be said for Ray's wife.

'Rita, you will welcome the guests and man the reception desk,' Marcus ordered and she quickly nodded in assent. 'Ray, you will take the guests' bags up to the rooms on arrival. Vincent will help you. I'll need you both working as quickly as possible, because I think people will start to arrive thick and fast.'

'No problem,' Ray answered, though his tone was nonchalant. He then looked to Vincent. 'Right, partner?'

Vincent gave a blank expression like he wasn't even listening. 'Yeah, I guess so,' he said, which hardly filled Ray with confidence. Still, he only had to last one more weekend, so he didn't mind picking up any of Vincent's slack if he needed to.

Ray had made a decision: no matter what Rita said come Monday morning, whether she was coming with him or staying, Ray was going to leave this place forever.

And he was going to take Chloe with him.

CHAPTER 34

CHLOE HAD BEEN GIVEN strict instructions for the weekend, and her mother had been firm and uncompromising when dishing out the orders.

Her father, however, had been a little gentler in his explanation: that the weekend was going to be extremely busy in the hotel, with lots of people wandering around. Lots of strangers. He'd told her it was very important that Chloe kept to her designated rooms.

She'd agreed to do as she was told. And she had fully intended to stick to that promise, too. However, the guests had been arriving in a constant stream for the past hour, and Chloe realised she was going to find it difficult to stick to her word.

The whole thing was just too exciting!

There was a buzz throughout the building, one that made it feel somehow *alive*. Chloe was used to experiencing the hotel as a big, empty, and even cold place. It always had the feeling of being an echo of the past. Large and grand, but somehow… lonely. Now, however, with the chatter and noise of people filling almost every room, the atmosphere was different.

Chloe couldn't help but constantly peek out of her room when she heard people walking close to it and passing down a nearby corridor. Adults dressed in the finest clothing—pressed suits and beautiful dresses—who all seemed thrilled to be here marched past her room in a never-ending line, all being shown to their rooms by her father. They chatted enthusiastically about what the weekend ahead would hold.

More voices approached, and again Chloe cracked open the door to her room and looked out. Through the gap, she could see her father pass by her line of sight, struggling with three large bags while sweating and red-faced. Then, she spotted an elderly couple follow behind. Chloe heard a brief snippet of their conversation.

'I don't think we'll see anything,' the man said. 'But it should be fun all the same.'

'Oh tosh,' the lady replied. 'I've heard a great deal about this house. So I'm hoping for the best.'

Chloe knew what they were referring to. Her father had prepared her for what was happening that weekend and the reason everyone was coming. Because, he'd said, it turns out that even some grown-ups like a good fairytale.

When Chloe had asked what that meant, he'd gone on to explain that the people who were coming all had one thing in common: they believed in things that simply didn't exist.

Ghosts.

Chloe knew what ghosts were, but her dad had gone to great lengths to make sure she understood they weren't real.

'Then how come some grown-ups believe in them?'

He'd paused. 'It makes handling certain truths easier.'

She'd asked what that meant, but he said he'd explain it another day, when she was older. What was important now, he'd said, was that there was nothing to be scared of in the house.

But Chloe wasn't scared at all. She'd fallen in love with the house since the first day they'd moved in.

Still, she wished she could be a part of what was happening right now. Fairytales or not, everyone seemed excited, and the house was full of happy sounds—it seemed like one big party. She wanted to be a part of it, not hidden away in her room while everyone else had fun.

So... would it really be so bad if she snuck out again to see what was going on? She'd become quite adept at that in her time living here, and it had worked well for her so far. Sure, with more people around there was much more chance of her getting spotted. But, considering most people wouldn't even know who she was… was that really a problem?

Chloe just had to make sure her mum, dad, Uncle Vincent, or Mr. Blackwater didn't see her.

After a few moments of deliberation, she made up her mind. She *would* be part of what was happening this weekend. And, if she got caught, then so be it, she'd accept the punishment. With a tingle of excitement, and after waiting to make sure her father was far enough away to not be a concern, Chloe left her room and pulled the door closed behind her.

CHAPTER 35

To say that Patricia Cunningham was looking forward to the weekend ahead was an understatement.

Everyone had gathered downstairs in the great hall, and what a hall it was—an impressive space with a high, ornate ceiling, stone flooring, and aged but elegant wallpaper. Patricia could practically *feel* the history seep out of the surroundings. Tables had been set with plates and cutlery ready for the evening meals, but one table in particular looked different from the others, which were draped in tablecloths. This one looked very old, made from fine oak, and was much bigger than the others. If possible, she aimed to be sitting there when the food was served.

Patricia had been enamoured with the building from the moment she and her best friend Betsy had been chauffeured down the driveway and had seen the three peaks of the proud, old house come into view. Such a magnificent and stately home would not have been out of place in her native Scotland.

She and Betsy had travelled down to the hotel from their home on the borders. It had been a relatively short trip, made easier thanks to their chauffeur Norm, who was staying a few towns over and would be back on Monday morning to take them home.

Patricia had first heard of the event through a paranormal society she was a part of. What lay beyond death was a subject that had always interested her, but it had become something of an obsession since the passing of her dear husband fifteen years ago. Betsy, too, was in a similar position, having lost her partner six years prior. Patricia was not a naïve person and knew one of the main draws the subject held for her was one of comfort; she wanted to know that maybe her Andrew still existed out there somewhere, instead of just having been snuffed out of existence completely.

Both Patricia and Betsy had worn their finery tonight—it seemed like the occasion for it—with Patricia in a royal-blue, strapless gown, one that suited her busty frame and hung down to her feet. It was embossed about the chest with a delicate floral pattern over see-through netting that showed a little skin beneath. Despite being in her mid-sixties, Patricia thought she was ageing well and was pleased with how the new dress looked on her, especially when complemented by her makeup and greying-blonde hair styled in an elegant and sweeping bun. She was relatively short, standing at around five-foot-six in the heels she was wearing, but she always ensured her posture was confident. Her mother had always taught her that a straight back and high chin would make her appear taller in other peoples' eyes.

Betsy, who was taller and thinner, was dressed a little more conservatively, with a silk blouse and a long, ankle-length black skirt. The outfit matched well with her dyed, curly dark hair.

People were chatting and mingling and enjoying a few glasses of complimentary champagne. It was nice to be surrounded by people who shared her interests and beliefs. But as good as this socialising was, Patricia was eager to kick the weekend off proper; they were all waiting for the owner of the hotel—Mr. Marcus Blackwater—to make an appearance and officially welcome them. They had been told he was going to give a speech to go over what they could expect in the coming days.

She and her friend were currently talking to a nice couple who had travelled up from Newcastle in the north-east of England. Their thick Geordie accent was sometimes difficult to understand—with lots of abbreviations that confused her—so she found herself smiling and nodding a lot.

Finally, Patricia detected a sudden change in the atmosphere and the talking around her dulled. Heads started to turn, and Patricia looked in the direction everyone else was. She saw a well-dressed man making his way through the crowd. He had dark, brushed-back hair, a smart black suit, and piercing blue eyes. He was certainly attractive, though he had a quality about him that seemed a little... tired. He was gaunt, with an ashen pallor. The man carried a glass of champagne, gripped at the stem.

She knew it was Mr. Blackwater.

He was followed by the young lady that had checked Patricia and Betsy into the hotel earlier that day. The woman carried a footstool lined across the top with plush red velvet. She was a very pretty girl, though she seemed afflicted by the same weariness as her boss.

Perhaps they were all working too hard here.

Mr. Blackwater moved close to the rear door that looked out over a courtyard, and the lady put down the footstool. Mr. Blackwater then stood atop it, elevating himself above everyone else. He was handed a butter knife and, though it wasn't needed, he tapped his glass with it, signifying he was about to speak. The last of the small murmurs in the room faded to silence, and an easy and charming smile crossed Mr. Blackwater's lips.

'Ladies and gentlemen,' he began, 'welcome... to the Blackwater Hotel!' A polite round of applause rippled around the room. The owner waited for it to peter out before carrying on. 'I'm so glad you could all join us this weekend, and I trust your surroundings are to your liking. But as fine a building as this is, I think we all know the reason you are here... and what you hope to see.'

A few people cheered, and there was another smattering of clapping. Patricia could sense the energy in the room. That everyone here could all get so excited over their shared passion was nice, and it gave a sense of camaraderie that, in truth, Patricia hadn't experienced a whole lot of in her life. It made her feel like she belonged.

'Now,' Mr. Blackwater continued, 'some of you may know a little about the building already, and some of you may not. But the history of the stately home is a long and extremely interesting one. It was built all the way back in the twelve-hundreds but has seen much in its lifetime, including more than its fair share of death. It is supposedly cursed, and well known in certain circles for being one of the most haunted houses in the country. Well, after living here for a while now, I can confirm that to be true. I have personally experienced things here that I still can't quite believe. I am not just talking about creaking doors or unexplainable noises, either. I have actually *seen* the spirits of the dead walking the halls.'

There were a few gasps, and Patricia felt her buzz of excitement grow. *This could be it.* She had been hoping this house could provide what so many other locations had failed to deliver.

Hoping... but not really believing it would be so.

However, if their host was to be believed, then maybe, just maybe, the weekend ahead would give Patricia the answers she so desperately sought.

'We have a whole host of activities for you to indulge in during your stay here,' Marcus went on. 'Those, however, will begin tomorrow. Tonight is about fun and getting to know each other. Food will be served shortly. So please, eat and drink your fill. But!' and he held up a finger of warning, 'make sure you are all fit and ready for what tomorrow brings.' He smiled. 'So no hangovers.'

The gathered crowd chuckled.

'Can't promise that!' someone called out, drawing more laughter.

'Well, don't say you weren't warned. Now, I've spoken enough. Speeches are boring, and there is fun to be had. I will be here for a little while longer for those that wish to speak to me, but I do plan on getting an early night. I ask that we meet here after breakfast is served in the morning, and from there I will lead a tour around the building and give you a little more of the history.' He then raised his glass. 'To a fantastic weekend.'

Everyone's glass raised in unison. 'Here here!' Patricia said, and took a sip of the delicious champagne, feeling almost giddy.

CHAPTER 36

Ray had to force a polite smile as the guests all toasted along with Marcus like he was some kind of celebrity. He also had to watch as his wife looked up at the man in admiration as well.

It turned his stomach. As did all the rubbish that Marcus had spouted about the house being haunted. Ray had lived here for two months short of a year, and despite a few odd things that could surely be put down to the building being old, he had seen nothing that would back up Marcus' claims.

It was all bullshit, said only to play to an eager crowd.

Ray stood out of the way at the back of the room. His body ached, especially his arms and legs after a hectic day of checking in guests and humping their bags up to their rooms. He'd then had to set up the great hall for the evening before serving drinks.

Vincent was locked away in the kitchen, doing some last-minute preparations to the banquet of food for that evening, so he had been no help. And Rita had been following Marcus around like a little lost sheep. Ray felt like he'd had to handle the bulk of the manual work himself.

Only a few days to go.

He had arranged accommodation a few towns over and booked enough space for all of them: himself, Chloe... and Rita. Whether his wife would actually join him come Monday would depend on if she kept her word.

After a little while, people started to take their seats, and Marcus looked over to Ray, giving him a deliberate nod.

This was what Ray had to show for his thirty-seven years on this Earth—relegated to being a bloody waiter for a bunch of toffs, all at the behest of an egomaniac who had designs on his wife. Hell, maybe that man was fucking her already.

Ray swallowed his anger and went to fetch the first plates of food.

Only a few days to go.

CHAPTER 37

'Good night, dear,' Betsy said to Patricia before giving her friend a peck on the cheek.

They were in the corridor outside of their respective rooms, and the hour was just past midnight. It had been a most enjoyable evening, but Betsy could feel the effects of the alcohol she'd indulged in—perhaps *over*indulged.

Both women were staying on the ground floor, to the back of the house in one of the rear wings. Theirs were the only two rooms in the corridor that looked out into the courtyard. It was pitch black outside and a little unnerving, especially when juxtaposed with the great hall behind them that continued to give off the hum of life, with the last guests still chatting and laughing. The sound was dulled by the separating doors and walls, making Betty feel somehow like she was just on the edge of safety.

'I'll give you a knock just after eight,' Patricia said. 'Then we can go for breakfast.'

'Sounds good,' Betsy replied. 'Sleep tight.'

'And let's hope nothing goes bump in the niiiight,' her friend replied in a sing-song voice. They both laughed, the terrible joke made funnier by their inebriated state, and Betsy walked to her room at the farthest-most point of the wing.

Once inside, and with the door closed behind her, Betsy turned on the light. The room was certainly to her tastes, fitting of a grand stately home. The four-poster bed was a very nice touch and lent the décor a regal feel. She noticed that the room was cold, however, which it hadn't been earlier that day. She then walked over to the black cast-iron radiator that was positioned between two bay windows and put her hand cautiously onto the metal. Though not exactly hot to the touch, it was certainly warm and should have been enough to heat the room at least a little.

Still, the bedsheets looked thick and comfortable.

Betsy paid a visit to the en-suite and then readied herself for bed, switching off the main light to the room and leaving on only the bedside lamp while she tucked herself in. No sooner had she gotten into bed did something draw her attention. She turned her attention to the far wall to her left, where two windows looked out over the rear grounds. The heavy curtains that hung either side of the bay windows remained open and tied back, and Betsy scolded herself for not shutting them before getting into bed. Maybe she was a little tipsier than she thought.

And it was from one of those windows that she saw movement from outside, drifting past the aperture. From her position in bed, Betsy stared out into the night, but the blackness beyond the glass looked like a heavy, impenetrable blanket, and nothing moved within it. Still, she was curious, if a little spooked, so got up to investigate—and to close the curtains.

With the light from the room, she could see at least a few feet out into the courtyard, but there was nothing obvious there that would have drawn her attention, and certainly no movement. Betsy could only think it had been a bat flying past the window.

She grabbed one of the curtains to pull it closed, but paused when she heard something behind her from the connecting en-suite: a banging noise, which she quickly realised was the sound of the toilet seat dropping and hitting the porcelain rim.

But... she had left the seat down.

With her heart in her mouth, Betsy slowly made her way towards the bathroom door. Could it be? Was the very reason she had come to this house for the weekend about to present itself to her?

It was indeed what she had wanted, but now that she was on the cusp of possibly seeing something, Betsy was terrified. She instantly regretted not sharing a room with Patricia.

Finding enough strength to push on, she opened the door and flicked on the light.

'Hello?' she called out to the empty room. There was a slight buzz from the light above, but she couldn't hear any sounds other than that. And there was certainly no one visible inside. Her breathing quickened, and Betsy considered running next door to Patricia's room, silly as it may be.

Instead, after a while, she switched off the light again and pulled the door shut. Leaving it open wasn't an option, as she would have been constantly looking over to it from her bed and expecting to see something peeking back at her from the other side. While she dearly wanted to believe there was something after death, the idea of actually *seeing* it was now a scary one. Especially since she was alone.

She again walked over to the bay windows and reached for the curtains. Her hand found the fabric, but when she was about to draw the curtains closed, her body froze up.

A breath, from behind, loud and cold. It rolled over her bare shoulders. The smell that flowed with it was foul.

Betsy wanted to scream. She knew instantly that someone—or some*thing*—was standing directly behind her. She could feel a spiking cold and could hear steady and rasping breaths. She managed only a pathetic squeak.

A feeling of immense dread came over her, and Betsy realised at that moment that coming to the Blackwater Hotel had been a huge mistake. That was made blindingly obvious by the sinister chuckle she heard. The unseen thing in the room with her now was *not* benign. Betsy looked into the window before her, terrified of what she may see in the reflection.

It was difficult to make out the shape clearly, as it was a dark mass instead of a human figure. But something was definitely there, without doubt. Goosebumps lined Betsy's skin. She needed to get out of that room.

And quickly.

Her body started to shake, and tears welled up in her eyes. Deep within her gut Betsy thought she was going to die.

There was only one way out of the room, and that would require getting past whatever the black entity was that blocked the way. She reached down within herself and used every ounce of strength and bravery that she could find and turned around. But when she did, she saw the way ahead was clear. There was only an empty room, and nothing blocking her escape to the door.

Betsy didn't want to stop and doubt herself, to question if she had even seen anything behind her in the first place or if it was all imagined. She only wanted to get out and to run to her friend. While she still might not be safe in Patricia's room, at least she wouldn't be alone. She made to run, and had just taken her first step when there was a knocking on the window behind her. A deliberate *clink, clink, clink* on the glass.

Don't look. Don't look. Don't look.

But she did. How could she not? As she gazed upon the horror that stood outside, Betsy was finally able to push out the scream that had been trapped inside of her.

There was a man standing directly outside of the window, so tall that his head was close to the edge of the frame. He was completely naked, skin blotchy and pale, and his penis hung limply, dangling just above the line of the window sill. His abdomen was sunken so much that Betsy was surprised she couldn't make out the spine through the skin. Cracked ribs poked free from the dried flesh, and his arms and shoulders were so thin Betsy could read the outline of every bone. The man's eyes were a dirty, milky white, with no pupils, and they stared wildly at her, almost popping from the sockets. A thin mop of black, greasy hair sat atop his head, but the most striking feature of all was his mouth, where the man's jaw looked to have long since been ripped off, along with his top lip. Betsy could see the line of his teeth, and the jagged flesh where they should have met the jaw was dark and purple. The man's tongue flopped freely down to his throat.

He had one hand pressed against the glass, and he brought his head forward to rest on the window. She heard him moan, even above her own screaming. His other hand slowly moved to his penis, which he began to rhythmically stroke. The demonic person then slowly ran his tongue up the glass.

Betsy clutched her chest. Her heart felt like it was going to burst and hammered wildly.

She ran.

Though her legs threatened to buckle beneath her, Betsy was able to make it out of her room and across the hall, and she started to pound on Patricia's door, desperate for her friend to let her in. Even out in the hallway, well away from the window in her own room, Betsy felt exposed and vulnerable. Panic had overcome her, and she pounded and screamed.

'Let me in!'

It felt like she was standing alone in that corridor for an eternity. However, she eventually heard the click of the lock from the other side, and the door opened to reveal her friend looking both tired and confused.

'Betsy, what on Earth—'

Betsy didn't allow Patricia to finish. She fell into the room, and into the arms of her dear friend, sobbing and wailing and shaking uncontrollably.

CHAPTER 38

'Are you sure I can't persuade you to stay?' Patricia asked her friend as Betsy finished checking out.

Betsy firmly shook her head. 'Not a chance.' Her expression was as serious as Patricia had ever seen it. Betsy then went on to ask, 'But Patricia, are you sure I can't convince *you* to leave?'

Since Betsy had burst into Patricia's room the previous night in a state of panic and fear, she had been trying to get Patricia to leave with her, insisting the house simply wasn't safe.

Patricia had listened in awe—and a little bit of jealousy—at the story of what Betsy had seen outside of her window. Patricia could understand the fear her friend had experienced, certainly, but there was no way Patricia could leave now. What Betsy had experienced was the *precise* reason they had attended this event, and no amount of fear would sway her.

Patricia was staying.

Betsy had spent the night in Patricia's room, sharing a bed. Patricia knew the woman hadn't slept much, though nothing else had happened. As soon as Betsy had gotten up, she'd arranged her own transportation home.

The young lady—Rita—handled the formalities of the check-out and apologised for any distress the hotel may have caused.

A few other early risers had gathered around, listening in with great interest.

'I just don't want you to regret not staying,' Patricia said as the hotel manager finished the check-out. 'Scary or not, you've seen something we *all* want to see. Just think what else might be in store for us.'

But Betsy was unmoved. One of the hotel workers—a large man in a suit, whose nametag read *Ray*—gathered up her bags. Betsy shook her head. 'Patricia, I'm scared of *precisely* what might be in store, don't you see? And I think you should be, too.'

'Oh tosh,' Patricia replied. 'Nothing here can hurt us. We're perfectly safe.'

Betsy just gave her friend a sad look, then hugged her. 'I hope you're right,' she said. Betsy then nodded at the gentleman carrying her bags and walked outside with him. Patricia felt sad her friend was leaving, and even a little guilty that she wasn't going to follow to lend support.

But finding out what had happened only strengthened Patricia's resolve to stay and see how everything unfolded. It gave her hope that, after years of searching, she would see with her own eyes that there truly was something on the other side.

CHAPTER 39

AFTER PUTTING her luggage into the boot, Ray helped the lady into the taxi she had called.

She looked shaken. He was worried for her, though he didn't believe the story she had told. Maybe that was harsh—perhaps she *thought* she was telling the truth, but he figured she was likely confused or misguided somehow. Perhaps it was a nightmare that just seemed real?

The guest dropped into the back seat of the car and swung her legs inside. Ray saw tears build in her eyes, and her hands were trembling in her lap. He leaned in a little closer.

'Are you okay?' he asked.

The woman didn't look at him. He knew it wasn't because of any snobbery, but because she was just struggling to hold it all together.

'I'm... not sure,' she eventually said. 'What I saw in there will stay with me forever.'

Ray considered his next words carefully. 'Well, you are leaving now, so you're safe.'

He didn't actually believe she was in any danger, otherwise he wouldn't have allowed his daughter to remain inside. But at the same time, Ray didn't want to see the woman even more upset and scared.

It was only after he'd finished speaking that she finally turned to look at him, eyes wet and sad. 'Look after my friend in there, will you, sir? I'm just worried about what will happen.'

'She'll be fine,' Ray replied with a friendly smile. 'I'll make sure of it.'

The lady managed a half-smile and nodded her thanks. Ray then closed the door and banged on the roof of the car, signalling to the driver that he could set off. As the vehicle made its way down the driveway, Ray took a breath. He was enjoying being outside, if only for a moment. The weekend had been hectic so far, and only one night had passed.

Still, he was edging ever closer to freedom.

CHAPTER 40

CHLOE KNEW she had a few hours until her father came to check up on her. So she decided it was again time to sneak out of her room—which was feeling more and more like a prison—just as she had the previous day. Moving around the house when so much was going on was a huge amount of fun for her, and Chloe hoped today would bring the same amount of excitement.

She had taken no more than a few steps down the hallway when she heard many footsteps marching towards her. She heard a male voice, speaking like a teacher addressing a classroom. Chloe quickly ducked into her parents' room, but kept the door open enough to peek out. Mr. Blackwater passed by her view first, followed by what seemed like every guest staying in the hotel. It was a tour, Chloe quickly realised, and Mr. Blackwater was divulging some of the history of the house.

'...and it was in the eighteen-hundreds that Perron Manor became an orphanage,' he said as they all walked by. 'As is symptomatic of the house, there were a great many deaths here during that time, explained away as a cholera outbreak. However, there is a great deal of doubt about that, and much of the evidence I have found shows cholera was used merely as an excuse to disguise the truth.'

'And what was the truth?' one guest asked.

'That nobody could accurately explain the deaths. There were stories, spread by the children who lived here, about a strange, pale man who came in the night—one who brought with him a horrible stink...'

Eventually his voice faded out, and the words became unclear as the group moved farther away. Chloe took the opportunity to leave the room and slowly move in the opposite direction of the crowd. She was interested in the story Mr. Blackwater was telling, but she didn't want to get too close for fear of being caught. So instead, Chloe snuck downstairs... or tried to. However, she had to stop when she heard her mother and father talking in the reception area, hidden away from her view.

'Just don't forget what you promised,' she heard her dad say. 'Once this weekend is done...'

'I remember,' her mother said, but she didn't sound happy. In truth, she hadn't sounded happy for a *long* time. Chloe felt her heart drop a little. While it didn't seem like her parents were having a full-blown argument, they still weren't being friendly. They were speaking to each other like they were enemies, rather than being in love.

She didn't want her mother and father to be like that. It hurt her knowing their formerly happy life was now on a knife-edge.

'Good,' her dad said. 'I'm going up to check on Chloe to make sure she's okay. Feel free to go see her too, if you can carve out the time.'

'I can't, I'm too busy,' was the response.

Chloe clenched her teeth together. She knew her mum was working hard, and Chloe tried to be understanding, but to hear herself spoken about so dismissively caused her to feel sad. She started to silently cry, then quickly turned and ran back to her room.

CHAPTER 41

WITH SOME TIME TO spare as the lambs wandered the halls of his home, Vincent hid himself away. He heard them pass by outside. They were awed by the house and the stories Marcus was spinning.

Their awe would soon be replaced, however, with a terrible and horrific wonderment. It would be brought on by the very things they wanted to see, but things their minds would not be able to comprehend.

He had locked his door, and now sat on the floor of his small room, just in front of his wardrobe, the doors of which were pulled open. He didn't have many clothes inside—Vincent didn't have too much of anything anymore—but the clothes were not his focus. Instead, he leaned forward and brought his hands up to the back wall of the wardrobe, feeling the scratch marks on the wood. Things were building up inside him again. His head felt like it would explode.

While Vincent knew he couldn't stop what was going to happen, or even act on his own impulses anymore if the house did not wish it, there was still a rising feeling of guilt. After all, he'd condemned his own sister, bringing her here even though he'd known what lay in store.

And not only that, he'd brought his niece into this hell as well.

The poor, innocent child.

He pushed the tips of his fingers into the wood, applying as much pressure as he could withstand, and slowly dragged them down the back of the wardrobe. The imperfections and undulations poked at his flesh, causing ripples of pain to shoot up into his hands. That was just the beginning. He repeated the motion, this time applying even more pressure and speed. The previously scratched surface of the wood cut in deeper, and he felt his nails catch and pull on splinters. More pain seared through his fingers and it made him feel sick. But it also brought with it a twisted kind of relief. The stinging fire made him feel human and fought back against the numbness that normally absorbed him.

Vincent's scratching increased in intensity, and he felt the raw nerve endings become exposed as skin was ripped away. The nail of his middle finger tore back savagely, causing him to emit a small yowl. The pain was so severe that he couldn't carry on with that hand anymore. He looked at the ruined nail, which was bent back at ninety degrees across its middle, exposing some of the bed underneath. Blood started to pool up from the torn skin.

Still, his other hand could take more, so Vincent continued to scratch at the wood, the pain reminding him that somewhere beneath it all, he was still human.

CHAPTER 42

It had been a marvellous day, but Patricia was a little disappointed to have not witnessed anything personally.

There had been stories from several of the others, where some guests claimed to have felt a presence down in the creepy basement; others told of seeing a little girl sneaking around behind them during the tour that morning, but Patricia had no experiences of her own to treasure. The second-hand accounts were interesting, even thrilling, but they were not what she had come here for.

Night had rolled in, and the guests gathered down in the great hall again for their evening meal. Without Betsy, Patricia had to join with another party made up of three couples. They all knew each other, so Patricia felt like something of an outsider, which she supposed she was. It would have been so much easier, and far more fun, had Betsy just stayed.

Service for the food was a little slow, with only two gentlemen on duty: the one who had helped Betsy with her bags that morning, and a rather scruffy-looking man. Both brought out the food and drinks, though they struggled to keep up with the demand.

While the hotel itself was something to behold, it seemed the owner had scrimped on the service staff. Before long, Mr. Blackwater himself strode into the room. He was accompanied by the lady who had checked Patricia in, and both looked more than a little flushed. The woman had a certain glow about her as well—one that Patricia was all too familiar with, even if she had not felt its satisfaction for a number of years.

She knew *exactly* what the two of them had been up to.

The woman walked straight through to the kitchen, presumably to help with the food service, while Marcus Blackwater started doing the rounds and speaking to guests at each table. It didn't take long for him to reach hers.

'I trust everyone is having a fun evening,' Mr. Blackwater said to them all.

There were nods of confirmation, as well as an, 'Oh yes, we are indeed,' by one enthusiastic lady. Patricia's response was a little more antagonistic, however. 'To be honest, I was hoping to see a little more.'

Marcus raised his eyebrows. 'Really? From what I understand, there has been a lot happening already.'

'I've heard the same thing,' Patricia replied. 'My friend even saw something last night which scared her off completely. However, as yet, my experiences have been left wanting.'

'Your friend was the lady who left?'

Patricia nodded. 'That's right.'

'I hope she is okay.'

'I'm sure she will be,' Patricia confirmed. 'Just a little spooked.'

'Glad to hear it,' Marcus said. 'I'm sure your fortunes here will change.'

'I do hope so,' Patricia said. 'I have been looking forward to this for a long time, yet it seems everyone else here is having all the fun.'

Marcus laughed, then asked, 'Have you partaken in any of the events so far?'

Patricia nodded. 'I went on the tour, which was very interesting, and sat in on a séance.'

'Well, we have a lot more planned for tomorrow. A full day of it! So make sure you get involved.'

'I plan to,' Patricia said. 'Care to give me an idea of what to expect?'

'We will be running some Ouija board workshops, vigils, and we even have a few guests who believe they have psychic ability, so I'll be conducting more séances with them. I'm hoping those prove interesting. And, after midnight, we have a special surprise, one that I will not ruin just yet. Make sure you are well-rested and get plenty of beauty sleep tonight... not that someone as beautiful as yourself needs it, of course.'

Patricia smiled at the compliment. It was nice, though it hardly sounded genuine. Patricia got the distinct impression that what they were seeing from Mr. Blackwater was something of a practised facade.

Not that she cared, of course. She hadn't come here looking for new friends.

'You have me intrigued,' she said as their food finally arrived: roast potatoes, mixed vegetables, and thick cuts of beef drizzled in gravy. Not exactly high-class food.

'I'll leave you to your meal,' the host said. 'Enjoy the rest of your evening, and I'll look forward to seeing you again tomorrow.'

With that, he moved on to schmooze with the people on the next table over.

'Wonder what the surprise is?' one of the gentlemen in Patricia's new group mused.

She had no idea, but she was certainly looking forward to it. Tomorrow was their last full day, and it felt like time was running out for her.

CHAPTER 43

With the evening finally over, and the time pushing two in the morning, Ray was looking forward to whatever sleep he would be able to get before rising early again to help prepare breakfast for the guests.

He felt physically wiped out and was close to running on empty. *Just one more day.*

He sat up in bed, nightlight still on, his tired body screaming for sleep. But Rita was still in the bathroom, readying herself for bed, and he wanted to speak to her for at least a little while before closing his eyes. Her waiting for him to drift off before coming to bed had been something of a habit recently, and he didn't want it to happen again tonight.

Though his brain told him she was not going to keep her promise, his heart held out hope that she might come through for him.

Eventually his wife appeared, and she walked to the bed without even looking at him. 'Sorry I took so long,' she said. 'Thought you'd be asleep.'

You mean you wanted *me to be asleep*, Ray thought. But he simply asked, 'How was your day?'

'Fine,' she replied. 'Busy.'

'You disappeared for a good portion of it,' Ray went on. 'Right around the same time Marcus did. Where did the two of you get to?'

Rita got into bed and began her nightly ritual of applying hand cream. 'Dealing with guests,' she said as if it were the most obvious thing in the world.

Ray didn't believe it, but he had no way of proving what he suspected. He also knew confronting his wife about it directly would only lead to another blazing row. One he didn't have the strength to have right now.

Too tired to fight for your marriage? Pathetic.

He couldn't help but wonder if there was anything left worth fighting for. At the moment he just felt crushed and defeated, unsure of anything. All he knew for sure was that he was leaving on Monday. That much was a certainty.

'Fair enough. Big day tomorrow, then,' he went on, trying to draw a little more conversation from her. 'Grande finalé of the weekend.'

'Uh-huh,' Rita agreed but offered no more.

'So... what have you got planned for everyone?'

She shrugged. 'Same as today, really. Rinse and repeat.' She lay down and turned her back on him.

'Has the event all been a success?' he asked, pressing further. 'Has it given you the closure you needed?'

'I suppose so,' was all Rita said, and then she reached out a hand and flicked off her nightlight. 'Goodnight.'

Ray couldn't believe it. The total dismissal of him left him furious. He actually shook with anger. Was she *trying* to enrage him? Was this just a tactic to push him further away?

Any fragile hope that their marriage was salvageable evaporated in that instant. Ray knew that they were done.

He could do nothing else other than switch off his own light and lie down as well, even though what he *wanted* to do was to yell and scream, to unload all of his frustrations and let her know what she was doing was unacceptable.

But he didn't.

He sat on his anger—stewed on it. If Rita wanted to stay here permanently with Marcus, then she could.

Fuck her.

CHAPTER 44

IT WAS another early start for Chloe, and she couldn't help but yawn as her father got her dressed and brushed her hair.

'Only one more early morning,' he said from behind her as he wrapped an elastic hair-bobble around the ponytail he'd formed. 'Then, things will change. I promise.'

'I don't mind being up early,' Chloe said, but she had to stifle another yawn—which would have given away the small fib she'd just told. 'But I don't like being stuck in my room all day.'

'I know,' her dad replied. 'That isn't fair on you. In fact, there's a lot that isn't fair about living here, don't you think?'

Chloe cocked her head to the side. 'What do you mean?'

She felt his hands fall on her shoulders and slowly turn her around. He was kneeling down, so his eyes were level with her, and he looked sad. 'I don't think we've been very good parents since we moved into this house, kiddo.'

'Yes, you have,' she replied, even though what he'd said rang somewhat true, at least in part. But Chloe knew her parents had been really busy, and were working hard to keep them here.

Her father just shook his head. 'We haven't. Not really. And I want you to know that things are going to change.'

Chloe paused, then asked, 'How?'

He smiled. 'I'll explain later. Now come on, I'll get you some breakfast before the guests start to wake up.'

She followed her father down to the kitchen, more than a little confused at what he'd said. She wondered what exactly was going to change for them.

CHAPTER 45

'But I want you now,' Rita said to Marcus, pulling him towards her, her mouth finding his. They were in his study on the top floor, hidden away from everyone else.

'I know,' he said, though he held her firmly at bay. 'But we must wait. The time isn't right.'

'The time's always right,' she told him, and he could only smile. *Poor little puppet.* Marcus wondered what it was like for her to be so controlled. Was there a part of her that existed somewhere inside, screaming to be let out while she was forced to act without her own agency? Or was she completely oblivious to it all, believing her actions were her own?

He gripped her shoulders tightly and looked into her eyes. 'Now, Rita, I need something from you.'

'Anything,' she said.

'After midnight tonight, forget whatever it is you're doing and come up here, to this room. I'll be waiting for you. Then… you can get what you want.'

'Okay,' she agreed readily. After a moment, she added, 'You know, I think my husband suspects something.'

Marcus chuckled. 'He'd be a fool not to. But it doesn't matter. Because, after tonight…'

'I can be with you forever?'

'Yes,' Marcus lied. 'Now, I need you to go and keep things moving downstairs. I will be along shortly, but I need to speak to Vincent up here first. Can you find him and send him up for me?'

'Okay,' she said, then brought one of his hands up to her mouth and slipped his index finger inside. He felt her hot, wet tongue massage the digit as she slowly sucked on it while holding firm eye contact.

Once finished, she flashed him a naughty smile. 'Until tonight, then,' she said and sauntered from the room.

Marcus shook his head and started to pace while awaiting Vincent's arrival. He had decided that it was this room, this study, where the ritual would take place. It wasn't the most comfortable space in the building, granted, but then again, Marcus had no real concern for comfort.

The book was already here, along with the translations. And it had enough space for what he needed.

However, things also needed to be put into place. A pentagram needed to be drawn—a task he would delegate to Vincent. That would be the last seal required, since the rest were already in place around the building. The host, too, was ready. It was obvious she was under the influence of the house now, of the power that flowed through the Devil's Door. Which was a relief, as she had initially proven quite resistant.

Everyone fell eventually, if you didn't have the intelligence and guile to keep those forces at bay.

Like Marcus did.

With the possession in place, Marcus had moved quickly to complete the trickiest step in the preparation phase. A step not guaranteed to work. Thankfully, however, he knew that it had.

He could smell it on her. The stink of life grew in her womb.

'You wanted to see me?' Vincent asked as he entered the study. Marcus stood in the centre of the room, hands behind his back, standing tall and proud. But his physical appearance was at odds with the confident and powerful posture, and he seemed to look more and more exhausted and haggard with each passing day. Vincent wondered if Marcus was even aware of the changes.

'Yes, I need a little more from you, old friend,' Marcus said.

Vincent just nodded. 'Of course.'

'The ritual will take place here, in this room,' Marcus said, holding his arms out to either side. 'The room needs to be appropriately set. I have instructions here'—he pulled a sheet of folded paper from his breast pocket—'that need to be followed. A number of seals need to be placed to protect the room, just in case. If you would be so kind as to prepare everything?'

'Of course,' Vincent agreed, and walked over to the other man to take the paper from him. After unfolding it, Vincent read through what was written.

'This all needs to be ready before midnight,' Marcus said. 'Then things can begin. After tonight, you will be in charge of the house. But, you will not be alone here. I need you to watch *her*, Vincent. That is your role now.'

Marcus went on to divulge further instructions to Vincent, and also outline *exactly* what would be needed of him.

'You can rely on me,' Vincent said.

Marcus smiled gratefully. 'I'm very glad to hear that. And I appreciate it, old boy. Now, I have lots to attend to, but feel free to make a start in here.'

Marcus then left Vincent alone in the room, and Vincent finally started to feel the gravity of what lay ahead. His fingers began to itch.

The day was finally upon them. Everything was set.

Now Vincent just had to navigate what remained of the pantomime downstairs. But only until midnight. However, that meant the rest of his day would no doubt consist of running after the snobbish guests, who were all keen to indulge in a world they knew nothing about. They were lambs to the slaughter, destined to fill the belly of the beast. To feed it.

To make it strong enough for what lay ahead.

Vincent had felt the energy in the house change recently. It was almost electrified, yet heavy and oppressive at the same time. He had also seen more and more of the spirits inside, all watching as the weekend's events unfolded.

They were waiting—held at bay for the time being while things continued to build.

Vincent still had more to do. He had his orders.

Ironically, Marcus' instructions were the least important ones on his list.

CHAPTER 46

THE GREAT HALL was full and bustled with life as all the guests sat down for their final meal.

The food was much improved, which pleased Patricia. While the meal was not huge, she was of the opinion that less was more. The dish was smoked chicken and blue cheese salad, which in and of itself could have been seen as quite basic. However, it was served with a beetroot sorbet, and that was something Patricia had never tried before. By rights, the combination shouldn't have worked. As it was, every element sang in harmony, and the meal was absolutely delicious.

Patricia had gotten word that Marcus himself had prepared tonight's dinner, which she thought was a nice touch.

The mouth-watering food was welcome, considering it had been another disappointing day. There had been a flurry of stories regarding experiences and sightings from some of the other guests, but Patricia always seemed to be in the wrong place at the wrong time.

She just hoped the weekend wouldn't pass without giving her a story of her own to take away.

Even though Betsy had been terrified to the point of fleeing the hotel, at least she had answers; she had something she could cling to for whatever remained of her life. She'd found proof that there was more after death.

Patricia didn't have that. Not really. Because secondhand accounts just weren't enough.

What was more, she now felt like something of a third wheel among her fellow attendees. She'd tried to mingle and join other groups, but never felt quite welcome, and the earlier camaraderie she'd experienced at the event had eroded away. Sure, people were polite and welcoming, but it was always at arm's length.

With an empty plate before her, and guests on either side who talked to each other rather than her, Patricia concentrated on what remained of her glass of red wine. She started to people-watch, noticing a certain buzz in the room. A lot of the chatter centred on the upcoming secret surprise Marcus had promised.

Patricia brought the glass up to her lips and inhaled, taking in the aroma of the wine, one that was infused with fruits and slight hints of pepper. She swirled the liquid, ready to take another sip, but paused when her vision switched from the deep red liquid to the face of the glass itself. Or, more specifically, the reflection in it.

Someone was standing behind her—a woman, pale and naked, with saggy and deflated breasts on show.

Patricia spun her head around with a gasp. Those nearby looked over to her, confused at the minor outburst. The only thing Patricia saw behind her, however, was the other patrons, all talking, laughing, eating, and drinking. There was no naked woman. Patricia quickly looked back to her glass—back to the reflection—but the pale woman was no longer there. Patricia cast her eyes about the room, feeling an unnerving sensation creep up on her.

What had she just seen?

The reflection in her glass had been quite clear, even down to the wide, milky eyes staring at Patricia. Despite her unease, excitement ran through Patricia's veins. Was that her first genuine experience?

'Are you okay?' a lady seated next to her asked.

'I'm fine,' Patricia responded. 'I just... think I saw something.'

'What?' the woman asked, her eyes widening in obvious interest.

Patricia held up her glass. 'I swear I saw the reflection of a ghostly woman in this.'

'Fascinating,' the woman said and elbowed the gentleman who sat on the far side of her. 'Peter, this lady here has just had an experience.'

Patricia then regaled her new captive audience with what she had just seen, brief though it had been. *Perhaps this is the start of something,* she thought to herself, feeling her excitement grow.

The night wore on, the drinks flowed, and—spurred on by what she had seen—Patricia started to have fun, mingling with others more easily. Before she knew it, the hour was close to midnight.

People began to ask where Mr. Blackwater was, and when they could expect this special surprise to take place. Patricia was deep in conversation when a commotion over near the rear door drew her attention. Cries of fright rose up from the people gathered there, and all in the great hall turned to look.

Intrigued, Patricia cut her conversation short and made her way over to the door. Two women—both in their later years—looked shaken, and one was close to tears. They were being comforted by those around them.

'What happened?' Patricia asked to anyone that cared to answer. A man next to her leaned in, and Patricia realised it was one of the hotel workers, the one she had seen running around tirelessly.

'They saw something outside the doors,' he said. 'A monk, apparently. He was just standing there, peering in from under his hood.'

Patricia could scarcely believe what she was hearing. 'Did anyone else see it?'

The man shrugged. 'I don't think so.'

It may just have been due to the excitement in the room, but Patricia felt a change in the energy around her—like something was building.

Soon after, people's attention turned again, this time to the other side of the room as Marcus Blackwater entered.

'Ladies and gentlemen,' he announced grandly. 'The time is almost here. I am going to ask you to remain patient for a little while longer. Feel free to look around the house again at your leisure. You may well see that, soon, things will become a lot different. And you will *all* find what you are looking for. I guarantee it.'

He then cast a look through the crowd, focusing on one person in particular—the hotel manager. Marcus gave her an almost imperceptible nod, which Patricia found intriguing.

Without fielding any further questions, the host turned and walked from the room, leaving everyone utterly confused. Excited chatter started to build, and the hotel manager also began to weave her way through the crowd to the exit. She was stopped by Ray, who took hold of her arm.

'Where are you going?' he asked her.

'I have things to attend to,' was the curt answer.

'Can you check on Chloe? Things seem... weird tonight.' There was an element of concern in his voice. The way the man spoke made it sound like Chloe was his child. Patricia then realised that these two were a couple, though clearly not on the best of terms.

She instantly felt pity for the man, knowing what she had seen between the woman and Marcus Blackwater.

'I don't have time,' she said, then pulled away from his grip and walked off.

He sighed.

'Are you okay, hun?' Patricia asked, laying a comforting hand onto one of his broad shoulders. The smile he gave was a weary one.

'I'll be fine,' he said. 'But if you'll excuse me for a moment, I need to go check on my daughter.'

He then walked from the room as well, leaving Patricia confused as to how any parent could let a little girl stay in a place as haunted as this one.

She checked her watch just in time to see the hand strike midnight.

CHAPTER 47

CHLOE WAS FINDING it difficult to sleep. She kept alternating between being too hot and having to kick off her covers, to being too cold and then having to duck back under them again.

She certainly felt tired enough to sleep, but lying with her eyes closed just made her feel restless, and the darkness in her bedroom seemed thick and heavy. That confused her, as Chloe knew darkness had no weight.

On top of that, even though she'd lived in the house for many months and had never once been scared by it, she was now on edge. She felt the need to constantly open her eyes to check the room around her.

Which was stupid, as there was nothing to be scared of.

However, no sooner had Chloe admonished herself for being silly did she hear the sound of the door handle to the room start to turn. She lifted her head off the pillow, breath held, and saw the door slowly start to push open. It swung into the room, and the light from the corridor streamed in, highlighting the silhouette of a person standing within the frame.

Fear surged through her and Chloe began to shake. However, she was soon made to feel even more stupid. Her eyes adjusted and she saw just *who* was standing there.

'Dad?' she asked, squinting.

'Sorry,' her father replied in a whisper. 'I didn't mean to wake you up. I just wanted to come and check on you.' He then moved into the room and closed the door behind him. 'Are you okay?' he asked.

Chloe quickly nodded, even though she didn't really feel okay. Not tonight... though she couldn't explain why. 'I'm fine.'

'Why are you awake so late?' he asked, sitting down on the side of the bed.

'I don't know. I just can't sleep.'

He smiled and tightened the sheets around her, which made her feel safer. 'Have you tried counting sheep?'

She just laughed. 'That doesn't work, Dad.'

'I know,' he replied. 'But people seem to suggest it a whole lot, so I figured they might be on to something.' He looked tired. Not in the same way Chloe's mother did—especially recently—but exhausted nonetheless.

'Where's Mum?' she asked, curious.

Her father's smile faltered. 'She's... a little busy at the moment, sweetie. So she asked me to check on you. You sure you're okay?'

Chloe gave him her bravest smile. 'I'm fine, Daddy. You don't need to worry about me.'

He tussled her hair. 'Kid, I'm *always* going to worry about you.' He then gave Chloe a hug and got back to his feet.

'It's gonna be a late night for me, I think,' he said. 'But you try and get some sleep.'

'Okay,' Chloe said, then added, 'night night.'

'Night night, kiddo. Sleep tight.'

He then left her alone, closing the door as he left. Chloe felt much more relaxed after his visit and was thankful for him dropping in. Her unease had disappeared completely, and it didn't take her long to finally drop off to sleep.

'What's that?' Rita asked, pointing to what had been drawn in chalk on the floor of the room.

'A pentagram,' Marcus replied as they both looked down at the symbol. Lighted candles were set at each point of the star; their gentle and flickering glow was the only light afforded to the room.

'Okay,' Rita went on. 'But why is it here?'

'Because we need it,' was his answer. Rita then felt his hands take hold of her shoulders, and the black suit-jacket she wore was pulled free. 'And it is where I'm going to fuck you. Isn't that what you want?'

Rita didn't much care for the symbol, but she certainly did want him inside of her. And she would do anything to make that happen again. Her husband and daughter were like distant memories. More accurately, they were inconveniences she wished were gone

Stop! What are you saying?

And there was that annoying and dissenting voice again from deep inside. One that just wouldn't go away. However, Rita had at least learned to ignore it.

She unbuttoned her trousers and wiggled out of them, then did the same with her blouse and stood before Marcus in just her underwear. He guided her into the centre of the pentagram.

Being surrounded by all of those old artefacts and books and then being laid down on the bare floorboards was hardly romantic, but Rita didn't much care. If Marcus wanted to get a little kinky, then she was game. Though, her abandon was momentarily brought into question when he pulled free a small switchblade from his pocket. Marcus unfolded the knife, and the flickering light from the candles made the metallic blade glint.

'Don't worry,' he said, standing above her. 'I need you to trust me.'

Marcus then undressed as well, completely. She smiled at him and raised a leg, nudging his dick with her toe. 'Come to me,' she said.

His smile bordered on a sneer, and he lowered himself towards her. Rita held her breath as he brought the knife to her shoulder and hooked it beneath the material of her bra-strap. He cut the material free and then repeated the process with the other side. The feeling of the sharp, cold metal on Rita's skin brought with it a flash of pain, but also excitement.

He then moved it down to her underwear and slid the blade in between the skin of her hips and the black fabric. This time, as he cut her lingerie away, Rita felt a fiery sting slide across her hip. She looked down and saw that he had drawn blood, which rolled down her leg to the floor below.

'Marcus!' she snapped, and put a hand to the wound, but he moved it away.

'Don't!' he shot back. 'Let it flow.'

Her initial reaction was to push back and tell him no, but something settled over her. It quelled her anger and fight, smothering it out like a thick blanket over a flame. Marcus squeezed her flesh around her cut, making more blood flow. The look in his eyes was animalistic, like a lion waiting to feed.

Marcus then brought the knife up to his own hand and placed the metal edge against his palm. Rita winced as he harshly slit his own skin, then wriggled his fingers to encourage the flow. The blood that poured free was much more generous than from her own cut, and Marcus made sure the small patch of red liquid that Rita had given up was completely covered by his own.

'That's it,' he said with an enthused grin. 'Perfect.' He then threw the knife away.

'Now what?' Rita asked, confused, but still willing.

He smiled, then tilted up his head before speaking loudly... though not to her. It was like he was issuing a command to the room itself. Or, rather, the house. The words Marcus spoke were lost on Rita. They were a language she wasn't familiar with.

'What was that?' she asked when he was done.

'An incantation,' was his reply.

Rita wasn't sure what to do with the information, but he then crawled on top of her. She felt his hardness press against her.

'Now,' he said, 'we fuck.'

Marcus was all over her, kissing and grabbing at Rita, devouring her. She arched her back and pushed up her hips, wanting him.

Rita let out a gasp of slight pain as he entered her; then she gave herself over to the ecstasy that was building.

CHAPTER 48

PATRICIA WAS mid-conversation with one of the ladies who had seen the 'monk' outside when she heard it—an incredible, all-encompassing noise that shook the very walls around them.

Shrieks of surprise rose up around her, even from Patricia herself. There were lingering vibrations from the sudden and terrible sound, but they slowly faded away.

The great hall was not as full as it had been, with many of the guests having taken Mr. Blackwater's advice to again explore the house. However, those that were still present began to panic.

'What the hell was that?' one man asked.

Patricia had no idea. Given the magnitude of the sound, she could only assume that it was perhaps a brief tremor in the earth, not that she'd ever experienced anything like that before, of course. She had to wonder if everyone else in the house had heard it as well. *Surely they must have.*

Another equally loud boom thundered around them all. Patricia felt her heartrate spike. It wasn't an earthquake, and it sounded more like something was striking against their very reality, the horrible booms like the impact of an immense, invisible object.

After fading out to silence again, the noise came back with a third crashing impact. The screams of the terrified guests echoed again, and Patricia was able to hear them from other areas of the house as well.

She expected another boom to hit and was braced for it... but it never came. There was only the whimpering and fearful sobs from the guests, with many asking, 'What *was* that?'

The relative quiet continued, and it was only after a few minutes without any further incident that Patricia felt confident the sounds—whatever they had been—were over.

'Was that something to do with Marcus?' one guest asked. 'Was *that* part of his bloody surprise?' Patricia noticed the man who had asked the question was talking to Ray, who was back in the room. She could tell from the man's shocked expression that he was just as in the dark as the rest of them.

It was then that a feeling of intense cold rolled through the room. Patricia was wearing a long, black evening gown, which was strapless, and her hair was pinned up so that her shoulders were exposed. Her skin tingled as the breeze flowed past her. She then began to notice plumes of misty clouds—people's breath as they exhaled. Her own breath hung before her, giving an indication of the sudden drop in temperature. She hugged herself, trying to keep in some of her own body's warmth.

'Something's wrong here,' she said, stating the obvious. Everyone else was deathly quiet, just waiting for something to happen. Patricia's eyes wandered around the room and she held her breath. Her focus then stopped on a large mirror mounted on one of the walls, and in it she could see the reflection of the guests, all with terrified expressions etched on their faces.

However, there were others in the reflection as well. People who stood between the guests—ones Patricia had not seen with her own eyes when scanning the great hall.

These strangers were all deathly pale and stood stock-still. And they seemingly went unnoticed by everyone else. In the time it took Patricia to scream, she had already taken in numerous horrible details about the things she instantly knew to be spirits.

The dead in the reflection were a mix of men, women, and children. Their clothing was mostly from a past era, and were all dirty and tatty.

Some were either completely naked or near-naked. All of their forms, however, were either mutilated or twisted in some way: withered arms, missing limbs, torn flesh, chests pulled open from neck to navel, and distorted and demonic faces that were frozen with blank, stony expressions.

When Patricia's scream actually tore free, those blank expressions suddenly changed to something much more insidious. It was at this point the other guests in the room turned in fright to see what had caused Patricia to cry out. It didn't take long for their focus to fall on the mirror as well.

Everyone in the room began to shriek in fright. Patricia turned away from the reflection, to see if those horrible things were actually standing between them all outside of the mirror as well.

But she couldn't see them. Only the other frightened guests.

However, when Patricia locked eyes with one particular gentleman, her heart froze. She suddenly wanted to shout a warning about the horrible thing that stood behind him: a rake-thin woman dressed in what looked to be old-style maid clothing. The left side of her head was completely crushed in, now little more than a concave mass of pulped black and purple flesh.

Her hand rose up and grabbed the man's neck from behind. He gasped in shock, and his eyes went wide. Patricia then noticed there were others around the group as well, just as she had seen in the mirror.

Patricia then looked back to the man, just in time to see his throat get ripped out completely.

CHAPTER 49

Chloe didn't know what to do. She was standing in her room, hands at her chest, tucked just beneath her chin.

Something was happening outside—through the whole house, in fact—but she had no idea what. A loud noise that she didn't understand had woken her. It was an almighty crash that seemed to come from all around her. Then, there was another, and another, and now people were screaming.

She heard running footsteps beyond the door to her room, and shouting, and there were other noises she couldn't place.

It sounded like chaos.

But Chloe wasn't sure if she should stay put in her room, or go outside and see what was happening. Staying inside felt like the safer, more sensible option, but what if there was a fire and she needed to get out? Chloe knew her mum or dad would likely come for her, but there was also a chance something had happened to them. Perhaps they were trapped or hurt… or worse.

She bit her lip and eventually decided to at least open her door and look out into the hall. At least then she might have a better idea of what was going on.

So, fighting through considerable apprehensions, she moved forward and slowly opened the door. While the short corridor outside was empty, Chloe could see people running back and forth through the adjoining hallway, all of them yelling in confusion.

She could tell people were scared, and the thought of staying in her room when something potentially dangerous was happening seemed stupid. So, she stepped out and began to walk down to the adjoining corridor. People sprinted past her view every few seconds. The sounds around her were constant and sometimes... bizarre. The screams, shouting, and crying, though worrying, were relatively normal in comparison. It was the other noises that she had picked up on: moaning, crashing, and... growling, that confused and terrified Chloe.

Just as she reached the intersection point, she noticed that no one was running past anymore. Though she could still hear pounding footsteps and shrieking, the way ahead now seemed clear, at least for the moment. Did that mean everyone had already fled the area?

Sensing she should get out of there as well, Chloe broke into a jog, suddenly desperate to find her parents.

Just as she turned the corner ahead, Chloe looked up, and her eyes went wide. She braced for the unavoidable collision as a large man in a suit barrelled towards her, running desperately and looking back over his shoulder. Even if he had seen Chloe, there was simply no time to stop.

She quickly closed her eyes, an instinctive reaction, and started to bring her hand up. But it was all in vain.

The impact from the much larger person took Chloe's breath away, and she felt herself thrown back with savage force. A searing pain exploded in the back of her head. Chloe had just enough awareness to realise she had struck a corner point of the wall behind her.

She then felt herself drop heavily to the floor like a rag doll, and was unable to move her arms or legs during the quick drop. The dizziness and pain she felt was overwhelming, and Chloe quickly fell into unconsciousness.

CHAPTER 50

Marcus was lost in his desires. He thrust hard against Rita, who lay submissively below him with her legs splayed.

But, he had to keep his composure, at least to some extent. The indulgence needed to keep going. It was, after all, the anchor that would allow *Impius Sanguis* to continue.

Sex was a sacred thing, despite what some people believed. It was the very act that created life. Indeed, with Rita, it already had.

This time, however, the sex was a subversion of that. It was an affront to God, and a staining of what grew within the host. Their blood had combined with the unholy seal below them, and now that he was inside of her, the ritual was in full flow. Above Rita's moans of pleasure, Marcus could hear cries of pain and agony echo from the lower floors of the house.

It was working.

Everything had built to this. The steady stream of bodies to the house had slowly built its power, while the protective symbols he'd placed had held it back. Now… everything was unleashed. Tonight, it was time for the house to break free from its shackles and gorge itself.

That was why he needed to hold out.

Marcus' own release would signal the beginning of the end, and he wanted the house to draw as much as it could before that happened.

CHAPTER 51

IT WAS CHAOS.

Ray was rooted in place, unable to comprehend or believe what was happening all around him in the great hall.

This isn't possible.

How could he accept what his eyes were showing him? There were strange people who had seemingly appeared from nowhere in the room with them. He knew those deformed and twisted 'others' were not human.

Ray had never believed in the things Marcus and Vincent had talked about—things that supposedly dwelled within the dark corners of the house. It was just a fantasy, believed by people who hadn't accepted what death really was.

But, as it turned out, it was Ray who had been naïve. The evidence was there for him to see, killing the guests and ripping them apart.

One poor attendee had his head torn clean off while he screamed, the wails getting higher before being cut short as his spinal cord became visible. The bone glistened with blood as it slipped out from the meat of his torn neck.

Another lady was gutted by two pale children, one of whom only had black pits for eyes, the skin around the sockets torn and ruined.

Ray also saw a man fighting against a horde of undead spirits. The swarm around him pushed the man closer to one of the stone walls, where Ray noticed the consistency of the wall begin to change—the wallpaper warped and morphed, turning into something else entirely.

Becoming more like... skin.

Then, something emerged from the fleshy substance, ripping itself free like a demonic child fighting from a womb.

The creature from the wall was different from the other ghosts in the room, however. Its skin was obsidian, and its wild eyes were a fiery yellow with vertical black slits for pupils. Long arms grabbed the man, and he was pulled back inside the fleshy expanse of the wall. The demon —if that's what it was—completely disappeared along with him, fully claiming its prey. However, some of the unfortunate soul's facial features remained on the stone surface: wide eyes and gaping mouth merging with the skin of the wall. A nightmarish prison, and one that Ray assumed would be for eternity.

That last horrible vision was enough to snap Ray back to life. As terrifying as all this was, Ray knew he had to act quickly.

Chloe.

The thought of anything like that happening to her filled him with dread the likes of which he'd never known before. He couldn't let his little girl succumb to this madness.

Ray didn't have time to try and make sense of what was going on. He just had to deal with what was before him and get to his daughter. His thoughts also ran to his wife as well, but Ray had no idea where she even was.

He felt an approaching cold behind him, one that grew stronger and more biting with each passing moment. He turned to see a tall man with no jaw shambling towards him, then reach out with pale arms and black fingernails.

Ray quickly broke into a sprint, fleeing from the approaching ghoul and weaving through the carnage in the great hall. His heart pounded in his chest, but the spike of adrenaline resulted in a kind of hyper-focus; every detail seemed to register, and Ray was able to duck and weave past clawing and reaching hands. Some were from the demonic entities, but others belonged to pleading guests who were being slaughtered.

Just as he was about to make it to the door, someone—or something

—did manage to grab him, taking fistfuls of his jacket in a desperate grip. Ray quickly turned, but was thankful to see it was one of the guests—a lady dressed in a black, strapless gown. She appeared to be in her sixties, and her eyes were wide with panic as she clung to him.

'Help me!' she pleaded.

While Ray was desperate to get to Chloe, he wasn't about to shrug off someone who so dearly needed his help. So, he put an arm around her and ushered the woman along with him. They broke through from the great hall and into the adjoining corridor, where they saw bodies lying on the floor. But at least there didn't appear to be any spirits barring the way, though Ray could still hear the hellish noises from the hall behind them.

'We need to get out of here,' the lady said as they set off running again. Ray slipped on something squishy underfoot. He managed to keep his footing, but he looked down to see something red and mushy on the ground. Ray pushed on, not wanting to know what he had been standing on.

'When we get to the entrance lobby,' he said, 'I want you to keep going out through the main door. Don't stop running.'

'And what about you?' she asked.

Ray kept his eyes dead ahead, teeth gritted together in determination. 'I need to get my daughter.'

CHAPTER 52

PATRICIA STRUGGLED FOR BREATH, running as fast as she had in a long time, which was made doubly hard since she was in heels. The exertion sapped her strength, but so too did the fear that overwhelmed her and pressed on her chest like a physical weight. That, combined with the running, made breathing difficult.

She had to keep going. Otherwise, she would wind up like those other poor guests back in the great hall. One *worse* than death.

But even as the intense panic threatened Patricia's sanity, the irony of finally seeing what she'd always wanted to was not lost on her.

Betsy had been right.

She should have left with her friend when given the chance.

The man that was guiding Patricia through the corridors ushered them both out into the entrance lobby. Body parts were scattered across the floor in rapidly expanding pools of blood. Thankfully, whatever massacre had taken place here now seemed to be over.

Patricia was turned and faced her guide, who stopped short.

'The door is there,' he said, pointing over to the exit. 'You just need to run through. Keep going to the road at the end of the driveway and don't look back.'

Patricia nodded, trying desperately to hold herself together for a little while longer.

Just long enough to escape.

'Good luck finding your little girl,' she told him, sucking in deep breaths. 'Go save her, and then get her the hell out of here.'

He gave half a smile, then turned and ran, making his way up the stairs. Patricia looked over to the door, towards her salvation, and drew every ounce of strength she had.

Just a little bit farther.

She ran. It was only a short distance to the exit, and she made it without incident. Judging by the wails and screams that sounded from other areas of the house, the entities seemed to be busy elsewhere. Patricia then pulled open the front door... and stopped dead.

On the porch outside a man was pulling himself across the stone ground. His bottom half was gone, and below his waist were only long, glistening red tendrils—intestines and guts that slithered behind.

One of his arms was twisted and deformed, a withered imitation of a limb. His head was a mess of cuts and lacerations, and there were bulging growths on one side. The skin of one of them was pulled down over one eye and connected to his cheek.

The withered hand reached out to Patricia, who shrieked in absolute terror. She took a step back, but there was something else blocking the way.

Arms suddenly wrapped around her. The skin was black and scaly, and the fingers of both were long and had talon-like ends. A sudden and overpowering sulphuric smell assaulted Patricia. She started to scream. The touch of the thing that held her burned.

Patricia was hoisted up into the air like a doll, then dragged backwards. She kicked her feet frantically in the air, causing her shoes to fall free, but it was futile. Whatever had her in its grasp was simply too strong. She turned her head and managed to see a little of the nightmare pulling her backwards.

It was a frightful creature, with a face that was a mix of human and inhuman features, all melded together like they had been made from wax that had started to melt. A mass of yellow eyes, all different sizes, lined the face and head. Behind the monster, Patricia saw the wall she was being moved towards had changed—it was now an expanse of pulsating skin, and her mind ran back to the man in the great hall who had been pulled into a similar flesh wall.

Patricia wailed, and she kicked against the shins of the entity, but succeeded only in cutting the thick flesh of her heel on the hard, jagged skin. Something cold and wet found her ear. A long, thin tongue that pushed inwards, secreting a viscous liquid deep into her inner ear.

With tears in her eyes, Patricia felt herself dragged inside the enveloping flesh of the wall. It was thick and warm and moulded around her form. The demon that held her suddenly released its grip, though she had no idea where it disappeared to. However, she was not able to turn her head to see, or even move her body at all. The only thing she could do was to roll her eyes and silently scream.

CHAPTER 53

VINCENT SAT on his bed with his hands over his head, pulling at his hair. He was desperate to block out the screaming outside.

He was also terrified of what could come into his room, either through the door… or by other means.

While the house had a purpose for him, Vincent knew it was difficult to control the poisoned and feral souls trapped within, even for something as powerful as Perron Manor. When not watched and controlled, those wild entities would always try to indulge in depraved acts against the living. Vincent could only hope the house could keep hold long enough for it to finish feeding.

A sudden rattling on his door caused him to jump.

'Help! Help me!'

'Go away!' Vincent shouted back. Tears were already streaming down his face, and his nose ran freely, with long strands of mucus dripping into his lap.

'Please! It's coming!' the person outside yelled.

The pounding on the door suddenly changed, becoming louder yet slower in frequency. He knew that whoever was outside was now kicking at the door, desperate to get in. Vincent was terrified that the person would also draw unwanted attention if they kept going like that. He needed to put a stop to it.

He got up, fists clenched, and strode to the door. 'I said fuck off!' Vincent then swung the door open, ready to confront the guest, but was met only by a look of surprise from a tall, rotund man in a suit. A rotted hand rested on top of the guest's bald head, and a young woman with long, stringy hair stepped from behind him. She wore a smile that, thanks to serrations at either side of her mouth, ran all the way up to her ears. She was naked, and her stomach had been cut open, with black, rope-like intestines bubbling free from the wound.

'Help,' the terrified man whispered. The entity behind him then thrust him forward, forcing him into the room. The screaming man crashed into Vincent and knocked him aside before falling to the floor. The manic spirit, screaming like a banshee, was quickly atop him. Vincent shrieked in terror as the ghoul's hand drew back its jagged and sharp nails. The hand then thrusted down. There was a crack, and the hand forced its way *through* skin and skull, destroying the back of the man's head.

Vincent then acted on impulse as his fight or flight instinct kicked in, very clearly favouring running for his life. He pushed himself to his feet once again and sprinted from the room, barging past anyone who got in his way.

The exit... I need to get to the exit.

But as he ran, Vincent was forced to stop when he spotted something up ahead: a small figure that lay in a crumpled heap on the floor.

Chloe.

The same demon that had first coerced Vincent into following its orders stood above her, looking down.

Pazuzu.

'Chloe!'

Vincent looked farther ahead to see who had called out, and saw Ray sprinting down the corridor towards them.

CHAPTER 54

RAY COULD SCARCELY BELIEVE what he was seeing. The madness from the great hall was terrifying enough, but he now experienced a whole new level of fear upon seeing that... *monster*... standing over his daughter.

He had no idea if Chloe was even alive. She was just a small, crumpled form on the floor, her hair covering her face.

The demon that stood close to her had black skin, and its knees were bent inward like the legs of a beast. Its stomach was sunken, pulled in tightly beneath a serrated, overhanging ribcage. The arms were disproportionately long, and its mouth was a mass of jagged, spindly teeth with no lips to cover them, resembling the mouth of a piranha pulled into a wide and hideous grin. And the creature's eyes were fleshy orbs of fiery yellow protruding out from the sockets. The skin of its face was like dark, melted wax.

The terrifying monster was not looking down at Chloe, however, but at Ray.

'Leave her alone!' he screamed.

There was another figure beyond the grinning nightmare as well. It was also stationary, but very much human.

Vincent.

The demon started to lean down and reach its taloned hands out towards Chloe's fragile form. Ray didn't even think, but simply ran forward towards it, desperate to protect his child. Just as he got close, the obsidian demon swung a hand faster than Ray thought possible. The impact across his face was so sudden and powerful that his head snapped back and he was physically thrown through the air, crashing down to the floor several feet from where he'd stood.

Ray's face burned and the back of his neck throbbed with pain. His vision spun. It was a struggle for him to lift his head and look back at the creature.

It now stood in front of Chloe, putting itself between Ray and his daughter as if in challenge.

Ray had to stop that thing from harming his daughter, even if it meant his own death. He got slowly back to his feet. He was unsteady and had to use the wall beside him for support. While sacrificing his own life to help Chloe was a given, what terrified him was the knowledge that it might not be enough. If he was dead, then the demon would just move on to her anyway. Unless...

'Vincent!' he shouted. 'Help! Please!'

However, his brother-in-law just looked scared and dumbfounded, and did not move at all. Ray couldn't blame him for freezing up, given the nightmarish situation they were all in, but this was his daughter at stake.

Vincent's own niece.

They had only really known the man for ten months, but surely family meant *something* to him?

The demonic entity turned its head towards Vincent, who shrank away under its gaze and took a few steps back.

'Leave... leave her alone.'

In response, the monster uttered a kind of chattering noise that, to Ray, sounded something like a chuckle. The demon clearly didn't see Vincent as any kind of threat. And why should it?

It took a step towards the man, and Vincent again backed up in kind. However, Ray was beginning to get his bearings again, and his vision had cleared. His head still throbbed, but Ray was at least now steady on his feet.

'Get away from me!' Vincent cried out.

In a flash, however, the monster was on him, moving with a speed that was almost impossible to comprehend. It suddenly had him in its grasp, and the long claws of one hand wrapped around his throat. Vincent wheezed, struggling for air, and his eyes went wide.

In that moment, Ray saw an opportunity. He quickly sprinted over to Chloe and scooped her up, holding his daughter in both arms. Though he was still a little wobbly, her light weight was easy to bear. She was breathing, and the relief he felt at her not being dead was overwhelming.

He knew he couldn't just leave Vincent. Not after the man had distracted the demon and allowed Ray to collect his daughter. But… what could he possibly do?

As it turned out, Ray didn't need to do anything.

The monster lifted Vincent from the floor, and his legs kicked wildly beneath him. Then, just as the demon's mouth opened and those sharp, spindly teeth moved closer to Vincent's terrified face, there was another thundering noise that boomed all around them. It was forceful enough that the vibrations ran through the floor beneath them. Ray even felt them run up his legs and into his gut.

There was another crashing sound, and the very walls around them shook. The demon, in turn, looked around in what Ray assumed was fright. The inhuman features actually appeared… scared.

Is it afraid of the house?

The creature looked like it was listening, though Ray had no idea to what. Another booming sound rang out and the walls shook again. The demon screeched, and dropped Vincent to the floor. The man began coughing and spluttering, rubbing at his neck as he sucked in desperate breaths.

He scuttled away while the ground beneath the demon's taloned feet started to discolour. It then changed, just like Ray had seen the walls downstairs change before…

The demonic entity wailed, but inhuman arms slithered free of the leathery skin that was the floor. They grabbed the shrieking demon. It fought against the monstrous arms, which were lined with bubbling black and red flesh, but the demon was overpowered. It was then dragged down into the ground beneath it. After letting out a final, hideous scream, the demon was pulled fully into the floor, the flesh swallowing it whole.

Ray's mind spun, unable to comprehend what had just happened. He, Chloe, and Vincent had just been saved. It was almost like the house itself had pulled the demon away from them, bringing a wild dog to heel.

Ray sprinted over to Vincent, holding Chloe tightly to him. He then helped his brother-in-law up.

'We need to go,' he urged. Vincent coughed and nodded.

Then they ran, all the way back to the entrance lobby. As they moved, it occurred to Ray that the screams around the house were dying out.

Either whatever was happening was drawing to a close, or there weren't many left alive to scream.

CHAPTER 55

Rita clawed at Marcus' back, digging her nails into his skin. She bit his lip as they kissed, and their tongues thrust against each other in a wild dance.

She was getting close.

'Keep going,' she said, panting. Their sweat mingled and intertwined just like their bodies.

The whole room was cold, but that just added to the sensations, and it helped give everything a sharpness. Her skin felt like it was on fire.

Through blurred vision, Rita looked up over Marcus' thrusting shoulder, and noticed shadows move about, seeing the forms of people floating close to her and looking down.

Watching.

She blinked the sweat away so that her vision cleared. What she saw there should have terrified her. But it didn't.

There *was* an audience of curious and pale faces. Milky eyes. Decayed flesh.

This is madness! Run!

Rita shook her head, trying to silence the voice that threatened to ruin everything for her.

'Keep going,' she repeated, pulling Marcus down into her. 'Harder!'

CHAPTER 56

VINCENT RAN ALONG BEHIND RAY, who carried Chloe while they navigated the stairs. They then fled out through the entrance door and into the night, their escape unhindered.

It was cold out, and Chloe—still unmoving—was only in a t-shirt and pyjama bottoms.

However, the more they ran, the more Vincent's stomach churned, and a fiery pain started to prickle over his skin. It became worse the farther away he got from the house.

In addition, his throat still burned from the icy-cold grip of the demon. Breathing was difficult, made worse by a panic that still ebbed inside of him; it had spiked earlier when Pazuzu had grabbed his throat.

Vincent had thought he was going to die back there at the hands of that vile, demonic entity—one that had been a constant tormentor to him in Perron Manor. However, the house had stopped it, and seen fit to spare Vincent's life.

That meant it still had a purpose for him.

He had an idea what that might be, but second-guessing the house was futile.

It seemed to perceive things in a different way, one he wasn't privy to. The plan to have Rita fall pregnant could not be a certainty, given the complications of conceiving.

Yet it had all fallen into place.

And the *Ianua Diaboli* had found its way to the house when the Blackwaters had taken ownership.

Marcus had met Vincent, who in turn had brought his sister to the house. She had then fallen pregnant exactly when she had needed to.

The right people at the right place at the right time, all bringing everything together. Just how far did the hellish tendrils from the house stretch? And how far into the future could it see in order to move its pawns on the chessboard as needed?

Was the future therefore set in stone, or could things be changed?

'Hold her,' Ray said after they stopped midway down the drive. He thrust Chloe into Vincent's arms and slipped off his jacket.

Ray then wrapped it around his daughter to give her some extra warmth before taking her back and checking her over. Vincent could see that the girl was breathing, so he hoped she was just unconscious with no serious injuries.

'Is she okay?' he asked.

'I hope so,' Ray replied. Vincent could hear the worry and anxiety in the man's voice. Ray then gently shook Chloe and started to stroke her hair as he cradled her to him. 'Wake up, kiddo,' he whispered.

Chloe remained unresponsive, and Vincent had a horrible feeling that she may be more hurt than he first thought. However, after a little more prompting from Ray, the young girl's eyes slowly flickered open.

'Daddy?' she asked, looking up at her father, clearly confused.

'It's okay, sweetie,' he said, hugging her tightly. Chloe winced and brought a hand up to the back of her head. 'Are you okay?' Ray asked.

'My head hurts,' she groaned. 'What happened?'

'You just had a little tumble, that's all,' he said. 'But you're fine.' Ray then turned to Vincent. 'Rita is still inside,' he whispered.

Vincent nodded. Surely she would still be safe? The house wanted her. *Needed* her. And though it was clear the spirits and demons inside could act on their own if left unchecked, Vincent didn't doubt that Rita would be protected.

Wouldn't she?

'I have to go back,' Ray added.

Better you than me, Vincent thought, knowing the house had no use for him, only his wife. While Vincent didn't want his sister to die, he himself didn't have the strength or bravery to go back inside to get her.

Not yet. Though when things calmed down, Vincent knew he'd be spending the rest of his life in that house. He couldn't get away. He'd fled this far, but the very thought of going any farther filled him with nausea.

Perron Manor still owned him.

Back inside, Pazuzu had clearly wanted Chloe, but the house had allowed Vincent enough freedom to save her. Maybe it was because she was inconsequential, or perhaps there was another reason. Regardless, it had protected him and saved his life. So there was no way it would let him leave.

'I'll take Chloe,' Vincent said, holding out his arms. Ray looked down at his daughter, then over to Vincent. Vincent could see deliberation on his brother-in-law's face. Eventually, Ray relented and handed Chloe over.

'What's happening?' Chloe groggily asked.

'Nothing,' Ray said as Vincent took hold of her. 'You just need to wait out here with Uncle Vincent for a little while, okay?' I'm just going to get your mother.' Ray then ran a loving hand over her hair and gently kissed her on the forehead. 'I'll be as quick as I can.' Ray then looked to Vincent. 'Keep her safe,' he instructed.

Vincent nodded. 'I will.'

Ray gave one last look to his daughter, then turned and ran back towards the house.

CHAPTER 57

He could hold out no longer; the building pleasure was just too great.

Marcus shuddered and let out an involuntary cry as he spilt his orgasm inside of the host. Finally, he flopped forward on top of her—completely spent and gasping for breath.

He had seen the 'others' gather in the room during the act, which had confused him. They shouldn't have been nearby, given Vincent had put the protective seals in place.

Don't worry about it. Your ascension is now.

With a satisfied smile, Marcus rocked back onto his heels and pulled himself free of Rita.

The cries of pain around the hotel had long stopped, so he hoped the house had had its fill. If so, some of the house's power should have been infused into Marcus during the Ritual, which in turn would have spread into the host. The life growing inside of her would now be tainted. More than that, it would be *clavis*—the key. And it would usher in something terrible to the world.

But the power Marcus had been blessed with still lingered, and it should stay with him long enough to cross over. He would gain eternal life, but at the same time keep his own free will. He would not be an eternal puppet like the other souls in the house, but an actual force in the dark and mirrored reality, possessing the ability to cross over at will.

Rita pushed herself up to her elbows. 'That was great,' she said. Her cheeks were flushed, and her smile was one of satisfaction.

But Marcus didn't care. She was just a means to an end. The house had gotten what it wanted—she would stay here now and birth its child.

And Marcus would get what he wanted as well.

After starting down the path his grandfather had been too fearful to tread, he was going to become more than a man. He would stand alongside demonic forces of the underworld.

Excitement filled him.

Rita then looked about at the silent entities watching them, all eerily motionless. However, she did not seem frightened, which was yet more evidence that the house still had its hold on her.

'What now?' she asked.

Marcus just smiled and pushed her from the pentagram. Rita backed up out of the symbol with a look of confusion on her face.

'Now' he began, 'I take the final step.' Marcus looked around for the knife he had used earlier. It surprised him that one of the gathered spirits—a small child with no eyes—stepped forward and held the blade out, offering it to Marcus.

He took it.

'Thank you, young one.'

The expression of the boy was as empty as his eye sockets.

Marcus then brought the knife up to his neck, ready to draw the edge over his throat. And he would do so under his own free will. Which was critical.

The metal sank into his skin, drawing blood. Rita gasped as Marcus felt the warm liquid dribble down to his chest. Pain spread like liquid fire and he yanked the blade horizontally.

Flicking his eyes down, Marcus saw other hands on the handle as well, covering his own. The child that had given him the knife was now standing behind him, and had reached around to take hold of the weapon. He felt the child's coldness and smelled its stench.

Why was the spirit helping him?

No matter, there was no reason to stop now. Marcus pulled harder and screamed in agony as he was forced to saw and slice at the tendons and thyroid cartilage. But he knew pain was only temporary.

The prior trickle of warm blood was now a stream, and it spilled from the gaping wound in his neck, wetting and warming his chest completely. He coughed, spraying the crimson liquid to the ground beneath him. His body instinctively fought and struggled for air, and he heard wheezing, gurgling sounds come from his open throat.

Marcus fell as the strength to hold his body up vanished. He slumped to the floor, and the dead in the room gathered around him.

Come see me die, he thought to himself. *I will soon rise up and control you all.*

Something was wrong. The souls that watched him die all started to smile.

It was only then that Marcus realised the truth. For his plan to succeed, he needed to carry out the ritual under his own agency, and not under the possession of the house.

Now, however, it became immediately clear that was *not* the case. He had no doubt Perron Manor had allowed him to realise that in his final moments, blowing away the veil of lies.

He had been a puppet of the house all along. And would continue so in eternal death.

CHAPTER 58

RAY WAS WALKING through the remnants of a massacre. Bodies of the dead littered the ground, and the floor was damp with blood.

But it was quiet. Horribly quiet. Ray's sloshing footsteps were the only thing to break the intense silence.

He was terrified—more scared than he could ever remember being. The things he'd witnessed only minutes before had been almost impossible to believe, yet he had seen them for himself. Having one's worldview completely shattered like that, on top of the horrific violence itself, was not something he was prepared to handle.

And to top it all off, there was a worry growing in the pit of his gut about Rita.

If any of the people inside had survived what happened, then surely they would have fled outside, just as Ray had.

To him, that meant no one else had survived.

Ray tried to push the thought from his mind, because he wouldn't stop searching until he either found her or found proof she was dead.

But it was hard not to think that he'd lost her, and keeping a lid on that realisation was difficult.

He carefully navigated the ground floor as quietly as possible, checking every room. Though the unexplainable activity had apparently now ceased, Ray was still on edge, certain that *something* still remained here. He knew it could simply be waiting to pounce.

However, the longer he searched without incident, the more he began to feel safer... relatively speaking. Eventually, he began to call out for his wife.

'Rita!'

But he got no response, and that made his worry grow. Surely there was no reason not to reply.

If the worst had happened, then Chloe would be without a mother, and he would have lost the only woman he'd ever loved. Their recent troubles suddenly seemed irrelevant, and an enormous surge of guilt came over him. He knew he should have done more to fix things between them before...

Ray began to quicken the pace and screamed her name again.

'Rita!'

She might still be here. She can't be dead. Can't be.

Cold logic was replaced with desperation, and Ray sprinted upstairs, searching that floor as well.

'Rita!'

Don't be dead. Don't be dead.

It had occurred to him that his wife could well be among the mushy, torn-up remains he'd already seen, or that she had been sucked into the house itself. If that was the case, he might not be able to find any physical proof of her death.

'Rita!'

With only one more storey to search, he turned the corner to the stairs—and immediately jumped. There was a figure standing at the top.

Ray braced himself, ready for the madness to start all over again.

But when the individual didn't leap down and attack him, and Ray's initial shock wore off, he realised just who it was that stood at the head of the stairs.

'Rita!'

She was alive.

'Ray?' she asked softly, sounding confused. Her eyes were wide with fear, and she looked as fragile as Ray had ever seen her.

He rushed up the stairs towards her as relief flooded through him.

Rita's legs felt like they were about to give out, and she was immediately thankful when Ray took her in his arms and pulled her into his chest. She cried into him.

'What happened?' she asked in between sobs.

'I have no fucking idea,' he replied, squeezing her tightly. 'But I'm so glad you're alive. I… I didn't think I'd find you.'

'What about Chloe?' she asked, pulling away from Ray. She was desperate to find out where her daughter was, but terrified of what he would say.

'She's safe,' Ray told her. Rita's tears flowed again, but this time she cried with utter relief.

The confusion that filled her was overwhelming. After seeing Marcus cut his own throat, it was as if a fog had been lifted from her eyes. She had stood motionless for a while, watching him cough and splutter as the life faded from his eyes. The strange entities around Marcus had then slowly dissipated away to nothing.

And then she was alone. And scared. And suddenly ashamed for all that she had done recently: ignoring her family, cheating on her husband, giving herself over so completely to Marcus, a man who had initially made her skin crawl.

When she then looked at his dead body—throat cut into a gaping yawn—similar feelings of revulsion quickly returned.

What have I done?

She'd run from the room, out into the hallway, and was met with a horrific sight.

Bodies were strewn around the corridor, though none were whole. A leg. An arm. Even a jaw.

'I'm so sorry,' she wailed, clutching Ray again. 'I don't understand why… how…' But she couldn't finish. She wanted to tell him that it was almost like someone else was controlling her, making her do those things. She even remembered screaming internally as she had flirted with Marcus before fucking him.

She realised that Ray was crying too. 'It's okay,' he said. 'It wasn't you.'

'What do you mean?' She looked up into his wet eyes.

'It was this place,' he replied. 'This *house*.'

Rita wasn't following, but it seemed there was no time to explain.

'Come on,' he said, taking her hand. 'We need to get out of here and back to Chloe. Let's go.'

Rita followed, desperate to see her daughter again. At the same time, she was ashamed at the prospect of facing her.

CHAPTER 59

'CHLOE!' Rita yelled and ran over to her daughter.

Ray watched, feeling something approaching happiness—as much as he could muster knowing there were many people dead back inside the house.

Rita seemed different. She reminded Ray of how she'd been a month ago, that one night where he thought he'd broken through to her, before she'd fallen back into whatever stupor that was controlling her.

But now, as she hugged Chloe as tightly as Ray had seen, and with such desperate love, he knew he was in the presence of his wife again.

That meant whatever had just happened in the house, Rita was now free of its pull.

Ray just hoped the change was permanent.

It was all so clear to him now. Perhaps he'd broken free of his own haze, but he was suddenly angry with himself for not seeing what had really been going on earlier. Hell, even his wife's *physical* appearance had changed.

Though, could he really blame himself for not realising that his wife had somehow become possessed by a haunted fucking house? It was insane to even think of.

'What's going on, Mum?' Chloe asked, still wrapped up in Ray's jacket.

Rita looked over to Ray with uncertain eyes.

'There was an accident,' Ray told his daughter. 'We have to leave here now.'

Chloe frowned. 'Will we be coming back?'

Ray paused for a moment, knowing how much the answer might upset her. But it wasn't something he could lie to her about. 'No, sweetie,' he said, as gently as he could. 'We're never coming back here.'

CHAPTER 60

1 MONTH LATER.

'Good news,' the lady on the other end of the phone said. 'The result is positive. You're pregnant. Congratulations!'

'Thank you,' Rita replied, feeling deflated. She then set down the receiver. That wasn't the result she'd been hoping for, though it was the one she had been expecting. She'd been late, and—worried about what it could mean—had gone to the doctor for a sample bottle so she could test for pregnancy. After returning the bottle, the five-day wait until she could make the call had been excruciating.

Now she had to tell Ray.

Rita pulled her coat tighter around herself and left the phonebox she was in. It was a short walk back to the hotel the family was staying in, but she planned to take her time. Chloe was at school, which was the only thing Rita could be thankful for at the moment.

How would she break it to Ray?

The issue of her cheating—if that was the word for it—was still raw. More so for her than for him, as Ray insisted he didn't blame Rita at all for what had happened. In his head, he was convinced she had been possessed by a supernatural presence, which was still something Rita was struggling to come to terms with.

But at the end of their time in Perron Manor, when Marcus had died, Rita had *seen* those spirits for herself. So it had to be true.

Regardless of how understanding Ray was being, however, and even if Rita wasn't to blame, the infidelity had still happened. And now there was a further repercussion to deal with.

Even though she dragged out the walk back as much as she could, Rita still reached the door to the hotel room far sooner than she'd wanted to. She took a breath and stepped inside.

Ray was lying on the bed, reading a magazine. He smiled upon seeing her and sat up. 'Hey, how was your walk?'

'Fine,' she said and closed the door behind her. She then slipped out of her coat and hung it up.

She felt nauseous.

Rita turned to him. There was no putting it off any longer… she had to get this over with.

'Ray,' she began. 'There's something we need to talk about.'

He sat up, and a frown crossed his face, no doubt mirroring the one Rita was wearing herself. 'What is it?'

She slowly padded over to the bed and sat near him, shaking, struggling to control her nerves.

She took a breath.

'I'm… pregnant.'

Ray's eyes widened. She could see him doing the mental arithmetic, something she had already done weeks ago.

Since getting out of the house, Ray had been patient with her, letting Rita try to recover both emotionally and physically from what had happened. For the first week after leaving she had done nothing but sleep and eat, and it had helped her body return to a healthier state. It was only in the past week that she had felt comfortable enough to again give herself over to her husband physically. Prior to that, however, the last time she had slept with Ray was months ago.

She saw the realisation quickly dawn on him, and Ray was unable to hide the expression of pain. The news hit him like a physical blow.

'I'm so sorry,' she whispered. Ray sat in silence for a while, and Rita was braced for him to explode—to scream at her for ruining their family.

But he didn't.

Instead, he reached out his hand and placed it on hers. 'It isn't your fault,' he said. 'I keep telling you that.'

'But... I'm pregnant,' she said again. 'With *his* baby.'

Ray shook his head. 'No. The baby is ours.'

Rita swivelled her body to fully face her husband. She was stunned. But a sliver of joy sprouted up from her gut like the green shoot of a plant breaking through the heavy, dark soil of her fear.

'Are you sure?' she asked.

He nodded and gave her the most genuine smile she had ever seen. 'You're damn right I am. That house nearly ruined us. Nearly *killed* us. But we beat it, and we got out. This isn't a setback, Rita, it's a blessing. And, if you agree, we'll have this baby together. Then Chloe will get a little brother or sister.'

Rita didn't know what to say. She'd been terrified of how Ray was going to react, especially since the idea of not keeping the unborn child was one that made her feel physically sick. It wasn't an option for her to do anything but keep it. But she had been scared of where that would leave the family unit.

So, hearing Ray understand the situation, and more than that, actually *want* to bring the baby into their family and love it like he did Chloe made her burst with joy.

She started to cry. She couldn't help it. The whole situation was just too overwhelming. 'I want that, too,' she said.

Ray smiled, tearing up himself. He brought her towards him and hugged her. 'Then this is a good thing—we're going to have another baby together. But promise me this: no matter what, we never tell either child what happened in that fucking house.'

Rita let out a small laugh. 'I *definitely* agree with that.'

Vincent lay on his bed in the foetal position. He rocked and pulled at his hair.

It had just gone three in the morning. He hadn't slept in what felt like weeks. The room was ice cold and the dead surrounded him. They *always* surrounded him now. Everywhere he went in the house, they were there watching him. And with them was Pazuzu.

It wasn't the only demon in the house, but was by far the most evil. It had decided to torment Vincent relentlessly since that night.

Pazuzu couldn't kill him. It wasn't allowed to. His job as the warden of the house was far too important.

But his comfort and sanity were not.

The demon stood over him, looking down on Vincent with that twisted and horrific face. It reached out a black talon as Vincent cowered and mewled. He then felt a sharp claw rake down his cheek, drawing blood. He screamed.

'Leave me alone! Please. Just leave me alone!'

But it wouldn't. This was his life now. The demon was angry at Vincent, and now it would have years of revenge on his mind and soul.

Even when Vincent was allowed to leave the house for a brief respite, to shop and gather basic supplies, he always had to return. Staying outside of the walls triggered an ever-rising pain and burning within him, which became unbearable after only a few hours.

Even if that were not the case, Pazuzu itself had said it would come for him if needed, no matter where he ran. And then, it wouldn't need to hold back.

Vincent almost wished that, after the night of Halloween, he had been arrested and forcefully taken from the house. Even if it had killed him, at least he would have been free of all this.

But that wasn't what had happened. The police investigated, and certainly suspected Vincent, Ray, and Rita, but could prove nothing. So, they were all set free, and Vincent was forced to return back to this hell.

Vincent knew that when the house was finally finished with him, and the time was right, Pazuzu would take his life... and Perron Manor would claim his soul.

Then, at long last, the unholy child created within these walls would be called home.

THE END

HAUNTED: PURGATORY

BOOK 3

CHAPTER 1

THE HAZELNUT COFFEE Sarah sipped was piping hot and full of flavour.

Her sister would have hated it.

The last time Sarah had been in the *Hill of Beans* was with Chloe. And back then, the man she was now due to meet had received a tongue lashing. All because he had delivered a warning Sarah and Chloe should both have heeded.

David Ritter entered the coffee shop and quickly spotted her. He was dressed in a dark t-shirt with the logo of a classic rock band blazed across the front, black jacket, blue jeans and scruffy trainers. He was of below average height, slightly overweight, with greying, brushed-back hair. However, he had a kind face and was as unthreatening as a person could be.

He spotted Sarah and gave her a sad, sympathetic smile—followed by a wave—and walked over.

'I'm sorry to hear about what happened to your sister,' he offered.

Sarah just gave a tight-lipped smile and small nod in return, then gestured to the empty chair opposite her. He took it.

'It was an accident,' Sarah lied. She didn't want him to know the full details of the story, nor the true danger Perron Manor actually posed. Not when she needed something from him.

It wasn't an accident. She had been killed. By something not of this world.

'So it *was* the fall that killed her?' David asked, seeming a little surprised. 'I'd heard that was the case, but thought maybe…'

'No, that much was true,' Sarah lied again. 'But before the fall, things happened we didn't tell the police about.'

David gave a solemn nod.

'So,' he started, 'you said in your message you wanted to talk to me about something?'

'Yes.' Sarah took another sip of her drink. 'Chloe and I got into a fight that day… before everything happened. She believed what you told her about Perron Manor, and I… well, I had a hard time with it. But Chloe did let something interesting slip. She said that, according to you, the only way to free the souls trapped at Perron Manor was… with an exorcism?'

'Possibly,' David said. 'But it was more an educated guess, to be honest. Why do you ask?'

Sarah took a breath. 'After Chloe died, I saw her again in the house. Upstairs. She seemed like she was in pain.'

David's eyes widened, but he then just nodded again. 'The house has her,' he stated.

That threw Sarah. She'd expected the revelation to be more of a surprise to him. *Does he know more about that place than he's letting on?*

'I believe it does, yes,' Sarah continued. 'But I can't let it keep her. I won't allow it.'

David paused for a moment. 'So… you want the place exorcised?'

'That's right,' she said, then added, 'and I need you to help me do it. Will you?'

David didn't consider the question for very long. 'Yes,' he said enthusiastically. 'I'll help you.'

Sarah felt a wave of relief, then smiled. 'Good.'

There was a momentary break in the conversation, and David used it as an opportunity to get himself a drink. When he walked back over, his face was a picture of seriousness.

'Do you think an exorcism is the best way to help Chloe?' Sarah asked.

He considered that for a moment, then nodded. 'I think so. As I said to her when I last saw her, there are no guarantees, and I want you to know that up front. However, I would say that is the best way to free her. Theoretically, it should release *all* the souls trapped inside.'

Sarah took another drink and considered his words. It all sounded so crazy. Ghosts, spirits, and demons? Those things shouldn't be real. However, Sarah's reality had changed now. She knew the truth. Things she had previously dismissed as make-believe were something much more real.

In fact, Chloe had been killed by a demon, and now her soul was trapped in the house she and Sarah had recently inherited.

Perron Manor.

'Can you help with the exorcism?' Sarah asked. 'I mean, is it something you can carry out?'

David's eyes went wide. 'Me? God, no. We'd need a priest, as well as the permission of the Church.'

'Okay. So how do we get permission and a priest?'

'We ask,' was David's response. 'I know of a priest local to the area, Father Janosch. He has experience in the supernatural and the occult. First, we need to convince him that you are telling the truth. He then convinces the Church. Hopefully, we can then get the exorcism officially sanctioned.'

'And what do we need to do to convince them? Provide proof?'

David nodded. 'Exactly. But it isn't always an easy thing to accomplish. However, I think I can help.'

'How so?'

'With my team. This is the kind of thing we do: investigate paranormal phenomenon and catalogue evidence of it.'

Sarah was vaguely aware of the team. After all, she'd read the book he'd written about Perron Manor, and in it there were details of a previous investigation in 2014 they had carried out there.

'Then,' David went on, 'I go to Father Janosch with what we have gathered. I know him pretty well, so I'm sure he'd help us. Plus, he's already aware of Perron Manor.'

'Has he had any experiences there?'

David shook his head. 'Not that I know of, but most people around here know of the house.'

Sarah drained the last of her coffee. 'Okay,' she said. 'That all sounds good to me. So... when do we start?'

'Well,' David began, 'I'll need to run it past the team to make sure they are all on board, though I can't see that being an issue. Considering the things we saw during our last investigation, I'd imagine they'll be chomping at the bit to get back inside. Then we need to arrange dates—'

'As soon as possible,' Sarah stated. 'We can get in there today if need be.'

Perron Manor was Sarah's now, and hers alone. However, she hadn't set foot back inside since the night her sister had died—three weeks ago. In truth, going back there scared the hell out of her. But she didn't have a choice.

David held up his hands and gave a friendly smile. 'Woah,' he said, 'that is a little too fast. It could be a few days at least, to be honest. Like I said, I need to get everyone on board; some of them have day jobs and they would need to request time off. How about we aim to start this coming weekend?'

'Fine,' Sarah replied, a little disappointed it wasn't all happening sooner. The fear of going back was overshadowed by the need to help her sister. 'How long will all of this take?'

David shrugged. 'That's the rub. There's no telling, really. As long as it takes to get what we need.'

'Then how long does it *usually* take?' she asked. A growing level of frustration started to rise up within her.

David gave her another sad smile. 'Hard to say. It depends on what we get from the house. Could be one night, or it could be much, much longer.'

'You'll appreciate the situation my sister is in, David. She's suffering, so time is of the essence.'

Sarah tried to keep a lid on her bubbling anger. However, it was difficult to do so given Chloe's death was so raw. Sarah was still in the early stages of grief, but that was only exacerbated by knowing Chloe's soul somehow lived on in torment. Sarah pictured in her mind what she'd seen that night at Perron Manor: Chloe, twisted and rotted, staring out from a window and mouthing the words *help me*.

'I get that,' David gently said. 'Believe me, I do. And I'm sorry I can't make things go any quicker. But we will work as fast as we can, I promise you that.'

Sarah could only nod in response. He was being perfectly reasonable, yet it was hard to be patient.

'Okay,' she said, repressing the urge to sigh.

'We'd need full access to the building. I assume that won't be a problem?'

'No, not at all,' Sarah replied. Then she asked, 'Would you all be living there while you investigate?'

David nodded. 'To an extent. My team are all volunteers, so they'd give as much time as they could. But some would need to take time out of the investigation to deal with their work and personal lives. Same with me. But we'd spend as much time as we could there, which would involve sleeping at the house for the foreseeable future.'

To Sarah, their personal distractions sounded like it would just slow things down. 'I could pay you all for your time,' she offered. The inheritance money she'd received along with the house was still sitting in her bank account, mostly unused.

David raised his eyebrows in surprise. 'That's... very generous of you. But you don't need to do that—'

'I insist,' Sarah cut in. 'Seriously, if it helps speed things up, it'll be worth it. I'll also pay for everyone's food the entire time, if that works?'

David took a moment. 'That's very kind,' he said. 'But... are you sure?'

Sarah gave an assertive nod. 'I am.'

'Okay,' he said, unable to hide his smile. 'I've never been paid for this service before. It's always been voluntary.'

'Well, help me save my sister, and I'll even throw in a bonus. When can you get everyone on board?'

'I'll call them straight away,' he said. 'Hell, even if it's just me and no one else, I'll still start this weekend. Will you be staying at the house with us?'

Sarah nodded. 'Is that okay?'

'Of course,' he replied. 'But... you aren't going to be living there in the meantime, are you? I wouldn't advise it. I think the house could be dangerous.'

'I'm at a hotel at the moment,' Sarah told him. There was zero chance of her staying in that house alone.

'That's good. So, I'll pull the team together and speak to Father Janosch as well, just to forewarn him.'

'And I'll see you at the house on Saturday. Does midday work?' Sarah asked.

'It does,' David confirmed. He then held out his hand to shake. 'I promise I will do everything I can to help you and your sister,' he told her. 'I mean that.'

'I know you do,' Sarah told him and shook his hand. She was appreciative of the sentiment, but she needed him to do more than just try. She needed him to succeed.

And she would do everything in her power to make sure that happened.

I'm coming for you, Chloe.

CHAPTER 2

The day was finally upon them and David was shaking with a nervous excitement. The team were all packed into David's transit van on their way to Perron Manor.

'I can't believe how anxious I am,' Ralph Cobin said from his position behind David. Ralph was a big guy, too, so for him to be feeling that way spoke volumes of what lay ahead. Though considering what had happened during their investigation back in 2014, David could hardly blame him.

The transit van was a six-seater. It was just big enough for all of the team and their equipment, but it was extremely cramped inside.

Jenn Hogan was seated up front in the passenger seat, which was apt considering David always looked upon her as his right-hand woman. Not that he ever admitted it to the rest of the group.

Ann Tate sat next to Ralph, and in the very back seats were Jamie Curtis and George Dalton.

David's vehicle had certainly seen better days. It was close to ten years old and there was an audible squeak down by the passenger-side wheel as they drove. However, the van had served David well, and he didn't have the money to upgrade yet. Though, perhaps the money he and Sarah had agreed upon would go some way towards changing that.

David was splitting the fee equally with everyone, of course, minus a little bit he insisted go towards upgrading their equipment. Their operation had thus far been completely self-funded—by *him*—and was a true labour of love. If things went well at Perron Manor, and they were successful in helping Sarah, then maybe, just *maybe*, he could turn the venture into something more.

Of course, that wasn't David's main reason for being here. Or why Perron Manor was such an obsession. He had personal business to settle with that house.

In addition, there was the incident from their last investigation in 2014, where a ghostly voice had sent him a message: *'Return here. Help another in need.'*

Another in need.

He'd had years to think on that, and to David it could only mean one thing.

'I think we're all feeling that way,' Jenn Hogan said, replying to Ralph's comment. 'But this time at least we know a little of what to expect.'

Jenn had been with David the longest out of everyone and was every bit as passionate about the subject of the paranormal as he was. She had a strong build to her—no doubt a product of her day job in a warehouse, humping around boxes for hours on end—wavy red hair, light freckles on her face, and brown eyes. She wore a thick blue jumper with the sleeves rolled up to the elbows.

'And how is the client holding up?' George Dalton asked from the back. He was the baby of the group at only twenty-three years of age. 'I mean, is it right to be doing this so soon after her sister died?'

'It's what she wanted,' David answered. 'You all know the reason we are here.'

'Yeah, but I mean... doesn't it seem a little farfetched?'

David frowned at him through the rearview mirror, but it was Ann who responded.

'How can you say that after what we saw in there?' she asked, bewildered. 'We *know* the house is haunted. We saw it with our own eyes.'

'I get that,' George said defensively. 'And I'm not denying it. But for her to see her sister so soon after death... I dunno, does that seem right to everyone?'

'There's no reason to disbelieve the client,' David stated. 'If we didn't have our own experiences with Perron Manor, then I get why we might be sceptical. But, come on… you remember what happened.'

George shook his head and shrugged before rubbing a thin hand over his patchy goatee. He had angular cheekbones, a long and sharp nose, pronounced upper front teeth, and was dressed in a smart, grey suit jacket with a black t-shirt beneath. While he shared the same love of the paranormal they all did, his other passion was the tech they used during their investigations. He was also a freelance IT consultant and worked a lot of jobs with David.

That was how they'd first met.

The weekend they spent at Perron Manor in 2014 had certainly left its mark on the group, and was the cause of the anxiety that now rippled through them.

Getting access back then hadn't been easy.

David had tried for years to arrange an investigation at that house, with no success, but had eventually managed to get the former owner— Sarah's uncle, Vincent Bell—to agree to let them stay for a few days. And while they had originally gotten some impressive results, it was the last night that would live in their collective minds forever.

They had used a demon board down in the basement in an attempt to communicate with the dead. And it had worked… a little too well, in fact, as it wasn't just the dead that had come through. There was something else.

A demon.

David believed it was the demon that was behind everything at Perron Manor, and the reason all the other souls were trapped there and unable to move on. By exorcising the demonic entity completely, David hoped the damned at Perron Manor would finally be able to move on.

However, trying to do that could be incredibly dangerous.

Sarah had told David that her sister had died when fleeing the house. A genuine accident, where she'd tripped and fallen down a flight of stairs.

But David had to wonder about that.

Still, it didn't change anything for him. The others might think differently if he shared his doubts, so he'd decided against that. It would have undoubtedly led to some of the team dropping out, which was not ideal. A place like Perron Manor demanded a full contingent.

Besides, they were experts in their field, and if proper caution and restraint were exercised, they were perfectly capable of handling whatever the house might throw at them.

'We're nearly there,' David said. He turned the vehicle off the winding country road they were on and down a narrower track. The house came into view up ahead.

'Starting to feel a little more on-edge now,' Ralph admitted.

'We'll be fine,' David assured him. 'This could be the start of big things for us.'

CHAPTER 3

SARAH STOOD with her back to the house, looking down the long driveway as the sound of a vehicle drew closer. She saw a blue transit van turn in through the open security gates.

The team had arrived.

She was relieved. Waiting out front on her own at the bottom of the entrance steps had been unnerving. Sarah had only been there for a little over ten minutes, but that was ten minutes too long to be standing alone at a place like Perron Manor.

Get a grip. You're going to be living back here, for a little while at least.

The cloudy sky was grey and accompanied by a drizzle of rain so light it was more like a blowing mist of precipitation. A musky, earthly smell from the muddy grounds around her permeated the air.

While standing and listening to the light wind, it had been hard for Sarah to resist the temptation to turn around and look upon the house again.

She knew what the building looked like well enough: stone construction and tall, narrow windows, with the most striking feature being the three peaks high up above that sat central along the length of the building and cut into the roofline. The building had an elegant if simplistic design, one Sarah had always liked.

However, the reason for not wanting to gaze upon the impressive architecture once more was a simple one—she was scared of what she might see looking back.

The last time Sarah had been at the house, her sister had been killed by the things inside. Sarah had held Chloe's lifeless body for a long time before finally dragging herself away, feeling utterly crushed and alone in the world. And, when outside, she'd had an overwhelming urge to turn and look back. It was there, in an upstairs window, she'd once again seen her sister.

Chloe had looked like a corpse that had been dead for years. And she'd mouthed a desperate plea for help.

That sight had plagued Sarah's nightmares ever since. It was the reason she was here again now, and the reason she'd enlisted the help of David and his team.

But she didn't think she was quite ready to see anything like it again, so she refused to turn her head and look back, despite a strong feeling of being watched.

The royal-blue vehicle drew closer, kicking up spray from the wet gravel it rolled over. Sarah noticed patches of orange rust around the wheel arches and edges of the doors, and there was a dent to the side near one of the front wheels.

The group didn't exactly travel in style. However, Sarah liked that. It seemed to suit David's personality somehow, judging by the brief interactions she'd had with him.

The van pulled to a stop in a covered car port which sat beside the house. Sarah's own car—a small, sleek, and sporty model—was parked there as well. She held her breath as the doors opened and the team emerged. She was surprised at the rag-tag appearance of them all.

For whatever reason, Sarah had expected them to be much like David: middle-aged white men, all with a nerdish quality to them.

But that was not quite the contingent standing before her. For one, there was one guy among them who was huge. He was tall, stocky, and relatively young—she guessed in his early thirties—with a thick but stylish black beard. His bulk was just about contained within a light-grey sports jumper with a logo she did not recognise stencilled in blue on the front.

A rather stern-faced lady with red hair jumped out of the front passenger seat, and David emerged from the driver's side.

There was also another woman, this one tall and thin with jet-black hair, matching black lipstick, and nose and lip rings. She wore dark eye shadow and her skin was as pale as moonlight. In addition, she was dressed in black trousers and a long purple coat with black patterns to it.

A pair of men completed the group. One of them had long blond hair pulled into a ponytail, an angular face with a serious expression, and brooding eyes. He also wore predominantly black, like the dark-haired girl.

The final man looked rather bookish, sporting a goatee and glasses, and he wore a grey suit-jacket over jeans in a smart-casual look.

David strode over to her first while the others spread out behind him. While their leader wore his usual friendly smile, none of the others really made eye contact with Sarah, instead either looking to the ground, to each other, or to the building behind her. All of them appeared awkward and uncomfortable.

Sarah knew why. It was a reaction she'd seen far too often in the three short weeks since her sister's death. People just didn't know how to act around someone who was grieving.

But Sarah didn't have time for that. She stepped forward and shook David's hand.

'Thanks for coming,' she said with as big a smile as she could muster, before lifting her head and standing tall to address the rest of them. 'Thank you *all* for coming. It really is appreciated. I take it you know why you are here?'

David paused, looked back to his team, then turned again to Sarah. 'They all know why they're here,' he confirmed. 'I briefed everyone.'

The woman with the black hair and purple coat stepped forward. 'And can I just say,' she began, her voice soft but even, 'I think you are extremely brave for doing this.'

Sarah quickly pulled her lips into a tight smile, more so to stop herself gritting her teeth in anger. The comment, while intended as kind and understanding, came across as patronising, like someone giving fake praise to a child for the most mundane of accomplishments. On top of that, there was an insincerity, almost a performance to the words.

'Thank you,' Sarah eventually said. The dark-haired woman gave a large smile in response.

Idiot.

'Well, let's get you introduced to everyone,' David said. 'That was Ann Tate. This,' he pointed to the big guy, 'is Ralph Cobin.' Ralph gave a polite smile and wave. After him was the redhead, Jenn Hogan, the guy with the goatee, George Dalton, and lastly, the tall man with the long blonde hair, Jamie Curtis.

Sarah did a double-take at that name but tried not to let her surprise show. Evidently, she failed.

'Don't worry,' Ralph cut in. 'His middle name isn't Lee.'

Jamie just shook his head and rolled his eyes. 'That got old the first seventy times you used it, Ralph,' he chided. 'I have a similar name to the girl from *Halloween*. Big deal.'

'Okay, I think we have more pressing matters,' David said in an admonishing tone. He then turned to Sarah. 'How about we go inside and start getting set up? Then I can go over what we have in mind.'

'Sounds good,' Sarah said.

But that was a lie. It didn't sound good at all, because it meant once again entering Perron Manor. Just the thought of that was enough to cause a stabbing pain in her chest. She took a breath and turned around, allowing herself to take in the details of the great house once again. She dug her hands in her pockets and pulled out the keys, waited a moment to try and compose herself, then started up the steps to the front porch.

She heard the footsteps of the others follow behind, drawing to a stop when she stood before the front door. The brass door knocker with the snarling lion's face looked back at her.

Ugly thing.

She slid the key into the lock and took a breath. *Here we go.* The door unlocked with a small squeak of sliding metal and she pushed it open, revealing the entrance lobby inside.

The very spot Chloe had died.

Sarah's gaze was immediately drawn to the floor at the foot of the stairs, and she remembered holding Chloe there as her sister grew colder in her arms. It had been all Sarah could think about for the last three weeks—being here now still felt like being punched in the gut. She had an urge to cry, one that was growing stronger by the second. However, she hated the thought of the others seeing her that way.

Keep it together.

Though a little more dust had gathered since her last visit, nothing else had changed: there was still grey marble-tiled floor with subtle whites and yellows, dark oak panelling to the walls, and a grand staircase that ran up to a half-landing, where it split off both left and right to walkways above. The air inside smelled stuffy, and the space had an oppressive feel.

'Just as you remember it?' David asked. Sarah turned around to answer but saw that he was instead talking to the rest of his team. They all looked anxious to varying degrees.

'Pretty much,' George said, his voice soft and almost feminine.

Sarah was aware they'd all had their own experience in the house. Not to the extent Sarah had, but she knew theirs was traumatic nonetheless. David had written a book about Perron Manor, one that detailed its storied history but also recounted his team's investigation in 2014. Sarah had read that book, so she knew most of what had happened to the group.

It was fantastical stuff, but now she believed it wholeheartedly.

The team fanned out, all taking in their surroundings. The entrance lobby was a grand space, but now felt small with seven of them inside.

'Where do we set up our headquarters?' Jenn asked. 'Same place as last time?'

'Makes sense,' David said. 'That seemed to work okay.'

'Headquarters?' Sarah asked.

David nodded. 'We'll have cameras mounted around the house, so will need a room where we can set up the monitors and computers, as well as store our equipment. A kind of base of operations.'

'I see,' Sarah said. 'So then, what... you capture something on video, send it to your priest friend, then they call in the exorcist?'

'Well, that's a very basic way of putting it, but not completely inaccurate. One video probably won't do it. We need to compile as much as we can and make our case watertight. Video is the best evidence we can hope for, but to be honest, everyone knows footage can still be doctored or faked. So, our best bet is to compile as much evidence as possible: video, audio, personal experiences, temperature fluctuations—we'll try and log everything. And, if we are lucky, it would be even better if Father Janosch witnessed something himself. That would carry a lot of weight.'

'Understood,' Sarah said. 'Do you know this Father Janosch well?'

'I guess.'

'So if he believes what you're saying, what are the chances he'd tell a little fib on our behalf? It would save us the trouble of gathering evidence.'

David paused, studying her face, probably trying to work out if she was joking or not. Sarah wasn't even sure about that herself.

'Lie?' David eventually asked. 'You *know* he's a priest. That... isn't exactly something he would be comfortable with.'

Sarah forced a smile. 'I'm just pulling your leg.'

David's eyes slowly widened in realisation. He let out a chuckle. 'I see. Very funny. Well, I suppose you could ask him that question yourself. I've arranged to meet him here in a little while, just to get things moving as quickly as possible. He knows roughly what we're doing, and has agreed to give the house a blessing. That's an important step. In truth, that alone *could* put an end to the haunting here. At least, in theory.'

'Really?' Sarah asked, surprised. 'Seems a little... easy.'

'I didn't say it would definitively work,' he replied. 'In fact, given the kind of activity we are talking about here, I think it is unlikely. But the blessing itself is an important first step. If it doesn't work, then it is still one required step chalked off. Which means we are closer to the exorcism. And, if it *does* work, then all the better... I suppose.'

Sarah narrowed her eyes. 'You don't sound like you want the blessing to be successful, David.'

'No, it isn't that. It would just be nice to get some verifiable evidence from the house.'

Sarah understood what he meant. In his book, David had told of some amazing events that had taken place during their investigation. However, the only 'proof' from it was his own word and testimony, as all the equipment had failed at the worst possible time. No video, no audio… no evidence. He'd had his most powerful experience ever in Perron Manor but had nothing to show for it.

This was a second chance for him.

'So,' George said, 'do we unpack everything now? It may take a while, so best to get started quickly, don't you think?'

'Yeah but… where are we all staying?' Jenn asked.

'I've been thinking about that,' David replied. 'It makes sense to use the beds already here, but I don't want anyone in a room on their own. So, I think we should double up.'

'Wait,' Ralph interrupted, 'does that mean sharing beds?'

'If everyone is okay with that,' David said.

'But there are seven of us,' Ann chipped in. 'That's an odd number.'

'True,' David began, 'but I thought it might be prudent if the girls take the biggest room here and we try and squeeze another bed in.'

For Sarah, being forced to cram into a room with two other women she didn't know wasn't exactly appealing, but she'd been through worse during her time in the army. While there, she'd had to bunk up with a lot of people—both men and women—so this was hardly a deal-breaker. In truth, it was far preferable to sleeping alone.

'I guess we'll have to,' Jenn said. 'After all, our rooms will just be a place to get our heads down for the night. It's not like we'll be spending a lot of time in there.'

'So then why don't we pick out the rooms first before we go get our stuff?' Ann suggested.

'Seems sensible,' David said. 'In fact, I think a quick tour to get ourselves reacquainted with the house would be a good idea.' He then looked over to Sarah. 'Would you be okay with that?'

'Of course,' she replied. 'A tour sounds good.'

CHAPTER 4

THE GROUP CARRIED out a lap of the ground floor first. For Sarah, it was a strange experience. It had only been a few weeks since she was last here, but in some ways, it felt like she had never been away. In other ways, however, it seemed as if a lifetime had passed.

The great hall was still impressive to see, with its high ceilings, antique dining-room table, and stone columns that ran down to a stone-tiled floor. There was an elegant, deep-green wallpaper to the walls as well as a plethora of oil paintings and a gold-framed mirror.

However, all Sarah could picture was the entities she had seen the last time she was in the room. The spirits of the dead: all pale, corpse-like, and distinctly demonic.

However, they were not as demonic as the thing that had killed her sister. The monster that *really* scared Sarah.

She knew it was still here in the house somewhere, hidden from them… but waiting. She could *feel* it. That creature was not just a ghost of the dead but something else entirely.

Something *more*.

'This is where a lot of people died in '82,' George announced to no one in particular. 'It was a massacre all over the house, but *especially* in here. Because this is where the chaos started.'

Sarah was aware of the events that took place back in 1982, and from what she understood 'massacre' was indeed the right word. It was strange to think her parents had been in the house when that had happened.

Chloe too, come to think of it, though her sister had remembered very little of that night.

They then moved on to the kitchen, which had been the hub for Sarah and her family. A place of laughter, food, drink, and bonding. Now it was silent. Sarah could practically hear her niece's babyish chattering and Chloe discussing her plans for their new home. Even Andrew's crappy jokes.

Next, Sarah found herself back down in the basement, and all the anxiety she was already feeling went into overdrive. It had never been a warm or welcoming place—the exact opposite, in fact—and the orange light above wasn't strong enough to illuminate the whole area, leaving large pockets of shadows around the perimeter. In addition, the ground consisted of uneven and dirty slabs, with the walls being thick stone blocks, some of which were streaked with watermarks. The biggest feature in the largely empty space, however, was the damn furnace.

Sarah would never forget that thing for as long as she lived. The first time she'd seen her brother-in-law start it up, the appliance had made a sound akin to a scream. They'd all thought it was just a quirk—a symptom of the furnace's age.

However, on the last night, Sarah had seen a man inside of it, practically burnt to a crisp. At the time, another entity—a horrible old man in a tattered suit—had tried to throw poor little Emma inside while the furnace was ablaze. She remembered the nursery rhyme he sang as he did.

Ring-a-ring-a-roses.

Sarah had saved Emma. She'd found an inner reserve of courage, one she really wished she could tap into now. Because, while walking around the house she used to live in, Sarah felt like a lost little child.

Thankfully, their time down in the basement was brief, and Sarah suspected David had picked up on her discomfort despite her best efforts to hide it. They all moved upstairs, which was easier for Sarah to deal with. After looking into bedroom after bedroom, with one bleeding into the next to her, they finally agreed upon their accommodations for the next several days.

Sarah had insisted no one use the bedrooms that had previously been hers, her sister's, or Emma's—doing so just felt wrong. But the rest were fair game.

So, the three girls claimed a front corner room, one of the biggest in the house, complete with an en-suite. Ralph and Jamie were paired in a room adjacent, with David and George taking the other front corner room. While the boys had agreed to share beds, it would have been tough to squeeze three to a single bed in the girl's room. Luckily, Sarah was fine with sleeping on the floor. She pulled a mattress from an unused bed into the room—a full bed and frame would have fit, but would have been a lot of work—along with some covers. Hell, she'd slept in hastily dug foxholes before while in Afghanistan. This would be a cakewalk.

After the rooms were assigned, the group finally went up to the top story, which was just more of the same: bedroom after bedroom. However, there was one area in particular David said he was interested to see, one he and his team hadn't been aware of back when they'd carried out their investigation.

The study.

As Sarah showed everyone around, she saw they were suitably impressed. Why wouldn't they be? The room contained a huge array of items and artefacts that were occult in nature: daggers, scrolls, sigils, even small animal bodies floating in a thick yellow liquid. Right up their alley.

'This is fucking unbelievable,' Ralph exclaimed.

'You didn't tell us about this place, David,' Jenn said with wide eyes. She turned to Sarah. 'How long has all this stuff been here?'

Sarah shrugged. 'Couldn't tell you exactly. It was locked off when we first moved in until we found the key. But I think it was here back in '82 at least. Probably before.'

George quickly spotted the somewhat faded pentagram on the floor. The one with a dark brown stain in it.

'What the fuck!' he exclaimed, pointing at the symbol.

'Weird, huh?' Sarah replied. It had freaked Chloe out when they'd first discovered this room as well. Despite talking about cleaning it up, they had never gotten around to it.

'It's more than weird,' George said. 'It's creepy as hell.'

David pulled out his phone and took a picture of it.

'Do you think this has something to do with what happened in '82?' Jenn asked David.

He shrugged in response. 'No idea. Possibly.'

'And what's that?' Ann asked before moving over towards a waist-high display case sitting central to the room. It had a glass top, and inside was a book that Sarah remembered all too well. It had previously drawn her interest to an almost unhealthy degree. Though why that was, exactly, she couldn't explain.

She also remembered the ledger, which sat on a writing table in the corner of the room. It had so far gone unnoticed by the others.

'It's just a book,' Sarah said. 'It isn't even written in English.'

David moved over beside Ann and put his hands on the lid of the case. '*Ianua Diaboli*,' he said, reading the title. He then looked over to Sarah and asked, 'May I?'

Sarah didn't really want him to, and her gut reaction was to tell him no. However, that was irrational, so she simply nodded her approval.

He lifted the lid and opened the book where it sat, staring at it in wonder. 'It's old,' he said. '*Really* old. And written in… Latin, I think.'

The others all gathered around as well and watched as David slowly worked through the pages.

'Funky drawings,' Ralph said while pointing to one of the sketches on the page. 'What the hell are they?'

'I think this is some kind of ritual book,' David said.

'Are you serious?' Ann asked, her mouth hanging open.

'I think so. I know a little Latin and can pick up some parts of it.' He then again looked to Sarah. 'Do you know where this came from?'

She shook her head. 'No. It was all here when we moved in.'

David's eyes drifted back down. 'I'll show this to Father Janosch as well. His Latin is much better than mine.' There was an obvious excitement in his voice. The room must have seemed like the find of a lifetime for him.

David then used his phone to take a few pictures of the book.

'How about we get set up?' Sarah asked. 'There will be plenty of time to look around here later.'

David seemed a little disappointed at the suggestion, but he slipped his phone back into his pocket. 'You're right,' he said. 'It would be good to at least have everything in the van unpacked before Father Janosch gets here.'

That brought the tour to an end, which Sarah was happy about. For the next hour, they unloaded the van and Sarah's car before starting to set up the equipment. Bags were dumped into the assigned rooms but were not unpacked. Sarah had decided to live out of her suitcase anyway, knowing they may well need to make a quick getaway.

They all gathered in the downstairs study accessed off the entrance lobby. It was not a room Sarah had spent a lot of time in. Looking at the walls, she saw a thick line of discolouration that ran up the full height of the room. It looked to her as if a bisecting wall had previously existed there at one point, separating the room into two spaces. Perhaps her Uncle Vincent's doing? There was a landline here as well, which Andrew had set up back when Sarah and her family had first moved in.

The computers had just been unpacked when the sound of a knocking on the front door drew the group's attention. Sarah felt a jolt of anxiety, and her mind instantly ran back to the night she and Chloe were terrorised by some unseen thing which constantly banged on the front door.

'That'll be Father Janosch,' David said.

'Of course,' Sarah added, feeling stupid and relieved in equal measure.

'Come on,' David said with a big smile. 'I'll introduce you.'

CHAPTER 5

FATHER LUCA JANOSCH stood waiting outside the entrance door to the house. His leather satchel dangled from his left hand and his long coat was pulled tightly around him, covering up his black robes. However, he had deliberately left the front zipper low enough so that people could see his white clerical collar.

In truth, he didn't really want to be at the house, but had never been one to turn his back on people who requested his help. He just hoped this was another one of David's wild-goose chases.

There had been plenty of them over the years.

Despite David's heart being in the right place—and insisting he was impartial when investigating—Luca had seen the younger man take leaps of logic that were, perhaps, overeager and misguided.

But Luca had heard many stories about Perron Manor. And even if only a handful were true, then he'd be stepping back into a world he'd not been a part of since his days back in Romania.

He heard movement beyond the double-door before him, and one leaf slowly opened. David was revealed first, wearing a big, friendly grin. There was a woman beside him, but not one of David's usual team. She had dark, wavy hair that hung just down past her shoulders, slightly tanned skin with a smattering of freckles, and piercing blue eyes.

Luca had a feeling he knew who this girl was, as David had briefed him on what was happening here. Also, Luca had heard the news around town as well, that Perron Manor had new owners, but one had died not long after moving in.

He assumed, therefore, that this was Sarah Pearson, the sister of the deceased Chloe Shaw. It had been Luca's own clergy that had carried out the funeral, though it was Father Roberts who had been in charge of the ceremony.

A terrible tragedy.

'Thank you for coming,' David said and shook Luca's hand before moving aside to let Luca enter.

'No problem at all,' Luca replied and stepped into the house. He turned to Miss Pearson and held out his hand to her. 'I'm truly sorry about the loss of your sister.'

Miss Pearson looked down at his outstretched hand for a moment. Eventually, she shook it as well, her grip firm and strong.

'Thank you,' she said. 'David tells me you're here to bless my house?'

'If that is okay with you,' he replied.

'It is. And if that doesn't work, then I understand we need to provide you with evidence that the house is...'

'Haunted,' he finished for her, nodding. 'That's right.'

'And you believe in stuff like that?'

'Ghosts?' he asked.

'Yeah. Because, if not, then you're gonna be kinda hard to convince, you know?'

Luca let out a chuckle. 'I see what you mean. But yes, I do believe in things of that nature. Though... I think they are less common than some people think. *Much* less common.'

He hoped it wasn't too obvious he was thinking of David.

'You don't need to worry about that here,' David said, oblivious, and still wearing an excited grin. 'This place is like nothing you've ever seen before. I promise you that.'

'So, what do we need to do to get started with the blessing?' Sarah asked. He could sense her eagerness.

'Nothing really. I just... start.'

'Great,' she replied. 'Then let's get to it.'

CHAPTER 6

DAVID AND SARAH accompanied Father Janosch around the house as the priest conducted the blessing. David had seen the ceremony before, but not in a house as large as Perron Manor.

He noted that Sarah had been a little curt with the priest and impatient to get things started. David sympathised, but her pushing could be a problem in the making. Even if successful, the whole process would likely not be quick. She needed to be patient.

Perhaps a delicately handled conversation was needed. But not now.

David was comfortable leaving the rest of the team to continue the set-up while he and Sarah again walked around the building, this time accompanied by Father Janosch. It was always an interesting experience watching the priest work, reciting passages from the gospel and sprinkling holy water from a flask.

David was interested to see if Father Janosch's rites invoked any anger or phenomena from the house.

He had known Father Janosch for a number of years, after requesting the holy man bless other locations he had been investigating. The priest was always friendly and amenable, and during some of these investigations, David had found out a little of the priest's backstory, learning he had been born in Romania but had moved to England with his parents when very young. The man had, however, gone back to

Romania for many years to work with the Church. David knew that *something* had happened over there that made the man amenable to the paranormal. It was something that troubled the priest, but not a topic he really spoke of in any great detail. All David knew was that it involved an exorcism at a Church in Hungary... and it had not gone well.

Father Janosch had the tiniest hint of a Romanian accent, likely picked up from his many years back in Romania as a young man.

At sixty-five years of age, he was in good physical condition, though he was quite a short man, standing at only five-foot-six. He had a pale complexion, short, brushed-back white hair, grey eyes, and a rather square face with a wide, letterbox mouth. His hands showed signs of ageing too, with pronounced veins and some liver spots on the back.

David noticed that as they progressed through the house, the priest's mood began to change. Especially after they ventured down into the basement.

'Interesting furnace,' he remarked as he splashed holy water on the ground.

'If you only knew,' David replied. 'Sarah has seen a spirit inside of it, when it was lit, no less.'

'Fascinating,' Father Janosch said. 'I have to say, the report you gave me on what happened here is quite astonishing.'

'Of our investigation, you mean? Well, what happened to Sarah's family here far outweighs my own experiences.'

'Shame you didn't manage to get any evidence during your investigation, though.'

'Tell me about it,' David replied. 'It would have been a game-changer for sure.'

'Let's hope you have better luck this time around.'

David felt Sarah's eyes fall on him. 'We will,' David replied with as much confidence as he could.

Father Janosch pulled his coat tighter around himself and continued around the basement.

'It's quite oppressive down here.'

'I noticed that as well,' David agreed. 'The whole house is the same, to an extent. You constantly feel like you are being watched.'

'But that isn't proof of phenomena,' the priest stated. 'Far from it.'

Sarah then cut in. 'I get the feeling you aren't one-hundred-percent sure you believe what we are telling you.'

Father Janosch stopped and turned to her. 'How so?'

'Just the tone of your voice,' she replied. 'I'm picking up on a little scepticism.'

'I can assure you I'm open-minded,' the priest replied, firmly. David felt the need to step in.

'Father Janosch is a believer, Sarah. He's seen things that not many people in this world have. Experienced the same things *you* have. He's here to help, I can promise you.'

Sarah held up her hand to quiet him and addressed the priest directly. 'I have no problem with you being sceptical about all of this, Father. In fact, I'd worry if you weren't. I imagine you deal with a lot of people who bend the truth when it comes to this kind of thing, so you need to weed out the crazies. I get it. But, at the same time, I know what I saw here. And I know my sister is trapped. So, if getting the house exorcised is the only way to free her, then that is what is going to happen. I'll walk to the fucking Vatican and drag the Pope here myself if I need to. Understand?'

David winced and he saw the priest's eyes widen in surprise. This wasn't something Sarah could bully her way through. Father Janosch would only take things forward to the Church if the evidence was indisputable.

'I sympathise with how you are feeling, Miss Pearson,' Father Janosch said in a kind voice. 'And I promise that I will judge any evidence I see impartially. *But*,' his tone took on a noticeable sternness, 'I will not lie to my superiors if I am not convinced myself of the validity of the claims. I hope that is clear?'

David stepped between the two. 'No need for things to get angry,' he said. 'We have our plan of action and we'll stick to it. We're all on the same side.'

Sarah kept her gaze on Father Janosch, her jaw set. She nodded, and Father Janosch did the same. 'Of course,' he said. 'I am just here to help.'

They didn't talk much more as they carried on around the rest of the house, and David made a note to have that conversation with Sarah sooner rather than later. She was grieving, he understood that, and so she could be forgiven for being short and agitated with people. However, everyone here was just trying to help, and David didn't want Sarah to push anyone away.

As they moved up to the top storey, and the last rooms to be blessed, David was eager to show Father Janosch the strange study. And, in particular, the book.

Once inside, David let the priest sprinkle his holy water and recite a passage, but could tell by the man's expression that he was surprised at what was in the room.

'Someone has quite the collection,' he eventually said.

'It belonged to a prior owner of the house,' Sarah told him.

'An Alfred Blackwater,' David confirmed. 'And it was then all passed down to his grandson, Marcus.'

After completing his blessing of the room, Father Janosch took his time inspecting the artefacts. He seemed troubled.

'I've not seen a collection like this before,' David said. 'I mean, I haven't had the opportunity to have a good look through it yet, but is it any wonder the stories of the house persist given all of *this* is sitting up here?'

Father Janosch took a moment before answering, looking through some of the books and journals that lined a shelf. He seemed much paler than he had downstairs.

'I… I honestly don't know what to think,' he said. 'I've actually heard of some of these books.'

'Well, you need to see this one in particular,' David said and guided the priest to the centre of the room where *Ianua Diaboli* sat in its case. The priest frowned as David opened the glass lid. 'My translation may be off,' David said, 'but isn't that Latin for *The Door to the Devil?*'

Father Janosch gave a small nod. 'Not far off. Translations aren't always straightforward, but I would wager it means *The Devil's Door.*' He then took hold of the book and lifted it up. '*The Devil's Door* is also a tome I have heard spoken of, but one I never thought was real.' He opened the book and started to go through the pages. As pale as he had looked before, David could have sworn he saw even more blood drain from the man's face. Before even getting to the halfway point, the priest closed the cover and dropped the book back in its case. He then laid his hands on the edges of the display unit to steady himself and looked up to Sarah.

'David tells me you saw many spirits in this house,' Father Janosch said. 'Not just one or two.'

'That's right,' Sarah replied.

'And something else as well… a demon?'

'I think that's what it was. Yes.'

David then cut in. 'It's my belief that the demon is the reason the spirits of the dead are trapped here. It is what's keeping them prisoner.'

Father Janosch was still staring over at Sarah. 'Can I ask—have you only seen the one demon here?'

That question gave David pause. Sarah nodded. 'I think so, yes.'

'There can only be one demon, surely,' David said. 'I didn't think more than one could ever co-exist in the same place.'

'I didn't either,' Father Janosch said, his voice weak. He again looked down to the book. 'Miss Pearson, how long were you and your family in the house before your sister died?'

'Not long,' she replied. 'About a month and a half.'

The priest nodded, but his brow furrowed. 'And during that time, did you ever personally feel… different?'

Sarah cocked her head to the side. 'Different how?'

'Like you weren't in control. Short-tempered. Angry.'

Sarah paused before shaking her head. 'No, not really. Don't get me wrong, the things that were happening stressed us all out, so I did fight with my sister more than I usually do. But it was nothing more than that.'

'And no one else in the house seemed different either?'

Again, there was a brief pause, before Sarah answered. 'No,' she said.

'I see.' Father Janosch then took a breath and straightened up. 'The blessing is done,' he declared. 'Now you will need to monitor the house and see if there are any further phenomena. I need to take my leave. However, David, you know where I am if you need me.'

'Erm… okay,' David said. He hadn't expected the man to be in such a rush to leave, as Father Janosch was generally quite social; he actually had to keep pace with the priest as they made their way back downstairs. They passed Jenn and George coming the other way on the stairs, each with small, mountable cameras in their arms. The pair moved aside to let the other three pass on their way down.

'You are more than welcome to stay a little while,' David offered.

'Most kind,' Father Janosch said as he stepped off the bottom stair and strode over to the entrance door. 'But I have things I need to attend to.'

Sarah opened the door for him, and David saw she was wearing a frown of confusion. Once Father Janosch stepped out over the threshold, he turned around and looked past both David and Sarah to the space behind them. He continued to stare beyond them as he spoke.

'Come to me with any evidence you have,' he said. 'But in the meantime, please be careful.' He then let his eyes settle onto Sarah. 'I mean that. If things start to get dangerous, don't force yourself to stay. You cannot help your sister if you end up just like her.'

He then turned and left. 'Wait,' David called after him. 'What spooked you so much, Father?'

'Nothing,' the older man shouted back, but he kept striding to his car. It did not take him long to start up the engine and disappear down the long driveway.

CHAPTER 7

Luca's hands trembled as they gripped the steering wheel tightly. He had an urge to put his foot down and ignore the speed limit of the winding roads ahead, just so he could get back home that much quicker.

But no matter how frightened he was, he knew that flipping his car and killing himself, or skidding head-long into an oncoming car and killing other innocent souls, would help nothing.

He'd felt a little uncomfortable after first entering the house, noticing its heavy atmosphere.

However, an oppressive feeling alone was not evidence of an evil presence. Not in his experience. It was just the human mind reacting to an environment. If said environment or building had a reputation already, then it was only natural a person would feel uncomfortable inside.

Still, that discomfort had grown the longer he'd been in the house, especially down in the basement. Luca didn't claim to possess 'the gift,' as he called it, but the sensation of things watching from the shadows was palpable.

A reminder of Zsámbék Church.

But none of that had compared with finding the book upstairs. *Ianua Diaboli*—it was a title he hadn't heard in years, and a book he didn't believe even existed beyond folklore.

However, if that tome back at Perron Manor was genuine, then David Ritter and his team could be in a lot of danger.

Luca had been hesitant to divulge what he suspected to David, knowing it would serve nothing other than to heighten the younger man's interest in the house.

Miss Pearson and her family had been in the house for a month and a half before Chloe Shaw died. That wasn't a long time. Supernatural activity usually took much longer to manifest to people in a haunted location. So that was strange in itself. And then the level of phenomena she claimed to have taken place—full-bodied apparitions interacting with the living, and even the demonic showing themselves—should have, theoretically, taken years to manifest, if at all.

Luca had always assumed David's stories about his investigation at Perron Manor were embellished. But what if they weren't? What if there was a reason things happened so quickly there. *Ianua Diaboli* might explain that.

Luca couldn't believe the book being in the house was a coincidence, either. His mind raced to add everything up, remembering what David had told him regarding Sarah and her story.

During their stay, Sarah and her family had apparently started to experience things they couldn't explain. That activity grew and culminated the night Chloe died. They had been woken from their sleep by something, and Chloe had fallen down the stairs of the manor as they'd fled, breaking her neck. A terrible accident. However, not caused *directly* by anything supernatural. Which meant the entities inside, if real, were not physically able to hurt anyone as yet.

It didn't appear that anyone had been possessed during that time, if she was telling the truth, which was another good sign.

All of that meant that even if things picked back up in the house where they had left off three weeks ago, the team inside shouldn't be in any immediate danger. Even if the house was what he suspected it to be.

On top of it all was Miss Pearson's claim that she had seen her sister inside the house immediately after death. That was troubling, but not exactly unusual. Luca had heard many similar claims over the years after the loss of a loved one, and the people who made them usually thought they were being genuine. But, in reality, it was just a figment made up from a grieving mind.

Regardless, he would need to work fast.

His mind swam, jumping around from one thing to the next: in one moment it tried to decide if Perron Manor could indeed be a Devil's Door, and in the next he battled his guilt for running out on everyone, justifying it to himself that he still had time.

However, it was fear that had driven him away.

Luca had looked into many supernatural occurrences for the Church over the years, but only once had he been truly terrified. Zsámbék Church. That was because it wasn't just his life that had been in danger, but his very *soul*. And that scared him more than anything else he could imagine.

Perron Manor could pose the very same threat.

CHAPTER 8

'Interesting start to the investigation,' Ralph said to Jenn. He was driving the van on the way to pick up food for the evening. Jenn was seated in the passenger seat next to him.

'Yeah,' she replied, looking out of the front window at the darkening skies. She felt a little tired as the adrenaline that had fuelled her for most of the day began to wear off. 'The priest didn't stick around for very long.'

'George said he practically ran out of the house.'

'Yeah, that's true,' Jenn confirmed. 'He just about knocked us over coming down the stairs. I think something spooked him.'

'Well, maybe that's a good thing and he'll take us seriously. Did David say what got the priest so freaked out?'

'Yeah, it was that book up on the top floor. Janosch took one look at it and apparently the blood drained from his face.'

'Crazy to think all that shit was up there back in 2014 when we were last here.'

'I was thinking the same,' Jenn replied. 'No wonder that part of the floor had been locked off.'

Jenn had been with David as part of his paranormal investigation team from the very beginning and was his longest-serving colleague. The work they carried out drove her and gave her purpose. Prior to

Perron Manor, she'd had experiences that were truly unexplainable, at least to her. They made her believe that death was not the end. However, despite witnessing some amazing things, nothing had ever quite made her truly, one-hundred-percent certain.

But 2014 had changed that. Now she had no doubt *at all* that the paranormal was real. It was also more terrifying than she had ever thought possible.

'You feeling optimistic?' Ralph asked as they eventually pulled onto a main road with streetlights and houses lining either side. It felt like they were finally getting back to civilisation after having been stranded out in the middle of nowhere. The trip would be a quick one, just long enough to pick up the banquet of Indian food they had ordered and Sarah had been kind enough to pay for. In fact, she had insisted upon it.

'About the investigation?' Jenn asked. Ralph nodded. 'I guess,' she said. 'If I'm being honest, I'm nervous about what we'll find.'

'Me too,' Ralph admitted. 'Truth be told, I almost backed out.'

Jenn chuckled. 'You aren't alone. George and Jamie told me the same. I think Ann is hesitant as well.'

'Our psychic?' Ralph asked with a big smile and a voice thick with sarcasm. 'What does she have to be scared of?'

Jenn laughed again. 'That woman is about as psychic as I am.'

'David believes it.'

'David can be an idiot at times. Anyway, I'm surprised *you* were thinking of bailing out. How big are you... like, six-four or something? And you're built like a fridge.'

Ralph shrugged and a look of slight embarrassment washed over his face. 'I don't think a fridge would do much good against what we saw there.'

'No,' Jenn admitted. 'I suppose you're right.'

'You ever think about that night?' he asked.

'All the time,' she said.

'Me too. It still scares the shit out of me. I mean, we found what we desperately wanted to find, but then... I dunno. It just left me with a lot more fear than excitement.'

Jenn turned her head to look at him. 'So why come back? No one would have thought any less of you if you didn't.'

'Pride, I guess. And the fact that I still need to know. Despite what we saw, do you *really* feel like you understand any of it any better? We have our little toys and we live for the snippets of evidence we get, but really we're just fumbling in the dark. It would be nice to learn a little more.'

Jenn understood that. The lust for knowledge—to have a definitive answer for what lay after death—was what drove her too. It had been that way ever since she was twelve and had woken up one night to see her recently deceased 'Nana' standing at the end of her bed.

Her parents had insisted it had just been a dream. Maybe they were right. But the experience lit something inside of Jenn.

All of the team had had similar experiences, something that had sparked their interest in what most people generally dismissed. Especially David, whose own story was tied directly to Perron Manor itself.

'What do you make of the client?' Ralph went on to ask.

'Sarah? She seems okay. I like her.'

'She's pretty intense, huh.'

'Maybe that's why I like her. She used to be in the army, you know.'

Ralph turned to look at her. 'I actually had no idea.'

'Yeah,' Jenn said, smiling. 'So I'd watch what you say to her.'

Ralph smiled and gave an exaggerated salute. 'Will do. But do you believe what she says?'

'About the house? Why would I not?'

'No... I mean about her sister.'

Jenn paused. She knew what Ralph was referring to—that Chloe Shaw had reappeared immediately after her death. Even for someone who believed in the paranormal... that was a stretch. Could a spirit really show itself so quickly after its body had died?

'I'm not sure what to make of it,' she admitted. 'But the way I see it, if we go in there and get the exorcism done, then everyone is happy. Whether the poor girl saw her sister or not, it should still give her some kind of peace.'

'I guess that's as good a way to look at it as any,' Ralph replied. 'Hell, we're even getting paid this time. She must be desperate.'

'The money will certainly help out,' Jenn said. 'The company I work for might make me take some unpaid leave as I'm nearly out of personal days.'

'I'm going to be in and out of the investigation,' Ralph said. 'Work is busy, so I'll need to spend some time away if things run on too long. Plus, things are getting more serious with Helen, so I need to make sure I spend time with her.'

Jenn could understand Ralph's need to balance his life with what they did. It wasn't a full-time job for any of them, including David. They all had their own responsibilities to fulfill. Ralph was a self-employed groundworker, she herself had a warehouse job, and David and George were in IT. Jamie and Ann were the only two who didn't have full-time employment.

Ralph pointed up ahead. 'I think that's the restaurant.'

Jenn gazed hopefully out into the night as her stomach started to growl. She saw a cluster of buildings about half a mile ahead, washed in pink and purple neon light. The sign above the door proved Ralph correct.

'Thank God,' Jenn said as they approached. 'I could eat a horse.'

'Gonna have to make do with chicken and lamb,' Ralph joked.

Jenn let out a chuckle. 'I guess that will work. Nice to have a feast like this together. We normally pick at sandwiches during our investigations, then sit up all night in the cold.'

Ralph pulled to a stop. 'Yeah, I was thinking the same. It'll be nice to have a little bit of comfort for once.'

Jenn got out of the car. 'Keep the engine running,' she said, feeling optimistic about the job ahead. 'I'll be back in a flash.'

CHAPTER 9

THE GROUP HAD GATHERED in the great hall, where they sat around the long table to partake in the banquet Jenn and Ralph had brought back. David had suggested that Sarah take a seat at the head of the table, but frankly, she didn't want the attention, so she insisted that David take it. Jenn, Ralph, and George were on one side of him with Jamie, Ann, and Sarah on the other. Sarah noticed that most of the team had handheld cameras with them, all set on the table.

Best to be prepared, she thought.

The food laid out was a mixture of chicken, lamb, and prawn dishes, accompanied by different types of rice, naan, popadoms, seekh kababs, and more. The normally stuffy odours of the hall were replaced with mouthwatering smells of onion, spices, cinnamon, and charcoaled chicken.

Everyone dug in, loading their plates with a mixture of the different foods on offer. Jenn and Ralph had also picked up some alcohol from the restaurant: some had beers and wine, though Sarah and Ann stuck with water. In truth, Sarah wanted a drink, but she wasn't sure she'd be able to stop after just one or two. Not with the way she was feeling.

Plus, she desperately wanted to keep her wits about her.

Despite her paying for it, the meal felt wrong to Sarah. There was a celebratory atmosphere between David's team as they sat chatting and went over old war stories. Though not quite a party, the atmosphere was close to it.

However, Sarah kept those feelings to herself and continued to eat. After all, she needed their help.

'Remember that place in County Durham?' George asked with a smile.

'Ah yeah, Birkley Close,' Jamie replied. 'That EVP we got... still freaks me out listening to it.'

'The voice definitely sounded like a child,' Jenn said.

'It *was* a child,' Ann confirmed. 'It communicated to us through me, remember?'

David nodded. 'That's right. It was really something to see.'

Sarah frowned. Did that mean Ann was a medium? She cast her eyes about and saw that Jenn and Ralph shared a look between each other, and Jenn rolled her eyes before giving a slight shake of the head.

That was interesting to note.

Sarah popped a piece of chicken into her mouth. Heat radiated from the rich, brown vindaloo sauce covering the meat. The intense warmth was a welcome sensation, and it was only intensified after she tore off and devoured a piece of chili-infused naan.

In her view, if the food wasn't spicy enough to melt your teeth fillings, it wasn't real Indian food. It was something Chloe had always disagreed with, as her pallet had always been more pedestrian.

The thought of her sister immediately made Sarah wonder if Chloe was with them now, watching them. If so, was she still in pain and torment?

She glanced over at the rear double-door that looked out over the courtyard. More memories from her recent-past flooded back, where Chloe had insisted she'd seen a man that looked like a monk, staring back in from outside. Sarah shuddered.

Over the course of the day the team had set up all of their equipment, a process made easier because of their last visit. They knew roughly where all cameras and sensors were to be positioned, and they had also shown Sarah where everything was. In addition, the group had demonstrated the computer equipment in their headquarters, so she now knew roughly how to cycle between camera views. They'd taught her how to work some of the EVP recording equipment, heat sensors, and motion detectors.

It was all fancy stuff, and Sarah just hoped they could get something usable that would convince Father Janosch.

She was worried about what had happened to the team's evidence the last time they were here. She'd read David's book, which covered that investigation, and in it he claimed the equipment had all failed at the crucial time. Either he was full of it, or more likely the house had decided not to let David have his proof.

If that was the case, what was to say this time would be any different?

Perhaps the only solution was to get Father Janosch back here so he could experience Perron Manor for himself.

'Sarah?' Jenn asked, pulling Sarah away from her thoughts.

She looked up. 'Yeah?'

'We've gotten a brief overview from David on the things you experienced here. But it might be a good idea to go over some specifics, if you don't mind?'

'Sure,' Sarah replied. She was thankful the topic of conversation was being brought back to the job at hand. 'What exactly do you want to know?'

'Well,' Jenn replied, 'I suppose the best thing to focus on is going over some of the things you and your family saw. And *where* exactly you saw them. I know on your last night the basement played a large role, so we'll concentrate a lot of our efforts down there. But beyond that, were there any other hotspots?'

Sarah thought about the question. The basement was probably the area with the most activity. It was also where one of those fucking ghosts almost threw her niece into the lit furnace. The entrance lobby played a part as well, since that was where Chloe had died. Sarah ran through the events in her head to think of any other locations where things happened.

'Chloe had some experiences in this very hall. She saw something standing just outside that door.' Sarah pointed to the rear, glazed door. 'And she saw something inside the room with her as well. She also claimed to have seen a woman in my room. An old hag, as she put it, who was crouched on my bed while I was asleep.'

'Creepy,' Ralph chimed in.

'I didn't see it myself,' Sarah told him, 'but it really creeped Chloe out. In truth, the last night was the only time I actually witnessed the things she had been talking about.'

'So everything was really focused on Chloe?' Jenn asked.

Sarah nodded. 'Yeah, I'd say that's accurate. I think the house focused on her because she got away back in '82… but now it has her.'

Jenn gave Sarah a sad smile. 'I can't imagine what you're going through,' she said.

There was an awkward silence between them all. It was the familiar, uncomfortable air that Sarah had noticed from people when they spoke to her about Chloe. She decided to press on. 'There is the entrance lobby, of course' she said. 'That's where Chloe died.'

Jenn leaned forward in her seat. 'And what exactly did you see in there, if you don't mind me asking? I know you were all running when Chloe tripped and fell, but I didn't realise there were entities in the area with you at the time.'

Sarah paused. She couldn't tell them the whole truth of what happened—where a demon had thrown her out of the house and then snapped her sister's neck. Sarah had already started the lie of her sister's death being an accident, and needed to continue it so as to not scare away the team.

'We were running from… ghosts,' Sarah said. 'There were scores of them, just standing watching us in the corridors and coming out of rooms. So we kept running as fast as we could.'

Sarah felt a pang of guilt in her gut for concealing just how dangerous the house was.

She knew it wasn't right. But she also needed to save her sister, and Sarah would happily damn her own soul to make that happen.

'Nothing in the study upstairs?' David asked. 'The one with the artefacts?'

Sarah considered the question, then shook her head. 'Not that I'm aware of.'

'Well, if everyone agrees,' Jenn began, 'I think we focus on the areas where there has been activity recently. We know where we saw things back in 2014, but with Sarah's experiences being more recent, I think we have to focus on the basement, the entrance lobby, Chloe's bedroom, and this hall,' she said as she gestured around the space they sat in.

'Makes sense,' David agreed. The others gave nods of confirmation as well. Sarah liked what she'd seen of Jenn; the woman seemed smart, straightforward, and practical.

'Sounds like a good plan,' Jamie said. He then looked over to Sarah. 'I know you weren't here back in '82 when all those people died, but did your parents or sister ever tell you anything about that weekend?'

Sarah shook her head. 'Not really. Chloe couldn't remember any of it, and my parents always avoided the topic whenever it was brought up. So you guys probably know more than me.'

'From what I've heard, you were lucky you weren't around,' Ann said. 'It was horrific.'

'Well, I didn't come along until the following July,' Sarah said. 'So I'm happy to have missed all the fun.'

'Understood,' Jamie replied. 'I've just always felt that weekend was important. It was the biggest known supernatural event in the house's history, after all. Any new insight might have helped us shape our investigation.'

Sarah just shrugged. 'Afraid I can't help you.'

Everyone suddenly stopped talking as the sound of thudding footsteps from the floor above them echoed. The fast, stomping footfalls directly overhead were soon followed by the sound of a door slamming shut.

Sarah's body locked up, and she looked over to the others with wide eyes. They all seemed equally shocked.

'Shit!' Ralph exclaimed. Nobody moved for the next few moments. Not until David suddenly slid back his chair.

'Let's go,' he commanded. 'Everyone upstairs now!'

Everyone leapt into action, springing to their feet and grabbing their cameras. The mood changed in an instant, and Sarah could sense the nervous anticipation and excitement radiate from the team.

They all quickly filtered out of the great hall and ran towards the stairs, Sarah bringing up the rear.

CHAPTER 10

DAVID LED the way as everyone raced up the stairs. He had his handheld camera pointing ahead, trying to keep it as steady as possible just in case it picked something up.

His heart was racing. The footsteps and slamming door had been unmistakable.

With the sounds coming from directly above the great hall, David knew which direction he needed to head.

Once they were up on the mid-floor, David led them to where he thought they needed to be, which was close to the stairs that led up to the top storey. Those stairs were flanked on either side by small rooms. He figured it *had* to have been one of those doors that had slammed.

David felt a swell of exhilaration mixed in with the nerves, realising they had a camera mounted close by that had likely picked up what had happened. He just hoped the camera was running okay and everything had been recorded.

If so, they may have already captured their first compelling piece of evidence.

The doors to both rooms were closed, and the stairs between them that ran up to the floor above were shrouded in darkness. The group stood in silence… waiting and listening. The narrow corridor had dark oak panelling to the bottom half of the walls and cream wallpaper above. The ceilings were high with ornate coving, and the lighting was cast by iron chandeliers.

David pointed his handheld camera up the steep stairwell, but couldn't make much out through the viewfinder. It was just too dark.

'Okay,' he said to his team. 'Given the great hall is directly below us, the slamming door had to be one of these two. Hopefully, we have caught the whole thing on that camera there.' He pointed to the end of the corridor, where the wireless camera was fixed to a wall bracket and pointed back towards them. David then turned to the first storage room, the one just to his left.

'Let's check it out,' he said and took a step towards the heavy oak door. David reached out a hand and slowly opened it. The door swung inwards, and he held his camera up. The room inside wasn't very big at all, about four feet by four feet, and the back wall was lined floor to ceiling with bare shelves.

A storage room.

He could see most of the room thanks to the light from the corridor outside, but still reached a hand inside and found the light switch. The extra light revealed nothing, however, as the room was totally empty. He let the others peek their heads inside to see as he moved on to the next door.

In truth, David didn't expect to see anything. Not now. He felt the activity they'd heard was just the house warming up, and it would likely be all they encountered for a while. That was how these things tended to work: little bursts of activity that were sparse at first, but that sometimes grew into something more substantial.

The second room was identical to the first, and just as empty.

'We need to go check the footage,' Jenn said after everyone had looked into the second room for themselves.

She was right, but David couldn't help but again look up those stairs that led to the floor above, and how they vanished into darkness at the halfway point. As he looked, an awful sensation came over him that something was staring right back.

'Agreed,' he eventually said in response to Jenn. 'Let's go.'

'Not to be that guy,' Ralph started, 'because I'm as excited as the rest of us to look at the footage. But we have a hell of a meal waiting for us downstairs that's just going to get cold.'

David turned to Ralph with a look of bewilderment. The others stared at him as well, all sharing the same expression. Ralph's cheeks flushed red and he held up his hands.

'Fair enough,' he said. 'We check the camera feeds first, *then* we can eat the cold food.'

CHAPTER 11

Sarah stood over the shoulder of David, who was seated at the computer in the room designated as their headquarters. The other team members were present as well.

David pulled up the camera view from upstairs that focused on the corridor and the two storage room doors. It also showed the first few steps of the stairs that led up to the top storey.

The image on the laptop screen was in colour, though the reds of the carpets and dark browns of the oak panelling to the walls were washed out. The video feed wasn't high definition, either, with a slight grainy quality to it.

'The noises we heard happened about ten minutes ago,' David said and rewound the footage. As the feed skipped backwards, they all saw the moment where the door had closed, though in reverse it looked like it opened.

'There,' Jenn said, excitement in her voice. 'We caught it!'

But David kept going back, and Sarah soon saw why.

'I knew it,' David said as he paused the video. 'I was certain both doors up there were closed when we looked around earlier. So something opened the door first, then slammed it shut.' He started the footage again, playing it forward at normal speed and turning up the volume to full.

All Sarah could initially hear was some faint feedback and a slight crackle. Eventually, however, the door to the storage room nearest the camera slowly drifted open with an audible creak.

Sarah felt a tingle run up her spine.

The video kept playing for a minute longer before they all heard it, loud enough through the tinny speakers of the laptop that Ann jumped. The thudding footsteps they'd heard from downstairs thundered down the corridor over to the open door, which was promptly slammed shut.

'Did anyone else see that?' Sarah asked.

'Of course,' George replied, 'how could we miss it?'

Sarah shook her head. 'No, I'm not talking about the door closing. David, can you rewind that bit again, to just before the footsteps.'

David did as she asked, then played the video back. Yet again, the heavy running of some invisible person was audible from the laptop.

Only, they weren't quite invisible. Sarah put a finger close to the screen. 'There, do you see it?'

David leaned forward and squinted his eyes. He rewound and played it again.

'I see it!' he then exclaimed. Everyone else leaned in close.

It was a faint shadow of a humanoid shape, and translucent enough to be almost undetectable. It moved quickly and disappeared inside of the storage room moments before the door was closed.

'Oh wow,' Jenn said as David played it yet again.

'Definitely looks like a person,' Ralph added, then turned his head to Sarah. 'Nice catch.'

She smiled, feeling pleased with herself.

'I agree,' David said. 'I think we really have something here.'

'So then let's call that priest!' Sarah suggested. 'We can get him back here to see this.'

'Well,' David started, 'we need a bit more. Don't get me wrong, this is a hell of a start, but for an exorcism we really need the evidence to be overwhelming.'

'And this isn't?'

'Not quite. Like I said, it's great, and something to really build off. I *will* call Janosch and give him an update tomorrow, but let's see what happens tonight. Who knows, we might even get more.'

Sarah felt herself deflate. Just what did the Church need as proof, a personalised fucking message from a ghost? She sighed. 'Fine.'

David reached up from his seated position and put what was supposed to be a comforting hand on her forearm. As he did, Sarah had to resist the urge to flinch away.

'I know it's hard to be patient,' he said. 'Hell, it's bad enough for us, so I can't even imagine how impatient you must be feeling. But if we don't do everything right, then it will just delay things in the long run. The last thing we need is the Church to look at what we send and just dismiss it. This,' he pointed at the screen, 'is only one incident. We need to give them—and pardon my French here—a *shitload* more of the same.'

Sarah nodded. He was right, but that didn't make having to wait any easier.

Everyone watched the video again a few more times, following it through to when they all appeared on camera to investigate the slamming door, just to see if there was anything else of note.

There was not.

Eventually, they all went back down to the great hall to pick through the remains of the cold food. It was hardly the tasty feast it had started out as, but everyone needed the energy. A little after ten, David suggested they all turn in, since it had been a busy day and he wanted everyone well-rested. They could begin again in earnest the following day.

Sarah readied herself for bed with her two new roommates without saying much. The lights went out, and she pulled the duvet tightly around herself. She then fell asleep thinking about Chloe.

CHAPTER 12

Jenn's eyes fluttered open, and she was met with darkness. She felt tired, like she hadn't gotten a full night's sleep.

She blinked and let her vision focus, taking in the details of the bedroom—the window on the far wall with its heavy blue curtains pulled closed. A dresser. A side table where her phone and a nightlight lay.

It was cold in the room as well, even under the covers.

Jenn was lying on her side, facing the far wall, but she could hear Ann's gentle snoring from directly behind her. Jenn also felt Ann's cold foot on her leg. She kicked it away and groaned, leaning over to check her phone. The screen lit up and showed it was just after three in the morning.

Why the hell have I woken up so early? And why the fuck is it so cold?

She rolled to her back and pulled the duvet tighter around herself. Then, she looked down to the foot of her bed.

Jenn's breath caught in her throat.

She could see part of someone crouched over where Sarah lay, though she was just able to make out the head and shoulders, the rest of the body disappearing below the edge of her bed.

It was hard to make out in the dark, and the form was like a shadow, almost translucent.

Jenn fought through her fear and forced her body to move. As she did, the head that had been looking down quickly spun to face her.

In a panic, Jenn quickly leaned over and switched on the nightlight. It kicked out a dull orange glow that, while not strong enough to completely illuminate the room, was enough to let Jenn see.

There was nothing there. Nothing at the end of the bed sitting atop Sarah, who now began to stir, along with Ann.

'What's going on?' Ann asked wearily as she sat up, eyes squinting and her black hair a wild mess. Jenn saw Sarah sit up as well and look over the frame of the bed, confusion evident on her tired face.

'I...' Jenn trailed off. For a moment, she was unsure if she should share the experience. What if it was nothing? She was in the game to get *true* evidence of the afterlife, not confused accounts that could well have been the remnants of a dream.

'Well?' Ann pressed. Jenn decided it was best to share regardless, just in case.

'There was something crouched over Sarah,' she said.

Ann then sat upright.

'There was what?' Sarah asked in shock.

'A shadow, a faint one, like we saw on the video feed earlier. It was just crouched over you, but when I put on the light, it vanished.'

Sarah looked around. 'I can't see anything.' She then hugged herself. 'It's fucking cold, though.'

'The whole room feels cold,' Ann added. 'Which is a sign of activity.'

That was true, however Jenn actually felt like the room was warming up a little compared to when she had first woken up.

'But how do we know for certain it *was* something?' Sarah asked. 'How do we prove it?'

Jenn shrugged. 'I'm not sure we can. There are cameras in the corridors outside, so we can check those in the morning to see if anything has been picked up. But in here, we don't have anything recording us.'

'But why?' Sarah asked. 'We need to get everything.'

'It's a privacy issue,' Jenn said. 'David is pretty strict on that. He isn't comfortable with having video footage of us sleeping or changing clothes. He says it isn't right.'

'And he has a point,' Ann added. 'I wouldn't be comfortable being naked on camera. That's not what I signed up for. Imagine if the footage got leaked.'

'I don't think it would be a national scandal, Ann,' Jenn replied, though she knew Ann wasn't exactly being unreasonable.

Sarah shook her head and looked exasperated. 'Are you serious? We could be missing way too much. I'm going to speak to David in the morning.'

'I'm *not* being recorded while I sleep,' Ann insisted.

'Then go home!' Sarah shot back. Ann looked insulted, her eyes wide, but instead of firing back she just sat in silence, sulking. They all stayed that way for a little while, waiting for something to happen.

Eventually, Ann lay down and angrily pulled the covers over herself. It was clear she was still annoyed at Sarah's comments.

Sarah cast Jenn a look, as if asking 'is she for real?' She then shook her head and lay down herself. 'You can switch off the light when you're ready, Jenn,' she said. 'I guess we can talk about this more tomorrow.'

Jenn did as she was asked, smiling a little at Ann having thrown a tantrum. It was nice to see the princess brought down a peg or two, even if Jenn didn't wholly disagree with her in principle.

While trying to get back to sleep, Jenn kept glancing down to the edge of the bed to see if the shadow had returned. She remembered how it had turned to face her just a moment before it vanished. It sent a chill up her spine.

Perhaps Sarah had a point. Could they really let modesty get in the way of capturing indisputable evidence?

CHAPTER 13

'Nope,' David said. 'I'm not seeing anything.'

Sarah sighed in disappointment.

The team were again in HQ, poring over the computer monitors. The first thing that morning, Sarah had knocked on David and George's bedroom door, and then told them what had happened the previous night. David's eyes lit up. Everyone was quickly rounded up and brought downstairs, still in their sleeping clothes and robes.

They checked the footage outside the girls' bedroom around the time of the incident but came up short. Whatever had happened inside the room had been isolated.

'Damn it,' Sarah said. 'How much is Jenn's experience worth to Janosch without evidence?'

David looked up at her from his seat. 'He may well believe her,' he said, 'but it won't hold too much water on its own. However, we will document it and add it to everything else.'

That wasn't good enough for Sarah. Two things of note had happened since they'd arrived yesterday, but only one had been caught. Batting at a fifty-percent success rate was going to make the whole process take much longer.

'We need cameras in the bedrooms,' Sarah said.

'We don't have enough for all the bedrooms,' David said. 'We already have them in a few, your sister and your niece's for example, as well as your old room, but we'd run out pretty quick if we tried to monitor every bedroom.'

'No,' Sarah said. 'I meant the bedrooms we're using.'

David paused, then shook his head. 'We can't do that. People should be allowed their privacy.'

'What does it matter?' Sarah pressed. 'I mean really, is anyone here going to use any of the footage for anything other than proof? It's not like videos of us sleeping are going to get leaked online like some seedy sex tape. It's nothing. Plus it just seems stupid not to monitor ourselves while we sleep. Everything here seems to happen late at night, often in the rooms that are in use. Those things focus on *us*.'

'We all have handheld cameras,' David argued. 'Those can be used.'

'But look what happened last night,' Sarah countered. 'There was no time to get the camera before whatever the hell it was disappeared.'

'I'm not comfortable being recorded like that, David,' Ann cut in. Sarah gritted her teeth but took a calming breath.

'I understand,' David said. 'I would never ask you to do anything you aren't comfortable with.'

'Then switch rooms,' Sarah insisted. 'Hell, I'll go sleep in a room on my own.'

'That isn't happening,' David stated. 'We can't get reckless... or impatient.'

'Actually,' Ralph said, sounding hesitant, 'I think Sarah makes a good point.' Everyone turned to him, and Sarah felt a small pang of relief. *Finally, some back-up.* 'We could be missing a hell of a lot. I get what Ann is saying, but let's face it, it isn't like we're waltzing naked around our rooms all the time. And we obviously wouldn't record bathrooms. So... is it really such a big deal?'

David looked around the group. 'How does everyone else feel about it?'

There were a few nonchalant shrugs before George chimed in. 'I'd be fine with it. We can just get dressed in the bathrooms if we need to, like Ralph says.'

'I'm okay with it, too,' Jenn added.

Jamie then chipped in. 'Me too, I guess.'

Ann threw her arms up in the air. 'David, no!'

However, Sarah had a solution.

'Look, given that shadow was close to *me* last night, it stands to reason to monitor the room I'm in. So, if anyone is game, I'll share a bedroom with someone else, and Ann and Jenn can stay where they are… without being watched.'

'But that would mean bunking up with a guy,' David said.

'I know, but that isn't a big deal. For God's sake, when I was in the army I bunked with men all the time. I think *you're* making a bigger issue out of it than it really is.'

David paused and chewed at his lower lip. 'I guess that would be okay, as long as you have no issue with it?'

'I don't,' Sarah insisted.

Then Jenn cut in. 'I have no problem being filmed. I'm happy to share a room with Sarah for this.'

Ann's eyes went wide. 'And leave me on my own? Because I am *not* sharing a room with one of the boys. I'm sorry, but *I* wasn't in the army, and I'm not comfortable with it.'

'Sleep on your own, then,' Jenn replied with a grin.

'Enough,' David said, raising a hand into the air. He again looked up to Sarah. 'If you're okay with it, I'll share a room with you. We can pull another bed into one of the rooms and I'll take that.'

Sarah smiled. 'Works for me. And we'll get a camera set up?'

'Yes,' David said. 'But we'll do that after breakfast. I'm starving, and right now I need coffee.'

Sarah was happy with that, and she was pleased David had finally seen sense. It would hopefully move things on at a much quicker pace.

While Sarah hadn't seen what Jenn had, the fact the shadow was over *her* meant she was potentially a target for the things in this house—much like her sister had been.

However, Sarah had another theory about that shadow. Maybe it was the same one they had seen running down the hall. It was entirely possible that *this* entity was not malicious.

Perhaps it was Chloe.

CHAPTER 14

'Very interesting,' Luca said into the phone pressed against his cheek, trying to block the concern from his voice.

He had blessed the house only yesterday. Now, if David was to be believed, there had been more activity already.

Luca was in his study and seated at the pine desk, which held his laptop. The study was his place of refuge—somewhere he could hide away, close the door, and block out the world. It wasn't a huge room, and that only helped convey a welcome sense of solitude. The window beside him gave a view out over the rear gardens of the clergy house, which had a neatly trimmed lawn and high conifer trees around the perimeter. A bookshelf sat behind him, packed with reference books and scripture, some of which were devoted to a subject on which he had become a reluctant specialist.

'We caught something on video,' David said, 'but missed the incident in the girls' bedroom last night. However, I'm very confident we'll see more soon. Can I ask, is there any way you can forewarn your superiors, so they know what's coming? It might speed things up, and our client is quite… impatient, as you can imagine.'

'I appreciate that,' Luca replied. 'But there really is no rushing these things, unfortunately. We will have to go through the appropriate channels, but only when we have a strong enough case.'

'Fair enough. I had to ask.'

'I understand. While I have you, I would be interested in looking at the book again, if that is okay. The... *Ianua Diaboli.*'

'Of course,' David replied eagerly. 'When can you come over?'

Luca paused for a moment, searching for the best way to frame his words. 'Well, it might be beneficial if you actually bring it to me. I think it would be easier to study it that way. I'd therefore be able to spend a bit more time with it, you know?'

That was an exaggeration at best. *You're afraid, Luca. You know you are.*

It was David's turn to pause. 'Well... I'd need to check with the client first. It's her book, after all, but I think she would be okay with it.'

'Could you find out and let me know?'

'Sure. Is there something interesting about that book, Father? Anything I need to be aware of?'

'Not really,' Luca said. *Is it really a lie if I'm protecting someone?* Luca hoped not, because that was his only justification. 'However, its age and subject matter are of great interest. That book might even help make the Church take notice of our situation.'

'There are tons of rare artefacts up there,' David said. 'We could catalogue them all if need be. Would that help?'

'Well, let's look at them after I've finished with the book. One step at a time.'

The other things in that study might indeed be valuable, and significant, but Luca could not look past *Ianua Diaboli*—if, of course, it was the real deal.

He sincerely hoped it wasn't.

CHAPTER 15

DAVID HUNG up the phone and scratched his chin. The conversation with Father Janosch had been interesting, and thrown up something of a curveball. Perhaps it was an opportunity, as Father Janosch had said; a reason for the Church to take a closer look.

The priest had indicated the book was of interest, but only because of its historical significance. However, David got the feeling Father Janosch may have been hiding something, which made him want to check out the book again.

He slipped his phone into his pocket and stood up from the ornate lounge chair he had been sitting on in the library. The ground-floor room was beautiful, with the walls filled with bookshelves that almost touched the high ceilings. Each shelf was neatly stacked with thick books. The space had a musty smell of old leather, and the tall window that looked out over the front grounds let in plenty of natural daylight, making the space feel light and airy... if a little dusty.

It was a little after midday, and while the others were finishing lunch in the great hall, he had left them to make the call. He quickly returned to them. As he entered the hall, Sarah looked up.

'Well,' she asked, 'what did he say?'

'He was interested to hear our experiences,' David replied and walked over to the table. All eyes were on him. He took a seat and felt a small pull in his back, a resulting twinge from when he and Sarah had earlier rearranged the bedroom they would share.

'And...?' Sarah asked.

'We have to carry on as we were, like I thought,' David replied. He saw Sarah's shoulders drop. He understood her disappointment, but it was what he had been anticipating before making the call—they simply didn't have enough yet.

Sarah took a deep breath. 'Okay. We carry on as we are. So what's next?'

'Well, before we get to that,' David said. 'There was something that came up in the conversation that was interesting. The book upstairs, in that weird study... Father Janosch would like to study it?'

Sarah frowned. 'Why?'

He shrugged. 'I'm not certain. He said it could be valuable.'

'Valuable?' Sarah asked. He saw her jaw clench. 'I'm sorry, but we have more pressing matters than finding out how much an old book is worth. What... is he planning to sell it on eBay and make a little money or something?'

David held up his hands. 'Sarah, it's nothing like that,' he said. 'Given what that book deals with, and also finding it in a house like this... he says it warrants investigation, and that it might help make the Church take notice of what we're doing here. I got the impression—though he didn't say it directly—that there's more to it than just monetary value. And think about it... if it interests the Church, then you have a bargaining chip.'

A look of realisation washed over her. 'I see,' she replied. 'Clever. Okay, he can come here and have a look. But only for a few hours. If he wants to see more, we need this place exorcised first.'

'There may be a problem with that,' David said.

'Which is?'

'He didn't want to come to the house to study it. Said he'd prefer we take the book to him so he'd have more time with it. Apparently it would be easier for him to study in his own home.'

Sarah let out a humourless laugh. 'I bet it would be. But then I'd never see it again.'

'He isn't a thief, Sarah,' David stated. 'He's a *priest*.'

'Let's not pretend that those things are mutually exclusive,' she shot back.

David shook his head. 'We can trust him. Father Janosch is a good guy. He's on our side.'

'Maybe you think so, but I don't know him from Adam. And I *certainly* don't trust him enough to loan him my stuff. Look, it's my book, and my decision. If he wants to study it, he does it here.'

She folded her arms across her chest, and though David wanted to try to make her see reason, he knew her mind would not be swayed. Besides, having Father Janosch spend some time here certainly wouldn't hurt their investigation.

'Fine,' David said. 'I'll speak to him again and let him know.'

'Great. So… what's next for today?' she asked.

CHAPTER 16

WITH THE NIGHT-VISION MODE ENGAGED, Jenn looked through the viewfinder of her camera. It was focused on Ann. The tall, raven-haired woman stood with her eyes closed and arms held out to her sides, attempting to contact the dead.

That woman is about as psychic as a doorstop. Why is David taken in by her bullshit?

It was approaching mid-afternoon and they were down in the basement. All of the lights were off, and the only source of illumination was the two bright beams from the torches Ralph and George carried.

'I'm getting something,' Ann said, cocking her head to the side.

'What?' David asked eagerly.

Ann was standing in the middle of everyone as they formed a crude circle around her. There was a chill to the air and a musty, moldy smell.

They had been down there in the dark for ten minutes, watching Ann through their viewfinders as she paced around, looking off into the shadows like she could see something the rest of them couldn't.

'Over there,' she said and pointed to a corner of the room. Ralph and George cast their torchlights over to where she was pointing, but all Jenn could see was the point where the two stone walls met. Nothing else. 'I feel a presence,' Ann went on. 'A child, I think.'

Jenn had to force herself not to roll her eyes.

It's always a fucking child with Ann.

That was her go-to. Jenn knew why: the ghost of a dead child would always pull at the heartstrings, so it helped keep any scepticism in check the others may have. Jenn fully expected the child would be a girl.

'It's a little girl,' Ann added.

Fucking bingo!

'Is she aware of our presence?' David asked.

'She is,' Ann confirmed with a slow nod. 'She's curious as well.' Ann then took a step forward and addressed the empty corner in soothing tones. 'Don't be scared, little one; we aren't here to hurt you. Do you have a message for us?' Ann cocked her head to the side as if listening.

After her pause continued for too long, David asked, 'Is she saying anything?'

Ann held up a finger to silence their leader. She then gave a slow nod. 'She says we have to be careful. There is something here that means to do us harm.'

'Some*thing*?' David asked. 'Not some*one*?'

'That's right. She was very specific about that.'

'The demon. It has to be.'

'I agree,' Ann said.

David shook his head in awe. 'That is amazing.'

Jenn gritted her teeth together. It was *not* amazing in the slightest. They all knew about the demon here already, because they'd *seen* it in 2014, and this non-incident had provided nothing in the way of true evidence.

This was the kind of bullshit nonsense that was far too easy to dismiss, and it made them all look like idiots or charlatans.

But Jenn knew she had to push through. For whatever reason, David believed in what Ann said and what she claimed she brought to the table.

Away from that nonsense, however, Jenn was convinced they were doing good work with their investigation. And *that* was the important thing to her. So she just had to accept Ann as she was, at least for now.

'Is she saying anything else?' Ralph asked. Jenn could hear the faintest touch of exasperation in his voice.

'She's just saying the same thing again: that we need to be careful. Wait... now she's saying she needs to leave us.'

Thank God.

'Can't you ask her to stay?' David asked.

'I'm afraid she's already gone,' Ann replied, before adding, 'travel safe, little one.'

They spent another ten minutes waiting for something else to happen before Ann eventually said, 'There is nothing down here with us anymore. I can't feel anything.'

And, instead of trying something else, David took that as evidence enough to leave the location. 'Let's head upstairs,' he said. 'I think it would be a good idea to try some vigils. We'll split up into teams and spread out.'

Everyone started to head out, and Jenn checked the battery on her camera as she walked. It was then she felt a cold hand grab hold of her shoulder. Jenn assumed it was Jamie, who had been standing close to her.

As she raised her head, she lifted the camera up as well, and as she did she saw through her viewfinder that the other six members of the team were all in front of her... including Jamie.

She was bringing up the rear alone.

The cold hand clamped tighter and Jenn's body stiffened in fright. Her breath caught in her chest. She wanted to turn round and face whatever was behind her, but she struggled to move. The others carried on trudging over to the steps.

'Guys...' she managed to squeak out, but no one heard. A foul, rotting smell flowed from behind her. Jenn began to shake. There was no question she was in the middle of an encounter, but fear had seized her, and she was terrified at the thought of turning around.

Instead, she held the camera out before her with one hand and slowly rotated it towards herself, flipping the viewfinder as she did. In the small screen, illuminated with the blue hue of night vision, she could see herself come into focus. Her eyes were wide and pupils were like pin-pricks. She studied her shoulder on the image before her but could see nothing. It was then she noticed she could no longer feel the cold touch.

'Guys!' Jenn shouted as she found her voice. She was suddenly blinded by torchlight as the others turned to face her.

'What is it?' Ralph asked, quickly lowering his beam from her eyes. Jenn momentarily saw stars and swirling motes. She blinked quickly to clear her vision.

'I felt something,' she said. 'A hand... on my shoulder. I'm sure of it.'

A moment of stunned silence was quickly broken by the sound of running feet over the stone ground. Everyone came over and crowded around Jenn.

'Can you still feel it?' Sarah asked.

Jenn shook her head and finally felt her body relax. 'No,' she said, rotating her arm at the shoulder a couple of times. The two torch beams flicked around the room but no one could find anything.

'George, go put on the main light,' David ordered. 'Quickly.'

George did as instructed and trotted over to the steps that led up to the floor above. The switch was situated on the wall just next to them, and he flicked it on.

The lights slowly blinked to life, giving off a brief strobe effect as they powered up. The team searched the basement but came up short.

'Are you certain about what you felt?' David asked.

'One hundred percent,' Jenn stated.

David then turned to Ann. 'I thought you said that whoever was down here had left?'

Jenn had to stop from shaking her head in disbelief. *Get a clue, David.*

'I thought they had,' Ann replied. 'But someone else must have come through just as we were leaving.'

Jenn ignored their conversation and pulled up her camera, skipping back through the footage to when she had felt the hand. She played the footage back, but all Jenn could see on the screen was her own terrified face. And behind that was only darkness.

No... wait.

There *was* something else there: two small glinting objects, which could easily have been floating dust particles if not for them being perfectly parallel. Jenn paused the footage and went into the settings menu of the camera. She started to increase the contrast, washing more light into the image. Click by click, the blacks behind Jenn on screen were forced back and replaced by a dull blue, making more and more of the space behind her visible. When the contrast was turned up to its fullest Jenn could make out the far wall behind her, as well as the black form of the furnace.

There was something else, too—something she could see more clearly now: a man standing flat against the wall.

Though the image was grainy and pixilated, he looked to be wearing dark robes. His face was a blank stare and his eyes glinted like reflecting pennies.

'Holy shit!'

CHAPTER 17

THE EVIDENCE SEEMED to be falling into their laps.

First was the shadow moving across the hallway, and now the footage from the basement, of something standing behind Jenn. While neither piece of evidence was completely clear, in Sarah's mind both were undeniable.

And on top of that, there had been the experience during the night.

The house is still alive.

David had warned Sarah that things might be slow to pick up because the building had been empty for three weeks. Spirits and demons drew on the energy of the living. It fuelled them and allowed them to make themselves known.

However, in the space of a single day, it seemed like the house hadn't missed a step at all.

David had given everyone some free time before they ate, so people had paired up and gone off to different rooms to conduct some vigils. From what Sarah could tell, a vigil just consisted of sitting in a room and asking the spirits to show themselves.

However, Sarah was interested to see what David was up to. He had disappeared off somewhere on his own.

After searching the ground and middle floors and not finding him,

Sarah then moved up to the top storey. She circled the corridor and made her way to where she suspected he was: the study.

As she turned the corner to the room, she saw the door was open and a light was on inside. While it wasn't dark out just yet, daylight was beginning to wane.

She poked her head inside the room and saw David was in the centre, and he had *Ianua Diaboli* out and resting on top of the cabinet's glass display lid. The book was open and David was scribbling something down into a small notebook that lay on the case as well.

'Hiding away?' Sarah asked, and David jumped in fright.

'Jesus,' he exclaimed, holding a hand over his chest. 'You just about gave me a bloody heart attack.'

'Sorry,' Sarah said, though the chuckle that followed probably showed her lack of sincerity. 'Are you supposed to be up here on your own? I thought we were always meant to be in pairs at least.'

'Fair point,' David replied. He then took a deep breath and lowered his hand from his chest. 'I figure with it still being daytime I should be okay for a little while.'

'Interested in my book?' Sarah asked, nodding to the artefact he was studying.

'A little,' he replied. 'I'm curious as to why Father Janosch is so focused on it.'

'Did you call him back?'

David nodded. 'I did, though couldn't get hold of him. I left a message saying he would need to come down here if he wanted to study the book.'

Sarah made her way over to David. She didn't like the study the first time she had seen it, but the longer she stayed, the more Sarah found herself spending time up here, always drawn back to *Ianua Diaboli*. She couldn't explain why, but there was something alluring about the book.

'If he's interested enough, he'll come around,' Sarah said. And she dearly hoped that he *was* interested enough, though she was prepared to use every dirty trick she had at her disposal to get this fucking exorcism finally underway.

'I also mentioned what happened last night, and about the footage we got down in the basement, too. I said that things really seem to be ramping up already.'

'Things haven't taken long to get going,' Sarah said, looking down at the book.

'No, they really haven't. Which is both good and bad.'

Sarah blinked, then lifted her head to him. 'Bad? How do you mean?'

'Well, I mean it could be a sign that things are going to become dangerous. I've never had so much activity in such a small space of time before. Well, not since I was last here.'

'But that's a good thing!' Sarah said. 'That means we will get our evidence much quicker.'

'Or everything gets out of hand and someone gets hurt,' he replied. 'Remember, things don't tend to end well for people in Perron Manor: the events in 1982, for example. And my own investigation in 2014 got a little dangerous at the end. Then, of course...' he trailed off.

'Then my sister died.'

He gave a sad nod. 'Exactly. Sorry, I don't bring it up to upset you, just to a make a point.'

'Which is?'

'That we have to be careful here,' David replied.

'I get that. And I'm with you. We'll be careful.' There was a brief look of hesitation on David's face, and he sighed. 'Something wrong?' she asked.

'I... I don't quite know how to put this, but I think we do need to have a talk.'

Sarah smiled. 'David, are you breaking up with me?'

He frowned. 'What do you mean?'

She just chuckled. 'That's pretty much how every break-up speech starts. *We need to have a talk.*'

'Oh, I wouldn't know about... I mean, that isn't what I'm getting at. Look, I know it's hard for you, but I just think you need to be a little bit more patient with how things are going. And a little more patient with the people here.'

'I *am* being patient,' Sarah insisted, her smile falling away. 'I've been nothing *but* patient since we got here.'

'Sarah... come on. I'm not trying to start a fight, but pushing Father

Janosch like you did, insisting on the camera in the bedroom despite Ann being uncomfortable, and getting annoyed when we don't get every little thing recorded...'

'Every little thing? David, according to Jenn there was something sitting on me last night. That's a pretty fucking *big* thing.'

'I know,' he said, holding up his hands. 'I just mean... this whole process is going to take time. I know that must be killing you, but there's no way around it. I just need you to go a little easier on everyone. They're giving up their free time, after all. And Father Janosch will do all he can for us, I know it.'

'And I'm grateful,' she said, her voice cold as ice.

But David just pointed to her hands, which were down by her sides and clenched into fists. 'Really? Look at how angry you're getting now.'

Sarah looked down and lifted her hands. The fingers had started to turn white, and her palms stung as her nails dug into the tender skin.

Perhaps David had a point. Sarah relaxed her hands and lowered them. She took a breath. 'Maybe you have a point.'

He gave Sarah a mournful smile. 'Again, I don't want to dismiss what you're going through with the death of your sister, and I don't blame you at all for being anxious. Just... please remember that everyone here is trying to help.'

'I get it,' Sarah said, meaning it this time. 'I guess I have been a little forceful. It's just, when I saw Chloe up in that window... she wasn't herself. She was *wrong*. All twisted up and rotting. She looked like she was in pain, and she was begging for my help. I just know she's suffering. I think all the spirits of the dead trapped here are going through the same thing. It's killing me knowing Chloe is trapped in that purgatory and I can't help her.'

'I get that,' he said. There was a look on his face she had never seen before. Serious, sad, even a little angry. 'I get that more than you...' He shook his head and went on. 'Never mind. Look, we'll free her, Sarah, I promise. We'll free *all* of them.'

Sarah smiled at him. 'Thank you. And I'll try harder to be a little more patient.' She then looked down to the book. 'Find anything interesting?'

David nodded. 'Plenty... I think. My Latin isn't great, but it seems to be a book of rituals, curses, rites, ceremonies, and God knows what else.'

'Sounds ominous,' Sarah said.

'Maybe. But the interesting thing about it is the constant reference to something called a Devil's Door, or Door to the Devil, and other variants on that.'

'And you don't know what a Devil's Door is, I take it?'

David shook his head. 'Not something I've ever heard of. Father Janosch seemed to know. I got the impression this book spooked him. He practically ran out of the house after seeing it.'

'I think we may need to have a talk with Father Janosch,' Sarah said. 'Sounds like he's holding out on us.'

'Agreed. I do think he's on our side, but I'd really like to know the full story about the book.'

Then something clicked in Sarah's mind. *The ledger!*

Sitting in the corner of the study was an antique writing desk that held a ledger with a brown leather cover. Sarah remembered looking through it weeks ago and realising what it contained: transcriptions of *Ianua Diaboli*.

'What are you smiling at?' David asked.

'I think I have a way to find out more about the book.'

CHAPTER 18

'WHERE ARE YOU GOING?' Jamie asked Ann as she got to her feet.

Ann turned back to him. 'I need to spend a penny.'

Jamie frowned in confusion. 'Spend a what?' Ann rolled her eyes.

Do I need to spell it out for you?

Thankfully, Jenn did it for her. 'She needs to go pee,' Jenn clarified with a chuckle.

The three of them were up in one of the mid-floor bedrooms carrying out a vigil. They all had their cameras with them, and Jenn also had an audio recorder as well as a device that detected any sudden changes in temperature. They had been in the room for close to an hour with no activity.

Ann was certain the room had nothing to offer and had told the other two they should all move on; she could feel no presence in the room. However, Jenn wouldn't listen… just like always. She said she wanted to be thorough.

'Oh,' Jamie said in response to Jenn's clarification. He then looked up to Ann. 'Should you really go alone?'

Ann appreciated his concern for her, it was sweet, but she didn't need babysitting. However, they'd picked one of the few rooms without an en-suite, meaning she'd have to find a toilet elsewhere. 'I'll be fine, Jamie,' she said. 'My room's just down the corridor.'

'Just go to the main toilet across the hall,' he said.

'No,' Ann replied, shaking her head. 'It's cold as hell in there.'

Jamie looked as if he had more to say, but relented. 'Okay,' he said. 'Just be careful. And shout if you see anything. We should be able to hear you from here.'

Ann smiled. 'I will.'

It was nice that he always looked out for her. Jamie was cute as well, and at least he believed in her abilities—unlike some of the others, who Ann felt were just jealous.

She left the room and strode down the corridor, back to the room she was sharing with Jenn. Sarah had moved over to David's room now, so Ann's bedroom felt bigger without that extra mattress crammed inside. It was still messy, however, and most of that was her fault. Her case was open beside her bed, and her dark clothes were strewn about the floor. She knew she wasn't the tidiest, but what did that matter when they were living out of suitcases?

The room smelled funky, and she wondered if perhaps there was some standing water in the radiator or pipes. She had some incense with her that she'd wanted to light, but Jenn had objected, saying that she hated the smell, and also that she didn't want it burning if they were out of the room with no one to watch it. It was a fire hazard, apparently.

Ann was certain the woman just wanted to disagree with her on principle. If Ann claimed the sky was blue, Jenn would argue it was pink.

Ann walked through into the en-suite, which was smaller than the main toilet on the floor, but more cosy and with a nicer décor.

The floor was tiled white, as were the walls. However, there was a thin band of turquoise tiling halfway up the walls which broke up the expanse of whiteness. A thick blue rug lay next to a cast-iron bath, and there was also a beautiful, old vanity unit and sink sitting below a large mirror. There were no windows in the room, but the small chandelier fixed to the ceiling was sufficient to fully light the space.

Ann gently swung the door closed behind her and heard it catch on the latch. She took a quick look in the mirror to check her hair, then walked over to the toilet.

A slow creaking sound made Ann turn, and she saw the door drift open.

She frowned, feeling her heart quicken. However, she soon caught herself. *You didn't fully close the door, so it obviously just blew open. Nothing to be scared of.*

She closed the door fully this time and waited, just to make sure it stayed closed. When satisfied, she then went to answer the call of nature, and after that stood to wash her hands in the sink. Ann again heard the click of the latch, and the long, drawn-out creak as the door slowly swung open.

Ann froze.

There was no way a simple draft could have opened the door again this time. *Could it?* She watched with bated breath as the door opened, revealing the bedroom behind. Ann expected to see someone standing on the other side—human or otherwise—but nothing was there. The bedroom appeared to be completely empty.

'Hello?' she croaked out, her throat feeling tight. Nothing.

Not knowing what else to do, and feeling a creeping dread climb up from her gut, Ann kicked out a booted foot to shove the door closed.

She waited. The door remained closed.

Ann finished washing her hands and turned off the tap. While towelling off, and facing away from the entrance to the room, she heard the ominous click of the latch again, as well as the drawn-out creak.

Feeling that sense of dread rise farther, Ann reluctantly turned her head to see the door opening yet again, as if it were taunting her.

But again, there was no one on the other side.

What the fuck is going on?

'Is there something you want to tell me?' she asked, deciding direct communication with the entity was the most appropriate course of action—because there *was* something here with her now, she had no doubt about that.

Ann just hoped it wasn't malicious in nature. Perhaps a benevolent spirit wanted to make itself known. Maybe even Sarah's sister.

'Chloe… is that you?'

Again, nothing. Just an unbearable silence. Ann thought about what to do next as her anxiety levels rose. Closing the door to see if it opened again was an option, or she could just try and leave to go get the others.

If Ann was honest with herself, the experience was unnerving her.

Another option would be to just scream. That would get the others to come. But how could she live that down? She could just imagine Jenn's smug face at seeing Ann so scared.

She then cursed herself for leaving the handheld camera back in the bedroom with the others. This was the *exact* reason David always insisted they take the cameras everywhere they went.

However... Ann did have her smartphone, which she could record video on. Sensing a chance to capture some evidence all on her own, and maybe prove to Jenn that she was a valued member of the team, Ann pulled out her phone and set it to record. She initially filmed herself as she spoke into the camera.

'This is Ann Tate, and I am in one of the mid-floor bedroom en-suites in Perron Manor. While in here, the door to the room has been consistently opening of its own accord. It has happened three times now, so I'm going to try again.'

She then hit a button to flip the camera view so that it now looked ahead, rather than back at herself. She took a breath, then stepped forward and closed the door again. Then... she waited.

Seconds went by, then a minute. Nothing. After waiting for close to four minutes, Ann was ready to give up. Perhaps her visitor had left her.

However, just before she put her phone away, the door opened again. This time much quicker than before.

Yet again, there was nothing on the other side.

'See,' Ann said for the benefit of the recording. 'That is the fourth time, and no one is here to open the door.'

She started to walk into the bedroom, wanting to film the room to prove it was indeed empty. However, as soon as she took a step forward the door quickly slammed shut, hard enough that it reverberated in the frame.

Ann let out a gasp and backed up again. Whereas before she had felt unnerved, now she was outright scared. Through the fear, however, she managed to keep her recording going, determined to come through for the team and prove her worth.

But Ann knew she needed to be out of that room. She reached forward and grabbed the brass door knob, trying to twist it. It didn't budge.

She tried again and shook it as hard as she could, growing desperate.

'Come on,' she pleaded, now terrified. Ann was trapped in the room and the temperature in there suddenly plummeted.

She continued to try to force the door. 'Please,' she cried, pulling and twisting again and again.

Finally, the door freed up and swung inwards, and as it did Ann lost her footing and fell to the floor, dropping the phone in the process.

She hit her back hard on the tiled floor. After letting out a groan, she rolled to her front and scrambled over to retrieve the phone, which had bounced and skidded off to her side, facing up.

Ann then ran from the room, the air around her still ice-cold. As she ran, she had a horrible feeling some unseen force would stop her and drag her back inside.

Thankfully, her escape was unhindered, and she thundered down the corridor and into the bedroom where she had left Jenn and Jamie. They both looked up to her in surprise.

'What happened?' he asked with a concerned frown.

'Something... something trapped me, in the bathroom,' Ann managed to wheeze out, lost for breath after sprinting for her life. The others quickly sprang to their feet.

'What do you mean?' Jenn asked. Ann took a moment to regain her composure.

'Something had me trapped!' Ann went over the full story, the words tumbling out of her without pausing for breath. When she finished, Jamie was wide-eyed in shock.

'Let me see the video,' Jenn said. 'We might have more evidence there.'

Ann was annoyed Jenn was more concerned with what was on the video rather than Ann's safety. Regardless, she pulled out her phone and played the footage for them.

They watched Ann on the playback telling who she was, where she was, and what had just happened. The view flipped to point ahead and

Ann closed the door. Minutes passed by and eventually the door was thrust open again.

'Jesus,' Jamie said. 'That's incredible.'

'It is,' Jenn agreed. 'But it could have been opened from the other side, by someone out of the shot.'

'Jenn!' Ann snapped. 'I can't believe you think I'd fake this. Who the hell else was there with me to even open it?'

'That isn't what I mean,' Jenn said, shaking her head. 'I know you're telling the truth. But to someone looking from the outside in, who would want to debunk our evidence, that's exactly what they would say.'

The door on the video then slammed shut.

'No way you can fake that,' Jamie said. 'The door was open and no one reached in to grab the handle.'

Jenn nodded with a smile. 'I agree. That part is indisputable, I'd say.'

Ann felt relieved.

'Must have been terrifying,' Jamie said as they watched the rest of the footage. He laid a hand on Ann's shoulder. She smiled at him, appreciating the gesture.

'It was a little,' she admitted.

The video footage then shook and jostled as Ann dropped the phone. It came to a stop facing the ceiling, but picked up quite a bit of the room in the frame. Everyone drew in a breath before Ann's hand appeared on screen and snatched up the phone.

Something had been in the shot.

Ann looked first to Jamie, then to Jenn, as the footage played out.

How did I miss that?

Ann realised she was shaking.

'Did you see it?' Jamie questioned, pointing to the screen.

They both nodded. Jenn then asked, 'Did you notice anything in the room with you at the time?'

Ann shook her head.

'No... but I didn't look behind myself when I was in there. Was... was *it* there the whole time, do you think?'

'No idea,' Jenn replied.

'Play it back,' Jamie said. 'We need to see it again, then tell the others.'

Ann rewound to the point she was trying to force the door open.

The footage started again. They watched as the door released and the phone fell. When it came to a stop, and the spinning picture finally settled, Ann hit pause.

On the still image, a dark, slightly blurred figure was standing against the far wall of the bathroom. His hands were down by his sides, and the man with the pale face wore an expressionless gaze. He looked to be wearing a dark suit and had black, brushed back-hair. There was a gash of red across his throat.

'Holy shit,' Jenn muttered. 'We need to show the others.'

CHAPTER 19

'Fascinating,' David said as he looked at the image on Ann's phone.

Everyone was back in HQ again after being called by Ann, who had insisted there was something important the whole group needed to see.

David had been up in the study with Sarah. She'd been about to show him a ledger she claimed would shed more light on *Ianua Diaboli*.

However, before they managed to look at the book, Ann had shouted up the stairs for them.

'Let me see that,' Sarah insisted, leaning closer to the phone. Her eyes grew wide. 'I think I recognise him,' she said, pointing at the man on screen.

David turned to her. 'Recognise how?'

'I think we saw him one time in the house—me and Chloe. I'm certain of it. I recognise the wound across his throat, and I'm sure he even spoke to us.'

'What did he say?' Ralph asked.

Sarah squinted her eyes in thought. Then, however, she shook her head. 'I can't remember exactly. But it was aimed at Chloe. Like he knew her, somehow.'

'How could he...' David started to say, then trailed off. Something clicked in his mind. 'Wait.'

He walked over to one of his many backpacks that were stored in a corner of the room, and pulled out an old scrapbook with a ring binder. David had used this to collect cutouts and notes when researching Perron Manor to write his own book.

Within the scrapbook were a variety of cuttings from newspaper articles glued onto the pages—not originals, but photocopies that he'd made at the local library and historical centres. He flicked through to the page he was looking for: an article about the formerly abandoned house finally being bought again. There was a picture of the new owner.

Marcus Blackwater.

David set the scrapbook down on a desk and asked Ann to put her phone down next to it, which she did.

'What do you think?' David asked. 'Same guy?'

'Holy shit,' Ralph exclaimed. 'It could be!'

The image from the phone wasn't perfectly focused or clear, so exact details were difficult to make out. However, there was definitely a likeness: the hair, the facial structure, and the dark clothes.

'If it is Marcus Blackwater,' David said to Sarah, 'then it would explain how he knew Chloe. She was living here when he died, right?'

Sarah nodded. 'Yeah, that's right.'

'*And* he cut his throat,' David added, pointing to the neck wound of the man on the phone screen.

'This is unreal,' Jenn cut in. 'Are we saying Ann may have captured footage of Marcus Blackwater?'

'I think so,' David replied. 'And if we have identified one of these spirits, maybe it will be more compelling to the Church.' He turned to Ann. 'Way to go, kid.'

'Yeah,' Jamie added. 'Nice work.'

Ann beamed with pride.

It must have been a terrifying ordeal, but she had come through it with something tangible for them to use. David was proud of her.

'We need to get the video from the phone and onto our system,' George said. 'Ideally as soon as possible so we can get it properly logged.' He then dug through a bag of his own and pulled out a white connector cable. 'May I?' he asked Ann.

'Of course.'

George got to work transferring the data. As he did, David felt a hand touch his elbow. He turned to see Sarah signalling for him to step away with her. They both moved over to the corner of the room.

'Has Father Janosch called you back yet?'

David shook his head. 'Not yet. I'm guessing he's just busy.'

'Okay,' Sarah said with a sigh. 'Still, things seem to be progressing pretty quickly, huh?'

'You can say that again. I'm not making any promises, but I wouldn't be surprised if we have all we need soon.'

'So what's the plan for tonight? I think it would be prudent to try and capitalise on the momentum.'

'I agree,' David said. 'Jenn and I were discussing this earlier. We have something with us, called a Demon Board—'

'I remember that from your book,' Sarah cut in. 'You used it down in the basement during your last investigation. Didn't it spark a lot of activity?'

David nodded. 'Probably too much. So I was considering using it tonight, but honestly I think we should hold off on that for now.'

'But why, if it's the best way to get results?'

'Because the way things are going, I don't want to push too hard and put us in danger,' David explained. 'And I think the Demon Board could do just that. Let's think of it as a last resort.'

He hoped Sarah understood and she was able to rein in her enthusiasm. Thankfully, she smiled and nodded. 'That makes sense. So, if not the Demon Board, then what?'

'Well,' he began, 'we talked about carrying out more vigils. At night I think we might get more activity from them. So, we'll split into two groups and see what happens. You up for a late night?'

Sarah smiled. 'Sounds good to me.'

CHAPTER 20

It had been a hectic day for Luca, but he'd had only one thing on his mind throughout it all.

The book.

Sarah Pearson's refusal to let him take it was an annoyance. No, it was more than that, since it meant he had to go back.

Luca had received David's voicemail not long after it had been left. However, he'd wanted to consult someone higher up the chain of command for advice before replying. So, he'd sent an email to the Bishop of Newcastle. Normally, it would have taken a few days to garner any kind of response, because the Bishop was a busy man.

After sitting back down at his desk in his study, following a community event which ran on longer than it should, Luca checked his email. There was a response from the Bishop, and it was not from his normal email address, but a private one.

I escalated your concerns and the response back to me was almost immediate. You are to determine if the book is indeed genuine. Also, you are to investigate the house to validate the owner's claims. If true, and if the house is what you believe it to be, then we must act quickly.

All of your other responsibilities are to be delegated. This is your sole concern until resolved.

Please update us daily with reports on your findings. And be careful.

Regards,

Bishop Turnbull.

Luca leaned back in his chair and let out a sigh. He brought a shaking hand up to his face and rubbed his mouth, which suddenly felt dry. The instruction to investigate was expected, but the speed at which he had received it was not.

That likely meant someone higher up knew what a Devil's Door truly was and had taken notice.

Luca considered his next step, and knew he should really call David straight away and arrange to go back to the house. But that could wait for tonight. He got up from his seat and walked into his lounge, pouring himself a large measure of single-malt whiskey. Luca downed it in one mouthful, then poured himself another.

CHAPTER 21

David readied himself for bed, feeling utterly exhausted. The vigils had run late into the night and proven uneventful.

The cameras had been positioned and were rolling, one mounted up in one corner that covered most of the room, and another on top of a wardrobe that focused on Sarah's bed. After all, she was the likely focus of any activity that might occur.

Sarah took her sleeping clothes out of her suitcase and started to pull off her t-shirt. David immediately turned around, feeling himself blush.

'You can use the en-suite to change,' he suggested.

He heard her chuckle. 'Would that make you feel more comfortable?'

'Well... I was thinking more about you.'

'I bunked with lots of guys in the army, David. I honestly don't care.'

He turned back to see Sarah standing in her bra and immediately looked away again.

'I know, but that was... I mean, this is...'

She laughed again. 'It's fine, I'll spare your blushes and change in the bathroom. I need to brush my teeth anyway.'

Sarah then gathered up her stuff and walked into the en-suite, casting David a sly grin as she did. She was clearly less reserved than he was. He wondered if he had been too quick in agreeing to share a room with her.

While Sarah was in the bathroom David quickly changed into some jogging bottoms and a t-shirt. As he was putting his old clothes back into one of his bags, he noticed the compact mirror he'd packed for the trip. It was something of a good-luck charm.

Katie's.

He lifted the mirror from the brown leather bag and held it. In truth, it was more than just a good-luck charm. He'd learned over time that mirrors could play a large part in investigations. Often, you could see things in them that you couldn't otherwise. Shadows, orbs, outlines of people: it was like the reflective surface bounced back an image of what was *really* there, not just what the naked eye could see.

The mirror was a compact one, sitting roughly the size of his palm and circular in shape. The lid was brass and had a raised pattern of swirling leaves that came together at the centre. It was old, a hand-me-down, and clicked open via a small button on the side. He pressed it, causing the lid to release and open a little, allowing his thumb to push it the rest of the way and reveal the reflective surface beneath. He saw his own face looking back.

David was reminded of some of the details Sarah had shared from her time in the house, such as when Chloe saw a woman in a reflection, sitting above Sarah while she slept.

Or the reflection Chloe had seen in the downstairs rear door, moments before a ghostly man made himself known.

It was something to think about, and David resolved to keep the mirror with him during their next vigil or investigative session.

He set the mirror back in his bag, slotting it in next to a first-aid kit that he'd also brought with him. He did that for every investigation.

Can't be too careful.

He was trained in first aid, something he felt was important when he'd decided to make the investigations a regular thing, Fortunately, those skills had yet to be called into use.

David sat on his bed waiting for his turn to use the bathroom. He looked up at the camera mounted in the corner, wondering if it would get anything of interest during the night. The investigation had started well with lots of activity, but the latest vigils were a bust. He hoped there was more to come from the house.

His mind wandered, again casting back to the investigation in 2014, and to the message he'd received from that ghostly voice. *'Return here. Help another in need.'*

He was finally back, and he hoped the meaning of that message would reveal itself.

It was also bothering David that Father Janosch hadn't gotten back to him yet. The priest was normally quick to reply, so David decided to try and contact him again the following day.

He was also aware he hadn't had the chance to follow up on what Sarah was going to show him up in the study: a ledger that would apparently shed more light on the book in the display case. The excitement of the day had pushed that particular issue down the list of priorities, but David made a mental note to speak to Sarah about it the following day.

Eventually, Sarah emerged from the en-suite and walked over to her bed, wearing only a vest top and some pyjama shorts. David again felt the need to avert his eyes as she sat on her bed and started to flick through her phone.

'I'll go use the bathroom now,' he said and got up.

'Uh-huh,' she replied, still looking at her phone. David left her to it and went into the bathroom.

It was close to one in the morning. Late-night sessions were required, but so was getting enough rest so they could stay alert. It was a fine act to balance. However, there was no time limit to their investigation here, so there was no reason to push themselves to exhaustion.

David finished up with using the toilet and brushing his teeth, then started to wash his face in the sink. He scrubbed his skin with a washcloth and soapy water, keeping his eyes screwed shut.

As he scrubbed, David started to feel a cold sensation wash over him from his left and roll over his cheek like a sour-smelling breath.

David paused, though his eyes were still closed tightly. Had it just been in his mind? The sensation had quickly passed, as had the smell, and all David could hear was the running of the tap.

After a few moments of nothing else, David dunked his hands into the full sink.

Something grabbed his wrist.

The grip was so strong and cold David let out a gasp. He instinctively opened his eyes and pulled his arm away. The soap stung as it seeped between his lids and David blinked quickly.

His hand was now free, with nothing grabbing his wrist any longer. Though his vision was blurry, David couldn't see anyone around him. He quickly rinsed his hands and splashed water on his face, washing away the last of the soap. With clear vision, he looked around again.

Nothing.

He brought up his arm and looked at his wrist. There was a noticeable red mark around it, with three distinct lines. He rubbed at his skin, trying to rid himself of the lingering cold.

David waited to see if anything else happened. His heart rate had quickened and his adrenaline levels had risen as well. He felt on edge. The sensation was something he was used to during investigations when things were happening, and it was controllable. He took deep breaths.

'Hello,' he said, hoping to draw out whatever was in here with him. Then he cursed himself: both his handheld camera and his phone were in the bedroom. Though he'd only expected to be in the bathroom for a couple of minutes, it was still a novice mistake.

A knock on the door made him jump.

'Did you say something?' Sarah called from the other room.

David didn't respond; instead, he just walked to the door and opened it, seeing Sarah standing on the other side.

'You okay?' she asked with a frown.

He nodded. 'Yeah. Just… something grabbed my arm, I think.'

'Really?' Sarah asked, eyes going wide. She then looked past him into the bathroom.

'There isn't anything here that I can see,' David said. 'It was just a quick experience. Over as soon as it happened. But look…' He held up his arm again.

Sarah squinted and leaned her face forward. Then a look of surprise came over her. She grabbed his forearm. 'Holy shit, look at the marks! They look like fingers.'

'That's what I thought. Only three of them, though.'

'Did you see anything?'

David shook his head. 'I was in the middle of washing my face, so I had my eyes closed. There was nothing around me when I opened them, though.'

He then moved fully into the bedroom with Sarah, closing the door to the en-suite behind him. Sleep would not come easy now, but they had to try. The cameras were running, so there wasn't much else they could do. And besides, if Jenn had been correct about what she'd seen the previous night, then an entity had come to visit Sarah while she slept. Perhaps tonight would see a repeat performance.

David switched off the main light, leaving only Sarah's nightlight on, and they both got into bed.

'Goodnight, Sarah,' David said as he lay down and pulled the duvet up over himself.

'Goodnight,' she replied, switching off her nightlight and plunging the room into darkness.

It was eerily quiet, and David could hear only the sound of Sarah's breathing. Though he didn't know why, he felt the need to speak to her rather than just rolling over and going to sleep. He wanted to make sure she was okay and felt safe. In reality, he knew she was tougher than he was; when it came to the spirit world, though, bravery and toughness could not replace experience.

In the end, he stayed silent and tried to focus on falling asleep.

'Kill him.'

David blinked himself awake, his mind in a state of confusion at being pulled from sleep.

'Kill him.'

The room was cold and dark, and everything was quiet... except for the voice he'd heard. It was a horrible, low, hoarse whisper, but he couldn't be sure if it was real or just a remnant of his dreams.

David rolled over and saw something standing over him, and immediately let out a cry of fright.

There was a woman, completely naked, standing motionless in the dark just next to his bed.

Sarah.

She had her eyes closed and her face was expressionless, but her head was tilted down towards him.

'Sarah?' David whispered. No response. He quickly came to the conclusion that she was asleep. Which made him wonder if it was *she* who had uttered 'kill him,' but in her sleep. He sat up and looked beyond her and around the room, to see if there was anything else present. But he could see nothing.

He turned back to Sarah, who must have been freezing, considering the temperature in the room. He had no idea why the hell she was naked, but quickly got out of bed and walked past her, grabbing her duvet up from the bed and making a mental note to ask her in the morning if sleepwalking was a common thing. When he turned back around with the thick quilt gathered up in his arms, he saw that Sarah had turned to face him.

She was still motionless, still asleep, but she had silently turned her body in his direction while he wasn't looking. Which was... strange. A creeping feeling of unease worked its way up David's spine.

Was it she who had uttered those words?

Kill him.

It was hard not to take in her full, naked body, even though it made him uncomfortable. It was just... there. And she was undeniably an attractive woman. David quickly walked over to Sarah and dropped the duvet around her, wrapping it tightly around her front.

'Sarah?' he said. He kept his voice even and gentle. She didn't move or acknowledge him. David didn't want to shake her awake, so he tried something else instead. He took hold of her hand and attempted to lead Sarah back to bed. Thankfully, she came with him, and David guided her down to a lying position on her mattress and dropped the quilt back over her, covering her naked body completely.

He then moved back over to his own bed. The room had a cold bite to it so he quickly hopped under the covers. He then looked back over to Sarah with a feeling of trepidation, half expecting to see her sitting up again, facing him.

But she was just as he'd left her: lying down and unmoving, except for the slow rise and fall of her chest.

David checked his watch which was next to his bed. It was close to three-thirty, which was something to remember. It would help him determine what time to focus on the next day when reviewing the camera's footage. Hopefully, it would make for interesting viewing.

CHAPTER 22

THE SMELL OF COOKING EGGS, frying bacon, and sizzling sausages filled the kitchen, making Sarah's stomach grumble in anticipation. She was ravenous.

The team were all sitting around the kitchen table sipping tea, coffee, and orange juice while Ralph cooked a traditional English breakfast.

'Can't hunt ghosts on an empty stomach,' he'd insisted.

While the group had brought some supplies and food, it wouldn't last them long, and Sarah knew she would need to fund a shopping trip soon to stock up.

The kitchen was full of noise and activity as the seven of them chatted and laughed. The room felt alive, like it had when Sarah lived in the house with Chloe, Emma, and Andrew. It was a nice feeling and lent a little warmth to Perron Manor, which had so far felt cold and unwelcoming.

It was just after nine in the morning, and Sarah was still wrestling with what David had told her, about how she had been standing over his bed in the night.

Her mind ran back to a few weeks ago, where her sister Chloe had told her she'd done the same thing.

The team hadn't checked the footage of the previous night yet, but

Sarah was interested to see what it would show. It would be interesting to see her sleepwalking in action, as she had no memory of it happening.

Jenn got up and moved over to one of the sets of drawers, then began digging through them.

'What are you looking for?' Sarah asked her.

'Some mats and coasters,' she said. 'Don't want to leave marks on the table.' She moved onto the second drawer down in the set. 'Do you have any? I can see candles and matches here, so we are set for a blackout.'

'It's fine,' Sarah insisted. 'Don't worry about it.'

Through the noise of chatter and cooking, Sarah thought she heard something else. A knocking.

She tilted her head to try and focus in on the sound. She soon heard it again. It was coming from the front door.

Then she heard the doorbell, which carried over the din in the room and made everyone stop talking.

Sarah got to her feet.

'Are we expecting someone?' she asked David, who was standing against the kitchen units with his mug of coffee.

He shook his head and frowned. 'Not that I know of,' he replied and followed her out of the room.

Sarah and David made their way to the entrance lobby and, through the glass in the door, saw the shape of someone standing outside. Sarah cast David a confused look before she pulled open the door.

Father Janosch stood outside.

'Father!' David said in surprise.

The priest gave a smile. 'Good morning to you both,' he said.

'I… I left you a message,' David went on. 'I wasn't sure if you got it.'

Father Janosch's expression grew serious and he took a moment before answering. 'I did,' he confirmed. 'But I was just so busy yesterday that I didn't really have the chance to call you back, not until the hour was late, anyway. So… I thought I would come by this morning instead. I hope I'm not intruding at all?'

Sarah wasn't a mind-reader, but she knew when someone wasn't being completely honest, and Father Janosch's story didn't exactly sound genuine.

'It's no trouble,' Sarah said. 'We were just about to have breakfast. Have you eaten?'

'I've had some toast,' he replied.

Sarah stepped aside. 'That's not exactly a hearty meal to start the day. You a vegetarian?' The priest shook his head. 'Good,' Sarah said. 'Why don't you join us? There's plenty to go around.'

'That sounds agreeable,' Father Janosch replied and stepped inside. As he removed his long grey coat, Sarah noticed him look nervously around the entrance lobby, particularly to the walkways above.

He doesn't like being here, Sarah said to herself. That wasn't a newsflash, as he had practically sprinted out after his last visit. In truth, she was surprised he'd come back so quickly.

Sarah then thought about her own attitude towards the house.

When she first arrived, she'd felt on edge and constantly scared. Now, however, while she was far from feeling at ease, that constant dread wasn't there anymore. Had she acclimated so quickly? That didn't seem right, especially not after seeing what happened to Chloe.

Sarah took the priest's coat and draped it over an arm. She then led them back through to the kitchen as David continued to question their new guest.

'So have you come to study the book here at the house?' he asked.

Father Janosch was a touch slow in responding, then said, 'I have, yes, if that is okay with you, Miss Pearson?'

Sarah turned her head back over her shoulder. 'Of course. Sorry if it is less convenient, but I really don't want the book getting lost or damaged, so I would prefer it stayed here.'

'I really would have taken good care of it,' Father Janosch said.

'I'm sure,' Sarah replied. 'But accidents happen that we can't predict, so I'm afraid I need to insist.'

'Understood,' he responded, though he didn't sound happy about it.

'Well, you might be interested to know that things have been progressing quickly here,' David said. 'A lot of activity. Some we've even managed to catch on tape. I'd like you to have a quick look while you're here. It'd be interesting to hear your thoughts on what we have.'

'I'd be happy to,' Father Janosch replied.

They walked through into the kitchen and all eyes fell on them.

'Looks like we have a visitor,' David said to the others with a big smile.

The priest simply stood in the doorway and gave an awkward wave. 'Hello, everyone.'

Ralph was the first to respond. 'How do you like your eggs, Father?'

'However they come,' he replied as Sarah showed him over to the table. There weren't enough seats for everyone, but Sarah was more than happy to stand and use the kitchen counter while she ate.

Ralph soon began to plate up the food and Sarah fixed the priest a coffee—one of her hazelnut roasts. She set it down and he took a sip. The worry he had been carrying on his face seemed to melt away.

'Oh, I say, that is delicious,' he remarked.

At least he has taste.

Everyone then tucked into their food. Sarah had to hand it to Ralph —while he hadn't exactly prepared fine cuisine, as far as hearty breakfasts went this wasn't bad at all. The bacon was nice and crispy, the sausages full and juicy, and the scrambled eggs were light, fluffy, and flavourful.

There were even fried tomatoes and mushrooms as well.

Initially, the only sounds in the room were the clinking of cutlery on plates and the wet chewing noises of people devouring their food.

'Can I ask,' Sarah began, directing her question to Father Janosch, 'why are you so interested in the book?'

He took his time in answering—chewing his food and swallowing before wiping his mouth. Sarah suspected he was playing for time.

'Well, it seems extremely old, for one. And from first glance, the text within looks to deal with some dark subjects, ones that specifically go against God. So, of course, it is going to be of interest.'

'When we were upstairs,' David cut in, 'you mentioned that you had heard of the *Ianua Diaboli* before?'

Father Janosch just nodded in response, offering no further narrative. However, Sarah didn't want to let the thread go so easily.

'So come on,' she pressed. 'How come you've heard of it?'

Yet again, Father Janosch paused, this time to take a long sip from his coffee.

'Just whispers, really,' he eventually replied. 'Stories from my time back in Romania.'

Sarah waited for him to keep going, but he fell silent. She chuckled and shook her head. 'Come on, Father, you're going to have to give us more and stop your ducking and weaving. I don't know why you are being so coy, but if you don't start being completely honest, I'm not sure I want you looking at the book at all.'

His jaw tensed and the priest made strong eye contact with Sarah. Not a threatening stare, but certainly a displeased one.

'Sarah,' David started, 'I'm sure Father Janosch isn't holding back anything—'

'It's okay, David,' Father Janosch said. 'I understand where Sarah is coming from. And I apologise if I seem a little evasive. Would it be possible to speak with the two of you alone for a moment?'

Sarah frowned and turned to David, who looked just as surprised as she was.

'Something you need to keep from the rest of us?' Ralph asked.

'Not really,' Father Janosch replied. 'But it would only be right to speak with Sarah and David first.'

'That's no problem,' David said. Father Janosch got to his feet.

'We can go to the living room,' Sarah added.

'Actually,' Father Janosch replied, 'it would be better to go upstairs and see the book. Things might be easier to explain that way.'

'Fair enough,' she said, then led the way upstairs, extremely interested in what the priest was about to tell them.

CHAPTER 23

ONCE IN THE STUDY, David, Sarah, and Father Janosch stood around the display case. David looked to Father Janosch expectantly.

'First of all,' the priest began, 'I want to apologise. Miss Pearson was correct… I *was* being evasive with regards to the book. I am sorry for that.'

'It was pretty obvious,' Sarah replied. 'But thank you.'

David felt a little ashamed. He hadn't picked up on Father Janosch's reticence. In truth, because David trusted the man completely, he never would have thought Father Janosch would withhold anything important.

'So… what is the issue with the book?' David asked.

The priest gazed down at it, lost in a stare. Eventually, he spoke. 'The reason I haven't been forthcoming with everything is… well, first because I'm not one-hundred-percent sure this book is genuine. However, if it is, then that poses certain… difficulties… with what you are all doing here.'

'What? With us gathering evidence?' David asked.

'Yes. You see, *Ianua Diaboli* was something I first heard about back in my youth just after being accepted into the Church. At the time, it was an off-the-cuff comment about a rumoured book which held great power. The priest who made the statement was not of sound mind, so I didn't put much stock into his words. The title always stuck with me, however.'

'And when did you next hear about the book?' Sarah asked.

'Years later, when I was in Hungary. I had an... experience there. I was assigned to assist an older priest on a case. It took a lot out of me and opened my eyes to what really exists in our world. Even beyond it.'

'Did that experience involve *Ianua Diaboli?*' Sarah asked, but Father Janosch shook his head.

'No. However, the priest leading the investigation was so overwhelmed with the activity at that Church, he wondered if the location was something he referred to as a 'Devil's Door.' Obviously, I pressed him on what that was, and he stated it was just a rumor based around a mythical manuscript.'

'*Ianua Diaboli,*' David said.

'Yes,' Father Janosch confirmed. 'But, in the end, as bad as that location ended up being, I don't think it truly was a Devil's Door. After the case, I tried to investigate the rumours regarding the book. I found out a great deal, but not much of it could be backed up with actual evidence. So I assumed it was just an urban legend.'

'So,' Sarah began, 'the obvious question to ask... what the hell is a Devil's Door?'

Father Janosch took a deep breath before beginning. 'The theory goes that a Devil's Door is a point in our world that is a direct link to Hell.'

'Are you being serious?' Sarah asked.

The priest nodded. 'Again, it was just a legend as far as I knew, but many of the stories regarding those gateways always linked back to a certain book.' He looked down to the display case.

'So you're saying the book I've inherited could prove the existence of a Devil's Doorway?'

'Only if it is genuine,' Father Janosch stated. 'We know this thing is old, but that doesn't mean what is written inside is true, or if it even holds any power. It could just be an old book full of lies.'

'Like the Bible,' Sarah added with a smile.

David's eyes went wide in shock and his head whipped around. A look of horror drew over Sarah's face, surprised at her own outburst. Her cheeks flushed red.

'Sarah!' David snapped.

'Well,' Father Janosch said with a nervous chuckle. 'I guess some people may think that way.'

'I'm so sorry,' Sarah said in reply, holding up a hand to her chest. 'I... I don't know what came over me there.'

'It's quite alright,' Father Janosch insisted, but David felt embarrassed on the priest's behalf. He couldn't understand why Sarah had said that to a *priest* of all people. Even if she did believe it, it seemed unnecessarily mean-spirited.

'No, it isn't alright,' Sarah insisted. Her cheeks were still red. 'There was no need for me to say something like that. I'm sorry, Father. Really, I am.'

'Honestly, it's fine,' he stressed. 'Please forget it. Also, moving back to matters at hand, the validity of this book is only part of the issue. What also concerns me is the *reason* it is here in this house.'

'What do you mean?' David asked.

'Well, you probably know more than I do, but Perron Manor has quite the disturbing history, correct?'

David nodded. 'More so than any other house I've heard of.'

'And if the stories of the more... supernatural... elements are true—'

'They are,' Sarah insisted. 'I've seen them myself.'

'Well, if so, that would mean the house has a power that is unusual, even among haunted locations.'

'You're saying that Perron Manor may be a Devil's Door,' David stated, connecting the dots.

Father Janosch paused for a moment, holding eye contact, then he gave a small nod. 'Perhaps. The power of the house, and the presence of *this* book, seem to be more than just a coincidence to me. It may be that whoever found the book and brought it here was well aware of what Perron Manor *really* was. But I could be wrong about that. I could be wrong about everything I'm saying.'

'You aren't wrong,' Sarah said. Both men turned to look at her.

'What do you mean?' David asked.

Sarah didn't respond. Instead, she walked over to an old writing table in the corner of the room and picked up a ledger from it. Suddenly David remembered what she had told him the last time they were up in this study, about the ledger being able to help them learn more.

She set it down on top of the glass display cabinet so the others could see. The cover was plain brown leather except for symbols that were drawn in each corner. To David, they replicated those on the cover of *Ianua Diaboli*. In the top left was an eight-pointed star, and opposite that was a cross. The lower left was a triangle with a separate, inverted triangle within it, and the final symbol resembled the eight lines of a compass, pointing off in their respective directions.

Sarah opened the cover to the first page. There was a handwritten note, and both David and Father Janosch leaned in to read it.

These transcriptions from Ianua Diaboli *are as accurate as I can make them, given the use of 'Old Latin' in with the more classical use of the language.*

While the original author of the book remains unknown, its purpose, and the purpose of the texts therein, are very clear. They all pertain to a very specific phenomenon that is able to exist in our world, one that is very relevant to Perron Manor.

This house is special.

It is, I believe, alive. And Ianua Diaboli *could very well be a way to harness what exists here, for those brave enough to do so.*

- A. Blackwater.

'Someone transcribed the book,' Father Janosch stated. He sounded far from happy.

'I think so,' Sarah replied.

David shook his head. 'This is unbelievable. The person who wrote the passage, this A. Blackwater, I think it's Alfred Blackwater. The grandfather of Marcus. And if he *did* translate the full book, then we have everything in this ledger that we need... right? I mean, it will tell us exactly what *Ianua Diaboli* really is.'

'Perhaps,' Father Janosch said with a frown. 'Latin isn't an easy language to translate, and there is certainly room for error.'

'But you are fluent in Latin, aren't you?'

He nodded. 'To an extent. But that note from Alfred Blackwater is worrying. It seems to imply what I feared, that Perron Manor is indeed a doorway to Hell.'

David felt both excited and terrified in equal measure. This was huge, far beyond what he'd ever hoped the investigation would yield. On the other hand, he felt woefully ill-equipped to deal with something of this magnitude.

'So what does it really mean if this place is a Devil's Door?' Sarah asked. 'Does that change anything we're doing here?'

David had no answer, so he looked to Father Janosch for support.

'There are no existing procedures in place that I am aware of,' Father Janosch said. 'No one really believed in their existence. However, I need to first determine what we are dealing with and see if it is genuine. To do that, I need to study the *Ianua Diaboli*. If Perron Manor is what I fear, then I will inform my superiors so they can escalate matters.'

'And then they will exorcise the house?' Sarah asked.

Father Janosch shrugged. 'In truth, I am not certain. You see, we don't know if that will even work.'

'What do you mean?' Sarah shot back. 'It *has* to work. The whole point of what we're doing here is to free the dead that are trapped. You know, like my sister!'

'I understand,' Father Janosch replied. 'But if we try that and it doesn't work... we could end up making things worse. For *us* as well as for those trapped here.'

David's mind was reeling. 'Why didn't you tell us this as soon as you found out?'

Father Janosch fell silent and he slowly looked down to the floor. He took a breath. 'Well, at first I had to raise the issue with my superiors and wait for their guidance.'

'Are we all in danger here?' David asked as his stomach sank.

The investigation was everything to him. He just *knew* it could be the making of him as a respected paranormal researcher. More than that, it would help someone long lost to him.

He felt like that hope was about to be pulled away from him. Was this the end of what they were doing here?

Father Janosch nodded. 'Potentially.'

'Hold on,' Sarah said, shaking her head. 'That doesn't add up. If you thought we were in danger, you would have just told us straight away. I mean, you're a *priest*, for God's sake… excuse the expression.'

'I only received my orders last night.'

'Your *orders?*' Sarah asked.

'Yes, from my superiors within the Church.'

'And those orders,' David interjected, 'are what… to investigate the book?'

'As well as the house,' Father Janosch confirmed.

'But *before* that,' Sarah said, 'when you were here two days ago, you saw the book and freaked out. You suspected the house was dangerous even then, didn't you.'

'I wasn't certain,' Father Janosch replied defensively. 'All I knew when I first arrived was David claimed the house was haunted. Then I saw a book and recognised the title. I wasn't sure about anything.'

Sarah shook her head and folded her arms across her chest. 'You're lying.'

Father Janosch's face hardened, but only for a moment. He cast his gaze once again down to the floor. 'Well, if I'm honest… I *was* scared. I've seen a lot in my years, but only once before have I ever been truly terrified to my core. I knew if this house was what I believed it to be, then I would be re-living something I dearly did not want to.'

'So you ran without warning us?' David asked. He was struggling to make sense of what he was hearing. He'd always known Father Janosch to be a good, honest man.

The priest still did not look up. 'I needed to be away from the house,' he said. His voice was small, like a child's. 'I know what happens if your soul is trapped in purgatory. It is a torment that never ends. After I was out of the house, I tried to take stock of the situation. Again, I didn't know if I was overreacting, and I was embarrassed about how I'd acted. So, I sought guidance from those above me.'

'And they led you right back here,' Sarah stated.

Father Janosch finally lifted his head to face them again. He nodded. 'They did.'

'And how do you feel about that?' Sarah asked.

'Terrified.'

David then brought the discussion back to what was weighing on his mind most, besides everyone's safety. 'So we need to stop what we are doing, don't we? We need to leave?'

'Why?' Sarah asked.

David shook his head in disbelief and turned to her. 'Because it's dangerous.'

'It was dangerous anyway, wasn't it?' Sarah shot back. 'We knew that coming in.'

'Not to this level.'

Sarah obviously didn't want things to end, and David could appreciate that. He didn't either, despite what he'd just heard. However, he couldn't put people's lives at risk.

'Well, I'm staying,' Sarah said, glaring at him.

David turned to Father Janosch for guidance. 'Father, what is your position on this. Do we have to leave?'

The priest took his time in answering. 'I cannot dictate what any of you do, I can only advise. It *might* be dangerous here, if we are actually dealing with what we think, but we still don't know for certain. So whether you stay or go… that is up to you.'

'What will you do?' Sarah asked.

'The Church wants me to investigate the house and the book, so I would ask that you grant me access.'

'And you'd be happy to stay here on your own to do that?'

David watched Father Janosch's face when asked the question. He looked horrified at the thought of it.

'I would stay on my own if I needed to,' he replied, though his tone was not convincing in the slightest. David could tell the priest didn't want them to leave him on his own here, but he had no right to ask them to stay, either.

'Tell me,' Sarah went on. 'Say you determine that the house *is* a gateway to Hell. Then what happens?'

'I inform the Church.'

'And then what?'

'That is for my superiors to decide.'

'Take a guess, Father. What do you *think* will happen?'

He thought for a moment. 'I'd assume they would try and figure out how to close the gate. I can't imagine the Church would want such a thing to exist.'

Sarah nodded. 'Okay. And how quickly would that happen? I get the feeling having an exorcism sanctioned is a slow process.'

'I think something like this would be more of a priority,' Father Janosch said.

'Yeah, I suspected as much. Last question, say the gate was closed... what would happen to the souls trapped in the house? Would they be freed... or would they be stuck?'

'I... honestly don't know,' he said.

David saw Sarah's jaw clench and she glared at the priest for a moment. Then she looked down at *Ianua Diaboli* and the ledger. 'Maybe there is a way we can find out.'

CHAPTER 24

'And that's everything we know,' David said to the team.

Sarah watched their faces to get a gauge on their reactions. They looked to be equal parts engrossed and worried.

David had pulled everyone into the great hall to go over what he and Sarah had learned. David stood at the head of the table with Sarah beside him, while the others were seated.

'Holy fucking shit!' Ralph stated. 'Are... are you being serious?'

David nodded. 'Afraid so.'

Silence.

Sarah could sympathise with them. She still hadn't quite gotten her head around the whole thing herself.

How the fuck am I going to help Chloe now?

'So... what does that mean for the investigation?' Jenn asked.

That was the pertinent question. Sarah was glad someone had asked it so quickly.

David turned to Father Janosch, then over to Sarah, and finally back to the others. 'Well, that's up to us. The decision is ours to make.'

'And if we stayed,' George began, 'is the objective the same as before? I mean, would we still just be gathering evidence?'

This time Father Janosch spoke. 'Regardless of what this house is or is not, we still need evidence of any paranormal activity. The Church requires proof to act. So, in effect, nothing changes. However, the severity of activity will be a key indicator of what is truly happening.'

Ann's hand went up. 'But how will you know if the book is real?' she asked. 'I mean, you said the existence of *Ianua Dia*... whatever it's called, was little more than a rumour anyway. It's not like there's going to be a certificate of authenticity or anything. So how will you *know*?'

Ann raised a good point. It was something Sarah had been wondering herself.

'Firstly, I need to study what's written inside of it,' Father Janosch responded. 'Once I fully digest the text, I will have a better understanding of what we are dealing with.'

'And you'll know for certain?' Ann asked.

'Hopefully,' the priest responded. He didn't sound convinced.

'There is a way to know for sure,' Sarah said. All eyes fell on her.

'How?' David asked.

'The book is supposed to be full of rituals and the like, right? Well... we can try one.'

Sarah was met with silence, as well as looks of confusion and astonishment.

'You *can't* be serious,' David eventually said.

'That would not be wise,' Father Janosch added. 'Playing with such things is not advisable. We could end up making a bad situation worse.'

Sarah shrugged. 'Fair enough. But it's one way to know for certain. And I wasn't talking about summoning a fucking demon-god or anything like that. Just trying one of the smaller rituals.'

'Like just summoning a demon-imp?' Ralph asked with a smile.

Sarah was glad of the levity he offered. 'Exactly,' she said. 'I'm sure we could all handle an imp.'

'Imp or not,' Father Janosch said, 'I don't think we mess with the rituals in the book.'

'Well, it's an option to keep in mind,' Sarah said. However, she decided not to push it any further. Instead, she changed the subject to how they would move forward. 'Anyway, we need to figure out what we do now. Everyone is obviously free to make up their own minds, but we can stay here and carry on, knowing what we do, or people can leave and call it a day. So... what does everyone think?'

The rest of the team just cast each other confused glances, each looking for someone else to take the lead. Sarah could understand their hesitation. It was a lot to drop on them and expect an instant decision.

'David, what do you think?' Jamie asked.

David took a moment. 'I'm unsure,' he replied. 'On the one hand, what we've found out definitely changes things. On the other, we've already carried out an investigation here before, and while it was tense, no one was hurt. *And* we've been here for a few days now with no real danger.'

'It's important to remember,' Sarah cut in, 'that we don't know for certain the house is actually one of these Devil Doors. It could all be bullshit.' She then turned to Father Janosch. 'Excuse the French, Father.'

He smiled. 'I've heard much worse.'

'Look,' David went on. 'I can't tell you all what to do. You have to decide for yourselves, individually.'

'But what are *you* going to do?' Jenn pressed. 'Are you staying?'

They all waited for an answer. It was slow in coming.

Eventually, David nodded his head. 'I am,' he confirmed. 'I know the risks, but I want to see this thing through. I just think the evidence we might get here would be game-changing for paranormal research as a whole. Even more so if the house turns out to be what Father Janosch suspects it is. However, I can't speak for any of you, and I don't want people staying on my account if they aren't truly comfortable with it.'

Sarah had suspected David would stay, but it was good to hear it out loud. Regardless of what anyone else chose to do, that meant things would still continue on in some fashion, and she still had a shot at helping her sister.

'Well,' Ralph began, 'I need to duck out for a few days after tomorrow regardless, since I have work commitments I can't get out of.'

That was one man down. Though not entirely unexpected, as Sarah had already been aware Ralph was going to be ducking out of the investigation due to work. The responses from the others would be a little more interesting.

'I'm staying,' Jenn firmly said. 'I haven't come this far to duck out when things get tough.'

'Not just tough,' David cut in. 'Dangerous.'

'*Potentially* dangerous,' Sarah corrected.

No, Sarah said to herself, *not potentially dangerous. It is dangerous and you know it.*

Chloe had been killed by the things inside Perron Manor; Sarah had seen that herself. She'd even lied to the whole team about it in order to get them here in the first place. And now she was adding to the deception.

'I don't care,' Jenn stated. 'You say the choice is mine to make, David? Well, I've made it.'

He smiled. 'You sure?'

'I am.'

'What about everyone else?' Sarah asked.

'I'm not sure,' George cut in. 'I mean, I'm all for what we're doing here, but this sounds like stuff we shouldn't be messing with.'

'I... tend to agree,' Ann added. 'To be honest, I think this is beyond what we are capable of handling.'

'I understand,' David said. 'And I don't want anyone to feel bad about leaving. You aren't letting anyone down if you do.'

'Well, I didn't say I was *definitely* leaving,' George clarified. 'I'm just... not certain if I'm staying yet.'

'Me too,' Ann added.

David then looked over to the last remaining team member. 'What are your thoughts, Jamie?'

He shrugged. 'I'm not sure yet, this is a lot to take in. Part of me just says *'fuck it*, let's keep going.' But I need to give it some more time.'

'I get that,' David replied. 'So what do people think about taking some time away from the house until they've made up their minds? No point in staying if you are hesitant.'

The reluctant trio of Jamie, George, and Ann turned their heads to each other, yet again all waiting for someone else to speak.

'How about this,' Jamie said to the other two. 'We stay for another night, then see how we feel in the morning when we've had time to think on it.'

Ann nodded in agreement.

'I'm okay with that,' George said. He then looked up to David. 'I guess it's decided. We're here for another night at least.'

CHAPTER 25

THOUGH HE TRIED NOT to show it, Luca allowed himself to breathe a sigh of relief as everyone agreed to carry on with the investigation for at least a little while.

Before he'd gotten to the house earlier that day, he had been torn on whether to broach his concerns with David and Sarah, and he wasn't sure how much to tell them even if he did.

His solution had been to ease his way in by hiding the truth, just to see if he could get to the book without alerting them too much to what was going on. However, he'd quickly been called out and forced to divulge everything.

Well... *almost* everything.

He was just thankful that revealing the truth hadn't restricted access to the book. It had crossed his mind that everyone, including Sarah, could have fled, and then she may have refused to let him study the book any further. Or worse, she let him stay, but Luca would be on his own.

While he didn't feel safe in Perron Manor, Luca certainly felt better having others around him.

However, he still felt bad about keeping one last thing from everyone. It wasn't something they needed to know necessarily, as it wouldn't impact what needed to be done. But it was important.

If Perron Manor truly was a Devil's Door, and those things actually existed in the real world, that meant other things he'd heard about the phenomenon could be real as well. And one story in particular terrified Luca.

If it was true… the Church had a lot of work to do.

CHAPTER 26

IN ALL THE excitement of Father Janosch's visit, checking the footage of the previous night had almost slipped their minds. It wasn't until Sarah had mentioned it again to David that he'd remembered about her standing over him last night.

After the meeting, he, Sarah, and Father Janosch gathered in the makeshift headquarters to sift through the video footage, with David sitting at the computer and the other two standing over him.

Thankfully, Sarah had said she was fine with him seeing all the footage, including the video of her standing naked over David. However, David had insisted that only the three of them be present for it.

David lined up the footage so the timestamp showed three in the morning. Thanks to the night-vision capability of the camera, the image was awash with black shadows and shades of blue. David and Sarah could both be seen in their beds from the camera's high vantage point. He pressed play, and for the longest time neither of them stirred.

'You say you checked your watch at three-thirty?' Sarah asked.

'Yeah, but I don't know how long you were standing there before I woke up,' David replied. 'So I thought it best to go back a while.'

'And you don't remember it at all?' Father Janosch asked Sarah.

She shook her head. 'Not a thing.'

'And have you ever done anything like it before?'

David noticed Sarah pause for a moment. 'No, not that I know of,' she finally said.

Many minutes passed until there was movement. The three of them watched on as, on screen, Sarah slowly got out of bed completely naked. She stood for a few minutes, just swaying gently on the spot, facing in David's general direction.

David felt uncomfortable watching.

'Are you sure you're okay with this?' he asked.

She just nodded. 'I'm fine, honestly.'

'Odd that you're just standing there like that,' Father Janosch added.

'Not really,' Sarah replied, and David picked up on the defensiveness in her tone. 'It's just sleepwalking. That's hardly paranormal.'

'No,' the priest replied. 'But the *cause* of it could be.'

Eventually, Sarah on screen began to move forward, taking steady steps and looking decidedly unsteady on her feet. She reached David's bed and tilted her head down towards him. From the vantage point of the camera, it was just about clear to see that her eyes were still closed.

'There!' Father Janosch suddenly exclaimed, loud enough to make David jump. The priest thrust a finger towards the computer and pointed at the edge of the screen to a corner of the room that was drenched in shadow. 'What is that?' he asked.

Everyone leaned in. After squinting, David saw it too, and paused the playback.

Just on the edge of the darkness in the corner was a noticeable outline of a person. Nothing was exactly clear due to the pixilation and the distance of the camera. But it was definitely there.

The person looked female to David; he could make out a tall, slim build and long hair. She looked to be naked as well.

'That... that's Chloe,' Sarah said while pushing her way closer to the screen. Her eyes were wide. She then brought a hand up to the screen and touched the image with her fingertip.

'Are you sure?' David asked. He didn't know how she could be; to him, the image just wasn't clear enough.

David had met Chloe a few times, but he would never have guessed the person on the footage was her. It *could* be, he supposed, but then again it could be just about anyone.

'It's her,' Sarah stated. The conviction in her voice was absolute, but David had to wonder if that was hope rather than certainty.

He looked back to the screen, where his attention split between Sarah and the figure in the corner of the room. The shadowy stranger blended in and out of the background around her. There were times when she was clearly visible, and other times it was like she wasn't there at all as she bled into the wall behind her. Not once did the stranger move.

As the half-hour mark approached, David remembered what had awoken him the previous night.

Kill him.

An audio device had been set up in the room along with the camera, and George had already overlaid the sound against the footage for them. David turned up the volume, raising the level of feedback and background static.

After a while, he heard it. The sound was crackly, almost like a blast of static, but the words spoken were clear.

'*Kill him.*'

'Oh my,' Father Janosch said.

David took a breath. It *hadn't* been a dream. What was worse, he'd been watching Sarah's face on screen the whole time. Her lips didn't move. It wasn't her.

In the footage, David began to stir as the words were repeated.

'*Kill him.*'

It was a horrible sound. Hoarse and almost pained.

'That didn't come from you, Sarah,' David said.

'I know,' she replied, her voice flat.

David watched himself on the video footage as he turned over in bed. 'Sarah?' he'd asked.

As he was watching, David flicked his eyes over to the edge of the screen, to the dark figure that stood watching. Yet again, she bled out of view, the pixels merging into the wall behind her. This time, however, she didn't reappear.

On the footage, David then got up and moved over to Sarah's bed, where he gathered up her duvet. He returned and draped it over her before leading her back to bed and laying her down.

After that, David spent a little time skipping forward through the footage to see if he could spot anything else, playing the video at four times its normal speed. But there was nothing of note. Of course, it would all need to be reviewed in-depth at a later date, as there could be something he had missed in their brief viewing. However, he felt like he had enough for now.

'Thoughts?' he asked the other two.

The response wasn't immediate. 'Interesting,' Father Janosch eventually said. 'Especially the person in the corner... I don't know what to make of that.'

'Pretty clear evidence of the paranormal, I'd say,' David suggested.

'I would agree,' Father Janosch replied. 'Sceptics might say the footage was doctored, but we know that not to be true. However, we do need to consider something else.' He then turned to Sarah. 'You say you have never had issues with sleepwalking before?'

She nodded. 'That's right.'

'In that case, we may need to consider that Sarah is becoming susceptible to the house.'

'Susceptible?' Sarah asked, incredulous. 'Care to explain?'

Father Janosch smiled politely and held up his hands. 'It is only a possibility. Given we saw you walk over to David, and then we heard that voice... to me, it sounded like an instruction.'

Sarah shook her head. 'Rubbish. You're implying that I'm... what? Becoming possessed? Well, I'm not.'

'Okay,' Father Janosch said, relenting, hands still up. 'I just said it for consideration. We all need to be vigilant and look out for each other.'

'Isn't it a bit quick to succumb to possession, Father?' David asked. 'We've only been here a couple of days.'

'True, but Sarah was here for a little while before that, living here with her family. Correct?'

'I was,' Sarah said. 'But I wasn't possessed.'

'And she wasn't here for very long,' David added. 'A month and a half or so. I didn't think someone could be broken down so quickly. And Sarah is pretty strong-willed.'

'I would normally agree, but we might not be dealing with a *normal* haunted location here. I don't think we can know *what* to expect.'

David thought it was certainly worthy of consideration. However, Sarah did not appear amenable to the suggestion, so David decided to move things on, though he made a mental note to follow the point up with Father Janosch privately.

'We have other evidence to look at as well,' David said to Father Janosch. 'I'd like to show it to you and get you completely up to speed.'

The priest nodded. 'Okay. But after that, I think it's important I begin studying *Ianua Diaboli*.'

'That's fair,' David replied.

'You two do what you need to,' Sarah said. 'I'm going to find the others.' She then turned and left the room, but not before glaring at Father Janosch on her way out.

David went after her, stopping her in the corridor outside.

'Sarah,' he called, grabbing her arm.

She spun around quickly.

'What!' she snapped. David noticed her hands were balled into fists, and he took a step back.

'Easy,' he said. 'Calm down a little, would you?'

'I *am* calm,' she replied, though she was clearly anything but.

'Look, I know how that must have sounded, but please just think about it logically. He's only airing a concern. One he may be wrong about, granted, but we still have to be honest with each other if we are concerned. And we can't get defensive.'

'David, he's implying that I'm fucking *possessed*. How am I supposed to react?'

'A little less angrily?' David suggested with a hesitant smile. He hoped injecting some humour would help calm Sarah down. However, she just took a step towards him.

'Do I seem possessed to you?' she asked. Her voice was low and steady.

'Not possessed, but certainly agitated,' he said. 'And come on, is it really such a leap for Father Janosch, considering what we saw on the video?'

'Yes.'

David let out a sigh. He wasn't going to get anywhere with her, though he wanted to keep trying.

'Sarah, come on. Please look at this impartially. No one is trying to offend you, here. I mean, don't you remember when we first got here two days ago? You were completely on edge, which I could understand given what you went through here. But now, the place doesn't seem to scare you anymore. Don't you think that's odd?'

Sarah paused. 'I'm just getting on with what needs to be done,' she said.

'And you feel totally safe here now?'

She looked away. 'I don't know.'

'Look,' David went on, 'I'm not saying the house has you under its control or anything, but we need to be careful. That's exactly what happens here: Perron Manor seeps into your skin and into your soul. And you likely won't even know it's happening, so we have to look out for each other. You might not be possessed right now, but it could have already begun.'

Sarah's eyes then turned to meet his. She looked calmer now, though sad. 'Can I tell you something?'

He nodded. 'Of course. Anything.'

She took a breath. 'When I was living here with Chloe, there may have been a few times when... I don't know... I wasn't quite myself. I didn't see it then, but looking back...'

'Can you give me some examples?' David asked.

'For one, I considered running away and leaving my family when they were in danger. Purely because I was scared. That isn't me. I'm not saying I'm normally a hero or anything, but I would never do that. And I fought with Chloe *a lot*.'

'You mentioned that before,' David said.

'Yeah, but it wasn't just normal bickering. I also don't think it was brought on by stress. There were times when I really wanted to hurt her with the things I said. No matter how much we ever argued in the past, we never stooped to personal insults.'

'So... you think you *were* possessed?'

Sarah shook her head. 'No... I don't know. I didn't think so before, but after what you've just said, how would I truly know for certain, right?'

David nodded. 'Yeah, I understand. Look, to me, given what you're going through and the loss you've just suffered, I think you're acting fine. Sleepwalking aside, that is. But—'

'That's another thing,' Sarah cut in, looking embarrassed.

'What is?'

'The sleepwalking,' she said. 'I don't know why I wasn't honest in there, maybe I'm embarrassed or worried, but I *was* doing something similar when I lived here. Chloe told me she saw me walking around the house at night, though I had no memory of it.'

The confessions were a lot to take in, and David was more than a little annoyed Sarah had lied to him. It made him wonder just what else she was lying about. Still, he had to keep his annoyance in check; she had levelled with him now, and this was still her house. It wouldn't do much good to piss off the host too much.

'Okay,' he eventually said. 'I appreciate you telling me all that. But from here on out, I'm going to need you to be as honest as possible with me, okay?'

She nodded. 'Yeah.'

'Appreciate that. And don't worry, I promise to keep an eye on you and step in if I think you are acting... strangely.'

Sarah smiled. 'Thank you,' she said. 'Are *you* okay staying here after what Father Janosch told us about the house?'

'I think so,' David replied. 'It does change things a little, I suppose, but I can't just walk away from an opportunity like this. Are you okay with us staying?'

'I have to,' Sarah said. 'Chloe's still trapped.'

'I thought you might say that,' he replied. 'But I have to ask: do you really think that was Chloe on the footage we just saw? Because, if I'm honest, I couldn't see it. The girl could have been anyone.'

'I know it was Chloe. I just *know* it.'

'Fair enough,' David replied. However, if that were true, then there was a problem. 'Doesn't it concern you, though? If it *was* Chloe, and *she* was the one telling you to kill me, I mean... does that really sound like your sister?'

'No, Chloe would never say something like that.'

'Maybe the house is controlling her, like it does all the other souls in here.'

She quickly shook her head. 'I refuse to believe Chloe is a puppet. Anyway, it doesn't matter. We just need to free them all, regardless. Every last soul trapped here.'

'Yes, but we also need to be careful. Perron Manor could end up using your sister to get to you… if you let it.'

Again Sarah paused. She took in a breath. 'Fair enough. I get what you're saying, and I won't let it affect me. I promise. Okay?'

David nodded. 'Thank you.' However, he wasn't certain if he'd truly gotten through to her or if she was just saying what he wanted to hear.

And he was troubled by what she'd just admitted.

'So what's the plan now?' Sarah asked.

'I'll show Father Janosch the rest of our evidence,' David said. 'Then, if people are up for it, we can split into two larger groups and run some experiments. But I'd like to help our priest up in the study. It isn't a good idea to have anyone working alone. You're free to join me.'

'I might come find you later,' Sarah replied. 'But for now, I'll go with the others and work with them. I think I need a break from the book and Devil Doors and all that stuff.'

'No problem. I'll walk you to the team.'

Sarah laughed. 'It'll take me less than a minute, David. Stay here, I'll be fine.' She was already turning around so as not to let him argue the point. She gave him a brief wave, and David watched her walk away.

CHAPTER 27

Luca was back in his study at home.

It was close to eleven at night, and he sat before his laptop with an unfinished email on the screen.

With his left hand he swirled a half-finished tumbler of whiskey. It was his third of the night.

The email was to the Bishop of Newcastle, and Luca was updating him on the progress of that day.

Luca had spent most of his time at the house studying *Ianua Diaboli*, and he'd been accompanied by David. What he'd found were pages upon pages of rituals and writings regarding the phenomena of the Devil's Door. However, there had been no indication of the author, or the date the book was written. It was therefore hard to judge the book's authenticity or true age.

Translating everything inside the book would have taken more time than Luca had available—months, he imagined—so the presence of the ledger and its transcriptions was welcome, if a little troubling. If someone had successfully translated the pages of *Ianua Diaboli*, what had stopped them carrying out one of the rituals?

Luca had found some very worrying things in the book that, if real, worried him. Particularly references to *Portae Septem*.

He'd also skimmed to the back and found the last section was titled *Claude Ianua*. Close the Door.

That ritual could prove vital. Luca remembered a sinking feeling of dread after reading it. Though it seemed surprisingly simple in its execution, the danger it also presented was worrying and required opening the door farther in order to then close it. He only read the ritual briefly, but knew it was important—a way that allowed his own world to re-establish dominance over the mirrored 'otherworld.'

That ritual needed to be carried out by a holy man, using the four elements.

No, five.

Luca shook his head and then went back to his keyboard, making mention of *Portae Septem* and *Claude Ianua* in his email to the Bishop.

Luca then took another long sip of his whiskey, which turned into a gulp as he finished what was left. He set the tumbler down and unscrewed the lid on his bottle, refilling his glass.

The buzz from the alcohol was welcome. He'd been feeling guilty ever since he'd left Perron Manor earlier that evening. David had wanted him to stay the night, but Luca had used the excuse that he wasn't prepared, and had no change of clothes. In addition, he'd said that he had duties to attend to the following day.

However, none of those reasons would have really stopped Luca from spending the night if he'd truly wanted to. After all, he'd been expressly told that Perron Manor was his priority now, and he could have easily returned home to get a change of clothing if it was that important.

Fear had kept him away.

He'd have to go back the following day, of course. All he'd bought himself was one night's reprieve.

Luca set his glass back down and started typing.

It is my suspicion that the book discovered at the house could well be the Ianua Diaboli, *previously thought to be a myth. I also suspect the house itself is therefore likely a Devil's Door. Though I cannot be sure, I feel the previous owners were aware of just what the house was. Whether they discovered this and then tracked down the book, or came into possession of the book first before making the connection, I cannot be sure. But it is too much of a coincidence.*

As you will no doubt be aware, if my assumptions are correct, we have to consider that other stories regarding the Devil's Door could also be true.

And we therefore have to consider the existence of the Seven Gates...

When he finally finished the email, Luca reread it twice. He wanted to make sure he sounded measured in his assessment and wasn't letting his fear of Perron Manor cloud his judgment. After all, they were dealing with myths and legends here.

He took another drink and then hit send. Luca eventually decided that he'd rather be accused of overreacting than not acting at all.

He then leaned back in his chair and closed his eyes. Luca was tired, and dearly wanted to sleep. Maybe another whiskey first, though.

However, after only a couple of minutes, a chime sounded from his laptop. He checked his inbox.

It was from the Bishop.

Get the book. Bring it to us. Call me on my direct line to keep me informed.

CHAPTER 28

Sarah's body was being pulled down, sucked into the earth around her. The soil and rocks that surrounded her pressed into her skin as she dropped. An unseen force dragged her lower and lower.

The temperature rose, as did her own screams. However, those cries were overpowered by those around her.

Below her.

The earth and rock were replaced with something else. Something wet and warm.

Flesh.

It ran with blood. She heard a new voice, one that rose above other agonised wails.

'*Kill him.*'

Sarah continued to scream and struggle as she was helplessly pulled farther down. She recognised the feminine voice that was audible above all others. It was Chloe's.

'*Kill him and come home, Sarah.*'

CHAPTER 29

DAVID ROLLED OVER, suddenly wide awake, though he wasn't sure why. He blinked and waited for his eyes to get used to the dark. The room around him was cold, more so than usual, and that alone set his mind on high alert.

As his vision adjusted, David was able to see Sarah's bed. She was sitting up and facing him with her eyes shut.

David immediately sat up himself, then cast a glance to the corner of the room, just in case a mysterious figure was again present.

This time, however, he saw nothing.

'Sarah?' he asked. He got no response.

David leaned over and grabbed his phone from the floor. When he activated the screen, he saw it was three-twenty-six in the morning.

Something had woken him. Possibly the cold, or maybe it was something else... something more instinctual.

He swung his legs out of bed, then stood with his fists clenched, readying himself.

David picked up his handheld camera and flicked open the viewfinder. When putting Sarah back to bed the previous night, he hadn't seen that mysterious figure. It was only when the footage played back that she had become apparent. With that in mind, he pointed the camera over to the corner and zoomed in.

There didn't seem to be anything out of the ordinary. He then began to slowly pan around the room and stopped on Sarah.

He could see her chest moving quickly in line with her rapid, shallow breathing. There was also a sheen of sweat over her skin, causing it to glisten. Thankfully, she was clothed this time, wearing a tank top.

Do I wake the others?

Nothing had actually happened to warrant it. Sarah was just sitting up in bed in her sleep, which was indeed odd, but not something dangerous in its own right. Although, now that David knew a little more about the house—and what it *could* be—everything was now significant. He only wished Father Janosch had stayed the night.

David suspected the priest had been scared, but he couldn't exactly force the man to stay, though Father Janosch had promised to return the following day and remain at the house for a few nights if required.

David started to turn the camera again, slowly panning around the room in an arc. He adjusted his feet and slowly swivelled so that he could capture the room behind him as well.

It was then, as he turned a full one-hundred-and-eighty degrees, he stopped and drew in a sharp breath. A female figure stood on the other side of his bed, not four feet away from him.

David didn't have time to scream before she leapt at him.

Jenn felt her body shaking.

'Wake up, Jenn,' a whispering voice pleaded. It was Ann's voice, and she sounded scared.

'What's wrong?' Jenn asked, sitting up and rubbing her eyes. She felt the sting of cold air, as if a window had been left open during the night.

Ann was squatted down next to her, dressed in just a dark purple nightie. She was shivering, and her dark hair was a wild mess, sticking up in all directions. Without her makeup, heavy eyeliner, and black lipstick, Ann looked like a completely different person. She had a cold hand resting on Jenn's shoulder.

'There's someone in here with us,' she whispered, sounding terrified.

George woke suddenly. He was moving. It felt like he was being dragged. Something had an ice-cold grip on his ankle, and he was pulled across his bed.

Panic filled him as he struggled to make sense of what was happening. He then felt himself drop off the edge of the bed and hit the back of his head on the floor.

He quickly scrambled up to a sitting position and looked around in the dark. His heart raced and his skin tingled from the cold, causing it to break out in goosebumps.

Ralph sat up in his own bed and rubbed his face.

'George?' he asked. George could see Ralph's squinting, confused eyes. 'What happened? Did you just fall out of bloody bed?'

'Something pulled me,' George said.

'It *what?* Are you sure?' Ralph's voice suddenly had more urgency to it. He quickly got out of bed and paced straight over to George to help him up.

'What's going on?' Jamie asked, now in a sitting position himself. He rubbed his shaggy blond hair and yawned. 'Something happening?'

'George was just pulled out of his bed,' Ralph replied.

'He was what?' Jamie asked as his body stiffened up. He looked quickly around the room, head swivelling from side to side. There didn't appear to be anything in the room with them.

After grabbing his phone, George shone the light from its screen onto his ankle and saw a red mark around it.

'Look,' he told the others, and they leaned in.

'Holy shit!' Ralph exclaimed. 'Wait, let me get my camera. We need to document this.' As he did, George looked up to Jamie, who had his own phone in hand as well. 'What time is it?' George asked.

Jamie checked. 'Three-twenty-six.'

'Witching hour,' Jamie added.

Ralph returned with his handheld camera and aimed it at George's ankle. 'Keep the light on it,' Ralph instructed him. Then, he addressed the camera. 'It's three-twenty-six in the morning, and our colleague George Dalton has just been pulled out of bed by something we cannot see. There is a visible mark on his ankle, which was not there before we turned in for the night.'

A slow, drawn-out creaking sound caused all three to look up. The door to the adjoining en-suite was gliding open.

Ralph lifted the camera up to capture what was happening, but George felt a creeping sensation work its way up his spine. He shivered, and it wasn't just from the cold.

'Hello?' Ralph called out. George heard the uncertainty in the big man's voice.

The door finished its swing and remained fully open. George could see nothing through the darkness inside the bathroom from his vantage point. He held up his phone, flashlight still on, and aimed it at the doorway. Now they could see a little farther into the en-suite.

Something was there.

George saw a woman, just at the edge of the beam of light. She was naked, short, and in her later years. Her greying blond hair was scraggly while her pale skin was marred with purple and yellow blotches. She wore a sinister grin and her eyes were wide with a manic, wild stare. The woman didn't move an inch.

'Fuck, fuck, fuck,' Jamie exclaimed.

They suddenly heard a scream from another room. George whipped his head around to the direction of the noise.

'That was Ann,' Jamie said.

Then, there was another cry, this one coming from a different room. 'Help me!'

David.

George quickly looked back to the en-suite, but the woman was gone. An ice-cold aura suddenly radiated from behind him.

'*Come to Patricia, dear,*' a throaty voice said. George didn't have to turn around to know the woman was now standing behind him. He felt cold, clammy hands grip his neck.

CHAPTER 30

ANN HAD FIRST SEEN the man after she'd woken. At least… she *thought* she had. She'd looked over to the curtains and her breath had caught in her throat: a man stood there with his stomach pulled open, holding his own innards in his hands. She'd scrambled out of bed, panicked, before turning to look back.

He was gone.

Ann had then quickly snuck over to Jenn and woken her up.

No sooner had she told Jenn they weren't alone was the man there again, and he lurched forward from the shadows.

With a scream, Ann pulled Jenn away from the lumbering nightmare. Escaping to the door was out of the question—they would have to go *past* him to get to it. So, instead, Ann and Jenn huddled in the corner. Now she feared for her life, and the man with skin as pale as ash took one unsteady step after another. He lifted his hands, showing them his intestines—thick chords of meat that glistened red.

'*Please… help,*' he wheezed. The expression the man wore was one of pain and sorrow. However, that quickly darkened and a sneer crossed his lips. He raised his intestines higher. '*Let me… strangle you.*'

'We need to get out of here,' Jenn said while squeezing Ann's hand.

Ann shook her head frantically. 'No! It'll get us!' She couldn't run past him. They would die.

'We *have* to!' Jenn shouted.

Part of Ann knew her colleague was right. Surely it was better to at least try to escape than just wait to let that... thing... kill them. But her feet refused to move.

The man took another heavy footstep closer to them. He started to chuckle. '*You'll like it here with us.*'

'Fucking run!' Jenn screamed and shook her. That jolted Ann to life. They both dashed away, holding hands, and Ann felt fear like never before as they attempted to weave to the side of the horrific stranger.

The man raised his hands higher and attempted to drop his rope-like guts over Ann. She felt cold blood drip onto her cheek, but the pair managed to duck to the side and avoid his attempt to grab them. They then sprinted over to the door. Jenn pulled it open as Ann cast a look back.

The man was gone.

Ralph watched George drop to his knees as the woman behind him squeezed her grip tighter. She tittered and ran a black tongue over her lips.

George's face was twisted into a grimace. 'She's crushing my neck,' he said. His words were strained.

'Do something!' Jamie shouted, his own voice full of panic. For half a second, Ralph was annoyed that Jamie had laid all responsibility of helping their friend at his feet. However, he didn't have time to dwell on that—George *did* need help, even though the thought of moving closer to that woman terrified Ralph.

Her eyes were milky white, with no visible pupils, and her stomach was sunken and pulled in beneath her ribcage.

'*Stay... here... forever, dear,*' the woman said. Her words were strained but had a certain sexualised lust to them. '*I'm oh... so... lonely.*'

George let out a cry of pain.

It was then Ralph acted. He lunged forward and grabbed hold of George's arms as the hag stared and grinned manically. With a heave, Ralph was able to pull George free of her grip and George fell forwards, hands on the back of his neck. Ralph then quickly pulled his friend up and dragged him to the door with Jamie leading the way. They were soon out into the corridor while the woman stood her ground, stock-still, and chuckled.

As Jenn and Ann barrelled down the hallway, Jenn saw a door open up ahead and braced herself for some kind of horror to reveal itself. However, she was surprised to see Jamie, George, and Ralph emerge, with George holding his neck and wincing in pain.

She ran over to them. 'What happened?'

Ralph looked up in surprise, his body tense, but Jenn saw him relax when he realised it was them. He quickly pointed back into the room. 'There's a ghost in...' but he trailed off.

With her heart pounding in her chest, Jenn looked inside. There was no one.

'There *was* someone in there,' he said. 'I swear, and George almost...'

'I believe you,' Jenn replied.

'We have to get out of here,' George said. 'It was a mistake to stay.'

Jenn could sense fear ripple through all of them, and though part of her wanted to argue, it was only a small part, overshadowed by what she and Ann had just seen.

Then, she heard another voice cry out from a nearby room. 'Help me!'

It was David. She had heard him yell for help once before already.

What the hell is happening to him?

'Let's go,' Ralph said and led the way as the others followed.

Jenn tried to push away the fear she felt as they ran to help their leader.

'I don't like this,' Ann said, her voice quaking.

Me either, Jenn thought. They reached the door and Ralph thrust it open—they all froze in shock.

David was struggling on the floor with a naked woman mounted on top of him. She had brown, matted hair, sunken, pale flesh, and twisted features that were almost demonic—as was the snarl on her face. The woman grappled with David, trying to keep his hands on the floor.

Sarah stood above them both, looking down in a trance-like state, her eyes only half open.

David turned his head to the others. He looked horrified and was clearly overpowered.

'Help me!' he yelled again. The nightmarish woman turned to look at the others as well, locking her milky eyes on them.

Then she was gone.

Jenn wasn't sure how, but one moment she was there; the next she seemed to just bleed into the surroundings, melting away to nothing and leaving David lying alone on the ground, panting and sweating. Sarah still watched, unmoving.

'What happened?' Jenn asked as she squeezed into the room. Ralph took a few steps forward and allowed the others to enter as well.

'I'm not quite sure,' David said and got to his feet. He looked scared, which was understandable, but there was something else to his expression. Confusion, perhaps. 'I woke up and something attacked me. And Sarah was...'

They all turned to look at Sarah, who still had her glazed eyes fixed on David.

'Is she asleep?' Ann asked.

'I think so,' David replied.

'It doesn't matter,' George said. 'We need to get out of here. Now.'

'No, it's okay,' David replied, waving a dismissive hand. 'I'm honestly fine.'

'I'm not,' George stated.

David frowned in confusion.

'Look, David,' Ralph began, 'stuff happened to us as well. A woman attacked George in our room.'

'Almost killed me,' George added.

'Something attacked us too,' Ann then threw in. Ralph, Jamie, and George turned to look at her.

In the confusion of what was happening, Jenn realised neither she nor Ann had told the others about the man in their room.

'What was it?' Ralph asked.

'Something with its stomach torn open,' Ann replied. Her bottom lip quivered and she hugged herself.

It seemed like everyone had had their own experience at the same time. Jenn realised they were damn lucky no one had gotten hurt, and with reluctance accepted they should stop tempting fate.

Ralph spoke first. 'Look, David,' he said, 'I... agree with George. I don't think we should be here. I know you wanted to stay, but tonight changes things. We need to leave. And not in the morning, but right now.'

'I see,' David said. He took a deep breath then gave a solemn nod. 'You're right. We can't put our lives in danger anymore.'

'What about her?' Jamie asked, motioning to Sarah.

David turned to look at her. 'We wake her, then all get the hell out.'

'She might not come willingly,' Ralph pointed out.

'Then we'll have to make her see sense,' David responded. He then moved his hand towards Sarah's shoulder. She followed his arm as it moved, eyes still only half open with a blank expression. David gently shook her.

'Sarah?'

He got no response, so shook her a little harder. Still nothing.

'Sarah!' Ann shouted.

Jenn and everyone else jumped at the sudden noise. 'Jesus, Ann, I just about shit myself,' Ralph scolded. However, when they looked back to Sarah, they saw her eyes blink a few times, then fully open. Her pupils started to focus. Jenn watched confusion draw over her face.

'What... what's going on?' she asked.

'Long story,' Ralph said. 'But we need to get out of here.'

Sarah frowned. 'What, why?'

'We've all been attacked,' Ann said. 'We nearly *died*.'

When she thought about it, though, Jenn wasn't so sure that was correct. *Had* they nearly died? They'd all had experiences, but they'd escaped. Even David, who had been pinned down and at the mercy of that savage woman. How long had he been stuck like that before they'd all run into the room? Could he really have fought off a spirit if it didn't want him to?

Jenn glanced over to Sarah and saw that she was clearly reeling, trying to catch up with what was going on. Sarah looked back over to her bed, then to the floor, clearly confused as to why she had woken standing up like that.

'Was I sleepwalking again?' she asked.

David nodded. 'Afraid so. A woman was attacking me and you walked over, then stood there and watched it happen.'

'Jesus,' Sarah exclaimed.

'Can we not go over everything now?' Ann asked, seeming full of agitation. 'That can wait. We need to get the hell out of here quickly!'

'Okay,' David said. 'I hear you. But we can't very well run out of here in our sleeping clothes, so we should quickly get changed, pack the essentials, and then we can leave.'

'I'm *not* going back to my room,' Ann insisted.

'We'll go together,' David replied and grabbed some clothes from his suitcase. 'It'll be safer if we stay in one big group. Sarah,' he said, turning to her. 'Get dressed. Hurry.'

But Sarah didn't move.

'Sarah,' Ann snapped. 'Move it!'

'And where are we all going to go?' Sarah asked.

'Anywhere but here,' Ann shot back. 'We all have homes we can go to.'

'At this hour? I'm guessing it's late.'

'About three-thirty,' Ralph said.

'So?' Ann replied. 'Who gives a shit?'

'You all came in one van,' Sarah went on. 'By the time David drops you all off, what time would it be? Some of you live out of town.'

'That doesn't matter. I'd rather be stuck in a car for a few hours than stay here. Even if we're dog tired. I honestly don't know why you're making this an issue.'

David, who was almost finished changing, cut in. 'Look,' he said, 'we can all just go back to my house for now, to pull ourselves together. It isn't a big place, and it'll be cramped, but I have a spare bed, a sofa, and some inflatable beds as well. We can get a few hours of sleep, then decide where we go from here.'

'What's to decide?' Ann asked. 'We leave here and never come back.'

'We get it, Ann,' Jenn said. 'You're done here. Fine. You don't need to repeat yourself over and over.'

'Well clearly I *do*,' Ann snapped. 'Because we are *still* fucking standing here arguing!'

'Sarah, please get ready,' David said as he finished tying his shoes.

'I'm not going,' Sarah replied, folding her arms over her chest.

Great, Jenn thought. *Just what we need.*

'Then fucking stay!' Ann shouted and stamped her foot. She then turned to their leader. 'David, would you just *do* something!'

'Look, the rest of you go and get ready,' he said. 'Stick together and be quick. We'll meet in the corridor, then head down to the van.'

'Let's go,' Jenn said, taking the lead. She walked from the room and the others filed out behind her. They made their way to the girls' room first, where Jenn and Ann quickly started to get dressed.

'What do you think David's saying to Sarah?' Ann asked.

Jenn shook her head. 'I have no idea.'

CHAPTER 31

'You have to come with us,' David said to Sarah.

'No, I don't,' she replied. Her voice was flat and cold. 'And you can't make me go. Unless, of course, you want to try and force me out of my own house.'

'I know I can't force you,' David said. 'And I would never try. But please, I'm just asking you to see sense. At least for one night, so we can process what just happened.'

'I didn't see what happened. I'm just going off what you've told me. And I still can't make sense of it all.'

'So... you think we're lying?' David asked.

Sarah's body relaxed a little and her eyes turned downward. 'I honestly don't know *what* to think.'

'I can easily fill you in. After waking a little while ago, I saw you sitting up in bed again. Given what happened last night, I was worried something was in the room with us. And I was right. There was a woman, and she leapt on me. If it wasn't for the others, I don't know what would have happened, because you weren't waking up. You just stood there, watching it all.'

Sarah was silent for a moment. She looked embarrassed.

David felt for her; none of this could have been easy for her, but she needed to stop being so stubborn.

Sarah lifted her head and her eyes widened a little.

'The woman who jumped on you,' she went on. 'Did you recognise her?'

David paused.

He was hoping she wouldn't ask that question, because he knew *exactly* who the ghostly apparition was. He'd known it as soon as he'd seen her in the viewfinder. It had become even more apparent when she was atop him. Even though her body was rotted, and her face twisted into a demonic snarl... he knew who it was.

Chloe.

She'd looked so full of hate and anger. However, he didn't want to admit that to Sarah, fearing it would only make her desire to stay even stronger. So, he shook his head and lied. 'No, I didn't recognise her.'

David hoped he sounded believable. Sarah narrowed her eyes at him, and he felt like he was being studied.

'You sure?' she asked.

He nodded. 'Of course I'm sure.'

Sarah stared at him a moment longer, then nodded. 'Okay,' she said. 'But it doesn't change the fact that I'm staying. If the rest of you want to leave, so be it, I can't stop you going any more than you can stop me staying.'

David wanted to scream at her. *Why is she being so stupid?*

He knew why, of course. Because of her sister.

David sympathised—more than she knew—but surely there was a point where self-preservation had to come first.

'Listen,' he went on. 'Just leave with us now, if only for a night, and then if you feel the need, I'll bring you back here myself tomorrow. But just get away from this house for a little while. Please.'

'Chloe can't leave, can she?' Sarah asked as if that were answer enough.

'Maybe not,' he admitted. 'But would she want you suffering like this? Or putting yourself in danger?'

'She wants my help,' Sarah said. 'And she's going to get it.'

'Not if you end up dead!' David snapped. He took a breath and ran a hand through his hair. 'Look,' he said, 'I'm sorry for yelling. But I just want you to listen to reason. Staying here on your own will do no good. And it certainly won't help Chloe if something happens to you.'

'I... don't know,' she said, looking down to the floor.

David could see the struggle within her. It was etched on her face. '*One* night,' he said. 'Just to clear your head.' He held out his hand to her. 'Please.'

She didn't move and instead looked at his waiting hand.

Please, Sarah, just listen.

Finally, she took it, and David breathed a sigh of relief.

'One night,' she said. 'Then you bring me back here tomorrow.'

'Deal,' he said.

CHAPTER 32

'COFFEE'S UP!'

Sarah opened her eyes at the call, though her body fought against waking. Her head pounded. She felt like she'd gone a week with only a half hour of sleep.

She was fairly sure the voice was David's, and could also faintly smell cooking meat.

The bed beneath Sarah sank as she rolled over, so much so that her hip touched the floor. It was then she remembered taking an inflatable last night, which had now lost a lot of its air. She lifted her head to see the bedroom around her. It was small and basic, with old white wallpaper, beige curtains, and a matching carpet that didn't seem to have any underlay. There was a single bed in the room as well, which Jenn and Ann had squeezed into together.

'What time is it?' Ann asked. It was more of a whining complaint than a genuine question. Sarah felt for her phone on the floor to check.

'Almost midday,' she replied.

'I'm making breakfast as well,' David shouted. 'I hope a traditional English fry-up is okay with everyone?'

It sounded good to Sarah.

'Coming,' Jenn shouted. She yawned, then added, 'I feel like crap.'

'Crazy night,' Sarah said.

Jenn turned to look at her from the bed. 'How are you feeling today?'

'I'm okay,' Sarah replied. 'My head's a little all over the place.'

'I can imagine.' Jenn swung her legs out of bed. 'I've never seen anything like last night before in my life.'

'What about back in 2014? I heard your investigation got pretty crazy.'

Jenn thought for a moment, then nodded. 'I guess. But we didn't stick around Perron Manor long after that, either.'

'So you're definitely done?' Sarah asked.

'I... don't know.'

Ann sat up as well, an angry frown on her face. 'Are you serious, Jenn? We *can't* go back.'

But Jenn just held up her hand. 'Lecture me later,' she said. 'First, I need coffee.'

Coffee sounded good to Sarah, too.

The breakfast David had served up was surprisingly good. He'd even fried up some mushrooms and poached everyone eggs.

All seven of them were crammed into an open living and dining space. The living room had a three-seat sofa as well as an old, scruffy armchair. Ann, Jenn, and Sarah had squeezed onto the couch, while Ralph took the chair, and all of them had their plates balanced on their knees.

The dining area was only around five-feet wide with a small pine table and matching chairs, but the table only accommodated two people. George and Jamie sat there, devouring their food.

David elected to sit on the floor, just in front of an old electric fireplace with a glass front. Inside of the glass panel were fake pieces of decorative coal.

Sarah didn't think it looked too comfortable down on the floor, since the carpet underfoot didn't appear to have underlay either, just like the ones upstairs. In some places the carpet-piles had worn thin.

'I'll need to call Father Janosch,' David said. 'Tell him we aren't at the house anymore. He was planning on heading over and joining up with us today.'

There were a few nods of acknowledgement, but no-one spoke. The topic of potentially going back was clearly the elephant in the room, and it couldn't be ignored for long. Sarah had thought of nothing else since waking that morning, constantly deliberating what to do.

The house was indeed dangerous; however, Chloe was still there… suffering. Sarah's sweet, caring, pain-in-the-arse sister, whom she had loved more than anyone else in this world. Sarah pictured Chloe's smiling face and then thought about Emma, who would grow up without a mother.

How could she ever again look her niece in the eye knowing she had abandoned Chloe's soul to damnation? Sarah realised tears were building in her eyes, so she subtly wiped them with the back of her hand, hoping that no one had noticed.

She saw David looking at her as he chewed his food. He offered her a solemn smile. She averted her eyes from him.

Enough, she told herself. *You can mourn later. Keep focused. Get back to the fucking house.*

However, without the others, what could she really do to help her sister? David and his team were the experts here… or so they said.

Sarah's mind ran back to the book up in the study, as well as the accompanying ledger. Perhaps there was something in the translations that could help.

In addition, there was Father Janosch. She had already been introduced to him now, and *he* was the one who could get the Church to help. So… did Sarah really need the others?

That's harsh, Sarah. They've given a lot to help you.

She took a breath. It was time to acknowledge the elephant.

'Have you all decided what you're doing?' she asked. 'You know, about going back to the house?'

The clinking of plates and chewing of food stopped. Silence briefly descended over them, which David eventually broke. 'Have *you* decided?' he asked.

'Yes,' Sarah said. 'I heard what you said before, and I get that the house might be dangerous. But I've lived with danger most of my life, it was kinda my job. I don't say that to be brash, but you all know why I need to go back there. You know what's at stake for me. So, I've made up my mind. I'm going back.'

More silence. Sarah went on. 'I don't expect any of you to come with me if you don't want to or don't think it's safe. You've already done enough.' She then looked up to David. 'I'd just ask that you give me Father Janosch's contact details and get him to speak to me. I'm still moving forward with the plan, because it's the only one I have. I need his help.'

She saw Ann shake her head. 'You're crazy,' Ann said.

Sarah let the comment go. *She's still freaked out about the previous night.*

Sarah saw the others cast nervous glances at each other. It was clear not everyone had come to a firm decision yet, which was to be expected. So, it was time for them to make up their minds.

'Look,' Ralph began. 'I gotta admit, I don't know which way I fall on this. Part of me was terrified, I'll admit, but another part of me feels like we are on the cusp of something big with the house. The proof we could get there, I mean... it's why we do what we do. *But*, I also gotta work and pay the bills, and I need to take a few days away at the very least. I gotta spend some time with my girlfriend as well.'

Sarah understood that completely. Their own lives had to come first.

'Take as much time as you need,' Sarah said. 'And if you want to come back when you are able, that's great. If not, no problem.'

She then looked around the room for someone else to voice their thoughts. No one did, so Sarah forced the issue and focused on Jenn. 'What about you?'

Jenn finished her mouthful of food. 'I honestly don't know either. I got scared, but... that house is confirming everything I've ever believed in and everything I ever hoped was true. But... I dunno, I think I need more time to decide.'

Sarah nodded. 'That's fair.' She then turned her attention to Ann, who had a face like thunder.

'Don't even ask,' Ann snapped. 'I'm out. I've made that perfectly clear.'

'You have,' Sarah replied, raising her hands defensively. 'And again, that is no problem. Thank you for the time you've given me already. I really mean that.'

Jamie and George both sat at the small dining room table looking at their plates.

'Any input from you two fellas?' Sarah asked. They looked up at each other, neither wanting to go first. It was Jamie who eventually spoke.

'I think I might be out as well,' he said and hung his head. 'Sorry.'

'Don't be sorry,' Sarah replied. 'I mean that. You've nothing to apologise for.'

'Yeah, I'm not so sure I'll be back either,' George added. 'Don't get me wrong, that house could be a game-changer. I'm just not sure we are the right people to study it.'

'How so?' David quickly asked with a frown.

George shrugged. 'I mean, come on, we all love what we do, but this is just a hobby for us. Is it really worth us putting our lives on the line?'

'*Just* a hobby?' David asked. 'I don't know about the rest of you, but I take this very seriously.'

'It's fine,' Sarah cut in. She sensed a disagreement coming, which could possibly turn into an argument she didn't have time for. 'And what about you, David?'

David held steady eye contact with Sarah for a few moments. His face was serious. 'I've given it a lot of thought,' he said, then paused and took a breath before finishing. 'I'm coming with you.'

Sarah smiled. She couldn't help it. While she was certainly prepared to go back alone, knowing David would be there was a huge relief.

He stood up and pulled out his mobile phone. 'I'm going to make the call to Father Janosch now,' he said, 'I'll update him on what happened and tell him to meet those of us who are going back later.'

As he walked from the room, Sarah caught his eye and mouthed, *thank you.*

He smiled and kept walking. She heard his footsteps ascend the stairs to the floor above.

Jenn sighed. 'Fuck it,' she said. 'I'm coming too.'

'You sure?' Sarah asked. 'You know you don't have to.'

'I know,' Jenn replied. 'But I want to see it through.'

'Appreciate it,' she said, still smiling.

Ann rolled her eyes. 'Jesus Christ… you three are fucking crazy, you know that?'

'Maybe,' Jenn said. 'But I need to do it. Same as David.'

'No,' Ann argued, '*not* the same as David. You know as well as I do the real reason he's going back.'

'Drop it, Ann,' Jenn snapped.

Ann shook her head and turned away. 'Fine,' she said and got to her feet. She walked off with her plate, taking it to the kitchen.

'What did she mean by that?' Sarah asked.

Jenn looked a little uncomfortable. 'It… doesn't matter,' she replied. 'Ask David. Not really my place to say.'

CHAPTER 33

THE PHONE RANG AND RANG. David assumed the priest was busy and expected the call to go to voicemail. However, he was pleasantly surprised when Father Janosch picked up.

'David,' the priest said. 'Is everything alright?'

'Father, I'm glad I caught you. Everything is… okay, I guess. But there has been a development.'

'What happened?'

'Well, there were multiple occurrences last night. All of them happened at roughly the same time, about three-thirty in the morning…'

David proceeded to recount the events of the previous night, making sure to give detail about each of the three experiences.

'…to be honest,' David went on to add, 'it was quite dangerous. George could have been seriously hurt.'

'That is most upsetting to hear,' Father Janosch said. 'Where are you now? Still at the house?'

'No, most people didn't want to stay, as you can imagine. So we all left and are at my place for the moment.'

'That's sensible. The severity is troubling. Not many normal hauntings manifest in such a serious way.'

'No, but we've always known Perron Manor wasn't just a normal haunted house.'

'I suppose you are right, but I had hoped that maybe its history was false. Or at least exaggerated.'

'Well, I think we have our answers on that point,' David said.

'So I assume you are done with the investigation now?' Father Janosch asked. 'If that's the case, could I ask a favour? It would be most helpful if Miss Pearson would let me borrow *Ianua Diaboli* for study. With the house out of bounds, it may be the only way to help her sister—'

'Actually,' David said, cutting off the priest. 'Some of us have decided to go back.'

There was a pause. 'Go back? Are you serious?'

'We are,' he replied.

'But David, if the house is so dangerous, then why?'

'I want to help my client,' David said. 'And I want proof that everything I've devoted my life to is not just make-believe.'

That wasn't the whole truth, but it was as much as he was prepared to give.

'Well, maybe there is another way. The book. David, if Sarah lets me have it to study and report on, I think the Church would act. So, really, there isn't a reason to go back to the house.'

'I thought you said the Church still needed substantial evidence to act?'

'I would count what happened last night substantial, wouldn't you?'

'Of course,' David said. 'But the trouble is, we didn't capture any of it. It would just be our testimony. Not really irrefutable proof to an impartial adjudicator.'

'I'll vouch for you,' the priest said. David picked up a hint of desperation. He knew Father Janosch was scared of the house—they all were, to an extent, but he wondered if the priest was letting his fear cloud his better judgment. Or, on the other hand, was David letting his need to get back there cloud his own?

After all, even though he'd persuaded Sarah to leave temporarily, David knew he was just as guilty of wanting to return. He wanted the exact same thing. The difference was, his desire to help a loved one in need had been stretched out over thirty-five years.

'I will speak to Sarah,' David said, 'but I already know the answer. She's single-minded in what she wants to do, and won't let the book leave Perron Manor if she thinks it could delay things.'

'How would it possibly—'

David cut in. 'Because if the book is gone for you to study at your own leisure, then the urgency is gone, Father. Sarah will have no guarantee on how long things will drag out, or how quickly the Church will act—if they even choose to at all. If you need *Ianua Diaboli,* I think you will need to come to the house.'

'I assure you,' Father Janosch replied, 'I would work as fast as I possibly could. And it would be quicker that way, too, as I could work late into the night from home.'

'Well, like I say, I'll speak to her for you.'

'No need,' Sarah's voice said from the open doorway of the bedroom. She walked over to David and held out her hand, requesting the phone. He gave it to her.

'Father Janosch?' she said. 'This is Sarah Pearson. Forgive me, but I overheard a little of the conversation you were having. And I can tell you that David is correct. I'm sorry, but I won't be letting that book out of my sight. It's not like I think you're going to take off with it or anything, but I just don't have time to fuck around. You are welcome to come over and help us; in fact, I'd like it if you could. But that's final.'

David listened intently as he heard the mumbles of a reply come from the priest, but he couldn't make out the exact words.

Sarah shrugged. 'It might well be irresponsible and dangerous, Father, but that's where I'm at with the whole thing. If you want to make sure we don't accidentally summon the Devil or something, I suggest you get your arse over to the house and help us.'

David's eyes widened in surprise. Sarah then smiled and nodded a few more times as Father Janosch replied.

'Okay,' she eventually said. The phone was handed back to David. 'He wants to talk to you.'

David held the phone up to his ear. 'Yes?'

'Fine,' Father Janosch said. 'I'll come.'

David looked up to Sarah and she flashed him a smile and a wink. 'Just gotta play hardball,' she whispered.

David said his goodbyes and finished the call with Father Janosch. 'Well played,' he said with a chuckle to Sarah.

'Thank you. I figured we could use his help, but he's been entirely too evasive for me.'

'Yeah. I think he's terrified of Perron Manor, to be honest.'

'Understandable. But he needed to make a decision, just like the rest of us. I just hope he follows through with it.'

'Were you serious?' David asked.

'About what?'

'Accidentally summoning the Devil. I mean, I know it was kind of a joke, but would you really be willing to attempt some of the rituals in the book? I remember you suggested something like that a little while ago.'

'I don't know. Maybe, I guess. I mean, if there is something in there that could help us, wouldn't you?'

'It's awfully dangerous,' David said. 'We might not summon the Devil, but we could very easily get something wrong and cause a great deal of harm. We really need to be careful.'

'Fair enough,' Sarah said. 'We'll be careful.'

David didn't know what to make of the answer. It was decidedly... ambiguous.

'I wanted to ask you something,' she went on.

'Shoot,' he said.

Sarah paused for a moment. Her eyes flicked to the side, as if she were considering her words carefully.

'What's the deal with you and Perron Manor?' she asked.

David cocked his head to the side. 'What do you mean?'

'Like... why are you so interested in it?'

He wasn't sure where the questioning was coming from. 'Because of what it is,' he replied. 'It's like the holy grail to people like me.'

'Paranormal investigators?'

'Right. It's what I live for. I've always believed that if I could carry out a prolonged investigation in the house, I'd get indisputable proof that death isn't the end.'

'And that's the only reason?'

He frowned. 'Should there be another one?'

Sarah was obviously pressing for something. *What exactly does she know?*

'Well,' she went on, 'Ann made a comment downstairs, about why you are so obsessed with the house.'

'*Obsessed?*'

'Okay, maybe she didn't use that word, but you know what I mean. She made it clear there was something beyond just your interest in the paranormal. Jenn wouldn't tell me anything, though, and said it was best to talk to you about it. So…' she held her arms out to her side, 'here I am, talking to you about it.'

David looked down to the floor and tucked his hands into his pockets. He let out a breath.

Shit.

He was annoyed Ann had let that slip after specifically telling his team not to do so. David wanted to appear professional—hell, he *was* professional—and not like someone who had lied just to get inside the house to further his own agenda.

Still, if anyone could understand his true motivations, surely it would be Sarah. At least he hoped so.

'You read my book on Perron Manor, right?' he asked.

Sarah nodded. 'Of course.'

'Well, do you remember the part in Chapter 17, where I mention a girl named Katie Evans?'

He saw Sarah squint as she thought about the question. However, she shook her head.

'Sorry, not really. Should I?'

'Probably not,' David said. 'It was only one line, about a girl that went missing in 1985. She was last seen at the house.'

'Okay, so what's so significant about that?'

'Well, I kept the details vague on purpose. Thing is, I know more about that incident than any other in the book. Katie Evans was my stepsister.'

Sarah's mouth hung open. 'Wait… are you serious?'

David nodded. 'Yeah. My mother got together with Katie's father when I was young, and Katie and I grew up together.'

'Jesus,' Sarah uttered. 'I... had no idea.'

'There's no reason you should have. She was a little older than me, but we did everything together. We used to stay up late at night telling ghost stories, usually ones involving the creepy house in town. We'd hike up to the grounds sometimes, always in the daytime, and dare each other to run up to the gates and touch them.

'One evening, she was going out with friends, and I'd overheard them talking. They were heading up to the house. I could tell Katie was excited and a little nervous. I wanted to go as well, but she wouldn't let me. And when she left that night, it was the last time I ever saw her... kind of.'

'What do you mean?' Sarah asked, tilting her head to the side. '*Kind* of?'

'Well, this story will probably sound familiar, but a year or so later when the investigation died down and she was never found, I wandered up to the house myself one day. I just *knew* Katie was inside. I hopped the boundary wall and walked up to the house. I was terrified. But, in one of the windows upstairs, I saw someone staring back at me.'

'Katie,' Sarah said.

'Yup. She looked horrible. Almost like a corpse. And she appeared to be in pain, too. I was so scared I just ran. But ever since, I've been trying to get back here to learn as much as I can in the hopes that I can help her one day.'

Sarah looked astonished. She shook her head, trying to find the words. 'I... um... don't know what to say. If it was in 1985, wouldn't my uncle have been living there?'

David nodded. 'Yeah, but he always said no one entered the property that night. Said there were a bunch of girls hanging around out front, but he went out and told them to scram, which he says they did. Katie's friends said the same thing, but they also swore that Katie turned back and was adamant she wanted to at least get over the wall. Apparently,' his voice cracked a little, 'she said to one of them that it would really impress her little brother. But the police searched the house and didn't find a thing. After a few years, they gave up looking. Just another missing person in this town. But that's not all.'

'Go on,' Sarah said.

'In 2014, when we carried out our investigation, we unleashed something in the basement...'

'I remember that part.'

'Right. Well, whatever was down there had a message for me. Not the group, just me. 'Return here. Help another in need.' I'll never forget that. I've always assumed it was about getting back to help Katie.'

'David... how come you didn't tell me any of this before?'

'I don't really know,' he said. 'I wanted you to think we were serious about what we were doing, not that I had an ulterior motive for helping. I didn't want to piss you off.'

'But your motive is the same as mine,' she said. 'Why the hell would it piss me off?'

He shrugged. 'Again, I don't know. I guess I'm just not used to sharing that story.'

'But the team all know about it?' Sarah asked.

He nodded. 'Jenn pieced it together a while ago, before our investigation in 2014, so I told everyone what had happened. But, to be honest, every person in the team has their own story of why we do what we do. That just happens to be mine.'

Sarah shook her head but smiled. 'You should have just told me, you know. Although I... do have another question.'

'Again, shoot,' David said, feeling relieved.

'Given what's on the line for you at that house, how come you were so quick to convince me to leave last night? I mean, I get you were scared, I think everyone was, but didn't you want to stay? You know, for Katie.'

'Of course I did!' he replied. 'But I also know how dangerous things can be if you push yourself too much. Running away last night didn't have to be the end, but if something happened to us in that house... well, who would help Katie then?'

'Fair point,' Sarah said. 'I just get a little impatient with the whole thing. Knowing Chloe is stuck there, suffering...'

'Yeah, I get it. So let's make sure we don't mess up and that we both set our sisters free. Agreed?'

He held out his hand. She laughed, then shook it. 'Agreed.'

'Okay, then. I suppose we need to get the others home, and then we can head back to the house.'

'Sounds good,' Sarah said. 'Jenn is still in as well, by the way. She's coming with us.'

'Really?' he asked. 'That isn't too surprising, I guess. I've never seen her shy away from anything.'

'She's a trooper,' Sarah agreed. 'Now come on, I'd like to be back at the house while it's still daylight. I want to find out more about that bloody book, because I'm willing to bet it has some answers.'

CHAPTER 34

THE VAN AMBLED down the long gravel driveway, causing Sarah to bounce in her seat. When she peered out through the front window, she could again see those distinct three peaks of Perron Manor.

While she had been desperate to return, Sarah couldn't deny it had felt good to be away from the oppressive house, if only for a little while.

David drove, and Jenn sat up front with him. Sarah was in one of the seats behind, looking over their shoulders. She saw her car parked outside in the carport where she'd left it. It had occurred to her to take it last night when everyone was fleeing, if only to turn around when the others were out of sight and come back on her own.

Now, she was glad that David had convinced her to get in his van with the others.

Gazing out at the house again, Sarah was reminded of the first time she'd laid eyes on it, only a couple of months ago. And yet, it seemed like a lifetime. Perron Manor had become such a big part of her life recently. All dominating. All consuming.

Hopefully, she would soon be free of it. As would Chloe.

They pulled to a stop in the carport, and David killed the engine. No one moved. The tension in the van was palpable, and Sarah was sure they were all thinking the same thing.

Are we crazy coming back here?

But she knew they couldn't just sit out in the van all day. There was work to do—namely, looking more closely at *Ianua Diaboli* and the ledger. Previously, Sarah had been happy to let other people worry about the book, but now it was time to take more of an interest herself.

As they waited, the sound of another car engine from behind alerted them.

David checked his side mirror and let out a laugh. 'He showed up quick.'

Just before they had set off, David had called Father Janosch to tell him they were on their way. The priest had said he'd join them as soon as he was finished with what he needed to do. Yet here he was, arriving only five minutes after them.

The three of them exited the van and Sarah turned to see Father Janosch's small, light-blue hatchback approach. It was a basic, unassuming car, which suited his role. She could hardly see a priest racing around in a sports car or a Bentley. They waited for him to pull up next to them before getting out.

'Hello, everyone,' he said with a bright smile, though it looked rather forced. Still, Sarah appreciated the effort. He *was* here helping them, after all, and she had to be thankful for that. He had a leather case with him that dangled from one hand, and a rucksack over his shoulder. He wore a long black coat, jeans, and white trainers.

Sarah held out her hand to him and gave a big smile of her own.

'Thanks for coming, Father,' she said. 'I know I put the pressure on you a little, but I'm grateful you're here.'

He shook her hand. 'Just remind me never to haggle with you in the future,' he joked. Father Janosch turned to David and Jenn. 'Just the four of us, I assume?'

'Yes,' David replied. 'The others decided against it for now.'

'Very well.' Father Janosch then looked to the house, and his happy expression faltered.

'Do you have a plan of attack?' David asked.

The priest shrugged, not taking his eyes off Perron Manor. 'Spend as much time as I can with the book and the ledger, and keep the Church updated.'

'Just tell them it's real,' Sarah said. 'The book, the house, the fact that it's a Devil's Door. We know that's true anyway. Tell them what you need to so they can send in the cavalry.'

'I wish I could,' Father Janosch said with a hint of sadness. 'And believe me when I tell you they *are* taking this seriously, but they need to know for certain before they act.'

'Does it matter?' Sarah asked. 'If they turn up here and Perron Manor just turns out to be a regular old haunted house, they can still help us, can't they? They can still sanction an exorcism and all that. But if it *is* what we think, then we'll have saved them time. So again, does it matter?'

'It matters,' Father Janosch confirmed. 'Because if we are correct, then we have more to worry about than just…'

'Than just what?' Sarah asked.

Father Janosch shook his head. 'Forget about it. It doesn't change what we need to do here. So, I suggest we start as soon as possible.'

He then walked off towards the house. Sarah cast David and Jenn a confused look, which they returned.

More to worry about?

Sarah wanted to push Father Janosch on that point, but there would be time for that later. For now, they needed to get started. The priest was right about that.

Sarah unlocked the main door, and they all entered and stood quietly in the entrance lobby. The house was silent. She looked to the floor at the foot of the stairs and remembered the sight of Chloe's body as it lay there in a crumpled heap—her head twisted and neck broken after that… monster… had killed her like she was nothing.

But Chloe *was* something. To Sarah, she had been everything. And now she was gone.

No, not gone. She's still here… suffering.

'I don't like how quiet it is,' Jenn said. 'Last time we were here, we were running for our lives.'

Sarah remembered the panic of their escape as well, even if she hadn't seen what the others had.

She felt on edge just being here, and she was sure David and Jenn were as well. It was like they were just waiting for something to happen.

Father Janosch spoke up. 'Should we go upstairs and get started?'

'As good a plan as any, I guess' Sarah replied. 'It's what we're here for. But why don't we bring the book and ledger down here, to somewhere more comfortable?'

'That would be appreciated,' Father Janosch said.

'And don't forget the rule,' David added. 'No one goes off alone. That was true before but *especially* after last night.'

The group took off their coats and Sarah noticed that Father Janosch wore a blue denim shirt underneath, one that was tucked into his jeans. However, despite his casual look, he still had his white clerical collar on show, as well as a small, silver crucifix that hung around his neck on a thin chain.

The four of them made their way up to the top floor and over to the study. Sarah approached *Ianua Diaboli* and looked down through the display glass to its leather cover.

Could it be true? Could this book hold power over the house? She noted again the strange symbols at each corner. Those were replicated —if a bit more crudely—on the ledger.

'Father Janosch?' she asked. He walked over beside her.

'Yes?'

She pointed down. 'Those markings on the book... what are they?'

'Protective seals, I believe. Markings that prevent anything from happening to the book.'

Sarah turned to him and frowned. 'Seriously? Are you saying I couldn't destroy it, even if I wanted to? Like, some spell would stop me?'

'They'd only stop you if you were possessed,' Father Janosch said. 'If not, you could destroy it without any problem. You see, the protection doesn't extend to the living.'

'So what does it protect from?'

'Well, to put it bluntly, the supernatural.'

She looked back to him. 'What, so ghosts don't rip it up?'

Father Janosch laughed. 'Kind of. You see, that book—if legitimate— could contain great power. The power could work against certain insidious forces here at this house. And they may want to destroy it. These markers prevent the dead, or undead, from doing so.'

'Undead?'

Father Janosch nodded. 'Just my term for things that have never truly lived. At least, not in the sense we know it. Demons and things like that.'

Sarah shook her head. 'That's crazy. Not that I don't believe you, of course, I've seen too much to be blind anymore. But I always took that kind of thing… spells, occult, demonic symbols… as horseshit.'

Father Janosch laughed again and patted her on the shoulder. 'I do love your way with words, Miss Pearson.'

'Just call me Sarah, Father. Please.'

'Okay, then I insist you call me Luca.' He then turned to David and Jenn. 'That goes for both of you as well, if you would. No need for formalities.'

David nodded as he and Jenn moved beside them.

Sarah's mind started to turn over as she looked back at *Ianua Diaboli*. An idea came to her.

'What if we *did* destroy the book?' she asked.

Father Janosch's head whipped round to her. 'Destroy it… why?'

'Well, if the book is linked to the house, and the Devil's Door, would destroying it close the door?'

Father Janosch shook his head vigorously. 'No, certainly not. At least, I don't think so. The thing is, if Perron Manor is a gateway to Hell, then it has been that way long before the book was brought here. So if we destroyed *Ianua Diaboli*, the door would simply remain open, but we would have lost a truly valuable weapon.'

'Understood,' Sarah said. 'We keep the book safe. But do we even know if the house has always been a gateway? I mean, has the land just been that way since the dawn of time, or was the door opened at some point?'

Father Janosch scratched at the back of his neck. 'Hard to say. You have to understand, what I do know of these phenomena are all based on rumours and stories. Until I saw *Ianua Diaboli*, I didn't believe there were such things as physical gateways to Hell in the first place. I *believe* the doorways have to be opened, but I can't be certain of it.'

'So how was *this* one opened?' Sarah asked, but then shook her head. 'Never mind,' she said. 'I appreciate you are as much in the dark as we are here.'

'Not quite,' David said and turned to the priest. 'Your knowledge of the occult and paranormal is going to be invaluable.'

'So he knows even more than *you?*' Sarah teased with a smile.

David laughed. 'Yeah. Consider him the Yoda to my Luke.'

'And what does that make me?' Sarah asked. 'And don't say the princess, or I'll smack you!'

David held up his hands. 'But Leia is awesome! Fine, you can be Han.'

'I'm okay with that,' Sarah said.

David then turned to Jenn and narrowed his eyes while he chewed his lip.

'I swear to God, David,' Jenn said, 'if you make me the big hairy thing I'm going to be furious.'

Father Janosch just looked confused and completely out of his depth. He leaned in toward Sarah. 'Who on earth is Yoda?'

CHAPTER 35

AFTER THEIR CONVERSATION UP in the top-floor study, the group retired to the dining room with the books.

The ground-floor dining room was David's idea, as the room was smaller and more intimate than the great hall at the back of the house, but had a large enough table for them all to fit around.

A single chandelier hung above them, lighting the room, and the only other piece of furniture of note was a chest of drawers set against the far wall.

Father Janosch sat at the head of the table, with David on one side of him and Sarah and Jenn on the other.

'So then,' Father Janosch said. 'Let's begin.'

'How are we going to do this?' David asked. 'Is there anything we can do to help?'

Father Janosch slid *Ianua Diaboli* over, so it was directly before him, and traced a finger down the cover. 'I think the best course of action is for me to read a section, then cross-reference it with the ledger here.' He tapped at the book next to *Ianua Diaboli*. 'I can then determine if I think the translations are accurate. Having a copy of *Ianua Diaboli* already in English would be a great help. However, I think the process will be slow and laborious, unfortunately.'

'Did you learn much from the time you had with the book yesterday?' Sarah asked.

'Some,' he replied. 'But I tried to take in as much as I could, flicking back and forth through its pages. Now is the time for completeness. But as you can see,'—he held up *Ianua Diaboli* with a groan, and pointed to its thick spine—'it will take a while.'

The process Father Janosch suggested made sense to David. The priest was by far the most fluent in Latin, and so was the best-placed person for the work. Of course, that would make David and the others little more than bystanders.

'We could read from the ledger,' Sarah suggested, as if reading David's mind. 'That would at least give us something to do.'

'Sounds like a plan,' Father Janosch said.

'Wait,' Jenn interrupted. 'I'm still not clear on something. I get why we're doing this, reading through the book and all. But at the end of the process... how best to word this... *so what?* I mean, even if you study all the book's contents, would that prove one way or another if it was legitimate? Or if Perron Manor really was one of these doorways to Hell? It's just words on a page. Not proof.'

The question gave David pause. It was a valid point. All they would know for sure was if the translations were correct or not.

He briefly thought of Sarah's earlier idea of testing out one of the rituals themselves, then quickly chastised himself for even considering such a thing. It would be stupid and dangerous to try.

Still, at least they would *know*.

'Well, that is why we need to keep gathering evidence,' Father Janosch said. 'From what I have seen, we have a good amount already. If we get more, and present it all along with the *Ianua Diaboli* and the translations, I think the Church will act.' He then leaned over to Sarah. 'However, I do want to reiterate that if you allow me to take the book home to study, and then show them in person, it will move things on much quicker.'

David looked to Sarah as well and waited.

She shook her head firmly. 'Sorry, Luca, no can do. I've made my position clear on that. But, since we are covering old ground, I want to again ask, would you bend the truth for us? Just tell them what they need to hear so they act. We all pretty much know what we are dealing with anyway, right?'

'But we are not *certain*,' Father Janosch said. 'And lying isn't something I'm in the habit of doing, being a priest.'

Sarah crinkled her nose. 'Really? You've been a little loose with the truth with us, wouldn't you agree? What with saying you couldn't stay here last night as you had duties to attend to, yet you magically showed up straight away after David's call?'

Father Janosch's face turned a deep shade of red. David wasn't certain if it was from anger or embarrassment. The priest then looked down to the table in front of him.

'Sarah,' David said, 'we don't need to go over that again.'

Sarah held up her hands. 'Fair enough,' she said. 'I don't want to fight. I just don't like the insinuation that I'm the one being difficult by insisting my own book stays in my possession.'

David addressed Father Janosch. 'Look, Fath—sorry, Luca... I'm sure Sarah didn't mean—'

But Father Janosch just raised a hand and cut David off. 'She's right,' he said with a sigh. 'I haven't been completely honest with you. And given the sacrifices you are all making by being here, I think I owe you that much. But please understand, what I am about to tell you is sacred knowledge. It is something I was expressly *forbidden* from sharing with you.'

David's heart began to quicken. Father Janosch, someone David had known for years, looked like a broken man. What knowledge was he about to impart?

'You don't have to tell us if it will get you in trouble,' David said, drawing a scowl from Sarah, which he ignored.

However, Father Janosch just shook his head and raised his eyes back up to them. 'I *have* been bending the truth. Or at least, I've been hiding some of it, which is just as bad. However, one thing I cannot do is lie to my superiors about this. If I get it wrong and we aren't dealing with what I suspected, then I would be finished. The idea that Devil's Door could really exist is a serious concern—'

'We get that, Luca,' Sarah said. 'That's why we're here.'

He shook his head. 'I mean beyond just Perron Manor. You see, if this one exists, there could be more.'

'Okay,' David chipped in. 'I understand that could be bad...'

'No,' Father Janosch replied. 'I don't think you *do* understand. Not really. One of the stories told along with the Devil's Door, was about the Seven Gates, or the Seven Doors. I've heard it called different things, but the idea is always the same.'

'Which is?' Sarah asked as she leaned forward.

'That if seven of these doorways are open at any one time, then... well, then it is all over.'

'What's all over?' David asked.

Father Janosch took a breath. 'Everything.'

David looked over to Sarah, and then to Jenn. They both seemed to be just as confused as he was.

'You're going to have to explain that more,' Sarah said. 'What do you mean everything is over?'

Father Janosch took a deep breath. 'It is said that if seven of the gates are open, then the connection to Hell is complete and at its strongest. Hell and our own world would merge.'

'Armageddon,' David added as his body slumped back onto his seat. He felt as though the wind had been knocked out of him. 'But surely that is just a story,' he went on. 'All religions and societies have their own tales about the end of the world, and that doesn't make any of them true.'

'No,' Father Janosch conceded. 'I know of many such stories, and to be honest, none keep me up at night. Indeed, the Seven Gates was never something I was concerned about, either. Like you said, just another myth and legend. Until this...' He tapped on *Ianua Diaboli*.

'But it could still all be bullshit,' Sarah said.

'And I hope it is,' Father Janosch replied. 'But you can see now why I need to be certain that, firstly, the book is genuine, and second, Perron Manor is actually a gateway. Because the resources the Church will then need to put into place would be... well, I can scarcely comprehend it.'

There were a few moments of silence between them all. It was Sarah who eventually spoke up, evidently trying to be the voice of reason. 'Well, even if this *is* all true, surely we know there can't be seven of those doors already open. Because, you know, we're all still here. It isn't raining fire or brimstone outside. So nothing has changed from what it was before we learned about the book. And nothing likely will change—the world has survived for this long without being sucked into Hell, so it's hardly something to be concerned about... right?'

No one answered. How could they? Each and every one of them was fumbling in the dark here. The gravity of the situation was overwhelming, and David had no idea what to say next. Part of him wished the priest had kept that information to himself.

Only a few days ago David had been excited at the prospect of getting back inside Perron Manor, to find indisputable proof of the afterlife, and also help his long-lost stepsister.

But things had moved on. Gateways to Hell had never been on David's agenda when he'd agreed to help Sarah, and now they were even talking about the end of the world. It was just too much for him to get his head around.

He realised that no one else had answered Sarah's question, and she shook her head in annoyance. 'Look,' she began, 'we need to just continue as we are. If the Seven Gates thing is real, then fuck it, we deal with *this* gate for now. That's the mission.' She looked over to David. 'Chloe and Katie still need our help.' Then, she pointed to the book. 'And that is still our best shot at finding out what the hell is going on. So, I think we should get started.'

She folded her arms over her chest, sitting with her back straight and head slightly tilted up. Her little speech was an attempt at a rallying cry, and she was absolutely right in what she was saying.

David still felt overwhelmed, but he nodded in agreement. 'You're right.' He turned to Father Janosch. 'Luca, I think we get to work.'

CHAPTER 36

JENN'S HEAD swam as Father Janosch began reading aloud from *Ianua Diaboli*. The Latin he was speaking sounded beautiful and exotic, despite her knowing the actual words likely had sinister connotations to them.

End of the world. Armageddon. Seven Gates.

What the hell had she gotten herself involved in?

Sarah had insisted on pushing on, but Jenn had remained silent, fading into the background as she fell deep into thought.

Jenn had believed in ghosts for as long as she had lived, and often thought about Heaven and Hell. As contradictory as it seemed, she'd always had trouble believing in those two things, though she couldn't explain why.

Others had suggested that surely the paranormal and things like Hell were one and the same. To Jenn, however, they had always seemed like separate ideas. She believed ghosts were a mere function of the universe —that our souls continued on in some form after the human body failed.

But that didn't mean heading off to eternal bliss and sitting on fluffy clouds while playing harps. Or being thrown into pits of fire to be immolated for eternity.

Jenn now hoped the book and the idea of portals to Hell were, to quote Sarah, horseshit. She could then go back to EVP sessions, Ouija boards, and ghost hunting: the things she signed up for.

They were clearly all ill-prepared to handle apocalyptic prophecies.

Father Janosch finished his reading and sat back. No one had followed along with the ledger, so Jenn had no idea what the first passage he'd read meant.

'Well?' David asked. Father Janosch looked ashen. He then sat forward and pulled the ledger closer.

'Please give me a moment,' he said, raising a finger. 'That was a lot to process, and I want to check the translation.'

Jenn braced herself. She wasn't sure she wanted to know what he'd read.

After a few minutes, Father Janosch sat back again. 'Okay,' he said after letting out a long sigh. 'The first section answers a question we all had about the gates: whether they have always existed, or if they have to be opened. Turns out, it is the latter.'

'What does it say?' David asked.

'It goes into detail about how the doors are opened,' Father Janosch responded. 'It is very... graphic, and against God. Human sacrifice. The spilling of innocent blood, and things that are...' he made a face like he was going to vomit, 'not something I want to repeat. But, according to this, gates *can* be opened, as long as a number of steps are met. So if that is true, then it means someone opened the door here. Either when the house was built, or before.'

'I would think before,' David added. 'During the research for my book, I discovered that the people who first built the house had to disperse a group of nomads from the area. The only descriptions were that those people didn't speak the King's tongue and, apparently, worshipped ungodly things. The document I found also claims those people were 'strange to look at,' though there was no other information on them to be found. I'd wager the land Perron Manor was built on was sacred to these people. And sacred for a good reason.'

'You think they opened the door?' Sarah asked. 'That's a bit of a leap, isn't it?'

Jenn had to agree.

'Depends how you look at it,' David replied. 'It's not like the tragic events that have happened at this house took a while to get going. They started pretty much straight away after the building was opened as a monastery. One of the monks went mad and killed his brethren. The horrific events just escalated from there. It makes sense to me that the land was already tainted.'

'But how could a group of nomads open a gate to Hell?' Sarah asked. 'They wouldn't have had *Ianua Diaboli* or anything like that.'

'Well,' Father Janosch began, 'I don't think this book here is the precursor to the existence of these doorways. The book is written in such a way as to impart a previously learned knowledge. The author, I think, is somebody who studied these gateways in great detail. So it is likely that the doors existed before *Ianua Diaboli* was written.'

'Okay,' Jenn started, finally finding her voice. 'So how did people back then figure out how to open these gates?'

Father Janosch slowly shook his head. 'As yet, I don't know. And that is something we may never know.'

'But,' Sarah began, 'if these nomads were able to do it, then *something* must have shown them how. I'm guessing the steps in that passage aren't just something you could stumble upon?' she asked Father Janosch.

'Correct,' he replied. 'But that mystery is probably irrelevant for the time being. There is a lot to get through here, and we have just scratched the surface.'

CHAPTER 37

Sarah yawned and rubbed her eyes. It felt like granules of sand were trapped beneath the lids. Her body ached from sitting down for too long.

Empty bowls sat at the far end of the table, having been pushed back out of the way. Tinned food was just about all Sarah had left in the cupboards since her time living there with Chloe, and no one had stopped to think about going out for more supplies.

Sarah drained the last of her lukewarm coffee, hoping the caffeine would help keep her energised. It had been a long afternoon.

After setting her mug back down to the table, she looked at the open book in front of Father Janosch. Despite working for hours, the pages they'd completed were dwarfed by the ones still to come.

This is going to take forever.

The information gleaned from the book so far had been interesting, and mainly covered rites and rituals that could summon different entities. Apparently, there was a demonic presence known as Pazuzu that often travelled through these doorways, and was described as an evil and detestable being that hated the living. He was considered vile and uncontrollable, even in the realms of Hell.

However, Sarah didn't know how much more she could listen to. If

Father Janosch had the translations covered, shouldn't the rest of them be trying to gather more evidence?

'We should be doing more,' Sarah said to David.

He frowned. 'In what way?'

'Well, Luca seems to have this in hand, so shouldn't we be carrying out some investigations?'

'Too dangerous to leave Luca here alone,' David replied while firmly shaking his head. 'And I don't like the idea of splitting into two groups. There aren't enough of us here.'

'And when do you think we're actually going to get the evidence we need, then? Because Luca himself said the book on its own isn't enough.'

'She's right,' the priest agreed. 'We still need more to present to the Church.'

David took a moment, and Sarah could see his mind working behind his narrowed eyes. 'Okay, how about we take a break from the book and go check the footage from last night, see what we caught there. I'd rather not try and draw anything out tonight, at least until we know a little more.'

'But we have a priest,' Sarah said. 'Fix him up with some holy water and surely we have a ghost-hunting Rambo.' She smiled as she said it, hoping to add some levity. Thankfully, she got a laugh from Father Janosch.

'I wish I were so brave,' he said. 'Or so useful. Though I do have my Bible.'

'See,' Sarah said to David. 'A Bible is practically an assault rifle in situations like these.'

'How about this,' Father Janosch offered. 'I finish up the section I'm working on, then we spend a little time trying to gather evidence?'

David sighed. 'I guess that makes sense. But everyone needs to be careful. No unnecessary risks.'

They waited a little while longer for Father Janosch to reach a natural break, then cleaned up the bowls from the table and carried them through to the kitchen. It seemed ridiculous that such a simple task needed all of them, but David had insisted they all had to stick together. Sarah had to wonder how that would work at night when they needed to sleep. She didn't know if there was a room big enough to squeeze four beds in, so Sarah guessed she would be sharing with Jenn, while David and Father Janosch would probably bunk together.

Sarah took a moment to look around the kitchen. The room had been the heart of the house when she had lived there with Chloe, Emma, and Andrew. She could almost see Emma sat at the table in her highchair, while the rest of them sat around chatting, with Andrew panicking about the next job that needed doing at the house.

'First, we'll check the cameras,' David said, pulling Sarah from her thoughts. 'We need to make sure they're still running. And we can have a quick look over last night's footage.'

'Isn't there anything else we can be doing?' Sarah asked. 'Something a bit more proactive?'

'After we check, yes,' David said, much to her annoyance. 'But to be honest, our best successes have come in the dead of night anyway, between three and four o'clock. That seems to be the time when the house is most alive. I think we need to be ready for that.'

'Plus,' Jenn said to Sarah, 'checking the cameras from last night is important. If we caught that woman attacking David, then that would be huge.'

She was right. They could have something just waiting for them that could be sent on to the Church straight away.

However, something was off. David's face was clouded with worry as he made eye contact with Sarah.

'There's... something I need to tell you first,' he said to her.

Sarah frowned and cocked her head to the side. 'Okay. Anything I need to worry about? Because you look like you've seen a... well, wrong choice of words.'

'It's about last night,' he said. 'When I was attacked. Remember when you asked me if I recognised the woman in our room?'

Sarah slowly nodded, and a feeling of dread came over her. She had an idea where this was going.

David lied to me.

'Who was it?' Sarah demanded through gritted teeth, though she suspected she already knew. Even so, she wanted to hear him say it.

He took a breath, then let out a long exhale. He looked like a schoolboy about to be chastised by his teacher. 'It was Chloe,' he eventually said, and his head hung low.

Sarah began to shake. Her hands balled into fists. 'Chloe?' she asked, teeth still clenched. 'So when I asked who it was before… you just lied to my face?' He nodded. 'Why?' she asked.

'Because I didn't know how it would affect you. You're here *for* her, and if you knew that she'd attacked me, I…' He shrugged. 'I honestly don't know. I guess I just didn't want you worrying about what she's become.'

'She hasn't *become* anything,' Sarah shot back. 'Chloe wouldn't attack you. That was something else. It must have been.'

David didn't reply, and just stood in silence with his head still hung low. Everyone else was quiet, trapped in awkward silence.

Sarah wanted to step forward and tear David's head off.

How could he keep something like that from me?

Regardless, he had to be mistaken.

'That couldn't have been Chloe,' she went on. Tears welled up in her eyes. 'She would never hurt anyone. It had to be the house playing tricks: another spirit made to look like my sister or something.'

Father Janosch slowly walked over to Sarah and laid a gentle hand on her shoulder.

She turned to him, trying to keep from breaking down completely. The thought of Chloe turning into one of those monsters was starting to dawn on her.

'He's wrong,' Sarah said to Father Janosch. 'That wasn't her. He's *wrong!*'

Father Janosch smiled. 'He is,' the priest said. 'And… he isn't.'

'I… I don't understand.'

'Places like this are evil, Sarah. And the souls of the dead who are trapped must obey the will of the house. I know this isn't going to be easy to hear, but I feel you must. The spirits are puppets, used as needed. *But* that isn't who they really are. The good person your sister was still exists. So, if David is correct and it *is* your sister we see on the footage, then you have to remember that the house is using her. Chloe's actions are not her own.'

That image of her strong sister, so utterly helpless and without agency being used against her will, broke Sarah.

What had Father Janosch called her... a puppet?

Sarah couldn't hold back the flood of tears anymore. What had been a steady flow suddenly erupted and she broke down sobbing, bending double as pain and anguish suddenly overwhelmed her.

Whether Sarah had fully admitted it to herself or not, she had always known deep down the kind of purgatory Chloe was in. Their last night at the house, when Chloe had died, they had both seen scores of spirits meaning to do them harm. In life, those people could not *all* have been evil or murderous. They were just being used—manipulated on strings by a master behind the curtain.

Helpless.

However, Sarah had not allowed herself to think of Chloe being used the same way. It was too painful.

She felt a hand on her back and realised the others had gathered around her. Someone pulled her upright and hugged her tightly. It was Jenn. Sarah continued to cry, the dam now completely broken.

'Why didn't I believe her?' Sarah asked between sobs. 'She told me about the house and I... I just wouldn't listen.'

Chloe had tried *so* hard to make Sarah see the truth, but Sarah didn't want to hear it. She'd thought she knew better—knew that Chloe was just stressed or worrying over nothing. She knew that it all had to be in Chloe's head.

And then Chloe had been killed. She had been right, and it was Sarah's fault she was dead.

The house had wanted Chloe all along, ever since she'd escaped it as a child. Now it had her.

Another death. More blood on Sarah's hands.

Just like Tania—Sarah's best friend who had died while they served together in the army. Sarah had been supposed to take point, but an overwhelming feeling came over her, gripping her with a fear she wasn't used to. Tania had filled in... then stepped on a landmine.

It should have been Sarah.

Two people she should have protected; two people she had failed.

'It's okay,' Jenn whispered. 'Just let it out.'

But Sarah didn't want to let it out. She didn't want to feel weak and helpless. She wanted to help Chloe. She wanted to put right, in some small way, one of the many wrongs in her life.

The biggest one.

Sarah pulled away and wiped her face with the sleeve of her jumper. 'I'm fine.' She shook her head, trying to clear away the hurt.

Then something drew her attention. A scent… one that was very familiar to her.

Lavender.

Sarah turned in the direction the smell was coming from, but there was nothing there—the scent evaporating just as it had become noticeable.

Chloe?

The last time Sarah had smelled lavender like that, she had been cradling Chloe's lifeless body, nuzzling her cheek to Chloe's head and taking in Chloe's familiar shampoo.

Was it just in her head? Thoughts of her sister triggering a phantom olfactory sensation?

Or was it something more?

'What is it?' David asked.

'Nothing,' she said, then once again wiped her face. 'Let's go. I want to see that footage.'

'You don't have to,' David began. 'We can review it for you and—'

'David,' she said sternly. 'I *want* to see it.'

CHAPTER 38

THEY WERE BACK in the makeshift headquarters, once again gathered around one of the laptops. David sat before it and lined up the video.

Sarah, Father Janosch, and Jenn all stood behind him, looking over his shoulder.

David felt terrible.

He was pretty sure Sarah hated him because of him hiding the truth.

Hiding the truth is still a lie, David.

He couldn't blame Sarah for being angry. It wasn't his place to keep something like that from her in the first place, even if he thought he was doing the right thing.

In his mind, Sarah had displayed certain tendencies during their time here, which were understandable but worrying: being overzealous, careless, and sometimes antagonistic with people. She was suffering loss, so her attitude was understandable, but David had tried to handle the situation and guard Sarah from… well, from herself.

But that wasn't his place.

He played the footage from 3am. On it, he and Sarah were in the room alone. Both were asleep.

David sped up the video while nothing was happening, then set it back to normal speed when Sarah sat up in bed. The timestamp showed three-twenty-two.

Sarah simply stayed in a sitting position, watching David.

'Can you remember this?' Father Janosch asked.

'No,' Sarah replied. 'Not at all.'

It wasn't long before David started to move on the video, rolling over and looking towards Sarah. He then sat up and moved his head to look around the room.

There didn't appear to be anyone else in the frame.

On the recording, David got out of bed and grabbed his handheld camera, panning around the room with it.

'This is where it happens,' he said to the others. 'Keep your eyes peeled. It wasn't until I'd turned to look behind me that I saw...'

He trailed off as he heard Jenn draw in a gasp.

Something had bled into the image. A figure, standing behind David on the other side of the bed. He felt goosebumps form on his arms as he watched. From the vantage point of the camera, it was hard to make out any definite details, other than the long, scraggly hair on the naked form of the woman.

There was no way to tell from this angle that it was Chloe.

On screen, he slowly turned around. As expected, the figure dove atop him.

'Jesus,' he heard Jenn utter from behind.

There was a struggle, and the woman forced David to the ground. She mounted him, lashing out with her arms, which he managed to grab in an effort to push her off. But she was a wild animal. The struggling continued as, on screen, Sarah got out of bed and walked over. She stood above David and his attacker and looked down—not moving or making an attempt to intervene.

'You still don't remember any of this?' Father Janosch asked.

'I don't,' Sarah replied.

'I remember your eyes were half-open,' David added, 'but you didn't seem awake. It was like you were in a trance.'

They continued to watch for a few minutes before the door to the room on camera opened. That was when the others filtered in. Just before they did, the savage woman looked up to the doorway... then disappeared, fading out into her surroundings as David lay alone on the floor.

The rest of the footage played out as David remembered, with him being helped to his feet and Sarah coming to from her sleepwalking state. But the footage offered up nothing that David wasn't already aware of. He paused the playback.

'Did that look like your sister to you?' Father Janosch asked Sarah.

'I... don't know,' she replied. 'It's hard to make out.'

'There is a way we might know for sure,' David offered, then pointed to the paused image, specifically to the handheld camera on the floor. 'I saw Chloe on that as I turned around. It scared the hell out of me. But... the footage on it might be a little more clear. It was certainly closer.'

David spun around in the swivel chair to face the others.

'Is the camera still in the bedroom?' Jenn asked.

'Should be,' David replied. He then looked to Sarah. 'Are you sure you want to see it?'

After a moment's pause, she nodded. 'Yeah. I'm sure.'

They all walked upstairs to the bedroom. As David opened the door, they were met with darkness. All the natural daylight was blocked out due to the thick curtains still being drawn. David reached in and flicked on the light. There, on the floor, was the camera.

Sarah strode into the room first and retrieved it. She flipped the viewfinder open, and the others crowded around.

'You will need to rewind it,' David said. 'When I dropped the camera, it would have just kept recording until the tape stopped.'

Sarah did, and they saw nothing but the dark bedroom from the camera's vantage point on the floor. Eventually, in reverse, the camera moved quickly up from the floor, and there was a flash of a person in view. By the time Sarah had hit the pause button, the footage had skipped farther back and was now focused on her own image as she sat up in bed.

'Play it again and try to pause the image as soon as you see the person behind me,' David told her.

She hit play, and the camera panned. The woman came into view and dove forward just as Sarah hit pause.

The image was a little blurry, given the lunge of the woman on camera, but there could be no denying who it was. Her skin looked decayed and her face was twisted up into a hateful snarl, but it was Chloe.

Sarah quickly snapped the camera closed and let it drop to the floor.

'I'm sorry,' David said.

'It's fine,' Sarah replied, though her voice made it sound anything but.

'Remember what I told you,' Father Janosch said. 'She is being controlled. Don't let that image be the way you remember her.'

'Hard to think of anything else now,' Sarah said. She then turned around and looked at David. 'I suppose there's something I need to tell you, too,' she said. 'Something I should have been honest about from the beginning.'

David frowned. 'Okay... what is it?'

'It's about how Chloe died. I told the police she fell down the stairs when we were running and broke her neck. I told you the same thing.'

David nodded. 'Right. But that's not what happened?'

Sarah shook her head. 'No. *Something* caught her. I don't know what it was, exactly, but it wasn't like the other spirits we saw that night.'

'A demon?' Farther Janosch asked.

'Possibly,' Sarah said. 'It broke her neck right in front of me. Just snuffed out her life like she was nothing.'

David was silent for a moment. They all were. By rights, he should have been mad at the deception, the same way Sarah had been at him. However, David had always suspected there was more to Chloe's death than Sarah had shared. He'd never pressed her on the issue because it suited his needs to think there was less of a danger in the house.

'That is worrying,' Father Janosch said. '*Very* worrying. In fact, it changes quite a lot.'

'I'm sorry,' Sarah said. 'I was just nervous that if I told the truth, David and his team wouldn't help, and I'd be helpless to save Chloe.'

'So we've been in more danger than we thought the whole time?' Jenn asked, obviously annoyed. Sarah turned to her with a genuine look of regret.

'I'm sorry,' she repeated.

'If the house was able to physically hurt someone and kill them after only a month and a half,' Father Janosch started, 'then that is beyond anything I've ever heard of as far as demonic activity goes. It's just too quick.'

David knew what he was driving at. 'Proof that the house is indeed a doorway to Hell?'

The priest took a deep breath. 'I think so. That knowledge would have been *very* useful upfront.'

'Seems like we've all been holding back the truth,' David said.

Sarah had lied to him; he'd lied to her; Father Janosch had been keeping his own secrets…

The whole thing was a mess.

No one spoke for a long while. Eventually, David broke the silence. 'We keep going then,' he said. 'As far as I see it, we still have a job to do.'

'Unless you have enough evidence now?' Sarah asked Father Janosch. 'What happened last night, plus how Chloe died, as well as everything else… is that enough to take to the Church?'

'Possibly,' Father Janosch replied. 'I'm going to call the Bishop to update him, see what he says. If it is enough, can I please take the book and the ledger away from the house?'

'I guess so,' Sarah said, finally relenting. Her face was still tear-streaked. The poor girl looked broken.

It had been a difficult day for all of them, made worse by the recent revelations. David felt punch-drunk.

'Come on,' Jenn said to Sarah. 'Let's get you cleaned up.' She took Sarah's hand and started to lead her off to the en-suite.

Sarah stopped her. 'I really am sorry,' she said yet again.

'I know,' Jenn replied, but didn't say anything else. The two disappeared into the bathroom, and David felt Father Janosch touch his elbow.

'We need to talk,' the priest said in a whisper. 'Privately.'

David shook his head. 'I don't think it is the time for any more secrets.'

'This one is needed. Trust me.' He then ushered David from the room, closing the door behind them.

CHAPTER 39

Luca stood close to David out in the hallway. He didn't want to risk the others overhearing if they came back in from the bathroom.

'I'll be brief,' Luca said. 'I think we have something else to be concerned about.'

'Something *else*?' David asked with wide eyes. 'How much more can there be?'

'It's Sarah,' Father Janosch went on. 'I'm worried about her.'

'Why?'

'What we saw on last night's video. And the previous one. It's the sleepwalking.'

'Okay,' David said. 'Are you thinking it's a sign that the house is trying to take hold of her?'

'I do,' Luca replied.

'I've been thinking the same thing, but it's something I've been keeping an eye on. I really don't think we are at the stage of possession yet. Not even close.'

Luca shook his head, trying to hide his frustration. David was too naïve. Though, perhaps he himself had been as well. 'I think things may be further progressed than you think,' he said. 'That's twice now I've seen her in a trance-like state. And she admitted that kind of thing happened back when she lived here with her sister, correct?'

David nodded. 'Correct.'

'Well, given what we know now about how Chloe died, that is proof of how quickly things can escalate in this house. I'm just concerned Perron Manor may have more of a hold on Sarah than even she is aware of.'

'You think it's possible to become fully possessed in such a short space of time?'

'Normally no, not at all. It would take a few months at least. But we are not in a normal situation. Either the forces behind Perron Manor are able to take hold of people quicker than I've ever seen, or there is another factor at play. Regardless, I'm worried the situation could get out of hand.'

'Then we'll keep a close eye on her,' David said. 'Unless you have another idea?'

Luca did not. He still needed to complete his work with the book, as ordered.

He let out a sigh. 'Fine. But make sure you don't let her out of your sight.'

David gave a firm nod. 'No problem.'

'You best go back inside,' Luca continued and retrieved his mobile phone from his pocket. 'I'm going to call the Bishop and update him. With any luck, he might agree that we don't need to be here any longer.'

'You're going to stay in the corridor on your own?' David asked with a look of concern.

'I'll be fine, David,' Luca replied. 'I'm right outside the door and will be straight back in after I've finished the call.'

David hesitated, but soon relented and went back into the bedroom, closing the door behind him. Luca unlocked his phone, scrolled down to the Bishop's private number, and hit dial.

It rang a few times then clicked to voicemail.

'It's Luca,' he said into the phone. 'There have been some developments. Activity in the house is... severe, and though I'm not certain yet, I am confident the book in Miss Pearson's possession is the real *Ianua Diaboli*. I also believe the house is indeed what we feared it to be. Again, I can't yet be one-hundred-percent certain, but I can see no other explanation for the level of activity we've seen here. Not only that, it has become apparent that the sister of Miss Pearson—Chloe Shaw—was killed by a demonic presence after only a month and a half inside the house. Please call back and advise. Until then, I will continue as ordered.'

He then ended the call and stared at his phone, hoping the Bishop would quickly get back to him and end the investigation. Then Luca could be free of this accursed house forever.

Bishop Turnbull strode down the hallway of the Cathedral Church of St Nicholas on his way to his meeting. The marble floor echoed his footsteps as he walked, the ceremonial purple robes he wore billowing around his legs. He had a file gripped in one hand, and his mobile phone was wedged between the document and his thumb. The phone lit up, showing he had received a voicemail. He stopped with a frown.

Strange it didn't ring first.

Bishop Turnbull placed the phone to his ear and listened to the message. However, he heard nothing but a few seconds of static. The Bishop then checked his call log. The only call he'd received had been that morning, but there had been nothing recent.

So he listened to the voicemail again, hearing the same static, and at the end he selected the option to ring back the caller. As soon as he did, it clicked to a voicemail of its own, and he heard Father Janosch's voice:

'You have reached Father Janosch. I am unable to come to the phone right now, but if you would please leave a message, I will get back to you as soon as I am able.'

'Luca, it's me,' Bishop Turnbull said. 'I think you tried to leave me a message, but I couldn't make anything out. Get back to me if you need anything. Also, I am keen to get an update. We *all* are, Father. So please carry on and get what we need. There can be no mistakes.'

He ended the call and carried on to his meeting. It would have been good to speak to Father Janosch before going in, as there were some important people waiting to hear what Luca had found out.

CHAPTER 40

Jenn was exhausted.

They all were. She could see it on the faces of everyone as they again congregated in the dining room and watched Father Janosch work.

Thoughts of running any sessions to gain further evidence had gone out of the window. After David and Sarah's confessions, the mood was grim. Everyone was wiped, and setting up another activity seemed like too much work. At least for tonight.

Instead, Father Janosch had insisted they keep going with the book, so the others had joined him.

However, as well as being tired, Jenn was angry. She kept it to herself for the good of the group, but the fact Sarah had lied to them about what happened to her sister enraged Jenn.

She was also angry that David hadn't told anyone else that it was Chloe who had leapt on him the previous night. Jenn had seen the face of that crazed woman; however, she had never met Chloe in life, so she hadn't made the connection. But it seemed like important information they all should have been privy to.

Apparently everyone had been harbouring their little secrets. Everyone except Jenn.

In truth, she just wanted to go home now. She needed sleep.

Evidently, she wasn't alone in that respect. A light snoring beside her drew her attention. David's head had dropped forward and his eyes were closed. Everyone turned to look at him.

'Is he asleep?' Sarah asked.

Jenn chuckled. 'It's been a long day.'

'Quite,' Father Janosch agreed. 'Perhaps we should all call it a night.'

He checked his phone again, something he'd been doing a lot in the past few hours, always followed by a look of disappointment.

Expecting a call, Father? Jenn wondered.

'That sounds like a good idea,' Sarah said. She pushed her chair back and rose to her feet, stretching her arms up above her head and letting out a groan.

'Where are we all sleeping?' Jenn asked. Her gear was in the room she had been sharing with Ann the previous night, but she'd be damned if she was staying in a room on her own tonight.

'I'm not sure,' Sarah replied. 'Do you think we'll all fit into one bedroom?'

Jenn thought about that, and she doubted it.

Father Janosch stood up as well and laid a hand on David's shoulder, giving him a gentle shake. David's eyes snapped open and he straightened up in shock. He looked up at the others in obvious confusion.

'I fell asleep, didn't I?' he asked.

Father Janosch laughed. 'You did. Come on, it's time for bed.'

David ran a hand through his hair, shook his head, then got up. 'Yeah, I think that's wise.'

'Jenn has raised a good point,' Sarah said. 'I'm not sure if four of us will fit into one room. Unless we clear out all beds and just use mattresses. But that's gonna be a lot of work.'

'I don't want us splitting into two rooms,' David stated.

'Okay,' Sarah went on. 'The biggest room is the one Jenn and Ann were using. I'll share a bed with Jenn'—she looked over to Jenn—'if you're okay with it? And then we can pull in some mattresses for you two,' she then pointed at David and Father Janosch.

'Makes sense,' David said. 'Yeah, let's do it.'

Jenn wasn't sure how happy she was with that, especially given Sarah's penchant for sleepwalking. The idea of waking up to see Sarah standing above her made Jenn shiver. Was it too late to just back out of the whole thing entirely? Jenn subtly checked her watch and saw it was close to midnight.

Come on, she said to herself, *you're here for a reason. Get on with it.*

While that was true, how far did her desire to find out the truth really go? After all, she probably had all the evidence she really needed now. Of course, there was still the issue of Chloe and the whole fucking Devil's Doorway business.

And also David's sister…

He was her oldest friend. Could she really abandon him when he needed her most?

After brief consideration, she decided she could not, and that realisation gave Jenn extra resolve to continue.

The group got to work rearranging the room as needed and pulling in the extra mattresses. In the end, the room looked like it was hosting a kid's sleepover. Everyone brought in their clothes and bags, and when finished, it was a tight fit.

'There aren't any cameras in here,' Jenn said.

Father Janosch, who was sitting on one of the mattresses on the floor, frowned. 'What do you mean?'

'We set up cameras in the other room to film Sarah and me during the night,' David clarified. 'But we don't have one mounted in here.'

'Do we need to get one ready?' Jenn asked. It was David's turn to check his watch now.

'It's going on twelve-thirty,' he said. 'That might take close to another hour.' He chewed his lip for a few seconds. 'We'll leave it for tonight,' he finally said. 'With four of us in here, we should be okay. If Sarah does try to sleepwalk, she'll probably trip over someone before she gets very far anyway.'

With that decided, everyone got themselves ready for bed, each using the adjoining bathroom to change into their sleeping clothes, though they kept the door open as they did. Finally, everyone settled down, but Jenn couldn't shake how uncomfortable she felt lying next to Sarah.

Stay in fucking bed, she silently pleaded. *Just for tonight.*

CHAPTER 41

Sarah was sinking into the earth again, getting dragged lower and lower through the soil and rock.

Kill him.

Farther down.

Kill him and come home.

Farther.

I'm waiting for you... Sis.

The earth around her changed the lower Sarah got. It eventually became flesh. Warm and wet. She saw faces grafted into the meat.

Some of them were strangers. One she knew.

Tania.

Tania's face was fixed into a scream.

The flesh around Sarah contracted, pressing into her.

Tania spoke. *'Release me. Kill him and release me.'*

Lower and lower.

Come home, Sis.

Sarah's eyes slowly opened. She felt cold and exposed, and it was dark all around her.

Her eyes slowly started to adjust, and through the thick shadows she was just able to make out her surroundings. Sarah quickly drew in a panicked breath.

She was down in the basement. Alone. Instinctively hugging herself in a vain effort to ward off the cold, she turned around, taking in as much of the area around her as she could. Everything was quiet, with only her own jagged breathing breaking the silence.

How the fuck did I get down here?

She knew the answer almost as soon as she'd asked the question. Her sleepwalking had taken her farther than usual. And, evidently, she hadn't woken the others when leaving the bedroom. They were likely still asleep. Unless, of course, something had happened to them.

Get a grip and stay calm, she ordered herself. *You've been in worse situations.*

Sarah closed her eyes and slowly brought her breathing under control, taking long inhales and letting out slow exhales.

Calm. Keep focused.

She opened her eyes again. There didn't seem to be any immediate danger, despite the strangeness of the situation, so all she had to do was get to the steps and head back upstairs. Simple.

A hoarse, gravelly, feminine... and familiar... voice cut through the silence.

'Hi, Sis.'

Sarah gasped and turned her head towards the furnace, which she could barely see due to the lack of light. The archaic heating device was almost completely covered in shadow.

Almost.

Sarah could, however, just make out its front, where the grills were open. There was no one inside.

It turned out Chloe was not inside of it, but on top of it. Her decayed face came forwards, swimming out from the darkness, as she crouched on the metal structure.

Her eyes were a dull white with no pupils, her skin was mottled grey, and her brown hair was thin and greasy.

My beautiful sister, reduced to this.

Chloe opened her mouth into a grin, revealing cracked and yellowed teeth, as well as blackened gums. A purple tongue slithered from her mouth and ran across her dry lower lip.

Sarah couldn't move, rooted to the spot in fear. Her sister then pulled back and once again disappeared into the darkness.

'We've been waiting for you,' Chloe said from the shadows. *'But you're home now.'*

A giggle. Chloe's voice was not her own, not quite like Sarah remembered it. It had a strained and almost distorted quality to it. Sarah then heard a noise from behind her, a sound that was something between a growl and a laugh. Not human. Sarah turned to the old cells that lined one of the far walls. The growl had come from one of them, though whatever had made it was hidden away.

'Don't worry about him,' Chloe said. *'You'll meet him soon enough.'*

Sarah snapped her head back towards the furnace.

'What do you want?' Sarah asked.

Another giggle from Chloe. *'Stop fighting, Sarah. Give yourself to us.'*

There was a skittering sound of something crawling over metal. Then Chloe emerged from the shadows again, this time standing next to the furnace. Sarah was now able to take in all her horrible, naked form: her sagging breasts, concave stomach with overhanging ribs, peeling and dry skin, and black fingers.

Chloe took a step forward.

'Stay back,' Sarah said, though her voice was a whimper.

This can't be Chloe. It can't be.

'Our mother was alone in this basement once as well, just like you. The house took her.'

'Leave me alone,' Sarah said, taking a step back.

'And then the house made *you*, Sarah. Can't you feel the connection to it? To Mother. And to your dear Papa... Marcus?'

Chloe stepped forward again. Another growl sounded from behind Sarah.

It occurred to her that she could break for the steps and take her chances, but the overwhelming fear that held her would just not let go.

'You're special, Sis. And we're going to take you now. You've been resisting, but no more. We need you to do something for us.'

'Get away from me!' Sarah bellowed.

'Kill him, Sarah. Kill him and come home to me.'

Chloe then dropped to all fours and let out another horrible giggle. Sarah screamed as the twisted version of her sister quickly scuttled forward with her belly pressed low to the ground. She moved like a spider, and cackled while wearing a manic grin.

Sarah turned, managing to overcome her fear enough to finally move. However, she screamed again as she turned straight into the thing that was looming behind her; it was tall and black, with a hideous mouth full of nightmarish teeth as well as melted facial features. A sickening smell of sulphur overpowered Sarah.

Despite the terror she felt when the monster grabbed her, Sarah recognised what it was—the demon that had killed her sister.

And now it had her too.

It lifted her easily from the ground, talon-like hands gripping her upper arms, and brought her closer.

Sarah kicked and flailed as the demon's mouth opened, then closed it over her own.

CHAPTER 42

Jenn opened her eyes, disturbed by movement in the room.

It was still dark. She could hear something shuffle about at the end of her bed and lifted her head, peering through the darkness.

'Sarah?' she asked.

Sarah seemed to be bending down, but quickly straightened back up and looked at Jenn.

'Yeah?'

'What are you doing?' Jenn asked.

'I needed the toilet,' Sarah whispered in response. 'It's a bit tricky climbing over everyone to get back to bed.'

'Okay,' Jenn said. 'What time is it?'

'Not sure. About four, I think.'

Jenn watched as Sarah stepped over David, moved back around to her side of the bed, and got in. As she did, Jenn felt a coldness radiate from the woman, enough to make Jenn tense up and shiver.

'Jesus,' she said. 'Have you been sitting in a fridge?'

Sarah gave a light laugh. 'No, but it's fucking cold in here.' Sarah then lay down and pulled the covers over her body.

Jenn wrapped her side of the duvet tightly around herself as well, hoping to ward off some of the cold Sarah was generating.

Despite the chill, Jenn was just glad Sarah hadn't been sleepwalking again.

Sarah had almost had her hands around David's neck when that bitch Jenn had woken up and ruined everything.

Still, it was a lesson. With the four of them together, could she really have gotten the job done without anyone else intervening?

She would need to get him alone.

Then, Sarah would be allowed to come home. For now, however, she had to be patient.

CHAPTER 43

LUCA TOOK another sip of his coffee.

They'd had a full day at it and evening was drawing in again, darkening the skies outside. They were in the dining room with *Ianua Diaboli* and the ledger. A constant *tap, tap, tap* of rain hitting the window could be heard.

Yet again, Luca was at the head of the table, with David and Jenn on one side of him and Sarah on the other.

It had been another long day and they had not left each other's sides. They had continued researching the book for a while, and Luca had noted references to the Seven Gates. That troubled him greatly. They also ran some sessions to try and draw out the spirits of the house. However, the results had been… disappointing. Luca had still not seen anything in the house with his own eyes.

The only thing of note was the phone call from Ralph, where he'd told David that he and the others were coming back to the house to get the rest of their stuff. They wouldn't be staying, however.

Sarah was certainly eager to get things moving. Though she physically looked exhausted, she moved with enthusiasm and energy, like a madwoman. She had been like that all day.

'We should split up into two groups,' she said at the table. 'It'll be fine. Jenn can stay here with Father Janosch to work on the book; David, you can come with me and we can run a vigil or EMP experiment or something.'

Luca could tell by David's expression that he wasn't about to go along with her idea.

'No,' he replied. 'We should stick together as much as possible.'

'But we need to be doing *two* jobs,' Sarah argued. 'Luca needs to do his thing with the book, but we also still need to be cataloguing any evidence we can. Last night was a bust, so we need to be proactive.'

'Then we'll just keep alternating,' David argued.

'We were going to do that last night,' Sarah said. 'But then we just ended up back in here, twiddling our thumbs while Luca carried on with the book. The rest of us are nothing more than third wheels.'

'Sorry, Sarah, but that's final.' David folded his arms over his chest. 'We need to be cautious here. You heard what Luca told us yesterday about what this place *could* be. I'm not going to put people at any more risk than we absolutely have to.'

Sarah shook her head in disgust. Luca could feel the anger radiate from her. Thankfully, she stayed silent and sat back in her chair, folding her arms as well.

David looked over to Luca. 'Please carry on.'

Luca started to read from the ledger.

He had picked up an unclear voicemail earlier from Bishop Turnbull. It seemed the message had been left the previous day, though Luca had been unaware of it until now.

The message was mostly just static but cleared up at the end, where Luca heard the Bishop state: *'So please, carry on and get what we need. There can be no mistakes.'*

Though the rest of the message was lost to a bad line, the intent of it had been clear: keep going.

That made sense. While he acknowledged the evidence David had shown him was compelling, as was *Ianua Diaboli*, Luca had seen nothing for himself as yet. It was all secondhand accounts, along with the footage. It was certainly enough to convince *him*, but could he claim with absolute certainty that what he'd been shown wasn't doctored or manufactured somehow? There was a chance the others were all in on it together in an attempt to gain some kind of plaudits.

He didn't believe that, of course. Not one bit. But other people might. And he knew the Church would be reluctant to involve itself in something that could damage its reputation—especially since that reputation had already eroded immensely over the last few decades. Attendance at sermons across most European countries was at an all-time low, and people were turning away from God in droves. So now the Church was nothing if not careful.

Luca had spent the previous day cross-checking the ledger against *Ianua Diaboli* to ensure the translations were accurate. Everything he'd seen indicated they were. So, feeling a desperate need to speed things up, he decided to focus purely on the ledger itself, which he could get through much quicker, only checking *Ianua Diaboli* to reference some of the hand-drawn sketches within its pages.

Whoever had written that book seemed to have a deep knowledge of what a Devil's Door was, and also how to leverage its power. If it was all genuine, Luca had to wonder about the book's author. How could he—or she—know so much? Where had that understanding come from? And what was the purpose of writing it all down? Who was the author looking to share his knowledge with? So many unanswered questions.

There was another mystery as well. Because the ledger and *Ianua Diaboli* had been at the house for such a long time, at least before Marcus Blackwater took ownership, Luca wondered if the book was somehow related to the horrible events back in 1982. The massacre had long been unexplained.

The others sat in silence as Luca worked. It was a little uncomfortable, having all eyes on him, and he could indeed sympathise with Sarah. It *did* seem like a waste of resources to have everyone sit and watch him read from the ledger when they could be doing something more productive. However, David was ultimately right—splitting the teams into smaller groups was just asking for trouble.

As he continued to read, Luca found himself skimming the pages, satisfied once he got the gist of each particular section, whether it be a ritual, a curse, even a rite. One part even detailed how it was possible to reanimate a dead body using a soul or demon via a Devil's Door. That was something Luca didn't want to think about for too long.

He moved quicker, only scanning the titles of each section in order to get an idea of what was ahead. After another hour of reading, he hit on something interesting.

Luca quickly cross-referenced what he saw against *Ianua Diaboli*, just to satisfy himself. The title of that chapter in the old book read *Impius Sanguis*.

Accursed Blood.

As Luca read through the pages of the ledger, a growing sense of unease worked its way up from his gut. The point of the ritual was to impregnate a host, one that was possessed by the forces that flowed through the door. The reward for the man giving his seed was free will after death, along with great power. The only requirement was the man himself was not under the control of any supernatural forces.

One phrase stood out: *Enim sanguis clavis est*. The blood is the key.

The ledger stated that the newborn child would be *clavis*—the key—and would unlock *Portae Septem*, the Seven Gates.

Luca's stomach tightened up. To complete *Impius Sanguis*, it said the doorway needed to be opened wider to draw power, and it needed souls to do that.

His mind immediately ran back to 1982 and the massacre on Halloween. How many people had gone missing that night? Luca couldn't remember exactly, but possibly enough to further open the door.

Could *Impius Sanguis* have been carried out that night by someone at the hotel? And if so, was an unholy child created?

He kept reading as the passages went on to detail the role of the Accursed Blood. After reaching adulthood, they needed to return back to a Devil's Doorway so their minds could be 'soured.' Then, when under possession, they had to offer up the soul of an innocent—killing someone by their own hand.

Their transformation would then be complete. If all Seven Gates were open during or after the Accursed Blood's transformation, the merging of Hell and Earth would begin.

Luca sat back in his chair, feeling all energy drain out of him.

'Are you okay, Father?' David asked.

However, Luca was not really paying attention, instead staring at Sarah. He knew her age, so could work out her birth year from there.

1983. *Could it be?*

'Sarah?' he asked.

She looked up. 'Yeah?'

'This might sound like a strange question, but could you tell me what month you were born?'

She paused, then her face fell. Her jaw tensed up and her eyes narrowed.

'Why is that important?' she asked.

Luca felt a knot in the pit of his stomach.

'Didn't you say you were a July baby?' Jenn cut in.

Nine months prior to July would put the conception at around October 1982.

'Why is that important?' David asked.

'Do you realise you may have been conceived at this house, Sarah?' Luca asked, keeping his eyes firmly on her. He saw her jaw tense again.

She slowly nodded. 'Yes, of course. I've always realised that was a possibility. I *can* count, for God's sake.'

Sarah made his question sound like a ridiculous one, but Luca could tell from her hate-filled glare that she knew he knew.

'And your father,' Luca went on to ask. 'Did he ever take in interest in *Ianua Diaboli*, or the ledger, when he lived here?'

Sarah shrugged and slid her empty coffee mug over towards herself. She cupped it in her hands and started to slowly rotate it on the table. 'How could I possibly know that for sure?' she said. 'But I doubt it. Dad was never one for that kind of thing. He was a simple man.'

Luca wasn't sure whether to believe her. If Sarah was the key, either her dad *had* to have used the book... or her father wasn't who she thought.

Luca's mind raced. *What do I do?* The book said that the key needed to be possessed again before taking a life. So... was Sarah possessed at that moment, or was the house still working on her?

He brought up a hand and took hold of the crucifix he wore, rubbing it between his fingers. He always did it absent-mindedly when nervous. And he was *definitely* nervous.

Jenn spoke up. 'I'm confused here, are you two angry at each other over something? You could cut the tension with a knife. What's going on?'

'Not angry,' Luca said. 'Just curious. How are you feeling, Sarah? Like yourself?'

She smiled. It wasn't a pleasant one. 'I'm fine, Father. Just eager to move things along. So how about we put those books away and go and gather some evidence? You can come with me if you want? Then we can talk more.'

'We don't split up,' David said. 'You *know* that, Sarah.' He turned from Sarah to Luca, then back again. 'Seriously, what the hell's going on here? It's like you two are having a stand-off.'

'Care to tell them, Sarah?' Luca asked.

'I have no idea what you're talking about... *priest*,' she said, the final word spoken with pure hatred. Her face suddenly twisted into a hideous snarl and, in the same instant, she raised her coffee cup and drove it down onto the surface of the table. The ceramic mug shattered. Luca instinctively pushed himself back from the table, as did David and Jenn.

'What the...' was all David managed to get out before Sarah snatched up a long, jagged shard. With frightening speed, she hopped up onto the table and lunged at Luca, who held his hands up to stop her. He managed to wrap his fingers around the wrist of her leading arm.

Luca fell backwards to the floor and Sarah on top of him. She screamed like an animal and tried to force the point of the shard down into his throat. Luca cried out, pushing up against her with everything he had. However, she was too strong, and the makeshift ceramic weapon lowered slowly until the point found his neck.

He felt the skin puncture.

No! Not like this!

Luca sensed movement around them both. Sarah was then yanked off him and thrown back. David and Jenn stood above Luca, looking horrified. Luca quickly brought his hand to his throat and felt a sting.

He looked at his fingers and saw spots of blood, but knew the wound wasn't deep or serious.

He had been lucky.

'Sarah, what the fuck are you doing?!' David screamed.

Luca pulled himself to a sitting position, where he was just able to see Sarah over the top of the dining room table. The horrible snarl was still etched on her face. She looked at him, then at the other two. Luca saw that the shard was no longer in her hand, but now on the floor close to him.

Would she attack again without a weapon?

'Stay back from her,' Luca said as he climbed to his feet. 'She's possessed.'

David and Jenn both looked shocked. 'What… when?' David asked.

Sarah began to laugh. 'You're all fucking pathetic, you know that? You'll die tonight. Every last one of you. By *my* hand.'

She then turned and ran from the room.

'What the fuck is going on?' David asked with urgency.

'It's true,' Luca replied, trying to take deep, slow breaths. 'There can be no doubt any more. The book, the house, everything is as we'd feared. Sarah is at the centre of it all.'

'I still don't understand,' David said.

So Luca explained as quickly as he could. About *Impius Sanguis, Portae Septem,* and about Sarah being the key. He also told them how she needed to take a life while under the control of the house.

'If she kills one of us, then the results could be… unimaginable,' Luca finished.

Jenn slumped down to a chair. 'I… I don't fucking believe this.'

'I understand,' Luca said. 'But you need to come to terms with it quickly. There may still be hope, but we need to be very careful.' He lifted *Ianua Diaboli* from the table. 'The first time I looked at this, I skimmed the very end of the book, just out of interest. There is a ritual there, *Claude Ianua*. It could help us.'

'Phone the Church,' David stated. 'This is too much for us. You have to get someone else here quickly.'

'I can try,' Luca said, 'but time is of the essence. If Sarah manages to kill one of us—'

'Then we run!' Jenn snapped. 'We get the hell out of here and leave Sarah alone until someone better equipped can get here.'

'And what if she got to someone else in that time?' Luca asked. 'Dragged them back here after we ran?'

Luca didn't want to disagree with Jenn. He wanted to run every bit as much as she did. To stay could mean not just the end of their lives but also eternal damnation for their souls. It would be pain and unimaginable torture... forever.

But what were their own lives compared to the lives of everyone on Earth? They had to try.

'Shit,' David said and ran a hand through his hair. He looked ashen. Jenn did as well. And Luca couldn't blame them. The situation was madness.

But they had to get through it.

'I'm scared,' Jenn said.

'I am too,' Luca admitted. 'But if we stick together, then the three of us should be able to hold her off if we need to.'

'But what about the house?' Jenn said. 'We wouldn't just be fighting against Sarah. We'd be fighting everything else inside this place.'

'Then we need to be quick,' David said. Luca saw that his hands were trembling. 'The ritual you mentioned, *Claude*... whatever it was. How does it work?'

'I'll explain later,' Luca said and set the book down, flicking through the pages to the back. He then opened the ledger up to the same place and started to read. The other two had their eyes fixed on the open door to the room.

He was thankful that *Claude Ianua* was not a complicated ritual to carry out. It brought with it great danger, but if everything went well it would be relatively easy to set up and follow. It surprised him that closing the doorways could be so straightforward, but then again, it could well have been a safeguard—a way to quickly cut off the book's power if needed.

A sound drew their attention. The low rumble came from a distance, but was getting close.

It was an engine.

'Shit,' David said. 'It's Ralph and the others. We have to warn them. If Sarah gets to them first... They don't know what's happening here.'

Luca gathered up both books, and the three of them sprinted towards the front of the house. As they broke through to the entrance lobby, Luca saw the front door was already open.

He heard Ralph's voice outside. 'Hey, Sarah, how have things been? Any other... Sarah! What the hell are you doing?!'

Ralph screamed.

CHAPTER 44

JENN'S MIND was in overdrive trying to catch up with what was happening. She had heard Ralph scream, followed by the panicked voices of the rest of the group outside. David got through the front door first, with Jenn, then Father Janosch following close behind. Jenn heard a thud on the marble floor beside her while still in the entrance lobby, and turned to see that Father Janosch had dropped the books. She didn't need to ask why. The rain outside was heavy, and could damage or ruin *Ianua Diaboli*.

Jenn ran out onto the front porch and into the driving downpour. The scene before her was one of chaos. Sarah was being dragged off Ralph, and he lay on the ground writhing in agony as the rain hammered down on him. George and Jamie wrestled with Sarah as she fought like an animal. The two men were clearly struggling but managed to push her to the ground. Jamie had an obvious gash across his forearm, and it was then Jenn saw that Sarah was holding a long kitchen knife which glistened with blood. Her hair was matted to her head.

Jenn's eyes snapped back over to Ralph as they ran towards him. He was clutching his stomach with his teeth clenched together in a pained expression. Though he was wearing a dark blue hoodie, Jenn could see an even darker wet patch pool out from beneath his hands.

'What the fuck are you doing?' George screamed to Sarah as Jamie cradled his arm.

Sarah took a step towards them with the knife raised. Her teeth were clenched and her eyes were filled with fury and hatred.

'Sarah!' David screamed. She turned to see David, Jenn, and Father Janosch advance. At first, she stepped forward towards them, seeming ready to take them all on. That terrified Jenn. However, a look of hesitation flashed over Sarah's face. She then turned and ran, sprinting over to the van the others had arrived in. Sarah thrust the knife into the front tire. Once, twice, three times.

'What the fuck are you doing?' Jamie screamed at her. However, neither he nor George dared to get to close. Sarah moved on to the other front tire and slashed at it wildly before running off again.

'Leave her,' David ordered to Jenn and Father Janosch. 'Get to Ralph.'

The three continued over to their fallen friend, the wet gravel crunching underfoot. Ann knelt next to Ralph and had his head on her lap.

'Help,' Ralph wheezed. He looked terrified, clutching his stomach. The rain hammered down on him.

'What do we do?' Ann asked, close to tears.

George was suddenly next to them, and he already had his mobile phone out. 'We need to call an ambulance.' He typed the emergency number into his keypad and put the phone to his ear. Jenn surveyed the area around them, but was unable to spot Sarah.

'She ran,' Jamie said to them with a hand clutched around his bleeding forearm. 'Over there.' He pointed over to one side of the house where the carport stood, covering the vehicles inside in shadow.

'She's going to slash the tires!' Jenn yelled.

David lifted up Ralph's hoodie to see a gash, the width of a knife blade, in his lower left side. Blood ran freely.

'Shit!' George yelled. 'I can't get any reception. What the hell! Anyone else?'

Jenn tried her phone but got a similar result to George. 'How can that be? Reception isn't great here, but we've never had this happen before.'

'It's the house,' Father Janosch said. Jenn heard a bang over in the carport.

Sarah was getting to work.

'We need to get Ralph inside,' David said, 'and out of the rain. I have a first aid-kit in there. Come on, help me.'

Jenn didn't want to go back in the house, but they were out of options. They couldn't use any of the vehicles to get away, Sarah had seen to that, and it had proven impossible to get through to the police or an ambulance.

She again looked over to the cars and saw Sarah standing watching them, smiling. The woman then slowly turned and ran into the shadows, towards the back of the grounds.

'Help us!' David yelled at Jenn. The others had crouched around Ralph, ready to lift his bulky frame. Jenn squatted down as well.

'On three,' David stated. 'One… two… three!'

They all strained. Ralph was even heavier than Jenn had been expecting, but they managed to lift him.

'What the hell is going on here, David?' George asked, panicked.

Jenn felt her fingers straining under Ralph's weight.

'I'll explain inside,' David replied. 'But we have to be quick.' They then shuffled their way back over to the door, accompanied by Ralph's screams of pain.

CHAPTER 45

'Take him to the dining room,' David said as they re-entered the entrance lobby. He was drenched to the bone and struggling with Ralph, his arms aching as the large man's weight became difficult to handle. 'We'll put him on the table.'

It was the best place he could think of. Already David's mind was racing through what to do next. If they couldn't get Ralph to a hospital, or get an ambulance out to the house, David would need to do his best to keep his friend alive.

However, his first-aid training probably wouldn't be enough.

Ralph's weight grew heavier as Father Janosch broke away from them.

'Father!' George snapped.

But the priest simply ran over to the corner of the room and picked up *Ianua Diaboli* and the ledger, which had been discarded on the floor.

'We need these!' he insisted and led the way over to the dining room. His head was on a constant swivel as if expecting something to leap out.

When David and the others were finally able to lower Ralph down to the dining room table, David felt relief in his arms. He lifted Ralph's hoodie again and saw the blood still running from the wound. David moved his hands over the gash and pressed down, applying as much pressure as he could, and drawing out another yowl of pain from Ralph.

Shit. This is beyond me.

'I need some blankets and my first-aid kit,' David ordered the others, while still trying to keep his focus. Blood pooled on the table below Ralph, and it seeped out quickly along the polished surface. David just hoped that no major arteries had been cut. 'The kit is in my room,' he said. 'Just grab the brown leather bag up there.'

Father Janosch had moved to the far end of the table and set both books down, opening them towards the back. He scanned the pages, mainly looking at the ledger.

What the hell is he doing?

'I'll go,' Jenn said to David. She looked pale and terrified, but David was glad she was brave enough to offer. There was zero chance of her going alone, however.

'George, Jamie, you two go with her.'

Neither looked enthused, though Jamie appeared to be the more hesitant of the pair. He had his own injury, still holding his bleeding forearm. The long cut was across the top, however, and away from the veins beneath the wrist.

'Wait!' Father Janosch said. 'We need some other things as well.'

'What are you talking about, Father?' David asked, still pressing down on Ralph.

'We need to stop what is happening here. If Ralph dies, you know what that means.'

George threw his hands up in the air. 'Can someone please explain what is going on?!'

Father Janosch ignored the frantic question and again addressed David. 'I need my Bible. And I also need some salt, candles, water, and some soil. A mirror, too.'

'For what?' David asked.

'Something I'm ill-prepared for... but we have no other choice. There is a ritual in *Ianua Diaboli* that I think closes the door. But it is dangerous.'

'Ralph is in trouble,' Jenn said. 'We need to—'

'I know how this is going to sound,' Father Janosch cut in. 'But if Ralph dies before we close the door... the consequences could be dire.'

'What the fuck is going on?!' Ann screamed in utter frustration. Her voice bellowed so loudly it momentarily drowned out the sound of rain outside.

'David can explain it to you,' Father Janosch said. 'I'll go with the others to get what we need, and I'll update them as best I can as well. But we all need to hurry.'

'Go,' David said to him.

'And everyone remember,' the priest added. 'If you see Sarah, avoid her. Run. Do *not* let her harm you.' He took a breath. 'Kill her if you must.'

'You can't be serious,' Jamie said in disbelief.

David felt for Jamie. For all of them. They had walked into a nightmare that he himself could scarcely wrap his head around.

'There is a mirror in the bag with my first-aid kit,' David said.

Katie's mirror. His good-luck charm.

'My Bible is up there, too,' Father Janosch said. 'And I have a flask we can use to collect the water. But we also need soil, candles, and salt.'

'You can get soil from the gardens,' David said. 'But candles… I don't know.'

'The kitchen,' Jenn said. 'There are some in the kitchen.'

'Be careful,' David added. 'All of you.'

Father Janosch nodded. 'Protect the books,' he said and motioned towards *Ianua Diaboli* and the ledger.

Father Janosch, Jenn, Jamie, and George then all walked from the room, leaving David with Ann and Ralph.

'I need something to cover the wound,' he said. Ann looked terrified but slipped off her coat. She then ripped at the arm of her net top that covered a purple blouse beneath. The material tore easily, and she handed it to David. He clamped it down onto the seeping cut in Ralph's stomach.

'What… did he mean, David?' Ralph said, struggling with his words. 'About closing the door before I die?'

David let out a sigh, and began to tell them everything.

CHAPTER 46

LUCA STRODE through the hallways of Perron Manor, keeping his hands clenched into fists, if only to stop them from trembling. He was on edge, and as alert as he'd ever been in his life; his eyes darted about and checked all corners as they moved. Sarah was in the house somewhere, lurking and waiting.

I can't do this. I'm going to fail.

En-route to the stairs, the group quickly ducked into the ground-floor study to try the landline there. It was dead.

Unless they ran off into the night, they were trapped at Perron Manor. However, there was no way they would be able to take Ralph if they did run, not without exacerbating his injury. And if he died before they got off the grounds…

As much as Luca hated the idea, he knew that closing the door was the only option.

I can't do this!

He was terrified, and the task ahead overwhelmed him.

They had been careless and hadn't taken the danger the house posed seriously enough.

He should have just followed Sarah's advice and told the Church that Perron Manor was indeed what they feared, even if he hadn't been certain. Consequences be damned.

If he had, then someone far more capable could have come to handle things. The rest of them could have gotten Sarah out of the house before she was turned. But no, Luca had hesitated and second-guessed himself. His handling of the whole situation had been terrible.

Now they could all lose their lives because of it. No, not just their lives. They would be prisoners of Perron Manor for eternity, stumbling among the dead in pain and agony—forever suffering the rot of their decaying souls.

Undead puppets to an unknowable master.

'Spill it, Father,' Jamie said as they started up the stairs. 'You owe us an explanation. Why was Ralph attacked? What the hell happened to Sarah?'

'She's possessed,' Luca replied. 'The house has her now. However, there is more...'

He managed to briefly explain their situation—at least, as best as he could in such a short space of time: Perron Manor *was* a Devil's Door, Sarah was under its possession, and she was also born of the house—her bloodline tinged with evil.

'Impossible,' George said after the explanation. 'That can't be true.'

'It is, George,' Jenn said.

But George shook his head. 'I'm sorry, but there is no way this whole thing has devolved into the possibility of the world ending.'

'Not ending,' Luca replied. 'Merging with Hell.'

'Same difference.'

True enough.

They entered the bedroom, where everyone had earlier dumped all their belongings, George ran over to grab David's bag as Luca retrieved his flask and Bible from his satchel. Luca then ran a hand over the front of the holy book. It had a burgundy leather cover with gold writing and a black embossed cross in the centre. The flask was glass and fit comfortably in the palm of his hand, with a plastic screw cap at the top.

'We need to get the first-aid kit to David before we get the rest of the stuff,' Jamie said.

'I really think we need to gather the other items we need first,' Luca insisted.

'And why the hell do we need all that? Candles and earth and whatever?'

Luca strode from the room first as the others kept pace.

'*Claude Ianua*,' Luca replied as they moved back towards the stairs. 'The ritual to close the door.'

'It needs candles and water?' Jenn asked.

'Fire, water, earth, and air,' Luca confirmed. 'The four elements. They need to be blessed by a holy man, and used as part of the ritual. The elements come together to join our own world to the other, to Hell, so we can then close the door.'

'Sounds insane,' Jamie said.

It was. The whole thing was insane.

Once they reached the bottom of the stairs, Jenn spoke up. 'There are candles and salt in the kitchen,' she said. 'But we need earth from outside. Do we split into groups?'

'It's dangerous,' Luca said.

'I know,' Jenn replied. 'But we don't have a lot of time. If we do split up and we're quick, we can all meet back up in the dining room in no time at all.'

Luca was torn. David would no doubt insist they stick together, given the group was already split, but Jenn was right: speed was of the essence.

He couldn't risk it.

Luca shook his head. 'You might be right, but if we thin our numbers any more and Sarah is hiding, there's a higher chance someone could lose their life. Come on, let's get to the kitchen.'

They ran as one and cut through the house. Luca hated the waiting. Their passage had been easy so far, which meant Sarah wasn't likely close, but that in itself unnerved him. He would prefer to know for sure where she was hiding. In addition, Perron Manor itself hadn't tried to hinder their progress at all. Was it just leaving them to Sarah, or biding its time?

In the kitchen, Jenn dug through a set of drawers. 'The candles are in here,' she said. 'Matches too. How many candles you need?'

'Grab as many as you can carry,' Luca said, and Jenn tucked a bundle of them under her arm. The packet of matches was thrust into her pocket. The candles were short and wide, but would do for what Luca needed.

Luca himself rifled through the cupboards and found some table salt, and he also grabbed a Tupperware container, knowing he would need something to carry the soil in. Lastly, he filled his flask with water from the tap.

He hadn't yet told the others that the ritual couldn't be done in the dining room. They would need to get as deep in the ground as possible.

That meant getting everyone down to the basement.

Hold out, Ralph. Just a little longer.

When they had everything they could get from the kitchen, that left only one element: earth.

'Out the back,' Luca ordered.

They ran through to the great hall and continued over to the rear door. Luca stepped outside first, and a security light flicked on, pushing away the darkness. The rain hammered down onto the uneven paving, leaving stretches of puddles.

No one was out there.

Where are you, Sarah?

The others stepped outside as well. They all slowly made their way through the courtyard to the gardens beyond, getting drenched by the rain once again. Luca still expected *something* to happen.

But there was no attack and no spirits blocking their way.

'Quickly,' Luca ordered the group. They ran over to a flower bed and he filled the Tupperware container with black mud, then pressed the lid down.

That was everything they needed. He stood up and turned around.

Sarah was there, standing on the patio, knife in hand.

'Hello, Father,' she shouted over the sound of the falling rain. 'Care to come over here? I have something I want to show you.'

She had discarded her jumper, now wearing only a tank top and jeans. The wet and cold didn't seem to bother her at all.

'Let us pass, Sarah,' Luca shouted back. 'This isn't you. You're being controlled. Surely you know that?'

Sarah shook her head and gave a humourless laugh. 'No, priest, I am finally free. No more worry, no more doubt, no more pain... and no more guilt. It's a beautiful thing, Father. True freedom.'

'You're a puppet, Sarah,' Luca shouted back. 'A puppet to the house.'

'Better a puppet to something real than a servant to a false god. You're ruled by fear, little wretch. That's all you have in your life.'

She took a step forward.

Luca tensed up. With Jenn, George, and Jamie beside him, they had numbers on their side. But Sarah was an army girl, and she held that glistening knife. She didn't have to beat them in a fight—she just had to bury that blade into one of their throats.

And Luca was the oldest and slowest.

'If only your sister could see you now,' Luca yelled. 'How do you think she'd feel?'

'She *can* see me,' Sarah shouted. 'And I can see *her*. She's proud of me. If I plunge this blade into your flesh, then I can come home to her and be with her forever. She's waiting for me.'

'No,' Luca stated, shaking his head. 'The *real* Chloe exists here somewhere, yes, but *beneath* the evil. And she's horrified at what you're about to do. Don't you see? She wants you to fight this, Sarah. She *needs* you to. We all do.'

Sarah laughed, then tilted her head back to let the rain fall on her face. She lifted the knife and traced the blade down her throat, over her chest, and towards her crotch.

'There's nothing to fight, priest,' she said, dropping her head back down. 'Chloe tried to get away from this place, but it wanted her. *Needed* her. It called her back. She couldn't get away from it. Perron Manor always gets what it wants. So why resist?'

Something clicked into place for Luca.

'No, Sarah. It was never about Chloe. The house wanted *you* back. It almost had you, too, but Chloe managed to convince you to leave. So it took her, and showed her to you to lure you in. Don't you see? Perron Manor needed to keep you here just a little longer in order to finish what it started with you. If you give in to it, the house wins.'

It was all so obvious to him now. Chloe was never the focus of the house. It had always been about Sarah. Both sisters had been called back when needed, and it had gotten to work on Sarah, even killing Chloe to keep Sarah there longer.

Luca had always been confused at how quickly she was showing signs of succumbing to the forces here after only a few days during their investigation, and after only a month and a half when she'd lived here with Chloe. But she was the key. She was born of the house. She was one with it.

It was troubling to think how far into the future the tendrils of Perron Manor could reach in order to manipulate things. Did that mean events were already set in stone?

No, he couldn't accept that.

Sarah had stopped advancing, and he saw a flash of something on her face. Resistance. The real Sarah *was* in there. Perhaps he'd gotten through to her.

'Fight it, Sarah! For your sister!'

She gritted her teeth together and brought a hand up to her head. She winced. Luca could see the conflict and fight going on inside her.

'Sarah, please,' Jenn yelled over to her. 'Just stop this. Ralph could die. Let us help him.'

Sarah's eyes then opened wide. Her hand fell back down to her side and a hideous smile crossed her lips.

Sarah shook her head. 'No, you're planning something. You want to close the doorway. I can't allow that.'

Another step forward.

'What do we do?' Jamie asked Luca. Luca had no clue.

CHAPTER 47

Where the hell are they?

The others were taking their time and it was worrying David.

Ralph was struggling. He was still conscious but in tremendous pain. He looked pale. So very pale.

Ann had raided the chest of drawers at the far end of the room and found some tablecloths that they had used to press onto Ralph's wound in an attempt to stem the flow of blood. David still pushed down with as much pressure as he could safely exert.

But he needed his first-aid kit.

Quick footsteps outside of the room drew his attention—a pitter-patter of someone running past the open doorway. A shadow had passed as well, but it moved too quickly for him to see anything clearly.

Ann's head swivelled around. 'What was that?' she asked.

'Hello?' David called, hoping it was one of the others coming back. Deep down, he knew it wasn't.

He heard a feminine giggle from the hallway outside.

Ann quickly moved over to stand next to David. The table, with Ralph atop it, was between them and the door.

'I don't fucking need this right now,' Ralph said.

David took Ann's hand and put it on the blood-soaked rags over Ralph's stomach.

'Keep pressing down,' he ordered. He then walked around the table to the other side. As scared as he was being closest to the door and whatever was out there, David didn't like the idea of Ralph being the one nearest to the danger.

'Show yourself,' he demanded.

Another giggle.

'Are you sure... you want that... Brother?' a voice said. It was crackly and gravelly... like the voice of the dead.

David's heart froze. While the voice was horribly twisted, it did trigger a pang of recognition within him, like a long-lost memory suddenly pulled to the fore through the mists of time.

It was Katie's voice.

He heard the slap of a bare foot outside. Then another. A shadow was cast on the floor of the hallway, and it moved closer with each step.

He trembled in fear and anticipation, and David was quickly reminded of his time back in 2014, when a disembodied voice had delivered a message to him: *Return here. Help another in need.*

David had always assumed that the 'other in need' was Katie, as he knew she was trapped at the house. Now he'd found her.

However, David was ill-prepared for the horror that stepped out from behind the door frame. He'd seen ghosts in the house before. Even a demon back during their first investigation, so David thought he was ready for anything...

He let out a scream and backed up into the table, banging into it and causing Ralph to cry out.

The thing that stood in the doorway was little more than a walking corpse: decay, rot, and death given form. The flesh on the woman's spindly frame was dry, wrinkled, and a mix of browns and greys. Some areas of skin were missing, showing bone beneath; ribs poked through the paper-thin flesh, shins had no covering, and the jawbone was also stripped bare, giving the woman a skeletal grin.

One eye was missing, just a dark pit boring into her cranium, and the remaining eye was cloudy and milky with no pupil. The only hair she had was a few wispy strands. On top of that, the horrific girl was completely naked, with sagging, punctured breasts drooping low.

Yet despite the disfigurement, the rot, and the ruin, David knew it was Katie.

'Hi, Brother.'

Though her jaw moved, the voice didn't seem completely in-sync, as if it were coming from another space behind the walking nightmare.

A black tongue rolled out from Katie's mouth and licked her dry upper lip. It then moved over the bottom teeth of the exposed jaw. Her hand came up to one ruined breast and squeezed.

'Am I still beautiful?'

She was mocking him. No, it wasn't her. This wasn't Katie. It was the house. *Perron Manor* was mocking him, trying to make him feel as much horror and revulsion as was humanly possible. And it was succeeding. However, David hoped Katie—the *real* Katie—was somewhere beneath it all and that she could hear him.

'I've come back for you, Sister,' he said. 'I never gave up. And I'm going to help you. The message: 'Return here, help another.' That was about you, wasn't it?'

The hideous woman just threw her head back and let out a humourless cackle.

'Idiot,' she said with hatred in her voice. *'That message was* never *about your dear sister.'*

David shook his head. 'Lies,' he replied. 'I won't let you fool me.'

Katie took a step forward, her motions jerky, like her body was on fire and she was walking on hot coals. *'I don't need to fool you. Perron Manor delivered the message, but the person you were supposed to help? That was never me.'*

David frowned, unsure of what to believe. If the message was never about Katie, then could it have been about…

'Chloe!' he exclaimed, as something suddenly made sense to him. 'Is that who I'm here to help?'

Katie slowly shook her head.

'Sarah?'

A nod.

He tried to make sense of it all. Was that the truth, the message was about Sarah? If so, it kind of made sense, given the circumstances of how he'd returned to Perron Manor. He *was* here helping Sarah in what she needed to do.

'It was Sarah that needed me,' he stated in realisation.

Katie laughed again. *'You still don't understand. The message was just the bait. A worm on a hook, and you bit into it. We kept you dangling on the line until we needed you. Sarah was always going to return home. But we knew her sister would convince her to leave before we had taken her completely. So... we took her sister and gave Sarah a reason to come back, though she was never going to come back alone. She needed help. An 'expert.' Someone we had dangling on a line, just ready to reel in.'*

Katie laughed again. David's head swam. That couldn't be true. 'Bullshit!' he snapped, feeling his anger rise. 'That's impossible.'

Katie then started to fondle her other breast, and David heard the crunch and crackle of dried skin. Dust fell to the floor from beneath her squeezing hand.

It's trying to sicken you, David said to himself. *To get under your skin. Don't let it.*

'Afraid not, little brother. That's why it first took me, you see. *The pieces for this night were put into place a long time ago. This house... it knows things. Sees time differently. We all do now. And it is... horrifying.'* She cackled and squeezed harder. *'Not something your simple brain would be able to comprehend. But know this: you're a pawn, David. You and all your friends. Now you're where we want you. There's nothing you can do about it. You'll join me soon enough, Brother.'* She then pulled her hand away from her now-crushed breast and waved her fingers at him. Katie backed up, one step after the other.

She wasn't quite finished. Her hand quickly found its way between her legs and she let out a moan. *'Then we can do what I know you always fantasised about. Isn't that right, Davey-boy?'*

David clenched up. His hands squeezed into fists and his teeth ground together. 'That isn't true!' he snapped, eyes wild in anger. 'I was too young. Not once did I ever—'

'Sure, sure,' Katie said, her tone one of pure condescension.

She then disappeared from the room.

David was motionless, trying to make sense of it all. He had been horrified at her final words.

He hadn't. Ever. Not once!

Not... once.

David quickly ran out of the room to again confront the horror, but found only an empty hallway.

CHAPTER 48

We have to charge her, Jenn thought to herself. *We're just standing and waiting.*

Sarah slowly advanced on them. All it would take was one swing or stab from that knife. Even if they all tried to flee and scatter in different directions, the likelihood was that only three out of the four would get past her.

And it only took one.

Sarah kept moving forward at a slow and steady pace.

'We need to tackle her,' Jenn said, hopefully only loud enough for the others to hear over the rain.

'We need to *what?!*' Jamie asked.

'You heard me,' she replied. 'We rush her. Better than waiting for her to come over and swing at us with that knife.'

'That's insane,' Jamie shot back.

But it wasn't. It was dangerous, certainly. Jenn knew it would take all of them to subdue her, but it was still four against one.

'She's right,' George added.

That was a relief—at least she wasn't alone. And Jenn had an idea of how to make it work. She pointed to the house behind Sarah, up to the top floor.

'Chloe!' she yelled. 'She's there, in the window!'

Father Janosch, George, and Jamie all looked up there to see nothing. Thankfully, Sarah turned her back on them to look up as well.

'Now!' Jenn cried and charged forward. It took the other three longer than she would have liked to figure out her plan. However, they soon ran as well, with Jamie and Father Janosch bringing up the rear. George kept pace with Jenn, and the two of them bore down on their target, who then started to turn back around.

Jenn leapt. She and George barrelled into Sarah, knocking her to the ground. The knife slipped from her grasp and skittered along the paved ground. Jenn grabbed one of Sarah's arms, and George seized the other. Both dropped their weight down onto her to keep Sarah pinned.

Jamie and Father Janosch soon reached the melee, but Jamie looked terrified. Sarah kicked and bucked wildly, exhibiting more strength than Jenn had expected, making holding her down difficult.

'Your belt!' she shouted up to Jamie. 'Tie her ankles together!'

Jamie looked confused for a second as Sarah continued to fight. She snarled and swore.

'Fuck you all! I'll bite your fucking throats out and watch you die!'

Eventually, Jamie snapped into action and removed his belt. Father Janosch, his hands still full of everything they needed for the ritual, dropped his weight down onto Sarah as well to keep her hips and legs from writhing.

After struggling for a few minutes, his hands slipping in the rain, Jamie managed to wrap the belt around Sarah's legs, tighten it up, and then tie it into a knot.

'We need to restrain her arms,' Jenn said.

'Jamie,' George shouted while straining. 'Get my belt, too. Quickly!'

Jamie once again sprang into action and pulled George's belt free.

'We need to get her onto her front, then tie her arms behind her back,' George said.

'I'll kill you all!' Sarah said. Her face was twisted into a furious and hateful glare. 'I'll tear your fucking guts out with my bare hands.'

Jenn tried to ignore the threats. 'On three we roll her,' she said, then began the count. The rain continued to hammer down, soaking Jenn to her core. 'One, two... three!'

She and George worked as one and flipped Sarah over, driving her face-first into the paving slabs of the courtyard. The hand George had been holding managed to get free, however, and Sarah managed to quickly grab him by the balls.

George let out a pain-filled shriek, but Father Janosch and Jamie were quick to force Sarah's arm behind her back, where it met the one Jenn was fighting with. George, with tears in his eyes and wincing in pain, then wrapped his belt around Sarah's wrists and tied a strong knot in it.

The four then backed away from Sarah, who lay on the ground, still writhing and swearing, but stuck.

'I'll fucking kill you all!' she bellowed.

'We need to move quickly,' Father Janosch instructed. 'Back to David. Now.'

CHAPTER 49

Back in the dining room, Jenn handed off the first-aid kit to David while Luca set down everything they had gathered.

The salt, for drawing out the protective symbol.

The Bible, for reciting the words of God.

Candles, earth, and water, which combined with the air around them to make up the four elements.

And the mirror, as well, to reveal the otherworld. It would be the anchor that held everything together. It would need to be broken in order to end the ritual.

While Ann removed Ralph's hoodie, David opened the first-aid kit and pulled out an alcoholic wipe—it wasn't much, but it was all he had. He used it to clean Ralph's cut as the big man screamed in pain. Ralph moaned as he bled onto the dining room table, his blood staining the wooden surface beneath him.

However, Luca concentrated on the ledger, reading through the ritual again and again to make sure he could commit it to memory. It was relatively straightforward, which was good, but unbelievably dangerous.

He added some of the salt to his flask of water, then recited a prayer over it in order to bless it and create holy water. He repeated the same prayer over the mud in the container.

Air and fire would need to be blessed downstairs when inside the seal.

David applied a thick layer of gauze over Ralph's wound and took out a roll of tape from the first-aid kit. He stretched a length over the gauze, crudely sealing it down.

Ralph looked pale, and in a great deal of pain. However, he was very much conscious. Luca wasn't a medical expert, but he was sure that was a good sign.

Luca noticed David looked odd as well. He almost seemed distracted somehow. Ann too. Luca had to wonder if something had happened while the rest of them were away gathering supplies.

'We ran into Sarah outside,' Jamie said to David and Ann.

'What happened?' Ann asked.

'She tried to attack us, but we managed to subdue her,' George answered. 'We tied her up, but I don't think it will keep her down for long.'

'We had our own run-in,' Ann replied.

'Don't,' David quickly snapped. 'We don't have time.'

Ann looked surprised at being shut down so abruptly, and more than a little annoyed, but she didn't press the point.

Luca was keen to hear their experience but didn't have time to probe it either. They needed to work quickly.

'Okay,' he said to the rest of the team. 'We need to get down to the basement.'

All of them, even Ralph, turned to look at him.

'Are you serious?' Jamie asked. 'Why?'

'We need to get to the lowest point that we can. It will help speed up *Claude Ianua*.'

'Why does that make any difference?' George questioned. 'Why can't we do it here?'

'The farther down we are, the stronger the connection with the doorway. That's what it says in *Ianua Diaboli*, and we need all the help we can get. So we need to move.'

'What about Ralph?' Jenn said. 'We can't risk moving him.'

'We have to,' Luca replied. He hated pressing the matter, as Ralph was clearly struggling, but the result of them failing in their task didn't bear thinking about. Their own lives, though he didn't say it outright to them, had to be expendable.

The realisation caused Luca to pause. It was hard not to be overwhelmed by how quickly the stakes had risen.

'I'll need you all to help carry me down there,' Ralph said. 'But if that's what we need to do, let's go.'

Luca was worried about the big man. His pallor was not a healthy one, and a film of sweat covered his face. However, Ralph seemed to be aware of the urgency of the situation, and Luca was thankful for the support.

Of course, Luca sincerely hoped Ralph *didn't* die. But more critically, he really hoped Ralph didn't die before they closed the door. That was all that was important.

Perhaps that made Luca a terrible priest. However, it was a guilt he would have to wrestle with another day. They needed to move, but the others also needed to know their roles going forward as time would be of the essence when downstairs.

'When we get to the basement we need to keep together so that I can mark out a protective seal with the salt. Then I'll put the mirror at the centre of the seal. Lastly, I'll need to spill my blood on both. Once that is done, we should be safe inside the seal. Step one will be complete, and the spirits here will not be able to reach us.'

'Could Sarah get to us, though?' David asked.

Luca didn't have the answer. 'I... don't know. Because of that, we need to be alert. Regardless, we then light the candles and place them around the perimeter. I will sprinkle the earth and the water there as well. These are the elements we use to re-establish the dominance of our reality: fire, earth, and water, and even the air we are breathing. Then I will recite a passage from *Ianua Diaboli* to start the ritual. Doing so will create a temporary merging.'

'A fucking *what?*' Jamie asked. 'Are you serious, you're going to join our world to... Hell?'

'I will only be merging Perron Manor, but yes, that is correct,' Luca confirmed. 'Doing that will give the house much more power, so it will be a very dangerous time. That is why we need the seal. Once the door is fully open, we smash the mirror, the anchor, and it closes the door permanently.

'Is that it?' David asked. 'Seems simple.'

'It is,' Luca replied. 'Opening the doors is more difficult. They require sacrifice, but closing them is only about re-establishing the Earth's dominance. At the moment, Perron Manor exists with a foot in each reality. Closing the door changes that. But remember that the house will be fighting us. As will Sarah, if she gets free.'

'Then we need to get moving,' Ralph said, pushing himself up to a sitting position.

David and the rest of the group quickly moved over to Ralph and helped him from the table, while Luca gathered up what they needed for the ritual, including the books and his Bible.

He just hoped his faith was strong enough.

Claude Ianua had to be initiated by a holy person. The specific faith did not matter, as long as the person had turned their back on darkness and dedicated their life to the light.

Once the merger was in full flow, Luca would need to keep reciting words from a holy text—in this case, the Bible—to fight the power coming through the Devil's Door. However, if his belief was not absolute… they were in trouble.

'Okay everyone,' he said. 'Let's go.'

CHAPTER 50

I can't fail.

Sarah continued to roll and slither over the wet pavement, feeling the rain soak through her clothes. She was cold and angry, and had to resort to wriggling across the ground like a worm.

She had been stupid—tricked far too easily. Now the others were inside and had locked the door behind them.

But they had also been stupid. Very stupid. Sarah's knife, which had fallen from her hand after Jenn and George had tackled her, had been forgotten.

All she had to do was reach it, and then use it to cut herself free. Doing so while tied up with her arms behind her back would be difficult but doable. She would just have to be careful not to accidentally slice her wrists in the process.

Fight it!

Sarah shook her head to try and exorcise that dissenting voice. She had to ignore it and listen to the will of the house.

Her skin tingled, feeling alive and almost on fire. It had felt that way since the previous night. On top of that constant sensation, she could now also feel an anger radiate from the house. It was aimed directly at her.

'*Get up!*'

Sarah quickly rolled over to her back and squinted through the cold rain that cascaded down onto her face.

'Chloe?'

Sarah's sister stood above her, naked and rotted. Her milky eyes burned with anger.

'You need to kill to come home to me,' she said in a hoarse, pained voice. *'If they succeed and close the door, you'll lose me forever. Get up and kill!'*

'I will,' Sarah promised. Before her very eyes, the form of her sister started to dissipate, then blew away like dust in the wind.

Just before Chloe did, however, Sarah noticed something; the hateful expression faltered, if only for a second, and was replaced by something entirely more mournful.

Sarah shook her head and rolled back over, again making her way towards the knife. She planned to get free of her bonds and gut every single person inside the house.

Then she would be home. Back with Chloe forever.

CHAPTER 51

DAVID WAS STRAINING under Ralph's weight. He had one of the man's arms draped over his shoulder while George held the other.

Ralph had insisted he could walk, but needed aid. That helped, as there was no way they could have carried his full weight down the narrow stone steps without dropping him.

The big man was in a great deal of pain still, made worse by being moved around, but he was still conscious and alert. It gave David hope that the stab wound might not be fatal… as long as they could get him medical attention soon.

Father Janosch and Ann led the way through the corridors towards the great hall, with Jamie and Jenn bringing up the rear.

'Jesus, Ralph,' George exclaimed as they neared the hall. 'How much do you weigh?'

Ralph managed a laugh as he winced. 'That's a bit of a personal question, George.'

As they moved, David kept his eyes peeled. It was hard not to expect something to leap from one of the doorways they passed, but they managed to get to the great hall unhindered.

Once inside, however, all of the lights blinked off and plunged them into darkness.

'Shit!' Ann said.

David was scared but not surprised. Did he really expect the route down to the basement to be a simple one?

'Ring-o-ring-o-roses,' a throaty, distorted voice called out from the far side of the hall.

Through the darkness, David could make out the form of a tall, pale man standing against the far wall. He was dressed in a dirty suit, and his eyes were little more than black pits.

'Shit!' Ann said again. 'Shit, shit, shit! What do we do?'

'We keep going,' Luca said and held out his flask of holy water before him, the top unscrewed.

The door to the steps was on the same side of the hall as they were, so the ghostly watcher was not blocking their path, though it was certainly a worrying presence.

David cast a glance out through the rear glazed door. He knew the others had tied Sarah up out there. However, he could see no sign of her. The security light was off, limiting how far he was able to see, which in itself was strange. If Sarah was in the courtyard and moving—even wriggling—she should have activated the light's sensors.

Ralph's weight was starting to cause David's neck to cramp up, but he kept on going. Soon they were at the door, with the pale man doing nothing but watching. Father Janosch pulled it open.

Ann screamed first.

George quickly stepped backwards, pulling Ralph and David with him as David nearly lost his footing. Father Janosch instinctively raised his hand again, holding the holy water out before him like a weapon.

Chloe stood on the other side of the door.

She was naked, her body resembling a decomposed corpse—just as Katie's had—and her face was twisted into something demonic. Her mouth was wider than it should be, and her teeth were sharper and blacker than they had been in life.

'Back!' Father Janosch commanded, but even David could sense the older man's fear.

Chloe giggled. *'You're all going to die here.'*

Luca quickly flicked his arm forward and sprayed Chloe with a mist of water from his flask. It coated her face. Her milky eyes went wide, and she dropped her head back then screamed.

It wasn't a human noise, too high-pitched and animalistic, and David could have sworn he picked up the sound of a bleating goat mixed in with the cries.

The spirit of Sarah's sister then backed up, bringing her hands up to her face as she continued to shriek. Father Janosch doused her again and again.

Chloe then looked up. David was startled to see she now looked different. Though her body was still ruined, her face was more reminiscent of when she was alive. The skin was smoother and pale, with red cheeks, and her eyes once again had their brown irises.

Most importantly, she no longer looked hateful. She looked... terrified.

'Help me,' she said before quickly vanishing right before their eyes. Her voice still echoed even after her form had disappeared.

'What the hell was that?' Jamie asked.

However, there was no time to deliberate. A light had drawn David's attention, and he turned again to the rear door. Sarah stood outside, soaked to the bone, with wild eyes and a knife in hand.

He hoped to God the others had locked that door after coming inside.

'We need to go,' Father Janosch instructed. It was then the tall, pale man finally moved, drifting over to the door. David couldn't help but watch the slow, silent glide.

A long, spindly hand rose up and touched the glass of the door. It shattered in an instant, exploding outward and coating Sarah, who didn't take her eyes off David the whole time.

'We need to go *now!*' Jenn then yelled. She grabbed hold of David and George, pulling them all forward towards the steps. Jamie slammed the door shut behind them, but there was no lock to hold Sarah back.

As a group, they all thundered down the narrow stone stairwell but were moving too quickly, and supporting Ralph proved impossible. He fell from their grasp, pitching forward into Father Janosch and Ann. David tried to grab at Ralph again but succeeded only in being dragged forward as well.

David tumbled down with the others, with the slapping of bodies on the hard stone steps ringing out along with the groans of pain from his team.

CHAPTER 52

JENN RAN down the steps with Jamie and Ann beside her, looking on in horror as the others lay in an intertwined heap.

'Are you okay?' she shouted.

The replies were groans of pain. Ralph held a hand to his stomach, where Jenn could see fresh blood wet his t-shirt again.

'Everybody up!' she quickly demanded. Sarah wouldn't be far behind, so they needed to move. Jenn carefully stepped over David and entered into the dark basement, helping Father Janosch up, who looked unsteady on his feet.

The items he needed had fallen to the floor and were strewn about the area.

'Quickly!' Jenn ordered. She helped up David and George, before finally assisting with Ralph.

Father Janosch began gathering his things. Then, the door above them opened with a long, slow squeak.

'Move!' Ann yelled.

As one, they all shuffled farther into the basement and were swallowed up by the dark. It was bad enough upstairs in the great hall, but at least there had been moonlight seeping in through the windows. Down here, they were underground, with no natural light to help them.

'I... I'm missing something,' Father Janosch said, panicked. Jenn felt the toe of her shoe strike something, and she bent down to retrieve a container she had kicked. It was the salt.

Jenn could hear slow and steady footsteps make their way down the steps. Suddenly, a burst of fire erupted from the furnace at the far side of the basement, powerful enough that it sounded like an explosion, blowing open the doors on the front. The flames continued—a roaring inferno with a figure caught inside.

A man with blackened, melted features leaned out from the metal structure, glaring at them with his one good eye.

The flames from the furnace cast a flickering glow over the whole basement, and Jenn could see that other spirits of the dead were also there with them. They stood around the perimeter of the area, watching: a man holding his own insides; a short, stocky blonde woman of advanced years; and the man with brushed-back hair and an open throat, whom they had earlier identified as Marcus Blackwater.

There was also a corpse-like woman with a crushed breast, and half a man who writhed around on the floor in a pool of his own blood, his bottom half completely missing. In fact, the more Jenn looked around, the more other spirits seemed to appear.

But it was not just spirits. There were tall, spindly forms in amongst the dead, with elongated arms, twisted faces, and obsidian bodies.

Demons.

One in particular was taller than the others, with a large mouth full of nightmarish teeth and facial features that had melted like wax. She had seen this thing before, back in 2014.

Pazuzu.

Jenn thrust the container of salt into Father Janosch's hands. 'The seal!' she shouted. 'Hurry!'

'I need the book!' Father Janosch shouted back, looking around frantically.

The spirits around the edges of the room started to slowly advance.

'Here,' George said and passed *Ianua Diaboli* to the priest.

Father Janosch set the book down on the ground, turning the pages to the back to study the illustrations shown in *Claude Ianua*.

'Get the other things,' Father Janosch demanded. 'Quickly.' He started to pour the salt out into a crude circle wide enough to fit everyone in it.

The ghosts continued to move closer, and Sarah emerged out into the basement from the steps. She walked at a leisurely pace.

With Ralph lying on the floor within the salt circle, the others quickly stepped inside as well, now with all the elements they needed. Jenn double-checked to make sure they had everything.

Father Janosch then started to work around them, drawing out additional lines inside the circle.

'Is that... a pentagram?' Jenn asked.

'It is,' Father Janosch replied. 'The tip needs to point north. Then it is a symbol of protection. If it is inverted, that's when it invokes the demonic.'

He worked quickly. However, Jenn was concerned. Sarah didn't seem to be in any rush, and neither did any of the horrific entities that slowly closed in as well.

Why?

'It's done,' Father Janosch said. He positioned the mirror in the centre, shuffling Ralph aside, then grabbed at the thin, silver crucifix he wore around his neck, yanking and snapping the chain.

Jenn winced when she saw the priest drive the edge down into the flesh of the back of his hand, piercing the skin. With gritted teeth, he sliced the bottom of the crucifix down over his hand, cutting through the prominent veins and drawing blood.

Father Janosch was clearly in pain, but he pinched the skin together along the cut to force out more blood, then let it drip down onto the mirror and the salt outlines of the seal.

He let out a visible sigh of relief.

'It's done,' he said. The closest spirits to them slowly moved to the outer edges of the symbol and stopped. There, they just watched. More and more gathered around, and Jenn felt panicked as they became trapped and surrounded. But just as Father Janosch had said, it seemed that they could not gain entry. Pazuzu and the other demons all stalked their way to the front of the crowd, bearing down on the team and glaring with eyes that burned yellow.

'Leave us alone!' Ann yelled as she cowered in fear. David looked horrified... but also defeated.

Father Janosch was still working, setting up the candles around the inside edges of the seal. Jenn pulled out the box of matches she had earlier jammed into her pocket and began to light the candles.

She saw movement through the crowd. Sarah was pushing her way through to them, wearing a condescending smile.

'Ignore her,' Father Janosch said. 'She can't hurt us now. We are safe.'

Regardless, Jenn still stepped back away from the edges as Father Janosch sprinkled dirt from the container on the ground, followed by holy water from his flask.

With everything set, he grabbed his Bible and began to recite words from its pages.

'I will bless the Lord at all times; praise shall be always in my mouth.'

Sarah laughed.

Something's wrong, Jenn thought to herself. *She's too confident.*

'Are you sure you are so safe, *priest?*' Sarah asked. Her voice dripped with malice.

Father Janosch kept going for a little while longer, reciting more from his Bible. When finished, he turned to Sarah.

'I am quite sure,' he said, staring her down. 'The elements are blessed. Fire, water, the earth, even the air around us. And the fifth element, too: the souls within the circle. We are protected, and *Claude Ianua* has begun.'

He then bent down and retrieved *Ianua Diaboli,* and he started to read from the open pages, loudly uttering Latin verses from the ritual.

'Oh Father,' Sarah said, waving her hand to get his attention. 'Your little seal will only hold me back if the faith of those inside is strong enough. I wonder... are you confident of that?'

'We all believe!' Jenn snapped and stepped forward. 'How can we not? Look at all the souls trapped here—damned and in purgatory. If Hell is truly real, then Heaven and the Lord *have* to be.'

Sarah shook her head. 'Not necessarily. And besides, David over there knows you are all fucked, don't you, David?'

David said nothing; he just scowled at Sarah. Father Janosch continued with his rites.

'And,' Sarah went on, 'your priest has about as much true faith as I do. He's a liar, a coward... a wretched excuse for a so-called 'holy man.''

Father Janosch continued unabated, repeating the same phrases over and over.

'Aperi ostium conjungere mundos. Infera et terra inter se illigantur. Vera forma revelatur ut ancora auferatur.'

'Keep going,' Sarah said. 'Open the door wider. Give me more strength.'

A rumbling sound from all around them drew shrieks of fear from the team. The thundering increased to an intense booming sound, as if something massive were striking the very reality of their surroundings.

'What the hell is that?' George asked as he moved his hands over his ears. Father Janosch kept going.

Jenn knew what was happening. The door was opening.

She happened to cast her eyes down to the mirror and drew in a breath at what she saw.

Instead of the concrete beams of the ceiling above, the reflection in the mirror showed something else. No longer concrete, the surface was made up of... flesh—red, glistening meat. And worse, it writhed and moved as human bodies emerged from within it, all of them trapped and screaming.

The souls of the dead.

It occurred to Jenn that *this* was how they existed in Hell. Fused to the form of the house.

The booms continued, getting louder and louder.

'Look!' Ann screamed, pointing to the walls.

What the fuck... Jenn could scarcely believe what she was seeing. The walls, floor, and ceiling of the basement were all changing, matching what she had seen in the reflection.

The walls bled as they turned to meat. Withered, human forms partially broke free, arms and legs flailing. Some were only faces, trapped within the fleshy surface around them and screaming manically. The noise around Jenn and the others rose dramatically, with the cries of agony becoming deafening.

'David!' Father Janosch yelled. 'Grab the mirror.' David was slow in moving, but eventually picked up the mirror from the ground.

Father Janosch turned to Sarah and gave a forced smile. 'It worked,' he shouted at her.

Though what was happening might have been part of the plan, he still looked as terrified as Jenn felt.

'It has indeed,' Sarah replied, just audible over the chaotic cacophony. 'As I said, your seal may keep out my brothers and sisters,' she motioned to the watching dead and demons that surrounded the circle, 'but now that you have opened the door and infused me with power, you can only keep me out if your faith is absolute.'

'My faith *is* absolute,' Father Janosch shouted back.

Sarah shook her head. She then picked up a foot and dropped it onto the salt line of the circle. With a swipe of her leg, the seal was quickly and easily broken.

Jenn was shocked.

What the fuck?

Sarah quickly stepped forward, lunging towards Jenn, who was unable to react in time.

She felt the knife penetrate her gut and bury itself right up to the hilt.

'No!' Father Janosch yelled.

Sarah yanked the knife sideways across Jenn's stomach. Jenn screamed, feeling her insides bubble free.

CHAPTER 53

DAVID WAS IN SHOCK.

Jenn dropped to the ground, holding her stomach as blood poured free through the slash in her t-shirt. She looked utterly surprised, eyes wide, not really comprehending what had just happened.

Fleshy red intestines pushed their way out through her split skin.

Sarah stood above her and raised the knife again. At the same moment, with the seal broken, the masses of the dead, along with their demon brothers, advanced onto the helpless team.

They were dead. All of them. They had failed.

Something inside of David snapped, and he bellowed out a roar born of both fear and fury. He threw himself forward and crashed into Sarah, forcing her down to her back and landing on top of her. The mirror he held fell from his hand down beside them. He saw her knife drop as well, clattering down close to the mirror.

David was vaguely aware of Father Janosch screaming something at him, but he was so focused on hurting Sarah that he didn't take the words in.

However, just as he positioned himself atop her, Sarah's hands reached up and grabbed his throat. A leg then snaked its way up in front of him, and she drove the sole of her foot up, connecting with the bridge of his nose.

David felt cartilage break and crunch beneath her driving heel. The world spun and pain erupted in his face.

Before he knew it, Sarah had reversed their positions, and he was easily forced to the ground. She quickly rolled on top of David, straddling him.

As chaos erupted around him, and he saw his team dragged away by the hordes of the dead in the basement, he heard Jenn spluttering and wheezing from somewhere close, gasping for breath.

Sarah stared down at him with a look of wild glee on her face.

CHAPTER 54

I'VE DONE IT!

Jenn was going to die; she wouldn't last long with her stomach cut open like that. Sarah's role was complete.

She could then forever be with the one person she had failed most of all—Chloe. They could be together forever at Perron Manor. Sarah's skin still tingled, and it made her feel alive. A constant, buzzing sensation seemed to emanate from her very molecules.

What are you doing? Stop this! Fight it!

She shook her head. That dissenting voice needed to be quashed. It had been lingering in the back of her mind since the previous night, when she had been fully turned. That was when her eyes had been opened.

Killing David would finally snuff out the annoying remnant of her former self.

Sarah reached down towards the knife beside her, using her fingers to push the mirror out of the way.

'Don't!'

It was a voice she recognised, and Sarah gazed up to see her sister standing before her. However, Chloe looked different than she had out in the courtyard.

While much of her body still exhibited the exquisite rot and ruin bestowed by Perron Manor, her face now seemed almost... human.

And she appeared to be in great pain. Chloe was clearly fighting against something, as her body was locked and shaking. Straining.

'Don't do it. Fight it.'

'I'm coming home to you, Sis,' Sarah said. 'There's no need to be scared.'

Chloe was crying. *'This isn't you. Fight it. You're a warrior. Fight it!'*

Sarah paused. What the hell was Chloe saying? She couldn't go against the house.

Screams from the others drew Sarah's attention as her fingers felt around for the knife. She turned her head and saw that Jenn lay on her back, holding her stomach, taking short sharp breaths. Her eyes were wide and staring at the ceiling.

Death was coming for her.

Father Janosch was being pulled to the ground, helpless as the spirts of the damned clawed for a part of him.

Jamie screeched in pain when Pazuzu, the stubborn and rebellious one, the opener of gates, took hold of his jaw in one long, talon-like claw. The jaw was ripped clean off. Then long fingers of the other hand bored through his eyes.

You're doing this. Jamie is dead because of you. Jenn will be soon. And Ralph. Listen to Chloe. Fight it.

Sarah looked down to David, who looked utterly defeated. He was crying.

But this was good. It was what the house wanted. All was right.

'Fight it!' Chloe yelled.

Fight.

Sarah clenched her teeth together. Her body tensed up and her mind swam with confusion, like it was about to split in two.

She just had to kill David. Grab the knife that was close to her hand and drive it down into his throat. Then all would be well.

Fight it.

Obey.

Fight!

Sarah let out a scream as her body shook. Her fingers found what she was looking for.

She brought the object up high above her head, gripping it in both hands. David turned away and closed his eyes.

Sarah thrust her arms down as she continued her scream.

The mirror in her grasp crunched and broke on the hard ground next to David's head. The lid snapped off and the glass shattered into small pieces.

Everything stopped.

The chaos that had previously surrounded Sarah drew to an immediate halt. All eyes turned to her.

The pale faces of the dead stared in confusion, as did the demonic entities. Pazuzu, with a blood-stained hand, dropped Jamie's lifeless body and stepped closer to her. It tilted its head. Even the previously writhing bodies trapped within the walls stopped moving and crying in pain.

Pazuzu let its head drop back and bellowed out a horrible, deafening screech.

Sarah's mind, previously so clouded and confused, suddenly became clear, like a terrible and painful fog had suddenly dissipated. Her skin still tingled, like pins and needles across her entire body.

She looked again to Jamie, then to Jenn.

What have I done?

Sarah quickly backed off David and pulled her knees up to her chest.

Oh God, oh God, oh God. No, no, no.

Jenn's breathing was growing slower, becoming more laboured. Still none of the dead moved. David quickly scrambled over to his fallen friend.

'Jenn!' He took her hand and cupped her face. 'Jenn!'

No, no, no.

The walls around them began to change yet again. The wet flesh melted away, running down to the floor and disappearing to reveal once again the stone structure behind. The bodies within the walls fell free. Their appearance softened and became more human.

So too did the appearance of the gathered dead who stood in watch.

All their deformities and disfigurements were stripped away. The rotted bodies changed, soon looking much more healthy and normal.

Then, the dead slowly started to disappear. The sensation Sarah felt on her skin, that tingling, started to fade away with them.

Pazuzu let out another roar before it melted into the darkness that swallowed up the room once again when the furnace dampened out to nothing. Sarah felt something approach her.

She turned her head up to see Chloe. However, her sister didn't seem pained anymore. She looked beautiful, without pain or worry.

Chloe was flanked by Jamie... and Jenn.

Sarah quickly turned to see David crying over Jenn's motionless body—blood still spilling out to the floor below her.

No!

Sarah looked up to her sister, Jenn, and Jamie. They were smiling. Jenn just gave Sarah a sad wave, took Jamie's hand, and then moved away into the darkness.

'I'm sorry,' Sarah said. 'I'm so, so sorry.' Tears fell from her eyes. Her heart was broken.

I caused this.

She had lied in order to bring the team here in the first place, and then she had killed Jenn with her own hands.

Chloe knelt down in front of her, and Sarah picked up on the familiar scent of lavender. A warm hand touched her shoulder.

'I'm sorry for everything, Chloe,' Sarah said. 'It's all my fault. Chloe... I'm so sorry.'

'Sarah?' a soft voice asked. It was Father Janosch, who was sitting up, his clothes in tatters and his hair a mess. However, he looked unharmed. 'Who are you talking to?'

She looked back to Chloe. 'Don't you see her?' Sarah asked.

He shook his head.

Ann was sobbing on the floor, and George had moved close to Jamie, his face a picture of revulsion and shock. David continued to cry over Jenn's body.

Chloe leaned forward, and Sarah felt a flood of warmth radiate out from the lips that touched her forehead.

'Thank you,' Chloe said. Her voice was little more than a whisper.

Chloe then stood up and turned around.

'Don't go!' Sarah cried. 'Please, don't go! I can't cope without you!'

Chloe's eyes were sad, but she stepped away into the darkness, disappearing from Sarah forever.

CHAPTER 55

Luca stood to his feet. Everything was a mess. Jamie and Jenn were clearly dead. Ralph's breathing was growing more laboured.

It had been close to twenty minutes since Sarah had broken the mirror, and everything had ceased in an instant.

The house around him felt different. He knew without question they had done it: completed the ritual of *Claude Ianua*.

The Devil's Door had been closed permanently.

But at what cost?

Everyone sat numb. Ann still cried loudly. Sarah's sobs were soft. Ralph stared up to the ceiling; if they didn't get him help soon, he would die as well.

Luca walked over to David, his legs shaking beneath him as he did. He knelt down. Jenn's terrified expression was frozen on her face, eyes wide open, hands on her stomach. Luca moved a hand over to her eyes and closed them.

'David,' he whispered. 'Ralph still needs help. We need to call an ambulance if we can. Or get him to a hospital somehow.'

David didn't look away from Jenn.

'What the hell happened here, Father?' he asked. His voice was so full of pain that Luca's heart broke for him. It broke for them all.

'I don't know,' Luca replied. 'It's hard to comprehend. But we did it. We stopped what was happening. That's something.'

'Two of my friends are dead,' David said angrily. There was a silence between them for a few moments. Eventually, David turned to Luca. 'I saw someone I knew here, you know,' he said. 'Just before we came down to the basement. It was my stepsister, Katie. A long time ago she went missing in this house. That's... that's what has always drawn me to it. Katie—or the thing pretending to be her—told me that the house had a plan. Something it had been orchestrating for a long time. Apparently that's why my sister was taken in the first place. And why Chloe was killed, too. All to get Sarah here to... to do what she almost did.'

'I know,' Luca said. He hadn't known about Katie, that was a surprise to him, but he was aware the house had been manipulating events for many years prior, even if he could scarcely comprehend *how* that was possible.

'What I don't get,' David went on, 'is if the house was able to line things up like that... how were we able to stop it? How could we stand in the way of a force like that?'

It was a good question. 'Perhaps,' Luca replied, 'because there was a force working with *us* as well.' The words made sense as soon as he said them. In fact, he got an overwhelming and unexplainable feeling that he was absolutely correct, despite making it up on the fly to help make his friend feel better. After all, what were the chances of a priest with a prior knowledge of the Devil Door's and *Ianua Diaboli* being called to Perron Manor to give aid? 'Maybe that other force helped the house align everything and make sure we were where we needed to be. Just not in the way the house wanted.'

'All so that Jenn and Jamie could die?'

Luca paused. How could he answer a question like that?

The truth was that, unfortunately, the sacrifice *was* worth it, given the stakes. But as a survivor, did he have any right to feel that way?

'David,' Luca went on, 'if we don't act quickly, Ralph could be next. And we don't want that to happen, do we?'

David, still looking at Jenn, shook his head.

Luca held out a hand to him. 'Come on, let's go.'

CHAPTER 56

THE RAIN HAD EASED. Everyone except Ralph and Ann was outside. Sarah stood on her own as Father Janosch, David, and George all huddled together away from her, speaking in hushed whispers. Ralph lay just inside the entrance door with a coat over him. Ann knelt by his side.

Sarah hugged herself, pulling tighter the coat Father Janosch had handed her on the way out.

As numb as Sarah felt, she was aware of the disgusted glances she was getting from David and George. And every time she turned around to look at Ann, she was met with a furious death stare.

Sarah couldn't blame any of them.

She had killed Jenn. She was the reason Jamie was dead.

More blood on her hands.

Luca had insisted they all come outside to try and call an ambulance. This time, the call connected straight away. He had told the operator there had been a terrible accident, but when he divulged the nature of the injury—a stab wound—the operator said the police would be sent as well.

Luca then told the operator that there were also two dead bodies. After all, how could he hide something like that?

Sarah could only imagine how many police would now show up.

More death at Perron Manor, the creepy old place in the middle of nowhere. More souls to add to its legend.

'Devil's House has struck again,' the locals would say.

However, Sarah knew the truth. This would be the last tale about Perron Manor. Its story was finished.

She saw Father Janosch turn from the others and make his way over to her.

'How are you holding up?' he asked.

It was a ridiculous question considering what they had all been through, as she was holding up the same as the others: in a total state of shock.

Though she had more weighing on her than the others, as *she* was the one who had taken a life. Possessed or not.

However, Father Janosch had asked the question from a place of concern, and Sarah was appreciative of it.

'I honestly don't know,' she whispered.

Father Janosch nodded in understanding, then waited for a little while before he went on. 'Sarah, down there in the basement, when everything ended... you were talking to someone. Chloe, I think you said.'

Sarah nodded. 'She was down there, but she looked normal again. Like she did in life.'

'We didn't see her,' he said. 'After you broke the mirror, it was like a snap, and then all the madness around us was gone in an instant.'

'I saw things a little differently,' Sarah said. 'The world slowly changed back to normal. All the spirits shifted as well, turning into something more peaceful. I think they're finally free. All of them. In fact, I'm sure of it.'

'And did your sister speak to you?'

'A little. She said 'thank you.' I know how this is going to sound, but I saw Jenn and Jamie as well. They were next to Chloe.'

Father Janosch drew in a deep breath. 'Okay.'

'Do you think I should tell the others?'

He looked over to them, then back to Sarah. 'I'm not sure. Maybe not at the moment... it would be a lot to take in. What happened to Chloe and the others when she finished passing on her message?'

'They turned and all walked away into the darkness. They left. I don't know exactly where they all went, but they're gone now. I know that for certain, because I can't feel them anymore.'

Father Janosch cocked his head to the side. 'Feel them?'

Sarah bit her lip, thinking how best to put her experience into words. 'Ever since I woke up under the control of the house, my skin... it almost felt like it was on fire. A tingle, or an itch, over every inch of me. It's not something I've ever felt before. But when the door was closing down there in the basement, and the spirits were leaving, the sensation dulled. And when Chloe left, it stopped completely. That's when I knew the door was fully closed... I just *felt* it. And now I know there are no more souls trapped in the house.'

'Because you can't feel them anymore,' Father Janosch said.

'I suppose that sounds stupid.'

The priest smiled. 'Not at all. Considering what we've been through, nothing sounds stupid.' He then narrowed his eyes and rubbed his chin. 'I wonder if being under the possession of the house has left its mark on you.'

'How do you mean?'

'Well, you saw things the rest of us did not. And you sensed when the door had been closed. Perhaps you are left with a gift: seeing and sensing things others can't.'

Sarah shook her head, dismissively. 'I don't think that's true...' But she paused. It wasn't the first time in her life that notion had entered her mind.

'What is it?' he asked.

'Back in the army,' she replied, 'when I lost my best friend. I was supposed to be on point that day, but an inexplicable fear took over me. I just couldn't do it. I've never been able to explain why that happened. My friend took over the duties that day and died for it. I lived. I could never understand why.'

'The house,' Father Janosch said. 'It kept you safe, so that it could call you back. Perhaps you've always had the gift, because of who you are and how you were born. And now it is... I don't know, amplified?'

'So I'm a freak,' Sarah said angrily.

He shook his head. 'No, not a freak at all. None of us can help how we are born; all we can do is control our own decisions in life.'

'I couldn't even do that,' Sarah said. 'I was a puppet.'

'But not anymore,' Father Janosch stated firmly.

They both heard the police sirens in the distance. 'Actually, Father,' Sarah said, 'I don't think I'll be making any of my own decisions for a long time.'

'What do you mean?'

She was surprised at how naïve the priest was being. Hadn't he thought it through?

Sarah again looked over to David and George. 'They're never going to forgive me, are they?' she asked. 'Any of them.'

'Well, they're a little bit shellshocked at the moment. We all are. But they'll come around. You weren't acting under your own power, Sarah. It was the house, not you. In fact, you even managed to beat it. Don't forget it was *you* who broke the mirror and completed the ritual. *You* closed that door and *you* released all the souls inside Perron Manor... including David's sister.'

'It was *me* that brought everyone here because of a lie. *I* got Jenn and Jamie killed.'

'And if you didn't bring them, how many more lives would this house have taken in the future? It would have brought you back here eventually. Who knows, it might have succeeded and turned you completely. Perhaps everything that happened here played out as it was supposed to.'

'If that's the case, it's only going to finish one way now.'

'The police,' Father Janosch said with a slow nod. So he *had* thought about it.

'Yes. Jenn's stomach has been cut open. Ralph's been stabbed. My fingerprints will be all over the knife, because I was the one wielding it. Jamie's injuries are not going to be easily explained, but the police will want answers.'

'We'll tell them the truth,' Father Janosch said.

'The truth is insane. They won't believe us.'

'I will seek assistance from the Church, then. They can help us and—'

'It was *me*,' Sarah said as the siren drew nearer. She saw vehicles heading down the drive.

'What was?'

'When the police ask who did it, you tell them *I* did. All of it. I stabbed Ralph. Killed Jenn. Did… *that* to Jamie. Tell them I was driven mad at the loss of my sister or something. No sense in any of the others ruining their lives over this.'

Father Janosch shook his head. 'I can't lie about that, Sarah. I won't.'

'Then they'll think you're nuts too. Just tell the others to go along with it. They won't speak to me and I know they'll never forgive me. I don't blame them. But I can do this much for them. They shouldn't be hard to convince.'

'Sarah, I—'

'Tell them!' Sarah yelled.

Father Janosch jumped in shock and took a step back. An ambulance and two police cars pulled up.

'Please,' she begged with tears in her eyes. She then turned and walked over to the police, though not before turning her head to give Perron Manor one last glance. She looked at the window where she had seen Chloe only a few weeks before, begging for help.

The house was clear.

CHAPTER 57

Two weeks later...

Luca sat in one of the back offices at Newcastle Cathedral—officially called the Cathedral Church of St. Nicholas.

With the room's polished hardwood floors, dark wooden panelling to the walls, and high ceilings with ornate coving, for a moment Luca thought he was back in Perron Manor. It was unnerving that a house so evil could have so much in common with the house of God. Thankfully, Luca just had to look out of one of the high windows at the city of Newcastle outside—and not the landscape of rolling hills and countryside—to know he was back in civilisation.

Perron Manor was behind him now. But the effects and fall-out were not.

Bishop Turnbull sat opposite him, on the other side of a large, mahogany meeting table. The Bishop was flanked by older men, four on one side and three on the other. Luca had no idea who the other people were, but they carried an air of authority about them. Each was dressed in a cassock, as was Bishop Turnbull, and they looked at Luca intently.

He felt like he was sitting down for a job interview.

'Thank you for coming in,' Bishop Turnbull began. He was a thin man in his late fifties, and his bald head had some liver spots showing. He wore rimless glasses which were perched on a long, thin nose, with dark-brown eyes behind them. 'I passed on your report and debriefing to my superiors.' He gestured to the men that flanked him. 'We owe you a great deal of thanks.'

'Not just me,' Luca was quick to point out. 'Miss Pearson, David Ritter, and also David's team did just as much as I. Probably more. Some even gave their lives.'

Bishop Turnbull nodded. 'Yes, we appreciate that. Truly. And we will make sure those who are still here with us are thanked as well. I take it Mr. Cobin is recovering well?'

'Ralph? I believe he will be okay, yes.'

'We need to talk about the others, actually,' Bishop Turnbull said.

'Is that so?'

'Yes. We need to discuss what they experienced. I understand they captured a great deal of footage and evidence as part of their investigation.'

'That's right,' Luca confirmed. 'I'm sure some will still decry it all as fake, but it is there nonetheless.'

Bishop Turnbull looked uncomfortably to the three men sitting to his left. One of them nodded to him, and Turnbull turned back to Luca.

'That evidence can never come out,' he said.

Luca frowned in confusion. 'What do you mean?'

'Exactly what I said. They can't make what they've found public.'

Luca didn't know what to say to that. 'I... don't follow. It's *their* evidence, how are we supposed to stop them doing what they want with it? And more importantly, *why* should we stop them?'

'Because of what the house was. There can be little doubt anymore, given your testimony.'

'And?'

Bishop Turnbull shook his head. 'If word spread of the existence of these doorways—and worse, they were backed up by actual evidence— what do you think the reaction of the public would be?'

Luca thought about it. His answer probably wasn't what they expected. 'Scepticism,' he replied. 'I honestly don't think many people would believe it anyway.'

'No, maybe not everyone. But enough people would. And what if the wrong kind of people or organisations found out about these doors, and tried to use them for their own gains?'

Organisations?

'So you want to keep the truth hidden,' Luca stated.

'We *have* to,' Bishop Turnbull replied. 'Because we still don't know enough. For example, with regards to the Seven Gates—were all open prior to you closing the door at Perron Manor? And who opened the gates in the first place? Can more be opened? Surely you can see our concern and what's at stake.'

Luca could.

Not *everyone* needed to believe what David and his team might announce to the world for it to be a problem, only a few of the wrong sort. Especially if word of *Ianua Diaboli* got out as well. For the Church, it was easier to hide something that no-one knew existed in the first place.

He realised what they were going to ask in regards to the book as well.

'You need *Ianua Diaboli*, don't you.'

'Of course,' Bishop Turnbull said like it was the most obvious thing in the world. Perhaps it was. 'The book is still at the house, I presume?'

'Yes,' Luca replied. 'And the owner is still locked up awaiting trial, as I'm sure you are also aware. So, if you want it, you would need to speak to her and ask her to give it up. Miss Pearson can be… difficult… to deal with at times.' He smiled fondly as he said it.

'Luca,' Bishop Turnbull went on, 'we want you to ask her to donate the book to the Church. You know her already, so we hope you can convince her.' His voice then took on a grave tone. 'If not, we will have to get the book by other means. But we *will* get it.'

Luca sat back in his chair. 'Wait… you're admitting you would *steal* someone's possession? The Church would stoop that low?'

The man to Bishop Turnbull's right leaned forward, lacing his fingers and setting them on the desk before him. He had a full head of grey hair, a square face, broad shoulders, and grey eyes that showed no emotion. 'You think the Church is above that, Father?' he asked with a gravelly, Eastern European accent. 'Do you not know how our history was built?'

Luca was dumbfounded. 'Of course, but I would have thought we'd moved on from mistakes of the past.'

'Then convince this woman to give us the book,' he stated, and slowly sat back.

Luca looked to Bishop Turnbull for support.

What they were threatening was ludicrous. Had they forgotten just who they were and who they served? Stealing was not something that should be permissible.

And despite Luca asking the Church for assistance in helping Sarah, they had ignored him. It looked like she was going to rot in prison while everything else just moved on.

Bishop Turnbull just looked down, embarrassed. He wasn't calling the shots here, Luca realised. Whoever these men were, they had Turnbull dancing on their strings like a puppet. Turnbull was only the mouthpiece for the meeting, and nothing more.

'We also need to discuss Miss Pearson,' Bishop Turnbull went on.

Luca had no idea what to expect anymore, so he just shrugged. 'Go on.'

'You say that she is now *clavis*—The Key?'

Luca shook his head in exasperation. 'Yes, but she is no longer controlled by anything other than her own free will. The door at Perron Manor is closed now. It has no hold over her. In fact, she beat it. She fought against the possession and defied it long enough to save us all. So she isn't a danger.'

'But she is still the Accursed Blood,' Bishop Turnbull said. 'Whether at Perron Manor or another of these gates, she could still be used as The Key.'

That much was true, but Luca still had no idea what they were implying. 'And...?'

'You say you believe she is now "sensitive," after her ordeal?' the Bishop asked, sounding like he was changing tack.

'Well, I believe she always has been sensitive to a degree, given who she is and her bloodline. However, I think the recent possession, where she touched the other side, has heightened those... abilities.'

Bishop Turnbull looked to the man at his side with an uncertain expression. The man beside him did not look back.

'We think she may be able to help us find out if there are other doorways open,' Bishop Turnbull finally said.

Luca frowned in confusion. 'Excuse me?'

'We believe that her 'sensitivity' could help establish whether a suspected location is normal, haunted... or something worse.'

Luca sat forward. 'But she is more susceptible now to the influence of the other side. Yes, I do believe she might be able to sense if a certain location is actually an open gate, but she would also be extremely vulnerable to its power. She would be a double-edged sword.'

'One we would need to wield carefully,' the man with the Eastern European accent said.

'Luca,' Bishop Turnbull went on, 'the Church is worried about these gates. *Very* worried. The order has been given to try and find the existence of any more. If there *are* others, we must close them all. The thing is, we were lucky this time. If all the gates were open prior to closing Perron Manor, who knows how close we came to the end. And until you found that book, we had no idea such things really existed. The Church *will not* be in the dark anymore. We are going to be proactive and seek these things out.'

'I can understand that,' Luca said. 'But Miss Pearson is incarcerated. She—'

'We can see to that issue,' Bishop Turnbull said. 'In fact, we've already put things in motion to help her.'

Luca shook his head, incredulous. 'She's been through enough,' he said.

'She is a soldier,' the Eastern European man said, sternly. 'One now without a cause. Or a family. Make her see, Father Janosch. Show her she could once again have a purpose.'

'But isn't it dangerous putting her into these situations? We are taking the key right to a lock that should not be opened.'

'Well,' Bishop Turnbull went on, 'for now we know that Hell is at least one gate down. And we only need her help to find the gates. She will not be involved in closing them.'

'Sounds like you have it already planned out,' Luca said.

'To an extent. We need Sarah, David Ritter, and the others to remain silent. However, we understand what we are asking here, so we can offer something in return. They will be offered the chance to participate in our investigations, Church funded, and led by you.'

'Me?!' Luca asked, incredulous.

'Of course. You've already closed one gate; you have prior experience with a serious paranormal incident in Hungary; and you have studied *Ianua Diaboli* and the ledger already, if only briefly. You are perfectly placed.'

'If I refuse?'

Another man sat forward, the oldest looking of them all. His face was painfully thin, almost skeletal, save for his sagging jowls. 'I'm afraid it is an order,' he said. His accent was English, but with no regional dialect Luca could pick up on.

'From what we understand,' Bishop Turnbull said, 'David Ritter and his team are not coping well after the incident. And since we are going to need to insist on their silence, we can offer them a job in return. One that would be very well paid.'

'So in effect, you are buying their silence,' Luca said. 'Only, you don't have the dignity to just leave it at that. You're also going to insist they work for you and help you as well.'

'No, Luca. They would be helping *you*. Use them as you feel they are needed. If any of them aren't up to it, fine. We can let them go and come to another arrangement with them. But your role now, with Miss Pearson as a guide, will be to find out more about these gates and hunt down any that exist. When one is confirmed, Sarah and her friends will be immediately pulled out. They will be safe.'

'This is madness,' Luca said, feeling his chest tighten. He wanted to be done with the Perron Manors and Zsámbék Churches of this world. He didn't want to risk his soul any more... but now he was being ordered back into the mouth of Hell. 'You're putting their lives in danger. They're just ordinary people; they aren't trained for this.'

'*No one* is trained for this,' the Bishop said. 'That's the point.'

'So they're pawns?' Luca asked.

'Think of them more as willing volunteers.'

'What makes you think they'll volunteer?'

'Because you'll convince them, Father,' Bishop Turnbull said. 'Just like you'll convince Miss Pearson to give us the book. Make them see it as an opportunity. Tell them to do it in the name of their fallen friends. For Sarah, it can be in the name of her sister, or her lost sense of purpose. Whatever it takes.'

Luca slumped and looked down to the table. 'I'm not comfortable with this,' he said. 'Not at all. And I won't be strong-armed into tricking people. It isn't right.'

Bishop Turnbull looked to his right again. The large man nodded. 'I understand, Father. This is not easy to hear, I am sure. And it certainly isn't easy to ask. But think of what is at stake here. Is this calling really something you can turn your back on?'

Luca clenched his teeth together as he glared at the man opposite. Other than Bishop Turnbull, he had no idea who these people were. And yet they were asking him to go against his morals and better judgment.

But what choice did he have? Turning his back on the request—no, the *order*—would be turning his back on a world that needed his help, even if it didn't know it. How could he live with himself if he ran away?

Luca brought up a hand and ran it over his face. He let out a long, defeated sigh.

'Fine,' he eventually said. 'I'll do it.'

THE END

THE HAUNTED COLLECTION VOLUME 2

Haunted Collection Volume 2

See how the story continues with Books 4, 5 & 6 of the Haunted series.

Haunted: Possession: A haunted cathedral. A possessed priest.

Haunted: Mother Death: An investigation into one of Britain's most haunted houses.

Haunted: Asylum: This haunted asylum holds secrets that could change the world.

Buy the Haunted Collection Volume 2 now.

ABOUT THE AUTHOR

Lee Mountford is a horror author from the North-East of England. His first book, Horror in the Woods, was published in May 2017 to fantastic reviews, and his follow-up book, The Demonic, achieved Best Seller status in both Occult Horror and British Horror categories on Amazon.

He is a lifelong horror fan, much to the dismay of his amazing wife, Michelle, and his work is available in ebook, print and audiobook formats.

In August 2017 he and his wife welcomed their first daughter, Ella, into the world. In May 2019, their second daughter, Sophie, came along. Michelle is hoping the girls don't inherit their father's love of horror, but Lee has other ideas…

For more information
www.leemountford.com
leemountford01@googlemail.com

ACKNOWLEDGMENTS

Thanks first to my amazing Beta Reader Team:

James Bacon/Christine Brlevic /John Brooks/Carrie-Lynn Cantwell/Karen Day/Doreene Fernandes/Jenn Freitag/Ursula Gillam/Clayton Hall/Tammy Harris/Emily Haynes/Dorie Heriot/Lemmy Howells/Lucy Hughes/Marie K /Dawn Keate/Diane McCarty/Megan McCarty/Valerie Palmer/Leanne Pert/Carley Jessica Pyne/Justin Read/Nicola Jayne Smith/Sara Walker/Sharon Watret

Also, thanks to my editor, Josiah Davis (http://www.jdbookservices.com) & my cover designer, Debbie at The Cover Collection (http://www.thecovercollection.com). The last thank you, as always, is the most important—to my amazing family. My wife, Michelle, and my daughters, Ella and Sophie: thank you for everything. You three are my world.